James Siegel is Senior Creative Director and Vice President of the BBDO advertising agency in New York. He has won numerous awards, including three Gold Lions at Cannes. He lives on Long Island.

Also by James Siegel

EPITAPH

JAMES SIEGEL OMNIBUS

Detour

Derailed

James Siegel

sphere

This omnibus edition first published in Great Britain in 2007 by Sphere

Copyright © James Siegel 2007

Previously published separately.

... first published in any Charge ... ... Warner Books

First published in Great Britain in 2003
Time Warner
Paperback edition published by Time Warner Paperbacks in 2006
Copyright © James Siegel 2003

Derailed first published in the United States ... Warner Books
First published in Great Britain in 2003
by Time Warner Books
Paperback edition published by Time Warner Paperbacks in 2004
Copyright © James Siegel 2003

The moral right of the author has been asserted.

*All characters and events in this publication, other than those clearly in
the public domain, are fictitious and any resemblance to real persons,
living or dead, is purely coincidental.*

A CIP catalogue record for this book is available from the British Library.

ISBN: 978-0-7515-4019-2

Papers used by Sphere are natural, recyclable products made from
wood grown in sustainable forests and certified in accordance with
the rules of the Forest Stewardship Council.

Typeset in Berkeley by M Rules
Printed and bound in Great Britain by Mackays of Chatham Ltd.
Paper supplied by Hellefoss AS, Norway

Sphere
An imprint of
Little, Brown Book Group
Brettenham House
Lancaster Place
London WC2E 7EN

A Member of the Hachette Livre Group of Companies

www.littlebrown.co.uk

Detour

To Sara Anne Freed, a remarkable editor and an even better human being, who took a chance on me, for which I'll be eternally grateful.

I'd like to thank Richard Pine, a remarkable agent, Rick Horgan for his editorial wisdom, and Larry Kirshbaum for getting into the trenches with me. Also, all my Colombian friends who took the time to tell me where I screwed up.

PROLOGUE

It's an old saying. An adage. A reassuring word to the wise. Or actually, to the scared. It's meant to mollify, to calm, to show one the utter silliness of their thinking.

You say it when someone's frightened to do something.

To travel, for instance.

To ride the rails. Hop a plane. Charter a boat.

To scuba dive. Jet-ski. Rollerblade. Balloon.

They're frightened a terrible *something* will befall them, that they'll set out to experience an enjoyable afternoon, a day, a vacation, a life, but instead, they'll end up dead.

And what do you say to them?

There's more chance you'll get hit by a bus while crossing the street.

Because how often does *that* happen, huh?

He kept a secret file in his bottom drawer, buried beneath his myriad charts, pulled out and dusted off for special occasions, as a kind of reminder.

J. Boksi, thirty-eight, about to be engaged. He was walking out of the jewelers, admiring the sparkling oval-cut two-carat ring set in filigreed white gold.

S. Lewes, twenty-two, newly earned MBA in business administration from Bucknell University. She was coming from her first job interview and staring up at the grandest buildings she'd ever seen.

T. Noonan, seventy, doting grandfather. He was taking a walk with his four-year-old grandson and explaining why Batman could not beat Superman in a fair fight, never ever, not on your life.

E. Riskin, sixty.

C. Meismer, seventy-eight.

R. Vaz, thirty-three.

L. Parkins, eleven.

J. Barbagallo, thirty-five.

R. and S. Parks, eighteen-year-old twins.

They'd all been hit by a bus while crossing the street.

Every single one of them.

They were all dead.

It reminded him that despite what you think, it can happen.

It can.

It can even happen to you.

The Insurance Actuary calculates the tipping point between risk and probability, thereby hoping to reduce the likelihood of undesirable events.

– The Actuary Handbook

Chances are, your chances are, pretty good.

– Johnny Mathis

ONE

Buenas tardes.

When they got to Bogotá, the first thing Paul and Joanna saw was a man with no head.

A picture of the man in question, apparently once the deputy mayor of Medellín, was plastered across various table-sized posters stuck to the walls in El Dorado Airport, all of them advertising different Bogotá newspapers. The man was carelessly sprawled in the middle of the street, as if he were just taking a much-needed rest. Except his shirt was stained with dried blood, and he was clearly missing something important. It had been blown off by a car bomb, which had been set by either the leftist FARC or the rightest USDF – depending on which theory you chose to believe.

Paul thought it was a hell of a welcome. But all in all, he still felt like saying *thanks*.

Glad to be here.

That's because flight 31 from JFK to Colombia had lasted eighteen hours, which was eleven hours longer than it was supposed to. There'd been a five-hour delay in

5

Kennedy and an unscheduled stop in Washington, D.C., to pick up baggage belonging to a Colombian diplomat who'd remained nameless.

They'd sat on a broiling Washington tarmac for hours – with no Bloody Marys or gin and tonics to cut the boredom or beat the heat. Serving alcohol during ground delays was apparently an FAA no-no. That was probably a good idea. The general disposition on board had grown angry and mutinous – with the possible exception of Joanna and the passenger to Paul's right, who calmly stared straight ahead into the seat back in front of him.

He was an amateur ornithologist, he volunteered.

He was used to waiting. He was off to the jungles of northern Colombia to hunt for the yellow-breasted toucan.

Paul kept looking at his wristwatch and wondering why it wasn't moving.

Joanna, mostly a bastion of calm, had reminded him that they'd waited five years. Ten hours, more or less, wouldn't kill them.

She was right, of course.

The New York delay, the eight-hour Washington layover, the increasingly fetid cabin, *wouldn't* kill him. He knew what would kill people and what wouldn't. After all, he was an actuary for a major insurance company, whose logo – a pair of paternal cradling hands – appeared regularly on sickly-sweet commercials twenty times a day. He could spin the risk ratios on all sorts of everyday activities, recite the percentages of accident and death chapter and verse.

He knew that the odds of dying in a plane, for example, were exactly 1 in 354,319 – even with the recent small bump due to men whose first name was *Al* and last name was *Qaeda*. A delay in takeoff would be in actuary-speak: *statistically insignificant*.

Plane delays couldn't kill you.

Car bombs could.

Speaking of which.

The sight of the headless man admittedly threw them just a little. As they walked from the gate in the general direction of baggage claim, Joanna noticed the first gruesome poster and immediately turned away, while Paul felt the first vague prickling of fear.

Worming their way through customs under the sullen eyes of soldiers with shouldered AK-47s didn't exactly help. When they finally made it through baggage, they were approached by a stooped white-haired man holding a crude hand-lettered sign over his head.

Breidbard, Paul, it said. Their last name was misspelled.

'I guess I'm considered luggage,' Joanna whispered to him.

The old man introduced himself as *Pablo* and timidly shook Paul's hand. He picked up all three of their suitcases in one swift motion. When Paul tried to wrest at least one bag back from this man who, after all, had to be thirty years older than *he* was, Pablo politely refused.

'Is fine,' he said, smiling. 'Please follow . . .'

Pablo had been hired through the local Santa Regina Orphanage. He would be their man in Bogotá, he explained. He'd drive for them, shop for them, and help guide them through the entire process. He'd accompany them everywhere, he told them.

It was reassuring to hear.

Pablo led them through the unruly and suffocating crowd. All airports were experiments in barely managed chaos, but El Dorado was worse. The crowd seemed like soccer fans who'd lost – loud, milling, and dangerous. Paul, who'd done a little boning up on his Spanish, forgot the word for *excuse me* and had to resort to a primitive form of sign language in an effort to get people to move out of the way. Most simply ignored him, or looked at him as if he were touched in the head. He eventually relied on out-and-out shoving to navigate their way out.

Getting through the crowd was just one of their problems.

The other was keeping up with Speedy Gonzalez, a.k.a. Pablo.

He seemed remarkably spry for a man who had to be pushing seventy. Even while carrying three bulging suitcases.

'Think he's chewing coca or something?' Joanna asked. Joanna ran three mornings a week and could do a good hour and a half on the StairMaster, but even she was having trouble keeping pace.

'Pablo!' Paul had to shout his name once, twice, three times, before Pablo finally turned around and noticed that the two people whom he was supposed to stick to like glue were out of breath and falling dangerously behind.

'Sorry,' he said almost sheepishly. 'I'm used to . . . how you say . . . *giddyap*.' He smiled.

'That's okay,' Paul said. 'We just don't want to lose you.'

They'd made it through the sliding front doors and were on the outskirts of a vast parking lot directly adjacent to the terminal. A sea of cars, dotted with small eddies of

8

slowly strolling passengers, seemed to stretch endlessly in all directions.

'What's that odor?' Joanna asked.

Paul sniffed the air; *motor oil and diesel fuel*, he was about to say. But Joanna possessed an uncannily accurate sense of smell, more an olfactory intuition, so he kept quiet.

'Ahh . . . ,' Pablo said. 'Wait.' He gently placed the suitcases on the cracked pavement, then walked a good twenty feet to what appeared, at least at this distance, to be some kind of ticket booth.

It wasn't. He returned holding two tightly wrapped packages trailing tiny plumes of steam.

'Empanadas,' he said, handing them to Paul and Joanna. *'Pollo.'*

'Chicken,' Paul whispered in Joanna's ear.

'Thanks,' Joanna whispered back, 'I've eaten at Taco Bell too.' Then she asked Pablo, 'How much do we owe you?'

Pablo shook his head. *'Nada.'*

'Thank you, Pablo – that's very generous of you.' Joanna took a bite of her empanada, then was forced to lick a dollop of red sauce which had trickled down past her lower lip. 'Mmmmm – it's *really* good.'

Pablo grinned. Paul thought that his face looked tender and tough at the same time – or, at the least, weathered.

'Wait here, I go for the car,' Pablo said out of deference to their obviously inferior constitutions.

'He's sweet, isn't he?' Joanna said after Pablo had disappeared into a row of Volkswagens, Renaults, and Mini Coopers.

'Yes, maybe we should adopt *him*,' Paul answered. He took her free hand and squeezed – it was sticky with perspiration. 'Excited?'

She nodded. 'Oh yeah.'

'On a scale of one to ten?'

'Six hundred and eleven.'

'That's all, huh?'

Two minutes later Pablo reappeared behind the wheel of a vintage blue Peugeot.

TWO

Their lawyer had booked them into a hotel with a French name, an American-style ambience, and an upscale Bogotá location. The area was called Calle 93, crammed with fashionable boutiques, high-rise hotels, and hip-looking restaurants with blue-tinted windows.

Their hotel was L'Esplanade, a name reeking of French chic, but its lobby coffee shop had Texas steerburgers and Philly fries on the menu.

Their tenth-floor suite had an unimpeded view of the surrounding green mountains. When Joanna pulled up the shades and made Paul look at them, he couldn't help wondering if armed insurgents were looking back. He decided not to share those feelings with his wife.

They'd been dutifully warned about coming to Colombia, of course.

Their original lawyer had urged them to try somewhere else.

Anywhere else.

Korea, he'd suggested. Hungary. *How do you feel about*

11

China? Colombia, he'd insisted, was too volatile. The sale of bulletproof glass was *a national growth industry,* he'd added.

But Korea or Hungary or China could take up to four years.

In Colombia it was two months. Max.

After waiting five long and agonizing years to become parents, four more years had seemed intolerable. Desperation arm-wrestled prudence and won hands down.

They were promptly steered to another lawyer, who specialized in Latin America.

His name was Miles Goldstein, and what he actually seemed to specialize in was enthusiasm. He was warmly effusive, seemingly indefatigable, and unabashedly committed. In this particular case, to bringing two dispossessed and suffering factions together. There were babies out there who needed homes; there were couples out there who needed babies. His mission was to make both parties happy. A handwoven sampler hung on the wall directly above his desk.

He who saves one child saves the world.

It was hard not to like a lawyer who subscribed to that kind of thinking.

Miles assured them that while Colombia wasn't an oasis of peace, the capital city was pretty much no problem. The struggle between leftists and rightists had been going on for thirty years – it had become just another feature of the landscape. But that landscape was mostly north, mountainous, and far away from Bogotá. In fact, according to a recent survey in *Destinations* magazine, a photocopy of which Miles produced from his desk drawer and handed to them, Bogotá was safer than Switzerland.

You've really got to watch your back in Zurich, Miles said.

PABLO HAD BEEN TRUE TO HIS WORD.

He'd driven them up to the doorstep, then flew inside with their luggage, forgoing the proffered help from an obviously pissed-off bellboy. When Paul and Joanna followed Pablo into the loud Art Deco lobby, a fawning concierge with dyed-blond hair and a slight lisp was waiting to show them to their room.

Pablo promised to return in three hours to take them to the orphanage.

After he had left, Paul laid himself out on the generously sized bed and said, 'I wish I could fall asleep, but I can't.'

Two hours later he woke up and said, 'What time is it?'

Joanna was over by the window reading the latest issue of *Mother & Baby* magazine. Paul couldn't help remembering that she'd begun her subscription over four years ago.

'Sorry you couldn't sleep, honey,' she said.

'I guess it caught up with me.'

'I guess.'

'Did you nap?'

'Uh-uh. Too jazzed.'

'What time is it?'

'One hour till Pablo comes back.'

'One hour. Well . . .'

Joanna put the magazine facedown and smiled at him.

13

The cover was a startling close-up of a newborn's eyes: baby blue. 'It's surreal, isn't it?' Joanna said.

'*Surreal*'s a good word.'

'I mean, in one hour we're going to meet her.'

'Yeah. Shouldn't I be pacing or something?'

'Or something.'

'Well, I would pace. But there's not enough room. Consider me mentally pacing.'

'Paul?'

'Yeah?'

'I'm so happy. I think.'

'Why just *think*?'

'Because I'm so scared.'

It wasn't like Joanna to be scared of anything – that was *his* department. It was enough to get him off the bed and over to her chair, where he shook off the pins and needles in his legs and leaned down to hug her. She put her head back on his shoulder and he smelled equal parts shampoo, Chanel No. 5, and, yes, the slightly acrid odor of fear.

'You're going to be great,' Paul said. 'Wonderful.'

'How do you know?'

'Because you've been babying me for ten years, and *I* don't have any complaints. Because I say so.'

'Oh well, if you say so . . .'

She lifted her head and he kissed her full on the lips. Nice lips, he thought. Beautiful lips. She was one of those women who look good falling out of bed – maybe better, since makeup seemed to cover up her features rather than do anything to enhance them. Pale, lightly freckled skin, with powder-blue eyes – the kind they hand-paint on

14

delicate porcelain dolls. Delicate, however, wouldn't necessarily be one of the adjectives he'd use to describe Joanna. Strong, smart, *focused,* was more like it. On certain occasions he'd been known to refer to her as *Xena, warrior princess* – always affectionately, of course, and usually under his breath. She'd be thirty-seven in less than two weeks, but she still looked, well, *twenty*-seven. From time to time he wondered if she'd always look that way to him, if generally happy couples tend to see each other the way they were back when, till they suddenly wake up around sixty or so and wonder who that middle-aged person is sleeping next to them.

'What if I'm completely incompetent?' she said. 'I don't have a degree in this.'

'I'm told it comes naturally.'

'You evidently haven't read *Mother & Baby.*'

'That's okay. You have,' he said.

'Fine. I'll stop panicking.'

'Great. Next time I panic and you reassure.'

'Deal.'

'I'm going to take a shower. I feel like I've been on a plane for two days.'

'You have been on a plane for two days.'

'See, I knew there was a reason.'

PABLO CAME TWENTY MINUTES EARLY. APPARENTLY, THAT WHOLE *mañana* thing was an ethnic stereotype without merit.

He knocked on their door, then politely waited outside, even after Joanna had virtually begged him to come inside and sit down.

Paul, who was only half dressed, had to hastily scramble into the rest of his clothes. Black linen pants and a slightly rumpled white shirt he'd neglected to take out of his suitcase. He took quick stock of himself in the mirror and saw pretty much what he expected: a face stuck somewhere between boyishness and creeping middle age, someone who was clearly the sum of his parts, none of which would've stood out in a crowd. Well, clothes make the man. He topped off his outfit with his red-striped *power* tie. After all, he was preparing for the most important meeting of his life.

The Peugeot was softly idling in front of the hotel.

Paul noticed the hotel doorman whisper something in Pablo's ear as he bent over to usher them into the backseat. A kind of rumba was playing on the radio.

'What did he say?' Paul asked Pablo after he had pulled away from the curb.

'He wished you *Many Blessings*.'

'Oh. You told him where we're going?'

'Yes.'

'Do you do this a lot, Pablo?' Joanna asked. 'With many couples?'

Pablo nodded. '*Happy* job, no?'

'Sure,' Joanna said. 'I think so.'

They passed a convoy of soldiers hunched together in an open made-in-Detroit Jeep. Paul couldn't help remembering the phalanx of armed sentries at the airport.

'Lots of soldiers around, huh?' Paul said.

'Soldiers? *Sí*.'

'How have things been?' Paul asked, a little hesitant to ask a question he might not like the answer to.

'*Things?*'

16

'The rebels? FARC?' It sounded like a curse, Paul thought. He imagined that to the vast majority of Colombians, it was. *The Revolutionary Armed Forces of Colombia.* The leftist guerrillas already holding much of the north, and most likely the group responsible for blowing the deputy mayor of Medellín to kingdom come.

Of course, there was always the chance the car bomb had been perpetrated by the right. FARC was embroiled in a long dirty war against the *United Self-Defense Forces,* or USDF, a rightist paramilitary organization of singular brutality.

On the way out of the airport, they'd passed a wall covered in red graffiti, which looked uncomfortably like fresh arterial spray, as if it had been written in blood.

Libre Manuel Riojas. Manuel Riojas was the reputed USDF commander, currently residing in an American prison for drug transgressions.

Pablo shook his head. 'I don't listen . . . No politics.'

'Yes. That's probably wise.'

'*Sí.*'

'Still, it must be scary sometimes?'

'Scary.' Pablo derisively waved a hand. 'I mind my business. Don't read the papers. It's all bad.'

Before departing, Paul had sent away for a video titled *The Colombian Way of Life.* After he'd watched the first five minutes, it was painfully obvious it had been created for schoolkids under the age of twelve. The video followed two teenagers, Mauricio and Paula, walking around sunny Bogotá, their intent being to show that *there's more to this modern South American city than coffee, cocaine, and guerrilla violence* – or so stated the back blurb.

17

Pablo was driving them past a street of sprawling mansions. At least Paul assumed there were mansions back there somewhere – you couldn't actually see them. An unbroken ten-foot-high stucco wall was in the way. Electronic gates periodically announced the demarcation of each new property, their names spelled out in tile mosaics embedded into the wall.

Casa de Flora.

Casa de Playa.

They passed a spotted dog with its ribs showing, urinating against the burnt-orange wall of the Casa de Fuego.

Something was unnerving about the scene. It took Paul a while to understand what it was.

Yes. The lack of people.

Except for several beggars, emaciated-looking women listlessly cradling babies in their laps, there was absolutely no one in view. Not in this neighborhood. They were all tucked out of sight, hidden behind a modern wall of Jericho.

La Calera, Pablo told them when Paul asked what the neighborhood was called.

Then, thankfully, their surroundings began to change.

Some scattered electronic and appliance stores, then small *cafeterías* advertising empanadas, *patatas,* and *huevos,* followed by a glut of news vendors, *lotería* shops, *supermercados,* various bustling places of commerce – the whole enchilada. A cacophony of smells wafted in through the half-cracked windows: bus exhaust, flowers, raw fish, newsprint – Paul was tempted to ask Joanna for a full rundown. They were clearly in the midst of the completely normal life of a capital city, just as Miles had promised.

18

And Paul wondered if there was a kind of conscious denial at work here – if there *had* to be an ostrichlike mentality in a country where deputy mayors had their heads blown off on a regular basis. If Colombians were able to wall off pieces of their conscious mind from the ongoing war, much as they carefully walled off poverty from the upper classes in the La Calera district.

He stopped musing; there was a sign just ahead tucked into a small grove of trees.

Santa Regina Orfanato.

'Here,' Pablo whispered. He pulled into a hidden driveway and stopped the car. A locked gate; a black buzzer set in brass.

Pablo turned off the ignition, got out, and pushed the button. *'Pablo,'* he said, *'Señor y Señora Breidbart.'*

The gate swung open ten seconds later. Pablo got back in and methodically started up the car. He drove into an inner courtyard shaded by tall, spindly pines.

'Come on,' Señor Breidbart said when the car stopped again. 'Let's go meet our daughter.'

THREE

Paul couldn't actually feel his legs.

He knew he had them – he was clearly and unmistakably *standing* on them, but they felt missing in action. Gone.

A second ago a short mestiza nurse in starched white had shuffled into the room hugging a pink baby blanket to her chest.

Inside this baby blanket, Paul knew, was a baby.

Not just a baby.

His baby.

When they'd entered the sterile anteroom, they waited a good twenty minutes for Santa Regina's director, María Consuelo, to come greet them. It felt longer than the plane flight. Paul stood up, sat down, walked around, looked out the window, sat down, stood up again. He counted the black tiles in the floor pattern, finding a familiar solace in numbers – there were twenty-eight of them. Occasionally, he squeezed Joanna's hand and offered her wan smiles of encouragement. Finally, María entered the room, a petite earnest-looking woman with jet-black hair wrapped tightly in a bun. She was followed by a small bustling entourage.

She greeted Paul and Joanna by their first names, as if they were old friends who'd come visiting, instead of prospective parents come begging. Then she dutifully introduced the members of her staff – the head nurse, two teachers, and her personal assistant – all of whom shook hands with them before departing in turn. María led them into her office, where they arranged themselves around a small table covered in neatly stacked piles of magazines, and then spent *another* twenty minutes sipping bitter coffee – brought in by a somber teenage girl – and making generally awkward small talk.

Maybe it wasn't small talk.

Paul felt increasingly as if it were the *oral exam*, the written part of the test having already been aced: employment checks, bank statements, stock certificates, mortgage slips, various recommendations from family and friends attesting to their good character and all-around worthiness. And the heartfelt letter it had taken Paul a solid week to compose, rip up, rewrite, painstakingly edit, and finally send off.

My wife and I are writing this letter to tell you who we are. And who we want to be. Parents.

María began by thanking them for the care package they'd sent the orphanage – diapers, bottles, formula, toys – a kind of authorized bribe Miles assured them was pro forma when adopting in Latin America.

Then she got down to business.

She asked Paul about his job – *an insurance man, isn't*

21

that so, Paul? Well, yes – though he didn't tell her that in his case, being an insurance man meant locking himself away in a small room and compiling the stats that set the rates real insurance men went and charged you. That his life's work consisted of calculating the risk in every known human activity, swimming through streams of raw data in an effort to reduce life to a semimanageable minefield. The definition of an actuary: *someone who wants to be an accountant but doesn't have the personality.*

'How long have you been employed there?' she asked.

'Eleven years,' he answered, wondering if that categorized him as a solid breadwinner or a working transient. Regardless, he knew she already had this information. Maybe she was simply testing his truthfulness.

Then things got a little stickier.

She asked Joanna about *her* job.

Human resources executive for a pharmaceutical firm. Only it became clear that María wasn't really inquiring about the nature of Joanna's job, as much as asking her whether or not she was intending to *give it up*, now that she had an infant daughter to take care of.

Good question.

One that Paul and Joanna had spent more than a few weekends debating themselves, without ever quite reaching a definitive answer. Paul could tell from María's tone of voice that she thought Joanna giving up her job would probably be a good idea.

For a moment Joanna said nothing, and all Paul could hear was the sound of the sputtering room fan, the electrical hum of the fluorescent lighting, and his own inner voice, which was screaming at Joanna to *lie.*

Just this once.

The problem was, lying wasn't really part of her M.O. She was awfully good at spotting them – lies, half-truths, gross misstatements of fact – but just about incapable of letting one pass her lips.

'I'm taking a leave of absence,' Joanna said.

Well, okay, Paul thought, true enough.

'How *long*?' María asked.

Paul found himself staring at the picture gallery that took up half the wall of María's office – multishaded adolescent faces peering out from backyard decks, swimming pools, playrooms, Little League fields, from under cocked college graduation caps – and wondering whether his daughter's picture would be gracing that wall.

'I'm not sure,' Joanna said.

Paul looked back at María and smiled. He must've looked like an overgrown child hoping for candy.

'I know I'll end up doing what's best for the baby and best for me,' Joanna said. 'I'll be a good mother.'

María sighed. She reached for Joanna's hand. It was a gesture Paul had seen doctors and priests make when they were about to impart bad news – one priest in particular, when Paul was eleven years old and it was his hand being reached for, patted, and held tight. The day his mom died.

'Joanna,' María said, 'I, too, am sure you'll be a good mother.' She smiled.

It took Paul a minute to understand that they'd passed.

Test over.

He felt a reservoir of pent-up anxiety flooding out of him. But only for a moment.

Because María said, 'I think it's time you met your daughter.'

María kept talking, but Paul pretty much stopped listening.

Her voice was being drowned out by the sound of his own heartbeat, which seemed raucous and dangerously irregular. And another sound too – heavy footsteps that were slowly but steadily advancing down the hall. Paul became preternaturally aware of the rivers of sweat virtually flowing down both arms.

Was that *her*?

The footsteps passed by and faded into silence.

Then, after a minute or two during which Paul found it difficult to breathe, a new set of footsteps appeared on his radar screen, grew in volume and texture and clarity, and seemed to stop just outside the door.

María said, 'I know you're anxious to meet her. She's *beautiful*.'

They'd received a tiny black-and-white photograph, that's all – passport-sized, dark, and maddeningly blurred.

The door slowly opened. The overhead fan was clearly spinning. Paul could swear the air turned stock-still.

The dark-skinned nurse walked into the room hugging a fuzzy baby blanket to her chest. Paul and Joanna shot up as Paul's legs lost all sensation, as if he were balancing on stilts.

Slowly, the nurse peeled back the top section of blanket, revealing spiky dark hair and two bottomless black eyes. The effect was a kind of infant *punk*, a beguiling mixture of innocence and attitude.

Paul fell immediately and terminally in love.

He was reminded of the first time he saw Joanna, across an airport waiting lounge filled with tired and frustrated people, wearily looking up to witness this pale-skinned and blue-eyed vision of loveliness haranguing an unforthcoming airline employee for information. Femininity and fearlessness seemed to meet in equal proportion, and he'd experienced something akin to a cocaine-induced rush, something he'd tried a few times in his frat days. That joyous but dangerous burst of pure exultation, which threatened to race your heart to heights of ecstasy, or break it in two.

Possibly both.

The nurse held their daughter out to them, and somehow Paul reached out for her first. The instant he pressed her to his chest, she felt as if she belonged there.

Joanna leaned in and softly brushed the baby's forehead with one perfectly manicured finger. The baby opened her tiny mouth.

'Look,' Paul said to no one in particular, 'she's *smiling* at us.'

María laughed. 'It's gas, I think. She's a beauty, though, no?'

'Oh yes,' Paul said, 'she's a beauty.' His daughter's skin was the palest shade of olive. Her nocturnal eyes seemed to express an intimate kind of understanding. That she'd finally come home.

Paul looked up at Joanna. Tears had reduced her eyes to two pale blue lakes.

María Consuelo beamed at them.

'I knew this child was meant for you,' she said. 'I *always* know. Have you chosen a name yet?'

'Yes,' Paul said. 'Joelle.' It was an amalgam of *Joseph*, Joanna's paternal grandfather, and *Ellen*, his mom. Both deceased. Both sorely missed, especially now.

'Joelle.' María sounded it out, then shook her head affirmatively. It had passed muster.

'Can I, honey?' Joanna put her arms out and Paul tentatively handed the baby over. She was so unbearably light, so ridiculously tiny, he was afraid that she might disappear at any second.

But no.

Joanna gathered her up in her arms and cooed.

'Ooooh . . . yes, Joelle . . . Gooood girl . . . Mommy's here . . .' She placed her pinkie into Joelle's tiny hand and Joelle fastened onto it.

A kind of circle had been formed, Paul thought: Joanna, Joelle, and himself. A circle is self-contained and self-sufficient.

It has no beginning and no end, forever.

FOUR

On the way back from Santa Regina, they passed a field of human heads.

Maybe they should've taken that as a sign, an omen signaling what was to come. But that's the *problem* with omens – they only become omens based on later events.

There was Joanna pressing a very sleepy Joelle to her chest.

There was Paul mentally traversing the newly discovered terrain of fatherhood.

There were twenty heads sticking up out of the ground.

Heads that were clearly and emphatically, well, *alive*. They were blinking their eyes, opening their mouths, slowly looking up and down, left and right.

'*Hambre,*' Pablo said, sighing.

'What?' Paul said. *Hambre* meant what? *Hunger.*

Joanna had seen them too. She'd instinctively brought Joelle closer to her chest as if to protect her, her maternal instinct suddenly pressed into action.

Pablo said, 'They are *protesta.*'

Hunger strike.

They'd buried themselves up to their necks in a section of unpaved road. Twenty or thirty of them, mostly young men and women. They looked like something out of Hieronymus Bosch, Paul thought, doomed penitents trapped in the third circle of hell.

'What are they protesting?' Joanna asked.

Pablo shrugged. 'Conditions,' he said.

'How long have they – ?'

'Long time,' Pablo said. 'Four, five weeks.'

Maybe not much longer.

The first thing Paul heard was the siren.

An ambulance, he guessed – because he saw a station wagon with *Ambulancia* painted on its side suddenly pulling up onto the sidewalk. Its roof light was conspicuously inert. No, the siren was coming from somewhere else.

Two police cars. *Urbano guardia*. One of them cutting right in front of them, causing Pablo to jam the brakes and veer suddenly to the left, where their car came to rest with its front bumper virtually touching a brick wall.

Joelle began crying.

She wasn't the only one.

The policemen used long black nightsticks.

It looked like that bar game where little plastic groundhogs pop their heads up in random order and you score points by bopping them on the head. Only in the bar game they can pop back down. They can lie low and hide.

Not here.

In mere minutes, minutes in which Joelle grew increasingly agitated and Pablo attempted to turn the car around, the ground turned scarlet.

Which is why the ambulance was there – the result of good civic planning.

Pablo finally managed to get the car in the opposite direction and take off down a ridiculously narrow side street, barely avoiding sudden streams of people running from all directions to watch.

The field of bloodied heads receded into the distance. It was harder for Paul to get the sight out of his head.

Joanna was shaking – or was that him? When he put his arm around her and hugged, it was hard to tell. He'd been here a day, he thought, *less* than a day, but he was increasingly convinced that Bogotá wasn't third world as much as fourth dimension.

Locombia, he'd overheard someone on the plane refer to Colombia: the mad country.

He had a pretty good idea now what they were talking about.

He was ecstatic that they were taking Joelle from here. They might've come to Colombia to rescue themselves – from loneliness, the doldrums, a life without kids – but they were rescuing her too. From *this*. Joelle would grow up in a place of relative safety and calm. Where she'd never see people buried up to their necks in a city street, and even if she did, policemen wouldn't be bludgeoning them half to death.

Pablo asked if they were all right.

'Yes,' Paul answered, aware that Pablo seemed remarkably undisturbed by the incident. Maybe when you lived in Colombia, it was just another day at the office.

When they entered the hotel elevator, Paul smiled at the middle-aged Colombian couple who walked in seconds later, expecting the smile *back* that seemed to be the right of new parents everywhere. No dice. He was greeted with cool and unmistakable hostility.

For a moment he wondered if it was simply their nationality. Weren't Americans targets of *everyone's* anger these days? But the man whispered something to his wife in Spanish, and among the Spanish words was a word Paul recalled from his high school foreign-language labors. *Niña.*

It wasn't because of who they were. It was what they were *doing*. Adopting a baby.

A *Colombian* baby.

They were just two more Americans doing what Americans had always done in countries not their own. Depriving it of its natural resources. First gold and oil and coal and gas. Now babies. Paul hadn't considered that point of view before. Now that he found himself in an uncomfortably frigid elevator, he did. It made him feel a little less like a rescuer and more like a pillager.

Luckily, their floor came first. He ushered Joanna out of the elevator and down the hall.

'Did you see that?' he asked Joanna.

'What?'

'Those people. In the elevator.' He slipped his key into the lock and opened the door.

'Talk low,' Joanna said. 'Joelle's sleeping.'

'That couple,' Paul whispered. 'They looked like they wanted to have us deported. Or shot.'

'*What?*'

Maybe Joanna had been trying to forget what she'd just seen on that street. She hadn't noticed.

'They *hated* us, Joanna.'

'You can't be serious. They don't even know us.' Joanna slowly settled into an armchair, where she looked close to collapse.

'They don't have to know us. They don't approve of us. We're taking their children from them.'

'*Their* children? What are you talking about?'

'Their country's children. Colombia's children. I'm telling you, they looked like I should be handing her back.'

'It doesn't matter. That's them. Everyone else has been perfectly nice to us.'

'Everyone else is taking our money. That might color things a little.'

Joanna wasn't listening anymore.

She was staring down at her child, busy doing what mothers do, he supposed – basking in that part of the unbroken circle where even fathers don't dare to tread.

FIVE

This is how they met Galina.

They'd fallen into a half-stupor by the armchair and awakened to a shrill, deafening alarm that turned out to be their daughter. They immediately knew they were in trouble.

They'd forgotten to sterilize the bottles they'd brought with them from New York.

They'd forgotten to sterilize the nipples.

All the things the nurse at Fana had gone over with them ad nauseam.

There was a kitchenette just off the sitting room. Paul threw a pot of water on the stove, then began frantically looking for something to open up the cans of baby formula. Joelle's screams reached heretofore unknown decibel levels.

Paul dropped two bottles and nipples into barely boiling water, but there wasn't a can opener to be found. Both kitchen drawers were starkly empty.

Joanna rocked Joelle while walking back and forth from the kitchenette to the bed, which only seemed to cause

Joelle to scream louder, if that were humanly possible. Joanna, fearless, indomitable, a four-year subscriber to *Mother & Baby* magazine, looked scared out of her mind.

There was a knock on the door.

Paul began rehearsing his apologies on the way to open it. *New baby, hungry, sorry for any—*

It was Pablo. And a woman.

'Galina,' he said, evidently the woman's name. 'She's your nurse.'

PABLO'S JOB DESCRIPTION PROVED TO BE A MODEST ONE. Technically, Galina might've been a nurse, but she was really a miracle worker.

Joanna, who still maintained at least a tenuous connection to the Catholic Church of her youth, was ready to nominate her for sainthood.

'Do you see this?' Joanna whispered to him.

Galina had managed to calm Joelle, retrieve the sterilized bottles and nipples, and locate a can opener for the formula, all in less than two minutes. At the moment, she was providing a startling display of ambidexterity, feeding Joelle in the crook of her left arm while arranging an impromptu changing table with her right.

Paul thought she looked pretty much like what a baby nurse should look like – anywhere from her mid-fifties to her mid-seventies, with a gentle face highlighted by pronounced laugh lines and soft gray eyes that seemed to resonate with the patience of, well . . . a saint.

'Can *I* do that?' Joanna asked her, but she was gently waved away.

'Plenty times to do this when you take your baby home,' Galina said. Her English was excellent. 'You watch me now.'

So Joanna did. Paul too, who'd vowed to be the kind of hands-on father that actually pitched in.

Galina finished feeding Joelle, then proceeded to demonstrate her burping technique, which was, of course, perfect. One firm pat on the back and Joelle made a noise that sounded like a bottle of sparkling Evian being opened. Galina gently placed Joelle down on the kitchen-counter-turned-changing-table and relieved her of her soiled diaper, with Paul acting as number one helper.

He was happy to note that the unpleasantness of changing a baby's diapers was mitigated by the baby in question being *yours*.

The hotel had placed a small white crib in the corner of their bedroom. Galina put Joelle facedown on the freshly laundered sheets and pulled a pink coverlet up to her neck.

'Um . . .' Joanna looked plainly uncomfortable about something.

'Yes, Mrs Breidbart?' Galina said.

'Call me Joanna, please.'

'Joanna?'

'Isn't . . . I thought a baby needs to be put on her *back*. When she sleeps. So she doesn't choke or get SIDS.'

'SIDS?' Galina smiled and shook her head. 'The stomach is fine,' she said.

'Well, yes, but . . . I read something, there were some studies done five years ago and they said –'

'Stomach is *fine*, Joanna,' she repeated, and patted her on the shoulder.

34

Now Joanna didn't look so happy at being called by her first name.

An uncomfortable silence suddenly permeated the room.

Paul thought that a kind of trespass had been committed, only he wasn't sure who'd trespassed upon whom. Joanna was Joelle's mother, true. Galina was her nurse. Her highly experienced and, by all evidence, *highly competent* nurse. A jury might have a tough time with this one.

Galina broke the silence first.

'If it makes you more comfortable, Joanna,' she said, and reached into the crib, gently turning Joelle over onto her back.

In the battle of wills the other guy had apparently blinked.

SIX

'You didn't say anything,' Joanna said.

Joanna wasn't sleeping. Paul wasn't either, but only because she'd just woken him.

Said anything *when*? He'd been in the middle of a dream involving a college girlfriend and a torpid tropical beach, and for a moment he was shocked to be on a bed in what was obviously a hotel room.

In Bogotá. Yes.

Consciousness continued to fill in like a Polaroid being furiously waved in the air. He was in a hotel room in Bogotá. With his wife.

And his new baby daughter.

Not with Galina, though. She'd departed for home after allowing them to go downstairs for dinner, where they couldn't find a single Colombian dish on the menu.

Galina was what Joanna was talking about. He hadn't said anything when Joanna accused Galina of putting Joelle to sleep the wrong way.

'I thought discretion was the better part of valor,' Paul said.

'I see. I read babies are supposed to sleep on their backs, Paul.'

'Maybe she hadn't read the same articles.'

'Books.'

'Right, books. She probably hadn't read those either.'

'You should've taken my side.'

Paul considered that one. That maybe he should've taken her side. He was tempted to point out that they were novices here, and that all things considered, he was inclined to go with empirical knowledge over self-help books and *Mother & Baby* magazine. On the other hand, if he agreed with her, he had a reasonable chance of being able to turn over and go back to sleep.

'Yes, sorry,' Paul said. 'I should've, I guess.'

'You *guess*? We're her parents now. We have to support each other.'

'You mean we didn't have to support each other before?'

Joanna sighed and rolled away from him. 'Forget it.'

It was clear that Joanna didn't actually *mean* he should forget it.

'Look,' Paul said. 'I didn't know who was right. Suddenly, this baby is ours. We're . . . *responsible* for her. Galina seemed to know what she's doing. I mean, it's her *job*.'

It occurred to Paul that the process of becoming a circle might involve some growing pains. God knows, they'd had enough of them trying to *have* a baby.

Take sex, for instance.

You could pretty much mark its decline from the moment they'd decided to start a family.

As Paul remembered it, they'd been lying on a nice

four-poster bed in Amagansett, Long Island, sloshed on California cabernet. When Joanna said *I don't have my diaphragm in*, he didn't say *okay, I'll wait*, and she didn't get up and get it.

They'd been married six years. They were thirty-two years old. They were drunk and horny and certifiably in love.

It would turn out to be the last spontaneous moment they'd have involving the act of conception.

When her period came a month later, they immediately decided to have another go at it.

This time there was no California cabernet and no Amagansett surf. The results were pretty much the same.

Her *friend* came right on schedule. Again. Only it wasn't a friend anymore, as much as an embarrassing if intimate relation she thought she'd booted out of the house, only to discover sitting back out on her front stoop.

In the Breidbart household, menstrual tension became decidedly *post*.

They soon began the exhausting roundelay of doctors in search of ever-elusive answers, as sex continued its slow and painful evolution from lovemaking to *baby*-making.

At one point he'd needed to shoot her with fertility drugs exactly one half hour before they performed sex. And it *was* a kind of performance – increasingly a *command* performance, summoned to do his duty at various times of the day and night. These times predicated on all sorts of physical factors, none of which had anything to do with actual lust.

A subtle kind of blame game ensued. When a thorough testing of Paul's sperm revealed that he had a below-average and barely serviceable sperm count, he'd sensed a slight shift in the air. The word *you* seemed to enter Joanna's conversation with greater frequency and with what he perceived as an accusatory intonation.

When a thorough testing of Joanna's ovaries revealed a slight abnormality that could, in some cases, inhibit proper fertilization, Paul had returned the favor. It was cruel and unforgiving.

It was also impossible to stop.

For both of them.

And it wasn't just each other who began getting on their nerves. Other people too. Lifelong friends of Joanna's, for instance, whose only crime was their apparently unlimited aptitude for getting pregnant. Including her best friend, Lisa, with two towheaded toddlers, right across the hall. Complete strangers began bugging them as well. Three seconds into meeting them, they'd invariably ask the k-question. *Have any kids?* Paul wondered why that wasn't considered unconscionably rude. Did *they* go around asking strange couples if they owned a car, or a decent bank account, or an in-ground swimming pool?

Eventually, their long road of futility inexorably led them to the new great hope of infertile couples everywhere. In vitro fertilization, otherwise known as *your last chance*. It was a kind of roulette wheel for high-stakes gamblers. After all, it was ten thousand dollars a spin. And Paul could've recited an entire actuarial table on its success rate – 28.5 percent, with the odds getting lower with each attempt.

They took Paul's sperm. They took Joanna's eggs. They formally introduced them. They sat back and hoped the romance would take.

It didn't.

They tried once.

They tried twice.

They tried three times.

They were up to forty thousand and counting when a remarkable thing happened.

It came the morning after a particularly bad night.

All their thinly nuanced charges had finally turned the air poisonous and explosive. Perhaps that wasn't surprising given that all exhalations are made of carbon dioxide; it had just been waiting for a match. In this case, a *shouting* match where they both said – okay, *screamed* – things better left unmentioned. Joanna had dissolved into tears, and Paul had sullenly disappeared into the den to watch some b-ball, which, given the general state of the New York Knicks, hadn't improved his mood any.

They were walking it off the next morning in Central Park, neither one saying much to the other, when they passed the playground off 66th Street. The sound of laughing children was particularly hurtful that morning, a lacerating reminder of what they couldn't have.

Paul was about to execute a detour when a small girl wandered past them in the futile process of capturing a runaway pink balloon. She was dark, Latin, and impossibly cute.

'Where's your mother?' Joanna had asked her.

But the more interesting question would have been, *who's* your mother? The woman who came breathlessly running up to them just a few seconds later, gently admonishing her daughter for running away. This woman was blonde, pale, and about their age. She picked up her giggling daughter, nuzzled her neck, smiled at Paul and Joanna, and retreated back to the seesaws.

Up to that moment they hadn't thought about it.

Adopting.

Maybe they'd just needed to see it in the flesh.

That afternoon when they got back to the apartment, Joanna asked Paul to take out the garbage. Surprisingly, this garbage consisted of syringes, thermometers, various fertility drugs, dutifully recorded journals, and everything else they'd accumulated in an effort to have a baby. Paul gladly dumped it all into the incinerator room.

When he got back inside, they'd ended up making love the way they used to – which, all things considered, was pretty terrific.

They went to a lawyer the very next day.

Now Paul could hear Joanna next to him in the dark. And the soft, soothing sound of Joelle's breathing. He rolled over and kissed his wife on the mouth.

'Next time I'll support you. Okay?'

He could sense her smile in the dark.

All systems were go for reentry into the land of Nod.

Except Joelle woke up.

And screamed.

SEVEN

It began the next afternoon.

Galina put Joelle in for her afternoon nap. She hummed a plaintive lullaby over the crib. Paul cocked his head from the bathroom, listening to Galina's lilting voice. When he came out, freshly shaven and only slightly sleep-deprived, Galina suggested that he and Joanna get some fresh air. The baby was asleep. Galina would be there for another few hours.

It was technically winter in Colombia, but even mountain-bound Bogotá was close enough to the equator to retain a dreamy warmth. Joelle *was* sleeping – a walk seemed like just what the doctor ordered.

They turned right out the hotel lobby and soon passed the kind of stores only tourists and one percent of the Colombian population could afford to walk into.

Hermès.

Louis Vuitton.

Oscar de la Renta.

They walked hand in hand, and Paul congratulated

himself on his tactical maneuver last night in bed. Things were clearly fine between them.

Joanna had fed Joelle this morning, while he'd pulled diaper duty. They'd taken turns babbling nonstop baby talk at her. That is, when they weren't telling each other how remarkably gorgeous she was. How unbelievably expressive her face seemed. What an unusually sweet disposition she had. Obviously, some natural law was at work here, able to turn two reasonably intelligent people into love-struck idiots.

Paul, though, was kind of enjoying idiothood.

Now he squeezed Joanna's hand as they waited at a curb. He kissed her neck when they stopped and lingered before an art gallery window. A Botero exhibition, the Latin American painter who portrayed everyone as grossly distended, fat, and swollen, like Thanksgiving parade balloons.

After they had strolled a few more blocks, he found he missed his daughter. This was a new experience – going somewhere and leaving a piece of yourself behind. He felt . . . *incomplete*. The circle needed to be closed again.

'Want to go back?' he asked Joanna.

'I was about to say the same thing.'

'I think I'm going to call her Jo,' Paul said after they had crossed the street and turned back toward L'Esplanade. Two couples on mopeds gunned their engines and surged past them, spitting out a thin cloud of blue exhaust.

'Ugh,' Joanna said; evidently, she wasn't referring to the noxious fumes.

'Something wrong with *Jo*?'

'When you tried to call me Jo, I threatened you with bodily harm. I think I *did* you bodily harm.'

'Yeah. Why was that again?'

'I dated a Joe, remember? He was unemployed and psychotic – not in that order. So all things being equal,' Joanna said, 'I'd prefer that you not call her Jo.'

'Fine. What about *Joey*?'

'Like in Buttafuoco?'

'Like in Breidbart.'

'How about we *start* with *Joelle*? Just so the poor kid learns her name.'

They were passing a toy store, its window stocked floor-to-ceiling with dolls, trucks, video games, stuffed animals, soccer balls, and some things he honestly couldn't recognize.

'What do you say?' Paul said.

'Sure,' Joanna said. 'Let's go buy some toys.'

WHEN THEY ENTERED THE HOTEL LOBBY, THEY NEEDED THE doorman to help them make it into the elevator. They'd gone a little overboard – *they'd* been like kids in a toy store.

There seemed to be so much more to buy than when *they* were children. It was pretty much G.I. Joes, Barbies, and Slinkys back then. Now there were vast new categories to contemplate, numerous subcategories too. Things that talked and walked and beeped and flashed and zapped and pirouetted and sang.

All of them seemed to have Joelle's name on them.

The doorman managed to get them into the elevator without a major mishap.

When they opened the door to their hotel room, Galina wasn't there.

'She's in the bathroom,' Joanna said.

Paul opened the bathroom door, stuffed giraffe in hand, but Galina wasn't in there either.

When Paul turned around with his hands up, Joanna turned an ugly shade of white.

It wasn't just Galina that was missing.

It was their daughter.

She was gone too.

'No, Mr Breidbart, I didn't talk to your nurse.' The concierge retained his air of helpful solicitude, but up against Paul's full-blown panic, it seemed woefully inadequate.

'They're not in the room,' Paul said. *Do you understand me?*'

'Yes, sir. I understand.'

Paul had come down to the lobby – after checking the rooftop pool, the restaurant, the hair salon, the game room. Joanna had remained up in the room in case Galina called.

'Perhaps she went shopping,' the concierge offered.

'Did you see them leave the hotel?'

'No. I was busy with several guests.'

'Well, did *anyone* see them leave the hotel?'

'I don't know, Mr Breidbart. Why don't we ask?'

The concierge led him over to the front desk, where he interrupted the registration clerk, who was in the middle of checking in a guest. He spoke to him in Spanish, gesturing to Paul. Paul heard him mention Galina's name, then *niña*, that word again. The registration clerk looked at Paul, then back to the concierge, and shook his head.

'He didn't see them,' the concierge said. 'Come with me.'

They walked outside the hotel where the doorman who'd just helped them into the elevator was flirting with a striking woman in a midriff-baring tank top.

The doorman immediately straightened up, deserting the woman in midsentence. After the concierge had explained the problem, he looked over at Paul and slowly nodded.

'Sí,' the doorman said. Apparently, he *had* seen Galina and Joelle leave the hotel. *'Hace una hora . . .'*

An hour ago. Which would have been just after he and Joanna had left the hotel.

'Ahh, mystery solved,' the concierge said, smiling stupidly. 'She is taking your baby for a walk.'

His baby had been napping.

Why would Galina take a sleeping baby for a walk?

Paul felt dizzy; the ground seemed to be tipping. The concierge was still talking to him, but Paul wasn't processing the words. There was a steady hum in the air.

'She's taken my baby,' Paul said.

The doorman and concierge were looking at him oddly.

'Did you hear what I said? *She's taken my baby.*'

'Yes,' the concierge finally responded. 'For a walk, Mr Breidbart.'

'I want you to call the police.'

'Policía?'

'Yes. Call them.'

'I think you are maybe too excited here . . .'

'Yes, I am excited.' The ground was tipping one way, then the other. The sun had gone cold. 'My baby's been taken. I'm excited about that. Call the police.'

'I don't think . . .'

'Call the police.'

'You are accusing your nurse of kidnapping, Mr Breid-bart.' It was said as a statement, not a question, and it seemed to Paul that the concierge's voice had somehow changed, gone from warm and helpful to cool and un-helpful.

'My baby was napping. The nurse told us to go get some fresh air. Then she left the hotel two minutes later and she's not back.'

'The baby woke up perhaps.'

'Perhaps you're right. All the same, I want you to call the police.'

'Maybe we wait a little and see if she returns, no?'

'No.'

'She has been used as a nurse many times here, Mr Breidbart.' Yes, the concierge's tone had definitely under-gone a transformation.

Paul was accusing a Colombian woman of a crime.

A sweet-looking Colombian woman with laugh lines and patient gray eyes who was taking care of a *Colombian baby*. A baby that he, an American, was spiriting out of the country because there evidently weren't enough American babies to go around.

'I don't care how many times she's been used. She took my baby without permission. She didn't tell us. I need to talk to the police.'

The concierge might not have agreed with him and might not have even liked him, but he was still a concierge.

'If that's what you want, sir,' he said stiffly.

He walked back into the lobby and up to his desk, where he lifted the phone with painful resignation and dialed out. Paul waited silently as the concierge said a few Spanish words into the receiver. He hung up the phone with undue force. The click echoed through the sterile lobby, causing several people to look up with alarmed and puzzled expressions.

THE POLICEMEN HAD THICK BLACK LEATHER BOOTS AND GUNS that looked like Uzis strapped to their hips.

Paul didn't notice any black nightsticks.

The concierge spoke to them in Spanish while Paul patiently listened. In the interim between the concierge's call and the policemen's arrival, Paul had called Joanna again.

No news.

One of the policemen spoke decent English. Even if he hadn't, his meaning would have been all too evident.

'Why you think your nurse *stole your baby?*' he said. He didn't look like he wanted an answer.

Paul explained as best he could. Joelle was napping, the nurse had suggested that they leave, then she'd left herself. She had neither asked permission nor left a note. They didn't know where she was.

'He says this woman is good.' The *he* the policeman was referring to was the concierge, who was standing off to the side with a semiscowl on his face. In the game of good cop, bad cop, it would've been hard to choose who was who.

'Perhaps you didn't understand me,' Paul said, and saw the policeman flinch. He remembered those bloodied heads sticking out of the ground, and for a moment he wondered whether he would already have been slugged on the head and hauled off to jail for making false accusations if he hadn't been an American.

He was in the middle of explaining the rightfulness of his position, of laying out all the reasons for his full-fledged panic, of carefully explaining why his nurse wouldn't simply have gotten up and *left* with their baby unless she had something bad in mind, when Galina walked into the lobby with Joelle.

EIGHT

Hours after Paul had apologized to the police, the concierge, and Galina – in that order – then apologized to Galina *again,* just to make sure she understood how sorry he was, he lay on the bed with Joanna and wondered aloud if paranoia wasn't part of the strange new province of parenthood.

'We're in a foreign country, Paul,' Joanna said, and Paul couldn't help thinking she was right figuratively as well. 'We came into our room and our baby was gone. She didn't tell us she was taking her. *No.*'

In point of fact, Galina *had* told them that she was taking Joelle. She'd left a note tucked under the cream-colored ashtray in the bathroom – when they got back upstairs, Galina had gone in and retrieved it. Perhaps if they hadn't been so quick to panic, they would've seen it. And known that Joelle had woken up from her nap just two seconds after Paul had closed the door. And that her forehead had felt just a little hot to Galina – not dangerously feverish, no, but a little hot, and that Galina wasn't the type to take chances. And they would've known that among the things they *hadn't* brought with them from New York was a thermometer. For which Galina had taken Joelle in search of a pharmacy. To purchase with her own money.

As it turned out, Joelle had a 101-degree temperature. Nothing to worry about with a baby, Galina reassured them, but something that had definitely needed to be checked out.

Galina forgave them, yet he noted an unmistakable glimmer of hurt in those soft gray eyes. Even anger. Something that said even saintly patience has its limits.

The next day Pablo took them to the U.S. Embassy.

When they entered the outer gate, where they were forced to walk through not one, but two metal detectors, they passed a familiar face coming the opposite way.

The bird-watcher. The somnolent man who'd patiently sat for eighteen hours on the plane with them.

'Hello,' he greeted them. He was already wearing the uniform of the bush. A safari shirt with large pleated pockets, khaki knee-length shorts, and thick brown hiking boots.

'Hello,' Paul said.

'Ahh,' he said, repositioning his glasses and staring down at Joelle as if she were a new species of Colombian finch. 'Yours?'

'Yes,' Joanna said. 'Her name's Joelle.'

'Well, congrats,' he said.

'Thanks,' Paul said. It was nice to run into someone from back home – even if it was someone he'd known for eighteen hours. 'We need to get a little paperwork done so we can take her home. How about you?'

'How about me what?'

'The embassy?'

'Oh, if you want to go into the jungle, you have to sign a release. They don't want your next of kin complaining they were negligent and didn't warn you. I think what they really don't want is anybody suing them.'

'Well, good luck,' Paul said.

'Yeah. You too.'

When they entered the spacious anteroom, they passed under a portrait of a smiling George Bush. It didn't really sound like an embassy, though, more like a nursery at feeding time. The room was crammed with couples holding, rocking, shushing, and changing a varied array of agitated Colombian babies. If running into the ornithologist was a welcome reminder of home, this was more like an actual homecoming. All the new parents were, of course, American. Joanna and Paul managed to find two seats next to a thirty-something couple from Texas. Paul *assumed* that they were from Texas because the man was wearing a T-shirt that said *God Bless Texas*. When the man said *howdy*, it was more or less confirmed. His wife was holding a baby boy with a noticeable harelip. Paul immediately chided himself, ashamed that his first impression of the boy hadn't been whether he was big or small or shy or friendly, no – he couldn't help zeroing in on the boy's physical imperfection.

He was kind of disappointed in himself. But as he looked around the room, he thought it was possible that he wasn't the only one doing some comparison shopping.

Every parent seemed to be mentally taking notes. Perhaps it was the nature of being handed a ready-made kid.

They were called into a fluorescent-lit room where a dour-looking Colombian woman asked them for Joelle's birth certificate. Which didn't, of course, say *Joelle* on it. Paul hadn't really known what the birth certificate said, since it was entirely in Spanish. Among the Spanish words was apparently the baby's name – the one given to her by her birth mother.

'Marti,' the woman said as she scribbled something down.

The biological mother was a complete unknown to them. María Consuelo had offered them information about her, which they'd promptly and politely declined. It was a kind of denial mechanism, they knew, a sophomoric one at that. It went something like this: If they didn't know about the mother, she wouldn't really exist. And if she didn't really exist, it would be easier to believe that Joelle was all theirs.

The woman asked them a few questions. Her manner was polite but aloof. Paul, on the lookout for any antipathy from the natives, was unable to read anything particularly malicious in her line of questioning. Still, he was relieved when the interrogation was over.

'YOUR BABY'S COMPLETELY HEALTHY,' THE DOCTOR SAID.

Their second stop of the day.

Adopted babies needed to undergo a medical exam before they were allowed to leave the country. Pablo had driven them to a pediatrician near the hotel.

Dr Dalliego was middle-aged, balding, and coolly efficient. He weighed, poked, and prodded Joelle with machinelike detachment as Paul and Joanna stood by with mute anxiety. Was it possible the physician would find something wrong with her? Her modest fever had disappeared this morning as quickly as it had come, but was there something that the orphanage had missed? Something that would necessitate returning her and leaving Colombia empty-handed and brokenhearted?

Occasionally, the nurse would interrupt the doctor with a telephone call, and he'd hand Joelle back to Joanna while he patiently listened to some other baby's mother or father pour out their fears. He'd calmly utter a few words of Spanish into the receiver, nod in a kind of affirmation of his wisdom, return the phone to the nurse.

Then back to the baby at hand.

After a while Paul grew tired of looking for clues in the doctor's expression. He decided he'd simply wait for the final verdict.

Which was apparently first-rate. *Your baby's completely healthy,* Dr Dalliego said. *She's fine.*

Which was more than you could say for her father.

Paul finally allowed himself to exhale.

NINE

They were back in the hotel room.

Galina had left for the day. Joelle was asleep in her crib. Slats of amber light were slanting in through the window.

He'd remember this exact moment for a long time. Just about forever. He'd remember the way it looked – how the rays of light crisscrossed the bedspread and seemed to cleave Joanna's naked leg in two. He'd take a photo of this moment and paste it into the album of very bad things.

Joanna was lying half in and half out of the bedsheets, staring straight up at the ceiling. She looked kind of morose.

Once upon a time Paul had resisted asking Joanna why she looked unhappy, because he always knew what the answer would be, and it always involved him. He was hoping things were different now – that the two of them were positively *suffused* with happiness – so he went ahead and asked.

'What's wrong?'

'You're going to think I'm crazy,' she said.

'No, I'm not.'

'Yes, you are. You don't know what I'm thinking. It's ridiculous.'

'Yes, I do. You're thinking I'm going to think you're crazy.'

'Besides that.'

'What, Joanna?'

'It's nuts.'

'Okay, it's nuts. Tell me.'

'She smells different.'

'What? *Who?*'

'Joelle. She smells different.'

'Different than what?'

'Different than . . . before.'

Paul didn't know quite how to answer that.

'So?'

'*So?*'

'So she smells different. I'm not –'

'Don't you understand what I'm saying?'

'No.'

Joanna rolled onto her side and faced him. 'I don't think it's *her*.'

'What?'

'*I don't think it's her,*' clearly enunciating each word this time so he'd know exactly what it was she was saying. Which was clearly and patently, well . . . nuts.

'Joanna – of course it's her. We took her to the doctor today. You were with her the whole day. Are you . . . ?'

'Crazy?'

'I wasn't going to say that,' Paul said. Of course, that's exactly what he was going to say. 'I just . . . I mean, it's just so . . . She's Joelle.'

56

'How do you know?'

'What do you mean how do I know?'

'It's a simple question. How do you *know* it's Joelle?'

'Because I've been with her two days. Because . . . it *looks* like her.'

'She's one month old. How many other babies have you seen here that look exactly like her?'

'None.'

'Fine. Well, I have.'

'Joanna, because she *smells* different? Don't you think it's kind of . . . paranoid?'

'You mean like when we thought Galina kidnapped her?'

'Yes.'

'Maybe we weren't being paranoid. Maybe Galina *did* kidnap her.'

'Do you hear what you're saying? Do you? It's ridiculous.'

'You didn't think it was ridiculous yesterday.'

'Yes, I didn't think it was ridiculous yesterday. That was before Galina came *back* with her. She had a fever, so Galina went to get her a thermometer. Remember?'

'Joelle didn't have a fever when we went for a walk, did she?'

'How do we know that?'

'Because I'm her mother. I held her before we left. She was fine.'

'Babies get fevers, honey.'

Joanna sat up. She took Paul's hands in hers – her palms felt cold and clammy.

'Look. Joelle had a beauty mark on her left leg. Right

57

here.' She reached over and touched his leg, just below the knee. It nearly made him jump. 'I saw it. I felt it. When you fell asleep the first night, I went to her crib and just . . . well, looked at her. I couldn't believe we *had* her. I woke up and thought I was dreaming maybe. I had to see her again. To know she was real. You understand?'

Paul nodded.

'Okay. When the doctor examined her today, I didn't *see* it. I told myself *maybe you're wrong, maybe you didn't really see a beauty mark before.* It was dark in the room. Maybe it was a speck of dirt, a smudge. Only . . . all day today I was thinking that she smelled different than she did before.'

'Honey . . .'

'Listen to me. Please.' She squeezed his hands, as if she were trying to physically press her belief into him, as if it were something that could be caught, like a disease. Only he didn't want her disease. He wanted her to stop this, to go back to being the ecstatic new mother who woke up in the middle of the night just so she could gaze at her daughter. 'Joelle had this . . . I don't know, musky smell. She had it when we picked her up at the orphanage, and she had it here. She stopped having it when Galina brought her back.'

'Okay. Why didn't you say anything then?'

'Because I knew you'd think I was crazy. Just like you're thinking now. I told *myself* I was crazy. But I didn't see the beauty mark today. So maybe I'm not.'

'Why would she switch babies, Joanna? Why? For what earthly reason?' Paul was trying to make her see how silly this all was. Belief was immune to logic; it operated by its own laws. And this scared him, if only because there was a tiny part of him that was, well . . . starting to listen to her. The fact was, Joelle *had* smelled a little musky. Now that Joanna had mentioned it, okay, yes, she had.

'I don't know why she'd switch babies, Paul. Maybe because of our fight.'

'What fight? You mean about putting her to sleep?'

Joanna nodded.

'That's ridiculous.'

'Okay, it's ridiculous. I'm ridiculous. I just think that two days from now we're going to be leaving this country with the wrong baby. Then it'll be too late.'

'What do you want me to do, Joanna? Even if I believed you. What would I tell the police? *What?* That I know we apologized to them for insisting our daughter had been kidnapped, but guess what, now we think she was *switched*?'

'We can go back to Santa Regina,' Joanna said. 'We can have them check her out for us.'

'And what do you think María would say about that? How stable would she think we are? How much would she want us to have one of her babies? Nothing's final yet, Joanna. They can still take Joelle back.'

'This baby's not Joelle.'

'I happen to disagree with you. Okay? I happen to think she is. Because the alternative makes no sense. None. Listen to yourself. You're basing this on a *smell,* for chrissakes. On something you *think* you saw in the middle of the night.'

'Let me ask you something, okay?' Joanna said.

No, he wanted to say – it's not okay.

59

'Let's say there's a one percent chance I'm right.'

'What?'

'That's fair, isn't it? One percent?'

'Look, I –'

'I'm asking you a simple question. You want to attack me with logic, fine, I understand. So I'm asking you a logical question. You love percentages, don't you? You're an actuary – pretend it's one of your insurance charts. Is there a one percent chance I'm right?'

'You want me to put a percentage on something I think is totally ridiculous?'

'Yes, I want you to put a percentage on something you think is totally ridiculous.'

'Okay, fine – there's a one percent chance she's not Joelle. And a ninety-nine percent chance she is.'

'Okay. Are you willing to leave the country with even the *chance* she's not ours?'

For a moment he was going to say Joelle wasn't theirs anyway – because in the usual God-given sense, she wasn't. But he couldn't say it. It wasn't true anymore. From the second he'd clasped her to his chest, she'd become theirs.

She was their daughter.

So now what?

TEN

It seemed an eternity before Galina opened her door.

Maybe because Paul was no clearer about what he was going to say to her than he was before, and so was standing there frantically trying to come up with something. In addition to hoping she wouldn't be home, that no one would actually answer Pablo's knock.

Pablo had driven the three of them to Galina's house in the Chapinero district, a working-class area of dun-colored apartment buildings and modest homes. When they'd slid into the backseat, Joanna hadn't taken their daughter from Paul's arms as she normally had in the two days they'd been with her.

She was making a statement.

This isn't my daughter. You hold her.

Well, Paul thought, they'd see.

'Hello, Galina,' Paul said when the door finally opened.

She seemed surprised to see them, but not in a way Paul construed as alarmed. In fact, she smiled, then leaned over and whispered a sweet hello to her very favorite baby. Paul felt like turning to Joanna and saying *see, satisfied now?*

Joanna didn't look any different than she had during the ride over, which was nervous and unhappy.

Galina invited them in.

The door opened onto a small living room. It had a brown leather couch and two worn but comfortable-looking chairs facing a television. A lumbering yellow dog barely shifted from its sprawled position on the floor. Galina had been watching a soap opera; at least Paul assumed that's what it was. A perfect-looking young woman was kissing a perfect-looking young man.

'Please sit,' Galina said, gesturing to the couch. *Do you see this,* Paul kept up his running, albeit silent commentary to Joanna, *she's inviting us in. She's asking us to sit on her couch.*

Galina brought out cookies and four cups of industrial-strength Colombian coffee in what must have been her fine china. She turned down the TV.

They made small talk.

'How did the baby sleep last night?' Galina asked.

'Fine,' Paul answered. 'She woke up once around two, I think, and then went right back.'

'You're lucky. She's a good sleeper.'

'Yes,' Paul said. Joanna remained conspicuously silent.

'You have a lovely house, Galina,' Paul said, continuing to search for anything to talk about except the actual reason for their visit.

'Thank you.'

'What's your dog's name?' he asked.

'Oca,' Galina said. At the sound of his name the dog lifted his head and sniffed the air.

'Did Pablo take you to the doctor yesterday?' Galina asked.

'Yes.'

'And what did he say?'

'Everything's fine.'

'Wonderful,' Galina said. She smiled; her laugh lines fairly cackled.

Then Joanna spoke.

'Her fever was gone.'

'That's good,' Galina said.

'I wonder what it *was*?' Joanna added.

'Who knows?' Galina lifted her hands up in the universal gesture of the human limitation to understanding the mysteries of the universe.

Which is what Joanna was trying to do, of course. Understand, at least, one mystery.

Paul knew that he was expected to take over.

If he sat back and said nothing, Joanna would accuse him of nonsupport, of aiding and abetting the enemy. Except the enemy was treating them to coffee and cookies and the general hospitality of her home. The enemy had run to a *farmacia* to buy Joelle a thermometer when she was sick. Still, he was counted on to do certain things. Support her, for example. Something he hadn't done when she'd insisted Joelle, the *real* Joelle in her mind, had been put to sleep the wrong way. Something he was firmly and unquestioningly expected to do now.

'Uh, Galina . . . we were wondering about something,' he started.

'Yes?'

'This is going to sound a little silly, okay?'

'Okay.' Galina repeated his American slang with evident amusement.

'My wife . . . both of us, really, have noticed this difference. About Joelle.'

'Difference. What do you mean difference?'

'Well, I said this is going to sound silly, but the fact is, she kind of smells different. Than she did before.'

'*Smells?*' She looked over at Pablo, as if for confirmation she'd heard him correctly. Apparently, she had. Pablo looked as confused as she did.

'She had this kind of musky smell,' Paul blundered on, 'and now she doesn't. It seemed to change after, uh . . . when we thought she was . . . when you went to get her the thermometer.'

'Yes?'

'We were just wondering about it,' Paul said. 'That's all.'

'All right.'

Evidently, Galina still had no idea what he was talking about.

'We were hoping maybe you can account for it?'

'Account for what?'

'Why she seems to be . . . different.'

Galina put her cup of coffee back down on its china saucer. The sound seemed to echo unnaturally. Maybe because the room had suddenly turned uncomfortably quiet, the only sound a vague murmur emanating from the lowered TV. If the five of them were on that soap opera, Paul thought, there'd be a dissonant organ chord now to signify the portent of something dramatic. In this case, Galina's growing realization that she was being accused, albeit clumsily, of something she still didn't understand.

'What are you saying?' she asked now. 'Are you suggesting . . . *what?*'

'Nothing, Galina,' Paul said, a little too quickly. 'We were just curious, that's all.'

'About *what*?'

'About why she smells different.'

'I don't understand. What are you asking me?'

We're asking you if you stole our baby, Galina. If you switched her.

'Nothing.'

'Then why are you here?'

Paul felt like asking Joanna that himself.

'We wanted to know . . . ,' and here Paul suddenly went blank.

'She had a beauty mark,' Joanna said.

'What?' Galina turned to look at Joanna.

'She had a beauty mark when we got her. It's not there now.'

'Beauty mark?'

'My daughter had a beauty mark on her left leg. And she used to smell like . . . well, like her. The beauty mark's gone. She smells different. *I want to know if it's the same baby.*'

Okay, Paul thought, Xena, warrior princess, was in full battle mode. The cat had been let out of the bag. Only it wasn't a cat as much as a Tasmanian devil, something large, carnivorous, and repulsive-looking. Probably the way the two of them looked to Galina right at this moment. After all, her back had physically stiffened – one of those clichés that evidently rang true. Her gentle gray eyes had turned hard as glass.

Paul found himself trying to look anywhere but at her, searching for a hole he might be able to hide in.

65

There was a box of cigars sitting on her mantel.

It had a photograph of a man in a white panama hat.

Paul wondered if Galina smoked cigars. A pair of brown slippers nestled like cats on her front welcome mat. The dog, who'd roused itself from its semicomatose state, had picked up one in his mouth, then dropped it by Pablo's feet, where it landed with an uncomfortable thud.

He forced himself to turn back to Galina. She still hadn't said anything – Joanna's accusation had turned her mute. She looked more or less horrified.

Later, much later, Paul would wonder if there's such a thing as peripheral hearing. Something that impinges on the ear but only announces itself later on.

He was trying not to stare at Galina's pained expression. He was wondering whether he should apologize to her. He didn't notice the muffled sound emanating from the inner recesses of the house.

Galina did. Which accounted for her expression.

Joanna had noticed it too.

Because she reached out and dug her fingernails into his arm. He almost cried out. Which would've made it two people crying in the house instead of just one.

Him and the baby.

There was a baby crying in the house.

He'd finally heard it.

He'd finally processed it. Because when he looked down at Joelle, she was sleeping. Which meant that there was a baby crying in the house, yes, only it wasn't this baby.

'Who's that?' That's the first thing he said. Stupid, okay, but then, he was obviously a little slow on the uptake today.

Galina didn't answer him.

'Whose baby is that?' he said, even though he was starting to have a good idea whose baby it might be.

'Pablo. Can you go see who it is?'

Pablo didn't move.

'Galina?'

She hadn't changed expression. Or maybe she had. The hardness in her eyes was still there, and there was something else now, a scary sense of focus and fortitude.

'Galina, is that our daughter? Is that *Joelle*?'

It took Paul a while to realize that Pablo *still* hadn't moved. That Galina still wasn't answering him.

Paul stood up with the baby in his arms – the question was, *whose* baby? He felt faint. 'Okay, I'm going to see who it is.' Announcing his plan out loud as if seeking approval.

He reached out to give Joelle to Galina and then, of course, stopped himself. Galina wasn't exactly his nurse anymore; it was possible this baby wasn't Joelle. He felt as if he were teetering on the edge of a deep and dangerous abyss – physically and emotionally hovering right over the edge. The room itself seemed to be swaying.

Then things flew into motion.

Joanna stood up and said *I'll go look,* and immediately began walking toward the sound of the crying baby. Pablo roused himself from his chair.

Paul offered up the baby in his arms so he could go join his wife, but it seemed to take an enormous effort to lift her.

'Sit down, Paul,' Pablo said gently.

He was offering to look himself. He was telling Paul to sit down and take care of the baby. Pablo was being Pablo.

Paul gratefully reclaimed his seat as Pablo followed Joanna into the hall. The baby was crying louder, screeching even. And Paul finally and completely acknowledged what Joanna had feared was true.

He *recognized* that crying.

He remembered it from the first day in the hotel room when their daughter had wailed endlessly for food. Until Galina had shown up and made everything all right again.

Galina was still stiffly seated in her chair – only she appeared to be physically closer to him than she'd been before. How was that possible?

For a minute or so nothing happened.

The baby continued to cry from somewhere in the house; Galina continued to stare at him with an odd and unsettling calm.

Then Pablo reappeared, walking back into the living room while supporting Joanna with one strong arm. She was leaning against him, her head laid back on his shoulder as if she were very close to fainting. Where was the baby?

Joanna clearly looked distraught, while Pablo appeared helpful. There was undoubtedly a causal connection between those two things, but Paul wasn't sure what it was.

Something was wrong.

Look closer.

Her head on his shoulder. It took Paul a few seconds – seconds in which the world changed from A to Z – to understand that the reason it was lying back on Pablo's shoulder like that was that Pablo had his wife's dark luxuriant hair wrapped tightly in his fist.

Pablo was pulling Joanna into the room by her hair.

Her mouth was open in a half-muted scream.

He threw Joanna down onto the couch, flung her backward as if she were a piece of luggage he'd thrown into the car at El Dorado Airport.

'*Sit,*' he said. The way one barks commands at a dog. A stupid, stubborn dog, a dog who should know better.

Paul felt rooted to the couch, a spectator to a horrifying drama that had suddenly and inexplicably become real. He was waiting for the intermission, when he could stretch his legs, shake the cobwebs out of his brain, and thank the cast for their stunningly convincing performance. The play continued.

Galina stood up.

She methodically began closing the wooden shutters on each side of the room as she talked to Pablo in a steady stream of Spanish. As if he and Joanna weren't even in the room. She seemed to be chastising him – Paul's Spanish was beginning to come back like a long-repressed memory, and it seemed like he could understand every fifth word or so. *You. Called. Not here.* For one regrettably stupid moment Paul wondered if she was yelling at Pablo for throwing Joanna down on the couch like that.

For not getting their baby.

For *turning* on them.

But that was like hoping you're asleep and dreaming when you're completely and terrifyingly awake.

Paul handed the baby to Joanna – the baby he'd thought was his daughter and that he now knew wasn't – and stood up to protest Pablo's treatment of his wife, to reason this out, to get Joelle and have Pablo take them back to the hotel this instant.

'I told you to sit down, Paul,' Pablo said.

Somehow he delivered this statement over Paul's prone body. This was an enormous surprise to Paul. That he wasn't standing. He was lying down on a wooden floor smelling of wet fur and shoe polish. *How had that happened?* He heard Joanna's sharp intake of breath.

'I'm okay, honey,' he said. Oddly enough, he didn't hear the words. His tongue was strangely obstinate; it had decided to lie down on the job. Just like the rest of his body, which felt absurdly heavy. There was a strange metallic taste in his mouth.

He tried to lift himself up from the floor. No go. He felt vibrations traveling through the floorboards, some kind of rebalancing of weight from one place to another. He heard heavy shuffling and sensed a quickening in the air itself.

They looked like marines.

Five men in mottled green uniforms who'd suddenly flowed into the room like a brackish river breaching its banks. Young faces with stolid expressions of dumb determination. Each of them carried a rifle.

'Please,' Paul said.

The room was eerily dark; Galina had closed all the shutters but one. It felt like the moment before everyone yells *surprise*.

The surprise is for us, Paul thought.

Then he passed out.

ELEVEN

Blackness.

But not completely. There were endless visions and dreams flickering through the blackness. Like being in a movie theater for a very long time.

He was eleven years old and suddenly afraid of the dark. He hadn't been afraid before, but he was *now*. Maybe because it was dark at the top of the stairs where his mother had recently taken up residence. Not just dark – a thick, suffocating blackness like a wool blanket pulled up over his head. *Your mother's resting,* his father told him. *She's sleeping. Don't disturb her.*

He crept up the stairs, where it smelled unpleasantly medicinal. He listened outside the door and heard the distinct sounds of a TV game show: a buzzer, a voice, phony audience laughter.

His mom wasn't sleeping, after all. It would be okay to open the door and crawl into her arms. But the darkness inside the room was even gloomier than the darkness outside in the hall. Only the soft glow coming from the portable TV with sadly bent rabbit ears made seeing possible at all.

It took him a while before he could make out the monster lying on the bed.

Last Halloween he'd gone trick-or-treating as a skeleton – all black, except for the white bones where his arms and legs were supposed to be.

It looked like that.

In the dream this skeleton lifted up a bony arm and waved for him to come closer.

Eventually, he woke up. Movie over.

'Morning,' the boy said.

Just as he'd said it every morning since they'd taught it to him. Not on purpose. When Paul had finally opened his eyes after losing consciousness on Galina's floor, the boy was there listening when he asked Joanna what time it was. Was it *morning*? The boy repeated it several times as if trying it out. Now he used it to greet them.

This morning, which was either the third or fourth morning they'd been here, the boy waited for some kind of verbal acknowledgment.

'Good morning,' Joanna said.

Then the boy placed their breakfast – corn cakes and sausage – on the floor and left.

They were in a house somewhere in Colombia.

It was impossible to know *where* in Colombia, since they weren't allowed out. The windows were boarded over. They could hear little from outside – the distant rumble of passing cars, occasional disembodied melodies trickling through from God knows where, a parrot squawking. All they knew was that it wasn't *Galina's* house.

72

They'd been transported somewhere else.

A claustrophobic room with a filthy mattress on the floor and two plastic chairs. There was a bucket in the corner.

That's it.

That first morning, Joanna had woken before Paul. When she couldn't rouse him – apparently, she attempted everything but jumping up and down on him – she'd tried opening the door. Locked tight. She managed to pry open a shutter, only to see solid wood staring back.

When Paul finally and groggily woke up, he was greeted with the sight of Joanna rocking herself back and forth in the middle of the floor. 'Oh God,' she was murmuring, 'oh God . . .'

He'd tried to comfort her, of course, even as he attempted to make sense of what had happened, to fight through a stultifying haze that seemed to have wrapped itself around his head. She seemed oddly distant, even with his arms enclosing her, as if she were obstinately holding a piece of herself back. He thought he knew why.

'I'm sorry, Joanna,' he said. 'For not believing you.'

'Yes. Okay. Great.'

'It seemed ridiculous. Switching babies. I couldn't imagine . . .'

'Where is she, Paul?' she cut him off. 'What do they want?'

It was a hard question to answer.

The first day they saw no one but the boy. He was dressed in mottled green camouflage like the others. He carried a rifle that seemed far too big for him. He might've been all of fourteen. Except for his *good mornings*, he remained mute.

The next afternoon they were finally visited by someone higher up the food chain. A man in his mid-thirties, a face Paul thought he recognized from Galina's house, just before he'd found himself staring at the ceiling.

'Look, we're not *political*,' Paul said when the man entered the room and locked the door behind him. 'I work in insurance.' This reminded him of something else. 'We aren't rich.'

The man turned and looked at him. 'You think we're *bandidos*?' His English was passable. He had what looked like a Kalashnikov looped around his shoulder, but he seemed neither violent nor unsympathetic.

'Where's my baby?' Joanna said. 'I want my baby back. Please.'

'I think I ask the questions here,' he said, not particularly rudely. Just as an unequivocal statement of fact.

'You've been captured by FARC,' he said, 'the Revolutionary Armed Forces of Colombia,' spelling it out for them in case they weren't up on their acronyms. 'We are the legitimate voice of the Colombian people.' Paul thought it sounded like a speech he'd made hundreds of times before. 'You are our political prisoners. *Comprende?*'

Paul said, 'We can't help you. I told you, we're not political. We have no *money . . .*'

He was interrupted by a rifle butt to his midsection. Delivered with enough force and precision to bring him straight to his knees.

'*Paul!*' Joanna recoiled, the obvious reaction when your husband is physically assaulted right in front of your eyes.

'When I ask a question, answer me,' the man said. 'You must remember this.'

Paul attempted to get up, for Joanna's sake, if not his own. He felt her fear as if it were a physical entity, cold and dense and implacable. But he couldn't straighten up; his stomach was on fire. His eyes were tearing.

'You are political prisoners of the Revolutionary Armed Forces of Colombia. *Comprende?*

'Yes,' Paul said, still on his knees, still gasping from the vicious blow to his solar plexus.

'You won't try to escape. *Comprende?*

'Yes.' Paul gave it one more try, gathered himself in an effort to scale what seemed like a sheer wall of pain, and finally managed to make it to a barely standing position.

'You step away from the door when we come in the room. You step away from the door when we leave. You stay away from the windows. Yes?'

'Yes, we understand.'

'How are you feeling?' He was addressing Joanna.

'I'm nauseous.' Her voice shaky if even-toned, as if she were desperately trying to maintain some semblance of composure, but pretty much failing. 'I feel like throwing up.'

He nodded as if he'd expected this. *'Escopolamina,'* he said.

'What?' Joanna asked, breaking the don't-ask-questions rule, this time apparently without consequences.

'A street drug. They use it to rob the *turistas* here.' He shook his head and uttered a dismissive sigh, as if that kind of thing – robberies and such – was beneath him. 'We were late – she was frightened, huh.'

Galina, Paul thought. He was referring to Galina.

'She put something into our coffee,' Joanna stated flatly.

The man shrugged. 'You'll feel better tomorrow. Pretty much.'

He turned and walked to the door, then hesitated there as if waiting for someone to open it. He turned and stared at them with an expression of clear expectance.

What?

'Oh,' Paul said. He took Joanna's hand and led her to the opposite wall.

'Good,' he said, as if addressing children who'd cleaned their room just like they'd been told to.

He walked out, locked the door behind him.

THEY SPENT MOST OF THEIR TIME ALONE REMINISCING.

They took turns remembering all the things they liked about New York. Even things that, oddly, they hadn't liked before – holiday crowds, for instance. The swarm of visitors that executes a stranglehold on the city from Thanksgiving to Christmas, creating bottlenecks from Times Square to Houston Street. Paul had always found the human traffic jams annoying and suffocating, only now he remembered them as joyous and even soothing. The inescapable smell of garbage waiting to be picked up was an aroma to be missed and cherished. The obstacle course of construction cranes, pothole barriers, and squat Con Ed vans every New York taxi was forced to navigate on its way from one side of the city to the other was a loop-de-loop of urban excitement.

It was all a matter of perspective. And right now their perspective was skewed through a rat hole in Colombia.

They remembered places outside the city too. They re-traced every single one of their vacations.

The rough-hewn cabin in Yosemite, where they'd gone when they were just dating but already moon-eyed. The Sea Crest Motel in Montauk that opened onto the whitest sand they'd ever seen. The ridiculously expensive but extravagantly lovely George V in Paris – honeymoon heaven.

They tried to reconstruct every great meal they'd ever eaten – Prudhommes to Pinks. Eclectic appetizers, bountiful entrées, sugary-sweet desserts.

They recounted their first meeting – two tired business travelers sharing the same gate. They theorized what the odds were of running into each other like that, of falling in love, of getting married.

They did all of this as a way to pass the time.

They talked about the past so they could avoid thinking about the future. There was an air of complete and utter unreality about this. Was this *really* happening to them – it couldn't be, could it? *Kidnapped?* Someone was going to yell *stop* and it was all going to end. It had to. It must.

Better to keep talking about the past.

ON WHAT MUST HAVE BEEN THEIR FOURTH DAY OF CAPTIVITY – IT was hard to keep count – Joanna said, 'Why do you think they told us not to go near the windows?'

Paul, who'd gradually descended into listlessness, barely managed a shrug.

'Because we must be where people could see us,' Joanna answered her own question. 'We must still be in Bogotá.'

'Okay.'

'We might be right on a street somewhere.'

Paul didn't like where this conversation was heading. Joanna had that *look,* the I'm-ready-to-tackle-something look. The one he'd seen when she was going up against an entrenched superior, a human resources transgressor, the very look she got when she'd decided that hell or high water, she was going to have a baby.

'There's just wood on the windows,' she said. 'We can pry it off.'

'With what?'

'I don't know. Our hands.'

'I don't think we ought to do that.'

'Really? What *ought* we to do, then? Sit around and do nothing?'

Yes, Paul thought. So far, they hadn't been told anything – why they were there, what was in store for them. The only thing that had actually been communicated to them was *not* to go near the windows. They'd been told *that.*

'Stay by the door and listen,' Joanna said. 'If you hear them coming, I'll stop.'

This was where he was supposed to volunteer for wood-prying duty. Or say *no* – it's too dangerous, forget it, let's just sit tight.

Joanna didn't appear ready to be talked out of it.

Okay, he'd give it a try. The wood looked pretty well nailed in. One good shake with no results would probably be enough to dissuade her, send her back to the mattress, where they could continue to reminisce about old times.

Paul said, 'I'll do it.'

Joanna took up sentry duty by the door. Paul moved the shutters back, revealing two solid planks of wood. He thought he could hear faint sounds of traffic out there.

He was able to grip one plank by its bottom. He pulled. There was some give there.

You could see the wood wobble before snapping back into place. Joanna could *certainly* see it.

'I *told* you,' she whispered.

Paul gave it another strong pull. This time the wood gave even more. He'd opened it a good half inch.

Yes, there was definitely traffic out there. Fairly steady too – they had to be close to a major thoroughfare. Somewhere people were going about their perfectly ordinary lives, shopping, eating, heading to work, all within earshot of two kidnapped Americans.

Paul resumed with renewed vigor, gulping in sudden streams of sweet-smelling air. He developed a steady rhythm, pull, rest, pull, rest. Slowly, bit by bit, the wood yawned open; he could see a red slate tile – a courtyard?

Joanna crouched by the door, a bundle of nervous energy urging him on with her eyes.

Suddenly, the wood snapped – broke right in half. It sounded like a gunshot, *louder*, and Paul stood there with half a plank of wood in his hands, waiting for the door to burst open with armed guards.

Joanna stiffened – put her ear to the door. Paul held his breath and waited.

After what seemed an eternity, Joanna shook her head. Nothing.

Paul allowed himself to breathe again.

He took his first actual look out the window.

Yes, it was the courtyard, all right. There was an adobe wall around it, holding several lopsided pots of cacti. A lone wooden table sat in the center of the garden with no chairs around it. And there was something else. A way *in;* a simple wooden gate led to the outside. Paul stared at it. There was a girl in a school uniform staring back.

Paul barely managed to stop himself from yelling *help!*

They were stuck in the room; the window was maybe two by two, and that was with *all* the wood removed. It was anybody's guess if they'd be able to worm their way out.

Paul spoke to Joanna without turning away. He was afraid if he stopped looking at the girl, she'd disappear, like a mirage or a really good dream.

'There's someone out there.'

Joanna immediately abandoned her guard duty, ran to the window.

For a moment the three of them simply stared at each other, as if seeing who would blink first. The girl looked to be eleven or twelve years old, clutching schoolbooks that appeared too heavy for her, and staring wide-eyed at what must have been two desperate-looking Americans staring back.

'*Hola,*' Joanna said to the girl – somewhere between a whisper and normal conversation.

The girl didn't answer.

'*Hola!*' Joanna tried again. She stuck her hand through the window and waved, like a desperate wallflower hoping to be picked at the dance.

She remained on the sidelines. The girl continued to stare at them without offering the slightest response.

It was agonizing. They were staring possible rescue in the face, only that face was decidedly and maddeningly blank.

Paul racked his brain, trying to remember the Spanish word for *help*, but came up empty. Maybe *help* was universal. Maybe the girl took English at school. Maybe . . .

'*Help!*'

He didn't recognize his own voice. It sounded high-pitched and desperate. 'Help,' he said again. 'Please . . . help us . . .'

The girl cocked her head, took a step back.

'We're prisoners,' Paul continued, pushing both hands out the window, wrists together as if they were tied, in a kind of primitive pantomime.

It looked like a glimmer of understanding passed across the girl's face. Then she turned to her left, as if someone had called out to her. She looked back at them, smiled sweetly, walked off.

'*No!*' Paul shouted.

He'd forgotten where he was.

In a locked room. Under armed guard.

It was just a matter of time.

He heard them seconds later. The sound of boots running on tile, of a key being jammed into the door lock, of nervous, angry jabbering.

He desperately tried to put the plank of wood back in the window, to shove it into place and hope they wouldn't notice. Like a child trying to glue a smashed vase back together before his parents make it through the front door. It was useless.

The first man through was the one who'd laid out the rules for them. It obviously didn't escape his attention that they'd broken at least two of them. *Thou shalt not go near the windows. Thou shalt not attempt escape.* For a moment

81

he simply stopped and stared at Paul, who was standing there holding the piece of shattered wood in his hand like a shield. It didn't provide much protection. The man made it over to Paul in three quick strides and smashed him across the face with the rifle butt. Paul's head snapped back and hit the wall. He tasted blood. The piece of wood clattered to the floor.

Paul could see Joanna's ashen face staring back at him. The man swung his rifle again, clipping Paul under the chin. He bit his tongue, tasted bits of broken tooth. He retreated against the wall, hiding his face behind both hands.

'Put them down,' the man said.

This was real power, Paul realized. There wasn't a need to force Paul's hands away; he was going to make Paul do it himself.

'*No,*' Joanna said. 'It's my fault. I *told* him to do it. Leave him alone. *Please.*'

'Put your hands down,' the man repeated.

'I said it's *my* fault.' Joanna tried to insinuate her body between Paul and his attacker. 'Hit me. *Me.*'

The man sighed, shook his head, gathered the neck of Joanna's dress in his fist, lifting her up off the ground.

'If you don't move your hands, I beat her. If you put them there again, I beat her worse.'

Paul dropped his hands.

TWELVE

Sometimes they were given newspapers.

They were allowed this small luxury by the powers-that-be. An *infinitesimal* luxury, since neither of them spoke Spanish. But things were coming back to Paul — dribs and drabs, words and phrases, sometimes entire sentences.

Anyway, it gave them something to do. Paul discovered you needed things to do to keep your mind off the unspoken question of the hour. *What was going to happen to them?*

The boy dropped off whichever newspapers their guards had discarded — mostly of the tabloid variety.

The back pages were filled with the local scores. After a while Paul understood that the front pages were too. It was as if Colombia were one big soccer match, both combatants going goal for goal, playing to the death. Guarding the left goal were their captors, FARC, and guarding the right one, the USDF, with the government ineffectually attempting to referee.

Kidnappings, bombings, and executions were how they kept score.

There was invariably a kidnapping story on the front page. A file picture of the snatched state senator, missing radio personality, or waylaid businessman. (The Breidbarts were conspicuously absent from the gallery of the gone.) There was generally an accompanying photo of the weeping wife, teary children, or somber family spokesperson.

The Spanish word for kidnapping was *secuestro*.

Bombings were only a little less frequent. For example: A ten-year-old boy named Orlando Ropero who liked soccer and *ventello* music was asked to deliver a bicycle by a teenager in the town of Fortul. He was given the equivalent of thirty-five cents as an inducement. When the bicycle and bicyclist, an excited and gratified Orlando, reached an intersection where two soldiers were stationed, he simply exploded. *Remote control,* said the papers.

Responsibility was placed at the doorstep directly to Paul's left. FARC. He decided to keep this particular article to himself.

Then there were the obligatory retaliatory bombings from the right: the paramilitary units of the United Self-Defense Forces, *self-defense* apparently consisting of killing as many people as possible with no particular regard for innocence. The generalissimo of this august organization for law and order was currently residing in a U.S. prison for drug smuggling.

Paul had read about Manuel Riojas in the States, of course.

Who *was* he exactly? Drug kingpin, legitimate politician, USDF commander, songwriter. He was one of those, two of those, or possibly all four. Certainly a songwriter. He'd reputedly written a number one hit for the Colombian songbird Evi, which had gotten some play in the States. A love song titled 'I Sing Only for You.' A title that took on ironic implications when she was discovered lying half dead on the floor of her penthouse apartment with her vocal cords surgically removed. Apparently, the lovers had experienced a falling-out. Evi had declined to press charges – *I don't remember,* she'd scrawled on a pad when she was asked to explain who'd done that to her.

Murder and torture were said to be Riojas' other vocations.

He was one of those people whose names were always followed by the word *alleged.* It was *alleged,* for example, that he had his own zoo on one of his many haciendas, used to *allegedly* feed his rivals to the tigers. That he *allegedly* enjoyed dropping people from a Blackhawk helicopter into a pool of writhing piranhas. That he offered human sacrifices in bloody and bizarre rites of Santeria – that was *alleged* too. He was clearly the stuff of tabloids; the tabloids took full and voracious advantage.

Paul and Joanna passed the newspapers back and forth till the ink stained their hands and their eyes grew blurry.

ONE NIGHT JOANNA WOKE PAUL AND ASKED HIM TO LOOK IN ON the baby.

It took Paul a moment to understand that she was deluded.

That they weren't in the hotel room sleeping next to Joelle, but in a locked room with no air.

His face stung where the man had repeatedly smashed him with the rifle butt, a beating that had lasted at least five minutes and felt much longer. He'd lost at least one tooth; his lip was split open and still covered in dried blood. Afterward, they'd had to watch contritely from the center of the floor as two guards came in and hammered a new piece of wood back into place, muttering at them the whole time.

'Shhh,' Paul whispered to Joanna. 'You're sleeping.'

She opened her eyes.

'I thought I heard . . .' She began to cry. Soft, muffled sobs that seemed even more nakedly pitiable with no other sounds around to cloak them.

Paul put his arms around her. 'Please, Joanna. We'll get out of this. They're not going to kill us – they had their chance when they caught us at the window. We're going to get out of here. We're going to get Joelle back. I promise.'

He wondered if promising Joanna anything was a good idea. But hope was the one commodity that hadn't been taken away from them. Not yet.

Then she did a strange thing. She stopped crying and disentangled herself from his arms. She put a finger to his lips.

'Listen,' she whispered.

'What? I don't hear anything,' he said. Only the sound of their breathing. Soft, regular, and strangely in sync.

'Listen,' she said again.

Then he heard it.

'It's the TV,' he said.

'Maybe it's real.'

'Probably not. No.'

'Listen, Paul. Listen. It's *her*.'

A baby crying.

Just like in Galina's house, only different than Galina's house.

'I know,' Joanna said. 'I just *know*.'

In Galina's house the sound of a baby crying had frightened them.

Here it had exactly the opposite effect.

She wrapped herself around him in the dark. She put her head on his chest, and both of them lay there and listened to the sound as if it were a beautiful rhapsody. As if it were their song.

IN THE MORNING THE MAN CAME BACK.

This time he wasn't alone.

Someone of evident importance was with him. Paul could tell from the way his attacker deferred to him. His role had changed; he was there to interpret now.

This became clear when the new man looked at Paul and Joanna and said something in Spanish.

'He asked you to sit down,' their original captor said.

Paul knew what the man had asked them to do. But he was still smarting from his previous beating. He thought it better to think things over before committing to even the simplest action. The man had asked them to sit, fine – maybe it was better to make *sure* he wanted them to sit. Joanna had remained stationary for another reason, he knew. Sheer willfulness, courage in the face of fire.

The man motioned them to the two plastic chairs. Once upon a time those chairs must've sat in the courtyard, that heavenly vista they'd fleetingly glimpsed before it disappeared again behind newly nailed oak. Dirt was ingrained in the white plastic, the kind that accumulates after too many winters spent outdoors.

They sat.

The man in charge spoke to them in soft, measured tones. He focused mostly on Paul, maintaining eye contact between puffs of a thick pungent cigar sending blue plumes of smoke drifting gently up to the ceiling. Paul recognized the brand: the box on Galina's mantelpiece. He had a scraggly beard; his skin was pocked from childhood acne. He spoke entirely in Spanish, at a pace leisurely enough to allow his lieutenant – that's how Paul thought of him now – to translate his words into English.

'This is what you are going to do for us,' the man said. And they finally learned why they were there.

THIRTEEN

There were three boxes of condoms on the table.

A French brand. *Cheval,* the boxes said, over the picture of a white stallion with fiery eyes and windswept mane.

An Indian woman wearing incongruous-looking bifocals was bent over the table, carefully stretching out the condoms one at a time. She was wearing black latex gloves and no top. Just a gray sports bra with a black Nike swoosh on it.

At the other end of the table, another woman wearing black latex gloves and sports bra was methodically chopping up blocks of white powder with a gleaming surgical scalpel. The lieutenant was leaning against the door, eyes fixed on the half-naked women like a man in love.

Paul was sitting against the wall, waiting.

They'd made him give himself two enemas spaced an hour apart. As he waited for the second one to take effect, he stared at the thirty-two bulging condoms already gathered in the middle of the table and tried not to feel sick.

He was reminded of one of those inane reality shows that had so recently swept the country. *Fear Factor* – wasn't that the one? Raw pig brains, bloody offal, cow intestines, laid out on a table before three or four greedy contestants. *Go ahead* – the smarmy host intoned every week – *whoever gets the most down wins.*

And didn't they dive in with unabashed gusto? Didn't they chow down to the last morsel, their eyes firmly on the prize? It helped Paul to think of them. They were his newfound role models. If they could do it, so could he.

After all, he wasn't striving for mere money here. The grand prize on this show was two lives.

His wife's and his daughter's.

Thirty-two condoms became thirty-three. The woman at the end of the table had just added to the pile.

He felt the familiar rumblings in his gut. He asked Arias – that was the lieutenant's name – if he could go to the bathroom.

Arias nodded and beckoned him forward. The women kept working without interruption, assembly line workers who hadn't yet heard the lunch whistle.

Arias opened the door and pushed him out. There was a bathroom just down the hall. Arias watched him as he went in and swung the door shut behind him.

The door didn't make it to the closed position.

Of course not. Arias' booted foot stopped it, just as it had stopped it the first time Paul ran to the bathroom.

The door swung back the other way as Paul sat down on the dirt-streaked toilet seat and tried not to notice Arias watching him. That was kind of hard. He closed his eyes and thought of his bathroom back home, where a dog-eared copy of *The Sporting News Baseball Stats* sat just to the right of the toilet. Not because he particularly liked baseball – he didn't. He liked *stats*. He visualized page 77 – Derek Jeter. Batting average, home runs, RBIs, stolen bases. Numbers *always* told a story, didn't they? It comforted him to think of numbers now. Numbers imposed order on the universe – you could lean on them, take comfort in them. They always added up.

For the second time in an hour, it felt as if every bit of his insides had come out of him. Then, with Arias still watching, he stood up and cleaned himself.

Back to the table. Where three more condoms had been added to the pile.

'*Sí,*' Arias said, staring at Paul and stopping the women in midmotion. 'Start swallowing.'

THIS IS WHAT THE FARC COMMANDER HAD TOLD THEM.

'We are a revolutionary army. We are involved in a long struggle against oppression. We are in need of financing this struggle, so we must do whatever we can.'

Whatever we can turned out to be exporting pure Colombian cocaine to the eastern seaboard of the United States.

That's how he began, as if he were seeking some kind of approval from them. Explaining the distasteful nature of the drug trade as a kind of necessary evil. A means to an end.

When he paused, Paul nodded, even nervously smiled, bestowing a kind of absolution on him. Perhaps that's all he wanted, Paul thought, someone to take the message back to the world.

Yes, we smuggle drugs, but only to further the cause.

Of course, that was stupid. They weren't going to kidnap them to relay their apologies. Of course, Paul hoped otherwise. Up to the minute the man told Paul he'd be swallowing thirty-six condoms stuffed with two million dollars' worth of cocaine and bringing it to a house in Jersey City.

He would do that if he wanted to see his wife and new daughter alive again.

Then and only then did Paul understand the full enormity of their predicament.

Yet there were still things Paul didn't understand.

The man asked him who knew they were here in Colombia – not *everyone,* just the people who kept tabs on them, who'd be expecting them to return on a certain date. Paul told him. Starting with his boss – Ron Samuels, head actuary of the firm he'd called home for the past eleven years. His in-laws, of course, Matt and Barbara, who resided in Minnesota and were due to fly in bearing gifts for their first grandchild. Finally, John and Lisa, their next-door neighbors and best friends.

Paul was ordered to write them letters, pretty much the *same* letter, three times.

Things are taking a little longer than expected down here and it will be a few more weeks before we can return with our adopted daughter – that was the general theme. They made him add a part about there being no need to call, since they'd be running from place to place with little time to chat.

Paul thought, *they don't want anyone to know.* Not yet.

They'd forgotten something, hadn't they?

'Pablo checked you out of L'Esplanade,' Arias said. 'The reservation clerk thinks you changed hotels. That's all.'

So they hadn't.

No one would know they were missing.

Not for weeks.

They gave him three sheets of paper and a blue ball-point pen that someone had virtually chewed the end off of. Paul wrote the letters with Arias hovering over his shoulder, evidently looking for any hidden messages, disguised cries for help.

When Paul finished, Arias read them out loud.

Later that afternoon, as Paul and Joanna sat on the mattress with their backs against the wall, Paul said, 'I think I know why they switched her.'

'What?'

He'd been thinking this through; he thought he understood now. 'Why they switched babies. Why they didn't just wait and take all three of us together.'

'Okay. Why?'

'Remember when Galina came back with the thermometer? You said we hadn't been paranoid, that we were in a foreign country. *Paranoia* is a foreign country, Joanna.'

'I don't understand.'

'Galina took Joelle that day so we would come back and find her gone. So we'd call the police. There was no note – remember, *she* went into the bathroom and found it.'

'Why would they want us to call the police?'

'Because they wanted the police standing there when Galina walked back in.'

'That doesn't make any sense.'

'Sure it does. You're in the country of *paranoia* now, remember? Think like a citizen. They wanted us to cry wolf. They wanted to make us look crazy.'

'Why?'

'Because crazy people have no credibility. Crazy foreigners have even less.'

'I still don't –'

'First we called the police and insisted our baby was kidnapped. Only she wasn't kidnapped. Then we noticed we had the wrong daughter – so she *was*. Only, if we called the police a second time, we would have looked more deranged than before. They *wanted* us to know they'd taken her.'

Joanna seemed to contemplate this notion. 'Okay. What if we *hadn't* noticed? I did – you didn't.'

Paul shrugged. 'If we'd never noticed, they would've called and told us. *We've got your baby – come and get her or else.* Either way, we couldn't have gone to the police without looking like lunatics. Maybe it was a kind of insurance policy: if one of us got away, if they botched the kidnapping, if I'd refused to drink that coffee and never passed out. Who knows? Maybe they were always going to make that call. We were *early*, he said, remember? Galina was yelling at Pablo about something – maybe it was *that*, bringing us there before she was ready.'

'Okay,' Joanna said. 'Why us?'

'Why *not* us? They must pick people they feel no one will bother at customs. The last time I looked, I didn't *look* like a drug smuggler.'

Joanna said, 'You're not a drug smuggler.'

'Not yet.'

She turned to look at him as if to gauge his expression for degree of seriousness. 'You're going to do it?' she asked. It sounded more like a statement.

Paul looked back at his wife. Her face had changed, he thought. Four days of mostly not eating or sleeping had sharpened her cheekbones and dug craters under her eyes. Yet even now when she was hollow-eyed and terrified, he saw something etched there on her face, as if the last few days had removed everything extraneous and left the only thing that really mattered. He'd like to think it was *love*.

'Yes,' he said.

'They'll arrest you. You can spend twenty years in jail for smuggling drugs. You're not a criminal – they'll see right through you.'

Yes, he thought, everything she was saying was true.

'What other options do I have?'

Joanna had no answer. Or maybe she did. She leaned her head against his chest, somewhere in the vicinity of his heart.

Thump, thump, thump.

'What if they're lying? What if they're lying about letting us go?'

Paul had been waiting for that question, of course. He gave the only answer he could.

'What if they're not?'

FOURTEEN

He would have eighteen hours.

Three-quarters of one day. One thousand eighty minutes.

That's it.

In those eighteen hours, he would have to swallow thirty-six condoms filled with two million dollars' worth of pure, undiluted cocaine, take a plane to Kennedy Airport, and get to a house in Jersey City, where he'd be expected to deposit them onto a dirty Newark *Star-Ledger*.

If he made it to the house one minute after the eighteen hours allotted him, Joanna and Joelle would be killed.

If he made it to the house and only thirty-*five* condoms came out of him, Joanna and Joelle would be killed.

If he didn't get the condoms out in time and one of them dissolved inside his stomach, *he'd* be killed.

His heart would go into cardiac arrest, his body into toxic shock.

He'd begin salivating from the mouth and shaking uncontrollably. He'd be dead before anyone knew what was wrong with him.

This was carefully and painstakingly laid out for him by Arias. To get his attention, to have him maintain focus.

A kind of pep talk.

Of course, if he made it to the house in eighteen hours with all thirty-six condoms still inside him, a call would be placed to Arias.

Joanna and Joelle would be set free to join Paul in New York.

They had Arias' word on it, as a FARC revolutionary in good standing.

THE NIGHT BEFORE THEY HAD BROUGHT HIM TO THE CUTTING house where mestiza women in sports bras worked tirelessly on Colombia's number one export, they heard someone singing that plaintive lullaby just outside the door.

Joanna, who'd been trying to grab some sleep on the ripped and dirty mattress, immediately woke and lurched to a standing position. The lullaby continued, seeped through the door like the irresistible aroma of a longed-for food.

The door opened.

Joanna put her knuckles to her mouth in an effort to stifle a sob, but she was only half successful.

'Please,' she said. *'Please.'*

Galina. Standing there with Joelle nestled against her chest.

'Please . . . Galina . . .'

Galina entered the room as someone locked the door behind her.

She met Joanna in the middle of the room, gently placing Joelle into her already reaching arms. Paul believed that gentleness like that couldn't be faked. That Galina was someone who loved children even as she kidnapped their parents, a dichotomy he found hard to reconcile.

There was no such dichotomy with Joanna. She folded her daughter against her chest and silently wept.

Paul stood next to her with his arm around her shoulders, the circle made whole once again. He couldn't help looking outside the circle. At Galina. He wanted her to look *back* – he thought that might be hard for her to do. He was wrong.

She met his gaze with perfect equanimity.

She even smiled, as if she'd just taken Joelle for another walk around the block and was ready to resume her duties as übernurse.

'See,' Joanna said to Paul. She'd rolled up the left leg of Joelle's blue stretchie and was pointing at an amber beauty mark just below the knee. Right where she'd said it was.

'Joelle,' she whispered, and kissed her daughter's face. 'Can she stay with us tonight?' she asked Galina. 'Please?'

Galina nodded.

'Thank you,' Joanna said.

And Paul thought how quickly captives become so grateful for any kindness from their captors. *Please* and *thank you* to the people who've snatched you from the world and locked you away in an airless room.

Galina reached into the pocket of her loose black shift. She brought out a baby bottle already filled with thick yellowish formula, and two diapers.

Paul took the bottle from her; he couldn't help remembering that the last time he'd accepted liquid refreshments from her, they'd been laced with *escopolamina*.

Galina turned to leave.

Paul wouldn't let her go without some acknowledgment of what she'd done to them. Some declaration of responsibility, even if it was defiant or angry or unpleasant.

'How many people have you done this to, Galina?' he said.

Galina turned back. 'It isn't your country,' she said slowly. 'You don't understand.'

Before Paul could answer her, before he could tell her that *understanding* and *kidnapping* didn't belong in the same universe, much less the same sentence, she turned around and knocked twice on the door.

The boy opened it and let her out.

JOANNA UNDRESSED JOELLE.

She looked over every inch of her body for any bruises, scratches, or suspicious discolorations. Any evidence at all that they'd hurt her daughter. Apparently not. Paul could sense the joy Joanna was experiencing just to be touching Joelle again, feeling her heartbeat, stroking her hair.

'It's going to fall out, you know,' Joanna said softly.

'What?'

'Her hair. It comes in like this when they're born, then they lose it.' Joelle's hair was ink black and soft as angora.

'When does it grow back?' Paul asked, even as he wondered if they would be around to see that. He sensed that Joanna might be asking herself the same thing.

'Six months, I think,' she answered. 'Around that.'

There was something surreal about their conversation.

As if they were having it back home in their apartment, two new parents just like any other new parents, wondering aloud at the miracle that's their daughter. As if the future stretched limitlessly ahead of them – preschool and kindergarten and grade school. Graduations, confirmations, and birthday celebrations. Girlfriends and boyfriends. Diaries and dance lessons.

Paul understood. They'd have this one night before he left. They'd treat it as normally as possible.

PAUL AND JOANNA SENSED THAT IT WAS MORNING WITHOUT actually knowing it. Their watches had been taken, the windows were boarded up tight. But their bodies had grown attuned to the different times of day, like blind people whose other senses compensate for lost sight. The morning *felt* different than the night.

This morning felt different than other mornings.

In a little while Paul would be leaving Joanna behind. He'd be leaving the country and leaving her *here*.

She'd fallen asleep with Joelle in her arms, and sometime later he'd fallen asleep with Joanna in his. When he opened his eyes, it took him several minutes to realize that Joanna was also awake – he could tell by her breathing, neither one evidently ready to face the other.

Not yet.

Then Joanna said, 'Good morning.'

'Back to you.'

His arms were numb from holding her all night, but he didn't dare move them. It might be the last time for a while. It might be the last time, period.

'At least they brought us Joelle,' she whispered. 'Maybe they're not so bad. They didn't have to do that.'

'They weren't being kind, Joanna,' he whispered back.

'No? Then why'd they do it?'

'To remind me, I think.'

'Of what?'

'What's at stake. What I'll lose if I don't get the drugs there – if I fuck up. I think they wanted to make her real again for me. That's all.'

Joanna pressed her back against him, as if trying to burrow right up inside of him.

'Paul,' she said slowly, 'if you get there and decide to tell someone, *do* it. I'll understand. Maybe they can be negotiated with. Maybe you can give them something in return.'

'Remember the pictures we saw on the airport wall – the deputy mayor of Medellín? They found his head two blocks from the car bomb. I think that's pretty much how they negotiate. I'm going to deliver the drugs and then they're going to make that call and they're going to let you go. You and Joelle.'

They lay there silently for a while.

Then she said:

'Sometimes I think we've been pretty unlucky. Sometimes I think just the opposite. We couldn't have a baby – that was tough, the toughest thing I've ever gone through. Before this. I mean who has to go through *this*? We're a newspaper story now, aren't we? But then, I've loved you. All this time I have. And I think you've loved me too – despite everything, I do. And that's lucky, isn't it? So who knows.'

It was her good-bye to him.

Just in case.

He was trying to think of *his* good-bye. He was trying to string together the right words to convey the ravenous ache that was gnawing at his insides. He was trying to articulate hope. He was trying to compose himself; to say good-bye without breaking down. There was a shuffle outside the door.

Then it swung open and Arias was there.

FIFTEEN

Retardo.

One of the eight million Spanish words he still didn't know. Sometimes Spanish words sounded like English words. The trick was to consider their context.

The context here was the huge black departure board in El Dorado Airport. And the words and symbols that preceded it.

Flt#345 a JFK. Nueva York.

That gave him some useful and solid clues.

Only Paul was attempting to ignore those clues. He was being willfully ignorant, a detective on the take who has no intention of putting two and two together.

He'd swallowed the thirty-six condoms two hours ago in a house outside Bogotá.

He'd been driven to the airport by Pablo, the very man who'd greeted him here just over a week ago.

He'd made it through security and customs.

The flight was *retardo.*

Okay, boys and girls, his Spanish teacher, Mr Schulman, used to say. *Any guesses?*

There was another clue here – one that was practically impossible to ignore. His gate companions. They were groaning, muttering, shaking their heads at each other with that same-old, same-old look of resignation.

Paul got up from his chair. He walked over to the check-in desk. He could feel the condoms sitting inside him with every step. It felt as if he'd swallowed a basketball. A lethal jump shot from Kobe, ready to drop through the net and kill off a possible rally in its tracks.

'Excuse me,' Paul said to the winsome-looking Colombian woman behind the airline counter.

'Yes, sir?' she said. She had that *look* – the one you saw at return counters on the day after Christmas. Defensive fortifications being readied for the coming onslaught.

'Is everything okay with the flight?'

He knew that everything wasn't okay with the flight, of course.

If everything was okay with the flight, the word *retardo* wouldn't be up there on the departure board. His fellow travelers wouldn't be uttering collective groans of frustration. But until the woman confirmed this, he'd stay dumb. He'd stick to the timetable in his head – the one that had him arriving in JFK approximately four and a half hours from now, and arriving at that house in Jersey City two hours later.

'The flight's delayed, sir.'

Suddenly, the only thing that felt heavier than his stomach was his heart. It sank like a stone.

There was still one more question to ask.

'How *long*?'

'We don't know. We'll make an announcement when we know more, sir.'

Paul felt like making an announcement himself. I'm carrying thirty-six condoms filled with cocaine inside my stomach, and if I don't get them out of me soon, they'll dissolve and kill me.

Then Arias will kill my wife and daughter.

A Colombian policeman was standing between gates. He was smoking and watching the legs and asses of every passing female – an equal opportunity leerer.

If you decide to tell someone, do it, Joanna had said. *I'll understand.*

What an easy thing to do. To talk. To tell.

He would unburden himself to the policeman, who'd stop scoping out the passing women and bring Paul to the nearest hospital, where they'd flush the drugs from his stomach. They'd take a report from him, including a full description of the kidnappers. They'd arrest Pablo and Galina.

How easy was that?

Only this was a Latin American country with an inflationary economy. Where everything was nominally expensive, but in actuality, cheap. Life, for instance. Life was cheap here. Joanna's was *dirt* cheap. If he opened his mouth, he was pretty sure he'd be closing hers forever.

The policeman threw the glowing butt of his cigarette onto the floor, where he ground it out with an impressive black boot.

And then walked away.

Paul sat.

Every fifteen minutes or so he got up and approached the check-in desk, where the Colombian woman he'd already talked to scattered for cover. She always seemed to find something to do, check the flight manifest or align the tickets into a neat little pile. He was getting on her nerves, an annoying suitor who refused to take no for an answer.

'We don't know anything yet,' she answered the second time he inquired when the plane would leave. He noticed she'd pretty much dropped the *sir*.

'I have to get to New York for an important meeting. I can't be late. Do you understand?'

Yes, she understood. But she didn't know anything, so if he would please take a seat again and wait for an announcement?

Fifteen minutes after waiting for an announcement that didn't come, he was back again. Then fifteen minutes after that.

'*Look,*' she said, 'I've already told you. We don't have a report yet.'

'Well, is the plane here? You can tell me if the plane's here, can't you?'

'If you'll just have a seat, I'll make an announcement when they tell us something.'

He didn't want a seat. He wanted answers. 'Who's *they?*'

'Excuse me?'

'Who's this mysterious *they?* The *they* that's going to tell you something?'

'Please sit down.'

'I'm just asking you a question. I'm trying to find out how long I'm going to be sitting here. I'd like a clue, a guess, *something*. Is that too much to ask?'

Paul realized that his voice was louder than normal. He sensed this because several tired passengers in the waiting

106

room had looked up from their crossword puzzles and newspapers and magazines to stare at him. They looked half alarmed and half supportive. Maybe because he was only doing what they themselves wished they were – venting a growing anger – even if he was doing it in a way that offended decorum. They'd keep their distance and silently root him on. He remembered another passenger who'd once upon a time harangued a different airline employee for information. Long ago and far away.

The woman behind this counter – *Rosa,* her name tag said – offered no such support.

'I *told* you. When they *tell* me something, I'll make an announcement. Now, I have to ask you to –'

'Fine, I'll sit down. If you tell me who *they* are.'

She decided to simply ignore him. She went back to her busywork as if he'd already turned around and gone back to his seat.

Paul felt something rise up his esophagus. For just a moment, he thought that a condom must have burst inside his gut, that in one moment he'd be down on the floor, drowning in his own vomit. But it wasn't cocaine. It was *rage* – all the poison he'd built up over the last five days of captivity. Rage at Galina and Pablo and Arias and the man with the cigar – it all focused on this woman who was refusing to tell him if he'd get out of Colombia in time to save his wife and daughter.

'I asked you a fucking question,' Paul said. Or shouted. *'I'd like a fucking answer.'*

Everyone pretty much lost the supportive look. Their faces registered pure alarm. Rosa's included. She stepped back, as if he'd physically assaulted her.

'There is no reason to use that language,' she said sharply. 'You're being abusive, and I'll call the authorities if you don't . . .' Paul lost track of what she was saying. Mostly because he could see several people in blue uniforms hurrying to the scene of the commotion. He wasn't sure if they were airline employees or a Colombian SWAT team.

If the police arrest me, I won't make the flight. This is what immediately went through his brain. *The flight might be delayed and it might be taking off God knows when, but if they arrest me, I won't be on it.*

'I'm sorry,' Paul said. 'Forgive me. I'm just under pressure because of this meeting. I'm sorry. Really.'

The blue uniforms were airline people. Three men and one woman who'd surrounded the counter in an impressive display of support. Airline people tended to stick together these days, now that they were operating on the front lines.

'Is there a problem here?' one of the men addressed Rosa.

She hesitated, then shook her head. 'No, it's all right,' she said. 'Mr Breidbart's going back to his seat.'

Mr Breidbart went back to his seat.

The plane was already one hour late.

He had seventeen hours left.

SIXTEEN

They were showing a comedy with Reese Witherspoon. Paul knew it was a comedy because several passengers were laughing.

He was watching the movie too. He had no idea what it was about.

Something was wrong with his stomach – other than the obvious. When he touched it, it felt tight as a bongo drum. He could play 'Wipe Out' on it. He was increasingly nauseous.

I will not throw up, he told himself.

If he threw up the condoms, he'd have to swallow them again; it had been hard enough to get them down the first time. Each swallow had triggered a reflexive urge to vomit. How had he managed it exactly? By using various and only half-successful stratagems.

First he'd pictured Joanna and Joelle sitting in that room – focused on the end benefit. That worked only for a while. So he'd changed tack, imagined each condom as a kind of local delicacy – a strange-tasting delicacy, even a repulsive one, but one that as a politically correct visitor he felt honor-bound to try.

When that didn't work either, when he gagged and almost brought everything back up, he'd thought of them as individual doses of *medicine*. Something prescribed to save his life – his life and theirs.

Somehow he'd managed to get all thirty-six down.

The hard part was keeping them there.

The plane had taken off two hours behind schedule. In order to avoid an unexpected turbulence over the Caribbean, the pilot had climbed to thirty thousand feet. This would add time to the flight, the pilot explained, but *better late than bumpy,* he added in that neutral midwestern twang every pilot in the world seemed to speak with. He was amending the flight path with their comfort in mind.

Paul's comfort was in negative integers.

Negative numbers had always fascinated him. They were the dark side of the moon, the antimatter of the numerical universe that he called home. He was traveling through this universe now.

'Are you all right?' the man next to him asked. Evidently, he wasn't watching the Reese Witherspoon movie. He was watching Paul. Paul looked weird.

'Just a little nauseous,' Paul answered.

The man seemed to pull back. Somehow he'd increased the physical distance between them without actually moving. Paul understood – *nausea* was the last word you wanted to hear during a long flight. Next to *bomb,* of course.

One of his industry's standard jokes: *Did you hear about*

the actuary who brought a fake bomb onto a plane? He
wanted to decrease the chances there'd be another bomb on the
plane.

Ha, ha.

'You want me to call the flight attendant?' the man
asked warily.

'No. I'll be fine.' Paul could feel individual beads of
sweat on his forehead. His stomach was rumbling like
thunder before a deluge.

'Well, okay,' the man said. He didn't look like it was
okay.

Paul tried to lose himself in the movie again. Reese was
a lawyer or something. She kept saying cute things and
smiled a lot.

He was going to throw up.

Paul stood and made his way to the business-class lavatory. Only it was occupied and someone else was waiting
to use it. A mother holding her four-year-old boy by the
hand. The boy was shuffling his feet and periodically grabbing at the crotch of his pants.

'He has to go,' the mother said apologetically.

Paul peered through the half-opened curtain leading to
first class. No one was waiting at that lavatory. He went
through the curtain toward the front of the plane.

'Excuse me, sir.'

A flight attendant had materialized out of nowhere. He
was slim, young, but very determined-looking. Right now
he was determined that Paul, a business-class passenger,
not make it into the first-class lavatory.

'We like you to use the lavatory in your section,' he
said.

'So would I. Only it's occupied. So –'

'If you'll just wait until the lavatory is available,' the man interrupted.

'I can't wait. I'm not feeling well.'

The first-class passengers were all looking at him. Paul could feel their eyes boring into his back. In the hierarchy of planedom, they were Brahmins and he was an Untouchable. This might have embarrassed him in his previous life. But in this life he was a drug smuggler about to upchuck his illicit cargo into the aisle, so he didn't care. He needed to get to that bathroom.

The flight attendant, whose name was Roland, was looking him over as if trying to ascertain if he was telling the truth. Was he really sick, or was he attempting to con his way into the glories of the first-class lavatory?

Paul didn't wait for him to decide. He moved forward, physically brushing past a defeated-looking Roland. He entered the bathroom and shut the door.

His nausea had reached a pretty much unendurable level.

He looked at himself in the mirror. His face was pasty and wet.

He closed his eyes.

He pictured Joanna shut in that airless room. Sitting on that filthy mattress. Alone. He wondered if she was praying for him, revisiting the faith of her youth, when she'd dutifully gone to confession every Sunday and renounced her girlish sins. He hoped so.

I will not throw up. He said this not just to himself, but to God. Okay, they weren't exactly on a first-name basis, but he was willing to give it a shot. He was ready to let bygones be bygones and become friends.

Don't let me throw up.

Rephrased now as an actual prayer, a plea from someone in need of a little godly intervention.

He took deep breaths. He splashed cold water onto his face. He clenched his hands into fists. He purposely avoided looking at the toilet, which seemed like a visual invitation to upchuck the drugs.

It worked.

He felt his nausea subsiding. He was still queasy, but he could actually imagine making it back to his seat without vomiting. Maybe there was something to this religious stuff, after all. Maybe even a jaded God had been moved to pity.

Someone knocked on the door.

'What's going on in there?'

Roland. Still sounding kind of indignant.

'I'm coming out,' Paul said.

'Fine.'

A minute later Paul opened the door and maneuvered past Roland, who smelled strongly of lavender. He made it back to his seat, where the man next to him eyed him suspiciously.

'Everything okay?' he asked.

Paul nodded. He turned onto his side and closed his eyes. He couldn't sleep, but he'd pretend to.

He had two hours left till customs.

THERE WAS A DOG AT THE BOTTOM OF THE ESCALATOR.

A German shepherd with a thick black harness around it.

Paul couldn't see who had hold of that harness, because the ceiling sloped to the angle of the escalator and restricted his vision.

It could be a blind person, he thought. A beggar with one of those white cups in his hand and a sign that said *I am blind. Please help me.*

Or it could be the other kind of person who would be holding a harnessed dog in an international airport. Waiting for a flight from Colombia.

He thought about turning around and heading back up against the flow. The escalator was packed – he'd never make it.

The escalator seemed to be moving at SLP speed, the slowest setting on your typical VCR. The person holding the dog was filling in by small increments, as if he were being drawn by a sketch artist in Washington Square Park.

First the shoes.

Black, sturdy, thick soles. Not necessarily a blind person's shoes, but not necessarily not.

Now the legs.

Thin and short and covered in dark blue.

Denim? Or the polyester weave favored by certain government agencies? It was hard to tell. The man's belt buckle rose into view, something substantial that seemed to serve some greater purpose than merely holding up his pants. The kind of buckle that made a statement.

The shirt began to materialize.

Paul was praying it would be a T-shirt.

Something that said *I Love New York.*

Or *My son-in-law went to Florida but all I got was THIS.* Really praying – like back in the first-class lavatory.

114

It was white and buttoned. There was some kind of badge on it.

A policeman. A customs man.

When Paul entered the last stage of the slowest escalator on earth, he saw he was right *and* wrong. It was a customs agent, all right, but a woman. She had dyed-blond hair tied into a tight ponytail, ostensibly to keep it from getting into her diligently steely eyes.

It didn't really matter what sex she was. He was focusing on the dog.

A sniff dog – isn't that what they called them?

The officer and dog were set up just to the left of the escalator. Paul tried to edge closer to the right railing. The dog was sitting on his hind legs with his quivering black nose pointed straight into the air.

He was wondering. He believed these dogs were capable of sniffing out drugs inside gas tanks, plastic dolls, even concrete canisters. What about *people*? Through layers of intestines and fat and condoms and skin?

Seriously sweating skin. Skin that had broken out in a veritable rash of sweat that threatened to turn him into a walking dishrag.

He stepped off the escalator. He could sense the customs woman staring straight at him. He could only *sense* this, because he was trying not to look at her. He was trying instead to look bored, blasé, nonchalant – to look this way in a direction that wouldn't bring his gaze in the vicinity of hers.

She must've been wondering what might cause a passenger from Colombia to be sweating bullets. No, more like an actual fusillade.

Paul could actually hear the dog sniffing; it sounded like someone with a bad cold. His chest tightened into a single painful knot. There were three supposed warning signs of a heart attack – excessive sweating, chest pain, and numbness – and he currently had all three. Only his numbness was more of the mental variety. He was so scared he couldn't think.

And then he did a very strange thing.

He petted the dog.

The shepherd had begun emitting a series of nervous whines, and Paul was convinced that in one second the officer would be asking him to step out of the line and accompany her to a special room where she'd X-ray him and then arrest him for drug smuggling.

He was facing his fear head-on. The way his father had once advised him to do when a seven-year-old Paul had confided his terror of roller coasters in the middle of Hershey Park. His father put him on the cloud-scraping Evil Twister, where Paul had promptly thrown up all over him.

Maybe blatant hubris would actually work this time.

The dog went stock-still and stared up at him with an eerily focused expression. His ears flattened – his educated nose quivered.

It was the customs woman who actually *barked* at him. 'Sir!'

Everything stopped. Other passengers turned around to stare at him – a teen with backpack, a family of four lugging loot from Disneyland, an elderly couple attempting to catch up with the rest of their tour group. Another customs officer began walking over from further down the terminal.

'*Sir!*' the customs woman repeated.

'Yes?' Paul felt as if he'd left his own body. As if he were looking down on this ridiculous if horrifying confrontation, which could only end with Paul Breidbart being led away in handcuffs. And disgrace.

'Sir. Please refrain from petting the dog, sir.'

'What?'

'She's not a pet, sir. She's a working animal.'

'Yes, of course. Sorry.' He took his hand away – it was clearly shaking.

Paul turned and walked toward the sign that said *Baggage This Way*. He silently counted his steps, thinking if he made it to ten, he would have gotten away with it.

He made it to eleven.

Twelve.

Thirteen.

The dog hadn't smelled the cocaine. He was okay.

SEVENTEEN

He took a cab.

The driver was Indian and spoke only broken English. Still, he had no trouble conveying his joy at getting a fare that would make his day. All the way to New Jersey would be double rate.

He took the Grand Central Parkway to the Triborough Bridge, while Paul looked at his watch approximately every ten minutes. Like a distance runner in the New York City marathon – so much real estate traversed in so much time.

So far, he was more or less on pace.

You're doing fine, the cheerleader in his head kept urging him on.

You're doing fine.

He was attempting to focus on the finish line. FARC's contacts in Jersey City would soon be clapping him on the back for a job well done and placing that call to Colombia. He'd be waiting by the gate the next day for Joanna and Joelle to disembark at Kennedy Airport to begin their new lives together.

Just an hour away.

Then the taxi slowed, crawled, stopped.

They were in a sudden bumper-to-bumper logjam, with no discernible movement up ahead.

Paul needed to get to a bathroom.

This feeling had been intensifying since he walked off the plane. At first just a slighter sense of fullness than he'd felt all day – exactly what you'd expect with thirty-six stuffed condoms sitting inside you. But then a growing and unmistakable need to void, every bit as ferocious as the need to vomit.

For the second time in a space of hours, Paul tried to will his body to listen up and desist. A simple case of mind over matter. His body, however, refused to pay attention; it was having none of it now. It had its own agenda, and it was demanding to be heard.

They hadn't moved an inch in five minutes.

The taxi driver was shaking his head and channel surfing through a sea of foreign-sounding radio stations. The resultant cacophony was harsh and physically grating. It was seriously hindering Paul's ability to concentrate on not going to the bathroom in the backseat of the taxi.

'Could you not do that?' he said.

'Eh?'

'The radio. Could you just pick one station?'

The taxi driver turned around as if he'd just been asked an astounding question. He peered at Paul through heavy-lidded eyes sunk into charcoal caverns of despair.

'What you say?'

'It's annoying,' Paul said. His stomach was beginning to seriously scream at him.

Find a bathroom. Any bathroom.

'*My* radio,' the taxi driver said.

'Yes, but –'

'*My* radio,' he repeated for emphasis. 'I play what I like. Okay.'

Okay. There was a boundary between taxi driver and passenger, and Paul had evidently crossed it.

His stomach was one unending cramp. Something was in there that desperately wanted to get out.

Hold it in.

The taxi driver honked his horn. He obviously meant it as a kind of protest, as opposed to something that might actually accomplish anything. It wasn't as if the cars directly in front of him could do something about it – they were as trapped as he was. He honked his horn again anyway – leaning on it this time, a long wail of frustration and anger.

The taxi driver seemed to enjoy letting off steam in this way. He smiled as if he'd told himself a good joke.

Until someone got out of the car in front of them – a Lincoln with a license plate that said *BGCHEZE*.

The man who walked over to the cabdriver's window seemed constrained by his own clothing, tight maroon sweatpants with a simple T-shirt that appeared more like a straitjacket.

He made a motion with his hand – *roll down the window*.

The taxi driver was in no mood to comply. He'd lost his smile, he was muttering in Indian.

'Roll down your fucking window,' the man said, now that his hand motions had gotten him nowhere.

The taxi driver now made a hand motion of his own. A wave of dismissal – *go away and leave me alone.*

The man didn't react well to this.

'Who you fucking waving at, huh? You like to blow your fucking horn at people? Open your window. I got something for you, you fuck!'

The taxi driver was not going to do that. No. He waved his hand at the man again and turned his head, banishing him from his presence.

'Hey, you fucking towel-head! You understand fucking English? You don't, do you? You don't understand a fucking word I'm saying. Here, I'll make it easy for you. *Roll. Down. Your. Goddamn. Window.*' He pounded the window on each word with a hand that appeared to be the size of Lower Manhattan.

The taxi driver had locked the doors. Paul realized this when the man began pulling on the door handle and it didn't open. This only seemed to make him angrier.

He began kicking the driver's door.

Paul couldn't tell whether the man had noticed that there was a passenger in the backseat. Even if he had, Paul didn't think it would've deterred him.

'Open the fucking door, you pussy!' he was screaming at a now seriously alarmed-looking taxi driver. The taxi driver in fact seemed to be looking around for help – first left, then right, then finally, inexorably, behind him.

'Maybe he'll just stop,' Paul said, staring into twin eyes of pure panic.

'He's goddamn crazy,' the taxi driver said.

Paul had to agree with him there. Two thoughts were racing through his brain. One: He was not going to be able to hold it in. Two: If the crazy man made it into his car, he was going to kill the taxi driver and Paul would not make it to Jersey City in time. Even if he *could* hold it in.

Paul rolled down his window.

'Look, could we just calm down?' he said to the man. His words sounded pained and filled with anguish – even to him.

His tone seemed to momentarily mollify the man. He looked at Paul as if he'd just come across an interesting artifact worthy of his attention.

'Tell him to open his door,' he said.

'Look, I'm sure he didn't mean to blow his horn. He was frustrated. All this traffic. Can we just forget it?'

The man smiled at him. 'Sure,' he said.

Then he reached into Paul's window and pulled the door lock up. He pulled the door *open* – accomplishing this in a matter of seconds. Before Paul could actually react, the man yanked Paul out of the taxi by his arm.

Paul stumbled, almost fell.

'Hey, come on, stop this,' he said.

Somewhere between *stop* and *this,* the man's fist connected with his chin.

Paul fell straight back onto the pavement. *Smack.* That wasn't the worst part. No.

He'd just spent hours fighting to keep the drugs inside of him, battling with his own body over this unwelcome and unnatural intrusion.

In one humiliating moment, he lost.

EIGHTEEN

They found an Exxon station somewhere in the Bronx.

A Middle Eastern man pumping gas pointed to the back of the station when Paul asked for the bathroom.

Paul had made it back into the taxi in the middle of the Triborough Bridge, with the assistance of a middle-aged woman who'd magically materialized from a white mini-van. He'd refused the woman's offer to obtain medical assistance. He'd told the taxi driver, who'd remained snugly in his front seat, that he wasn't interested in going to the police. No. Just 1346 Ganet Street in Jersey City.

First he'd needed a bathroom.

The taxi driver closed the plastic partition between driver and passenger as Paul sat half on his hip the entire way.

When he got into the stifling gas station bathroom – which wasn't so much a bathroom as a hole with toilet – he discovered pretty much what he'd expected.

Everything he'd swallowed back in Bogotá had come out. The condoms were still intact.

He dumped them into the filthy sink, washed them off with warm rusty water. He took off his pants and slathered

123

them with the yellowish gunk that came out of the soap dispenser, then soaked them under the faucet. He cleaned himself up as best he could.

He wasn't going to swallow the condoms again. He couldn't. He would get to the house in Jersey City and tell them what happened – that they'd come out just a few miles from delivery.

He carefully placed the drugs in the overnight bag he'd dragged into the bathroom with him. He went back out to the taxi and crawled into the backseat. The driver had aired it out during his bathroom break. Both doors were wide open, both windows rolled down.

At least the driver didn't say anything to him. Paul had taken one on the chin for him.

His gratitude must have outweighed his disgust.

Thirty minutes later they entered Jersey City.

Paul was looking on the bright side. Yes, there was a bright side. He'd made it *this* far. Consider the percentages.

He was blocks from delivering his cargo. From fulfilling his part of the bargain.

The taxi driver turned into an area festooned with Arabic signs. They passed a yellow mosque complete with gleaming minaret, an open-air market dripping with exotic-looking fruits and vegetables. They crawled past several women covered head-to-toe in black burkas, drifting down the street like shadows.

My name is Paul Breidbart. I have something you've been waiting for.

He pictured Joanna's face as she got off the plane. Still hollow-eyed and fatigued, but flush with gratitude and relief. She would have Joelle pressed to her chest. They would go home, where their best friends, John and Lisa, would've tied bright pink balloons to the doorknob of their apartment.

My name is Paul Breidbart. I've got something for you.

The taxi stopped. The driver was craning his neck, peering out the side window.

'Are we here?' Paul asked.

'Thirteen forty-six Ganet Street?' the driver said.

'Yes. Is this it?'

'This is Ganet Street,' he said.

'Good,' Paul said. They were in the middle of a block. A grocery, a drugstore, and two check-cashing places were situated on one side of the street. The other side looked residential, which must've been the side he was looking for.

Only something was wrong. The taxi driver was shaking his head and sighing.

'Thirteen forty-six?' he asked again.

'Yes.'

'It's not there,' he said.

'What?'

'It's gone.'

'I don't understand.'

'Look,' the taxi driver said. 'It's missing.'

NINETEEN

Morning.

Joanna could smell fried plantain and smoke. And the familiar musky odor of her baby. Her soft head was tucked under Joanna's chin as she guzzled the pale yellow formula provided by Galina.

Paul had left hours ago. Or was it days?

She'd tried to be brave about it. She'd tried to stay strong for Paul – he'd need it. When he left, when he actually departed from the room, it was as if hope had left with him.

This is what it feels like to be utterly alone, she thought.

And yet there was Joelle. So she wasn't.

Galina had come back soon after Paul left, and Joanna had latched onto her baby like she used to clutch her pocketbook in the face of a possible 84th Street mugger.

You will not take this from me.

And Galina hadn't.

'Would you like to feed her with me?' Galina asked.

'Yes.'

So they had. Side by side, like the young moms with

their foreign nannies who congregated on the Central Park benches every morning. Only no swings, seesaws, or slides.

There was another difference, of course. This nanny had kidnapped them.

Joanna didn't bother mentioning that particular fact. She was trying to hold on to the moment. *Don't upset the applecart,* her mother used to say to her when she'd complain about something or other. Meaning be happy for what you have. Why? Because it can always get worse.

If you let me hold her and feed her and be with her, I'll say nothing about what you did to us.

This, admittedly, went against every fiber of Joanna's character. She was used to speaking her mind. But she couldn't take the risk of Joelle being snatched from her a second time.

Galina asked Joanna how she'd slept. She commented on how good an eater Joelle was. She demonstrated the proper way to burp her. Talking to Joanna as if they were still back in the Bogotá hotel room.

And Joanna nodded, answered back, even *conversed.*

'Where were you born, Galina?' Joanna asked after Joelle had been fed and gently rocked into a semblance of sleep.

'Frontino,' Galina answered. 'In Antioquia. North,' she added, realizing that Joanna wouldn't know one Colombian province from another. 'On an orchard farm. A long time ago.'

Joanna nodded. 'What was it like?'

Galina shrugged. 'We were poor. Campesinos. I was sent to school by the fathers.'

At the mention of religion Joanna recalled the black

jacket and white collar you could glimpse through the confessional partition. The smell of mothballs, incense, and baby powder.

Joanna was intent on keeping the conversation going. Joelle was asleep, and any minute Galina might stand up and say *hand her over*. Besides, it was undeniably pleasant speaking with another human being.

There was another reason. Talking kept her from thinking.

Eighteen hours, they'd told Paul.

Galina reached over and gently and playfully caressed the spiky hair on Joelle's head.

It would be hard not to like a woman like this, Joanna thought. There must be two Galinas; this one you'd willingly hand your baby to.

'When did you come to Bogotá?'

'During the riots,' Galina said. 'When Gaitán was killed.' She explained to Joanna, described what Colombia was like in the 1940s. Jorge Gaitán was a man of the people – not lily-white the way the rest of the politicians were. Half Indian. The hope of campesinos like her father. Only he was gunned down by a madman. The country went crazy, dissolved into *La Violencia* that had never really ended.

Joanna listened, nodded, asked questions. She supposed she was not only interested in keeping the conversation flowing but interested in what Galina was saying. Maybe it would give her a clue.

You don't understand, Galina had said to Paul when he'd asked her how she could kidnap them. *It's not your country.*

Okay, Joanna thought, *help me understand.*

128

She reached for parallels from Hollywood. Colombia was like *West Side Story* – a movie she'd cried at as an eleven-year-old when she saw it on TV; the Jets versus the Sharks, with the bumbling and ineffectual Officer Krupke in the middle. Here it was leftists against rightists, with the government stuck in between.

Only there was no coming together in the end over death.

Just death.

She held Joelle even tighter within a soft rocking rhythm.

My baby, my own . . .

That song from *Dumbo* just flitting into her brain. Dumbo could fly away just using his enormous ears.

If an elephant could fly . . .

She tried to picture Paul on an airplane somewhere over the Atlantic. Or was he there already? How much time *had* passed since Paul departed?

She turned to Galina to ask her this question, but Galina was staring down at Joelle, seemingly lost in thought. Or was it memory?

'I had a daughter,' Galina said.

Joanna was about to ask what her name was, what she looked like, where she was. There'd been the undeniable use of past tense.

'What happened to her?' Joanna asked.

Galina stood up. She reached for Joelle.

When Joanna didn't hand her over, Galina said, 'I'll bring her back.'

Joanna had no choice; she handed her daughter to the woman who'd stolen her.

* * *

AFTER JOANNA HAD WOKEN THE NEXT MORNING, SHE PRESSED her ear up against the rough slats that covered one of the windows. She was trying to expand her universe by feet, even inches.

She heard construction sounds – scattered hammering and a muffled rhythmic pounding. She pictured a pile driver, a steam shovel. Two dogs were barking. An airplane passed overhead. Someone bounced a basketball.

Then Galina stepped into the room. There was no baby with her. This time she was bearing something else.

News.

'Your husband,' she said in a flat, emotionless voice. 'He didn't deliver the coca.'

TWENTY

There was a charred, blackened, and still-smoldering hole approximately a third of the way up the left side of Ganet Street.

Paul finally figured out that this used to be 1346.

'It burned down,' a resident in a white skullcap explained to them.

'When?' Paul asked.

'Yesterday.'

Paul felt something in his stomach – pretty much the opposite of what he'd felt before. The torturous sense of fullness had been replaced by an equally torturous sense of nothingness.

Call it a black hole, sucking in every particle of hope.

'The people who lived there?' Paul asked. 'Do you know where they are?'

The man shrugged.

It turned out that no one really knew where they were. No one really knew *who* they were either.

'Freakin' Ricans,' said a white man holding a beer can half submerged in a brown paper bag.

'Foreign people,' said another man, who appeared to be from Eastern Europe and spoke only a halting English.

The foreign people had kept to themselves. They'd been there only six months or so. They didn't mix much. There were two or three of them, depending on whom you asked. Men.

'No one died, though? In the fire?'

Apparently not. The firemen, at least, hadn't discovered any bodies.

By this time the taxi driver was growing impatient. He'd made his double fare, and he was anxious to get back.

'Keep the meter running,' Paul said.

'You okay?' the taxi driver asked him. He must've noticed Paul's ghostly reflection in the rearview mirror.

They crawled up Ganet Street and found a diner. Through the window Paul could see an empty phone booth in the back. He had left his cell phone at home.

They'd given him a number. Just in case.

He'd explain. *I have your drugs here, all thirty-six condoms. I just need someone to give it to.*

Paul told the driver to wait.

'Sure. Give me the money you owe me.'

Paul pulled $165 out of his wallet and handed it through the partition. The guerrillas had returned his cash and traveler's checks largely untouched.

Do you think we're bandidos?

No. Just kidnappers and murderers.

When Paul entered the diner, he heard the unmistakable sound of peeling tires. When he spun around, all he could see was a thin cloud of blue exhaust where the taxi should've been.

He used his phone card. After a minute listening to the series of dull clicks, the phone rang, but no one answered. One ring, two rings, three rings, four. Paul let it ring for approximately five minutes. They were like dog minutes – each minute the emotional equivalent of a week.

He hung up and tried again.

Still no answer.

He felt feverish.

He walked back to 1346. He searched each passing face for signs of recognition, but they moved past like speeding drivers.

He planted himself in front of the burned-out house, where thin, needlelike cinders were still suspended in the thick, humid air.

They must've been expecting him, he thought. Someone would come back for the drugs.

He stood there for a kind of eternity. People walked back and forth, in front of him, behind him. No one stopped to speak with him. No one asked him what was in the overnight bag.

Then someone did come up to him.

A kid, even though he didn't look much like a kid.

When he ambled across the street and sort of shuffled over to Paul, he thought that maybe this kid had been standing across the street for a long time. He looked familiar.

'Pssst,' the kid said.

'Yes?' Paul asked. He felt a first glimmer of hope.

'I know why you're here, chief.' He looked to be the right nationality – Latino anyway.

'You do?'

'Sure, Holmes.' The kid looked left, looked right, then

motioned to Paul to follow him. 'Just waiting for the all-clear.'

'I saw the building had burned down. I didn't know what to do,' Paul whispered, half a step behind him. The kid had turned the corner and was headed down a side street guarded by row houses all painted various uninspiring shades of brown.

'Uh-huh,' the kid said.

'I thought I'd wait till you found me.'

'Good thinking, chief.'

Halfway down the block, the kid turned toward an alley between two houses. They ended up in a backyard paved with cracked and spray-painted cement. Two empty windows with no shades stared at them from the back of the house.

'Let's see what you got in the bag for me,' the kid said.

They'd found him. He was going to make it, after all.

It took just two seconds after Paul had opened the bag to realize he was dead wrong.

It was the kid's expression. He'd looked in the bag and seemed, well . . . disappointed.

'What the fuck is *this*?' he said.

'This is . . . ,' Paul started to explain, then stopped.

'*Money*, Holmes,' the kid said. 'You scorin' or not?'

Not. It made perfect sense that the street where some Colombian drug dealers had been waiting for their cocaine might be a street where other drug dealers waited to sell it. He'd stumbled across one of them.

'No,' Paul said. He started to zip up his bag.

The zipper didn't make it to the closed position; the kid grabbed his arm.

'Wait a minute, Holmes.'

It was like showing meat to a dog.

The kid had recovered from the disappointment. He was starting to realize what it was that he *had* seen.

'Where's the fire?'

'I've got to go. I thought you were someone else, okay?'

'What's wrong with *me*?'

'Look, it's not mine. I need to give this to someone.' Paul was tugging at the bag, but it wasn't budging.

'*I'm* someone, chief.'

'Look, this belongs to some dangerous people, understand? They're going to be mad if they don't get this.'

There was someone else who was dangerous here. The kid had lost the easy demeanor of a salesman. His eyes had gone stone-cold; he'd tightened his grip on the bag.

'Tell you what,' the kid said. 'Let go.'

'No,' Paul said, surprising even himself. The old Paul would have spun the numbers, calculated the risks. He would've let go of the bag.

Not today.

If he lost the bag, it was over.

The kid reached into his pocket for something. Paul saw the dull gleam of metal.

'Look, boss, you want to let go of the bag, okay? You don't want me to hurt you any, right?'

'I can't let you have it,' Paul said.

'You ain't letting me have it. I'm taking it from you.'

Paul didn't let go.

He hardly saw the kid's hand move. It didn't seem possible a hand could launch itself into Paul's left cheekbone *and* make it back to the side of his body all in the blink of

135

a swollen eye. Paul felt as if he'd been hit by a high inside fastball – something that had happened twice in Little League, leaving a slight crack still detectable in X-rays of his orbital lobe.

Surprisingly, he didn't go down. He tottered, teetered, wobbled. Then he did something even more surprising.

He swung back.

The kid had loosened his grip – maybe it was hard to wallop someone with one hand and hold something with the other. Paul wrenched the bag clear away from him, then swung it forward in the general direction of the kid's head.

SMACK.

The kid went down. Hard. Hard enough to bang the side of his face on the cracked cement and look up at Paul with a hint of incredulity, if not outright fear.

Paul stared back.

Maybe it was Paul's expression – he had his game face on. A face that said *come on, just try it again. Just try.* Or maybe, and more likely, it was the police cruiser that slowly drifted into view between the two houses.

Whatever it was, the kid got up and ran.

TWENTY-ONE

Miles answered on the third ring.

'Hello?'

'Miles?'

'Yes?'

'This is Paul. Paul Breidbart.'

Paul was back at the diner. He'd tried the number in Colombia again. Six times. No answer. He could think of just one other person to call.

'Paul?' It seemed to take his lawyer a long time to flip through the Rolodex in his mind and actually place him. 'Well, how the hell are you? Are you and, uh . . . Joanna back?'

Paul wondered if he'd needed a real Rolodex to come up with his wife's name. He guessed, probably.

'No. Yes. *I* am.'

'You are? She's *not*?'

'I'm in trouble, Miles.'

'What's the problem? Everything okay with the baby?'

'Can I come see you?'

'Of course. Call the office tomorrow and make an appointment with –'

'I need to see you now,' Paul cut him off.

'*Now?* I was just on my way home.'

'It's an emergency.'

'This can't wait till regular office hours?'

'No. It can't wait for regular office hours.'

'Well . . . okay,' Miles said after a moment's hesitation. 'It *is* an emergency, right, Paul?'

'Yeah. It's an emergency.'

'You'll have to meet me at my house. You got a pen handy?'

'I'll remember.'

He gave him a street address in Brooklyn.

PAUL USED A LOCAL CAR SERVICE WHOSE NUMBER WAS POSTED ON a crowded bulletin board in the diner's stinking vestibule.

Jersey Joe's Limos.

Stuck between *Stanley Franks Psychotherapy* and *Wendy Whoppers Body Work – In Call and Out Call.*

Paul could've used a session with both.

He needed a limo more.

Although Jersey Joe's Limos apparently didn't have limousines. Ten minutes after he'd called, a forest-green Sable pulled up to the diner and honked its horn twice.

The grossly overweight driver offered to put Paul's bag in his trunk. Paul gripped the handle straps tighter and declined.

He wondered how much time he had. Had he been afforded an extension of sorts? When Arias called that house

138

in Jersey City, no one would answer. There'd be no ring because there'd be no phone. Maybe they'd know something was wrong – they'd take that into consideration. They'd restrain themselves.

They were coming off the ramp of the Williamsburg Bridge, and some very strange-looking people were coming into view. At least strangely dressed. It was summer, but the men wore enormous fur hats and long black jackets. The women wore even more.

He hadn't connected the address Miles had given him to Williamsburg, bastion of Orthodox Judaism. Clearly, that's where they were.

At every traffic light, sweating, bearded faces stared at him through the windows.

Miles' home was a handsome brownstone neatly festooned with pots of scarlet geraniums.

Paul paid the driver, then lugged his black bag out of the car, like your friendly neighborhood drug dealer.

He walked up the brownstone steps and rang the buzzer.

The door was opened by a stout, smiling woman who would've been pleasant-looking if it weren't for the thick black wig that sat on her head like a helmet.

'Mr Breidbart?' she asked.

'Yes.'

The woman introduced herself as Mrs Goldstein and led him into a wood-paneled study.

'He'll just be a minute,' she said. 'Please sit down.'

Paul chose one of the leather chairs facing a desk buried in an avalanche of paper.

After Mrs Goldstein had left, he wondered about the wig.

Cancer?

A sudden image of his mother came back to him, meticulously placing someone else's hair onto her head before the dresser mirror.

Paul gazed at the crowded bookshelves that lined two sides of the den, where books and pictures fought for space. Most of the photographs were of Miles. Shaking hands, posing with various Latin American kids. There was a picture of Miles and María Consuelo standing together in front of the Santa Regina Orphanage. There were several framed citations haphazardly mounted on the wall. *Latin American Parents Association Man of the Year.* Sitting just below an honorary degree from a law school and a certificate of service from a local hospital.

When a man entered the room and turned around to shut the door, Paul almost asked him when the man in the pictures would be coming down.

But it *was* the man in the pictures.

In disguise.

Miles was wearing a black felt yarmulke. He was in the process of detaching a small black object resembling a box from his naked forearm, unwrapping a tangle of crisscrossing leather straps. He was wearing a jet-black jacket that fell all the way down to his knees, looking very much like someone who'd wandered out of a *Matrix* movie.

'They're called tefillin,' Miles said after he'd shaken Paul's hand and sat down behind his desk. He'd added the strange black box with trailing straps to the rest of the clutter on his desk, where it lay like some exotic sea creature, an inky octopus maybe, now dead. 'They're kind of indispensable to morning prayer.'

'It's afternoon.'

'Yeah. I'm playing catch-up.'

'You're an Orthodox Jew?' Paul asked.

'Hey – you're *good*.' Miles smiled when he said it.

'You didn't dress like this at the office. I didn't know.'

'Of course not, why would you?' Miles said. 'Anyway, I'm *modern* Orthodox. And I'm kind of unorthodox about my orthodoxy. Wearing nonsectarian attire is a necessary accommodation I make for my career – it might frighten off the clients. Wearing a yarmulke at home is a necessary accommodation I make for my religion – if I didn't, God might get angry. Got it?'

Yes, Paul got it.

He was eager to get off the subject of Judaism and onto the subject of his kidnapped wife and daughter.

'So,' Miles said, 'you're here. Welcome back. What's the problem?'

'The *problem*?' Paul repeated it, maybe because it was such a hopeful word – problems could be faced and surmounted, couldn't they?

'Bogotá,' Paul said flatly. 'It wasn't safer than Zurich.'

'What?'

'I'm in trouble,' Paul said. 'Help me.'

PAUL WAS SIPPING A CUP OF GREEN HERBAL TEA GENEROUSLY provided by Mrs Goldstein.

Good for the nerves, Miles said.

Miles' nerves were evidently okay – he'd declined a proffered cup and was instead sitting at the desk with his hands clasped against his forehead.

He'd pretty much reacted the way a concerned lawyer should at the news that his clients had been kidnapped, with one of them still in Colombia and the other forced to smuggle drugs past U.S. Customs. Maybe more so. His face had dropped, become a puddle of concern, anger, and empathy.

He'd come out from behind the desk and clasped Paul around the shoulders.

'My God, Paul. I'm so sorry.'

Paul allowed himself to be comforted, to soak it in like a parched sponge. Up till now, the only person who'd felt sorry for him was him. Miles wanted details.

'Tell me what happened – exactly what happened.'

He told Miles about the afternoon they came back to the hotel and discovered their baby gone. About the next day, when Joanna had matter-of-factly stated that she was certain that the baby sleeping next to them wasn't Joelle. About the trip to Galina's, the cries coming from the back of the house, followed by Pablo's sudden brutality.

The boarded-up room. Arias. The man with the cigar. The burned-out house. Paul continued right up to the moment the taxi stranded him in Jersey City.

Miles listened intently, made a few notes on a yellow legal pad that magically appeared from the clutter on his desk.

'Pablo?' Miles asked him. 'This man was your driver?'

'Yes.'

'Uh-huh. And he was contracted through Santa Regina?'

'Yes. Why? Do you think Santa Regina had anything to do with this?'

'Not a chance. I've known María Consuelo for years. The woman's a saint.'

Paul peeked at his watch. 'They said eighteen hours. That's two hours from now.'

'Okay. Let's think about this logically.'

Paul was going to say that was easier said than done. That it wasn't *Miles'* wife and child in the line of fire. That time was running out. He remained quiet.

'Look, I know it looks pretty bleak, but we've still got something they want,' Miles said. He peered at the black bag on Paul's lap. 'In there, huh?'

Paul nodded.

'Maybe we should lock that up in my safe. I have kids running around.'

'Okay.'

Miles walked around to Paul's side of the desk. He unzipped the bag and looked inside.

He whistled. 'I'm no expert on narcotics, but that looks like a lot of stuff.'

'Two million dollars.'

'I'd say that constitutes *a lot.*'

Miles zipped the bag closed, then tentatively picked it up, holding it at arm's length the way dog walkers carry their pets' droppings to the trash can. He opened a liquor cabinet that wasn't; there was a stainless-steel safe inside.

After he'd locked the bag in, he settled back behind the desk. 'If you don't mind me asking, how did you manage to swallow all that?'

Paul was going to say that it's amazing how much you can swallow when your wife's life depends on it. You can swallow thirty-six condoms and your own fear and disgust.

'I don't know. I had to.'

'Yeah, guess you did,' Miles said. 'Okay, where were we?'

'The drugs. The something they want.'

'Right, the drugs. They're not going to do anything to your wife until they know where it is. Doesn't that make sense?'

Paul nodded.

'Of course it does,' Miles continued. 'That's *two million dollars*. Besides, I believe FARC's been known to hold hostages a long time. Years, even.'

Miles offered that particular fact as a palliative. It had the opposite effect; it made Paul sick to his stomach.

Years.

Miles noticed. 'Look, I was just making a point. They may have told you eighteen hours. I don't think they meant it.'

'How do you know?'

'Call it an educated guess.'

Okay, Miles was saying, you have more time. It's like those threatening past-due bills you get in the mail – they're just trying to scare you.

But Paul *did* feel sick to his stomach – in addition to feeling sweaty, filthy, and physically exhausted. He closed his eyes, rubbed his throbbing forehead with a hand that still smelled of gas station soap.

'You okay?' Miles said with evident concern. 'I mean *relatively*? Look, I need you to stay with me. We'll work this out, we'll find a way – but I *need* you, okay?' He looked down at his scribbled-on pad. 'Let's review our options.'

Paul wasn't aware that they had any.

'One – we go to the authorities.' Miles seemed to contemplate this notion for a moment; he shook his head. 'Uh-uh. Your first instincts were probably dead-on. I mean, which authorities exactly would we go to? The NYPD? The State Department? The Colombian government? They haven't been able to free their *own* people. Never mind a foreigner. Plus, if FARC finds out we've got people looking for Joanna and the baby, she becomes a liability to them. Then they might do something to her. And there's something else. You did smuggle drugs into the United States – *a lot* of drugs. Under duress, sure, the worst kind of pressure, but we're still talking narcotics trafficking, a federal offense. Okay, we don't go to the authorities. Agreed?'

Paul said, 'Yes.' He was enormously heartened by Miles' use of the *we* word. It made him feel a little less alone in the universe.

Miles held up a second finger. 'Two. We could do nothing. We could sit and wait for them to contact you.' He shook his head again. 'Not so smart. How do we even know they know *how* to get in touch with you? Odds are, they don't and who says your wife told them? Okay, scrap that. We can't sit on our hands. Now . . .' He held up a third finger, leaned slightly forward. 'Three. We can contact them ourselves. We can tell them we've still got their drugs. All we're looking for is someone to give it to. *We give you the drugs, you let Joanna and the baby go.* No Joanna and baby – no drugs. Drugs equal money, lots of money. They'll want the money.'

Okay, Paul thought, it sounded like an actual plan.

Perfectly logical, simple, even *hopeful*. Except . . .

'How are you going to contact them? They're not answering that number. I've tried.'

'The driver,' Miles said, snapping his finger. 'Pablo. I'll call Santa Regina. María must have his number somewhere.' Miles opened his desk drawer and pulled out a small phone book. 'Let's see . . .' He scanned down one page, then flipped to the next. 'Consuelo . . . Consuelo . . . here we are.'

He picked up his phone, punched in a number.

Some people chat on the telephone as if the person they're speaking to is right next to them in the room. Miles was like that. When he said hello to María, he grinned, smiled, shook his head, as if she were sitting there right in front of him.

Fine, Miles said, *and you?*

Yes, growing up. And how are yours?

That's wonderful – I'd love to see a picture . . .

They continued in this vein for a minute or two, small pleasantries, polite inquiries, general catching up.

'María,' Miles said, 'I wonder if you could give me the number of a taxi driver – Pablo. I'm not sure what his last name is . . . Yes, that's right. I'm thinking of using him for another couple . . . Really? Oh great.'

Miles gave Paul the thumbs-up. He waited, flipping a pencil back and forth between two fingers.

'Ahhh . . .' He scribbled something down. 'Thank you, María . . . Of course. Talk to you soon.' He hung up the phone.

'Okay.' He looked up at Paul. 'We have the number. Now . . .' He looked down at the pad and dialed again.

146

This time there were no hellos, no pleasantries exchanged, no small talk. That was because there was no talk at all. Miles waited, flipped the pencil, looked at his watch, stared around the room. Then he shrugged his shoulders, hung up the phone, and tried again.

Same result.

'Okay,' Miles said, 'no one's home.' He put the phone down. 'I'll try again later.'

Paul nodded. The question was, how much of *later* did they have?

'Look,' Miles said, 'I've been thinking about this. You probably shouldn't go home. Not yet. They didn't want anyone knowing you're back, correct?'

'Yes.' He'd been lifted up, borne along by Miles' optimism, but now that they'd failed to connect with anyone, he felt his spirits plummeting.

'Let's keep it that way, shall we? At least for the time being. You can stay here. Until we get through to them. That all right with you?'

Paul nodded again, willing to be reduced to childlike obedience. If Miles were recommending he stay here, he'd stay. *Yes, sir.* He was drained, dog-tired, in dire need of a pillow.

Miles made some explanation to his wife – Paul heard him whispering in the next room. Then he led Paul upstairs, past his children's room, where two boys with remote controls in their hands looked up from their Nintendo.

There was a small guest room at the end of the hall.

Miles clicked on the light.

'Make yourself comfortable. If you want to take a

shower, the bathroom's down the hall. There's pillows in the closet.'

Paul said, 'Thanks.' He *did* need to take a shower, remembering what had transpired in the middle of the Triborough Bridge. But he didn't have the energy.

Miles turned to leave, took a few steps, then turned back. 'I'll keep trying the number. If we don't get him today, we'll get him tomorrow. We're going to save them, okay? Joanna and the baby, both of them. We'll do everything we can.'

It was as good a good-night prayer as Paul could hope for.

He took off his shoes and socks and lay down on the bed without bothering to get a pillow.

PAUL WOKE UP IN THE MIDDLE OF THE NIGHT. HIS WATCH SAID 3:14.

There was that moment when he wasn't aware where he was, or even what had happened to him. When it was still possible Joanna lay next to him in bed and in the next room lay Joelle, softly sucking on her pacifier.

Then reality intruded. He knew where he was. He knew *why*. Understood that eighteen hours had come and gone and his wife either was or wasn't alive. He shut his eyes and dug his head into the mattress in an effort to get back to sleep.

He couldn't.

He felt suddenly wide-awake, infused with the energy of the seriously panicked. He turned one way, then another. He got a pillow from the closet; lay back and closed his eyes again. No dice. His mind couldn't stop racing.

Hello, Arias, nice to see you. How've you been?

Buenas noches, Pablo.

Galina, good to see you again.

He pictured Joanna too, locked up in that room. His wife, his warrior princess.

After an hour he gave up.

It was dead quiet, the time of the night when it seemed he might be the only one on earth.

Don't be silly. The darkness can't hurt you, his father used to say to him as he lay shivering under the covers.

Hard to believe that was true. After all, Paul had been assured that other things wouldn't hurt him, only to find out differently. Cancer, for instance, which he'd been told was nothing much, even though it had already reduced his mom to the human skeleton he'd discovered lying on her bed, before it killed her just three days past his eleventh birthday. His father was distant, and not home much. His mom was the nurturer in the family. He'd resorted to serious and constant prayer on her behalf. When she succumbed anyway, when the family priest fastened onto his hand as his mom – not his mom, her *body* – was brought down the stairs draped in a white sheet, he'd secretly renounced his belief in a higher deity. He'd embraced the cool logic of numbers. He'd carefully constructed a universe of structure and compliance. Where probabilities and ratios were your friends. Where you could statistically calibrate the odds of bad things happening to you, then take comfort in them.

It wasn't by chance that he'd gravitated to a career whose sole purpose was controlling risk.

In actuary-speak: *reducing the likelihood of undesirable events.*

His risk management skills seemed to be lacking these days.

He rolled out of bed and stood on his bare feet. The wooden floor felt cool and ancient. There was no television in the room, no radio.

He needed a diversion, something to keep his mind off things. Something to read.

He tiptoed down the staircase, but it still protested with creaks and groans. Having no idea where the hall lights were, he had to feel his way along from banister to wall.

He finally made it into Miles' office, where after some fumbling around he discovered the light switch just inside the door.

Click.

He shuffled over to the bookshelves. Okay, light reading was in order here. He seemed to be out of luck. The shelves contained the kind of books you might expect in the office of a lawyer. Law books, a veritable glut of them: thick, leather-bound, and singularly uninviting. There were a few other books there but nothing that looked particularly enticing. A Jewish Bible with a cracked, peeling binding. The *Kabbalah* – whatever that was. A biography of David Ben-Gurion. A wafer-thin volume titled *The Story of Ruth*.

It won by default.

He could use a good story. The story of *anything*. But when he pulled it out, not without some difficulty since it was wedged between *New York Estate Statutes* and *Principles of Trial Law*, a stack of papers fell out.

150

Paul reached down to scoop them up.

Letters, old ones by the look of them. Sickly yellow to off-white.

Dear Dad, Daddy, Pop, Father, the first letter began.

One of the video-game players from upstairs. Writing from summer camp maybe?

He felt like a voyeur, an intruder into the Goldstein family history. It made him think of his own family – or lack of one.

He felt a sudden and overwhelming sadness, mixed in with something he clearly recognized as jealousy. Miles was lucky. He had a wife who wasn't sitting in Colombia under armed guard. Two children who dutifully wrote him from camp, delighting in using every existing term for *father.*

Paul would've been happy with one.

Dear Dad, Daddy, Pop, Father: Remember when you took me to the zoo and you left me there?

Miles had taken his boys to camp and one of them was registering his unhappiness. Reminding his dad of another time he'd been taken somewhere and left behind. Momentarily separated in the crowd of monkey watchers while Miles went off to purchase some cotton candy. Paul was creating his own version of the Goldstein family history – what familyless people do to pass the time.

He might've continued in this inventive mode if it weren't for a sudden sharp sound at the door. One of Miles' boys, standing there in blue pajamas rubbing his half-open eyes against the glare. He looked about fourteen, Paul thought – that gangly, awkward age between childhood and teen. The boy's legs were too long for his

151

body; the faintest fuzz covered his upper lip like a lipstick stain.

'I heard someone on the stairs,' the boy said.

If Paul had felt voyeuristic before, he now felt embarrassed. Caught red-handed reading personal letters between son and father. As if it were perfectly okay, as if he had the right to.

'I pulled the book out, and they fell out,' Paul said lamely.

The boy shrugged.

Paul slipped them back into the book, wedged it back onto the shelf.

'Well,' Paul said, 'back to sleep.'

The boy nodded and turned as Paul shut the light and followed him out. They trudged up the stairs together.

'Did you go to summer camp?' Paul asked him.

'Huh?' The boy was still half asleep.

'Summer camp? When you were younger?' Paul said.

'Uh-huh,' the boy answered sleepily. 'Camp Beth-Shemel in the Catskills. It sucked.'

'Yeah,' Paul said, 'I didn't like sleepaway camp either.' Paul had been sent to camp the summer his mom died.

At the top of the stairs Paul said good night and went back to his room, where it took another two hours before he actually fell asleep.

BY THE TIME PAUL WOKE, IT WAS MIDMORNING AND MILES WAS gone.

'He left for work hours ago,' Mrs Goldstein told him. 'He said to please make yourself comfortable. So *please*' –

she smiled shyly – 'make yourself comfortable. He'll call you later.'

He'd found Mrs Goldstein in the kitchen after he'd put his shoes and socks on and ventured downstairs. One of Miles' boys was at the table reading a comic book – *Spider-Man Wreaks Vengeance*. This was Miles' other son – he looked about two years younger than his brother.

'Hello, I'm Paul,' he said to the boy.

The boy mumbled hi without looking up.

Mrs Goldstein sighed. 'Tell him your name. When someone introduces themselves, you introduce yourself back.'

The boy looked up and rolled his eyes. 'David,' he said, then immediately dived back into the adventures of a boy who introduced himself by entrapping and hanging you upside down in his sticky web.

Mrs Goldstein was still wearing her wig, but this time Paul noticed a tuft of her own hair peeking out of one side. It seemed thick and dark, and Paul suddenly understood it wasn't cancer, but religion, that dictated she cover her head.

'Would you like some coffee, Mr Breidbart?'

'Paul. Please.'

'Please you want some coffee, or please call you Paul?'

'Please to both.'

'All right. But you have to call me Rachel.' She pronounced it with a guttural *ch*, like Germans do.

'Yes, Rachel. Thank you.'

'Sit down. He doesn't bite.'

Paul sat down next to the boy, who didn't seem particularly surprised to have a strange guest sitting at the breakfast table with him.

The humidity seemed to be gone today. Butter-yellow sunlight was streaming in between the geraniums in the window box. If his wife and daughter were back home, the three of them would've strolled into Central Park today and spread out a picnic blanket in Sheep Meadow. They would've luxuriated in the newfound aura of family.

Later, after Paul had taken a shower, after he had dressed in one of Miles' crisply ironed shirts generously provided by his wife, after he had read two newspapers – one of them Jewish, which he dutifully leafed through without understanding one word – after he had basically done *anything* to keep from jumping out of his skin, Miles called.

'Okay,' he said. 'Brace yourself. I got through.'

'What?'

'I called a few more times last night – nothing. Ten times this morning – still nothing. I finally got him this afternoon. Our friend Pablo.'

'And?' Paul felt the vague stirring of hope.

'He was suspicious, of course. To put it mildly. First he denied even knowing you. Even when I told him who I was, that I know everything that happened there. After a while he said okay, he might know you a little, but he had no idea what I was talking about. He *drove* you places, that's it. I told him to relax – no one's going to the police. His memory seemed to come back then. I told him about the house being burned down. I assured him we've still got the drugs. I think it's going to be okay. He's going to get back to me. He's going to tell us how to deliver the bag. The where and when.'

'And Joanna? And my daughter . . . Are they . . . ?'

'They're fine.'

Paul felt the large knot that had lodged somewhere in the pit of his stomach slowly begin to unwind. At least, a little.

'I asked Pablo if he was absolutely sure about that,' Miles continued. 'I laid it out for him so there'd be no mistaking. No Joanna and Joelle – no drugs. I think he got it. It's like litigation. You have to make them think you've got the upper hand, even if you don't. Who knows? Maybe we do. We've got their drugs, right?'

'Okay.'

'*Okay?* What about *that's great, Miles? That's terrific? I'm positively overjoyed at the news?*'

'I'm positively overjoyed at the news.'

'You don't sound overjoyed at the news.'

'I'm worried.'

'Okay, you're worried. Of course you're worried. Who wouldn't be in your shoes? Have some faith, I'll lend you mine if you like – no charge. I told you. We're going to get this done. He's going to call back, we're going to deliver the coke and get out of Dodge.'

'It's something else.'

'*What* something else?'

'What if we give them the drugs?'

'Okay?'

'But they still don't release them?'

It was the obvious question, of course. The same question Joanna had asked him back in that room. The one he'd been avoiding looking at too closely or too often. Something that was easy enough to do when he was dodging U.S. Customs inspectors and drug-dealing kids.

155

Not now. Not when he was finally about to get two million dollars' worth of drugs into the right hands.

Miles shrugged. 'I don't know how to answer that. I think trusting them's the price of admission. Sorry, that's pretty much the way it is.'

TWENTY-TWO

They took her somewhere else without warning.

The middle of the night? The middle of the day? She didn't know. Only that she'd fallen into one of those bottomless slumbers and was happily in the middle of a sweet dream. The sweetest. She was home with Paul on what seemed like a lazy summer afternoon. A Sunday maybe, where they'd stumble out of bed around ten or so to secure a Sunday *Times* and two iced Starbucks.

The dream had that Sunday feel.

Then the door slammed open – she perceived it as a thunderclap outside their 84th Street apartment. Rainstorm to follow.

What actually followed was someone pulling her up off the mattress and directly out of her dream. Accompanied by the acrid odor of nervous, sweaty men. And the sound of harsh orders delivered in a quasi English they must've picked up from kung fu videos.

'Chop-chop,' one of the men – boys really – said to her. *'Vamos.'*

Then the ski mask came down over her head, only

backward, so that the eye holes were somewhere behind her, and all she could see was blackness.

She wondered if this was it. The end. The first steps on her way to a shallow grave in the middle of nowhere in particular. A candidate for one of those gruesome pictures in the newspapers. She tasted her own fear – a sour tang on the back of her tongue.

She'd been thinking a lot of her own death lately. Ever since Galina had summarily informed her of Paul's failure to come through. It had the power and solemnity of a death sentence being read by a hanging judge.

Not that.

Not *only* that. It was the demeanor of her guards. The boy who brought Joanna her daily breakfast no longer acted like a room service waiter hoping for a tip. There was no smiling *good morning*. Someone had gotten the message to him: She was no longer a cash cow, but a sacrificial lamb.

The other guards too. Gruff, sour, pissed off. They spoke to her with barely restrained anger and thinly disguised contempt.

She could smell the menace in the air.

Now this. She was being pulled out the door, along a hallway, then suddenly down some steps – one, two, three – she stumbled and nearly fell. They'd tied her hands together with rope – the harsh fibers dug into her wrists.

'I can't *see*,' she said. She hated the panic in her voice – the helpless-victimness of it.

She was a veteran of H.R. departments. She was used to victims parading before her desk, please-don't-hurt-me kind of girls – they were almost *always* girls, sobbingly relating one abuse or another. She would nod, smile, and comfort, but there was always a small part of her that wanted to say *why didn't you stand up for yourself? Why?*

Now she was like them, reduced to naked pleading. Her wrists were already burning and she was still inside the house. She could smell the odor of burned grease, butter, pineapple. They had to be walking through the kitchen. Not walking – stumbling, tripping, flailing.

No one had answered her. Or maybe they had. When she said *I can't see,* whoever was pulling her forward had tugged sharply on the rope. She banged her shoulder into the wall.

This was their answer. *Shut up.*

She knew she was outside from the sudden sharp smell of pine, the sweet scent of hibiscus, and the familiar if nauseating smell of gasoline. The air *felt* different – that too. It had the texture of night, already swollen with morning dew. It felt painfully sweet to be outside again. To breathe the cool air and feel a soft breeze against her throat. Only she was being taken away – from what she knew to what she didn't.

From Joelle.

A car door opened.

But it *wasn't* a door. She was pitched forward into a trunk. No gentle hands to break her fall. Her cheek met the car trunk floor flush. She cried out from the sudden pain in her jaw.

'*Silencio,*' one of them said.

The car trunk shut. Panic bound her tighter than the rope around her wrists. There was only so much air in a car trunk. She would run out of it sooner rather than later.

It didn't help that she was breathing too rapidly, her chest heaving, as if she'd just come back from a good morning run.

Slow down, she told herself. *Stop it.*

The car started with a loud rumble – she heard two car doors open and close. Then she was moving. Gently at first, like a boat drifting away from a dock. The car turned right, then left in a slow circle, before quickly picking up speed.

They seemed to be going more or less straight.

A highway?

To where? From where?

At least she wouldn't be dead of suffocation when they arrived; as soon as the car accelerated, streams of chilled air rushed in against her face. They'd removed something from the underside of the trunk so she'd be able to breathe.

This heartened her a little. If they were concerned enough to keep her alive for the trip, maybe they wouldn't kill her when they got there. Maybe.

Stay strong.

They traveled for at least an hour, possibly two. The worst part was her cramped position – her bound arms pinned underneath her body. They quickly went numb. Her shoulders were a different story – every time they hit a bump, a stabbing pain shot from her shoulders down the middle of her chest. The car needed new shocks almost as much as the highway needed new paving. A few times it felt as if they were falling into a hole.

The men had turned on the car radio. It sounded like some kind of ball game – a soccer match maybe.

Whatever it was, it had engaged the men's attention.

They were laughing, muttering, cursing. There were three of them, she thought – three distinct voices.

As long as she was surrounded by blackness, she could imagine somebody else was there with her.

Joelle.

She'd thought about having a child for five years, was consumed with it, yet when it finally happened, when she'd finally walked into the Santa Regina Orphanage and was handed this extraordinary little girl, she'd been humbled by the power of baby love. Umbilical cords were severed. This connection, she was certain, was for life.

I'll bring her back, Galina had promised.

What was a kidnapper's promise worth? Especially now that Joanna was being driven somewhere else? She felt tears running down her cheeks, only to be blotted up by the ski mask. The wool tasted like dust.

Stop it.

After a while she must've drifted off.

She was suddenly aware that the car had stopped moving. No rushing air. No stomach-turning bumps in the road. The car radio was off.

She heard a rooster crowing loud and clear.

The car trunk opened. A gray light filtered in through the wool fibers. She was pulled out by her legs. Her chin banged against the lip of the trunk. She could smell her own blood.

She was stood up. The man who did so took the opportunity to run his hands up over her breasts. *Bueno,* he said in a singsong way, and laughed.

A sudden chill gripped her. Of all the various ends she'd contemplated, of all the numerous indignities and

161

violations she'd envisioned in her darker moments, she hadn't thought about this one.

But why not?

The man stopped pawing her, began leading her somewhere. She could make out vague shapes through the wool. She was being taken into a house.

In through a door – a big step up which no one warned her about, causing her to trip and smack her knee against solid stone. She was yanked back up onto her feet again and pulled down what must've been a hallway. She could barely sense two walls on either side of her.

It smelled of *farm*, she thought.

Sheep, cows, chickens. Unvarnished wood beams. Baking bread.

Suddenly, they stopped and the ski mask was pulled off her head.

She was in a small room – not unlike the room she'd just left. The windows were boarded up just like that one. There was a dirty mattress on the floor – an identical twin to the one she'd just spent eight nights sleeping on. But there was a major difference.

People.

Two of them. Other women.

When the guards left, they came up and touched her as if they weren't quite sure she was real.

'*Hola*,' one of them said – a woman of about forty or forty-five.

'I'm American,' Joanna said. 'Do you speak English?'

'Not really. But then, neither do you,' said the other woman. And she smiled.

* * *

Their names were Maruja and Beatriz.

Maruja was a journalist – or had been one, till she'd been pulled out of her car just across the busy Plaza de Bolívar. Beatriz was a government official who'd recommended stronger action against the guerrillas. She'd paid for this by being stolen off the street in broad daylight and having to witness her bodyguard being shot dead before her eyes.

A morose-looking man the guards called *el doctor* appeared to be in charge. He appeared just minutes after Joanna was placed in the room. He told them they weren't allowed to speak to each other. *No talking*. He wagged his finger at them, like an exasperated mother superior at a convent school for girls.

The other guards were more lenient, Maruja said. Or at least more distracted. At night they mostly listened to soccer matches and soap operas on a small TV in the hall and didn't pay much attention to them.

Joanna had lost Paul, then Joelle. Now she was surrounded by people going through the same thing she was. They had husbands and children and parents. They understood.

The three of them whispered and signed. Maruja and Beatriz related their respective stories. They passed pictures of their children and spouses. Of their houses too, one in the fashionable La Calera section of Bogotá, the other nestled in the hills above the city.

When they asked Joanna if she had children, she told them yes. One. No picture, though, just the one she kept in her head. She told them what had happened to her and Paul. Maruja and Beatriz sighed, shook their heads in empathy.

The three of them slept on the one mattress, head to feet to head. Maruja, an unreformed smoker back in the real world, snored; Beatriz elbowed her in the ribs to make her stop. Apparently, sisterly affection only went so far.

They had to be in the mountains, Joanna thought. It grew icy cold that night – they breathed vapor and huddled against each other's bodies for warmth. In the morning Joanna saw tiny droplets of frost on the wooden slats covering the windows.

By the second day it felt a little like an endless pajama party. They braided each other's hair. One of the guards had procured Maruja a bottle of cheap nail polish – Purple Passion. They took turns doing each other's nails, pedicures too.

The man who'd felt Joanna's breasts kept his distance. Joanna's fear of rape faded, pushed aside by other fears. Death, of course. And another gnawing fear which was a kind of death too: Would she ever get out of there?

Maruja and Beatriz had the gray pallor of the confined and dying. Joanna wondered how long it would be before her own skin turned the same shade.

Occasionally, the guards let them watch TV with them, Beatriz confided. Maruja and Beatriz looked forward to the news shows. Sometimes their husbands would be on, offering messages of hope.

We are negotiating. We are in discussions. Stay brave.

Joanna knew there'd be no such comfort for her. Paul had left and vanished into the ether, as quickly and completely as her former life.

Her third morning, there was a knock at the door. That itself was unusual, since the guards tended to simply barge in on a whim. The three of them might be sleeping, whispering, even partially undressed and sponging themselves from a tepid bucket of water; a *whore's bath* – wasn't that the expression?

This morning they were sitting in the center of the room fully clothed, passing the time constructing lists of their favorite cities. Beatriz had picked Rome, Rio, and Las Vegas. Maruja, San Francisco, Buenos Aires, and Acapulco. It was Joanna's turn. All she could come up with was New York. The city she lived in, the one she was aching to return to.

The door opened and Galina walked in.

It was a measure of Joanna's desperation that the sight of her kidnapper gave her a rush of – what? Pleasure? Relief? Simple familiarity?

Maybe it was because Galina appeared different than the last time Joanna had seen her, when she'd solemnly informed her about Paul's failure to come through. She seemed more like the *other* Galina now – the one you wouldn't mind hanging out with on a sunny bench in the park.

She motioned for Joanna to come closer – she had something to tell her.

'We've heard from your husband,' she whispered, and squeezed Joanna's hand. 'It's going to be all right.'

And Joanna's heart, spirit – whatever that thing is that allows people to occasionally walk on air – surged. Not just because of the news. No.

Galina hadn't come to the mountains alone. One of the guards – a shy boy who looked all of thirteen – entered behind her.

He was holding Joelle.

TWENTY-THREE

They'd traveled over the Williamsburg Bridge, then through the Lincoln Tunnel, headed to a place somewhere outside Jersey City. It was five o'clock. They were on a mostly empty road flanked by fields of swaying cattails. *High as an elephant's eye.* The lyrics were from Joanna's favorite musical, *Oklahoma!* They'd attended the revival on their last anniversary, Paul told Miles.

The word *last* stuck in his throat.

It was three days and eighteen hours since he'd left his wife and child.

The swamp was throbbing with the steady hum of insects. Still, you could hear the Major League scores clear enough. Miles was listening with rapt attention.

'Baseball,' Miles said, 'is the hardest sport to handicap. Brutal.'

'You mean bet on?'

'Yeah, bet on. You've got to give runs, two, three, depending on the pitcher. The worst team in the world wins sixty times a year. Go figure. It's a sucker's bet.'

'You bet on sports?'

'Well, sure. Penny-ante. You know, twenty, thirty dollars – just to keep things interesting. It's my little rebellion against prescribed living. Orthodoxy has little rules for everything. It can drive you nuts.'

Paul guessed that going to work without his yarmulke was another one of Miles' little rebellions against prescribed living. 'Did you ever think about *not* being Orthodox?'

'Sure. But then what would I be? It's sort of like asking a black person if he ever thought about not being black. You can think about it all you like, but it's kind of who you are.'

'So? Are there rules about betting on baseball games?'

'Yeah – you have to stay away from the Padres.' Miles turned up the radio for the National League scores.

Paul felt like mentioning that he and his coworkers had spent more lunch hours than he cared to remember establishing risk ratios for specific pitches thrown to specific batters in specific parks. A bunch of regular Bill Jameses. He could've told Miles, for example, that throwing a down-and-in fastball to Barry Bonds in 3-Com Park had a risk-to-reward ratio of three to one. Every two times you got Barry, he'd launch one into the stratosphere.

He didn't, though.

Paul understood Miles was talking about sports so they wouldn't have to talk about something else. What they were doing. Meeting drug dealers in a swamp outside Jersey City. If they talked about it, they would be forced to acknowledge that they were hopelessly out of their element.

'Thank you,' Paul said.

'For what?'

'For doing this with me, I guess.'

Miles remained silent for a minute. 'I sent you to Bogotá. I told you you'd be safe. That makes me kind of responsible, doesn't it?'

'Great. Can I hire you to sue yourself?'

'Sorry. I don't do suits.'

'How long have you been a lawyer?' Paul asked after turning up the AC.

'How long?' Miles repeated, as if he'd never been asked that particular question before. 'Too long. Not long enough. Depends on the day.'

'Why did you want to be a lawyer?'

'I didn't. I wanted to be Sandy Koufax. God didn't cooperate. My fastball was more like a change. If you can't be Sandy, you get to be a doctor or lawyer. Indian chief wasn't available – it should be, we're a *tribe*, aren't we? I went for lawyer. Maybe not the kind of lawyer they expected.'

'They?'

'You know, all the wise men of the tribe. Everyone goes real estate, tax, or corporate. I went legal aid. Juvenile division.'

'What was that like?'

'Crazy. I had a caseload of about a hundred fifty. I'd get about ten minutes with each kid and a quick glance at their file before saying hi to the judge. That was it. And it's not like I could do any pleading-out there.'

'Why not?'

'You couldn't threaten the prosecutors with a long jury trial because there *are* no juries in juvenile, and kids don't really have any information worth trading. No one wants to deal. The best I could do was get them committed to a Bronx hospital, because it was safer than putting them in a juvenile hall.'

'Hospital?'

'Yeah, a mental hospital. They'd do their time popping meds instead of getting gang-raped. Trust me – it was heaven next to your average juvenile prison. For them it was the safest place on earth. Anyway, when I got to court and began mistaking Julio for Juan, and María for Maggie, I thought I might be in trouble. I told my supervisor he had to lessen my caseload – that I was committing borderline malpractice. He said *keep dreaming.* I left.'

'So you went from juvenile delinquents to Colombian babies.'

'Yeah. I thought I'd get involved at an earlier stage of development. It pays better. What about you?'

'Me?'

'Yeah. Hard to believe you always wanted to be an insurance man. What did you do – fall into it?'

No, not fall, Paul thought. *My mom died,* he wanted to say. *My mom died and I got scared.* He felt like explaining this to Miles, that like Einstein, he was merely trying to impose order and probability on a cold universe.

'More or less,' was all he said.

A dirt road appeared to the passenger side of the car – not so much a road as an indentation in the muck. A trail to nowhere in particular.

Miles slowed, then pulled over.

'They said a dirt road about three miles down,' he said, trying to peer ahead down the mostly hidden path. 'Oh well . . .' He turned the car into the opening, bouncing over a small hump.

Suddenly, cattails were scouring both sides of the Buick, making it feel as if they were traveling through a car wash. Paul, who'd hated roller coasters as a kid, hadn't liked car washes much either. His fervid imagination had attributed a malevolence to those stiff bristles, smothering sponges, and scalding jets of water.

He felt the same kind of vulnerability now. The car was safety. Outside in the swamp, who knew?

He peered through the windshield, which had quickly become a battlefield of slaughtered swamp bugs. Miles turned on the wipers in an effort to clear them – but it was as if they were beating against a monsoon.

When the road ended, they were in a small clearing all by themselves. Miles stopped the car.

'I guess this is it,' Miles said. He tapped the steering wheel, once, twice, peering nervously from side to side. Miles might've felt half responsible for Paul's predicament, but it seemed like he might be having second thoughts about actually accompanying him. 'What's the protocol with drug deals? Half-hour waiting time?' He looked at his watch. 'We're five minutes early.'

Paul said, 'Are you sure this is it?'

'No.'

'Great. Just checking.'

Ten minutes went by. Miles commented on the weather, then immediately ran out of small things to say. Paul understood. Making conversation when you're scared shitless was an effort. Paul rubbed his hands together and attempted to swallow his own dry spit.

Paul heard the car first.

'Someone's coming,' he said.

A minute later a blue Mercedes-Benz emerged out of the cattails and came to a lurching stop about twenty feet from them.

Both cars sat there, facing each other.

'Okay,' Miles said after a good minute went by, 'I guess we get out.'

Miles flipped the trunk switch, pushed his door open, and gingerly stepped out of the car. Paul followed.

They met at the back of the car.

'You want to hold it?' Miles said. 'Or me?' The well-traveled black bag was peeking out from under an old tarp.

'I'll take it,' Paul said. 'I'm the one who was supposed to deliver it in the first place.'

He pulled his bag out. No one had gotten out of the other car. It was still sitting there, its engine idling, no discernible movement from inside.

'Did you hear the one about the lawyer and the actuary?' Miles said.

'No.'

'Me either.'

They approached the Mercedes side by side. It reminded Paul of a western – just about every western ever made, where the two lawmen stride toward the gunslingers shoulder-to-shoulder in the movie's final showdown. As a responsible actuary he would be remiss not to mention that legions of western heroes had defied the odds – roughly fifty-fifty – of getting their heads blown off.

The Mercedes' driver's door opened. Two men stepped

out of the car. They might've been car salesmen. No mirrored sunglasses, heavy gold chains, or garish tattoos. Instead, they wore well-pressed chinos and golf shirts. One in a powder-blue Izod, the other opting for a striped Polo.

The driver – he was in Polo – nodded at them. 'You guys look a little nervous.'

Okay, Paul thought, give him points for being perceptive.

'Which one's Paul, huh?' he asked. He spoke with a noticeable accent – Colombian, Paul assumed. His voice was high-pitched, almost girlish.

Paul had to restrain himself from raising his hand.

'Me. I'm Paul.' They'd stopped about five feet from each other. The black bag seemed to be growing heavier by the second.

The driver nodded, slapped his neck. 'Fucking mosquitoes. I'm gonna get West Nile.' When he took his hand away, there was a blotch of bright blood on his neck.

He looked at Miles. 'Who are *you*, my friend?'

'His lawyer,' Miles said.

'His lawyer?' He laughed and turned to his companion. 'Fuck me, I don't have a lawyer.' He turned back to them. 'Are we going to have to sign papers or something?'

Miles said, 'No papers. If you could just make sure they give him his wife and daughter back.'

'Hey, don't know what you're talking about. *Not my job,*' he said, affecting a thicker accent for comic effect. No one laughed. 'I'm here to sight the white, okay?'

'Okay,' Miles said.

Paul remained silent. Good thing. He was too scared to speak.

'So, boss?' the driver said. 'You here to give me the bag or ask me to dance?' The other man laughed.

Paul held the bag out at arm's length.

'Open it,' the driver said. 'I like to see what's inside first.'

Paul laid it on the dirt ground and zipped it open. When he bent down, he felt light-headed and nearly tipped over. Something began humming in the swamp, an überhum, the biggest insect in the pond.

The driver stepped forward and gazed down at the bag.

'Huh? Looks like fucking *rubbers* to me.' He had a lazy left eye; he seemed to be looking in two directions at once.

Paul started to explain. 'They're filled with –'

'Shit, I *know* what they're filled with. I'm goofing with you, boss.' He smiled. 'Let's take one out and make sure, okay?'

When Paul hesitated, the man said, 'You do it. No offense, but they were up *your* ass.' He turned to his pal. '*Culero,* eh?'

The insect hum had gotten louder – Paul's ears were ringing. Paul reached into the bag and took out a condom, neatly tied in a knot by one of those women back in Colombia. He held it out in his now seriously sweating palm.

The driver pulled something out of his pocket.

Click. A sinuously shiny blade caught the light. Paul tensed, and Miles took one step back.

'Relax, *muchachos.*' He gripped Paul's hand, almost gently, and pointed the blade straight down. Paul wondered if the man noticed his hand was shaking.

He did.

'Don't worry,' he said to Paul. 'I've only slipped a couple of times.'

He flicked the blade at Paul's palm. When Paul twitched, he laughed and did it again. The other man – the one wearing the Izod with the little green alligator – said something in Spanish. He had a thin, almost whispery voice.

The driver jabbed the end of the blade into the condom, opening up a tiny slit. He was reaching down to scoop up some of the white powder onto his finger when something happened.

It was that hum.

It had grown even louder, *annoyingly* loud, as if it were causing vibrations in the ground itself. You wanted to shout *shut up,* to swat whatever it was with a newspaper, to crunch it under your shoe.

It would have been useless, though. Using your shoe.

The two cars plowed out of the cattails at about the same time.

Jeeps, the kind with fat, deeply treaded tires and juiced-up engines. They were belching black smoke and closing fast.

The man looked up and slapped his neck again. And just like last time, his hand came away with smeared blood.

'They shot me,' he said.

He grabbed the bag and ran. The other man too. They vanished into the cattails. Polo and Izod.

Paul felt frozen to the spot. It took something whizzing past his ear and puck-pucking into the ground about a foot from his left shoe to actually get him to move. That, and Miles, who grabbed his right arm and yelled, 'Run.'

He scrambled after Miles into the weeds.

He could hear this behind him: the sound of rumbling engines being shut off, of car doors slamming, of shouts and screams and war whoops. He thought westerns again: the outlaw band riding into town on a Saturday night intent on letting off a little steam, firing their six-shooters into the air. *Jeep Riders in the Sky.*

Only they were shooting semiautomatics, and they were shooting them in their direction.

Paul ran straight through the cattails, dry thin stalks whipping his face and arms. He followed the shape of Miles' disappearing body. The ground wasn't conducive to running for your life – it was wet, thick, and mucky. Ten seconds into the weeds his socks were soaked to the skin.

Behind him the men were still screaming. They were still shooting too – cattail heads were disappearing like airborne dandelion spores.

And something else, something that had become uncomfortably and chillingly clear.

The gunmen were *following* them.

The cattails, Paul gratefully noticed, *were* as high as an elephant's eye. Wonderfully, gloriously high. High enough, Paul thought, to completely swallow them. He could barely make out jittery patches of blue sky overhead. The dealers had chosen an impenetrable place that would be hidden to just about everyone.

They stood a chance.

He remembered something. In the childhood game of rock, paper, scissors – paper, the most fragile substance on earth, always won out over rock. Why?

Because paper can *hide* rock.

Somehow the thought didn't comfort him.

He kept running, panting after Miles as if he were a faithful hound out duck hunting. He tried not to dwell on the fact that they were the ducks. His feet churned up dollops of mud, his blood jackhammered into his ears.

The men were behind them and gaining.

Paul wasn't certain whom it occurred to first – Miles or him. It seemed like they both stopped running at almost the same moment. They turned and stared at each other and made the same unspoken decision more or less in unison. They dropped straight to the ground.

If they could hear the men chasing them, then the men could hear them.

Lie down and do nothing.

Their pursuers would have to get lucky.

Do the numbers. He imagined it as an actuarial problem that had been dropped on his desk. The square mass of two bodies, divided into the square mileage of this swamp, divided by six or seven people looking for them. What were the odds of being found? Substitute the cattails for hay, and they were the proverbial needles.

They hugged the ground.

It soon became apparent that Izod and Polo had different ideas.

They were still running. Somewhere off to the left – the sound of two small breezes whipping through the weeds.

But behind them a kind of tornado.

Run, Paul thought. *Run, run.*

They had the drugs. They were carrying Joanna's fate in their hands. They had to make it out of the swamp.

But the sounds of separate footsteps seemed to converge into one dull roar. Then someone screamed, and suddenly all sound stopped. Even the insects seemed to bow their heads in a moment of silence.

After a minute or so it picked up again, like a skipped record finding its groove.

What happened?

Paul received his answer almost immediately.

'Hey!' someone shouted. '*Hey!* We got your dancing partner here. He looks kind of lonely.'

They'd captured one of them. Izod or Polo. Just *one*. The other one was still out there. He was probably lying low like them – being a needle.

The sound of the gunmen searching wavered in and out, like a faulty shortwave signal. Once Paul glimpsed a red Puma sneaker about ten feet from him – that's it. He shut his eyes and waited for the bullet in his back. When he opened his eyes and peeked, the sneaker was gone.

He went back to the problem that had been dumped on his desk. Risk ratios had to be formulated, tabulated, and segmented for another potentially dangerous activity.

Plane Travel.

Driving a Car.

Construction Jobs.

Lying in a Swamp Being Pursued by Homicidal Gunmen.

'Tell you what,' one of their pursuers screamed. 'Got a deal for you, *bollo*. You come on in now, we won't kill you. How's that?'

Bollo. Pussy. One of the Spanish words eighth graders taught themselves, snickering, between classes.

Okay, Paul wondered, why were they only concentrating on the other drug runner in the weeds? Was it possible they hadn't seen Miles and him in the clearing? Was it?

Miles answered the question for him. 'He must have the bag,' he whispered. 'They want the *drugs*.'

The man with the high-pitched voice and lazy eye. Polo. He'd snatched Paul's bag when the shots rang out.

The gunman shouted for the lazy-eyed man to come in, called him a *bollo,* an *abadesa,* a *culo* – all not-so-nice things, Paul imagined. He repeated his proposition. If he'd only stand up and walk toward them bag in hand, he'd get out of the swamp with his life – honest injun.

Still no answer.

Paul assumed Polo didn't believe a word of it. They'd already put a bullet into his neck – if he wasn't going to die of West Nile, he might expire from that.

'Okay,' the man shouted, 'okay, that's cool. How about some music while you think it over? For your listening pleasure.'

Someone walked back to the Jeeps and turned on a CD player. Or maybe it was the car radio. Latin samba came wailing through the cattails. Screeching trumpets and a good steady beat. *Music, that's nice of them.* Only something seemed wrong with this music. It sounded shrill and off-key.

It took a minute or so for Paul to understand why.

At first Paul thought it might be a trick of the air, an aberration in sound waves caused by the thick cattails and even thicker heat. It wasn't.

It was a man screaming. Izod.

They were torturing their prisoner in time to the music.

To cover up the sound. Or because it made it more fun. Or because they liked samba.

One, two, three . . . scream.

They kept at it for an entire song – the longest song on earth.

'American Pie' might be nineteen and a half minutes. This song was longer.

Finally, it stopped. 'What ya think?' the man shouted. 'Celia Cruz, *mi mami*. A fucking scream, no?'

Paul turned to Miles.

'Who are they?'

When the Jeeps had burst through the weeds and the men surged out with guns drawn and firing, he'd thought *the police. Government agents. Narcs.*

Not now.

Miles didn't answer. Maybe because his hands were up over his ears. His eyes were closed as if he didn't wish to see anything either. A long bloody scratch went from one side of his forehead to the other. He'd done Paul a favor, he'd extended himself beyond the call of reasonable duty, and now it was very possible he was going to die because of it.

'Julio.' Another voice now, thin and whispery. *'Juliooooo . . .'*

There was something pitiful about this voice.

'They broke my fingers, Julio. They broke my whole hand. My hand, *Julio . . . You gotta come in! You hear me! I can't . . . Please . . . They want the* llello, *man, that's it. For fuck's sake, come in!'*

The torturer's deal had fallen on deaf ears. They'd changed tack. It was Izod's turn.

'Listen to me . . . They broke my fingers, all my fingers,

Julio ... every one of my fingers ... Bring in the hooch ... They're killing me ... Please, Julio ... please ... You hearin' what I'm sayin'?'

Julio remained mute.

They gave it another song.

Another samba, played with the volume cranked down, so the man's screams were louder, in your face, standing out even over the spanking rhythm and blaring horns.

Sometimes he screamed actual words.

Ayudi a mi madre!

Please help me, Mother!

The music stopped again.

Paul heard sniffling, a horrible mewling sound.

'Julioooo ... my ear. They cut my ear off. It hurts ... oh, it hurts, Julio ... oh, it hurts ... Come in ... Please come in ... Please ... You GOT to ... They cut my ear off, Julio ... You understand ...'

Julio might've understood – he would've had to be deaf, dumb, or *dead* not to understand. He wasn't coming in.

Paul pushed his head to the ground. It stank like rotting vegetables. If he were an ostrich, he would've stuck his head into the ground and kept it there.

It was hard listening to a man being tortured. Even one you didn't know. He knew him well enough to *see* him. Neatly pressed pants and a powder-blue Izod turned bloodred. There was a black hole where one of his ears used to be.

'No ... no, please no ... Don't ... No, not my balls ... please, not my balls, no ... Julio, don't let them cut my balls off ... Pleeeeease, Julio, no ... Don't let them do that ... No –'

A bloodcurdling howl.

It was so loud one of the torturers told him to *shut the fuck up*. The man whose testicles he'd just sliced off.

The man *did* shut up.

For a while there was mostly silence. Just the insects, the slightest breeze rustling through the cattails.

May I have some water?

It was him again.

I'd like some water. Please. Some water . . .

Softly and politely, as if he were in a restaurant talking to a waiter.

As if they might politely answer him back.

Sure, still or sparkling?

Eventually, he stopped speaking. At least actual words. All verifiable human language ceased. He reverted to a guttural, indecipherable whimpering.

His tongue.

They'd cut out his tongue.

Paul couldn't listen anymore.

He needed to stop hearing.

The odds of accidental death from being struck by lightning are 1 in 71,601 for an average lifetime.

The odds of dying from being bitten by a nonvenomous insect are 1 in 397,000.

The odds of drowning in a household bathtub are 1 in 10,499.

The odds of . . .

'*Maricón*, see what you made us do. Fuck – your boyfriend bled like a fucking *cerado*. All over my goddamn shoes. We gave you a chance, you cocksucking motherfucker.'

181

Their prisoner was dead.

Someone went back to the Jeeps. Paul could hear doors being opened, then slammed shut.

'What are they doing?' Paul whispered to Miles. But Miles still had his hands over his ears – his skin had turned the color of skim milk.

They were on the march again – one or two of them, slowly moving through the fields.

Paul smelled it first.

If Joanna were there, she would have sniffed it out minutes sooner, he knew. She'd have lifted her head and said *how odd, do you smell that?*

It was wafting in through the cattails. When Paul lifted his head again in an effort to make sense of it, he heard sounds of splashing.

'They're making a line,' Miles whispered, his first actual conversation in the last half hour. He'd finally taken his hands off his ears – was *all* ears now, but he clearly didn't like what he was hearing.

A line? What did Miles mean? *What* line?

'The wind's blowing that way,' Miles said. First an enigmatic pronouncement about *lines,* now the weather report.

'They're going to burn him out,' Miles said in a weirdly detached voice. 'They're going to make him run right *to* them.'

That smell.

Kerosene.

Okay, Paul finally understood. He got it. Much as he didn't want to, much as he wanted to remain dumb and clueless. They were laying down a line of *kerosene.* They

182

were making this line behind them, behind the wind itself, which was blowing away from them. Paul pictured it – a solid wall of flame. And he pictured something else – that house in Jersey City. What *used* to be a house in Jersey City. The place he was supposed to meet the two guys in the blue Mercedes, Polo and Izod. Only he hadn't met them, because someone had burned down the house – reduced it to a dark primeval hole.

Who?

The same guys who were circling them with kerosene in their hands. That was the logical conclusion – what the empirical evidence would lead you to.

Paul had twice tried to deliver the drugs, and twice he'd been stopped by the same band of arsonists.

Paul turned to Miles once again to ask him something, but the question flew out of his head at the sight of Miles edging backward on elbows and knees. He looked . . . odd. Like a white person trying to dance black. Like he was doing the *worm.* He was doing it double-time; moving at the speed of panic.

Paul saw why.

The odds of dying from smoke or fire are 1 in 13,561.

The first flame had shot up into the air about fifty yards behind and to their right. It looked biblical – like a solid pillar of fire. The line of cattails would light up like briquettes soaked in lighter fluid, then be spurred forward by the wind. If they ran from the fire, they would only wind up facing another kind of fire, the kind produced by semiautomatic weapons. Miles, who'd been known to bet on a baseball game or two, was betting that he could go the other way – that he could go *toward* it. That he could make it out before the entire line lit. That he could race the fire and win.

By the time Paul caught up to him, Miles had turned himself around. They shimmied through the weeds on their bellies just a few feet apart from each other, noses inches above the pungent stink of the swamp, an odor still preferable to its alternative.

Burned flesh, Paul couldn't help noticing, smelled sickly sweet.

The men had miscalculated – tried to get someone to run who was very possibly past running. *The bullet in his neck*, Paul thought. The man in the Polo shirt was dead.

They kept crawling.

Picture those half-fish creatures in the Pleistocene era, slithering out of the water onto dry land on their way to a better future. If they'd only known what awaited them, Paul thought, they might've turned around and gone back.

He felt only half human now. Covered in slime and mud, bleeding from the razor-sharp weeds and furiously biting insects. Breathing was next to impossible – sinewy lines of choking black smoke were already snaking across the ground.

He was traveling blind. His eyes were dripping – half from the smoke and half from the awful knowledge that he'd failed.

He could sense the fire to their left. How far away? Twenty yards? Close enough to feel the heat like a wave – the kind that tumbles you into the surf and just won't let you go. Faint blisters were rising up on his forearms.

Faster. Faster. Faster.

What were the odds they'd make it now? The actuary in him said: Nil. Zippo. *Nada.*

Give up.

He couldn't. Self-preservation vanquished self-pity. If his wife and child were going to make it out of Colombia, he had to make it out of the swamp.

Paul could see the first jagged slivers of fire flickering through the stalks. The cattails were crackling, snapping, literally disintegrating in front of his half-blinded eyes. It felt as if every bit of air were being sucked out of there. The men were screaming over the fire's deafening roar like college students before a pregame bonfire.

Miles collapsed to his right.

He lay there on his belly, wheezing, desperately trying to gulp in air.

'Come on, Miles. A little further.' It took an enormous effort for Paul to get the words out of his mouth. They tumbled out half formed and garbled, as if he were speaking in tongues. They had zero effect. Miles lay there, unmoved and unmoving.

The fire was making a beeline for them. It was almost there.

'I . . . can't . . . ,' Miles whispered between gasps. 'I . . .'

Paul grabbed his shirt collar – hot and steaming, like laundry fresh from the dryer.

He pulled.

It made no sense. It was merely symbolic, since he didn't have the strength to pull Miles from the fire, any more than he had the strength to stand up and take on the murderers who'd started it.

He pulled anyway.

Suddenly, Miles seemed to gather what little energy he had left. He moved. Just a foot or so. Then another foot. And after coughing up some black phlegm, a foot more.

It was too late.

They were in the mouth of the furnace. It was yawning open for them. They weren't going to make it.

Though I walk through the valley of the shadow of death, my . . . My rod and my . . . My rod . . . Where were the words when you really needed them? He was down to crawling on bloodied hands and knees. He was doing what any atheist does in foxholes. He was mumbling the magic words he'd abandoned as a sad and lonely little kid.

Miles was there beside him. The fire lit him up like someone in a flash-frame.

Paul's flesh began to sear – to literally burn off. He took one last lunge, then covered up his face, hoping it wouldn't hurt.

That was all.

TWENTY-FOUR

Nothing had been said to her. But she knew just the same.

Galina might've told her it was going to be all right, but it wasn't all right.

It was monotonous and deadening and endless.

Every moment, at least, that she wasn't holding Joelle in her arms. Those moments, by contrast, were achingly life-affirming.

She got to experience those moments only twice a day – for morning and evening feedings. Galina would bring her to another room in the farm – she was fairly sure it *was* a farm, since she could hear roosters and chickens and the bleating of cows and sheep. She could smell them too – mixed in with the unmistakable odor of freshly turned manure. She'd been born in Minnesota, farm country, and her olfactory senses had been honed on those earthy smells.

When she asked Galina what happened – whether Paul had delivered the drugs like he was supposed to – she shrugged and didn't answer.

No answer was necessary. He had or he hadn't, but Joanna knew that she needn't be packing her bags anytime soon.

It was the routine that saved her – those morning and evening feedings, waited for with a tingling anticipation. It was routine that was murdering her too, bit by bit. The sameness, the torpor, the sense of unyielding and unbroken siege.

Her emotions, raised to the sky by Galina's whispered assertion, were all dressed up with nowhere to go.

She was losing weight too – she'd become familiar with certain bones in her arms and rib cage she hadn't known were there.

One night she heard a furious slapping from somewhere in the house. Followed by someone moaning – a man.

She sensed Beatriz and Maruja awake and listening next to her on the mattress.

'Who's that?' she whispered.

'Rolando,' Maruja whispered back.

'Rolando,' Joanna echoed the name. 'Who's he? Another prisoner?'

'Another journalist who's become the story,' Maruja said.

'Like you?'

'No. Not like me. Bigger. His son . . .' And her voice trailed off as if she'd fallen back asleep.

'His *son*. What about his son?'

'Nothing. Go to sleep.'

'Maruja. What . . . ?'

'He had a son . . . that's all. Shhh . . .'

'What happened to him? Tell me.'

'He became sick.'

'Sick?'

'Cancer. Leukemia, I think. He wanted to see his papa one more time. Before he died.'

'Yes?'

'It was in the newspapers,' she whispered. 'On the television. A big kind of national soap opera. They let Rolando watch. The talk shows. He saw his son on TV speaking to him, pleading with them to let him go.'

Joanna tried to imagine what it must've been like for a father to witness his dying son on TV, but gave up because it was too painful to contemplate.

'People came forward – how do you say . . . *los famosos*. Politicians, actors, *futbolistas*. They volunteered to take Rolando's place. Take *us*, they said, so Rolando can be with his son. He had a few months to live.'

'What happened?'

Maruja shook her head – Joanna's eyes were getting used to the dark, and she could make out the vague outline of Maruja's pointy chin.

'Nothing happened.'

'But the boy . . .'

'He died.'

'Oh.'

'Rolando watched his funeral on TV.'

Joanna wasn't aware she'd begun crying. Not until she felt the wet mattress against her cheek. She'd never been much of a crier. Maybe because she spent most of her workday getting other people to *stop*, even as she secretly resented their public displays of weakness. But now she

189

thought it was both terrible and wonderful to cry. It made her feel *human*. Knowing that she was still capable of being moved by someone else's tragedy, even in the midst of her own.

'Rolando?' Joanna asked. 'How long has he been here?'

'Five years.'

'Five years?'

It didn't seem possible. Like hearing about one of those people who've survived for decades in a coma, kept alive in a kind of suspended animation.

'When his son died, Rolando became very angry with them. He doesn't listen. He talks back,' Maruja said, as if she were snitching on another child. Joanna wondered if Rolando's defiance made life difficult for Beatriz and Maruja. Probably. 'He ran away once,' Maruja whispered. 'They caught him, of course.'

Ran away. The very sound of it caused Joanna's heart to quicken – what a mysterious and exotic notion.

To run away. Was such a thing possible?

She heard some more slapping, yelling, what sounded like someone being slammed into a wall. Joanna shut her eyes, tried not to picture what was going on in that room. Rolando was *tied to the bed*, Maruja said.

She imagined what running away would be like instead – how it would feel. She pictured the wind at her back, the scent of earth and flowers, the dizzying sense that every footstep was putting distance between her and them. It was such a delightful dream she almost forgot whom she'd be leaving behind.

Joelle.

They had her baby.

The fantasy dissipated – *poof.* She was left with an empty ache in her chest, the hole that's left when hope takes off for parts unknown.

Eventually, the slapping subsided – a door slammed shut.

She had trouble getting back to sleep. Maruja and Beatriz were slumbering away, but she remained obstinately awake. In a few more hours it would be morning and Galina would bring Joelle to her, and together they would feed and change her.

It was something worth holding on to. Even in this place. Sleeping three to a bed, and in the next room a man tied up like a barnyard animal.

She dozed off but was awakened what seemed like minutes later by the crazy rooster who seemed to crow all hours of the day and night.

JOELLE HAD A COUGH.

When Galina placed her in Joanna's arms, her little body shook with each tiny eruption.

'It's just a cold,' Galina said.

But when Joanna tried to feed her, Joelle refused the rubber nipple. Joanna waited a few minutes, tried again, Joelle still wouldn't eat. She kept coughing with increasing and violent regularity. Each cough caused her deep black eyes to go wide, as if she were surprised and affronted by it. Joanna pressed her lips to Joelle's forehead – something she'd seen friends do with their own children.

'It's *hot*, Galina.'

Galina slipped a hand under Joelle's T-shirt to feel her chest, then laid her cheek against her forehead.

'She has a fever,' Galina confirmed.

Joanna felt her stomach tighten. *So this is what it's like,* she thought. Being terrified not for yourself, but for your child.

'What do we do?'

They were in the small room Galina always took her to for feedings. Four white walls with the faint impression of a crucifix that must've once hung over the door. They walked her there maskless now, something that had both comforted and terrified her the first time. It had seemed to make an astonishing statement to her: *You're in for the long haul.* There was no need to play hide-and-seek with her anymore.

When Galina put her hand on Joelle's forehead, she pulled it away as if it were singed.

'Wait,' she said, and left the room.

She came back waving something. A magic wand?

No. The thermometer she'd purchased for them in Bogotá. Joanna numbly let Galina remove Joelle's diaper – her thighs were chafed and red. Galina placed her stomach-down on Joanna's lap and told her to hold her still.

She gently eased the thermometer in.

When Joanna saw the mercury climbing, she said, 'Oh.' An involuntary response to naked fear. When Galina took it out and held it up to the light, it was nudging 104.

'She's sick,' Joanna said. This wasn't the little fever babies get from time to time. This was for real.

Galina said, 'We need to sponge her down.'

'Aspirin?' Joanna said. 'Do you have baby aspirin here?'

Galina looked at her as if she'd asked for a DVD player or a facial. They were obviously somewhere rural – a place where the guards were relaxed enough to watch TV at night and not really bother to stop Maruja, Beatriz, and Joanna from talking to each other. A place as far away from a stocked pharmacy as it was from the USDF patrols looking for them.

Her daughter's fever was sky-high. It didn't matter. They were on their own.

'Please.' Joanna heard the pleading in her own voice, but this time it didn't surprise or disgust her. She would beg on hands and knees for her baby. She'd offer to give her right arm or her left arm, or her life.

'If we sponge her, it'll bring her fever down,' Galina said, but she didn't sound very convincing. The worry lines in her face had taken on an aspect of true fear. Joanna found that far more terrifying than the sight of the soaring thermometer.

Galina left in search of a wet rag.

How strange, Joanna thought. That Galina seemed able to effortlessly change back and forth between kidnapper and nurse, first one, then the other.

She came back carrying a pewter bowl filled with sloshing water. Somewhere she'd found a small hand towel, which she liberally soaked while sneaking worried peeks at a still-screaming Joelle. She wrung it out and began gently sponging her down. Joelle didn't cooperate – she twisted and turned on Joanna's lap as if the touch of the rag were physically painful.

She was screaming in anguished, heartbreaking bursts. Her tiny body quivered.

Joanna grabbed Galina's hand. 'It's not helping. It's making it worse.' The wet rag hung down limply, drops of water softly hitting the rough wooden floor.

Pat, pat, pat.

'Look at her, for God's sakes. *Look at her.*'

'It'll bring the fever down,' Galina said. 'Please.' But she didn't attempt to yank her arm away. What would the guards think if they saw Joanna with her hand wrapped around Galina's bony wrist?

Joanna let go.

When Galina finished, she felt Joelle's forehead again. 'A little cooler, yes?'

But when Joanna felt it, it was like touching fire.

Galina diapered Joelle, lifting her off Joanna's lap, rewrapped her in a rough wool blanket. Joelle was still wailing away – her red face clenched like a fist – as Joanna rocked her against her breasts and shuffled back and forth in the small space allotted to them. She sang to her, barely above a whisper.

Hush, little baby, don't say a word,
Mommy's gonna buy you a mockingbird.
If that mockingbird don't sing . . .

Her mother used to sing that to her. She'd play the James Taylor, Carly Simon duet on the living room stereo and dance around the Castro Convertible with Joanna in her arms. It had always made Joanna feel safe and adored.

It wasn't working with Joelle.

She'd stopped screaming, but only because she'd cried herself out. When she opened her mouth, there didn't seem to be enough energy left to emit a human sound.

Galina said, 'I have to take her now.'

'No.'

'They'll get angry if I don't.'

Joanna was too scared to notice, but later she'd turn Galina's words over and over in her mind.

They'll get angry if I don't.

The first tiny admission that in the us-versus-them dynamic of the household – Maruja, Beatriz, and Joanna versus their guards – there might be another *them* too.

Galina and her.

Galina would've left Joelle with her, only she couldn't because *they'd* get angry.

In a world devoid of tangible hope, you grasped at verbal straws.

She gave Joelle back to Galina. She was led back to her prison, otherwise known as their room, where Maruja and Beatriz saw the expression on her face and asked what was wrong.

WHEN EVENING FEEDING CAME AROUND, GALINA SHOWED UP AT the door looking ghostly pale. That wasn't the alarming part.

She was Joelle-less – *that* was the alarming part.

'What happened? Where is she?' Joanna asked.

'In her crib. She finally cried herself to sleep. I didn't want to wake her.'

She took Joanna to the feeding room anyway, past two mestizo guards playing cards – one of them a girl with chestnut skin and shimmering black hair that fell to the small of her back. After Galina shut the door, she said, 'She has pneumonia.'

195

'*Pneumonia?*' The word resounded like a slap. 'How do you know? You're not a doctor. Why would you say that?'

'Her chest. I can hear it.'

'It could be a virus? Just the flu?'

'No. Her lungs – they're filled with *flúido*.'

Fear gripped Joanna and refused to let go.

'You've got to get her to a hospital, Galina. You *have* to. Now.'

Galina stared at her with an expression that under different circumstances Joanna might've termed tender.

It was the tenderness shown toward the hopelessly brain-addled.

'There *are* no hospitals,' Galina said. 'Not here.'

THAT NIGHT JOANNA COULD HEAR HER DAUGHTER SCREECHING.

It made the guards unhappy. It got on their nerves. In the middle of the night one of them pulled her off the bed, where she'd been holding Beatriz' hand to keep from running to the door and screaming at them.

'*Vamos,*' he said, shoving her toward the open doorway.

Beatriz got up to protest.

'*Para eso –*'

The guard, who was called Puento and was usually docile and amiable, shoved Beatriz against the wall.

A crying baby can test a new parent's patience, according to *Mother & Baby* magazine.

Where was Puento taking her?

After he'd locked the door behind them, another guard walked up to them carrying Joelle at arm's length. Later Maruja would tell her that FARC *guerrilleros* were particularly nervous about getting sick, since there were no doctors around to treat them.

The jittery boy literally dumped Joelle into her arms, then motioned her toward the feeding room. He ushered her in at a safe distance, giving Joanna a small shove in the back with the rifle butt. He slammed the door behind them.

Joelle was swimming in sweat.

Every breath produced a strangled, raspy gurgle. When Joanna put her ear to Joelle's chest, it sounded like someone dying of emphysema.

Where was Galina?

Joanna pounded on the door – once, twice, three times. Eventually, Puento opened it, looking intent on pounding something back.

Joanna asked him to get Galina to come immediately, right now, *this very second.*

No response.

She asked for a rag instead, nervously pantomiming the act of wringing one out. She couldn't tell whether Puento understood her, and if he did, whether he cared.

She'd say no. He slammed the door in her face.

Minutes later, though, he returned with a piece of filthy cloth. He threw it in her general direction.

She'd neglected to ask for *agua* – fortunately, the rag seemed damp enough without it. Joanna went through the now familiar ritual of unwrapping and undiapering her baby, trying not to notice her nearly blue skin and hummingbird shiver. She wiped her down the way Galina would have.

'It's going to be okay,' she whispered to her daughter.

'We're going to get home and see Daddy. You're going to like New York. There's a merry-go-round, and in the winter we can ice-skate. There's a zoo with polar bears and monkeys and penguins. You'll love the penguins. They walk kind of funny.'

She held her baby the entire night. Most of the time Joelle screamed and moaned and gurgled. Those were the good moments. The terrifying ones were when Joelle slipped into sleep and her breathing seemed to stop altogether.

Once, when Joelle was clearly and demonstrably alive, basically screaming her lungs out, Puento opened the door and looked in with a nearly murderous expression. He raised his ever-present Kalashnikov – that's what Paul said they were called, *Russian-made rifles,* ancient and unreliable – and pointed it straight at Joelle's head.

'I'll make her stop. She's sick. I'll get her to stop. I promise.'

He lowered the rifle and shut the door.

Joanna must've nodded off.

She woke up when someone shook her by the shoulder.

It was Galina.

The first thing Joanna noticed was the utter lack of crying, the absolute and shocking quiet. The second thing she noticed was that there was no Joelle in her arms. Gone. For one heart-stopping moment she thought her daughter hadn't made it through the night. That Galina had come to tell her that Joelle's body had been taken away, buried in some field.

She was about to start screaming when she *saw* her.

She was lying peacefully in Galina's arms.

She was breathing better, not normally, no – but absolutely, unequivocally *better*.

'I got her medicine,' Galina said. 'Liquid drops. *Antibióticos*. She's going to make it, I think.'

Galina had traveled over one hundred miles, Joanna would learn later. She'd called a doctor she knew – she'd gotten a *farmacia* to open up and give her the drops.

She's going to make it, I think.

Joanna's new mantra.

Joelle had grown noticeably cooler, her cough had quieted to manageable, she'd mostly stopped shaking.

Galina watched Joanna feed her. Galina seemed oddly transfixed, even mesmerized. Maybe it was lack of sleep, Joanna thought.

No, this was different, as if she were borne away by memory.

Joanna remembered.

I had a daughter.

'Galina?'

It seemed to take a minute for Galina to come out of her reverie and actually answer her.

'Yes?'

'Your daughter. What happened to her?'

Galina turned, cocked her head at an awkward angle, as if she were trying to hear something from the next room. Or maybe it was from somewhere further away.

'She was killed,' Galina said.

'Killed?' Joanna wasn't prepared for that word. Dead, yes, but *killed*? 'I'm so sorry – that's horrible. How, Galina? What happened?'

Galina sighed. She looked away, up at the shadow of

the crucifix still visible on the wall. She made the sign of the cross with a slightly trembling hand.

'Riojas,' she whispered. 'Have you heard of Manuel Riojas?'

TWENTY-FIVE

Galina was staring at mother and child.

She was thinking:

Holy Mary, Mother of God.

For just a moment it was like that picture on my bureau. Faded almost to black and white after so many years, but suddenly come to life. Yes.

It was me. And her. My child.

She was back in my arms. She was that young again.

Just a niña. *My* niña.

Was she ever that small?

Was she?

You can remember, can't you?

CLAUDIA.

Clau-di-a.

Her name was like a song. Scream it down the streets of Chapinero around suppertime, or down the stairs of their *apartamento* after school, and it was hard to keep its singsong rhythm out of your voice – even when you were good and mad. Even when you were *pretending* to be mad, because Claudia hadn't done her homework yet, or she was late to dinner.

It was impossible to *really* be mad at her. She was that kind of child. The gift from God. She always got around to doing her homework eventually, and she always did it well enough to get As.

She might be late for supper too, but when she arrived, out of breath and suitably contrite, she'd barrage them with a dizzying recounting of the day's events.

Turn down the radio and eat, Galina would say.

But the truth was, she enjoyed listening to the radio more than she enjoyed seeing her scrawny daughter eat.

Claudia was one of those oddly *aware* children. Precociously sensitive to the world and to most of its inhabitants. An unrepentant toy-sharer, even after her favorite doll – Manolo the bullfighter – had his leg torn off by the bratty girl down the hall.

She was the kind of child who wore out the word *why*. Why this, why that, why *them*?

In a country like Colombia, Galina always believed *why* was a word best avoided.

Maybe it was destined, then, that when Claudia got to La Nacional University – with honors, of course – she'd fall in with a certain crowd. That when she started getting answers to those persistently indignant questions – like why do one percent of Colombians control ninety-eight percent of the wealth, why has every program to alleviate poverty and hunger failed miserably, why were the same people saying the same things in the same positions of power, why, why, *why* – she'd align herself with those who might do something about it.

Or, at least, *talk* about doing something.

Simple political clubs at first. Harmless debating societies.

Don't worry, Mama, she'd tell Galina and her father. *We drink coffee and argue over who's going to pay the bill. Then we talk about changing the world.*

Galina did worry.

She had a reasonably developed social conscience herself; it had never done her much good. She could still remember the rallies for Gaitán – the half-mestizo leader determined to democratize Colombia – and recall with poignant fondness the feeling that had wafted through the streets like a spring breeze in the dead of winter. *I am not a man, I am a people.* She could remember his riddled body on the front page of her father's newspaper. After that, a kind of fatalism had set in – like hardening of the arteries, it came progressively with age. The young were inoculated against *that* particular disease; it took years of wear and tear before idealism crumbled like so much bric-a-brac.

Claudia began spending more time out of the house.

More late nights, which she'd attribute to one boyfriend or another.

Galina knew better.

Claudia was flush with love, yes. But not for a boy. That nervous agitation and those shining eyes were for a cause. She had a monstrous crush on a conviction.

Now when Galina warned her about becoming involved in *la política,* she was invariably met with stony silence or, worse, an exasperated shake of the head, as if Galina could have no concept of such things. Of what was wrong and needed *fixing*. As if she were an imbecile, blind and deaf to the world.

It was precisely the opposite. It was her very *knowledge* of the world – of how things worked in Colombia, or didn't, because in truth nothing worked in their country, nothing at all – it was *that* painfully accrued understanding that made her so frightened for her daughter.

When did Claudia first make contact with *them*?

Maybe when she told Galina she was going on a holiday excursion with girlfriends. *To Cartagena,* she said. When she returned ten days later, there wasn't a tan line to be seen. If anything, she looked paler. *The weather was awful,* she explained. Galina was sorely tempted to check the papers to confirm this. She didn't.

Cartagena was north. But so, she knew, was FARC.

These little trips became more and more routine.

To a university seminar, she'd explain.

To visit a friend.

A camping trip.

One lie after another.

What was Galina to do? Claudia was of age. Claudia was in love. What were Galina's options, other than to wait it out, hope it would pass like most first loves do. She was being handed a tissue of lies, and she was using it to dry her tears.

Claudia began dressing down. All kids did to some extent, but Claudia wasn't making a fashion statement. More a statement of *solidarity.* She began going days without makeup, without so much as peeking into a mirror.

She didn't know that it only made her more beautiful.

Had Galina mentioned how lovely Claudia was? How perfectly exquisite? Almost *feline*. Sinuous, graceful. Her eyes, of course. Oval, deep amber, and her skin what Galina's *madre* used to call café au lait. She must've inherited her looks from someone other than Galina. Maybe from her paternal grandmother, the chanteuse, a *ventello* singer of some renown who'd reportedly left broken hearts from Bogotá to Cali.

One day Claudia went away and didn't come back.

Another holiday excursion, a seaside jaunt with friends. But when Galina called these friends, frantic, panicked, two days after Claudia's supposed return had come and gone with no Claudia, they professed total ignorance.

What holiday trip?

Odd. She didn't feel surprise. Just confirmation. That, and simple, unrelenting terror. She sat by the telephone, trying to will it to ring. Trying to keep herself from picking it up and dialing the *policía*. She *knew* where Galina was; bringing the *policía* into it would've been worse than doing nothing.

Eventually, Claudia *did* call.

Galina ranted, raved, screamed. The way you admonish a child. How could Claudia not call, how *could* she?

Claudia wasn't the little girl late for dinner anymore.

I'm with them, because to not be with them is to be with the others, she said.

She spoke assuredly. Logically. Even passionately. It's possible there was a part of Galina, the long-buried part of her that once cheered beside her father for Gaitán, that might've even *empathized* with her.

In the end she said what mothers say. What they're allowed to say. Even to revolutionary daughters who've gone to the hills.

You'll be killed, Claudia. They'll call me to pick up your body. Please. Come back. Please, I'm begging you.

But Claudia dismissed her pleas – the way, as a little girl, she had scoffed at wearing rubber boots in the rain.

Then I can't feel the puddles, Mama.

Claudia, above all, was a girl who wanted to feel the puddles.

Her father was devastated. He threatened to go to the *policía*, to haul her back home. *You should've known,* he accused Galina, *you should've known what she was up to.* Galina knew he was speaking out of frustration and wounded love; he knew that going to the *policía* was dangerous, and going after Claudia useless, since he wouldn't begin to know where to look.

So they sat in their private cocoon of pain. Waiting for a spring that might or might not come.

Occasionally, friends would pass on messages. It's better if she doesn't call you, a certain young man explained, a fellow traveler from the university who sported a four-inch goatee and wore a black beret in the fashion of Che. She's all right, he told them. She's committed.

Galina was committed too. To seeing her daughter's face again. She needed to touch her; when Claudia was a child, she'd settle like a nesting bird in the billows of her dress. *I'm a kangaroo,* Galina would whisper, *and you're in my pocket.*

Now her pocket was empty.

One day they received another message from the young man.

Be at such and such a bar at eight tonight.

When Galina asked why, he said *just be there*.

She didn't ask again.

They dressed as if going to church. Wasn't this, after all, what they'd been praying for? They arrived hours early. The bar was uncomfortably dark and seedy, patronized mostly by prostitutes and transvestites.

They waited an hour, two hours, three. In truth, Galina would've waited days.

Then she felt a tap on her shoulder, no, *more* than a tap, a warm hand alighting on her shoulder like a butterfly. She knew that touch. Mothers do. It had *her* blood coursing through it.

How did Claudia look? Ragged, thin, sick?

If that had been the case, maybe they would've been able to talk her back – the way you talk someone down off a ledge. Maybe they could've simply lifted her off her feet and carried her back home.

Claudia didn't look ragged. Or thin. Certainly not sick. She looked *happy*.

What's your greatest wish for your children?

The wish you end each nightly prayer with?

The one you whisper to yourself when they tell you to blow out the candles for another birthday you'd rather not be celebrating?

I wish, you murmur, *for my child to be happy.*

Only that.

Claudia looked radiantly, unmistakably happy.

Was *beaming* too strong a word?

If she'd been in the throes of first love before, now she was clearly in the midst of a full-fledged affair. One look at her, and Galina knew they'd be leaving without her.

Claudia kissed Galina, then her father.

The three of them held hands, just like when Claudia was four and she'd coerce them into another game of dog and cat. Claudia was always the cat. And the cat was always captured.

Galina asked her how she was.

But she already knew the answer.

'Good, Mama,' Claudia said.

'Why didn't you *tell* us?' Galina asked, then began doing what she'd promised herself she wouldn't. Crying, crumbling, falling to pieces.

'Shhh . . . ,' Claudia whispered, daughter-suddenly-turned-mother. 'Stop, Mama. I'm *fine*. I'm wonderful. I *couldn't* tell you. You know that.'

No. All Galina knew was that Claudia was her heart. And that from now on life would consist of hurried meetings in transvestite bars and furtive messages from friends.

Claudia told them little of anything specific. Where she was. Whom she was with. She mostly asked about home. How was her cat, Tulo? And her friends, Tani and Celine?

For their entire time together, Galina refused to let go of her hand. She must've thought, in some primitive part of her brain, that if she never let go, Claudia would be forced to stay with them. That as long as they were touching, they couldn't be apart.

She was wrong, of course. Hours flew by, the opposite of all those days waiting to hear from her when she'd felt stuck in time.

Claudia announced she had to leave.

Galina had one last, enormous plea left in her. She'd been practicing it as Claudia asked about home, about relatives and schoolmates, as Galina sat and held her hand like a lifeline.

'I want you to listen to me, Claudia. To sit and hear everything I have to say. Yes?'

Claudia nodded.

'I understand how you feel,' she began.

She did understand. It didn't matter.

'You think I'm too old. That I can't possibly feel what you feel. But I do. There was a time, when I was very young, that I was just like you. But what I know, I know. FARC, the USDF – it doesn't matter. Both sides are guilty. Both sides are blameless. In the end they are each other. Just as innocent. Just as murderous. And everyone dies. Everyone. I'm asking you as your one and only mother in the world. Please. Don't go back to them.'

She might've been speaking Chinese.

Or not speaking at all.

Claudia couldn't hear her, and even if she could, she was incapable of understanding a word.

She patted Galina's hand, smiled, the way you do to those already claimed by senility. She stood up, embraced her father while Galina remained frozen to her chair. Then Claudia reached down, put her head in the hollow of her neck.

'I love you, Mama,' she said.

That's all.

On the way home, they sat in complete, numbing silence. They'd dressed as if going to church, but they returned from a funeral.

There were just a few messages from her after that.

From time to time the boy from the university called with news. Every time Galina opened the paper, she held her breath . . .

THE DOOR CREAKED OPEN.

Galina stopped talking.

Tomás – one of the guards – nodded at her, motioned for her to get up.

Joelle was out of danger now. Joanna would have to give her back, return to her room.

'What happened to her?' Joanna asked Galina, transferring Joelle to her, suddenly desperate to know the ending. 'You didn't finish the story.'

Galina simply shook her head, pressed Joelle to her chest. Then she headed to the door.

TWENTY-SIX

He didn't know he was alive and kicking until he realized that's what he was doing. *Kicking.* Moving his legs back and forth in an effort to put out the fire that was crawling up his skin.

He must've passed out from the smoke. He remembered the wall of flame bearing down on them like an act of God. Maybe it wasn't an act of God – because he seemed to remember he'd *prayed* to God just before everything went black and here he was *alive.*

So maybe he and God had made up. Maybe God said enough with numbers and equations and risk ratios and let's try blind faith for a change, okay?

He wasn't actually on fire. Not literally. His pants, what was left of them, were smoking. And the skin poking out from their tattered remnants appeared baby pink – the telltale sign of first-degree burn.

Somehow they'd made it past the line of kerosene.

Everything to his left was a charred, smoking black. The wind had taken the fire in a single direction. Meaning Miles was right. They'd headed *toward* the fire and won.

Or he had. Miles was missing in action.

What about *them*?

Paul tentatively raised his head and peeked.

It looked volcanic. Picture one of those Discovery Channel specials where islands of lush vegetation are reduced to boiling stews of smoke and fire. Here and there scattered bursts of flame still shot high into the air.

Overall it was lunar-empty.

They were gone.

With this ecstatic realization came an equally horrific one. They were gone; so were the *drugs*. They were interred in the black soot. His one and only chance of saving Joanna had vanished. *When God shuts a door, he opens a window,* his long-dead mother used to say. But going along with his newfound doctrine of faith, it was entirely possible the reverse was also true. That when God opened a window, he shut a door.

Paul was alive; Joanna and Joelle were dead.

Soon enough.

He collapsed back onto the still-steaming earth, as if shot.

Someone said hello.

A creature with a completely black face, save for the eyes, moon white like those of a minstrel singer, his whole person surrounded in rising wisps of smoke.

An *angel*? Come to earth to tell Paul he was wrong, sorry, he hadn't survived the fire, after all? Given Joanna and Joelle's probable fate, would the news be that unwelcome?

It wasn't an angel.

It was Miles.

*　*　*

THEY FOUND MILES' CAR PRETTY MUCH WHERE THEY'D LEFT IT. Both doors were yanked open and the windshield was smashed.

That wasn't what upset Miles.

Not that they'd trashed his car, but that they'd actually *seen* it, taken note of it, jotted down his license number or maybe his registration, which was stuck somewhere in the glove compartment. Now that the euphoria of actually surviving had worn off, Miles seemed to understand that it might not be for long. He retreated to somewhere inside himself.

That made two of them.

Paul had apologized to Miles on the way to the car – *sorry for almost killing you.* Miles reiterated that he was the one who'd sent Paul and Joanna to Colombia. Only this time he hadn't sounded very convincing.

Then they'd both shut up.

The spiderweb cracks in the windshield made driving an exercise in guessing. There either were or weren't cars in front of them, lights were either green or red, road signs were anybody's guess. On the way out of the swamp they passed four fire engines screaming down the highway.

Paul tried to navigate with his head out the window.

Somewhere between Jersey City and the Lincoln Tunnel, Paul said, 'Who were they?'

Miles didn't immediately answer.

'They must've burned down the house in Jersey City,' Paul added. 'It had to be them.'

Miles nodded. 'That makes sense.'

'So?'

Miles seemed lost in thought. Either that or he was still feeling too depressed to talk. They'd entered the white fluorescent glow of the Lincoln Tunnel – always a kind of sci-fi experience.

After a while Miles said, 'I don't know who they are. I can *guess*. The other side.'

'What other side? The Colombian government?'

'The Colombian government's not going to be shooting people over here.'

'Okay. Then who are we talking about?'

'The other side in the war. Those right-wing paramilitary nuts. Manuel Riojas.' He didn't appear to be very happy about this suggestion.

'*Riojas?* I thought he's in jail. They extradited him. To Florida.'

'Sure. *He's* in jail. They're not.'

'*They?* Who's they?'

'His people. His gang. His foot soldiers. You know how many Colombians there are in New York City?'

Miles tried to clean his hands by wiping them on the seat divider, but it only succeeded in making it black.

'They followed FARC's drug contacts?' Paul said, trying to work it out as he spoke. 'That's what you're saying? Found that house in Jersey City and burned it down? Then tailed them here?'

'Maybe. Why not? They're on different sides, but they pay for things the same way. Drugs mean money. Money means guns.'

Okay, Paul thought. He wondered if sometimes money just meant money.

'Consider it a two-for-one. They get to kill a few of

FARC's friends, and score some drugs at the same time. Just my theory.'

Given what Paul had read about Manuel Riojas, it was a theory you'd rather not spend too much time thinking about.

'What now?'

'I can bullshit you and say I've got a great idea. Would you believe me?'

MILES INSISTED THEY STOP AT HIS OFFICE IN THE CITY.

'I might have a hard time explaining to my wife why we look like we've just returned from Baghdad. There's a shower there. And some clothes.'

Miles' office was in a brownstone on the East Side. Three months ago Paul and Joanna had walked in there and been told they'd have a daughter in two months.

Miles parked the car in a single-car garage beneath the building.

When they exited the car, Paul could smell that peculiar odor of garages everywhere – mildew, dust, and motor oil. Joanna, he noted with a pang, would have been able to discern a few other things as well.

They entered the house through a side door, opening onto a hallway with gray cement walls covered in a sheen of condensation. A single naked bulb supplied what little light there was.

They took the stairs up to the first floor, which contained a modest waiting room filled with out-of-date magazines. Paul remembered sitting there with Joanna, flipping through a strategically placed issue of *Time*.

Infertility – the New Scourge was the cover story.

'Bathroom's upstairs,' Miles said. 'Want to go first?'

'Thanks,' Paul said. 'I have nothing to wear.'

'I'll lend you some jeans.'

When he turned on the shower, the water at his feet turned black. The skin on his legs and arms felt scrubbed raw, and he wondered if he needed medical attention.

When he got out of the shower, he examined himself in the bathroom mirror. His face seemed okay – a little pinker than usual, certainly more despondent-looking. There was nothing a doctor could do about that.

Miles had left blue jeans and a white button-down shirt just outside the bathroom on a chair. They were about two sizes too small. He waddled out to the hallway where Miles was patiently waiting his turn.

He wordlessly passed Paul on his way to the bathroom.

When Miles came out, he was back to more or less normal skin color.

'Let's go to my office,' he said without any particular enthusiasm.

Being in the very place where Miles conducted his business, where he pulled strings and conjured up babies, didn't seem to do anything to improve his disposition. He sat behind his desk and looked strangely lost there – as if he'd forgotten what it was he did for a living.

Paul only had to look above the desk to remind himself.

He who saves one child saves the world.

Okay, Miles. There's another child who desperately needs saving now. And her *mother*. Her too.

He scanned the rest of the room while Miles sat there silent and brooding. In between an honorary degree from

Baruch Law School and a citation from the board of a Bronx hospital was a poster he hadn't seen before. *The All-Nazi Baseball Team,* it said, a diamond grid with each player's name affixed by position. *Joseph Goebbels* was on the pitcher's mound. *Always threw curves* was the scouting report on him. *Hermann Göring* was behind the plate – *great defense,* it said. *Joseph Mengele* was in right – *lethal arm. Albert Speer* at third – *surprising power.* The ball girls were *Eva Braun* and *Leni Riefenstahl.* The manager? *Hitler,* of course: *a great motivator.* Not great enough: The poster reminded everyone that the team *Lost World Championship in 1945.*

Ha, ha.

Paul wondered if Jews other than Miles found that particularly funny.

'I don't suppose you have the kind of money to make it up to them?' Miles finally said. He was looking down at his hands where his fingernails were still black, even after the shower.

'Two *million*?' Paul said. It might just as well have been two billion.

'Okay.' Miles shrugged. 'Just asking.'

Paul had come to a decision of sorts. It wasn't an easy one, but it was clearly the *only* one. It didn't matter that he'd smuggled drugs into the country. Not anymore. The drugs were gone, the cupboard bare. His family was hanging by a string.

'I'm going to the authorities,' he said.

'The *authorities*?' Miles repeated, as if it were a strange and foreign concept. 'Okay. Which authorities are we talking about?'

'The police, the government, whoever has a chance of

doing anything. The State Department, the Colombians. Every authority there is – all of them. I'm going to tell them everything – throw myself on the mercy of the court. Isn't that the expression?'

'The mercy of the court? Oh yeah, that's an expression. Absolutely. That's pretty much all it is. I don't think mercy is allowed through the metal detectors. You might want to reconsider.'

'*Reconsider?* What do you suggest I do? Tell Pablo I lost two million dollars' worth of drugs, but if he doesn't mind, I'd like my wife and daughter back anyway? I've got to do something. It's the only thing left.'

'Maybe not,' Miles said.

'What are you talking about?'

Miles stood up, stared at the four walls, began pacing back and forth behind his desk, slowly, bit by bit, seeming to regain that can-do aura right before Paul's grateful eyes, until he stopped, looked up, and snapped his fingers.

'Plan B,' Miles said.

TWENTY-SEVEN

His name was Moshe Skolnick.

He was a Russian businessman, Miles said.

What kind of business? Paul asked.

'I have no idea,' Miles answered. 'But he's awfully good at it.'

Whatever the nature of his business, Moshe did a lot of it with Colombians. 'He's got contacts there,' Miles said. 'He flies to Bogotá at least three times a year.'

Plan B, going to Moshe, was preferable to Plan C, going to the authorities, Miles said, because Paul needed someone who knew the right people. Or, more accurately, the wrong people.

'Someone who's got credibility with both sides.'

Paul had agreed to give it one more shot. If Paul was fueled by sheer unadulterated panic, Miles seemed fueled by sheer stubbornness, as if giving up would be a personal affront. Once upon a time Miles had promised them a baby and he'd only half delivered. He seemed determined to finish the job.

They were driving to Little Odessa.

'How do you know him?' Paul asked.

'That's the thing about being in my line of work. You meet all sorts of people you wouldn't ordinarily meet.'

'He was a client?'

'More like a client of a client.'

'Not a friend?'

'You don't really want him as a friend. You don't want him as your enemy either. He owes me a favor.'

First Miles dropped Paul off at his apartment.

He needed his own clothes; Miles' pants felt like they were cutting off his circulation. He needed his own surroundings and his own life. Lying low didn't much matter anymore. He and Miles had decided that if he ran into his friends John or Lisa, he'd blame Joanna's absence on a visa screwup, something Paul had come back to work out from this end. With any luck he'd avoid seeing them.

He took the stairs to lessen the odds. He made it to his apartment without running into anyone he knew.

When he shut his door, very gently because he didn't want John or Lisa to hear, he saw a crib sitting in his living room. It had pink wooden slats and frilly bedding decorated with teddy bears. An oversize red bow was stapled to it, looking like an enormous hothouse flower. It was conspicuously empty.

He walked over and picked up the card Scotch-taped to the headboard.

Congratulations on our new grandchild! Figured you'd need this when you got home. Matt and Barbara.

Joanna's parents, making their first down payment on grandparenthood.

He felt a stab of pain somewhere under his heart. If heartache was a misnomer, if emotions resided somewhere in your brain and not lower down, why did it physically hurt *there*?

They should've been home by now. The three of them.

Friends would've come calling, toting bakery cakes, bottles of champagne, tiny pink baby clothes. Joanna's parents would've settled into the guest room for a solid week or so. The apartment would've been pulsing with life.

Its current emptiness seemed to accuse him of something. He knew what too.

All he had to do was look at the clock sitting on the living room TV, the time and date prominently displayed in numbers the color of blood.

Miles would be back in fifteen minutes to pick him up. He dressed in chinos and a T-shirt, threw his cellular phone into his pocket, and headed for the door.

His answering machine was pulsing green.

Oh well.

He hit the play button.

Hello, Mr Breidbart. I'm calling on behalf of Home Equity Plus. We're offering a special rate on refinancing good for this month only . . .

Hey, it's Ralph. When you get back, give me a call, would you? I couldn't find your charts on McKenzie. By the way, congrats on the baby. Cigars to follow.

Hiya! It's Mom, honey. Got your letter, but we don't know when you're coming back. The hotel said you checked into another one. Call us, please! Love ya! How do you like the crib?

Hello, Mr and Mrs Breidbart. This is María. I'm calling to check up and see how everything is.

María Consuelo, making that follow-up call she'd promised them.

This call was followed by two more follow-up calls from María. Then a *spectacular one-time-only offer* from a carpet company. Followed by an automated solicitation from an assemblyman up for reelection. Then another message from María.

By this fourth one she clearly sounded annoyed. She'd called them four times, *four*, and there was still no word. She'd appreciate it if they would do her the honor of calling back and letting her know how things were.

Hi, María. As a matter of fact, things aren't going so well. The baby you gave us was kidnapped by your nurse and driver. I smuggled drugs into the country to try to get them out, but we were attacked and almost burned to death. So, all in all, things could be looking better. Thanks for asking.

LITTLE ODESSA SEEMED LIKE ITS NAME. LIKE ANOTHER COUNTRY. The evening had turned gray and misty, and a strong wind was whipping in from the ocean. You could see flecks of white foam out there and little whirlwinds of sand dancing across the beach.

Half the store signs were in Russian. The street fronting the beach was crowded with nightclubs, most of them named after Russian cities.

The Kiev. The St. Petersburg. Moscow Central.

Lack of shut-eye was catching up to Paul. He'd nodded off going over the Williamsburg Bridge – only the combination of metal grating and worn shocks revived him, bouncing him awake to a scene of stark black and white. The little bit of sleep had been painfully sweet – once his eyes were open, the dread quickly returned.

Moshe worked at a sprawling warehouse.

Miles pulled into the back lot. Two men were leaning against the only other car – a maroon Buick – smoking cigarettes and jabbering in Russian.

When they got out, Miles waved at them, but they didn't wave back.

'Friendly guys,' Miles said. 'They love me.'

The parking lot faced a half-open loading door. They ducked underneath. The inside was astonishingly huge – the size of your average Home Depot. It might've contained just as much merchandise.

There were rows of washers, dryers, refrigerators, TVs, stereos, computers, and furniture. There were bicycles, basketballs, golf clubs, clothing, and tires. There were video games, books, lawn furniture, and gas grills.

A group of men were milling around the home appliance section. One of them turned and waved.

'That's Moshe,' Miles said.

Paul thought he was slickly dressed for a warehouse. He was wearing what looked like a thousand-dollar suit, complete with blue silk tie and nicely buffed shoes that came to a distinct point. He had a goatee and thick eyebrows, which seemed to give him a look of perpetual amusement.

He walked forward and grabbed Miles in a bear hug, bestowing a kiss on both cheeks.

'Heyyyy . . . Miles . . . my favorite lawyer.' He had a smoker's voice, husky and low, layered with a thick Russian accent.

After Moshe had put Miles back down – in his enthusiasm he'd actually lifted him a good inch or so off the ground – he turned to Paul and smiled.

'Paul?'

Paul nodded. 'Hello,' he said. 'Nice to meet you.'

Moshe shook his head. 'Not so nice, I think. Miles tell me your . . . situation. Catastrophe. My sympathies. Your wife and child, huh? Those guerrilla –' He uttered what must have been a Russian curse. 'You know what we do to guerrillas in Russia, huh? Remember that theater in Moscow – those Chechen bastards? Boom – boom – gassed them to fucking hell.'

As Paul remembered it, the Russian authorities had also gassed about two hundred innocent hostages to hell as well. He thought it better not to mention this to Moshe.

Instead, he asked Moshe if he could help.

Moshe put a large arm around Paul. 'Look, I know those bastards. Some of them. We see what we can do, okay? Sometimes things can be negotiated. They are about as Marxist as we were – everyone's a businessman, okay? Listen – they won't kill them. Not likely. I make some calls.'

'Thank you. Really.'

'Don't thank me yet. I haven't done shit.' He smiled. 'We see.'

He looked through the half-open loading door and shook his head.

'Hey, Miles, my fucking genius lawyer, how many times I tell you not to park there? You're blocking the door.'

Miles said, 'Oh, sorry. I'll move it.'

'Give your keys to one of my guys. He move it for you, okay? We go to the office and talk.'

'One of your guys dented my fender last time they moved it for me. I'll do it,' Miles said.

A man walked by, groaning under the weight of an enormous crate on his left shoulder. It looked in imminent danger of tipping over and smashing to bits. The man had *CCCP* tattooed on his arm – the letters of the old Soviet sports federation.

'Go ahead,' Miles said to Paul. 'I'll be back in a minute.'

'Park it on Rostow, okay, *meshugener*,' Moshe said. 'You park it on Ocean, they gonna ticket you.'

Miles said *okay*. He slipped back under the loading door.

'Paul.' Moshe motioned him to follow. They went through a side door and into a hallway where the walls were paneled in cheap imitation wood. Moshe's office was down the hall – *El Presidente*, it said on the mottled glass. Paul assumed that was a joke.

'We wait for Miles, okay?' The office had a waiting room with two couches. He pointed to one of them. 'Please.'

Paul sat down as Moshe slipped into the inner office.

RING.

Ring.

He'd fallen asleep. Apparently, his cell phone had jolted him awake.

How long had he been out?

His phone had stopped ringing – he remembered its ring like an echo. He fished it out of his pants pocket, flipped it open, and checked the number. An area code he didn't recognize.

Where was Miles?

The inner door opened and Moshe was standing there smiling. He looked down at his watch – a shimmering kaleidoscope of gold and diamonds.

'What the fuck,' he said. 'We get started.' He walked back into his office.

But Paul's cell phone rang again.

'Mr Breidbart?'

It was María Consuelo.

'Yes, hello.'

'I have been calling you for three days. Do you know that?'

'Yes, María. We've been –'

'I always make a follow-up call to the new parents. I told you and Mrs Breidbart this, yes?'

'Yes, you did. We were . . . staying at a relative's.'

'I was getting worried. We need to make sure our new families are settling in. How is everything? Is the baby fine?'

'Yes, she's fine.'

Moshe was just visible through the half-open door of his office. He was pointing at his watch.

'Just a minute,' Paul said to him. But Moshe couldn't hear him; he cocked his head and cupped his left ear like a comedian searching for laughs.

'What?' María said.

'No, not you. I was talking to someone else. The

baby's fine. I really have to run. I certainly will –'

'Can I talk to *Mrs* Breidbart, please?'

For a moment Paul couldn't bring himself to answer. 'No,' he said. 'She's not here.'

'Oh? She is well?'

'Yes, she's well. She's just not with me. Not at the moment.'

'Can she call me? I'd like to speak with her.'

'Yes. She'll call you.'

'All right. You're sure everything is good?'

'Yes, everything's okay. Couldn't be better.'

'All right, then.'

Paul was going to hang up, was just about to, but he suddenly couldn't resist asking a question of his own.

'María?'

'Yes?'

'I'm just curious. How long have you been using Pablo? How well do you know him?'

'Pablo?'

'Yes. The driver you gave us. Have you been using him a long time?'

'I gave you a driver? No.'

'No? What do you mean, no? I'm talking about *Pablo*. You hired him to take care of us in Bogotá.'

'No. I didn't hire him.'

'Okay, someone from your staff. Someone took care of it for you.'

'Accommodations and transportation are not supplied by us. The contract clearly stipulates this, yes?'

'So who . . . ?'

'Who? Your lawyer. Mr Goldstein, yes?'

Your lawyer, Mr Goldstein.

'Miles,' Paul said.

'Yes, certainly. It's his responsibility to provide accommodations and . . .'

'Transportation.'

'Yes.'

Moshe was still waiting for him in the office. He was still smiling.

'Mr Goldstein called you two days ago, María,' Paul said, keeping his voice low. 'Remember – he asked you for Pablo's number.'

'Called me, no. Mr Goldstein didn't call me.'

'He didn't call you. He didn't call you and ask you for that number? Two days ago – Wednesday night?'

'No.'

A vision came back to Paul. Miles on the telephone – smiling, nodding, laughing, *emoting* for someone who wasn't actually there in front of him. But someone *was* there in front of him.

Paul.

'Okay. Thank you.'

'Was there a problem with your driver?'

'No problem.'

'Please have Mrs Briedbart call me.'

'Yes. Good-bye.'

He was operating by rote – the way you can steer your car left or right, stop at lights, and accelerate on highways, even when your mind is somewhere far away. Paul's mind was far, far away, stuck in a place between terror and helplessness.

'Coming?' Moshe was suddenly standing right in front of him.

He was still smiling, but Paul understood that it was like Galina's smile when she'd opened her front door and welcomed them into her home.

'Is there a bathroom?' Paul asked. 'I need to use the bathroom.'

It's amazing how the survival instinct takes over.

How you can be frozen to the spot, your body positively numb with fear, and you can still move your mouth and ask for the bathroom – ask for *anything* that will prevent you from walking into that office. Because you know with absolute certainty that if you walk in, you won't be walking out.

Moshe seemed to contemplate this request for a moment.

'Back there,' he said, pointing with his thumb. 'Out the door to the left.'

Paul stood up. His legs felt like they had back in María's office, like soft jelly. He was trying not to let Moshe know that he was in on the big secret, that he understood he was the only actor in this charade who hadn't been given his lines.

'Down the hall,' Moshe said, but Paul noticed that he'd stopped smiling.

'Okay. Be right back.' He turned to go.

Moshe put his hand on his shoulder. Paul could feel sharp fingernails digging into his flesh.

'Hurry,' he said. His teeth were yellow and misshapen, something that hadn't been evident from a distance. Now that Paul was close enough to smell him, he could see the physical legacy of what must've been an impoverished Russian childhood.

229

'Sure. I just need to use the bathroom. Then I'll come right back.' It sounded like bad exposition – he was giving too much information.

'Good,' Moshe said, seemingly unawares. 'We got lots to do, huh?'

'Yes. Lots to do.'

Paul walked through the door, resisting the overpowering urge to run. It's what you do in the face of mortal danger, isn't it? It's wired into your system – this need to churn your legs and take off like a bat out of hell.

He could hear Moshe stepping out into the hall behind him, evidently making sure Paul was going where he said he was.

The bathroom was about ten yards down the hall. *Hombres,* the door said – perhaps it came with the El Presidente model in the Spaghetti Western Collection.

He didn't have a plan when he said he needed to go to the bathroom. He didn't have a plan now.

Just a goal. To make it out of there alive.

He could sense Moshe still there in the hall. Watching him.

He went through the bathroom door.

It had a sink, a dirty urinal, and two narrow stalls.

What now?

His *phone.*

He could call the police. He'd tell them he'd been threatened, that he was trapped, in physical danger.

He went into the first stall and locked the door. He sat down on the toilet seat.

Paul pulled out his phone and dialed 911 – a number

that was now and forever associated with the date of the same number.

Nothing. That grating three-note announcement heralding that he'd done something wrong. That his party has moved or changed numbers.

He checked the number in the display window: 811.

Okay, nerves. He dialed again – wondering if his cell phone was on vibrate and ringing, since it seemed to be shaking in his hand. Even as he asked himself this, he knew perfectly well it wasn't his phone that was shaking.

This time he got through.

'Emergency. How can we help you?' A female voice that sounded vaguely automated.

'I'm in danger,' Paul whispered. 'Please send the police.'

'What's the problem, sir?'

Hadn't he just told her what the problem was?

'These men . . . they're trying to kill me.'

'Is this a break-in, sir?'

'No. I'm somewhere . . . in an office. Not an office . . . a warehouse.'

'Have you been attacked, sir?'

'No. Yes. They're about to attack me.'

'Where are you located?'

'Uh . . . in Little Odessa.'

'Little Odessa. That's in Brooklyn, sir?'

'Yes, Brooklyn.'

'What's the exact address, sir?'

'I don't . . . Somewhere by the . . .' There were footsteps coming down the hall. Paul stopped talking.

'Give me your name, sir.'

The footsteps stopped just outside the door. The door opened. Two men walked in, one of them whistling 'Night Fever.' The faucet turned on, one of the men began washing his hands.

'Sir? Your name, sir?'

Someone coughed up phlegm, spit it into the sink. The men began talking. They spoke in a haphazard mixture of Russian and English, switching from one to the other seemingly at random.

The man washing his hands said something in Russian, then asked if someone named Wenzel made the vig?

The whistler stopped. 'What?'

'Wenzel. He pay vig or not?'

'Oh, sure thing.'

'Fucking GNP of Slovakia, right?'

The other man answered in Russian, and they both laughed.

Then some back-and-forth, mostly in English – *you see Yuri around, tell that motherfucker he eat me* – interrupted by the sound of one of the men urinating.

'Sir . . . are you still . . . ?'

Paul clicked the phone off. He suddenly realized that he'd been holding his breath ever since the men walked in. When he let it out, it sounded like the whoosh of a just-turned-on air conditioner.

Both men turned around and faced the stall. That embarrassing moment when you realize someone's there, has been there the whole time you've been speaking.

Paul could just make out their feet underneath the stall door. Those hybrid sneaker-shoes, felt with garish nylon racing stripes.

One of the men said something in Russian.

When Paul didn't answer, he switched languages.

'You whacking off in there, Sammy?'

'No.'

Silence. They didn't recognize the voice.

'Okay,' one of the men said. 'Just checking – we're with whack-off patrol.' They laughed, then turned and walked out.

Paul was about to press send again, but he could hear them through the closing door. Someone was out there speaking to them – Moshe?

He'd be asking them if Paul was in there.

Yes, they'd say. There was someone whacking off in the stall.

Okay, that gave him maybe five minutes. Less, before Moshe himself walked in or sent one of his men back. To do what?

Pull Paul out of the stall and finish him off.

The emergency operator had asked him for the address, but he didn't know it. They should hold seminars on this: If you're going to be killed somewhere, *note address*. Note *name* too; he'd forgotten the name on the warehouse roof.

He stood up and pushed the stall door open. There was one small window. He lifted it open. Almost. Halfway up it stuck tight. It looked like it hadn't been opened in years, at least not from inside – dead spiders were littered between the window and rusty screen.

And one not-dead spider. Black, fat, and stubbornly sticking to its fly-littered web. *Spiders* – stuck alphabetically between *retroviruses* and *ticks* on Paul's long list of things to be frightened of.

Paul flushed the urinal to cover the noise, then gave the window a monumental push. It flew open.

First things first. The spider.

He attempted to crush it against the screen with a wad of rolled-up toilet tissue, but the screen was so rusted it fell off.

Good. *Double* good – the spider disappeared with it.

Paul stepped onto the sink and, using it for leverage, began to push himself through the window. He was facing the back lot. Miles was long gone. Only that maroon Buick remained; the man with *CCCP* tattooed on his arm was leaning against the driver's side door, smoking a cigarette.

If the man turned just a little to his right, to scratch his arm or spit or just stretch his neck, he'd have a perfect view of a terrified man squeezing himself through a window.

It didn't matter. Going back wasn't an option.

It was a tight fit. The window was about the size of the window in the Bogotá house, the one he'd put his arms through in an effort to make that bewildered schoolgirl understand they were crying out for help. He was still crying *help,* but if the smoker saw him, he wouldn't get it.

Keep worming.

The window frame seemed to be scraping off layers of skin; he thought he might be bleeding. He remembered a startling scene from Animal Planet, an enormous python actually coming out of its skin. If only *he* could do that – leave his burned and battered self behind for something fresh and new.

The smoker threw his cigarette to the ground and

watched it for a moment, seemingly hypnotized by the little wisp of smoke undulating in front of him.

Paul was down to his lower half, but there was nothing to hold on to. His upper thighs were taking the entire weight of his body. It felt as if he were literally going to break in half.

He felt a tickle on the small of his back. He twisted his head back.

The spider.

Black, hairy, and back. It was taking a constitutional across his naked skin where his shirt had ridden up.

He pushed and strained with renewed vigor, keeping one jittery eye on the spider.

He should've been looking the other way.

When he finally turned around to check on the man with the *CCCP* tattoo, he was staring right at him.

He'd straightened up off the car; he'd begun to amble over as if he were trying to get a better look. What an odd sight – *a grown man crawling out of a window.*

Or not crawling. Paul was pretty much stuck. He could feel the individual prickly hairs on each of the spider's eight legs.

'The fuck you doing?' The man had stopped about ten feet from him. A Russian bear. He had serpentine stretch marks on his arm where his muscles bulged enough to give the tattooed letters an odd lilt. He looked like a poster child for steroid use.

'There's a spider on me,' Paul said. It was the first thing that flashed into his mind, probably because other than the giant standing in front of him, it *was* the first thing on his mind.

'Spider?'

'Yes. I panicked,' Paul said.

'Huh?'

'I jumped through the window.'

'Spider?' He began laughing. Real, gut-wrenching, roll-in-the-aisle laughter, like a laugh track on the WB. Any minute, tears were going to start copiously flowing down his cheeks.

'Scared of *spider*?' he said. 'Ha, ha, ha.'

Okay, at least he believed him.

'Can you get me out of here?' Paul asked.

The Russian sluggishly stepped forward and grabbed Paul by his arms.

Paul could feel the enormous strength in the man's muscles – like something inhuman, even mechanical. When he pulled, Paul thought either he was going to come flying through the window or his arms were going to come flying out of their sockets. Fifty-fifty.

Suddenly, he was on the ground, arms intact.

That might not have been a good thing.

The man had walked over to his left, where he made a show of picking up a large chunk of cement, which had broken off the base of a parking meter that for some reason was lying there in the yard. He weighed it in his hands, then looked at Paul with an odd smile.

Paul stepped back.

The man lifted the ragged chunk up over his head and began advancing toward Paul.

'Wait . . .'

But he didn't wait.

The Russian brought the cement block down with full

force. About six inches from Paul's right shoe.

He smiled, lifted it up, admired the ugly starburst of brown blood. Some of the spider's legs were detached but still twitching.

'No more,' he said.

Before Paul could move, there was a sudden sound from inside the bathroom. Moshe's face was staring at them from the open window.

No one said anything.

Moshe looked confused. Paul had evidently just crawled out his bathroom window – how else could he have gotten outside the warehouse? – but he must've been wondering whether Paul actually *knew*. He had to be undecided as to which Moshe he should be playing here. The concerned friend of a friend, out to help Paul save his wife and daughter?

Or the man who'd been asked to murder him?

'He was scared of spider,' Paul's benefactor said, still looking amused by the whole thing.

Moshe didn't share his amusement. He looked at Paul and said, '*What* spider?'

'On my back,' Paul said. 'I was standing at the sink and the spider landed on me. I have a kind of phobia. I panicked.'

'Phobia?' He evidently wasn't familiar with the term. He was probably very familiar with lying. He was staring straight into Paul's eyes – the way the gamblers on *Celebrity Poker* lock onto their competitors' faces in order to know whether they're bluffing. It felt *physical,* like an actual pat-down.

Moshe said something in Russian, out of the corner of his mouth.

What?

Paul decided not to wait to weigh its nuances.

The man with the tattoo on his arm could've easily moved, flattened Paul with one lazy punch, or simply knocked the cement block out of his hands. The one he'd discarded in the dirt but Paul had picked up. It must've been a complete and utter shock that someone scared of spiders was capable of committing a physical assault. The man didn't actually move until the cement block made contact with the top of his head. He went down with a sickening thud.

Paul ran.

'Paul!' Moshe shouted behind him.

He'd never make it out of the yard. He'd gotten rid of the steroid user, sure, but in a minute there'd be others. Lots and lots of others.

He heard shouting, the sound of the loading door sliding open.

He didn't have enough of a lead. It was hopeless.

Sometimes you get lucky.

As any good actuary could tell you, sometimes the odds are just that. Odds. Numbers. They don't matter. You can be absolutely certain that if you live long enough, one day they'll rise up and bite you in the ass.

Or kiss you on the mouth.

His path to the open gate took him right past the parked Buick. Even in a full-out sprint – okay, not much by Carl Lewis standards, but okay by your average weekend warrior's – he was able to glance inside.

The keys were dangling from the ignition.

He stopped short, pulled the front door open, and slid

in. He turned the key and put the pedal to the metal.

He whooshed out of the gate. Just as three men came running after him.

But their cars weren't in the lot.

They were parked on Ocean or Rostow so they wouldn't block the loading door.

TWENTY-EIGHT

In the early-morning light Miles' Brooklyn brownstone looked darker, even forbidding.

The black tower of fairy tales.

Paul had spent the night in his car, parked in a deserted lot underneath the Verrazano Bridge. He'd ruled out going back to his apartment – he was afraid someone might be there waiting for him. He'd woken to a street bum rapping on his window, staring at what must've been a mirror image of himself.

Paul peeked in the rearview mirror to check. Yes – a worthy candidate for bumhood. His skin was pasty. His eyes were rheumy and bloodshot. His head hurt.

He kept asking himself *why?*

It felt like he'd entered the bizarro world of the Superman comics he used to read as a kid. Where everything was upside down, inside out. Where people who looked like your friends, weren't. Where you didn't have a clue.

A piece of his rational brain kept asking if he could've been mistaken. About everything. If he might've misunderstood what María said on the phone. If he'd put two and two together and come up with five.

Maybe Miles *had* hired Pablo. Maybe Miles' Wednesday night call had simply slipped her mind.

And Moshe? Maybe what he'd whispered to the steroid user had been an innocent crack. Something about the spider – about actuaries with silly phobias.

And those men running after him? Why *not*, if he'd just clobbered one of their coworkers over the head.

Maybe.

Only he couldn't forget the way Moshe looked at him through the office door – that smile dripping with chilling insincerity. The way Moshe watched him walk down the hall to the bathroom, as if sighting his prey.

And something else. *Miles had gone to move his car but never came back.*

Things were beginning to stir in the neighborhood.

People were trickling out of their houses – young, old, even ancient. Unlike Miles, these were people who didn't dare offend God, even if he did scare off a client or two. The men wore long corkscrew sideburns falling down to their shoulders like Victorian ringlets. They all wore black skullcaps. They must be headed to worship, Paul guessed, suddenly realizing it was Saturday.

Eighteen hours and four days. Dread seized him and refused to let go.

Miles' house remained conspicuously quiet.

Paul waited twenty minutes – eight o'clock, a reasonable hour to be awake and functioning.

He got out of the car and walked up to the brownstone steps.

He thought he saw a flash of movement through the living room window, slight and insubstantial, like the shadow of a butterfly.

When he knocked on the door, he only had to wait ten seconds before Rachel opened it.

She was dressed in her Saturday best, wig firmly in place under a black wide-brimmed hat, evidently ready to join the throng making its way to prayer. She peered at him quizzically, giving a phantom glance at her watchless wrist.

Yes, it was kind of early for visitors.

'Hello,' Paul said as normally as he could muster. 'Is Miles here?'

It was an obvious question, Rachel's face seemed to say. Where else would Miles be at eight on a Saturday morning but in his home?

'He's not feeling well. I was about to take the children to shul, Mr Breidbart. Was he expecting you?'

Good question, Paul thought.

When Miles asked Rachel *who's there?* from behind the door and groggily walked into view without waiting for a response, Paul decided the answer was no.

He wasn't expecting him.

Miles looked surprised, even shocked. It wouldn't be amiss to trot out an overused cliché and say he looked as if he'd seen a ghost. He *didn't* look like he was feeling well, but the sight of Paul had evidently made him feel worse.

Miles recovered. Maybe his lawyerly instincts took over, reverting to the kind of expression he'd be expected to maintain if one of his clients had just confessed to murder on the stand. Of course Miles didn't practice trial law –

he'd gone into foreign adoptions. And a few other things you maybe didn't need a license for.

'Paul,' he said, a quasi smile plastered to his face. 'I said I'm always available, but this is ridiculous, no?'

Okay, Paul thought, give him credit for grace under fire.

Something was bothering Paul – besides the obvious.

Think.

Miles brought him to Little Odessa to have him killed. Paul had assaulted someone, hijacked a car, and escaped. Moshe would've called Miles with that piece of news.

So why was he so shocked at seeing Paul in the flesh and still standing?

'I ran into a little trouble,' Paul said.

Rachel was standing between them like a referee who doesn't understand the bout's begun. 'You should go upstairs and rest,' she said to Miles with just enough wifely edge to make her point. Business was business, but this was his day off.

'Trouble?' Miles responded, ignoring his wife. 'By the way, sorry I was called away yesterday. Did Moshe tell you?'

More to the point, Paul thought, did Moshe tell *you*? And if not, why? For the fiftieth time that morning, Paul asked himself if it was possible he'd gotten it wrong. He would've given anything for that to be the case.

Rachel cleared her throat.

'It's okay, honey,' Miles said. 'I promise that after I talk to Paul here, I'll take a nice long rest.'

Miles looked like he could use it. He appeared feverish and tired, as if he hadn't slept in days.

That made two of them.

Rachel clearly wasn't happy about Paul's intrusion, but she silently acquiesced. She called her sons.

They slipped through the front door and trooped down the brownstone steps behind their mother with no great enthusiasm.

It was just the two of them now.

Miles said, 'Come in.'

He led Paul into the familiar clutter of his office. 'So what did Moshe say? Can he help you?'

Paul still desperately wanted to believe Miles.

He wanted to apologize for braining that man with a cement block and for stealing a car.

He wanted to cling to the image of a Miles who'd braved death with him in the Jersey City swamps.

He couldn't shake Miles' initial expression at the door. His surprise at Paul's *aliveness*. Miles had known what awaited Paul in that warehouse. If Paul was wrong about everything else, he was right about that.

'What's the matter?' Miles asked, still the friendly lawyer out to help. 'You said you ran into trouble. What happened?'

'María called me,' Paul said, letting that simple statement hang there for a moment.

'María?' was all Miles said.

Paul noticed that the telephone Miles had used to call María Consuelo – or *not* call her – was lying off its hook. Then he remembered something.

Religious Jews weren't allowed to take calls from sundown Friday to sundown Saturday.

Orthodox rules.

Miles thought Paul was dead and buried, because Moshe hadn't been able to call and tell him otherwise.

'That night you picked up the phone and called María?' Paul said. 'You *didn't* call her. You just pretended to.'

Paul made sure to speak slowly so Miles would be able to grasp the full import of what he was saying – and because it was hard to actually get the words front and center. 'If María hadn't called and told me, I would've walked into that office with your friend. I'm pretty sure I wasn't going to walk out.'

Everything seemed to drain out of Miles' face. Paul remembered a Thanksgiving Day balloon he'd seen punctured on TV when he was a kid – the huge smiling visage of a cartoon sheriff running into a streetlamp and deflating into something wrinkled and insubstantial.

'You're an insurance actuary,' Miles said, 'right?'

'Yes.'

'Okay. What are the odds of you making it out of here alive?'

He was pointing a gun at Paul's head.

It had suddenly materialized from behind the desk; he must've pulled it out of a drawer.

'Let me give you the facts,' Miles said. 'It's how you guys work, right? Facts – then figures. This is an Agram 2000. Croatian made, machine action. It used to belong to an honest-to-God KGB assassin – at least that's what Moshe told me. They liked the Agram because it's small enough to stick in your pocket and highly accurate up to twenty feet. More facts. We're alone – my wife and sons are praying to a just and benevolent God. Also, that funny thing on the end of the barrel? A silencer. No one will hear

245

me shoot you. Okay, now, what would you say the odds are?'

'Poor,' Paul said. And getting poorer by the second, he thought. Miles was having trouble keeping his hand steady – the one gripping the Agram 2000.

'Why?' Paul asked.

For a moment it appeared that Miles hadn't heard him; he seemed to be listening to something else. He stood up, walked to the window, peeked out through the curtain – all the while managing to keep the gun trained on Paul.

'You see anyone out there?' he asked.

'Anyone? What do you mean?'

'What do I mean? I mean, did you see anyone out there? Anyone not wearing a yarmulke, for example? Never mind. Doesn't matter.'

He came back behind the desk, sat down.

'Why?' Paul asked again.

'Why? You sound like a child asking one of the four questions. Why do you think?'

'Money.'

'Money. Well, sure, money's *part* of it. You ever bet on anything, Paul?'

'What?'

'You ever bet on anything? Guess not. Stupid question. It's probably against the *actuarial* code. Remember the 1990 no-huddle Buffalo Bills?'

Paul was having trouble remembering anything except the gun pointed at his head.

'My first colossal blunder. You know you can bet straight up if you've got the guts. If you just *know*. None of those annoying points to deal with. Only you've got to lay three to win one. That's okay. I was sure. I *knew*. My religion prescribes one ritual bath a year. That was mine.'

'You lost.'

'Oh yeah. Sure you didn't see anyone out there, Paul? Someone driving by the house maybe?'

'No.'

'Good.'

'You said you bet thirty dollars here and there,' Paul said. 'Just to keep things interesting.'

'I fibbed. It's *more* interesting when you bet thirty thousand. I'll tell you how I got started. One day I was sitting and waiting by the phone. You know what for?'

'No.'

'Neither did I. Something. When it rang and I picked it up, the person on the other end said Mr Goldstein, *this* is your lucky day. It was a touting service. A Delphic oracle of the ESPN generation. They toss you the first pick for free, just to show what excellent prognosticators they are. They were excellent – *that* day. I won. I even won again. That's the problem. You start feeling kind of omnipotent. You forget that's reserved for the man upstairs. I began practicing a personal form of downside economics. I bet more than I actually *had*.'

Someone started up a car outside. Miles jerked his head toward the window, gripped the gun with knuckles turned suddenly white.

'It's just a car,' Paul said.

'Sure. It's just a car. Everyone *walks* on Shabbat.' He kept one eye on Paul, and the other on the window, at least until he heard the sound of the car engine slowly drifting down the street.

'Are you expecting someone?'

'Yes. I'm expecting someone. I'm just not sure when I'm expecting them. Sometime soon, I think.'

Miles closed his eyes, wiped his forehead.

'My bookie wasn't very understanding, Paul. About not having the money. What were the odds he'd say *no problem* and wipe the slate clean? Come on, Paul . . . numbers?'

'I don't know.' Paul was continuing to answer him, back and forth and back, as if they were in that car in New Jersey, just shooting the breeze. As if the pet weapon of the Russian KGB weren't trained on his head. Maybe something brilliant would occur to him.

'You don't know? Come on. You've *met* him. Moshe, the Russian businessman. By the way, he doesn't really do a lot of business with Colombians. He doesn't have to. He does perfectly fine taking bets from me.'

Paul remembered the conversation he'd overheard in the bathroom. Had Wenzel *made the vig*? one of the men asked. *Fucking GNP of Slovakia.* And they'd both laughed.

'By the way, you know what the Russians call the Colombians?'

Paul shook his head.

'Amateurs.' He smiled, wiped his forehead again. 'Moshe called me his favorite Jewish lawyer back at the warehouse? Because other Jewish lawyers *take* his money. I'm the exception. I'm the gift that keeps on giving. See, I owed Moshe what I didn't have. What were the odds I could wiggle out of that one?'

Paul was calculating other odds – trying to gauge the distance to the office door, wondering how long it would take him to make it to the front door of the house if he made it out of the office.

'You're still here,' Paul said.

'Yeah. I'm still here. You can have smarts and you can have luck. I needed both. I opened my arms and waited for manna from heaven. And I was delivered.'

'How?'

'*How?* That's what I've been trying to tell you.' The gun was still drifting – every so often Miles would notice with a slightly sheepish grin and attempt to re-aim it.

'You don't want to shoot me,' Paul said.

'I don't? That's odd. That's really odd. You see my neck's back in the noose again. Not from you – you're just *inconvenient*. It's those assholes with Uzis and kerosene I'm worried about. They looked through my car – they know I'm here. They're smelling blood. They're starting to put it together. I can *tell*. They're closing in.'

'Put *what* together?'

'Maybe they *are* amateurs next to the Russians, but not by much. In the pantheon of assassins, let's call them lower Division 1. I'm cooked.'

Miles looked cooked. His face was in full flop sweat. Paul couldn't help wondering if his trigger finger was sweating as well, if it might unintentionally slip.

'I don't understand,' Paul said.

'I know you don't.'

'The men in the swamp. You said they were Manuel Riojas' men. What does he have against you?'

'What are the odds poor little Paul's ever going to figure *that* one out? Let's just say no good deed goes unpunished.'

249

'What good deed?'

'Okay. No bad deed goes unpunished.'

'I don't –'

'He who saves one child saves his ass.'

It was as if Miles were speaking in fragments, Paul following a step behind, collecting each piece and desperately trying to glue them together.

'Joanna!' Paul nearly shouted it. Miles had lied about calling María. It suddenly occurred to him that he might have lied about something else. 'You said she's fine. Is she?'

It seemed to take Miles a second to refocus, to concentrate on the question being asked of him and actually answer it. 'Sure,' he said. 'Under the circumstances. Sorry about your wife and kid. Not my fault – sort of. It wasn't supposed to happen like this. Can't help you there. Wish I could.'

'Miles . . .'

'Uh-uh.' Miles waved his gun at him. 'My turn. I've got one more question for you. Last one, honest. It's not even an actuarial question. Ready – pencils out?'

Paul was preparing to launch himself at the door. Or across the desk. *Pick one.* He had nothing to lose.

'Know what's the worst sin in Orthodox Judaism – other than marrying a shiksa, of course?'

'No,' Paul said.

'Sure you do.'

Paul made it only halfway across the desk when the bullet exploded out of the barrel. It entered the cranial cavity, which governs memory and social skills, exiting below the neck and embedding itself into the cover of *New York State Adoption Statutes*. He'd gone *toward* Miles because he thought it might give him the element of surprise.

250

He was wrong about that.

Miles had surprised him first.

The worst sin in Orthodox Judaism?

It wasn't murder.

No.

I promise that after I talk to Paul here, I'll take a nice long rest, he'd told his wife.

He'd kept his word.

TWENTY-NINE

Joanna was granted one of those rare afternoon feedings where she was allowed to linger with her baby, rock her into sleep, and simply stare at her.

When she came back to her room, Maruja and Beatriz were gone.

There had been talk lately. Something in the wind. A possible prisoner exchange or straight cash ransom. The last time Maruja saw her husband on TV, he'd hinted at imminent release.

Joanna had caught Maruja praying with the rosary beads that had been given to her by one of the guerrillas – Tomás, sad-eyed and secretly religious, who'd fashioned them from cork and presented them to her after she'd asked him for a Bible.

The man they called *el doctor,* who periodically visited them like a dutiful concierge making the rounds, told Maruja and Beatriz that they might be taking a little trip soon and winked at them.

Joanna had felt like two people. One of these people was overjoyed for Maruja and Beatriz; they'd become like sisters and she felt their pain at being separated so long from children and family.

The other Joanna felt devastated, jealous, and abandoned.

Now Maruja and Beatriz were gone.

The room reeked of loneliness, of people who've packed up and left. It was freshly tidied – the mattress fluffed and turned, the floor swept. The meager clothing Maruja and Beatriz had accumulated over time – castoffs from the *kids,* as Beatriz called their guards, most of whom *were* kids – was conspicuously missing. Beatriz had fashioned a makeshift dresser from two milk crates – when Joanna looked inside, there was only the sweatshirt with the logo of the Colombian national soccer team that Maruja had graciously handed down to her.

Joanna sat in the corner and cried.

After an hour or so she knocked on the door and asked to see *el doctor.* It was opened by Tomás, looking even more melancholy than usual, who didn't respond one way or another. But a few hours later the doctor knocked on the door and walked in.

'Yes?' he said, flashing that magnanimous smile that Joanna found incongruous from the person imprisoning her.

'Where are Maruja and Beatriz?' Joanna asked him.

'Ah. Good news,' he said. *'Released.'* As if he'd been pulling for them all along.

'Oh,' she said. 'That's wonderful.'

'Yes.' His smile grew even wider. 'Next. You.'

Joanna allowed herself to believe him – for a moment she did.

'And my *baby*.'

'Yes, of course. Babies belong with their mothers.'

'What about Rolando?' she asked.

The doctor ignored her. Instead, he gazed at the surrounding sparseness. 'You have more room now, yes?'

Joanna nodded.

'Good.'

THE FIRST NIGHT A.B. – AFTER BEATRIZ – JOANNA HAD TROUble sleeping. The mattress, which had always felt crowded if snugly warm, now felt uncomfortably roomy and ice-cold. There was a strange, slightly nauseating smell in the air. She woke up thirsting for company. Somehow this translated into something more tangible.

She knocked on the door and asked for water.

The female guard with long black hair opened the door. She was watching the TV, where a somber news anchor was reading from a sheet of paper.

When she went to get Joanna water, she made a point of turning the TV off.

The water, which was tepid and acidic, did nothing to help Joanna sleep. She lay with eyes wide-open, staring up at the ceiling. Beatriz had drawn a multitude of stars on the plaster ceiling with a felt pen. A way to break down their prison walls and create a pathetic illusion of freedom.

Joanna dug her head into the mattress and selfishly wished Beatriz were back beside her.

That smell. *What was it?*

It seemed stronger now. She decided it had to be the mattress itself. They'd turned it over in a clumsy stab at neatness, but the side she was sleeping on – or attempting to – had been against the dirty floor forever. It was the *absence* of smell too, she thought – the familiar scent of departed friends.

She stood up, turned the mattress back over, then lay down again.

She didn't notice it right away.

The room was too dark. It took her eyes getting used to the blackness and the fact that the smell, instead of improving, grew exponentially worse.

It took Joanna turning first left, then right, even reversing her position on the bed. It took her placing her head facedown into the foam and nearly gagging.

She lurched to a sitting position and stared at the place on the mattress where her head had been seconds before.

It was like a Rorschach blot. Staring at an amorphous mix of color and shadow and finally finding the haunting image within.

A large, uneven stain.

She thought she knew what it was. A stain the approximate size of a human head.

She closed her eyes and pressed a finger into the middle of rusty brown. It felt damp, like cellar earth. When she looked at the tip of her finger, it was stained brown. Blood.

She staggered to a standing position. She lurched around the room as if drunk, chased by a growing panic.

She banged furiously on the door.

Tomás again. She wanted to say their names out loud – to state them clearly and unmistakably. But she saw something dangling out of the crook of his pants pocket.

The rosary made of cork. The one he'd given Maruja, the one she'd sworn to always keep with her as an eternal symbol of faith, hope, and dogged survival.

Joanna waited till he shut the door, till she slumped onto the floor and buried her face in her hands.

Then she screamed bloody murder.

THEY KNEW SHE KNEW.

About Maruja and Beatriz.

She probably told them herself, every time she jumped when one of them entered the room or came within two feet of her. She couldn't help wondering *which one* pulled the trigger, drew the knife. Was it Tomás, who seemed to mope about even more than usual these days? Or Puento, who'd pointed a rifle at Joelle when she was in the screaming throes of pneumonia? Or both?

She had to reassure herself each time that they hadn't come for *her*.

She was absolutely certain they knew she knew when *el doctor* came in and apologized for having to chain her to the wall.

He seemed genuinely remorseful about it but explained that it was for her own good.

'If USDF patrols begin shooting,' he said, 'you'll be safer like this, no?'

No. Joanna asked just once for him to not do it. Please.

He shrugged and sighed. It was out of his hands, he explained. It was just for nighttime – that's all.

They chained one end to a piece of a long-defunct radiator. The other went around her left leg.

It wasn't physically uncomfortable – the pain was psychic. It put a punctuation mark on her existence. She was now literally under lock and key.

One of them would come in to unlock her in the morning. Joanna wouldn't start breathing normally again until this ritual was actually accomplished. Then she'd know she was alive for at least one more morning. She could let herself look forward to feeding time. This living from hour to hour was taking its toll. She was generally jumpy, weepy, and exhausted. There were times she found herself unable to stop shaking.

When she told Galina that she was pretty positive Maruja and Beatriz had been murdered, Galina shook her head and said *no, they were released.*

'They weren't released,' Joanna said. 'Tomás has Maruja's rosary beads. She never would've left them behind. The girl turned off the news that night when she saw me looking. There was blood in the bed. I know.'

Galina wouldn't listen. She went deaf.

It was maddening. It was sickening.

It was clear that talking to Galina about certain things was like talking to a wall. Joanna knew what *that* was like, because she talked to her wall in lieu of talking to Maruja and Beatriz. She'd decided it was slightly more rational than talking to herself.

Sometimes the wall became someone she knew. Paul. From time to time she tried to imagine where he was – in a prison for drug smuggling? Dead? When she felt suffocated with fear, she'd place him right there beside her and fill him in on her day.

Sometimes Paul answered back.

What's wrong?

They killed my friends.

Maybe you're wrong about that.

No. There was blood on the mattress. I discovered it the day they left.

Maybe one of your friends cut herself.

No. It was a lot of blood. And Maruja left something behind.

Still.

You have to believe me. Sometimes I feel like I'm going crazy, but I'm not going crazy.

Okay. I believe you.

I'm scared now. Every day I'm scared.

Stay strong. You're Xena, my warrior princess, remember? Besides, I'm coming for you.

When? I want to be home, Paul.

Soon, honey.

When?

Soon.

SHE ASKED TOMAS FOR THE ROSARY BEADS.

'Maruja gave them back to you when you released her, I guess,' Joanna said.

Tomás didn't answer her. But when Joanna asked for them, he handed them over.

She'd been watching the way the door locked. A key turn from outside slid a small bolt into the lock. That's it. The wooden jamb looked ancient and wormy.

Joanna ripped off one cork bead from the rosary. The cork was barely malleable, like half-hardened clay.

When Galina took her out of the room for the next morning feeding, she pushed the small piece of cork into the lock hole, grinding it in with her thumb.

That night she watched as one of the girls left the room, closed the door behind her, and dutifully turned the lock. Joanna listened for the telltale click. She didn't hear it.

A growing excitement took hold of her. A warm glow, like a shot of aged brandy when you're really, really cold.

Beatriz had drawn stars to get out of prison, only Beatriz had been murdered in her bed.

This was better.

Only she was still chained to the wall. And she couldn't leave without her baby.

There was the question of what to do next. She didn't wake up one morning with an escape plan. She hadn't talked strategy with the wall. She took this first step and said *if it works, we'll take another.*

Then something presented itself, something that took care of two major obstacles at once.

Joelle got sick again.

Just a bad cold this time – enough to make her sniffly, irritable, and slightly feverish.

Joanna asked Galina if Joelle could stay with her. Not just for an hour or two, but all night, like the time Joelle had pneumonia and she'd walked her back and forth for hours on end.

Galina said yes.

Then Joanna asked her something else. Could they unchain her? What if Joelle needed to be rocked? Joanna might need to walk her around the room. It would be immeasurably helpful if she wasn't chained to the radiator.

Galina seemed less accommodating there.

Joanna pleaded her case, and finally, Galina said she'd talk to the guard.

It was Tomás. Maybe he liked her more now that she'd gotten religion. Maybe he was making amends for murdering her friends. He said fine. No chain tonight.

When he closed the door behind him and turned the lock, Joanna held her breath.

No click.

So here it was. She'd taken one step, then another and another, and suddenly, she'd reached a door. It was tantalizingly open.

For a moment Joanna wondered if she could actually walk through it.

The bloodstain on the mattress both prodded and held her back. If she failed, they'd kill her for trying. If she stayed, they'd kill her eventually.

Courage.

She waited for hours – till her internal clock placed the time at somewhere around two in the morning. She was reasonably sure there wouldn't be anyone outside the door – when she'd needed that rag in the middle of the night, she had to bang on the door for five minutes before Puento answered.

She tiptoed to the door and put her ear up against the wood. Nothing.

She turned the knob.

It didn't move. For just a moment she said *okay – I was wrong. The cork didn't work. The door's still locked. I'm stuck.*

Then she gave it a bit more pressure.

The knob turned.

The door edged open.

It was like the door in a haunted-house movie – the door you shouldn't open but do. The door that has something evil waiting for you on the other side.

There was nothing there.

Empty hall.

Since they'd removed her mask for walks to the feeding room, she'd learned enough to know where things were. To her right was the kitchen, the feeding room, the place they kept Rolando – if he was still actually there.

To the left – freedom.

Joelle was sleeping fitfully in her arms. She had visions of her waking up and screaming – the best alarm system a FARC guard could ask for. She'd have to move very slowly and very carefully. She'd have to inch along.

When she stepped out into the hall, it felt as if she were moving through something physical – a force field of science fiction. She stopped and breathed. Then she turned left and padded down the hall, one small shuffle at a time, till she came to what had to be the outside door – the one they'd brought her through blindfolded and terrified.

She was *still* terrified.

She pushed it open.

THIRTY

Trajectory.

Atoms have it. Electrons and neutrinos. Lives too.

The trajectory of the bullet that killed Miles, that left him slumped and oddly peaceful-looking with the Agram 2000 still glued to his hand, went through his neck and directly into one of the dusty legal tomes that took up most of his bookcase. *New York State Adoption Statutes*. The bullet's force sent several other books flying, scattering pages like confetti.

Paul ignored it at first. Trajectory.

Instead, he assumed a helter-skelter trajectory of his own. Nearly flying off a suddenly blood-splattered desk, then staggering around the room like a boxer on his last legs, unsure whether to go down or keep fighting.

He remained upright.

Clues, his brain nagged him.

Miles was his last link to what happened in Colombia.

Clues.

Miles had been right about the silencer. No one would've heard the gun go off – it sounded like the small pop you make by pulling a finger out of your cheek. Like a cartoon sound effect.

There was plenty of blood, though. The room stank of it.

Paul came around the side of the desk where Miles still sat – his *body*. He tried to ignore it – this lifeless lump of flesh that used to have a name and a voice and a family.

Know what's the worst sin in Orthodox Judaism?

Paul opened the desk drawer. Papers, staples, pencils, two half-empty packs of gum. Wrigley's spearmint. A calculator, ticket stubs, paper clips, envelopes. He had no idea what he was looking for.

Clues.

The question was, what *was* a clue? How did you divine clues from ordinary office things, the stuff of daily life?

They're starting to put it together. I can tell.

He looked through some of the papers in the desk drawer. A W-2 tax form. A solicitation for subscription renewal from a legal journal. A coupon from Toys 'R' Us – circled in red ink. *Chatty Cathy.* A New York Giants schedule from 1999.

A phone book.

The one Miles had looked through when he'd pantomimed calling María – when he'd snapped his fingers and said *the driver. Pablo. María must have his number somewhere.*

María's number was in there, of course.

Pablo's would be also.

Paul didn't know his last name – he'd just been Pablo the driver, Pablo the hired help.

Then Pablo the kidnapper.

He had to search through A, B, C, D, E, F, G, H, I, J, and K before he found it. *Pablo Loraizo.*

Odd, the last name seemed familiar.

He ripped out the page and stuck it into his pocket.

He was searching for clues, but he was clueless. About what to do. Call the police? Find the local shul and inform Rachel and kids that their husband and father had just blown his brains out?

Leave.

Leaving sounded good. When the police came to talk to him, he'd tell them they'd chatted, then Paul had left. *Suicide?* What suicide? Or he'd tell them everything – that Miles had sent him to Colombia to be kidnapped and his wife and daughter held for ransom. *What* ransom? Two million dollars' worth of uncut cocaine he'd dutifully smuggled through customs. Maybe he'd leave that part out.

He felt light-headed, like in Galina's house when he'd stood up to confront Pablo and ended up lying down instead. His thinking was all over the place, scattershot. Unlike the bullet that flew through Miles' head.

He took notice of it now – its trajectory.

It had made a mess. Book pages were scattered all across the floor. No, they weren't book pages. On closer look they were handwritten.

Letters.

Okay, Paul remembered.

The night he couldn't sleep and wandered down here to find something to read. He'd ended up reading that letter from summer camp – *Dear Dad: Remember when you took me to the zoo and you left me there?* Feeding his loneliness by gorging on someone else's family.

264

He was stepping over the sheets of paper to make his way out of the room when he noticed something else.

He read, bent down, stood there transfixed, hands on knees.

A bullet's trajectory is governed by physics, he thought.

By the forces of propulsion, drag, and gravity. And the position of the shooting hand itself. This is important. Which way the hand's pointing.

Maybe just before Miles decided to put a bullet into his brain, he'd reflected on the odds of *poor Paul ever figuring this out* and decided to better them.

He said *I'm pointing here.*

This way.

THIRTY-ONE

He was back in the comfy surroundings of home – he'd been unable to think of anywhere else to go.

Except it wasn't comfy. There were too many reminders.

He pushed the crib across the apartment and halfway into the closet so he wouldn't have to look at it, pink teddy bears grinning up at him on their ride across the room, as if amused by his childish attempt to hide the hopelessness of his situation.

Lisa must've heard it rolling across the floor, because a second later Paul heard a knock at the door. When he tiptoed over to squint through the eyehole, Lisa, Joanna's best friend, was squinting back, her puzzled expression causing her mouth to twist nearly sideways, an endearing affectation Paul had always found vaguely sexy. Not today. Either Paul and Joanna were back – suddenly and unannounced – or someone was burglarizing their apartment.

Paul *felt* a little like a burglar, an intruder into his own life.

Paul waited her out.

He had the visa story all ready to go, but he was in no mood to use it. Not yet.

After Lisa had knocked once more, then shrugged and left, Paul picked up the stack of letters he'd taken from Miles' office. If you sniffed them closely, you could still smell his blood.

He closed the blinds and turned off the phone. It would take Rachel a while to locate him. He couldn't remember whether she knew his last name, probably not. It didn't matter – at some point she'd look through Miles' phone book, with the police over her shoulder, and collect all the *Pauls*. They'd winnow it down to him. Eventually, they'd call.

I went to talk to Miles about my adoption problems. When I left the house, he was alive. Was he depressed? A little – he mentioned something about gambling debts. I'm so sorry to hear about this.

The letters weren't dated.

But he was able to organize them chronologically by color. From parched yellow to off-white.

The most recent was the letter he'd read that night, the letter Miles' son had written from summer camp. It was the other letters he was interested in. The other letters that had come tumbling out of *The Story of Ruth*. These letters were different. These letters weren't written by a child.

They were written *about* a child.

Dear Mr Goldstein, the first one began.

I have a child in desperate need of adoption.

Most people wrote to Miles wanting to adopt a child. Needing, asking for, even *begging*, for a child. This letter was different – it was offering one up.

Consider this a special request, this letter continued. *This has to happen immediately. There's no time to follow the usual paperwork. That's why I'm writing to you directly. That's why I need your help. I have to hear from you now. Today. Tomorrow. I beg you to answer me as soon as humanly possible.*

Paul went on to the second letter, then the third.

He read them slowly, carefully, sometimes going back to reread something before pushing forward through time. All the letters, of course, were written *to* Miles. He didn't have the letters Miles wrote back. It was like eavesdropping on one-half of a phone conversation. You had to supply the responses yourself. You had to fill in the blanks.

The letters went on to explain who this child was. A three-year-old girl. The letter writer insisted the child needed to leave Colombia now. It explained why. Her father was after her. The girl was in terrible danger. And finally and most tellingly, the letters explained how this was all going to take place.

After he'd read the last letter, he reread them all. And he remembered how Miles had spoken in fragments and how he – Paul – had followed behind trying to collect the fragments and glue them together.

What are the odds poor little Paul's going to put this together?

Bad, Miles, he thought now, *awful,* but it's just possible the odds were getting better.

The full name of the little girl's father never appeared. Just an initial. *R.* Somewhere between letters, his name must've been whispered in Miles' ear, then never mentioned again.

But the letter *writer* was there at the bottom of every page. That's what Paul had noticed exiting the room, blood in his nostrils – what had made him stop and look and read. The signature at the bottom of the page.

A lovely lilt to the letters, especially the *G*.

For Galina.

THIRTY-TWO

At first he thought the sound at his door was a dream.

Maybe because that's what he was doing. Dreaming, at least half dreaming.

About his wife and daughter.

About the little girl.

And that sampler that sat over Miles' desk.

He who saves one child saves the world.

Who was this little girl? Galina's granddaughter.

She'd clearly stated that in her second letter to Miles. And she'd written about the girl's father. *That* too.

Once I thought my own daughter was safe from him, she'd scrawled. *I was wrong.*

She'd begged Miles for help. Her granddaughter needed to get out of the country.

Her father is looking for her. He won't stop till he finds her. As you know, R has the power and means to do so.

She needed to be adopted by someone in America. This needed to happen fast.

As the letters continued, she told him a little more about the girl.

She's seen things no child should ever have to see, she'd written. *No one should have to see. She has nightmares.*

By the fourth letter it became obvious that Miles had said okay. That he'd help. More than help. He'd evidently made an offer of stunning generosity and selflessness. He'd agreed to adopt Galina's granddaughter himself.

Are you sure? she'd written him. *As overjoyed as I am, you must understand this is not a sometime thing. It's a forever thing. You won't simply be her parent. You'll be her protector. Her guardian. Her only hope.*

Yes, Miles must've written, he was sure.

But he'd wanted something in return.

What?

It was hard to say.

It was obvious Galina's joy had more or less vanished. Her letters had taken on the sober tone of a business negotiation.

Understand what you ask might not be possible, Galina wrote. *I don't know them. I don't speak for them. I can only ask them.*

Them.

Paul was like a two-year-old, beginning to understand that meaningless words stand for meaningful things.

Them said yes.

They must've, because Galina's last letter was a heartrending plea for her granddaughter's future.

I ask a few things of you, she wrote. *To comfort her when she wakes up frightened in the middle of the night. Please read to her — she likes stories about trains and clowns and rabbits. Teach her what she needs to know in her new country. Protect her. From time to time, I ask you to please let me know how she's doing. Not every week, not every month. Now and then. This is my last letter to you. The less contact we have after this, the safer it'll be. I ask just one more thing. It's the most important thing. For you and your wife to love her.*

There was someone at the door.

He was suddenly wide-awake, staring at the bedroom ceiling.

He heard it again.

A soft scratching. It sounded like a cat asking to be let in.

He didn't have a cat.

He continued to lie there on his bed; he wondered which door it was. The closed door of his bedroom, the apartment door itself? This was important. If it was the apartment door, he still had a chance. If it was the bedroom door, he was dead.

He concentrated; tried to fine-tune his hearing. Blood was pulsing into his eardrums; his breathing was tight and shallow and noisy.

The scratching sound seemed faint and muffled.

Okay, he thought, the *apartment* door.

He slid off the bed and resisted the temptation to crawl underneath it. The front door was locked. He was still master of his domain. He could keep them out – he could protect himself.

He was dressed only in boxer shorts. When he glanced at the full-length mirror against the wall, he looked comically vulnerable. He stood stock-still, craned his neck to listen.

Scratch, scratch.

It's those assholes with Uzis and kerosene I'm worried about.

The men from the swamp, he thought.

Or.

It's the man with *CCCP* tattooed on his arm.

He was at the front door. The one Lisa had squinted through, which, if memory served him correctly, was locked tight.

Even double-bolted.

He gingerly opened his bedroom door. He stepped out. He stared at the front door as if seeing it for the first time. Really *looking* at it. It appeared solid enough – in need of a paint job, sure, but strong as steel. This analogy comforted him.

He could swear he'd double-bolted it but couldn't remember whether the oblong knob was supposed to be vertical or horizontal.

He suddenly realized he hadn't heard a sound since he'd walked out of the bedroom. He realized this because he heard it now.

This much closer, it seemed raw and amplified. *The fog comes on little cat feet* – a poem he remembered from childhood. But this wasn't a cat, and this wasn't childhood.

A weapon.

His eyes zigzagged around the apartment, jittery, in circles, like a fly caught between windowpanes.

The metal paperweight from Sharper Image. Maybe.

The polished African walking stick Joanna's parents had brought back from Kenya. Possibly.

A dull glass egg sitting in the middle of the dining room table. No.

The dining room table.

Knives.

He stared at his kitchen, trying to remember where Joanna kept the steak knives.

He resisted the overwhelming urge to run there.

Walk. Tiptoe. Float like Muhammad Ali. They didn't know he was here. They were guessing. They might get tired of trying to jimmy the lock. They might give up.

Not if they knew he was in here.

He *drifted* to the kitchen, visualizing himself as light and noiseless, even though he felt heavier than lead, aware that the sounds at the door were growing louder and more insistent.

They were trying to fit something into the lock – that's what it sounded like. Frustration was setting in. They were trying to *force* it in, like date rape – first polite and consensual, then insistent and brutal. The lock was screaming *no*. The intruder didn't give a shit.

Paul opened a kitchen drawer. It squeaked.

The scratching stopped dead.

Silence.

You have to do something about these drawers, Paul. If Joanna had said that to him once, she'd said it a thousand times. And a thousand times Paul had told her to *hire one of those guys in the back of the Pennysaver.*

The handymen had remained unsummoned. The drawers continued to complain every time they were opened.

The people behind the door knew he was in here.

More bad news.

The open drawer contained Joanna's phone book, some pencils, paper clips, a take-out menu from Hunan Flower.

No knives.

The scratching came back. Harder.

The second drawer down, he hit pay dirt. It contained the entire Ginzu Knife Collection, for which they'd sent $49.95 in five easy monthly installments. Those remarkable knives you saw cutting through tissue paper in thirty-minute infomercials. Forged by actual samurai masters in Yokohama. He wrapped his fingers around a cool plastic handle and pulled one out.

He turned and faced the door.

Maybe ten feet from it. From *them*. It seemed inconceivable and ridiculous that a mere *door* could save him. He could almost smell their need. He was sure Joanna could've.

Call 911.

This time he could actually tell them his address.

He could summon a patrol car. Scare them away.

Make them think they were coming any minute.

The phone was on the other side of the apartment. It seemed as vast and impassable as the Sahara.

Wait. He didn't have to call. He just had to *pretend* to.

'Yes, is this the police?' he suddenly shouted. 'Yes, I'm at 341 West 84th Street, apartment 9G. Someone's trying to break in . . . Yes, that's right . . . You'll be here in two minutes? Thank God.'

Oddly enough, his fake phone call didn't cause the man or men to stop. No.

Maybe he should've asked himself *why?*

Maybe if it wasn't five in the morning, and if he wasn't scared out of his mind, and if he was just a little brighter about these things, he would've.

Then he would have understood that the only reason a

fake phone call to the police wouldn't deter someone from breaking into your apartment is if they *knew* it was a fake phone call.

And the only way they could know that is if they knew you didn't have a phone.

If, say, they'd taken the precaution of disconnecting it.

THIRTY-THREE

He felt his sheer strength at first.

The overwhelming, undeniable *there*ness of it.

The knotty muscle. As if the *door* weren't made of steel, but the man who'd burst through it was. *CCCP*, he thought.

One moment Paul was standing ten feet from the door with the Ginzu in his hand. The next, an amorphous black shape was hurtling straight at him.

He lunged at the black apparition with his knife, but the man deflected his arm with almost comical ease.

The knife went skittering off somewhere on the floor.

Before the man could kill him, Paul kept going.

Momentum carried him past the man's swatting arm and back into the kitchen, where he attempted to ransack the second drawer without slowing down. But he cut himself on one of the other Ginzus – perhaps the apple-corer they'd received free because they'd acted *now*. His hand came up bloody and, more important, *empty*.

The man was right behind him. He could hear him breathing hard, as if the exertion of kicking in the door had tuckered him out.

Only momentarily. Not enough to make him stop.

Paul zigzagged into the bedroom like a broken-field runner. He slammed the door shut.

No.

The man had made it to the other side of the door just before Paul could actually close it.

He was pushing back.

Adrenaline was a kind of drug, Paul thought. He could feel every single muscle crackling with energy. He felt powerful, relentless, even indomitable.

He didn't stand a chance.

Adrenaline could only do so much. The person on the other side of the door wasn't human. He was a freakish force of nature. The door was moving backward.

One inch.

Two inches.

Paul's hand was slipping in his own blood.

'Fuck!' Paul shouted. *'Fuck!'* Grunting, trying to summon a last reserve of strength.

He could bellow all he wanted. He could push and scratch and fight and pray. He was going to lose.

It ended with a bang *and* a whimper. The door slammed into the wall with a loud crack. Paul went backward; no – he flew, soared, catapulted. He careened off the bed. He grabbed for the phone – dead.

The man came for him.

Paul put his hands up to defend himself. He screamed. Nothing came out.

The man had put one hand around his mouth, the other against his windpipe.

He felt like a rag doll whose head was about to be smashed.

But the man didn't smash Paul's head.

He spoke to him.

Whispered even.

'Breathe,' he said. 'Nice and easy. That's it.'

There was no Russian accent. No Colombian accent either. That was the first surprise.

There was another.

LATER, AFTER PAUL HAD STOPPED SHAKING, THEY TALKED ABOUT old times.

Not really *old* times. Fairly recent in memory, just far enough away from now to be ancient history.

The delay in Kennedy.

The layover in Washington, D.C. Eight excruciating hours sitting on the tarmac with nothing to do.

Only it hadn't seemed excruciating for the man. No. He'd sat there with utter calm staring at the seat back in front of him.

He was used to waiting, he'd said. *Remember?* he asked Paul.

He was a bird-watcher.

THIRTY-FOUR

Jungle gym.
The Jungle Book.
In the jungle, the mighty jungle, the lion sleeps tonight.
Jungle boogie.

Joanna was reciting the entire known canon of jungle references. She was being her own google.com. Some of these jungle references were clearly sanitized, the jungle made friendly. Something to dance to, sing to, for four-year-olds to innocently clamber over.

There were other, scarier references.

The concrete jungle.
It's a jungle out there.

She would just as soon not think of those.

The real jungle, the humid infestation of invisible buzzing, shrieking things and rotting, tangled vegetation, was scary enough.

For one thing it was dark.

Darker than dark.

A suffocating canopy of branches blotted out whatever moonlight there was. It was like stumbling around a closet

280

– the kind children are convinced harbors hideous monsters.

There were definitely things going bump in the night. She could hear them directly above her head. Rustling branches, sudden growls. *Monkeys?* Or something worse? *Jaguars, ocelots, boa constrictors?*

Joelle had woken up soon after they'd made it down a small clearing and into the thick trees. She'd begun wailing for food – or because she was cold or just plain sick. Joanna didn't know. She was still learning the foreign language of infancy – something Galina seemed to have down pat. It didn't matter. She had no baby formula with her, and she couldn't do anything about the surrounding chill the baby blanket was doing little to counter.

'We're going home,' she whispered to her daughter, though it was solely for her own benefit. Speaking out loud helped pierce the darkness, let her know that *she,* at least, was present and accounted for. Of course it might've been doing the same for any animals in the vicinity. Human or otherwise.

Occasionally, invisible flying things smacked her in the face. She nearly swallowed an enormous moth – just managing to spit it out, then bending over and retching when she realized what had been fluttering around her mouth.

She had no idea where she was going.

She'd decided she'd maintain a straight line from the house. Even if she didn't know where she was headed, she'd know where she was headed *from.* There was a problem, though – as with all thought-out, rational plans of attack. The enemy had a vote.

The jungle wasn't cooperating. There were innumerable

obstacles in her way – massive tree trunks, several of which she almost walked into, sudden steep drops, a black stream complete with invisible waterfall that sounded, for one instant of comfort, like TV static.

She kept making detours till she felt like *it* in blindman's buff. She'd been spun around too many times to know which way was which. She desperately needed someone to tell her if she was getting warmer.

Right now she was getting colder. And hungrier. And more frightened.

The simple rocking motion of putting one foot before the other lulled Joelle back to sleep. Joanna was tempted to join her. In the morning she'd at least be able to see – survey her surroundings and make an educated guess where she was.

She was worried someone would peek in the room – Tomás or Puento. That they'd send out searchers who knew the jungle and, more important, knew how to *track* someone in it. She had to keep moving.

She stumbled into a large clearing.

It was as if someone had flicked on the room lights. She could suddenly see her legs, Joelle's sleeping face, the *sky*. She hadn't seen the sky since . . . well, she couldn't remember. She was momentarily stunned at the tapestry of glittering stars – so many of them that it seemed artificial, like an enormous disco ball. She stood there and caught her breath.

Odd. Here she was in the middle of a jungle, but if she didn't know any better, she would've sworn she was standing before a *field*. Something cultivated, regular, attended to. There was a dank but distinct odor in the air. What?

She stepped forward till she stood on its very edge.

Of course.

Coca. She'd stumbled across an illegal cocaine field, the kind they grew deep in the jungle to shield from government patrols.

Joanna felt a surge of – what? *Hope?*

She was trespassing on dangerous ground. But at least it was ground trod by humans.

If she waited till morning, someone might come – the farmer who tended it. But what if it wasn't a campesino looking for a little supplemental income? What if it was one of – *them*? Maybe they grew their *own* fields – maybe this was one of them. She felt caught between competing and equally compelling inclinations. She would do anything not to go back into the jungle. If she stayed, if she lay down and curled up till morning, she might end up having waited for the wrong people.

Go or stay?

Then it was decided for her.

The field itself was an indistinct blanket of mostly black. Even as her eyes grew accustomed to her moonlit surroundings, it stayed that way. Black.

It had an odor with an almost physical dimension – wet, pasty, and bitter.

Then she understood. The field looked black because that's what it was.

Black as ash.

It'd been burned to the ground. She could see it now – a tangle of five-foot coca plants reduced to shattered, twisted stumps.

A government patrol had discovered and torched it. Or

the USDF. Or the farmer who grew it. Maybe they practiced a kind of slash-and-burn agriculture.

Anyway, it was abandoned. No one would be coming in the morning.

She had to keep moving.

Which way?

It seemed like you should be able to tell from the stars. *How?* Paul knew this kind of stuff – she'd bought him a telescope for his thirty-fifth birthday that proved virtually useless on the roof of their apartment building. The bright lights of New York City didn't just blind starry-eyed newcomers – they did a pretty good job on amateur astronomers. Still, more than once Paul had tried to point out one constellation or another to her. She wished she'd paid more attention.

Okay, which direction?

She swung her arm in an arc and decided she'd stop it when it felt right. Like throwing darts blindfolded.

When her arm stopped moving, it was pointing left.

She kissed Joelle on the top of her head and moved back into the jungle.

Morning was coming fast.

The light had changed from deep black to charcoal gray. She stopped having to worry that each footstep might land her in quicksand, or into a hole, or on top of some animal's head.

That was the good part.

The bad part was that she could see some of the screeching, growling, slithering things that she'd only *heard* up to now. Imagination might be scarier than reality, she decided, but not by much.

What looked like a kind of baboon swung past her by inches, emitting a threatening screech that almost shattered her eardrums. It landed in the crook of a tree branch four feet above her head and shook a vine in her direction. It displayed its teeth – they looked large and frighteningly sharp.

Joanna turned to her right and stumbled through the underbrush, hoping the monkey wouldn't come after them.

It didn't.

Later, she saw a tree branch suddenly move right in front of her. Literally get up and begin detaching itself from the trunk of an enormous tree dripping lacy veils of green moss.

Of course it wasn't a tree branch. It was a *snake* – clearly enormous and clearly alerted to her presence. It was as thick as her arm, with dead yellow eyes and a black flickering tongue. Scared stiff and trying not to scream, she watched it uncoil for what seemed like minutes.

It slid off into a thick patch of ferns.

With the growing light came the heat. It covered them like a wet towel and left her drenched in sweat. The insects seemed attracted to perspiration; clouds of white gnats descended on her from all directions. She tried swatting them away, but they were as oblivious as New York City pigeons – short of actual gunfire, they weren't budging.

Then there were the mosquitoes – or their very large cousins. She was a movable feast for them – her bitten arms were covered in red bumps, as if she'd broken out in hives.

Joelle had started crying again and didn't seem in any mood to stop.

Even to someone unschooled in the lingo of infants, it was obvious that while Joelle might be hot and uncomfortable, it was all about hunger now. For the first time, Joanna wondered if she'd done the right thing. She should've planned – stockpiled baby formula. She was guilty of criminal lack of foresight.

Nothing seemed to calm Joelle down; soon Joanna needed calming as well. Fear lodged somewhere in the pit of her stomach and physically constricted her, as if her legs were bound by rubber bands. She was living through one of those dreams of being chased, where you can't, for the life of you, *move*.

They were as lost as lost can be.

The jungle had swallowed them whole – eaten them alive. They weren't going to get out.

She kept walking anyway – something inside her ordering her to lift one leg, then the other. Sheer stubbornness maybe.

Walking songs – front and center.

I'm walking, yes indeed, I'm talking, yes indeed . . .

These boots are made for walking . . .

Walk like a man . . .

She decided she'd keep walking till she couldn't. That was fair. Go as long as she could and then drop. Fight the good fight.

It was early morning – save for the brief respite by the abandoned coca field, she'd been walking six straight hours.

Then she smelled it.

She stopped dead, closed her eyes, crossed her fingers.

Sniff.

She smelled it again.

Sausage.

Was that possible?

Hot, sizzling, aromatic *sausage*?

Maybe it was some kind of plant? An animal? A jungle smell she was simply unfamiliar with?

She sniffed the air again, taking her time. No. It was clear as day. Someone was cooking breakfast.

Her heart leaped, soared, did pirouettes. She stopped rocking Joelle and brought her up under her chin.

'We made it. We're going home. We're free.'

She couldn't see anyone – the same panorama of trees, vines, stumps, and ferns. A massive dew-laden spiderweb refracted the sun into sparkling carats of fire.

She followed the smell.

Left, then right, then straight ahead.

Nose, don't fail me now.

The jungle seemed to thin – not all at once, but slowly, inexorably. The air lost its heaviness, her lungs eased, the insects drifted off.

The smell intensified, tickling her taste buds, reeling her in.

Now she could see patches of empty space through the trees.

She quickened her pace – if she'd been wearing sneakers instead of half-inch heels, she would've broken into a run.

Even Joelle seemed to sense a change in the air. Her crying lessened, then stopped altogether. She emitted a series of gurgles and hoarse sniffles.

Joanna skirted vegetation that had clearly been *stepped* on. Someone had walked here, snapping stems, grinding broad green fronds into the dirt. She thought she could make out an actual footprint.

The smell was intoxicating. She was nearly drunk on it. She lurched past a massive banyan tree and was suddenly staring into thin air.

A lone figure was standing there, backlit by a sun the color of marmalade.

The figure was saying something to her.

Joanna dropped to the ground, Joelle nestled in her arms. She hung her head, rocked back and forth, began weeping.

'No,' she whispered to herself, to Joelle, to the person standing in the clearing, maybe to God. *'No . . .'*

The clearing sloped uphill to a ridge where a modest farmhouse stood.

It had a smoking chimney, lime-green shutters, and a dilapidated back pen holding roosters, goats, and cows.

It was the first time she'd seen it from the outside.

'Quick,' Galina said, 'back to the room before they see you.'

THIRTY-FIVE

Galina snuck her back into the house. Not without being detected. The Indian girl with long black hair came out of the bathroom and nearly bumped into them. Galina had an explanation.

She fainted, Galina told her in Spanish, *she needed some air.*

The girl nodded, seemingly disinterested.

Once Galina ushered Joanna back into the room, once she closed the door and sat down, she said, 'It was stupid. You don't *know* the jungle.' She took Joelle from her exhausted arms, changed and fed her. 'You would've died out there.'

'I'm going to die anyway,' Joanna answered. It was the first time she'd uttered that thought out loud. It seemed to give it an awful legitimacy.

Galina shook her head. 'You shouldn't say that.'

'Why not? It's true. They'll kill me like they killed Maruja and Beatriz. You don't want to talk about it. They killed them in here – in this room. I can show you their blood.'

'Her cold's worse,' she said, referring to Joelle, continuing to avoid any mention of the two ghosts still hovering in the room.

'Yes, her cold's worse. And her mother's still chained to a wall. And we won't talk about two murdered women.' Joanna's own voice seemed alien to her now – flat, emotionless. It's *hope,* she thought – she'd lost it out there in the jungle.

'I'm going to put her to sleep,' Galina said.

'Yes. Wonderful idea. While you're at it, put me to sleep.'

Galina winced and rubbed her left arm.

Nurse. Kidnapper. Friend. Jailer.

'I don't understand you,' Joanna said.

'What?'

'I don't understand. You. Why you're here. Why you're with these people. Killers. Murderers. You were a mother.'

Galina had turned to leave, but now she stopped, looked back at her. It was that *word,* Joanna thought.

Mother.

'You never finished your story,' Joanna said. 'Tell me. I need a good story tonight. I do. I need to understand why.'

THIRTY-SIX

'I need a good story tonight.'

Just the way Claudia used to say it to me because she didn't want to go to sleep yet.

A story, Mama, she'd beg. A story.

Well, okay.

A story.

AFTER GALINA AND HER HUSBAND HAD LEFT THE BAR THAT night, they didn't speak to Claudia again.

Sometimes the boy from La Nacional would call them.

There was a firefight with helicopter-borne Special Forces in the mountains. A new initiative by a just-sworn-in president who'd promised to get tough with the *guerrilleros*. The boy said Claudia was there – army officers reported a beautiful young girl in camouflage fatigues. *Don't worry,* the boy said, *she wasn't hurt.*

These government forays were infrequent and entirely for show. Getting tough on the *guerrilleros*, everyone knew, was simple posturing. There might be two tough factions in Colombia, but the government wasn't one of them.

There was FARC, the Revolutionary Armed Forces of Colombia, on the left.

And on the right, the United Self-Defense Forces.

All names in these kinds of conflicts were exercises in irony. *Self-Defense* – as if they'd been punched in the nose and were simply defending themselves from a playground bully. Maybe that's what some of them believed they were doing.

Just not the man who ran it.

If you wanted to understand what happened to Claudia, you had to understand him too. If you saw Claudia tripping down the alleyways of Chapinero as a sensitive and easily bruised eight-year-old, you had to see *him* growing up in Medellín and doing a generous share of the bruising. They were counterparts. If Claudia was the light, he was the dark.

They were due to collide.

How do you explain a Manuel Riojas?

Bogeymen aren't usually born, they just are. They lurk in the swamp of human fear and misery. They don't have beginnings, just ends. But even then, they never go quietly, not before they leave behind desolate swaths of scorched earth.

Real bogeymen *do* have beginnings. They have birthdays and confirmations and school graduations. They live in neighborhoods, not swamps. Manuel Riojas grew up in the grimy Jesús de Navarona neighborhood of Medellín.

Galina had visited relatives there once. She remembered how a steady gray rain washed the garbage downhill. It was possible she'd driven by Riojas himself – later she'd wonder about that. If he might've been carjacking by then. If he might've picked their car – pointed a pistol through the window and ended everything before it began.

It's said he grew up on the stories.

The legends of Colombia's *bandidos*. Desquite and Tirofijo and Sangrenegra. *Revenge, Sureshot,* and *Blackblood*. Galina came to believe that countries where much of the population is poor and oppressed are doomed to worship the wrong people. People who steal from the rich, even if they never actually give anything back to the poor. It doesn't matter – they *are* poor. Or were. They might be vicious, murderous, clearly psychotic. They're victimizing the victimizers. That's enough to make them folk heroes. Enough to make children who grow up in uncertain circumstances daydream of becoming them.

Riojas' criminal beginnings were murky. It's said he went back and had police files altered, court records erased, various acquaintances from his early life eliminated. It's known he was arrested at least once by the time he was fourteen – possibly for petty theft. It's believed he bartered fake lottery tickets, hijacked cigarettes, stole cars, before moving on to something infinitely more lucrative. The particular scourge of their godforsaken country: drugs. Specifically, coca. He started as a runner, a small dealer. He was apparently a favorite of the local *contrabandista,* who made the fatal mistake of trusting him, promoting him through the ranks. Somehow the severed head of this *contrabandista* ended up stuck on a pole on a mountain road outside Medellín. Somehow Riojas ended up in charge of the Medellín cocaine trade. This was generally acknowledged to be the first exhibition of Riojas' particular business ethos. He didn't compete with rivals. He murdered them. He did it in ways meant to discourage others. Children were murdered in front of their parents. Mothers were raped in front of their husbands. Enemies were tortured and mutilated, their freshly slaughtered corpses placed on public display. More fodder for the newspapers.

Property wasn't excluded. Warehouses, factories, competing cocaine fields, were torched and obliterated.

The stories grew; the legend took form and substance.

He rose to nearly unimaginable heights.

That's necessary for a bogeyman. To tower over the cringing. And they *did* cringe. Not just rival gangs, the Ochoas, the Escobars, who soon disappeared in a series of vicious and prolonged bloodbaths. But the *familias* who pulled the strings. They bowed down too. Riojas ate the heart of his enemies, then became them. He was elected state senator. They say he'd promised this to his mother. Respectability. They say he'd pledged this to the idols he kept in a secret chapel on one of his haciendas. *Santeria,* they whispered, the bastard religion practiced throughout much of the country outside Bogotá.

But rulers demand more than obedience. They demand armies. The one belonging to the government was toothless. It didn't take any particular intelligence to realize that the only army worth fighting lived in the mountains north of Bogotá and called themselves FARC. They spouted Marxist mumbo jumbo about toppling the *elite,* talked about the *people* as if the people actually mattered. Under different circumstances, Riojas might've sympathized with them, even *joined* them. After all, he came from the same impoverished background. Now he was another successful *capitalista* trying to protect his investments. They were the enemy.

He armed his own militia. He gave his most trusted executioners titles. *Captain. General. Major.* That made them more or less an army. He demanded money from the five *familias* to fund it.

Now they could have a real war.

Riojas could conduct it the way war was supposed to be conducted. When the USDF wanted to keep campesino villages from harboring FARC guerrillas – not that they had, not that they'd even thought about it, just that they *might* – they'd pick twenty campesinos at random. You, you, and you. They'd make them dig their own graves, then force their fathers or brothers or uncles to execute them. Whoever refused, joined them in the pit. This was the kind of muscular teaching a simple campesino could understand.

Claudia was captured by the USDF two years after she walked out of that bar.

The boy from the university called and told them.

After Galina had dropped the phone to the floor and stared at it as if it were something alien, after she had reluctantly picked it up and found her voice, she asked the boy if her daughter was dead. Only it wasn't *her* voice – it sounded like someone years older.

No, he said. She'd been captured alive.

He didn't add that it wouldn't be for long.

He didn't have to.

For one entire year Galina assumed Claudia was dead.

She thought of having a proper funeral but was always dissuaded at the last moment. Sometimes it was something she found as she cleaned the house. She cleaned all the time now. Ceaselessly, relentlessly, *religiously*. She'd trudge back from caring for someone else's daughter or son and immediately grab a mop, a sponge, a dustpan, desperately clinging to routine as a way to stave off thoughts of suicide. One day while vacuuming under Claudia's desk, she found a birthday card an eight-year-old Claudia had drawn for her in school. A stick-figure mommy holding a stick-figure baby in her arms. *Te adoro,* the baby whispered.

Galina said *not yet.* The funeral would wait.

Sometimes memory would be triggered by something completely ordinary. Stuffing a bedsheet into the washer and suddenly remembering Claudia's first period, how Galina had stood flustered and embarrassed before Claudia's soiled bed one morning before middle school. Even as her daughter remained oddly composed, even comforting. *I know what it is, Mama — it means I can have grandbabies for you.*

Galina pushed the funeral off again.

Everything that follows, Galina would find out later.

Claudia was captured in the town of Chiappa. They'd sent her there for supplies, and someone spotted her. Stories about her had been circulating for months. The beautiful university girl with the revolutionary fever. Someone was sitting and waiting for her. He followed her from town, called in reinforcements. When Claudia got back to the ravine where her fellow soldiers in the war against capitalism were holed up and waiting, a USDF brigade was already circling in for the kill.

When she opened the flap of their makeshift tent, just

a few shirts strung together to keep out the rain, bullets rained down on them instead.

Three of the *guerrilleros* were killed. Two made it back through the jungle, one of them dragging a shot-up right leg that was later amputated.

Why wasn't Claudia killed like the others?

Maybe because they were told not to.

Because Riojas had heard the stories and was curious to see her in the flesh. More than curious. *Desirous.*

He left a state dinner in Bogotá that night. Someone whispered into his ear, and he flew by helicopter to a hacienda in the north. When he entered the room where Claudia was on her knees, both hands tied tightly behind her back, he was still wearing his tuxedo.

He took his time. *Examining* her, the way you appraise horseflesh or hunting dogs. Apparently, he had plenty of both.

He must've liked what he saw.

You can imagine what happened during the next two days. You can close your eyes and say a prayer and peek. Riojas personally took charge of her *interrogation.* She came very close to dying. She prayed for it, hoped to God that the next time he beat her into unconsciousness she wouldn't wake up. Despite having joined the army of the godless, Claudia still *believed.* Somewhere inside herself she retained her Catholic core. She spoke to it now.

She'd heard the stories: prisoners pushed out of helicopters, fed to the tigers. It would happen to her.

But two days turned into three.

Then four.

An entire week passed.

No one came to take her off in a helicopter, or for a trip to the tiger cage. Yes, there *were* tigers. She squinted out her window through nearly beaten-shut eyes and saw them pacing back and forth like sentries. In the afternoon someone threw a live pony into the cage and the tigers ripped its throat out.

Then something odd happened.

One day Riojas came in and didn't beat her. He asked her something instead.

To open her legs for him. Politely requested it. Claudia said no, shut her eyes, waited for a fresh onslaught of pain.

Riojas left the room.

The next time he came in, he was bearing gifts.

French lingerie.

Riojas asked her to try it on for him. Claudia said no.

Again he didn't touch her.

By the third time, Claudia began to understand something.

She wasn't experienced with men; she'd had a casual boyfriend or two.

She could tell when someone was in love.

It had happened before – boys in primary school, then university, who'd begin acting stupid around her, wholly outside the realm of normal behavior.

It became increasingly clear that Riojas wasn't going to kill her.

He was going to court her.

Why?

Maybe because Claudia was Claudia.

Because he coveted what he couldn't destroy. *Love is strange* – isn't that what the songs say?

At some point Claudia began to understand that this adoration might save her. Maybe not forever. Just for a while. Somewhere she stopped wanting to die and began wanting to live.

When he asked her a fourth time to dress in French lingerie, to turn around and please kneel on the bed for him, she said yes. She understood it wouldn't do to *always* deny him. Eventually, he'd tire of that. Then he'd tire of her.

There's something truly pathetic about a captor falling in love with his prisoner. Claudia needed to *use* that to her advantage. She needed to hold something back. To sometimes give in, but always deny the one thing he wanted more than anything else. Reciprocity.

Her heart – as the poets say.

She began to dine with him, at an actual dinner *table*. Set with gleaming silver, translucent china. Dressed up in whichever five-hundred-dollar dress he'd picked out for her. Sometimes she'd wear something else, deliberately ignoring his wishes. He'd throw tantrums that subsided only after most of their dinner had ended up on the floor.

He delighted in telling her what he'd done to other women. Women who'd crossed him. That singer – Evi, the pop star who'd thought she could carry on with a musician while seeing *him*.

I went up to her apartment with my personal doctor. I held her down while he cut out her vocal cords, then I sat there and watched as he sewed her up. She no longer sings very well.

He was trying to evoke fear and obedience. Claudia would act bored. She was convinced if she did the opposite of what he expected, she could survive another day.

He loosened the leash a little.

She was allowed outside – always accompanied by one of his goons. She listened. She observed. She memorized things.

Where were they? She smelled salt in the air. Not all the time, just on the days when the wind blew hard from the north. They had to be on the coast. Even so, they were hopelessly isolated. There wasn't a single roof in any direction. Just lush palms, overgrown ferns, tumbling birds-of-paradise. Wild parrots serenaded her on her walks around the hacienda.

Then she observed something else.

Something horrible.

Riojas had always used protection with her. Lately, he'd become careless. He was usually drunk or coked up.

She missed a period. Then another.

One morning she woke completely consumed with nausea and spent half an hour on the floor of the marble bathroom, staring at her warped reflection in the gold-leaf fixtures.

She decided she would kill herself.

She came to this decision calmly and rationally.

There were knives in the kitchen.

There were two swords mounted above the fireplace in the den. She would put one of them right through her, through his *monstrosity*, before anyone could stop her.

Riojas was away. She cleansed her face, meticulously applied the French makeup Riojas had brought for her, dressed in a charcoal pantsuit she thought suitable for a funeral.

The armed guards he kept stationed around the house were fortuitously absent from the den.

The swords appeared to be ceremonial. Japanese, she guessed – delicately curved steel fixed to bright hand-painted hilts. They were hung on nails, crossed at mid-blade.

She was reaching for one of them when she felt it. Or maybe she just imagined she had.

Like a *kick in the gut.*

She'd touched the instrument of her own death, and something had moved in the pit of her stomach. She sank to the floor.

She understood. She knew what it was.

More than that. She knew she couldn't bring herself to kill it.

It was half her.

It means I can have grandbabies for you, she'd once whispered to her mother, Galina. Maybe she remembered saying it that morning. Maybe it gave that tiny movement in her belly a face, a place in the world.

She hovered between despair and worse.

She'd made a decision to live, but it was a decision impossible to live *with.* So she made another kind of decision.

When Riojas returned from Bogotá, Claudia feigned happiness, guiding his hand onto her stomach as if helping him claim new territory. Another piece of the world ready to be affixed with his monogram – those cartoonish-looking *R*s prominently displayed on every one of his handkerchiefs, napkins, undershorts – anything capable of bearing thread.

He began pampering her. Within limits, of course. She wasn't his wife. He had one of those back in Bogotá, in addition to three obscenely rotund children. He couldn't squire her around town. But he showed what might be termed *deference*. The leash grew looser. A captured rebel, even one showered with mink coats and five-hundred-dollar shoes, might run. But a girl carrying his child?

He stopped talking about the women who'd crossed him.

Except for the day she told him.

He asked for sex and she turned him down, pregnancy being a convenient excuse, one to be added to all the others.

Of course, he said, he understood. But before leaving her room he turned and spoke to her.

If you ever try to leave with my baby, I'll hunt you down and kill you. Both of you. However long it takes, no matter where you've gone. Do you understand?

She nodded, forced herself to smile, as if that were a sentiment worthy of admiration. A macho declaration of love.

Good, he said.

She began venturing further. Past the tiger cages. Down a twisting dirt path into the jungle. She *had* smelled salt air. The hacienda's property ended on a bluff overlooking the Caribbean, where a small fishing village sat directly below the cliff. Skiffs sat half beached on the sand, spidery nets drying in the sun.

A bodyguard still came with her, but the distance between them seemed to increase in proportion to her swollen stomach. He'd often leave her alone with a book, let her nap undisturbed on one of the hammocks overlooking the water.

She befriended the zookeeper; in addition to the tigers, there were ostriches, llamas, chimpanzees. His name was Benito, and unlike the other men in Riojas' employ, he seemed to lack the psychotic gene. He'd been trained in zoology. He let her know that feeding live horses to the tigers wasn't his idea. Feeding two-legged things to them wasn't either.

A job was a job.

He let her watch as he fed them freshly cut hunks of sheep and cattle, venturing into the cage dangling the day's lunch from a long hooked pole.

Claudia waited for Riojas to make one of his numerous trips.

She slipped out of bed at 3 a.m. She opened her top drawer, removed a change of clothes, wrapped them around the kitchen knife she'd slipped into the waistband of her pants.

She'd unlocked one bay window in the den before retiring. She opened it wide enough to slip out – no mean feat considering her swollen stomach. She stepped out onto the blue grass.

She'd rehearsed this at least a dozen times.

She could've walked the route in her sleep.

She waddled past the tiger cage to the zookeeper's shack.

She removed the keys from the bent nail. She pushed the sleeve of her shift back to the elbow, pulled out the knife, and placed it against her skin.

She used the extra clothes she'd taken from her drawer to soak up the blood. She walked back out to the tiger cages and pushed the bloody clothes through the bars.

Claudia carefully placed the keys into the cage-door lock and left them dangling there.

She turned to the path that led to the sea.

She was buying time.

In the morning they'd discover she was missing. They'd find the keys to the tiger cage still sitting in the lock. As if someone had let themselves in and locked the door behind them to ensure that there would be no way out. In case they lost their courage and changed their mind. They'd discover her bloody clothes. Shredded to pieces.

Riojas would be called in Bogotá. He'd think back to their last night together. He'd replay everything. Her smiles and laughter and demure assurances, and he'd see only lies. Had she killed herself? Had she *really*?

Eventually, he'd know the truth. They wouldn't find any ground-up bones. They'd understand the charade she'd perpetrated, and Riojas would start to make good on his promise.

If you ever try to leave with my baby, I'll hunt you down and kill you. Both of you. However long it takes, no matter where you've gone. Do you understand?

Maybe Claudia heard those words as she walked through the jungle that night and down to the sea. As she sat and crouched in one of the slowly rocking fishing skiffs and waited for the fishermen to appear like ghosts out of the early-morning light . . .

THE SOUND OF A CRYING BABY. IT STARTLED JOANNA BACK TO reality. Back from that hacienda and the tiger cage and the jungle.

Joelle had woken up.

It was her cold. Galina reached over and wiped Joelle's nose, cleared the crust from her eyes with a tissue. Joanna gave her the bottle, urged the nipple into her mouth, gently rocked her. Soon Joelle's eyes grew sleepy, fluttered, closed into two tiny slits.

Galina was hugging herself as if she were suddenly freezing.

'What happened, Galina?' Joanna asked. 'What happened to Claudia?'

GALINA SPENT THE EMPTY DAYS DUTIFULLY FEEDING AND BATHING and powdering other people's daughters.

She ritually and repeatedly cleaned house.

She discovered bits and pieces of Claudia and arranged them in a kind of shrine. Old birthday cards. Photographs. Letters. Half-burned incense candles. Little items of mostly cheap jewelry. She did what people are supposed to do at shrines. She prayed for a miracle.

Sometimes they actually happen.

Sometimes you wake up and dress yourself in the same dowdy shift as the day before. You sit down at the kitchen table and listlessly eat a breakfast of stale corn cakes and fruit, because you're supposed to eat, even if you have no appetite. You vacuum a carpet you've already vacuumed enough times to wear smooth. You dust every piece of furniture in the house. You rewash the dishes and scrub the floor. Then you sit back down at the kitchen table because it's time to eat lunch.

And sometimes you hear a soft knock at the front door.

You wearily stand up to answer it, not *immediately*, because you hope they'll go away and leave you alone. But they don't, so eventually you have to get up, shuffle over to the door, ask who it is.

And you hear a murmur from the other side. Something with an *M*. A voice you can't quite place that seems to touch some distant part of you. And you ask again. *Who is it?*

And now the *M* comes with other letters attached to it. It's no longer an orphan. You suddenly understand that the person on the other side of the door isn't telling you their name. They're stating *yours*. Only it's a name only one person in the world can use.

Your heart stops beating as if there's some kind of electrical short in your wiring. You turn the lock with trembling fingers. You fling open the door and the person whispers it again.

Mama . . . Mama . . . Mama.

And she falls into your arms.

THEY FOUND HER A HIDING PLACE.

Colombia was a big country.

Riojas was bigger.

Aunt Salma wasn't an aunt by blood, but by affection, a spinster who'd been semi-adopted by the family long ago and was from then on always present at holidays, confirmations, and funerals. Back in Fortul, where Galina was born.

They drove Claudia there the next day.

Claudia assured them Riojas didn't know her last name.

All FARC converts changed their surnames to save their families from retribution.

Galina knew that would protect her only so much.

Claudia was striking and pregnant. Riojas would be beating the provinces to find her.

It was a measure of Galina's manic joy that she hadn't noticed. Not immediately. Certainly not at the door, where she'd gazed teary-eyed at her; not even at the kitchen table, where they'd clung to each other like shipwreck survivors.

But when they finally separated and she checked her daughter for damage, she saw the kind she hadn't expected.

'You're pregnant.'

Two years ago Claudia might've had an answer for that – a comment on her mother's diminishing powers of observation. She simply nodded.

'Whose is it?'

Claudia told her. She was never going to speak about it again – just this one time. She held both of Galina's hands. She spoke slowly, softly, calmly. It was good she kept Galina's hands prisoner. Galina felt like using those hands. To hit something. To cover her ears. To wrap around her mouth to prevent herself from screaming. It was impossible for a mother to sit there and listen to this. It was beyond endurance.

The subject of abortion never came up.

It's possible the pregnancy was too far advanced by then. Maybe it didn't matter. It wasn't how either of them had been raised.

Aunt Salma lived near a dairy farm outside the city,

where it was possible Claudia might live in relative privacy and anonymity. At least for a while. At least until the baby was born.

They told Salma just enough to understand the gravity of Claudia's situation. They constructed a story for anyone who couldn't be avoided. An unfortunate love affair. An unplanned pregnancy. A girl who wanted to be left alone with the result of her bad choices.

Galina and her husband visited every two weeks, making sure to leave late at night, to stop several times along the way to check for any suspicious cars that might be following them. Any more than two weeks might be risky. Any less would be unbearable.

With the help of a local mestiza midwife, Claudia gave birth to a baby girl.

Galina had wondered how she'd feel. If she'd ever be able to embrace the baby as her actual *grandchild*. When the infant emerged headfirst, Galina saw Claudia in every facet of her features. She felt transported through time. To a hospital bed in Bogotá, the smell of blood and alcohol and talcum, a screaming baby who even then seemed to grab for something just out of reach.

She was named for Claudia's paternal grandmother. Sofía, the *ventello* singer. She was swaddled, baptized, showered with affection from the small circle of people allowed to know of her existence.

For a time, brief and fleeting, Galina allowed herself to relax and luxuriate in the peculiar pleasures of being an *abuela*. When she visited Fortul, baby toys in hand, she was like anyone else visiting their grandchild. She pretended that Claudia lived in Fortul because her husband worked for one of the refineries there. That Claudia never made the return trip because the baby wasn't ready to travel. That they always stayed inside because the weather was nasty or because Sofía was sensitive to the sun.

Then it became impossible to pretend.

Salma returned from the market one day looking nearly anemic. She told Claudia that people were asking questions. Someone was showing a *picture* around. Claudia remembered her first days of captivity when Riojas had interrogated her, when he'd posed her naked in various positions intended for maximum humiliation. Even with her eyes swollen shut, she could see bursting flashbulbs shooting out of the black like Roman candles.

They had to move them.

Another family resource was contacted and imposed upon. And it *was* an imposition. Whoever hid them was keenly aware they were putting themselves in the line of fire. A kind of ad hoc system developed. Claudia and Sofía were *shuttled*. Back and forth and back between whichever relatives and friends were momentarily able to swallow their fear and provide them with a temporary home.

It wasn't easy for Claudia to be passed around like an unwanted relative. But that's what she was. A burden, an albatross. Albatrosses meant death; so might Claudia. She'd spend a few weeks to several months at each house or apartment before leaving. Usually in the middle of the night. She became adept at packing quickly, bringing just enough from one place to another to make each new stop seem remotely like home.

Slowly, pressure eased. Stories of *paramilitares* inquiring after a beautiful girl with a small baby became more

sporadic, then stopped altogether. Claudia's stays length-
ened, routine replaced fear. Sofía grew from infant to tod-
dler – in an instant, it seemed to Galina, who only saw her
in carefully parceled-out increments. Claudia seemed to
grow as well, regaining pieces of herself that had been
taken away from her in that hacienda. She began venturing outside, baby in tow, disguised in sunglasses and an
enormous straw hat.

Galina accompanied her on some of these walks. She let
herself imagine that life might reach some kind of normalcy. It had been *four years*. If one read the papers correctly, Riojas had more than enough to keep him
occupied. They were threatening to extradite him to the
United States for narcotics trafficking. Maybe he'd forgotten about Claudia. About *them*. Maybe he no longer
cared.

When the three of them strolled hand in hand – lifting
a begging Sofía over the curb by both arms – it was easy to
imagine this was true.

Later Galina would understand that's what he'd wanted
them to think. So they'd begin to believe it was over. Become a little more carefree, even care*less*. So they'd stop
peeking around corners.

She never knew how it happened.

Not *exactly* how it happened. She would never know
that. She would have to *imagine* it, which was worse than
knowing. Because the imagination can conjure up every
nightmare never dreamed.

Someone spotted Claudia. That much she knew.

Galina received a panicked call from her daughter. Or
rather, her answering machine did. For the rest of her life

she would admonish herself for going shopping that day. For opening the refrigerator and somehow seeing the necessity for food. She would have hours and days and weeks and years to imagine what was being done to her daughter while she performed the mundane tasks of daily living. To ponder a single question. If she'd been home to take Claudia's call, would she have been able to *save* her?

When Galina *did* get home, when she casually pressed the button on her answering machine and heard her daughter's clearly terrified voice, she knew it was already too late.

She buried her panic, did what you're supposed to do when someone calls you. Call *back*. Claudia's uncle – the one she'd been staying with for the last month and a half – answered the phone. He didn't know where she was, he said. Her or the baby. They must've gone for a walk.

Someone saw me at the market. That's what Claudia had whispered into the phone.

She hadn't waited for her uncle to return home. Out of self-preservation, out of the desire to protect *him*, she'd gathered up Sofía and run. Later they'd notice some of her things were missing. Not everything; some of Sofía's clothes and a small picture of the three of them – grandmother, mother, and baby – she'd managed to tote from one hiding place to another.

Claudia had been spotted in the market, and in a near panic she'd called the one person she trusted most in the world.

Galina wasn't there. She was out shopping.

Claudia had decided she needed to leave *then*.

After that, who knows?

After that, you're left with the clinical police reports and a few eyewitnesses who may or may not have seen anything.

Mostly, you're left with the body.

She was found on the edge of a barrio.

No one was aware it *was* a she at first. It was an amalgam of flesh and bone, a jigsaw puzzle that took two police pathologists a solid week to piece together before proclaiming it was *her*. They knew this much. What had been done to her had taken time and patience. There were traces of rope found around her neck. What *once* was her neck. There were acid burns everywhere. *Every inch of her skin.* That's what the police report said. It was supposed to be kept confidential to spare the family, but it was leaked to a newspaper, which printed it as a small item on the weather page. She'd been burned and mutilated. The report didn't mention if she was alive and conscious during the ordeal.

It didn't tell Galina *who* did it either.

It was another unsolved homicide. To be added to the thousands of other unsolved murders in Colombia.

Had Riojas been there in person?

Had he gotten another one of those calls in the middle of a dinner, coolly whispered in his wife's ear that he had urgent business to attend to? Had he smiled, rolled up his sleeves, walked in on a bound and terrified Claudia, just like he had four years before? It's impossible to say.

But Galina *saw* him there.

When she pictured it, as she did over and over and over again, dulled by alcohol, pumped full of whatever pills she'd managed to wheedle from yet another doctor, Riojas was always there. Wielding the knife. Spilling the acid. Choking the life out of her daughter.

He was always there.

WHEN GALINA FINISHED, JOANNA COULDN'T THINK OF ANYthing to say. She sat in stunned silence.

It wasn't until Galina stood up to leave, till she whispered good-bye and turned to the door, that Joanna realized there was a missing piece of the story.

'Sofía?' Joanna said, hesitant to ask because she was afraid to hear Galina's answer. 'What happened to your granddaughter?'

Galina stopped just before the door. 'Dead,' she said without turning around. 'Like her mother.'

There were other questions – how had their deaths led Galina to FARC? But Joanna didn't ask. If she thought about it hard enough, she could probably fill in the blanks herself.

After Galina left, Joanna lay on the floor and curled her body around her daughter, as if to protect her from fatal harm.

THIRTY-SEVEN

From the outside it looked like a taxi garage. *Dial-a-Taxi*, it said in big yellow block letters.

Apparently not.

For one thing there were no taxis inside.

There were no taxi drivers.

There were dark hallways that seemed to lead nowhere. There was a big room with faint oil stains on the floor. Maybe it had been a taxi garage once, but not now.

This was where the bird-watcher took him.

He'd been escorted down his apartment stairway with the bird-watcher's hand on his arm, then bundled into a car with gray-tinted windows and driven outside the city by a faceless chauffeur. Queens, Paul thought – that vast unknown that Manhattanites traversed on their way to the East End, only stopping for gas or the occasional Mets game.

'You don't watch birds,' Paul said to him sometime during the ride.

'No,' the man said. 'I watch other things.'

* * *

IT TOOK PAUL A WHILE TO UNDERSTAND THAT HE WAS BEING interrogated.

They were asking questions and it seemed as if he was answering them. Yes, there were *two* of them. After a while he noticed that one of the men always stayed out of sight and directly behind him – the two of them switching off like beach-volleyball players rotating between net and serve. He wondered if this was a tactic meant to scare him. One of them hiding behind him, doing God knows what. If so, he felt like telling them they needn't bother – he was scared enough already.

When they got to the garage, the bird-watcher had slipped on a blue vinyl jacket. No, *slipped on* was too casual a description. He cloaked himself in it, like a Masters champion displaying the green jacket.

This jacket had *DEA* prominently displayed in white letters, each half a foot tall. Paul imagined that was so there'd be no mistaking who was bursting through the front door of some walk-up in Spanish Harlem. Apparently, the bird-watcher hadn't felt the need to announce his affiliation when he'd burst into Paul's Upper West Side co-op.

'Know what this spells, Paul?' the bird-watcher asked him.

'Yes,' Paul said. 'Drug Enforcement Agency.'

'Wrong.'

'D . . . E . . .'

'Wrong.'

'I thought DEA is –'

'Wrong. This jacket spells *Paul is fucked*.'

Yes, Paul thought, okay. 'Do I get to call a – ?'

'You know *why* it spells that, Paul?' the bird-watcher interrupted him. 'Can you guess?'

'No. Yes.'

'*No. Yes.* Which is it?'

'Excuse me. Can I call a lawyer?'

'Sure you can call a lawyer. How about *Miles Goldstein?* He's a lawyer, isn't he?'

Paul didn't answer. The bird-watcher had shed his glasses, and with them any suggestion he was involved in the gentle and scholarly pursuit of ornithology.

I watch other things.

'Paul, I asked you a question. Perhaps you're not familiar with the dynamics of DEA interrogation. That's okay. I'll explain. We ask. You answer. It's pretty simple. So what do you say – we clear on this?'

Paul nodded.

'Great. Terrific. So what did I ask you before? Hey, Tom, you remember what I asked Paul?' He was addressing the man lurking behind him. Paul turned to peek, but immediately felt the man's arm on his shoulder forcefully turning him back.

'You asked him if Miles Goldstein was a lawyer,' Tom said.

'Yes,' Paul answered. 'He's a lawyer.'

'Wrong,' the bird-watcher said.

'He's an adoption –'

'Wrong.'

'We went to him because –'

'Wrong. Miles Goldstein is *not* a lawyer.'

Paul shrugged, stuttered – he felt like the dumb and picked-on student unable to divine the right answer.

'Miles Goldstein *was* a lawyer. Was. His brains are splattered all over his home office. But you know that, Paul. Do we have to review the dynamics of DEA interrogation again?'

'No.'

'No? Okay, Miles Goldstein was a lawyer. What else was Miles Goldstein? Besides a cocksucking Jew bastard. You think Jews have infiltrated the corridors of power, Paul? Do you think they've co-opted our foreign policy? Hijacked the banks, corrupted our corporations, polluted our bloodline? You think that, Paul?'

'No.'

'No? It's okay, Paul — we're just shooting the shit. You can tell me — some of your best friends are Jews, yada yada yada . . . but come on, you mean to tell me you don't curse the Yids every time you open the paper? You think Osama picked *Jew York* because he hates the Yankees?'

'I don't know.'

'Well, sure, you don't *know*. But you can *guess*. You can have a sneaking suspicion. Come on, Paul: Jews — yea or nay?'

'Nay,' Paul said, surrendering to peer pressure. He wanted the bird-watcher to smile at him, pat him on the back, hail-fellow-well-met. He wanted to get out of this garage and save his wife.

The blow to the back of his neck drove his face straight into the table. He came up sputtering blood.

'Paul. *Paul* . . .' The bird-watcher slowly shook his head, but the image became increasingly blurred — Paul's eyes were tearing up. 'I'm surprised at you. *Tom* is a Jew.

You offended him deeply. Why would you want to go and insult Tom like that?'

Paul tried to tell him he didn't mean it, he was just trying to be liked. He was in too much pain to speak. Initial numbness had given way to a searing and excruciating agony. Thick drops of blood were leaking onto the table.

'Try to avoid offending us from here on, Paul. Just a word of advice, okay? One friend to another. Me, I'm the calm type, but Tom's been up on more brutality charges than the LAPD. Now, where we? What *else* was Miles Goldstein?'

He got Paul a tissue, then waited patiently until Paul cleared enough blood from his throat to answer.

'I don't know,' Paul whispered. 'He was a kind of drug dealer, I think.'

'Ya *think*?' The bird-watcher smiled, but it wasn't the kind of smile Paul had been seeking. No.

'Yeah, Miles Goldstein was a drug dealer. You're right. Absolutely. Who did the dirty work for him? Who were his couriers?'

Me.

Paul said, 'Really. I want to call my lawyer.'

'Really. You really, really want to?'

'Yes.'

'No.'

'You haven't . . . I'm supposed to get a call. You haven't read me my rights.'

'There's a reason for that, Paul.'

'What reason?'

'You don't have any.'

'What?'

'See, we could read your rights to you, but you don't have any rights. Where've you been? It's Giuliani time.'

'I'm not a terrorist,' Paul said.

'No, Paul, you're not a terrorist. You're a mule. You're a *culero*. You're an up-the-ass FedEx package. We know what you are. But Goldstein was playing ball with those crafty little left-handers in *Che* Stadium. You know, FARC is a federally designated *terrorist group*. Yeah – they're on the list – the one with Osama and Hezbollah. That's why we supply Colombia with Special Ops nuts and really cool hardware. So if Goldstein was in business with terrorists and you were in business with Goldstein, well, that makes you . . . let me see, what does that make him, Tom?'

'That makes him subject to the newly drafted laws of national security. Or, as we like to say, rat-fucked by Ridge.'

'Yeah,' the bird-watcher said, 'that's about the size of it. No, Paul, you don't get a call. You don't get a lawyer. You don't get three hots and a smoke. You don't get *out* of here. Not unless we say so. And speaking of your fucked situation in life, I'd love to know how Miles and you walked into his office in Williamsburg and only *you* walked out.'

THEY PUT HIM IN A CELL, WHICH REALLY WASN'T ONE.

It didn't have a toilet or a sink. Unlike the room in Colombia, it didn't have a bed. It was just empty space surrounded by bare wall and what looked like a newly installed metal door.

If he wanted to lie down and sleep – and he did, desperately – he would have to lie directly on the concrete floor.

He tried, lay on his back and stared up at a single caged bulb, which didn't appear to be shutting off anytime soon. It was enclosed in metal so he couldn't reach up and break it, use it as a weapon, even against himself. No suicides on their watch.

Before throwing him in here they'd badgered him with questions – the majority of which he'd tried to answer. Mostly, he'd tried to explain what had happened. The kidnapping in Bogotá, the awful position in which he'd found himself, forced to choose between his wife and daughter and breaking six different federal drug statutes.

He couldn't tell whether they believed him or whether they thought he was making it all up.

They asked him a lot of questions about Miles. Interrupted by an occasional change of pace: What school did Paul go to? What does an actuary make? Which company did Joanna work for?

Every time he mentioned his wife's name, he felt a dull ache in the center of his chest. Everything he'd done, he'd done for them. Jo and Jo. He was no closer to freeing them. They were receding into the distance. It was as if he were pulling them up the side of a mountain, really putting his shoulder to it, only the rope kept slipping through his hands, dropping them further and further away.

AFTER A FEW HOURS IN HIS CELL THE BIRD-WATCHER CAME FOR him again.

Tom was missing in action.

'You know what really aggravates me, Paul?' the bird-watcher said. He was inhaling deeply on a Winston, holding in the smoke till the little vein in his forehead throbbed, then letting it out in a blue wispy stream.

'No,' Paul said.

'That was a rhetorical question, Paul. I appreciate you finally grasping the nuances of DEA interrogation, but I wasn't actually seeking an answer. What really aggravates me, what sticks in my craw, is that I worked this asshole for a year and a half, and now he's dead. A really bad case of coitus interruptus. I've got blue balls the size of grapefruits. Know what that feels like?'

Paul kept quiet this time.

'It doesn't feel good, Paul. It hurts. All I've got to show for it is lots of free miles on American – and I've got to put those back into an agency pool. You believe it? All those boring trips to Bogotá watching *Bruce Almighty* and sitting next to shitbags like you, and I get a trip to San Juan next Christmas – if I'm lucky. And I don't *feel* lucky. I mean, a year and a half and I end up with *you*? The last round-tripper on the Goldstein Express.'

Paul had been the last of many, the bird-watcher explained. It had taken him a long time to figure it out. He'd patiently followed the money trail. From Goldstein to Colombia and back. This close to wrapping it up, *this* close, and then . . .

'So what happened in his house, Paul? Monetary disagreement? Contractual dispute?'

'I told you,' Paul said. 'He shot himself.'

'Maybe. Only I'm inclined not to believe you. You've got the bad luck to be the one left holding the bag. Sucks, doesn't it? I need my pound of flesh, and you're it.

He shot himself? Maybe. Maybe not. Maybe I don't give a shit.'

'I keep telling you, they *kidnapped* us. Miles set us up with a driver. And a nurse . . . *Galina*. She switched babies, and when we went to confront her . . .'

Paul stopped here. The whole thing sounded implausible, even to him. The bird-watcher seemed to be in no mood for any story providing Paul with even a shred of innocence. He was busy lighting another cigarette and staring off into space.

There was another reason Paul stopped speaking.

A few things were penknifed into the table. Some dirty epithets, a couple of crude drawings, and a heart cleft in two.

Paul was looking at the letter carved into the larger half of the jagged heart.

It was the letter *R.*

It reminded him of something.

The letters from Galina. And the granddaughter she was determined to protect at all costs.

Her father is looking for her. He won't stop till he finds her. As you know, R has the power and means to do so.

R.

And Paul finally understood.

THIRTY-EIGHT

They called it a *fault tree*. The moribund boys in the loss adjuster department called it that.

When tragedy struck, something was lost, a building burned to the ground, a plane felled from the sky, a bridge collapsing into a river – you needed to apportion blame.

So you worked backward.

You created a fault tree.

You started with the *twigs* – all the little facts you knew, everything. Then you tried to ascertain which ones led back to the *branches*. To the *trunk* itself. If you were lucky, if you did your homework and took your time, you made it all the way back to the *roots*.

There was nothing much to do in his cell but clear wood, attempt to untangle the branches, and put it all back together.

That's what he did.

He cut and pruned and sawed and snapped, and in the end he made a tree.

It began with a Colombian baby nurse.

She helped American couples flooding her country in

search of instant families. A good woman really, someone who knew what it's like to desperately want a family, because she had one once, a *daughter*, at least, who might've looked much like Joelle.

The Colombian nurse worked for an American lawyer. Maybe not all the time, a lot of the time. An *adoption* lawyer, sending couples who'd tried everything short of baby-snatching to a country whose first export was cocaine and second was coffee, but third was children. A country with almost as many unwanted kidnappings as unwanted kids.

This lawyer had rejected tax or corporate law and entered the ranks of legal aid, where general disillusionment had eventually led him into foreign adoptions. He put needy babies together with needy families, and he got to pat himself on the back and make a good living at the same time.

Just not good enough.

One day he picked up the phone and a tout whispered in his ear. He was off to the races. Or the hard court, the domed stadium, the baseball diamond, the hockey rink, whichever and wherever men in uniforms played games for the lure of the money, the pleasure of fans, and the deliriousness but mostly agony of the bettors.

With the lawyer it was agony.

He was a respectable man with a dirty habit. And a dangerously ballooning debt. He owed the wrong guys.

Back to the baby nurse in Bogotá.

Her daughter had a daughter with someone.

Let's call him *R.*

Let's imagine he was the wrong kind of person, the guy

you wouldn't want your daughter bringing home from a date. Someone dangerous and abusive. Even criminal.

Definitely criminal.

Once I thought my own daughter was safe from him. I was wrong.

Something happened to the nurse's daughter.

She was killed, kidnapped, made to disappear, *something,* because suddenly, it was just the baby nurse and her granddaughter. The daughter was gone, yes, but the little girl – she survived.

Only there was a problem.

Her father is looking for her. He won't stop till he finds her. As you know, R has the power and means to do so.

The nurse needed to act. Fast.

She needed to get her granddaughter away from R, and the only way to do that was to get her out of the country.

How?

By going to the one person who could help her. The one person who knew how to get kids out of the country because, after all, that's what he did for a living. She appealed to the adoption lawyer for assistance. One more Colombian child he needed to help *el norte.*

Only this child was different. This child had a price on her head. Oddly enough, there was price dancing around the *lawyer's* head too. All that money he owed to the wrong guys – the Russians with yellow teeth and CCCP tattoos on their arms.

Sure, he wrote, I'll help. You came to the right guy. No problem.

Just one little stipulation.

Money.

Not the usual legal fees. No.

Enough to get him out of hock to the Muscovites and enable him to keep all those professional sports prognosticators in business. Lots and *lots* of money. And then he told her how to get it.

Here's the deal, he told the baby nurse. Here's how.

I send you couples looking to adopt, just like before. Every so often – not every time, not even every *other* time, just now and then – one of these couples will have the bad misfortune to be kidnapped. It's endemic in your country, isn't it? What can a lawyer do about that?

Who's going to kidnap them?

Those Marxists in the hills, the ones who've helped kidnapping surpass soccer as the Colombian national pastime.

And what was FARC going to do with these kidnapped couples? Easy. Everyone knew that FARC made their money the old-fashioned way – they *earned* it. *How* they earned it was through the sale and smuggling of pure, uncut Colombian cocaine.

Mules were their method of choice, but they fit a prototype that must have been summarized in every U.S. Customs training film. Colombian, poor, and disreputable. For every two mules who got through, one was snagged, vacuum-cleaned, and exported back home.

What if these mules could be middle-class, American, and thoroughly respectable? What then? What if the unfortunate husbands could be sent through customs packing millions of dollars of cocaine in order to rescue their wives and babies?

The baby nurse simply had to take this idea, this piece

of pure brilliance, to FARC. Oh yes, and assist here and there in the kidnappings. There was *that*.

Everyone would get their heart's fondest wish. The nurse would get her granddaughter to safety. FARC would get a foolproof, surefire pipeline to New York. And the adoption lawyer? He'd get the money to keep the Russians off his back and bet the over-unders *and* the points.

He who saves one child saves his ass.

And for a time it worked. A *long* time, if you judged by the age of the letters.

Something happened.

Paul. The actuary's actuary, who always figured the odds, but never considered the odds of his nurse leaving the hotel with one baby and returning with another. *The last round-tripper on the Goldstein Express.*

Suitably duped, doped, and dumped in front of a burned-out safe house. And then almost slow-roasted to a crisp in the New Jersey swamps.

How did that happen?

Remember what the lawyer told him before extinguishing his own life?

It's those assholes with Uzis and kerosene I'm worried about.

They're starting to put it together. They're closing in.

And earlier, after they'd driven back from the swamp, when Paul asked him who their near murderers were?

Those right-wing paramilitary nuts. Manuel Riojas, he said. *He's in jail. They're not.*

And remember what the nurse wrote in that letter?

He won't stop looking till he finds her. R has the power and means to do so.

They seemed to be talking about two different people.

Unless, of course, they weren't.

Miles was scared enough to put a gun to his head and blow his brains out.

Galina was scared enough to send her granddaughter off to another country and to never see her again.

One scared of R. One scared of Riojas.

Think of this *R* carved not into the desk of a defunct taxi garage, but right into the trunk of the fault tree. And then you understand.

R is for Riojas.

He had the power and means to find her, and slowly and surely, that's what he did. Those men in the swamp weren't looking for drugs or money – not *simply* drugs and money. They were looking for someone's daughter. They were putting it together. They were closing in.

There it was in all its awful glory, the fault tree.

But when Paul looked at it, he thought he just might be able to use it to find shelter from the storm. Shelter for *all* of them – Joanna and Joelle and himself.

Just one question.

The girl the lawyer promised to adopt as his very own. Galina's granddaughter.

Where was she?

THIRTY-NINE

The bird-watcher bit.

Paul was offering a look at a rare bird. At least the elusive progeny of one. He was offering to lead him to the nest.

'That's an interesting story,' the bird-watcher said. 'How would you catalog it? Fiction or nonfiction? Maybe *science fiction.*' Paul could tell he was more interested than he was letting on. For one thing he slipped the cigarette he was just about to light back into its crumpled pack. He straightened up and peered at Paul as if he were finally worth looking at.

'On the other hand, I'll admit you've created a willing suspension of disbelief, Paul,' he said. 'Of course Manuel Riojas isn't my case. He's case-*closed.* He's sitting in a federal prison on twenty-four-hour butt-bandit alert. So I ask you, why should I give a shit?'

'Because Riojas might be in prison, but his men aren't.' He was echoing a certain lawyer, now deceased. 'They killed two men in New Jersey.'

'Colombian shitbags like themselves. So I ask again, why should I care?'

'Because if he's still sending men to kill people, he's still smuggling drugs. His men are. Isn't your job to stop it?' He was practicing a dangerous kind of role reversal – lecturing his jailer on the right and proper path. Any minute he expected his head to be driven back into the table. Only Tom was still absent, and his back was clear.

'Well, that's a matter of debate, Paul. What my job is. It's usually what the U.S. government says it is. Right now it says my case is Miles Goldstein, which means my case, what's left of it, is you. Not Manuel Riojas. I'll admit he's a lot sexier than you are. But that doesn't mean I can turn cowboy and go riding off in a posse of one. Think what that would do to internal structure – if we all decided to do what we wanted. Think of the *paperwork* involved.'

'Riojas is still awaiting trial. His daughter would be valuable to you.'

'Maybe. If there *is* a daughter. Which, let's face it, Paul, is kind of debatable. I'll admit it, though – I'm intrigued. I am. Riojas' *bandidos* aren't my area of investigation, but if you're telling the truth, they interfered with my money trail. They gummed up the works – which, one could interpret, has placed them into my area of investigation. So maybe I have quasi license to widen the net. Maybe. I'm still not sure how this impacts on your general welfare.'

'I can help you.'

'So you say. How?'

'I was the last person to see Miles alive.'

'Congratulations. Who cares?'

'Rachel. His wife seems like a very decent person. I don't believe she knows.'

'Knows what?'

330

'What he did. The deal he struck with Galina. The drugs, the kidnappings. The *girl*.'

'Okay, then. If she *doesn't* know . . . ?'

'She knows *something*. She probably doesn't know what it means. She'll talk to me. She'll want to know what Miles said before he killed himself.'

'While we're on the subject, what *did* Miles say before he killed himself?'

'Whatever I say he did. Whatever will get her to lead me in the right direction. To the girl. To whatever money Miles managed to stow away.'

'Paul, you have the perfidious heart of a DEA agent. Who would've *thunk*? Let's review. You want me to let you loose to probe and pry the poor widow. And in return for your government's generosity?'

'No charges. And you help me get my wife and child back.' There. This was his chance, this was his last best hope.

'Sorry. I think you're forgetting your current status as a stateless person. Let's say, however, that charges will be *reviewed*. Let's say that any said help provided by said defendant being held under the Patriot Act will be taken into utmost consideration. That any possible help within the normal channels to extricate defendant's wife and baby will be extended.'

It was the best Paul could get.

Yes, he said.

SHIVAH.

The Jewish version of a wake.

Various members of the Orthodox community were entering Miles' house in a steady stream of black, like ants bringing crumbs back to the queen. Crumbs of respect, condolences, and coffee cake.

The bird-watcher had rummaged through Paul's closets and brought him back a suitably dark suit. He looked like just another mourner.

The first thing he noticed when he walked through the door was the odor. The smell of too many people packed too tightly together in a too-little room. There was no air-conditioning – perhaps it was considered disrespectful to the dead. There was enough disrespect already. Paul sensed a glowering uneasiness in the room, as palpable and uncomfortable as the heat. *Know what's the worst sin in Orthodox Judaism, Paul?*

Yes, Miles, now I do.

Paul felt himself being prodded forward, slowly being sucked into a suffocating sea of black.

He found himself standing in front of three backless wooden chairs, containing the remains of Miles' family. His two sons in black suits and even blacker yarmulkes, sitting rigid and tight-lipped as if they wanted to be anywhere but there. And Rachel, accepting whispered condolences with bowed head, as if they were unwanted flattery.

The older boy listened to Paul's *I'm sorry for your loss* with silent resignation. Despite his father's sins, Paul felt only compassion. Maybe because if you threw out the yarmulkes, it could have been his house when he was eleven years old. Numbly welcoming a parade of strangers who kept asking him if there was anything they could do for him, when all he wanted them to do was to give him his mother back. He knew Miles' sons would spend the next few years wondering if God was an underachiever.

When Rachel saw him, it seemed to take her a long while to place him. She looked up, down, then slowly back up again, squinting at him as if trying to focus.

Then she pretty much fainted.

A GENERAL GASP WENT UP WHEN RACHEL FELL.

Poor thing, Paul heard someone murmur. *It's the stress.*

Both boys jumped from their seats as if ejected, clearly fearful that they were going to be made full orphans today.

Rachel was carried to another room by committee, Paul tentatively following in their wake.

When her eyes fluttered open, when she made it back to a sitting position, she saw Paul standing there.

The bird-watcher had made some calls. The story – there *had* to be a story – was that Paul had left Miles alive. That he'd finished his business with him – this unfortunate visa screwup – shook Miles' hand, and went on his way. That all this had already been related to the police.

Paul, in other words, was in the clear.

Still, the sight of him had proved too much for her.

'The last time I saw my husband, you were standing there,' she said. 'I half expected Miles to come walking out of his office. I'm sorry.' They were sitting more or less alone now.

'I'm the one who should be apologizing,' Paul said. 'I didn't consider what it might do to you – seeing me here. I just wanted to pay my respects.'

'Yes, of course. Thank you for coming.'

He wondered how long it would take her to begin asking questions. Knowing that she might've been the second-to-last person to see her husband alive, but that Paul was the *last*.

Not long.

'You have to understand this came as a complete shock,' Rachel said. Her wig had been knocked slightly off-kilter. It gave her the look of someone who'd been blindsided, not just by life.

'I imagine every wife feels the same way. Every *widow*.' She looked down, as if mentioning that word for the first time had made it real. 'Really . . . he didn't seem depressed, or angry, or desperate. He seemed . . . like *Miles*. Maybe a little more harried the last few days. I assumed it had to do with helping you. He said the Colombian government had screwed up royally this time, that your wife and baby were stuck in Bogotá.'

'Yes, it's a big mess,' Paul said.

'Did you sense anything? Did you see something I didn't?' She'd dropped the *Paul,* opting for more formality. But then, what was more formal than death? 'That day when you talked to him, when we left you alone? Did he seem unhappy, upset about something, *suicidal*?' Her eyes were moist, red-rimmed – she probably hadn't slept much lately. She must've lain in bed staring at the same question until it imprinted itself on her eyelids: What had she missed?

'He mentioned something about gambling debts,' Paul said.

True enough.

'*Gambling*? Betting?' Using a different word didn't seem

to make it any more comprehensible to her. 'He'd bet ten dollars. He'd look at the sports pages in the morning and say there goes my allowance. *Ten dollars.* How big a debt could that have been?'

'Gamblers lie, Rachel. It's an illness, like alcoholism. He might've told you it was only ten dollars. It's more likely it was ten thousand.'

'*Ten thousand?* It can't be. I would've known. We weren't in debt. I would've seen it.'

No. You didn't know about Miles' other little business. You didn't see the money going out because you didn't see it coming in.

'Maybe he had more money than you knew about. Who did the finances, wrote the checks? You or him?'

'Miles did.'

'See. If he wanted to hide money from you, he could've.'

Rachel seemed to contemplate this notion for real. A new mourner stepped into the room, reached down to take her hand, and whispered something in her ear.

'Thank you,' Rachel whispered back.

The man nodded solemnly and retreated from the room backward, as if it would have been disrespectful to turn around. Paul remembered: the uncomfortable awkwardness displayed in front of family survivors. What to say to a kid whose mother's died of cancer? What to say to a wife whose husband has just shot himself?

Rachel looked up at him. 'I can't *comprehend* it. I would've understood. It's just money. I would've said okay, we'll get you help, we'll deal with it. He would've had the support of the entire community. It would've been okay.'

No, Paul felt like saying. It wouldn't have been okay. The community might've rallied around a gambler, not a drug smuggler. Or a kidnapper.

'To kill himself because he owed some money. It doesn't make sense.'

Again, Paul felt like setting her straight. It wasn't money, it was fear. Not just for himself – for them. In the end a selfish person had committed a selfless act. He must've believed if he wasn't around anymore, his family would be out of harm's way. But Riojas wasn't someone who'd shrink from ordering the murder of a woman and children.

'A lot of people kill themselves over money,' Paul said. 'Themselves or other people. I know. I work in insurance.'

Rachel looked down at her hands. She still wore her wedding ring, Paul noticed. He wondered how long it would be before she took it off and relegated it to the bureau drawer.

'What else did he tell you? He seems to have chosen you to tell all his secrets to,' she said with just a trace of bitterness.

No, Paul thought, not all.

'He talked about his family. How important you were to him.'

'Not important *enough*. I think you're telling me what you think I want to hear. Don't.'

Paul shook his head. 'I got the distinct feeling family was it with him. It made me wonder why you never adopted a child yourselves. Being that it was his life's calling.'

Rachel hesitated before answering. 'I'm not sure a Colombian child would be welcome in this community.

We're an insular bunch, Mr Breidbart. That's an understatement. It's not a particularly flattering thing to say. It's true.'

'Miles had a kind of love-hate relationship with his community and religion, didn't he?'

'It's not a religion. It's a way of life.'

'I know. I'm not sure Miles felt entirely comfortable with that way of life.'

'You're not supposed to feel comfortable. You're supposed to please God. It's a hard thing to do.'

Someone peeked in, saw the two of them talking, withdrew.

'Did you ever meet any of them?'

'Meet any of *who*?'

'The babies. The adopted children. Did Miles ever bring any of them home?'

'No.'

Then someone did come into the room. An older woman, who leaned down and said something in Yiddish. Rachel nodded, stood up. Paul reached out to steady her, but she waved him away. Paul got the feeling she was stronger than first impressions might lead one to think – strong enough to weather her husband's suicide and the long, lonely nights sure to follow.

She wouldn't be fainting again anytime soon.

PAUL HUNG AROUND FOR A BIT.

He became increasingly uncomfortable. The heat, sure, but more than that, the sideways glances, the whispered conversations in Yiddish, the islands of mourners that seemed to offer him no harbor.

Then, much to his relief, someone as out of place as him. An honest-to-goodness black man walked in.

For a moment Paul assumed he was there to clean up. To gather the empty platters, the crumb-filled cake boxes and squashed and lipstick-stained paper cups, and cart them out to the curb.

The black man was wearing a suit – ill-fitting, not very expensive, but nonetheless a *suit*. He was a bona fide mourner.

One thing was painfully obvious. If the Orthodox crowd had considered Paul an interloper, they stared at the black man as if he were an *intruder*.

The black man seemed immune to the reaction he'd caused. He went up to Rachel, sitting again on one of the uncomfortable backless chairs – Paul supposed discomfort was the point – reached down, and shook her hand. He said something to her. She looked slightly dazed, no doubt still digesting everything Paul had just told her. Still, she managed to find the energy to nod and say something in return.

When he moved off into the room, staring down at the last cracker topped with chopped liver, no doubt wondering what it was, Paul walked over and told him.

'*Liver,* huh?' the man said. 'Hate liver.'

'It's *chopped* liver. It tastes different . . . It's pretty good.'

'Still don't think so. Not a liver guy,' he said. 'My name's Julius.'

Paul shook his hand. 'Paul Breidbart.'

'Well, hey, Paul, looks like you and me are the only people here not wearing beanies.'

'Yarmulkes,' Paul said, unable to resist the temptation to correct him.

'Yama-*what*? Whatever.'

'Were you a friend of Miles?'

'Friend? Nuh-uh. We crossed paths, like.'

'Professionally?'

'Huh?'

'Are you a lawyer too?'

Julius seemed to think that was funny. 'Nuh-uh. I was on the other side, you might say.'

'What other side?'

'He was representin' me.' Julius had a long scar that trailed down his right hand and onto his wrist.

'Oh. Miles was your lawyer.'

'Thas right. Juvenile court. Going back some now. I was one *badass* then, okay? I was *into* shit.'

'He helped you.'

'Sure. He helped keep my ass out of juvenile jail.'

'He got you off?'

'Kinda. Why you so curious?'

'I'm just making conversation.'

'That's *what* you're doing, huh?'

'I don't really know anybody here.'

'Really? I'm real tight with them.' Julius smiled.

'Why'd you come?' Paul asked.

'Told you, Miles worked his juju, kept me out of juvenile prison.'

'So he *did* get you off.'

'You want the whole 411, huh? Hey, I was into shit. I shot somebody. He got me *classified*. Antisocial *gangsta*. They stuck me in the loony bin till I turned eighteen and walked.'

'That was *okay*?'

'Okay enough. Not bad. You zoned on lith and drew pictures. No one bothered you too much. I read a lot. Hung out in the library. I got my degree. When I walked, I had somewhere to go. Saved me from the fucking wolves.'

'How long were you there? In the hospital?'

'Long enough. Walked into the zoo at fifteen.'

'*Zoo?* You said it wasn't that bad.'

'Nuh-uh. We called it the zoo 'cause it was across the street from the Bronx Zoo. You could hear the elephants at night, man. Sometimes the lions. In the spring they took us there on retard patrol. Got us llama food – half the kids *ate* it. That was fucking hysterical.'

One of the mourners, an old Jewish man with a thick gray beard, was staring at them disapprovingly.

'Back in the 'hood that's known as *disrespectin*',' Julius said.

Paul gently steered Julius to another part of the room, ostensibly in search of edible food.

'You kept in touch with Miles?' Paul asked after a suitable platter had been scoped, located, and raided.

'Kinda. Now and then. After I made good, I called – just so he'd know we all didn't end up dead. He was cool.'

'Yes,' Paul said.

IT WAS TIME TO GO.

Julius had left a few minutes after talking to Paul, announcing his departure at the front door.

Julius is leaving the building, he said. No one seemed particularly unhappy about that.

Paul was wondering what he was going to tell the bird-

340

watcher. A vague progress report hinting at promising leads and imminent results.

He said good-bye to Rachel and the boys. She seemed relieved to see him go.

On the way down the brownstone steps he bumped into someone going up.

He glanced up to say *excuse me*, then stopped himself.

'If you can tell me where the car is parked?'

Moshe was dressed in impressive funereal attire, black silk suit with charcoal tie and a knit wool yarmulke attached to his hair with a bobby pin. He wasn't alone.

The man that Paul clobbered over the head was standing in Paul's face. He had a freshly stained bandage wrapped around his forehead.

Paul could feel his physical menace like a disturbance in the air.

'The car, Paul? Where is it parked, please?'

'Queens,' Paul said.

Paul had abandoned the car in Long Island City before taking the train back into the city.

'Queens,' Moshe repeated. 'Any particular part? Near Corona Ice King, maybe? Best ices in the city, you would not believe it. Which part of Queens are we *speaking* about here?'

'Long Island City. Twenty-fourth Street off Northern Boulevard.' Paul was keeping the man with the CCCP tattoo firmly in view. It was hard not to – he was still in his face.

'Good of you to tell me. Appreciate it.'

A moment of silence. Not that it was *quiet*. The air was humming with possibilities, most of them unpleasant.

'You seem nervous, my friend,' Moshe said. 'Spider land on you again?'

Paul stood still as Moshe moved past him up the steps. Paul managed to stand his ground as the Incredible Hulk followed. When Moshe reached the door, he turned around.

'You should relax a little. I'm in cash business, my friend. No cash, no business. Understand?' He nodded at the door. 'The man I was doing business with is deceased. A shame.' He smiled, turned, then looked back as if he'd forgotten something. 'Maybe you should not relax *too* much. My comrade here is righteous pissed at you.' He laughed out loud and went into the house.

FORTY

Paul found himself walking around in a constant cold sweat.

He could hear his wristwatch ticking.

He dreamed Joanna was dead. He was at her wake, talking to Miles.

One morning he thought he heard her voice behind him on the street. When he turned around, it was a young mother pushing a carriage and talking on her cell phone.

Interrogations were called *debriefings* now. They felt the same. Paul's progress report was derided for what it was – the essay portion in a test he hadn't studied for.

'In other words, Paul, you got *ugatz*,' the bird-watcher said. 'It's back to rat school for you.'

'I need a little time,' Paul said.

There was a problem with needing a little time. There *wasn't* any.

He needed to come up with something if the bird-watcher was going to save his wife. If she was still savable.

Now that he was an unofficial DEA rat, he was allowed

343

to sleep in his own bed. Not sleep. Toss, turn, stare wide-eyed at the ceiling.

Two seconds after he'd entered his apartment, someone was knocking on his door.

Lisa again.

This time he couldn't pretend no one was home.

When he opened the door, she practically fell into his arms.

'Where is she?'

Paul was momentarily confused as to which *she* Lisa was referring to. Neither one, of course, was currently available.

'Where's the baby?' Lisa said, scanning the four corners of the room like an eagle-eyed real estate agent, which, in fact, she was.

'There was a problem,' Paul said, ready to trot out the story he and Miles had concocted for general use.

'Problem? *What* problem? Where's Joanna?'

'Bogotá.'

Lisa pushed her blond hair back with one hand. She was one of those East Side women who'd crossed the park – born to money that had inexplicably dried up, but still looking very trust-fund.

'Joelle's visa wasn't in order.'

'In order? What does that mean?'

'It means it wasn't functional. We couldn't get her out of the country.'

'Oh, Paul. That's *terrible*. So what's going on? What are you doing about it?'

'I'm working it out from this end.' Now that Paul was actually trying out the story, he thought it held up pretty well. He himself was a different matter. He wasn't holding up pretty well. Fatigue seemed to have settled into his bones.

Lisa must've sensed this, because she went to embrace him again, bestowing a comforting hug and lingering there long enough for Paul to lean against her.

She smelled like home.

LATER, WHEN JOHN RETURNED FROM WORK, LISA CALLED A babysitter and they both came in, toting a bottle of cabernet.

It was wonderful to see John.

It was terrible to see John.

He was Paul's best friend, the guy with whom he'd spent more time than he cared to remember, sitting in various West Side bars, relating the ups and downs of babymaking. The guy who'd bucked him up and, on more than one occasion, dried him out.

So while it was enormously comforting to see John's face, it was discomforting having to lie to it.

Paul was forced to create details on the spot, to make all of it seem convincing, coherent, and perfectly logical. The trick was to mix in enough truthful stuff – everything he remembered about his daughter – to give it the ring of authenticity. Downing two glasses of wine proved only mildly helpful.

It didn't do anything to alleviate his guilt. Or his fear.

Chatting about Joanna as if she were simply waiting for him back in a Bogotá hotel room felt horrifyingly callous. Joanna might be waiting in a room, but it lacked maid service and you couldn't pick up a phone and order a burger and fries at 2 a.m. She might not be waiting for him at all.

There were hidden pitfalls in the thicket of lies.

'Give me her number, for Christ's sake,' Lisa said. 'I haven't spoken to her for ages. Why hasn't she called me?'

'You know what long distance costs from Colombia?' Paul said. A ten-minute call to New York from L'Esplanade had cost him $62.48.

'Okay, I'll call *her*,' Lisa said. 'Got the number?'

'I have to look it up,' Paul said.

The room went silent as Lisa and John waited for him to do just that.

And waited.

'Frankly, I'm exhausted,' Paul said. 'I need to turn in. Promise I'll find it for you later.'

Lisa and John reluctantly stood up. They hugged him, told him that if there was anything they could do for him, he shouldn't hesitate to ask.

HE COULDN'T SLEEP.

He called Rachel Goldstein.

He was still hoping she might lead him out of the rabbit hole.

'Yes?' Rachel said after he'd identified himself.

'I wanted to check and make sure you're okay.'

'Why?'

'*Why?*'

'I hardly know you. I appreciate your concern, but I'm kind of baffled at it. You're not a relative. You're not a friend.'

'I *felt* like a friend,' he said. It's true. For a while Miles had felt like his only friend on earth.

Rachel didn't bother disputing him.

'How are you holding up?' Paul asked.

'I'm holding *on*. Eighteen years of marriage and I'm finding out there was a husband I didn't know. How would you feel?'

One of her sons must've come into the room. *It's all right*, Paul heard Rachel murmur. *I'm fine*. Then the sound of a door gently closing.

'Who *was* he? That's what I keep asking myself,' Rachel said, her voice sounding unbearably weary. 'How do I even remember him?'

'The way you want to, I guess. What's wrong with that?'

'The way I want to,' Rachel repeated, then said it again. Either because she thought it made sense or because she was ridiculing its stupid sentimentality. 'Okay. I'll give it a try.'

Silence.

'I met one,' she said.

'One what?'

'One child. You asked me today if I had met any of the adopted babies, remember?'

'Yes.'

'I did. Once. Not a baby, though.'

'No?'

'A little girl.'

A little girl.

'I think I'll remember Miles like *that*. Why not? Walking through the front door with a little Colombian girl in his arms.'

Okay, Paul thought, *slowly*.

'Do you remember her name?'

'Her *name*? It was over ten years ago.'

'You sure? If you thought about it a little.'

'Why do you care what her name was?'

Good question.

'Before we adopted, we talked to a couple who used your husband. They adopted a daughter. She looked, I don't know, around thirteen. I was wondering if it might've been her.'

Rachel went silent again.

Think, Paul urged her, *think*.

'Something with an *R* maybe? Sorry, I don't remember.'

R, Paul thought, like her father.

'What about her parents? You remember them? Why weren't they there?'

'I have no idea. Maybe they couldn't pick her up till the next day.'

'That's odd. You're required to go to Colombia and bring your baby back with you. That's the way it works.'

'Maybe they ran into problems. The girl, as I recall, had some problems of her own.'

'What kind of problems?'

'Emotional stuff. Something was just a little bit wrong with her.'

'What?'

'I'm not sure. She cried and screamed a lot.'

'She was probably scared. Don't you think that's normal?'

'I have two children who've been scared occasionally. Even terrified. They're terrified now. Finding out your father killed himself will do that to you. This was different. The girl was afraid of the dark, afraid of the light – afraid of everything. Something was, I don't know, *off*. I remember Miles going into her room in the middle of the night trying to calm her down.'

'Did he?'

'I don't know. Maybe. In the morning he took her to meet her parents. That was that. She had beautiful eyes – I can still remember them.'

'Well,' Paul said, suddenly anxious, even desperate, to get off the phone. Something had been buzzing around his brain, something someone said. 'You should get some sleep. If there's anything I can do.'

She didn't bother saying good-bye.

FORTY-ONE

He couldn't hear the elephants.

Or the lions.

Certainly not the llamas.

He could hear the industrial-strength air-conditioning. The clink of metal trays being loaded onto a wheeled lunch cart. The intercom system marred by sudden bursts of static. The insistent banging against the meds window – a bathrobe-clad teenager demanding his caps *now*.

He could hear the voice in his head too – the many voices banging around in there.

For instance, there was Julius' voice, the kid from Miles' days in legal aid.

Walked into the zoo at fifteen. We called it the zoo 'cause it was across the street from the Bronx Zoo.

And there was Galina's voice. Hello, Galina.

She's seen things no child should ever have to see. No one should have to see. She has nightmares.

And while we're at it, add Rachel's voice to the mix.

The girl was afraid of the dark, afraid of the light – afraid of everything. Something was, I don't know, off.

And then, finally, the last voice, the one shouting to be heard over all the others. The one in the letter that Paul had first attributed to Miles' son, but now knew better.

Dear Dad, Daddy, Pop, Father: Remember when you took me to the zoo and you left me there?

And suddenly, he was listening to his own voice.

'Yes, from the insurance company,' Paul was saying to the matronly woman behind the admissions desk. The woman who admitted you to Mount Ararat Psychiatric Hospital, the redbrick, barred-window, linoleum-floored institution that stood directly across the street from the Bronx Zoo. *Two* zoos, side by side, human and otherwise.

The woman was staring at Paul's business card as if it were a lotto ticket that had miserably failed her. Paul wondered if Julius had looked into the same face at fifteen.

If *she* had?

'What's her name?' the woman said.

'Name?'

'The name of your client's daughter?'

Paul hesitated just a second.

'Ruth,' Paul said. 'Ruth Goldstein.'

Okay, it was a shot in the dark. Or maybe it was more like *twilight*, just light enough to make out the title of that book crammed full of letters.

The Story of Ruth.

Something with an *R*, Rachel had said.

'Uh-huh,' the woman said, staring into a computer screen that seemed to be having trouble waking up. She slammed the mouse with a beefy hand.

'Damn system,' she said to no one in particular.

It might've been an indictment directed at everything,

not just the computers. The system, for instance, that made a mental institution smelling faintly of urine a safer alternative to juvenile prison. That warehoused children in trouble, kept them ignorant and medicated, until they could be loosed on the world at eighteen.

Damn system. Yes.

The computer finally responded, either to the vicious assault on the poor mouse or to the woman's tongue-lashing. It sprang to life with an ear-grating hum. A few, this time *gentler* taps on the mouse elicited the asked-for information.

'Uh-huh, okay,' the woman said. 'Ruth Goldstein. What *about* her?'

For a moment Paul didn't answer. A part of him had expected to be told there was no such person here by that name. That he'd been misinformed. That the door was *that* way.

'I told you,' Paul said, equilibrium regained. 'My client recently passed away. It was sudden and unexpected. There's a certain amount of paperwork that needs to be processed. A reevaluation of who's paying what. Obviously, we need to ensure that Ruth continues to receive the same good care.'

Paul doubted the word *good* was warranted. But he wasn't here to offend anyone. He was here on a rescue mission – though oddly enough, the about-to-be-rescued weren't in Mount Ararat Psychiatric Hospital, but three thousand miles away. He could only cross his fingers and pray they were still breathing.

'So you want the *Financial* Department. Why didn't you say so?' the woman asked.

'I'd like to see the girl first.'

'The girl? Well, I'd have to ask a doctor about that. You haven't been properly vetted, have you?'

Paul thought *vetted* was an appropriate term, given that he was standing in *the zoo*.

'Well, could you ask, then?' Paul said. 'I assume her father was pretty much the only one who visited her, but he's gone. Someone's got to tell the poor girl what's happened.'

When the woman didn't immediately answer, he said, 'He did, right?'

'Did what?'

'Visit her?'

The woman looked down at the computer, hit the mouse a few times.

'*Miles* Goldstein?'

'Yes.'

'He was on the list. Doesn't say whether he visited her.'

'Well, can you talk to the doctor – explain the situation?'

'Okay. I can only do one thing at a time.'

Paul wondered what that *other* thing was that was conflicting with calling the doctor. Apparently, it was picking up a Styrofoam cup filled with coffee and slowly sipping it.

After she had swallowed some coffee, making a sour face in the process, she picked up the phone with extravagant lethargy and punched a few numbers into the keypad.

'Yeah,' she said. 'Dr Sanji? . . . Yes – I have someone from an insurance company here to see Ruth Goldstein . . . That's right. The father died . . . Yeah. He says . . . Uh-huh. Okay.'

She threw the phone back in its cradle – *there, take that.*

'Dr Sanji will come get you.'

DR SANJI WAS A WOMAN.

She was Indian. She looked harried, overworked, and pretty much no-nonsense.

'You say her father passed away?' the doctor said in a singsong Indian accent. They were sitting in the waiting room off the lobby. What did people wait for in a place like this? Paul wondered. For sanity? For the bats to leave the belfry?

'Yes. A few days ago.'

'I see. And you came to inform her of this?'

'Yes. And to make sense of the financial arrangements. We want to make sure the girl's still taken care of, just as her father would've wanted.'

Dr Sanji looked down at a folder. 'The mother is deceased as well.'

'Yes.' True enough. Miles had lied about everything else, but not about that. 'She's alone in the world.'

'Well, Mr . . . ?'

'Breidbart.'

'Yes, Mr Breidbart. I will tell you she is no more alone than she was before. Of course *psychically,* she is. Her father wasn't what you would describe as doting. He hardly visited. Birthdays, I think. The odd holiday.'

'How long have you been her doctor?'

'Not long, Mr Breidbart. Two years.'

'So you weren't here when she was admitted.'

'Most definitely not.'

'May I ask you how she's doing?'

'Relative to what?'

'Relative to normalcy.'

'*Normal* is a pejorative term. You'd be better off asking how she is doing relative to *her*. To how she was doing last year, or the year before that. It's like golf – a sport that regretfully I've just taken up. You play against yourself. You improve in increments.'

'Okay. Then how's she doing relative to her?'

'Ahh . . . there we have a problem. We speak in relative terms, but you, I'm afraid, are not a *relative*. You are, as you've clearly stated, merely her late father's insurance agent. As such, you are not privy to the information you are seeking. Sorry.'

'She has *no* one,' Paul said. 'Not anymore.'

'Legally, yes. Even, I suppose, literally. But I am bound by confidentiality laws, much as you are, Mr Breidbart. Until you or someone else is appointed her legal guardian, we have little to talk about. Let's simply say that she is no harm to herself or others. That, like Dilsey in one of your great American novels by Mr Faulkner, she endures.'

'Can I see her?'

Dr Sanji launched into another exquisitely presented argument detailing her rights, or lack thereof, in this matter.

Paul interrupted her.

'Look, I know I don't have a legal right to see her. I'm simply asking to. What's the harm? I'm going to be responsible for seeing that she continues to get care. That the bills are paid. And someone needs to tell her that her father's no longer alive.'

'The person who will tell her about her father's death is assuredly not going to be you. You have neither the necessary legal standing nor the necessary experience dealing with the emotionally handicapped. Secondly, these bills you speak of? It is my understanding that Mr Goldstein did little in the way of subsidizing *anyone*. His daughter's bills, I have been led to believe, are primarily covered by New York State.'

'New York State?'

'Yes, indeed. I can only assume that Mr Goldstein pleaded indigence at the time, something, it's clear from your expression, he may have merely pretended to.'

Okay, Miles had struck a business deal and, like most good businessmen, had striven for maximum profit. He'd wanted to keep his overhead costs low, and the fact that his overhead was the care and feeding of a sick little girl hadn't deterred him. Why pay when New York State will?

When had the whole thing occurred to him? Paul wondered. From the very moment he laid it out in that letter to Galina? Or later, when she was already on her way and he thought back to his halcyon days in juvenile court.

The best I could do was get them committed to a Bronx hospital. For them it was the safest place on earth.

Lies to Galina aside, it's clear he never intended to actually *adopt* her. He'd never once mentioned it to his wife. Had he considered – even for a minute – someone else? One of the many childless couples beating a path to his door? A home instead of a ward? Or, like the schizophrenics Paul could hear bellowing on the other side of the double-hinged door, had he deluded himself into a kind of justification? That the safest place for an emotionally disturbed child with a murderous father looking for her was a room with bars on the windows.

Maybe when he went into her room to calm her down that night, he whispered *stop crying, and tomorrow I'll take you to the zoo*.

'Look,' Paul said. 'I can leave, complain to someone, get a writ, come back. All I want to do is see her. I won't say a word to her. Promise.'

HE BROKE HIS PROMISE.

Not on purpose.

After Dr Sanji had relented, he followed her down one ward and up another. He found himself in a kind of day-room. Board games were scattered across several small tables like props – no one was playing. A TV in the corner was tuned to a talk show.

There were about twelve or thirteen kids there. It could've been the lunchroom in a local high school, various cliques engaged in vibrant discussion. If you looked closer, it was more like the conversations you hear in sandboxes – two- and three-year-olds talking *at* each other.

When an enchanting-looking girl of about fourteen stepped up to him and asked if it was true that hematite had been detected on Mars, he said *I don't know*.

He realized he'd broken his promise to Dr Sanji when the doctor said hello to her.

'Hello, Ruth, how are you today?'

'Fair to middling,' she said. 'And you? How did you play the back nine yesterday?'

'About as well as I played the front nine,' Dr Sanji said. 'Incompetently. Thank you for asking.'

Galina's granddaughter, Paul thought.

Ruth.

'I asked this man here about the recent discoveries on Mars,' she said. 'Hematite would suggest there was water at one time. Water would suggest there was life. Life on Mars, what a wondrous notion.'

She was dressed quite ordinarily, worn jeans and a T-shirt that exposed an inch or so of adolescent stomach. Her eyes, Paul noted, were still as beautiful as Rachel remembered them – wide, deep brown, and radiating an undeniable intelligence.

He'd expected that most kids on this ward *lived* on Mars.

Ruth apparently studied it – with the avid interest of an astronomer-in-training.

'And would you like that?' Dr Sanji asked her. 'Little green men?'

'I'm afraid little green men would scare the bejesus out of me,' Ruth said.

Okay, Paul thought, there was something odd about the way she spoke. Not just the evident smarts. *Wondrous . . . bejesus.* It was as if she'd learned human discourse from books. As if she'd wandered out of an old-fashioned novel.

'I would much prefer a few one-celled amoebas,' she said, smiling in Paul's direction. 'Say, I've got a knock-knock joke for you. Knock, knock.'

'Who's there?' Paul answered, the straight half of that new comic sensation, Breidbart and Goldstein.

'A,' she said.

'A who?'

'Amoeba.'

'That's very funny,' Paul said.

'The appropriate response would've been laughter,' Ruth said.

'I'm laughing inside,' Paul said, duly chastened. 'Believe me.'

'That's odd. I do the same thing *all the time*. Laugh inside.'

In another place, he thought, he would've found her precociously delightful. But here you were forced to look at things in a different light – the sickly fluorescence of a mental ward.

He'd followed his hunch and found the nest, but in it was an odd bird.

'Better to laugh than cry,' Paul said. 'Yes?'

'Oh, I do a fair amount of crying as well. Don't I, Dr Sanji?'

Dr Sanji said, 'Yes. You are one of our better criers, Ruth. For sure.'

'Want to see?' she asked Paul.

'Oh, I don't know,' Paul said. 'Maybe later. We can have a contest.'

'I'll win, hands down. What's the prize?'

'Hmmm . . . ,' Paul said. 'I'll have to think about that one.'

Dr Sanji shot him a look that said *time's up*. He'd broken his promise ten times over. He'd come, he'd seen, it was Ruth, he couldn't help thinking, who'd conquered.

Dr Sanji walked him to the door.

Outside the dayroom Paul said, 'She's quite remark-able.'

Dr Sanji nodded, smiled. 'Yes, quite.'

'She seems, almost . . . normal.'

'You said almost, Mr Breidbart. Why?'

'I'm not sure. I got the feeling, I don't know, that she was playing a part. Like a very good actress. Does she read a lot?'

'Volumes. Like the others *eat*. You're fairly perceptive about our Ruth playing roles. I call her the chameleon. She sometimes *becomes* what she reads. Or whom she's lis-tening to. Sometimes I honestly feel like I'm talking to myself. Ruth, of course, has never been anywhere near New Delhi. She could make you think differently.'

'Why does she do that?' Paul said.

'Why? Are you asking for a diagnosis, Mr Breidbart? I'm afraid you won't get one from me.'

'Because you don't know?'

'Because I'm not at liberty to discuss it. This is old ter-ritory, is it not?'

Paul nodded.

'I will ask you this,' Dr Sanji said. 'Why does a chameleon change its skin color to that of its surround-ings?' When Paul hesitated, she answered for him. 'Come, Mr Breidbart, it's Biology 101. A chameleon changes skin color to protect itself.'

'From what?'

'Predators.'

FORTY-TWO

A, a car backfiring.

B, a gun firing.

C, a firecracker.

D, none of the above.

Joanna was awakened by a series of loud, rapid bursts. In the moment when her heart took up temporary residence in her throat, she devised a multiple-choice test in an effort to divert fear from running rampant. She picked A, *a car backfiring,* because it was the only choice offering a modicum of comfort and plausibility.

Unfortunately, she was totally *onto* her act of self-deception.

Car? *What* car?

She couldn't help remembering that Maruja always feared that the forces of good – admittedly a relative term in Colombia – would try to rescue her and, in so doing, kill her. That they'd barge in guns blazing and set off a conflagration resulting in her bloody demise. It turned out she would've been better off worrying about the menace closer to home.

Joanna heard the bursts again. Louder, sharper, like the cracks of a bullwhip.

She hugged the wall – her one and only friend, if you didn't count *Galina,* that is, who'd smuggled her back into the house after her ill-fated escape attempt. The problem with gaining Galina as a friend was that you had to be kidnapped by her first. And there was her annoying habit of remaining blind, deaf, and dumb to the criminal flaws in her housemates.

The door swung open, slamming against the wall, causing little flecks of plaster to fly into the air.

Something else flew into the room. The guard Puento, propelling himself through the door like a man shot out of a cannon. His rifle was slung down off his hip in ready-fire position.

Okay, Joanna thought, *I'm dead.*

Puento scoped the room with nervous-looking eyes. By the time he located Joanna in the right corner, she'd stopped hugging the wall. She was still firmly attached to it, courtesy of her leg chain. Sitting straight regardless, shoulders back, ready to go with dignity.

She was going somewhere else first.

Puento began unlocking her leg chain, sweat dripping off his glistening forehead and causing him to periodically stop and try to wipe it out of his eyes.

'Qué pasa?' Joanna managed to get out, about the limit of her Spanish vocabulary.

Puento didn't answer. He was engrossed in the intricacies of putting key into lock, one ear evidently trained on the outside commotion. That was her explanation for his nonresponse, and she was sticking to it. The other explanation would be that he didn't want to inform Joanna that he was taking her someplace to kill her.

When he finally managed to release her from her chain, he roughly yanked her to her feet.

He dragged her through the door.

The house was in a kind of pandemonium. Panicked guards were racing down halls, springing out of doors, bumping into each other. One of the girls was attempting to load her gun as she ran – several shell casings falling to the floor, where they rolled around, sounding like roulette balls circling the wheel.

Someone was shouting. *El doctor,* she thought.

The shooting continued. Yes, it was *gunfire.* A backfiring car or a few tossed firecrackers wouldn't be causing the house to undergo a nervous breakdown.

Count her among the nervous.

Not for herself anymore – someone else.

Where was her baby?

She was pulled through the outside door. It was early morning, that murky moment between night and day.

'Please . . . *por favor,*' she said to Puento, 'my baby. Joelle.'

Puento remained nervous and unresponsive. He dragged her behind him without looking back. They were clearly headed back to the jungle.

She felt a creeping panic the further they moved away from the house. She had no idea who was shooting at whom. It was happening someplace she couldn't see.

'My baby,' she tried again. 'Please! I want . . .'

And then she heard it.

The sound she found herself listening for now in the

middle of the night, the one she'd grown particularly attuned to, like Pavlov's dogs.

She twisted her head around, even as Puento continued to pull her into the jungle. *There.* Coming out of the house, the stooped figure of Galina. She was carrying a crying Joelle in her arms. Away from the gunfire, to safety.

'Wait,' she said to Puento, who seemed in no mood to listen. 'Stop. Galina has my . . .' She dug her feet into the soil, went limp, turned into dead weight.

Puento looked at her as if he couldn't quite believe what she was doing. He had a *rifle*. With actual bullets. She was his prisoner. Didn't she know what they'd done to her friends?

Puento swung his rifle off his shoulder and pointed it at her head. It wasn't the first time he'd pointed a gun in her direction – there was that night Joelle wouldn't stop crying. He'd been making a point then. Now he looked like he just might go through with it. He was clearly spooked.

They were under attack.

Camouflaged bodies were flying past them into the jungle.

'Up!' Puento shouted at her, putting the gun barrel up against her forehead.

Joanna closed her eyes. *If I don't see it, it's not there.*

She would wait till her baby joined them, until she knew Joelle was safe. It's what mothers do.

Puento screamed at her. The cool muzzle jabbed into her skin.

She heard an explosion, felt blood splattering on her face. When she opened her eyes, it was dripping down her

364

hand. *How odd*, she thought. There was no pain, none whatsoever.

When she looked up at her executioner, he wasn't there. He was lying on the ground next to her.

Galina caught up with them. Somehow she managed to avoid looking at Puento's bloody corpse. Joanna wished she had done the same. Galina gently lifted Joanna up from the ground.

One of the girls materialized like magic from the black edge of jungle. She stopped to make the sign of the cross over the prone body, then stared at Joanna with an expression of palpable hatred.

Murderer, her eyes said.

She must've caught Joanna's act of nonviolent resistance. It had cost Puento his life.

She motioned them into the jungle, jabbing her rifle hard into Joanna's back.

They hid in a grove of giant ferns.

Galina gave Joanna the baby. *Shhh*, Joanna whispered, rocking her gently. She could feel the tiny thudding of Joelle's heart against her own.

She wondered if Galina was thinking back to another jungle, to another mother and child who'd never really made it out alive.

The gunfire eventually sputtered, flamed out.

After twenty minutes of waiting, some of the FARC soldiers straggled back from what must have been the scene of battle. They looked shocked. For some of the younger ones – the fresh-faced kids from the boonies – it might've been the first time they'd ever fired their weapons in anger.

When they shepherded Joanna and Joelle back to the

farmhouse, their mood was black. Joanna was rechained to the wall, Joelle pulled from her arms. She could hear arguing going on through the door of her room.

She fell asleep listening to its surging rhythms, like the sound of angry surf.

WHEN GALINA CAME IN FOR THE MORNING FEEDING, SHE WAS pale and tired.

'What happened last night?' Joanna asked.

'A USDF patrol,' she said, shaking her head. She seemed to be having a hard time meeting Joanna's eyes.

'How many were killed? Besides Puento?'

'Four,' she said.

'I don't care about Puento. He killed Maruja and Beatriz – I *know* he did – him and Tomás. He got what he deserved.'

'*They* care about Puento,' Galina said, still averting Joanna's eyes.

'What were they arguing about last night?'

'Nothing,' Galina said.

'Nothing? I heard them. *El doctor* – some of the others. What's wrong, Galina? Why can't you look at me?'

'They're angry,' Galina said.

'About Puento?'

Galina shrugged. 'Not just Puento. They think . . . you brought the patrol maybe.'

'What does *that* mean? How could I have possibly brought the patrol?'

'They think they came looking for you.'

'For *me*? That's ridiculous. How would they even know

I'm here?' Joanna found that she was talking faster than normal, that her voice had taken on a slight air of desperation.

'Some of them . . . they're only boys. Almost children. They think maybe you're *unsafe*.'

'What happens when you're unsafe, Galina?'

Galina didn't answer. Instead, she reached down to slick back a stray hair on Joelle's head.

'What happens to you when you're unsafe?'

Joanna noticed Galina's hands were shaking.

'Were Maruja and Beatriz *unsafe*? Is that what they decided?'

'I didn't know about Maruja,' Galina whispered.

It was the first time she'd mentioned either of their names since Joanna discovered the bloody stain on the mattress. The first time she'd acknowledged out loud what had happened to them.

'I didn't know about Beatriz,' Galina continued. 'I'm sorry. It had nothing to do with me. I would never have . . .' Her voice trailed off.

Joanna stood up, using the wall for support. She needed it.

'Are they going to kill me?'

Galina looked up, finally met her eyes. 'I told them you're an American . . . Doing something to an American would bring more trouble.'

'Doing something? Killing. You mean *killing* an American. What did they say when you told them that, Galina? *You're right, Galina? Thank you for reminding us?*'

Galina lifted her hands together – fingertips touching. *Make a steeple,* Joanna's mom used to say. *Make a steeple and pray.*

'Promise me something,' Joanna whispered.

'Yes?'

'You'll find her a good mother.'

JOANNA SPENT MOST OF THE DAY TRYING TO MEASURE HER LIFE. Not too bad a life, she decided, but nothing exceptional either.

The thing she regretted most of all was not getting to raise her daughter. She thought she would've made a spectacularly good mom. It was *that* life she saw hurtling before her eyes – the one missed. Strolling on a carpet of leaves in Central Park on a fall afternoon, taking a spin on a hundred and one merry-go-rounds. All those mother-daughter chats they'd never have. Things like that.

That would've been lovely, she decided.

Toward the end of the day she noticed a tiny stream of amber light peeking through the boarded-up window. A small piece of wood was missing now, blown off in yesterday's fusillade.

She put her face against it, drinking in the smells.

Nightshade. Peat. Chickenshit.

She put one eye there.

Galina was standing outside with someone. She could only see half of them. But she had the strong sensation she knew the other person. Those brown shoes. The tan cotton pants with a sharp crease down the front.

Yes, she thought. Of course.

What was *he* doing here?

FORTY-THREE

He came home from the mental hospital, locked his door, and fished the piece of folded paper out of the bottom of his sock drawer. The page he'd ripped from Miles' phone book in an office reeking of blood.

He sat and stared at the number written in spidery blue ink.

Think of it as his lottery number.

Lotteries were a joke around the halls of his company – the kind of thing actuaries snickered at over morning coffee. These numbers were a one-in-a-million long shot that might just come in.

Cross your fingers.

He took a deep breath and dialed the long-distance number.

When they'd lost the two million dollars' worth of drugs in the New Jersey swamp, he'd thought he'd lost something more important. The only thing in the world he had left to bargain with. He'd been wrong about that.

He'd discovered he had something even better. When

he constructed the fault tree that day, he'd understood that its gnarly branches might save him. All of them.

That he might be able to bargain his family to freedom.

Only he wouldn't be bargaining with FARC. No.

This negotiation would be conducted with a party of two, and *only* two.

There was Galina. And there was someone else.

It had occurred to him only when he remembered back to that awful day it began, when they'd gone to Galina's house and woken up somewhere else.

Before their world turned topsy-turvy, while they were still making perfectly polite conversation over *escopolamina*-laced coffee, Galina's lumbering dog had picked up a slipper sitting on the doormat and dropped it at someone's feet.

Boom.

The sound of one shoe dropping, just before the other one did.

Dogs are creatures of habit.

Does Galina live alone? Paul had asked on the ride to Galina's house. And Pablo had hesitated a long moment before saying yes. Why?

Because she *didn't* live alone.

She had a husband.

'Hola?' Pablo's voice, clear and intimate, as if he were sitting right there.

'Hello, Pablo.'

He obviously recognized his voice. Yes. Otherwise there wouldn't have been the ensuing silence.

Paul took a deep breath. Then asked the question he'd been dreading since he'd picked up the phone – even before that, on the long ride home from the hospital.

'Are my wife and daughter still alive?'

Nothing else mattered but the answer to this question. Everything hinged on it.

'Yes,' Pablo said.

Now it was Paul's turn to be silent. Not entirely. He gave an involuntary half-sob, the kind of sound you utter when you make it out of a vicious undertow and discover you're surprisingly and gloriously alive.

Okay, go.

'I met your granddaughter today,' Paul said.

'Who?'

Pablo had answered the way Paul would've expected him to, but there was the slightest quaver in that one word that spoke volumes.

'Your granddaughter.'

'I don't understand what –'

'The little girl you sent to America so her father wouldn't get her. I don't blame you. Riojas wouldn't be my idea of an ideal son-in-law either. Are you following me so far, Pablo? If I'm speaking English words you don't understand, please tell me. I need you to understand everything I'm saying today. Every word. Okay?'

'Yes,' Pablo said. 'I understand.'

'Good. You sent your little girl to America because you wanted her to be safe. You arranged things with a lawyer we both know because you knew he could get her out of the country. And because he was going to adopt her as his own. That was the deal, Pablo. Am I right so far?'

'Yes.'

'You broke all contact with your granddaughter. You did this for her own safety. I understand. It made perfect

371

sense. And you took comfort in knowing that she was being raised in a nice home in Brooklyn. Far away from Manuel Riojas. Under a new name. Ruth. That Miles was keeping his promise. To raise her, protect her, even *love* her. Isn't that what Galina made him swear?'

'Yes.'

'After all, you were keeping your part of the bargain, weren't you? The *two* of you? Whenever he asked you to, whenever he gave you the word, you'd help kidnap some couple for your friends in FARC. Just like you agreed to. You did your part and Miles did his. Right?'

'My granddaughter. Where did you . . . ?'

'What did he send you, Pablo? Pictures? Birthday photos? Once a year, so you could put them in a secret album and look at them now and then? A little letter here and there so you'd know everything's okay? What did he tell you? That Ruth's just a typical American kid, living a typical American life? That she's popular in school, pride of the community, the apple of her father's eye?'

'What are you saying? Is something . . . ?'

'Let me tell you about Ruth. Listen closely. She's not a typical American kid. Not exactly. She's not pulling As in school. She's not on the cheerleading squad. She's not dating the captain of the football team. She won't be going to the senior prom this year. Or *any* year. She isn't doing any of the things Miles told you she was. None of them. That was fiction, that was made up. Do you understand?'

'Where *is* she?'

'Not in a nice house in Brooklyn. Not in a nice boarding school in Connecticut. She's in a hospital.'

Silence.

'What *kind* of hospital. Is she sick?'

'Yes. No. Not in her body – in her mind. I have no idea what she went through back in Colombia. I can guess. I have no idea whether she was sick enough to be put in that hospital, or whether *being* there made her sick enough to stay. I don't know. What I *do* know is that Miles never adopted her. I'm pretty sure he never intended to. The day after he picked her up, he dumped her there. She's spent most of her life looking through bars.'

Crying. Paul could distinctly hear the sound of Pablo sobbing.

'How is she?' Pablo asked.

'How's my *wife*?' Paul replied. 'How's my *daughter*?'

Silence again.

'What do you want?' Pablo said. Okay – he'd weathered the storm, he'd come through the other side, and now he was beginning to catch on.

'What I've always wanted. *Them*. On a plane to New York.'

Long ago Pablo and Galina had brokered a deal.

Now it was time for another one, for Paul to use the bargaining chip of all bargaining chips and implement the plan he'd hit on back in that DEA cell.

'Think of it as a prisoner exchange. FARC does exchanges all the time, don't they? With the Colombian government or the USDF? One of theirs for one of ours? Think of this as another exchange, Pablo. Your granddaughter for my wife and child. Okay, it's a little different this time. FARC won't be making the exchange. You will. You and your wife. My guess is, that won't be so easy. I don't care. You'll find a way to do it. *Fast*.'

There was one last thing.

'There's something I haven't told you. Are you listening? Good. Riojas might be in a federal prison here, but he's still *looking* for her. You don't want him to find her.'

FORTY-FOUR

They were on their way to the zoo.

Paul was riding in the bird-watcher's Jeep, just the two of them.

After Paul had hung up on Pablo, he'd needed to make one more call.

The bird-watcher had given him a number if Paul needed to reach him.

Twenty minutes later he showed up at Paul's apartment – *I was in the neighborhood,* he said.

Paul told him about the Bronx hospital. About Miles' little sentencing trick from his days in juvenile court. About finally standing face-to-face with Manuel Riojas' lost little girl.

The bird-watcher was suitably impressed.

'You want an honorary badge? We give them out to schoolkids who take the official DEA tour in Washington. You can be my real make-believe deputy.'

Paul declined. He was up to the hard part, what he needed the bird-watcher to agree to.

The exchange.

'Whoa, I don't know about that, Paul. You didn't mention anything about a *trade*. Last time I looked, that wasn't part of my job description.'

'My wife's an American citizen. You promised you'd help get them out. Here's their chance. Here's how. Miles must've gotten Riojas' daughter into the country illegally. Isn't that normal U.S. protocol – sending illegals back where they came from?'

'After suitable bureaucratic bullshit, which you cannot *begin* to believe. I imagine you're talking just a little bit faster here. And the girl might – and I reiterate *might* – be valuable to us. Wasn't that the nature of your enticement, Paul? The carrot you so artfully dangled in front of us?'

'She's not going to disappear. You can make whatever arrangements you want after you send her back. Put her someplace you can see her – stick her in another hospital. I don't care.'

He was lying, of course.

He did care.

Spending ten minutes with her in that awful place had made him care. If he could effect the trade, he'd be helping three people.

'I don't know, Paul. You're asking me to go outside normal channels. To put my cowboy hat on. I'd have to think about that one. By the way, did the weeping widow mention anything about illicit money? Assuming Miles didn't blow it all on the Cleveland Cavs? There's nothing the DEA likes better than bags and bags of ill-gotten gains. It's how we keep score.'

'No,' Paul said. 'She didn't have a clue about any of this.'

'Okay, fair enough. You've done a bang-up job, Paul. First-rate. At some point we'll have to do a full body search on his bank accounts. As far as your trade scenario, I'll have to get back to you on that one. I admit I'm kind of leaning toward helping you. I mean, fuck those little Marxists, right? They won't be very happy when Pablo kidnaps their hostages. It puts a smile on my face just thinking about it.'

This was two days ago.

One day later the bird-watcher called him with the good news.

He'd done some thinking, run it *up and down the flagpole a few times.*

He'd made a few calls to *overseas assets.*

He'd wangled the necessary papers.

In the end he'd put his Stetson on.

The plan. The girl would be taken to a debriefing house in Glen Cove, Long Island. How much she knew was probably negligible, but it was worth the effort to find out, and worth seeing what Riojas might do when he found out they had her. They'd make sure he knew. Maybe he'd send someone to try and get her. It's possible. They'd keep the girl there long enough to find out. To make sure Paul's wife and daughter got on a plane. To flush Riojas' men out of the weeds. Then, if all went according to plan, they'd reciprocate.

Paul, honorary DEA deputy and faux insurance agent of the late Miles Goldstein, would accompany the bird-watcher to Mount Ararat Hospital.

Plan on.

*   *   *

THEY WERE CURRENTLY ZOOMING OVER THE 138TH STREET bridge. Well, not zooming, moving in fits and starts, due to construction in the left lane.

Clouds were gathering over the East River. It was late morning, hot and humid.

'Looks like rain,' Paul said.

'Thank you, Uncle Weatherbee,' the bird-watcher said.

Paul realized he still didn't know the bird-watcher's name. When he'd asked him, the bird-watcher said he preferred to remain *an international man of mystery,* then asked Paul if he'd preferred *Austin Powers* 1 or 2.

Yankee Stadium was looming off to the left, its graceful arches bone white against the blackening clouds. *Twins vs. Yanks 7:30 tonight.*

When they got to the end of the bridge, they veered left.

'Not exactly prime real estate, is it?' the bird-watcher said. 'If I put my jacket on and yelled *DEA,* half the neighborhood would start running.'

The bird-watcher pointed out a restaurant – *best chorizo in New York.* He nodded at a kid in retro basketball shorts, nervously bopping up and down on a graffiti-scarred street corner. *Ten to one he's pulling guard duty for a skank house.*

Now they were headed up Hunters Point Boulevard.

'Ever been to the Bronx Zoo?' the bird-watcher asked.

He seemed relaxed and chatty today, as if Paul were his partner riding shotgun on a case, instead of an insurance actuary who'd taken an unfortunate detour.

'When I was a kid.'

For some reason Paul had never visited the zoo as an adult.

He knew the reason.

You go to zoos when you're a kid.

Or when you have kids.

THE HOSPITAL SEEMED MORE OPPRESSIVE TODAY.

It might've been purely physical – the air-conditioning was on the blink, someone said – but Paul thought it had more to do with just being there again. Seeing it a second time let him appreciate the full awfulness of the surroundings, what it must've been like for Julius to stare at these salmon-pink walls for three years.

What it was like for Ruth he could only imagine.

Now she'd be leaving it behind.

He felt as if he were at the end of a marathon. Exhausted, yes, but with an exuberance that felt like hope.

After the bird-watcher had presented his credentials, they were ushered into a wood-paneled office, where the hospital administrator offered them seats. The bird-watcher had called ahead. He'd pulled strings, twisted arms, pulled rank, produced papers, done whatever a high-level DEA agent does to get what he wants. Mostly, he'd played the national security card – which, like AmEx platinum, seemed capable of opening all doors and rebuffing all dissent.

The administrator seemed glad to see them, as if he were in the company of minor celebrities. At least *one* minor celebrity.

'I don't suppose you can tell me any details?' the man asked the bird-watcher in a tone of voice that suggested he was more than capable of keeping national secrets.

The bird-watcher declined.

'Let's just say if it wasn't crucially important, I wouldn't be here,' he said.

The man – *Theodore Hill*, the degree on the wall said – nodded knowingly.

'I assume you have doctors waiting wherever this place is you're taking her,' Theodore said.

'Of course,' the bird-watcher replied.

'Her meds are listed in her file. Lithium mostly. She's not much trouble.'

'Glad to hear it.'

Up to this point, Paul Breidbart, *insurance agent,* had remained silent. But curiosity got the better of him – that, and the assumption that what an insurance agent wasn't privy to, a DEA agent was.

'What happened to her?' Paul asked. 'Back in Colombia?'

The bird-watcher turned to look at him with an expression of mild disapproval. Asking questions wasn't his job today. Before the bird-watcher could interrupt, plead time constraints, or simply stand up, the administrator spilled some details.

'I wasn't here when the girl was admitted. Different administration. Naturally, I looked at her file when you contacted me. According to her adoptive father, she witnessed the torture and murder of her mother. Was apparently *made* to witness it. It went on for several days. Some kind of drug lord's idea of retribution – it's quite a country down there, isn't it? I imagine we're talking about a true sociopath with strong sadistic impulses. As you might assume, being forced to watch something like that would

380

have an unhealthy effect on a three-year-old. She evidently became too much for her father to handle.'

Yes, Miles had given it all of one day, Paul thought.

'Well' – the bird-watcher looked at his watch – 'we have to get this show on the road.'

'Of course,' Theodore said, a man glad to be of service to his country. 'They're bringing her down.'

Paul had one more question.

'Does she know her adoptive father passed away?'

'Yes. According to Dr Sanji – have you met our Dr Sanji?'

Paul nodded.

'She said Ruth weathered the storm quite nicely. He was pretty much a father in name only. On the other hand, he was all she had.'

No, Paul thought. She had a grandfather who'd cried for her. A grandmother who'd entered a pact with the devil in order to save her.

'What's she been told?' the bird-watcher asked. 'About where she's going?'

'Per your instructions, she was told she's going somewhere for treatment. Not permanently, just for a little while.'

The bird-watcher nodded. 'Good.'

IT SEEMED LIKE HER EYES WERE OPENED WIDER TODAY.

Maybe she was taking it all in. The surrounding world. Burned-out buildings and potholed highways, looming bridges with pigeon-covered underpasses, roving bands of restless kids trolling the mostly mean streets. Paul

381

wondered how many times she'd been taken outside the hospital — if they still conducted *retard patrols* across the street where they fed the llamas and threw peanuts to the elephants.

They'd made it out of the Bronx and were this moment coming off the ramp of the Throgs Neck Bridge. When Paul was a kid, he'd wondered what a *frog's* neck looked like.

Ruth remained mostly silent. Every so often she'd utter something that might've come from the pages of *Little Women* or a 1930s comedy.

'Ezooks,' she exclaimed when they passed a particularly huge man lolling against a stripped car, 'get a load of that gorilla.'

Her first sight of the Throgs Neck Bridge elicited a chorus of *gosh*es and *gee whilliker*ses.

Occasionally, the bird-watcher peered in his rearview mirror in an effort to see whether she was really saying what it *sounded* like she was.

Even with the looming rain, Long Island Sound was dotted with sails today.

'Quite a flotilla,' Ruth said.

The bird-watcher pulled a cigarette from his pocket.

'Think she'll mind?' he asked Paul.

'Why don't you ask her?'

'Darling,' the bird-watcher said, 'would it trouble you greatly if I partook of some nicotine?'

Ruth stared at him.

'A smoke? A cancer stick?' he said.

'Cancer is the second leading killer in the United States,' Ruth answered, sounding like an actuary in good standing.

'You don't say,' the bird-watcher replied. 'Well, I'll certainly keep that in mind.'

The bird-watcher lit up, sucked in a generous amount of cancer-causing nicotine, then blew it out, where it drifted to the backseat, causing Ruth to sputter and cough.

'Whoops,' he said, 'maybe I ought to crack open a window in deference to our friend.'

'I don't particularly like cigarette smoke myself,' Paul said.

'Yeah,' the bird-watcher said, 'me either.'

He opened the driver's side window, letting in pure humidity and the sound of a mufflerless beer truck to their left. It sounded like an entire pack of Hell's Angels.

'Lovely,' the bird-watcher said.

'No, it's not,' Ruth volunteered, obviously unfamiliar with sarcasm. 'It's raucous and revolting.'

'You're right,' the bird-watcher said. 'My bad.' He turned on the CD player. 'This ought to help.'

Latin music.

It sounded vaguely familiar.

Paul closed his eyes. *Was that what was playing in Pablo's car on the way to Santa Regina?* His heart had been beating so fast it hurt. About to meet the daughter it had taken eighteen hours and five years to find. He was already forgetting her face, he realized with a pang. How long had he really had with her – a *blip* in time – and yet they'd forged a connection strong enough to still tug at his emotions, to pull them clear across time and space.

He was a *father,* he guessed. That's all.

They were headed east on the Long Island Expressway. Which was decidedly better than heading west on the LIE, since that side of the highway was staying true to its moniker as the world's longest parking lot.

They were close, he thought. About to close the circle again.

He wasn't absolutely sure when it hit him.

But *hit* was the right word.

A realization that came with the force of a punch to the solar plexus. It *staggered* him.

The music.

It *wasn't* the music playing on Pablo's radio.

He'd heard this music somewhere else.

Suddenly, he was back on his stomach in a field full of cattails and screams. Trying not to listen as a human being was tortured to death just fifty yards from him. Hearing every excruciating whimper as they cut off his body parts one by one.

You could almost hear the sound of knife hitting bone. Even with that music blaring. Even with that pounding rhythm and screeching horns.

Even then.

Celia Cruz. Queen of Samba.

Mi mami, one of the men yelled. *A fucking scream.*

That's what the bird-watcher was playing on his car radio. Only it wasn't a car radio. It was a Jeep radio. A green Jeep.

Two green Jeeps had come flying out of the cattails that day.

Paul's eyes were wide-open. They must have matched Ruth's.

He looked at the bird-watcher sitting beside him. A bulge on the left side of his shirt. *Assume shoulder holster complete with loaded gun.*

The bird-watcher was still contentedly puffing away, considerate enough to exhale through the crack in the window. He was humming along to the late Queen of Samba, keeping one eye on the road.

At some point that eye wandered. He noticed Paul noticing him.

Or maybe it just took him a few minutes to suddenly realize he'd screwed up.

'Shit. That was kind of Homer Simpson of me.'

Paul felt familiar tentacles of fear wrap themselves around his newborn hope. And strangle it.

'Oh well,' he said. 'You were going to know eventually. Although I was kind of hoping it wouldn't be while doing eighty on the LIE. It kind of forces me to multitask. Not that I'm not up to the challenge.' He stubbed his cigarette out with his right hand.

Freeing it for other things.

'Okay. Let's get the lay of the land here. I have a *gub*.'

Paul was frozen to the seat.

'Come on, you saw the Woody Allen movie – *Take the Money and Run*? The bank heist – the note he passes to the teller? *I have a gub. Work* with me, Paul. I'm trying to protect our friend back there from needless anxiety. We can talk pig latin if you'd like. No? Okay, what the heck. We'll talk turkey.'

Paul remained mute. He'd already been deaf and dumb far too long.

'You'd probably like an explanation. Okay. It'll pass the time. Where in the world do I start? Oh yeah. Colombia. I can bore you with my trials and tribulations as a DEA agent in good standing. As *our man in Bogotá*. I can chart

385

for you the moment I went from gung-ho to who-are-we-kidding? The moment when I realized it was all a charade, politics, Vietnam with a different jungle. I *could* bore you with all that claptrap, but it would be like the whining of a child. So let's talk like adults.'

He looked into the rearview mirror.

'You okay back there, sweetheart?'

'I'm marvelously comfortable, thank you.'

'*Marvelously* comfortable. Glad to hear it. Not too much longer to go. I'm so used to kids asking *are we there yet?* He glanced back at Paul. 'Beretta. Bore-tip bullets. In case you're wondering.'

'Where are we going?'

'Metaphorically, to hell in a handbasket. Speaking of *we* as a nation, of course. I understand your concerns are more personal. We'll get to that. Do you know what a DEA agent makes, Paul? No? Let's put it this way – when Bush so generously decided to let the rich get richer and the deficit get larger, he wasn't doing *me* any favors.'

A police car was cruising up to them in the right lane.

The bird-watcher closed the two inches of open window. Cranked the music louder.

'Remember, Paul. I'm an official agent of the U.S. government and you're someone facing federal drug charges, not to mention indictment on several newly minted anti-terrorist statutes. Your only ally in this car is a mental case. Sorry, darling. Just calling a spade a spade. To be blunt, Paul, I can shoot you on the spot and get a couple of pats on the back from Nassau's finest. Understand?'

'Yes,' Paul said. The police car was almost parallel with them. A female officer glanced out the window at them. The bird-watcher had placed some kind of badge on the dash-board. The officer smiled, nodded, turned back around.

'Wonderful, well done. Still comfortable back there, darling?'

Ruth didn't answer.

'I'll take that as a yes. Oddly enough, I never actually ran into Mr Riojas in Bogotá,' he said. 'Not until our government decided in its infinite wisdom to have him exported to U.S. federal prison. Sometimes we need to show everyone how swimmingly the war on drugs is going. We need someone's head on a platter. He has a very big head. The fact is, he outlasted his usefulness, like Noriega. Back in the days when all we cared about were the little lefties in the hills, Mr Riojas was *very* useful. He was like one of those Colombian vampire bats – ugly as hell and God forbid one should ever show up in your attic, but boy do they do a number on the mosquito population. They perform a useful function. Until they don't. Someone decided Riojas had become a liability. We paid off who we needed to, and one day I get the call. Mr Riojas is coming home for trial. And who do you think gets picked to escort the notorious fugitive to justice?'

The bird-watcher reached forward, readjusted the radio. 'She's got a voice on her, all right, but frankly, it's hurting my ears. How are yours?'

'Working fine,' Paul said. He'd begun tumbling numbers in his head, numbers he summoned front and center for immediate review.

Accident ratios for a typical SUV.

'Great. Still good back there, sweetheart?' addressing himself to Ruth.

'The road sign said *Commack*,' Ruth said.

'Right you are. Commack. You're my official navigator, okay?'

'I'm not entirely confident I'm up to the task,' Ruth replied.

'Oh, sure you are. Just keep looking at the signs and you'll perform the task quite nicely. *What* a vocabulary,' he said to Paul.

'Where are we going?' Paul said. 'What are you going to do with us?'

In a typical year 31,000 occupants of passenger vehicles are killed in traffic accidents.

'Would it kill you to let me finish the story? Where was I? Oh, right. On a plane home, with public enemy numero uno. By the way, we're talking private jet – plenty of legroom and a shitload of cold Coronas. What we do for the *really* bad guys. It's amazing what you start talking about in the back of a plane when you have nothing else to do. He's not a terrible guy, really. A bit excessive on the violence thing, sure, but pretty much on a par with your typical Special Ops guy. Talk about *sociopath with strong sadistic impulses.* Those guys are *brutal.*'

'Riverhead,' Ruth said. 'One mile.'

'That's it, honey. Right again. You're doing a fabulous job. In case you're interested, Paul, I can get the Beretta out of my shoulder holster and into firing position in exactly 2.6 seconds. No lie. We hold tournaments when we start going wacky on surveillance. I'm the official DEA record-holder.'

Of all vehicular fatalities in any given year, sport-utility vehicles account for over 28 percent.

'I would say Mr Riojas was a bit dejected on the ride home. He could see the handwriting on the prison wall. He was clearly preoccupied with *loose ends*. There was a piece of unfinished business that seemed particularly top of mind. He'd made a *vow*, which he'd yet to fulfill. Vows are kind of sacred to these fellows, especially when they make them to their Santeria gods. Apparently, even drug lords imbibe the opiate of the masses. Regardless, he'd made a vow and damned if he wasn't going to see it through. You can guess what we're talking about, can't you, Paul?'

'Exit 70,' Ruth said.

'One more exit to go, people. Keep up the good work, Ruth.'

Most fatalities involving sport-utility vehicles are due to rollovers, of which SUVs have the highest rate among all vehicles, approximately 36 percent.

'It seems a certain ex-mistress of his had the temerity to leave him flat. Carrying his *child* too. What's a fellow to do? It's not like he didn't tell her what was in store for her if she ever ran away. He'd spelled it out. He swore it on a stack of chicken heads. Still, off she went. It took him three years to find her. When he did, he went, okay, a little overboard. He took his time, used all his formidable skills. I'm not condoning that kind of brutality. But it's kind of like charging a jungle animal with intolerable cruelty. It's their survival instinct, how they get to stay king of the jungle. He related it to me in a most matter-of-fact voice. How he decided things. Who'd watch whom? Who first: mother or daughter? He picked mom. He admitted how surprised and delighted he was at how long she lasted.

389

Only there was a fuckup. One of his executioners apparently had a crisis of conscience and went *vamos* with the kid. So now what? Riojas had only completed half the vow. He's not the kind to give up. He kept *looking* for her. Got to the point where he was pretty sure she'd been smuggled to America. Which didn't really discourage him. You know why he was telling *me* all this, Paul?'

Fifty-eight percent of SUV rollover crashes are caused by extreme turns.

'He sensed a man willing to listen. Not just to a story. To an *offer*. Think of me as Cortés hearing the first stories of Latin American gold. And what was he asking me to do, really? Not spring him – he was astute enough to realize that was out of the question. Simply to fulfill the promise of a doomed and shattered man. By the time we touched down in Miami, I'd agreed.'

Forty percent of SUV rollovers are caused by alcohol consumption.

'I went to work. It was the same work I'd always been doing. I just had a new paymaster. It's amazing what happens when you follow the money. You never know where it'll lead. In this case, to Miles Goldstein. And then you. You were kind enough to be my honorary deputy and help wrap it up for me. My signore salutes you. I've already cashed out. Just one thing left. Or two.'

'They tied her to something,' Ruth said.

'What?' The bird-watcher jerked his head around.

'My mother. They tied her to a pipe in the ceiling. They put me on a chair and ordered me to watch.'

Thirty-two percent of fatal SUV rollovers are caused by speeding.

'Now, sweetheart, we don't need to be talking about that, do we? You're my official navigator, correctomundo?'

'They burned her. She screamed and screamed. He showed me his knife – he made me touch it.' Her eyes were lost in time, Paul thought.

'Okay, I think that's enough of that, don't you? Just tell me when the exit comes, all right, sweetie?'

Twenty-two percent of fatal SUV rollovers are caused by driver inattention – e.g., changing radio stations.

'When she closed her eyes, they'd make her wake up again. They would start all over. I was in the chair. I saw it. They took her skin off.'

'Yes, you remember. I understand. No wonder Daddy dumped you in that bad place. Now, how about giving it a little rest?'

Ten percent of fatal SUV rollovers are caused by driver incompetence – e.g., pushing the wrong pedal.

'You're falling down on the job, Ruth. Here's the exit I'm looking for.'

The bird-watcher shifted into the exit lane, flicked on his right turn signal, began turning off.

'Seat belt on, Ruth?' Paul asked gently.

'Yes.'

Six percent of fatal SUV rollovers are caused by inadvertent action – e.g., lifting the emergency brake while the vehicle's in drive.

'Good,' Paul said.

He pulled the transmission into reverse just as the Jeep went into the apex of its turn.

It took probably less than 2.6 seconds, because the bird-watcher was unable to get his Beretta loaded with snub-nosed bullets out of his shoulder holster. It likely wouldn't have made a difference. The Jeep teetered violently to the left, partially righted itself, then went over.

Paul and Ruth were wearing their seat belts.

The bird-watcher wasn't, as cowboys are wont to do.

Nearly two-thirds of passenger fatalities in SUV rollover crashes are unrestrained.

There was that moment when the Jeep hovered between air and ground, when Paul could see asphalt looming like a dark wave he hadn't seen coming. Then it broke over him.

He heard glass shatter, a scream, the awful sound of shearing metal. He must've blacked out. When he came to, he was upside down and staring into a pool of blood. He was still in his seat, but the seat seemed half detached from the car, held there by a few flimsy screws.

Where was Ruth?

He turned his head around, half afraid he wouldn't be able to, that he'd discover he was paralyzed and dying.

No. His head pivoted around just like God intended it to.

The entire backseat had disappeared.

He looked out the shattered window to his right.

There.

It was a surreal photo, something that belonged on the wall at MOMA. The backseat was sitting upright in the grass perfectly intact, and so was the person sitting on it. Intact, seemingly whole, and demonstrably alive. She looked as if she were simply waiting for a bus.

That accounted for two of them.

Where was the bird-watcher?

The entire windshield was blown out. Gone.

The interior of the upside-down Jeep was beginning to fill with thick, acrid smoke. Something else. The putrid odor of gasoline.

He unclasped the seat belt that was digging into his gut. He used his hands to feel his way through the window and out onto the pavement. He pushed himself out. Every inch of movement left a trail of blood.

His face. Something was wrong with his face. Numbness had given way to searing pain. When he touched his cheek, his hand came away bright red.

He stood up, somehow made it to his feet, both arms out for balance like a tightrope walker.

A body was lying about twenty feet from the totaled Jeep.

Paul stumbled toward it.

The bird-watcher.

He wasn't moving. He was still as death.

And then he wasn't.

He moved. One hand at first. Slowly feeling around as if looking for something. Then the other hand, Paul about five feet from him, caught between moving forward and moving back. The bird-watcher lifted himself up onto his palms – executing a kind of half push-up, gazing around like a man appearing out of a hole.

He saw Paul frozen to the spot.

The bird-watcher *had* been searching for something.

He'd found it.

He stood up – one leg, then the other – smiled through an ugly matting of blood and dirt. He pointed his gun at Paul.

'Remember Rock-'em 'Sock-em Robots, Paul?' Something was off with his speech – he seemed to be missing part of his tongue. 'Had two as a kid. You could knock their blocks off, right off their bodies, but it didn't matter, they kept coming.'

He took a few steps forward, gun still pointing at him.

Ruth began crying. When he gazed back at her, she seemed caught up in a shower of green leaves.

Paul turned back to face his fate – one way or another it was going to end here.

The bird-watcher was still stumbling, unsteady, oddly loose-limbed, but inexorably boring in.

'That was some trick you pulled.' He was having problems with his *t*s. *Ha was some rick you pulled.* 'Learn that in actuary school?'

No. In actuary school you learned the difference between risk and probability. You learned that not wearing a seat belt during a rollover should kill you. *Should,* but not always. But you learned something else about life and its opposite number, something of a mantra around the halls of an insurance company.

If one thing doesn't get you, the other thing will.

A Dodge Coronado had come hurtling off the LIE onto the exit ramp. Safety rules recommend a slowing down of at least 50 percent while turning into a highway exit. The driver of the Coronado must've missed that class.

When confronted with the smashed and smoking Jeep sitting in the middle of the sharply curving exit road, he was forced to swerve dangerously onto the shoulder, then lurch back onto the road to avoid a weeping willow. That brought him face-to-face with another slightly swerving object.

The bird-watcher had no time to react.

He was sent flying into the air, looking like one of those circus tumblers performing a gravity-defying finale.

He came down with a loud thud.

Then lay still.

FORTY-FIVE

She needed to dream tonight.

She'd noticed the looks from Tomás. The fact she'd received no dinner for the first time she could remember. The frazzled look on Galina's face, and her trembling hands.

She'd kissed Joelle good night in a way that really was good-bye. She'd said her prayers, confessed her sins. She'd made peace with it.

She needed to dream.

If she was lucky, this dream would involve being woken in the middle of the night, not by a gun muzzle, not by the sharp blade of a knife, but by Galina's soft whispers.

It would involve Galina quietly opening the lock that chained her leg to the radiator. Whispering directions into her ear. Then slipping silently out of the room the way people do in dreams.

It would involve standing up and padding softly through the door.

Slowly making her way down the empty hall and then pushing open the door to outside, the way she did once before.

It would certainly involve following those directions whispered into her ear. Walking not into the jungle, but the other way entirely, down past the back pens where chickens were nervously pecking at the ground, then onto the one-lane road.

She would walk down this road as if floating, her feet barely touching the ground. She would walk without looking back. Without fear or rancor.

She would come around a bend, and a car would be waiting there for her. A midnight-blue Peugeot. Its engine would be softly rumbling, and its driver would slip out of the front seat to greet her, making sure to put a finger to his lips.

He would reach into the car and pull out a bundle of blanket and hair. Her baby daughter, whom he'd gently place into her arms.

'Thank you,' she'd whisper to Pablo.

Thank you. Thank you.

TWO YEARS LATER

Sunday in June and the Central Park merry-go-round was full.

Paul and Joanna sat on the bench holding hands.

You could smell cotton candy, roasting peanuts, and candied apples. A catchy calypso number drifted over from the circling horses. Something from a Disney movie, Paul thought. *Under the sea . . . under the sea . . .*

Occasionally, Joanna put her head on his shoulder and left it there, and Paul got the strong sensation that the world was, in fact, perfect.

It seemed light-years away from the events of two years ago.

From Bogotá. And Miles.

From that day on the exit ramp of the Long Island Expressway.

And yet, sometimes it wasn't far away at all. It was right there in the room with him, lurking around his office, riding with him in the car, sleeping in his bed.

Memory is like that, a friend from childhood that you never really lose contact with. Even when you desperately

401

want to. Popping up at moments in your life when you least expect it.

In the middle of a balmy Sunday in June, for example.

He wondered sometimes how much he'd tell his daughter.

Would he tell her, for instance, about the spectacular assassination of a certain Colombian ex-drug lord in the bathroom of a Florida courtroom? How Manuel Riojas was going through pretrial motions when he was escorted to the men's room to relieve himself and never came back.

Would he tell her that the assassin apparently gained access with the use of a DEA identity badge? This badge evidently genuine, if clearly defunct, having belonged to a DEA agent who'd been dead for more than two years.

An agent who'd been known to don other uniforms from time to time. The uniform of an ornithologist, for example, resolutely searching the jungles of northern Colombia for the yellow-breasted toucan.

A bird-watcher.

Would he tell her how the bird-watcher's badge came to be in the possession of a hired assassin?

Would he *explain*, refer to that day on the LIE when the DEA agent lay dead in the middle of the exit ramp, and the badge that he'd placed on the dashboard lay right next to him, virtually begging to be picked up for some future if undetermined use.

Would he tell her about that day later on, when he brought that badge to a familiar office in Little Odessa, Brooklyn? When he sat on the other side of a door with *El Presidente* stenciled on it. Talking business with Moshe.

You know what the Russians call the Colombians? Miles asked him the day he shot himself.

What, Miles?

Amateurs.

And maybe Miles was dead right about that. The Russians ran a *very* profitable cash business. Maybe because they were willing to do anything for the right price. Just about anything at all. Break-ins, heists, even assassinations.

Including truly spectacular ones, the kind others wouldn't even touch.

As long as you had the cash, of course. Lots of it.

But where could Paul possibly get *that* kind of cash?

Would he tell her? Would he explain where?

Would he go back to that day again? The smoking Jeep, the puddle of blood and oil. *I already cashed out,* the bird-watcher had said to him before he went tumbling into the air and took forever and a day to come down.

And when Paul looked back at Ruth, she was covered in a whirlwind of green leaves. But they *weren't* leaves. Because the bird-watcher *had* cashed out, received his wages from his new paymaster, from Riojas. And years of DEA training had given him the perfect place to stash it.

How many cars had he ripped the floorboards out of over the years? Looking for bags of coke, Baggies of pot, bricks of hashish? Enough of them to realize what a fine place it was for hoarding things you don't want found.

Only he wasn't counting on an *accident.* He wasn't factoring in Paul putting the transmission in reverse while they were doing sixty miles an hour.

The impact ripped the Jeep apart, blew out the

sidewalls, sending hundred-dollar bills hurtling into the air, where they settled like snow onto Ruth's head.

Would he tell his daughter how easy it was to stuff the money into his wallet, into his pockets, as they waited for the ambulance to arrive?

Would he *remind* her?

The merry-go-round slowed, stopped spinning, came to a halt. Accompanied by the bittersweet cries of disappointed children.

Two of them came toward the bench.

Joelle, of course. Looking quite the little lady in a pink jumper, her black hair pinned up with tiny pink barrettes, pink being her most very favorite color – at least this week.

And carrying her, dragging her away from the merry-go-round that she just *had* to take another spin on, was her big sister, looking every inch a *real* lady, almost sixteen, those astounding brown eyes widened with what Paul fervently hoped was happiness.

Or, at the very least, peace.

This was the daughter he thought he would have to tell everything to one day. Perhaps not. Maybe whatever he'd done to keep her safe would be better left unspoken and unacknowledged, part of a secret history she'd left behind for good. *Protect her*, Galina had once written to Miles. And finally, at last, someone had.

In the end, adopting her had seemed the obvious thing to do.

When Joanna and Joelle returned from Colombia, Paul had called Galina and Pablo to explain as best he could what happened. That completing his part of the deal was now uncertain, and very much on hold. They were once his kidnappers. Now they were simply distraught grandparents. And two people who'd risked their lives to return his wife and daughter to him. He was eternally grateful.

He told them what their granddaughter was like, sent them pictures, described how unusually sweet she was, that she was blessed with the special gift of endearment.

She was facing a statusless limbo – an intercountry wrangling that was going to leave her back in Mount Ararat Hospital for quite a while. Maybe forever.

Paul visited her, visited her again.

One day he brought Joanna and Joelle along.

It became a weekly routine. So did Paul's calls and letters to Ruth's grandparents in Colombia. This time, of course, the letters detailing her life weren't made up. They were genuine. So were the feelings of regret every time the three of them left Ruth at the door of the hospital. She'd stand there and wave at them until their car disappeared around the corner.

He honestly couldn't remember who brought it up first. Galina and Pablo? Or was it him?

Call it a tie. Colombia wasn't necessarily any safer for Ruth than it was before. It wasn't safe for anyone these days. Galina and Pablo were feeling their age. Suddenly, it was as if all parties involved knew the right thing to do. Where Ruth belonged.

Galina and Pablo gave their permission.

Paul and Joanna filed for adoption and were granted it one year later.

She wasn't out of the woods. It was entirely possible she might never be. She attended group therapy on a triweekly basis, remained medicated, and occasionally lapsed into periods of heartbreaking desperation.

Most of the time she smiled, even glowed. Paul was convinced that her family nourished her, every bit as much as it nourished him.

He'd gone from no family to a full one in the seeming blink of an eye. He'd abandoned the safety of numbers for the uncertain possibilities of life. Odds are, he thought, it would be a good one.

'Come on, sweeties, let's grab some lunch,' Paul told his daughters.

Joelle and Claudia.

Oh yes. On the day they officially gave Ruth their last name, she'd asked them if she might change her first one as well.

'To what?' Paul asked her.

What was my mother's name?

Joanna told her.

'Claudia,' she said. 'Claudia Breidbart. It'll do.'

Derailed

To Mindy, who tends to her family
as she tends to her garden – with
great love, ceaseless devotion,
and unflagging enthusiasm.

ACKNOWLEDGMENTS

I would like to thank both Sara Ann and just plain Sarah for their immense help in structuring this story, Larry for believing in it, and, of course, Richard, for unapologetically championing it.

Attica

I spend five days a week teaching English at East Bennington High and two nights a week teaching English at Attica State Prison. Which is to say, I spend my time conjugating verbs for delinquents and dangling participles for convicts. One class feeling like they're in prison and the other class actually being in one.

On the Attica evenings, I eat an early dinner with my wife and two children. I kiss my wife and teenage daughter goodbye and give my four-year-old son a piggyback ride to the front door. I gently put him down, kiss his soft brow, and promise to look in on him when I get home.

I enter my eight-year-old Dodge Neon still surrounded in a halo of emotional well-being.

By the time I pass through the metal detector at Attica Prison, it's gone.

Maybe it's the brass plaque prominently displayed on the

1

wall of the visitors room. 'Dedicated to the Correction Officers who died in the Attica riots,' it says. There is no plaque for the prisoners who died.

I have only recently begun teaching there, and I can't quite decide who's scarier – the Attica prisoners or the corrections officers who guard them. Possibly the corrections officers.

It's clear they don't like me much. They consider me a luxury item, like cable TV, something the prisoners did nothing to deserve. The brainchild of some liberal in Albany, who's never had a shiv stuck in his ribs or feces thrown in his face, who's never had to peel a tattooed carcass off a blood-soaked floor swimming with AIDS.

They greet me with barely disguised contempt. It's the PHD, they mumble. 'Pathetic Homo Douchebag', one of them scrawled on the wall of the visitors bathroom.

I forgive them.

They are the outnumbered occupiers of an enslaved population seething with hatred. To survive this hate, they must hate back. They are not allowed to carry guns, so they arm themselves with attitude.

As for the prisoners who attend my class, they are strangely docile. Many of them the unfortunate victims of the draconian Rockefeller drug laws that treat small purchases of cocaine like violent felonies. They mostly look bewildered.

Now and then, I give them writing assignments. Write something, I say. Anything. Anything that interests you.

I used to have them read their work in class. Until one convict, a sloe-eyed black named Benjamin Washington, read

2

what sounded like gibberish. It was gibberish, and the other convicts laughed at him. Benjamin took offense at this and later knifed one of them in the back over a breakfast of watery scrambled eggs and burnt toast.

I decided on anonymity there and then.

They write what interests them and send it up to the desk unsigned. I read it out loud and nobody knows who wrote what. The writer knows; that's good enough.

One day, though, I asked them to write something that would interest me. The story of them. How they got here, for instance, to Mr Widdoes's English class in the rec room at Attica State Prison. If they wanted to be writers, I told them, start with the writer.

It might be enlightening, I thought, maybe even cathartic. It might be more interesting than the story 'Tiny the Butterfly', a recent effort from . . . well, I don't know, do I? Tiny brought color and beauty to a weed-strewn lot in the projects until he was, unfortunately, crushed like a bug by the local crank dealer. Tiny, it was explained at the bottom of the page, was cymbollic.

I gave out the assignment on Thursday; by next Tuesday the papers were scattered across my desk. I read them aloud in no particular order. The first story about an innocent man being framed for armed robbery. The second story about an innocent man being framed for possession of illegal narcotics. The third story about an innocent man being framed . . .

So maybe it wasn't that enlightening.

But then.

Another story. Hardly a story at all (although it had a title); a kind of introduction to a story. An invitation to one, really.

About another innocent man.

Who walked on the train one day to go to work.

When something happened.

One

The morning Charles met Lucinda, it took him several moments after he first opened his eyes to remember why he liked keeping them closed.

Then his daughter, Anna, called him from the hallway and he thought: *Oh yeah.*

She needed lunch money, a note for the gym teacher, and help with a book report that was due yesterday.

Not in that order.

In a dazzling feat of juggling, he managed all three between showering, shaving, and getting dressed. He had to. His wife, Deanna, had already left for her job at P.S. 183, leaving him solely in charge.

When he made it downstairs he noticed Anna's blood meter and a used syringe on the kitchen counter.

Anna had made him late.

When he got to the station, his train had already left –

he could hear a faint rumble as it retreated into the distance.

By the time the next train pulled in, the platform had been repopulated by an entirely new cast of commuters. He knew most of the 8:43 crowd by sight, but this was the 9:05, so he was in alien territory.

He found a seat all by himself and immediately dived into the sports pages.

It was November. Baseball had slipped away with another championship for the home team. Basketball was just revving up, football already promising a year of abject misery.

This is the way he remained for the next twenty minutes or so: head down, eyes forward, brain dead – awash in meaningless stats he could reel off like his Social Security number, numbers he could recite in his sleep, and sometimes did, if only to keep himself from reciting other numbers.

Which numbers were those?

Well, the numbers on Anna's blood meter, for example.

Numbers that were increasingly and alarmingly sky high.

Anna had suffered with juvenile diabetes for over eight years.

Anna wasn't doing well.

So all things being equal, he preferred a number like 3.25. Roger-the-Rocket-Clemens's league-leading ERA this past season.

Or twenty-two – there was a good round number. Latrell Sprewell's current points per game, accumulated, dreadlocks flying, for the New York Knicks.

Numbers he could look at without once feeling sick.

The train lurched, stopped.

They were somewhere between stations – dun-colored ranch houses on either side of the track. It suddenly occurred to him that even though he'd ridden this train more times than he cared to remember, he couldn't describe a single neighborhood it passed through. Somewhere along the way to middle age, he'd stopped looking out windows.

He burrowed back into the newspaper.

It was at that exact moment, somewhere between Steve Serby's column on the state of the instant replay rule and Michael Strahan's lamentation on his diminishing sack total, that it happened.

Later he would wonder what exactly had made him look up again at that precise moment in time.

He would ask himself over and over what would have happened if he hadn't. He would torture himself with all the permutations, the what ifs and what thens and what nows.

But he did look up.

The 9:05 from Babylon to Penn Station kept going. Merrick to Freeport to Baldwin to Rockville Centre. Lynbrook to Jamaica to Forest Hills to Penn.

But Charles clearly and spectacularly derailed.

Attica

Two nights later after dinner, my four-year-old climbed onto my lap and demanded I do treasure hunt on his back.

'We're going on a treasure hunt,' I whispered as I traced little steps up and down his spine. 'X marks the spot . . .' as he squirmed and giggled. He smelled of shampoo and candy and Play-Doh, the scent that was clearly and uniquely him.

'To get to the treasure, you take big steps and little steps,' I murmured, and when I finished he asked me where this treasure was exactly, and I answered him on cue. This, after all, was our routine.

'Right here,' I said. And hugged him.

My wife smiled at us from the other side of the table.

When I kissed them all good-bye, I lingered before stepping out into the driveway. As if I were attempting to soak up enough good vibes to last me through the night, straight through the redbrick archway of Attica and into the

8

fetid rec room. Like a magic aura that might protect me from harm.

'Be careful,' my wife said from the front door.

When I went through the metal detector, it went off like an air raid siren.

I'd forgotten to take my house keys out of my pocket.

'Hey, Yobwoc,' the CO said while patting me down. 'Keys are like . . . metal.' Yobwoc was Cowboy backward and stood for Young Obnoxious Bastard We Often Con.

PHD was just one of my monikers here.

'Sorry,' I said. 'Forgot.'

As soon as I entered the classroom, I could see there was another piece of the story waiting for me at my desk. Eleven pages, neatly printed.

Yes, I thought. The story is just getting started.

Other sections soon followed like clockwork.

From that first day on, there would be another piece of the story waiting for me every time I entered the classroom.

Sometimes just a page or two – sometimes what would constitute several chapters. Placed flat on my desk and all, like the first one, unsigned. The story unfolding piecemeal, like a daytime serial you just can't pull your eyes away from. After all, it would end up containing all the staples of soap opera – sex, lies, and tragedy.

I didn't read these installments to my class. I understood they were solely for me now. Me and, of course, the writer.

Speaking of which.

There were twenty-nine students in my class.

9

Eighteen blacks, six Hispanics, five pale-as-ghosts Caucasians.

I was reasonably sure that none of them had ever ridden the 9:05 to Pennsylvania Station.

So where was he?

Two

An expanse of thigh – that's all at first.

But not just any thigh. A thigh taut, smooth, and toned, a thigh that had obviously spent some time on the treadmill, sheathed by a fashionably short skirt made even shorter by the position of the legs. Casually crossed at the knees. All in all, a skirt length that he'd have to say fell somewhere between sexiness and sluttiness, not exactly one or the other, therefore both.

This is what Charles saw when he looked up.

He could just make out a black high-heeled pump jutting out into the aisle, barely swinging with the motion of the train. He was directly facing her, his seat backward to the city-bound direction of the train car. But she was blocked by the front page of *The New York Times,* and even if she wasn't blocked by the day's alarming if familiar headline – MID-EAST BURNING – he hadn't yet looked up toward her face, only peripherally. Instead he was focusing on that thigh and hoping against hope she wouldn't turn out to be beautiful.

She was.

He'd been debating his next move: whether to turn back to his sports stats, for instance, whether to stare out the grime-streaked window, or scan the bank and airline ads lining each side of the car, when he simply threw caution to the wind and peeked. Just as *The New York Times* strategically lowered, finally revealing the face he'd been so hesitant to look at.

Yes, she *was* beautiful.

Her eyes.

They were kind of spectacular. Wide and doe shaped and the very definition of tenderness. Full, pouting lips she was ever so slightly biting down on. Her hair? Soft enough to cocoon himself in and never, ever, come out.

He'd been hoping she'd be homely or interesting or simply cute. Not a chance. She was undeniably magnificent.

And that was a problem, because he was kind of vulnerable these days. Dreaming of a kind of alternate universe.

In this alternate universe, he wasn't married and his kid wasn't sick, because he didn't have any kids. Things were always looking up there; the world was his oyster.

So he didn't want the woman reading *The New York Times* to be beautiful. Because that was like peeking into the doorway of this alternate universe of his, at the *hostess* beckoning him to come inside and put his feet up on the couch, and everyone knew alternate universes were for kids and sci-fi nuts.

They didn't exist.

'Ticket.' The conductor was standing over him and demanding something. What did he want? Couldn't he see he was busy defining the limitations of his life?

'Ticket,' he repeated.

It was Monday, and Charles had forgotten to actually walk into the station and purchase his weekly ticket. The time change had thrown him off, and here he was, ticketless in front of strangers.

'Forgot to buy one,' he said.

'Okay,' the conductor said.

'See, I didn't realize it was Monday.'

'Fine.'

Another thing had just occurred to Charles. On Mondays he stopped at the station ATM to take out money he then used to purchase the weekly ticket. Money he also used to get through the week. Money he didn't, at the moment, have.

'That's nine dollars,' the conductor said.

Like most couples these days, Charles and Deanna lived on the ATM plan, which doled out cash like a trust fund lawyer – a bit at a time. Charles's wallet had been in its usual Monday morning location, opened on the kitchen counter, where Deanna had no doubt scoured it for loose cash before going off to work. There was nothing in it.

'Nine dollars,' the conductor said, this time impatiently. No doubt about it; the man was getting antsy.

Charles looked through his wallet anyway. There was always the chance he was wrong, that somewhere in there was a forgotten twenty tucked away between business cards and six-year-old photos. Besides, looking through your wallet was what you were supposed to do when someone was asking you for money.

Which someone was. Repeatedly.

'Look, you're holding up the whole train,' he said. 'Nine dollars.'

'I don't seem . . .' continuing the facade, sifting through slips of wrinkled receipts and trying not to show his embarrassment at being caught penniless in a train of well-to-do commuters.

'You got it or don't you?' the conductor said.

'If you just give me a minute . . .'

'Here,' someone said. 'I'll pay for him.'

It was her.

Holding up a ten-dollar bill and showing him a smile that completely threatened his equilibrium.

Three

Of all the things they talked about – and they talked about all sorts of things – there was one thing they didn't talk about.

Commuting to work? Yes.

I was thinking the other day, she said, *that if the U.S. government was run like the Long Island Rail Road, we'd all be in trouble. And then I realized that maybe it is, and we are.*

The weather? Of course.

Fall's my favorite season, she said. *But where did it go?*

Baltimore, Charles answered.

Jobs? Absolutely.

I write commercials, Charles said. *I'm a creative director.*

I cheat clients, she said. *I'm a broker.* After which she added: *Just kidding.*

Restaurants dined in . . . colleges attended . . . favorite movies. All spoken of, discussed, *mentioned.*

Just not marriages.

Marriages, the plural, because she wore a wedding band on her left ring finger.

Maybe marriage wasn't considered an appropriate topic when flirting. If flirting was what they were doing, of course. Charles wasn't sure; he was kind of rusty at it and had never been particularly at ease with women to begin with.

But as soon as she'd pressed the ten-dollar bill into the conductor's hand, Charles protesting all the while – *Don't be silly, you don't have to do that* – as soon as the conductor gave her one dollar in return, Charles still protesting – *No, really, this is totally unnecessary* – he'd gotten up and sat in the empty seat next to her. Why not – wasn't it the polite thing to do when someone helped you out? Even someone who looked like her?

Her thighs shifted to accommodate him. Even with his eyes glued to her heartbreaking face, he'd managed to notice the movement of her legs, a memory that stayed with him as he spoke to her about the banal, trivial, and superfluous – a good name, he thought, for a law firm specializing in personal injury suits.

He asked her, for example, which brokerage house she worked for. *Morgan Stanley,* she answered. And how long she'd been there. *Eight years.* And where she'd worked before that.

McDonald's she said.

My high school job.

She was just a little younger than he was, she was reminding him. Just in case he hadn't noticed.

16

He had. In fact, he was trying to think of just the right word for her eyes and thought it was probably *luminous*. Yeah, luminous was just about perfect.

'I'll give you your money back as soon as we get to Penn Station,' he said, suddenly remembering he was in her debt.

'Tomorrow's fine,' she said. 'Ten percent interest, of course.'

'I've never met a woman loan shark before. Do you break legs, too?'

'Just balls,' she said.

Yes, he guessed they *were* flirting after all. And he didn't seem half-bad at it, either. Maybe it was like riding a bicycle or having sex, in that you never actually forgot how. Although it was possible Deanna and he *had*.

'Is this your usual train?' he asked her.

'Why?'

'So I know how to give you your money back.'

'Forget about it. It's nine dollars. I think I'll survive.'

'No. I've got to give it back to you – I'd feel ethically impugned if I didn't.'

'*Impugned?* Well, I wouldn't want you to feel impugned. By the way, is that an actual word?'

Charles blushed. 'I think so. I saw it in a crossword puzzle once, so it must be.'

Which got them onto a discussion about what else? Crossword puzzles. She liked them – he didn't.

She could make it through Monday's with *both eyes closed*. He needed both eyes and a piece of brain he didn't

17

possess. The one that provided focus and fortitude. His brain liked to roam around a little too much to sit down and figure out a five-letter word for . . . say . . . *sadness*. All right, all right, so that was an easy one. *Grief*. That place where his brain insisted on spending so much of its time these days. Where it had set up house and resolutely refused to budge. Except, of course, when it was imagining that alternate world of his, where he could flirt with green-eyed women he'd just met not five minutes before.

They kept talking about other mostly inconsequential things. The conversation a little like the train itself, moving along at a nice, easy clip, if briefly stopping here and there to pick up some new topic of discussion before gathering steam once again. And then suddenly they were under the East River and almost there.

'Well, I'm lucky you were here today,' he said, entombed in darkness as the fluorescent train lights flickered off and all he could see was the vague shape of her body. It seemed like he'd just got on, like he'd just been asked for nine dollars he didn't have, and she'd just untangled her thighs and paid for him.

'Tell you what,' he said. 'Take the same train tomorrow and I'll pay you back then.'

'You've got a date,' she said.

For the rest of the day, even after he'd shaken her hand good-bye and watched as she disappeared into the Penn Station crowd, after he'd waited ten minutes for a cab uptown and was greeted with his boss, Eliot, telling him to brace himself just two feet into the office, he'd think about her choice of words.

She could've said fine, sure, meet you tomorrow. She could've said good idea. Or *bad* idea. Or just mail it to me.

But she'd said: *You've got a date.*

Her name was Lucinda.

Four

Something was up.

Eliot informed him their credit card client was coming in to speak with them. Or, more likely, to scream at them.

Blown deadlines, poor tracking studies, unresponsive account executives – they could take their pick.

Even though the actual reason was the same reason it always was these days.

The economy.

Business simply wasn't good; there was too much competition, too many clients with too many options. Groveling was in, integrity out.

This was going to be a visit to the principal's office, a sit-down with Dad, an audience with the IRS. Where he'd have to stand and assume the position and say thank you, sir, too.

One look at Ellen Weischler's sour expression when he

walked into the conference room pretty much confirmed this.

She looked as if she'd just tasted curdled milk or sniffed something odious. He knew *what,* too. The last commercial they'd done for her company was a triumph of mediocrity. Badly cast, badly written, and badly received. It didn't matter that they'd recommended another one to them. That they'd begged and pleaded and, yes, even groveled in an attempt to get them to choose a different board. It didn't even matter that the first cut of the commercial had been almost good – clever, even hip – until the client, Ellen in particular, had meddled with it, changing copy, changing shots, each succeeding cut more bland than the previous one, until they'd ended up with the current dog wagging its tail five times a day on network buys across the country. It didn't matter because it was *their* spot, and the buck – or to be perfectly accurate, the 17 percent commission on the $130 million account – stopped there.

There being, of course, Charles.

He greeted Ellen with a chaste kiss on one cheek he thought better of halfway into his lean – thinking you should probably shake hands with she who was about to deck you.

'So . . . ' Ellen said when they'd all taken their seats. All being Charles, Eliot, two account people – Mo and Lo – and Ellen and hers. *So,* the way Charles's mother used to say it when she'd found a *Playboy* under his bed. *So.* A *so* that demanded explanation and certainly contrition.

'I guess you're not here to raise our commission,' Charles said. He'd meant it as a joke, of course, only no one laughed. Ellen's expression stayed sour; if anything, she looked worse than before.

'We have some serious issues,' Ellen said.

We have some serious issues, too. We don't like you telling us what to do all the time. We don't like being repudiated, belittled, ignored, screamed at. We actually don't like sour expressions. This is what Charles wanted to say.

What he actually said was: 'I understand.' And he said it with a hangdog expression he was perfecting to the point of artistry.

'It seems like we talk and talk but no one listens,' Ellen said.

'Well, we—'

'This is just what I mean. *Listen* to me. Then speak.'

It occurred to Charles that Ellen had transcended angry and gone straight to rude. That if she were an acquaintance, he would have already walked out of the room. That if she were a client worth significantly less than $130 million, he would've told her to take a hike.

'Of course,' Charles said.

'We all agree on a strategy. We all sign off on it. And then you consistently go off in other directions.'

Those directions being wit, humor, entertainment value, and anything else that actually might make a consumer sit up and watch.

'This last commercial is a case in point.'

Yes, it is.

'We agreed on a board. We said it was going to be done in a certain way. Then you send us a cut that's nothing like what we agreed to. With all this *New York humor* in it.'

If she'd uttered a profanity, c—t, say, she couldn't have looked more distasteful.

'Well, as you know, we're always trying to make it—'

'I said *listen*.'

She'd definitely entered *rude* and might actually be edging into *humiliating*. Charles wondered if this was something one was capable of recovering from.

'We have to send cut after cut back to you just in order to get it to the board we originally bought in the first place.' She paused and looked down at the table.

Charles didn't like that pause.

It wasn't a pause that was finally inviting a response. It wasn't even a pause meant to let her catch her breath. It was a pause that portended something worse than what preceded it. The kind of pause he'd seen from girlfriends before they dropped the axe and dashed all hope. From unscrupulous salesmen about to get to the fine print. From emergency room interns about to tell you exactly what's wrong with your daughter.

'I think maybe we need a change of direction,' she looked up and said.

Now what did that mean? Other than something bad. Was it possible she was firing the agency?

Charles looked over at Eliot, who, strangely enough, was looking down at the table now, too.

Then he understood.

Ellen wasn't firing the agency.

Ellen was firing him.

Off the account. Ten years, forty-five commercials, not an insignificant number of industry awards – it didn't matter.

The answer was no. You couldn't recover from this. Eliot could, but he couldn't. And it seemed to him that Eliot must've known, too. You don't take a step like this without informing someone in advance.

Et tu, Brute?

No one was speaking. The pause wasn't merely pregnant, it was pregnant with triplets – angry, bawling ones; something Charles was scared he himself was about to start doing – just lay his head on the table and begin crying. He didn't need a mirror to know he was turning bloodred. He didn't need a psychiatrist to know his self-esteem had taken a mortal hit.

Ellen cleared her throat. That's it. After repeatedly admonishing him for speaking out of turn, she was waiting for him to say something after all. She was waiting for his resignation speech.

'You don't want me on the business anymore.'

He'd meant it to sound emotionless and maybe even slightly defiant. But he'd failed. It sounded whiny and defensive, maybe even pathetic.

'We certainly appreciate all the great things you've done,' she began. Then he kind of tuned out. He was thinking that a ballsy company, a ballsy *president*, might've stood up to them – said we pick who works on your

24

business here, and Charles is the guy. Maybe. If the account were less significant, if business were better, if they all weren't spending so much time on their knees.

But Eliot was still staring down at the table, doodling now as a way to give him something to do while Charles was being publicly eviscerated. Or perhaps he was just doing the math – $130 million versus Charles Schine – and coming up with the same answer every time.

Charles didn't let her finish.

'It's been fun,' he said, finally striking the right note, he thought. World-weary cynicism with a touch of noblesse oblige.

He exited the conference room engulfed in a kind of hot haze; it felt like walking out of a steamroom.

And into an entirely different climate. Word had spread. He could see it on their faces, and they could see it on his. He barely acknowledged his secretary, walked into his office, shut the door.

Later, after everything fell apart for him, it would be hard to remember that it all began this morning.

In this way.

As for now, he sat behind closed doors and wondered whether Lucinda would be on the train tomorrow.

Five

She wasn't.

He took the same train, stood on the very same spot on the platform.

He walked the train from car to car – first back, then forward – scanning each face the way people do in airports when they're expecting relatives from overseas. Faces they know but don't know, but long to know now.

'Remember the woman who bailed me out yesterday?' he asked the conductor. 'Have you seen her?'

'What are you talking about?' The conductor didn't remember him, didn't remember her, didn't remember the incident. Maybe he was used to berating commuters on a regular basis; yesterday's drama wasn't worthy of recall.

'Never mind,' Charles said.

She wasn't there.

He was a little amazed that it mattered to him. That it

mattered to the point where he'd walked the cars like a rousted homeless man seeking warmth. Who was she, anyway, but a married woman he'd harmlessly flirted with on the way to work? And that's what *made* it harmless – that they hadn't done it again. So why exactly was he looking for her?

Well, because he wanted to talk, maybe. About this and that and the other thing. About what happened to him at the office yesterday, for instance.

He hadn't been able to tell Deanna.

He was all ready to. Honest.

'How was work today?' she'd asked him at dinner.

A perfectly legitimate question, the question, in fact, he'd been waiting for. Only Deanna had looked tired and worried – she'd been peering into Anna's blood sugar journal when he walked into the kitchen.

So Charles had said: 'Work's fine.'

And that was it for talk about the office.

When Anna first got sick, they'd talked of nothing else. Until it became apparent what the future held for her, and then they'd stopped talking about it. Because to talk about it was to acknowledge it.

Then they created a whole *canon* of things they were not to talk to each other about. Anna's future career plans, for example. Any article in *Diabetes Today* involving loss of limbs. Any bad news in general. Because complaining about something other than Anna diminished Anna.

'I was monitored by Mrs Jeffries today,' Deanna said. Mrs Jeffries was her school principal.

'How did it go?'

'Fine. Pretty much. You know she always throws a fit if I deviate from accepted lesson plans.'

'So did you?'

'Yes. But the composition I gave out was "Why we like our principal". So she couldn't really complain, could she?'

Charles laughed. And thought how that was something they used to do a lot of. The laughing Schines. And he looked at his wife and thought, *Yes, she's still beautiful*.

Dirty blond hair – with a little help from Clairol, maybe – tousled and curly and barely constrained by a white elastic headband; dark brown eyes that never looked at him without at least a modicum of love. Only there were tired lines radiating out from the corners of those eyes, as if tears had cut actual tracks into the surface of her skin. Like those lines crisscrossing NASA photographs of Mars – *dry riverbeds*, the astronomers explain, where torrents of water once surged across the now dead landscape. Which is sometimes the way he thought about Deanna – all cried out.

After dinner they both went upstairs. Charles attempted to help Anna with her eighth-grade social homework – the separation of church and state, something she was trying to do with MTV tuned to the volume of *excruciating*.

'What steps did the United States take to separate church and state?' Charles said, only he mouthed the words so that maybe Anna would get the point – that there should be a separation of homework and TV.

She refused to take the hint. When he finally stood in front of the television so she'd stop sneaking peeks at Britney or Mandy or Christina and concentrate on the business at hand, she told him to move.

'Sure,' he said. And jerked his arms and legs in a reasonable facsimile of the funky chicken. *See, I'm moving.*

At least that elicited a smile, no small accomplishment from a thirteen-year-old daughter whose general demeanor ranged from sullen to dour. Then again, she had good cause.

When he finished helping her, he gave her a kiss on the top of her head and she grunted something that sounded like *Good night* or *Get lost.*

Then he entered his bedroom, where Deanna was lying under the covers and pretending to sleep.

The next morning he ran into Eliot by the elevators.

'Can I ask you something?' Charles said.

'Sure.'

'Did you know they were coming in to ask me off the business?'

'I thought they came in to *complain* about the advertising. Asking you off the business was how they registered the seriousness of their complaint.'

'I just wondered if you knew it was coming.'

'Why?'

'*Why?*'

'Why do you want to know if I knew it was coming? What's the difference, Charles? It was coming.'

When the elevator doors opened, Mo was standing there with two legal pads and the new head creative on the business.

'Going down?' she said.

Six

'Lucinda,' he said. Or yelped.

That's what it sounded like to him – the noise a dog makes when its tail is stepped on.

She was back on the train.

He hadn't seen her when he sat down; he'd opened his paper and immediately burrowed into the land of the Giants: 'Coach Fassel lamented the lack of pressure by his front four this past Sunday . . .'

Then that black pump, the stiletto heel like a dagger aimed at his heart, as he looked up and bared his chest for the kill.

'Lucinda . . .'

A second later, that perfect face edging out into the aisle to peer at him, eyes sheathed in black-rimmed spectacles – *she hadn't worn glasses before, had she?* – followed by a full-wattage smile. No, more like one of those soft-glow bulbs,

31

the kind of light that takes the edge off and makes everything look better than it actually is.

And she said: 'Hi.' Such a sweet 'hi', too, as genuine sounding as they come, a woman who seemed glad to see him. Even though she was four rows and three days away from their scheduled assignation.

'Why don't you come over here,' she whispered.

Yes, why not.

When he reached her, Lucinda pulled her impossibly long legs off to the side to let him pass.

'Just in time,' she said. 'I was ready to call the police and report the nine dollars stolen.'

He smiled. 'I looked all over for you the other day.'

'I'll bet,' she said.

'No, really, I did.'

'I was *kidding*, Charles.'

'So was I,' he lied.

'So,' she said, hand out, impeccably manicured fingernails polished bloodred, 'pay up.'

'Sure.' He reached for his wallet, opening it up to a picture of Anna and hiding it immediately, as if it were an admonishment he didn't wish to hear. He placed a crisp ten-dollar bill in her hand, the tips of his fingers grazing her flesh, which felt slightly moist and hot.

'Your daughter?' she said.

He blushed, was sure he blushed, even as he answered, 'Yep.'

'How old?'

'Too old.' The wise-guy-ish you-wouldn't-believe-the-travails-of-fatherhood tone. The good-natured *I love her and all, but I wouldn't mind wringing her neck on occasion.*

'*Tell* me about it.'

So she had children, too. Of course she did.

'Daughters?' he asked.

'One.'

'All right, I showed you mine, now you show me yours.'

She laughed. *Score one for Charles, the cutup.* Then she reached into her bag, one of those cavernous things you could've gone camping with if it wasn't made of such obviously expensive leather. She fished out her wallet and flipped it open for him.

A very photogenic little girl of about five, blond hair flying in all directions, caught in midair on a playground swing somewhere in the country, maybe. Freckle faced, knobby kneed, and sweet smiled.

'She's adorable,' he said, and meant it.

'Thanks. I forget sometimes.' Mimicking his tone of parental weariness. 'Yours looked lovely, too – what I could see of her.'

'An angel,' he said, then immediately regretted his choice of words.

The conductor asked them for their tickets. Charles was tempted to ask him if he remembered the woman *now*. After all, he was doing everything possible to sneak peeks at her legs.

'Here,' she said to Charles after the conductor managed to pull himself away and move on. She'd put a dollar bill in his hand.

'I thought I owed you interest,' he said.

'I'll let you slide. This time.'

He wondered about *this time*.

'I didn't remember you with glasses,' he said.

'Getting new contacts,' she said.

'Oh. You look great in them, by the way.'

'You think?'

'Yeah.'

'Not too serious for you?'

'I like serious.'

'Why's that?'

'Why do I like serious?'

'Yes, Charles. Why do you like serious?'

'Seriously . . . I don't know.'

She smiled. 'You're kind of funny, aren't you?'

'I try.'

They were passing Rockville Centre, the movie theater where he often took Deanna plainly visible from the train car. And for one surreal moment, he imagined he was looking out on his past life. That he was firmly ensconced in this new universe of his – snug as a bug in *Charlesville*. Just Lucinda and him, newly married and on their way to work. Still chitchatting about their recent honeymoon – *where* had they gone, exactly? Kaui – yes, two weeks at the posh Kaui Hilton. Already starting to think about having kids, too – after all, they weren't getting any younger, were they? One of each, they'd decided, though it didn't really matter. As long as they were, of course, healthy . . .

'Busy day today?' she asked him.

'Busy? Sure.' Busy fending off disgruntled clients looking for his head and bosses looking to betray him. And for a second, he felt like telling her exactly what had been going on there and finding a nice soft spot on her shoulder to cry on.

'Me too.'

'*What?*'

'It's going to be a busy day for me, too.'

'I imagine you're getting a lot of angry calls these days.'

'Well, if you consider death threats angry.'

Charles smiled. 'You're kind of funny, too.'

'You think?'

'Yes. Clients must have loved you when times were good.'

'Are you kidding? Then you weren't making them enough money. They all had a cousin or brother-in-law or grandmother whose stock split sixty-four times. Why couldn't I sell them one of *those*?'

'Well, admit it. It was kind of like throwing darts.'

'Sure. Now they're throwing them at me.'

He thought he detected the slightest accent. What, though?

'Were you born in New York?' he asked her.

'No, Texas. I was an army brat,' she said. 'I grew up everywhere and nowhere.'

'That must have been tough.' The usual platitude one was supposed to offer at that kind of statement, he guessed.

'Well, your best friend changed identity just about every six months. On the other hand, it was kind of neat because *you* changed identity, too, if you wanted to. If you screwed up in Amarillo, they didn't have to know about it in Sarasota. You were able to start clean.'

'I can see the benefit of that,' Charles said. The man across from them was pretending to read the paper, but what he was actually doing was the very same thing the conductor had done. That is, taking every opportunity to stare at Lucinda's thighs. Charles felt a certain pride of ownership – even if ownership consisted solely of the forty-five-minute ride into Penn Station.

'Did that happen a lot?' Charles asked.

'What?'

'You screwing up?'

'Once or twice,' she said. 'I was rebelling against authority.'

'Is that what you called it?'

'No. That's what *they* called it. I called it getting lit.'

'Who's they? Your parents?'

'Yeah. And the army psychiatrist they made me go to.'

'How was that?'

'Have you ever *met* an army psychiatrist?'

'General incompetence? Major malpractice? No.'

She laughed. 'See, I told you you were funny,' she said.

Yes, an absolute laugh riot. 'Maybe you wouldn't mind calling my clients up and telling them that.'

'Sure. How *are* things at the office?'

'Fine.'

'You said you were in what . . . advertising?'

'Yes. Advertising.'

'So? How is the ad biz these days?'

'It has its good days and bad days.'

'And . . . ?'

'*And . . . ?*'

'These are the bad days?'

'Well, no one's threatening to kill me.' No, just to demote him into insignificance.

'Come on, I complain about my job – you complain about yours. Fair's fair . . .'

And so, what the hell. He did tell her.

Initially not intending to reveal much more than that he'd had a little trouble with a client, but once he started he found himself more or less unable to stop. Listening to himself spill out the details of office *Sturm und Drang* with genuine amazement at his utter lack of control. Seething Ellen Weischler. Backstabbing Eliot. The unfairness of it all.

He supposed she could have stopped him at any point. She could have said enough, or do you really want to be telling me this, or even begun to laugh at him.

She did none of those things, though. She listened. And when he finished, she said:

'And they think brokers suck.'

'I don't know what made me tell you that,' he said. 'Sorry.' Although he wasn't, actually. Embarrassed? Sure. But at the same time *purged*. As if he'd finally thrown up last night's rancid meal and could finally get back to the table.

And then she did more than just listen to him. She reached out and massaged his right shoulder. More like a soft, soothing pat, a friendly rub, a supportive and sisterly squeeze.

'Poor baby,' she said.

And Charles couldn't help thinking that certain clichés are belittled out of nothing but jealousy. *Her touch felt electric,* for instance. A cliché knocked as pure hokum by people unlucky enough not to be feeling it. Which, at any given moment, was *most* people. Because, well, her touch *did* feel electric; his body was suddenly humming like one of those power lines they string across the dry Kansas plains.

They blew into the East River Tunnel – *the tunnel of love,* he thought – and for just a moment he was afraid he was going to lean over and do something stupid. That he'd end up being taken away in handcuffs for this stupid thing on the platform at Penn Station.

Then something happened.

The train car went pitch black, the lights zapping off as they always did when the train burrowed under the East River. It felt as if he were sitting in a darkened movie theater waiting for that phosphorescent glow to come rescue him. Or for something else to rescue him; he could smell her there in the darkness. Lilac and musk.

And then her breath was by his ear, soft and humid. Her mouth was close enough to kiss as it whispered something into his ear.

Then the lights blinked on, blinked off, and settled back into full ghostly fluorescence.

Nothing had really changed.

The unrepentant voyeur sitting directly across from them was still peeking at Lucinda's thighs. The woman with varicose-veined legs was dozing across the aisle from them. There was the pinch-faced banker, the college kid slumped over his textbook, the court stenographer warily guarding her Teletype.

Lucinda also looked just like she had before, turned face forward like everyone else.

Wasn't she turning back to her newspaper, checking the Amex and the Nasdaq and the overseas indexes and municipal bonds?

He waited a while to see if she'd look over and resume speaking with him, then looked out the window, where they passed a massive billboard that said, 'Lose Yourself in the Virgin Islands.'

When the train settled into Penn Station, he asked her if they might have lunch sometime.

You're the sexiest man I've ever met.
That's what Lucinda whispered to him on the train.

Seven

'Okay,' Winston said, 'okay. Seven players who hit forty or more home runs with eleven letters in their last name.'

'Yastrzemski,' Charles answered, immediately going for the local boy made good, the BoSox star who'd been raised on a Long Island potato farm.

'Okay,' Winston said. 'That's one.'

Winston Boyko. Mailroom employee. Baseball fan. General raconteur.

He'd been stepping into Charles's office ever since he'd spied Charles in his faded Yankees T-shirt.

Charles had asked him if he wanted anything, and he'd said, *Yes, the starting lineup of the 1978 Yankees, including DH.*

Charles had gotten every one with the exception of Jim Spencer – first baseman – and that, more or less, had started a friendship. Of sorts.

Charles couldn't tell you where Winston lived or what his middle name was, or even if he had a girlfriend or wife. It was a let's-talk-baseball-trivia kind of friendship, a relationship conducted in the ten minutes a day Winston delivered the mail – once in the morning, once in the afternoon.

Right now, it was morning and Winston was grinning because Charles was having trouble coming up with any additions to the great Yaz.

Killebrew – sorry, nine letters.

Petrocelli – good guess, only ten.

'How about you give me till this afternoon?' Charles asked.

'You mean so you can look it up on-line and then pretend you didn't?'

'Yes.'

'Okay,' Winston said. 'Sure.'

Winston wasn't your average mailroom employee. For one thing, he was white. For another thing, he was easily smart enough to be writing copy.

Charles had wondered on more than one occasion why he'd ended up delivering office mail – but he'd never asked him. They weren't that kind of buddies.

On the other hand, you never knew. Wasn't Winston looking at him with a hint of genuine concern?

'You okay, chief?' he asked him.

'Sure. I'm fine.'

Only he wasn't fine. He'd been handed a pain reliever account from Eliot, his boss and betrayer. By note, too – 'Till

41

something better comes along,' he'd written at the bottom of the page. Only when was *that* going to be?

And he was thinking about what he was going to be doing for lunch today. Who he'd be having lunch *with*. The woman with the luminous eyes.

And Charles thought: *I have never cheated on Deanna. Not once.*

Not that he hadn't been tempted here and there. Sorely tempted, sometimes experiencing actual physical symptoms not unlike the warning signs of a heart attack – a faint sweat, a dull ache in the chest, a slight nausea. It's just that whenever he contemplated going further, he experienced the very same symptoms.

Only worse.

The problem was that he looked at infidelity pretty much the way he imagined Deanna did – not as a fling, but as a *betrayal*. And betrayal was the kind of word he associated with Benedict Arnold and the 1919 Black Sox. The kind of act that gets you either banned or executed. Besides, he was sure that he loved his wife. That he loved at least the constant unalterable presence of her.

Then again, this was before life betrayed *him*. Before he started dreaming about life in a more Charles-friendly universe.

'You look kind of sick,' Winston said. 'I'm worried it might be contagious.'

'It's not.' You couldn't *catch* what he had, could you?

'That's what Dick Lembergh said.'

'Dick Lembergh? Who's that?'

'Nobody *now*. He's dead.'

'Thank you. That's comforting,' Charles said.

'I'll give you a hint,' Winston said.

'A *hint*?'

'About the other six players. Three of them were American Leaguers.'

'Why didn't you say three of them were National Leaguers?'

'Hey, you're *good*.'

Winston might not have a blue-collar mind, but he had a workingman's body. That is, he looked like he could beat you up if he ever felt like it. He had a tattoo on his upper arm – *AB*, it said.

A mistake I made, he'd once told Charles.

Getting the tattoo?

Nah. Dating that girl – Amanda Barnes. I like the tat.

'By the way,' he said now, straightening up to leave, 'I'm not a hundred percent sure if it's seven players with eleven letters in their last names or eleven players with seven letters in their last names. A guy told it to me in a bar around two in the morning, so it's anybody's guess.'

They met at an Italian restaurant on 56th and Eighth where it was reputed that Frank Sinatra used to eat on occasion.

Lucinda was dressed for success – if success was making Charles's eyes water with adoration and arousal. A silk V-neck blouse that didn't hang, drape, or cover – it *clung*.

43

Of course, it could have simply been nerves he was feeling. It was like having lunch with a supplier, neither one exactly sure what to expect.

So Charles asked her what any friendly business acquaintance might ask another. What her husband did.

'Play golf,' said Lucinda of the lovely eyes.

'For a living?'

'I hope not.'

'How long have you been . . . ?'

'Married? Long enough to have to think about it. And you?'

'Eighteen years,' Charles said. He didn't have to think about it – didn't particularly want to think about it, either. On the other hand, wasn't talking about their spouses a sign that nothing untoward was going on here, that everything was pretty much innocent?

'Eighteen years ago I was in grade school,' Lucinda said.

He'd wondered how old she was – around thirty, he guessed.

'So,' Lucinda asked him, 'any new backstabbings to report?'

'Well, I have a new account.'

'Yes?'

'An aspirin. Recommended by doctors two to one over other aspirins.'

'That's great.'

'Except doctors don't recommend aspirin anymore. But if they did . . .'

44

'So what are you going to . . . ?'

'I don't know. It's a headache.'

Lucinda laughed. Lucinda had thin wrists and tapered fingers that she used to brush her thick dark hair out of her eyes – *one* eye, actually. He thought of Veronica Lake in *This Gun for Hire*.

'How did you get into . . . ?'

'Advertising? Nobody knows how they get into advertising. It's a mystery. Suddenly, you just are.'

'Kind of like marriage, huh?'

'Marriage? I don't follow.'

'Well, believe it or not, I can't remember actually *wanting* to get married. I don't even remember saying *yes*. I must've, though.'

She twisted her diamond ring as if to make sure it was actually there – that she was, in fact, married. Maybe it was Charles's charm that was making her forget?

'Your husband. Did you meet him in Texas?' Charles asked.

'No. I smoked pot in Texas. And hung out in backseats.'

'Oh, right – I forgot – you were a juvenile delinquent.'

'They call it *hell-raiser* in Amarillo. How about the teenage Charles? What was he like?'

'Oh. I was a heck-raiser, I guess.' The teenage Charles read a lot of books and handed in every homework assignment and term paper on time.

'Oh, right – you were the guy we made fun of.'

'Yeah. That's me.'

*

Charles was basking in the afterglow of lunch.

Unfortunately, he was also staring at a file that said 'Account Review' on the cover.

The thing about being given a pain reliever account was that you didn't necessarily want to accept it. Pain relievers, dishwasher detergents, deodorants. They were signposts to a kind of advertising Siberia. 'Downward Spirals This Way.' They existed in a place where no one much noticed what you did, save the clients themselves. And they made you test, retest, and test some more, even though odds were good you'd still end up with a housewife holding the product up to camera and telling you how it changed her life.

In addition to inheriting the account, he inherited a commercial that seemed to be well into the preproduction process. That is, it had already been tested, retested, and tested again and then sent off to three production houses for bids. One of them – Headquarters Productions, Charles noticed – had been recommended by the agency. He knew their rep – Tom Mooney, old style and annoying, a Fuller Brush man with reels.

The account executive on his new account, Mary Widger, had sent him the TV board for his perusal. As it turned out, it wasn't a housewife holding the pain reliever up to camera and telling the world how it changed her life. It was a housewife holding the pain reliever up to camera and telling her husband instead.

He called David Frankel, an agency producer he'd never worked with before, since David worked on the kinds of commercials he'd be doing from now on but hadn't up till now.

'Yeah,' Frankel answered the phone. 'Who's this?'

'Charles Schine.'

'Oh. Charles Schine.'

'I think we're going to be working together.'

'It's about time,' David said. Charles wondered if he was expressing friendliness or simply satisfaction at Charles's demotion into the land of analgesics.

He'd pick friendliness.

It was the agency producer's job to bid out the board, work the numbers to everyone's satisfaction, then go off and shoot it with you.

'This job seems a little high,' Charles said. He was referring to the bid price penciled in at the bottom of the page – already forwarded to the client for approval after factoring in editing, music, and all the other post-production costs. Plus agency commission.

Nine hundred and twenty-five thousand dollars for a two-day shoot.

'They always pay that,' David said.

'Okay. It just seems a little high for two actors and an aspirin bottle.'

'Well, that's the price,' he said flatly.

'Fine.' It wasn't as though money were something Charles was supposed to concern himself with – only if the clients themselves were concerned about it. And according to David, they weren't.

But it did seem high.

'Why don't we get together next week and go over everything,' Charles said.

'I count the minutes,' David said.

Charles guessed friendliness wasn't what David had been expressing after all.

Their second lunch date was still more *lunch* than date. Still just two people who found each other interesting, if unavailable.

When dessert arrived – two biscotti with cappuccinos – she said: 'You never mention your daughter. What's she like?'

'Normal,' Charles said.

'Normal?'

'Yeah. Normal.'

'That's it? I've heard gushing parents before . . .'

'Rude. Moody. Generally embarrassed I'm her father. *Normal.*'

Of course he hadn't told her *why* his daughter was rude and moody a lot of the time.

But she was looking at him with an expression that looked kind of reproachful, so he did.

'She's sick.'

'Oh.'

'Juvenile diabetes. And no, you don't just take insulin and everything's okay. Not this time.'

'Sorry,' she said.

'So am I.'

Lucinda was a first-class listener.

He realized this about ten minutes into his mostly uninterrupted monologue about just *how* sorry he was. How eight years ago he and Deanna had brought this normal little girl into the ER and left with someone else. A kid he had to give shots to twice a day and monitor closely so she wouldn't dive into hypoglycemic shock. A kid for whom he had to go buy special insulin made from pig cells because it was the only one she'd really respond to, but whose general condition was in free fall anyway. A kid like that.

His kid.

She listened with empathy and concern. She shook her head, she sighed, she politely asked him questions when she didn't understand something. *Pig insulin – why was that?*

He answered her as best he could, and when he finally finished spilling his guts, she resisted feeding him even one moronic platitude. He appreciated that.

'I don't know how you manage,' she said, 'I really don't. How's Anna dealing with it?'

'Fine. She's renting herself out as a pin cushion.'

One of the ways *he* was dealing with it, of course, was this way. The lame joke, the stale bon mot, laughing in the face of disaster.

'How's that working out for you?' Lucinda asked him after he mentioned *needling* Anna about taking her pig's insulin on time.

'How's what working out?' Charles said. Playing dumb.

'Nothing,' Lucinda said. 'Never mind.'

*

49

What do you talk about when you can't talk about the future?

You talk about the past.

Sentences begin with 'Remember when . . .' or 'I passed Anna's old nursery school today . . .' or 'I was thinking about that vacation we took in Vermont . . .'

After he and Deanna spent dinner reminiscing about the heatless ski shack in Stowe where Anna's milk bottle had frozen solid, after they finished eating and stacked the dishes and Charles went upstairs and checked Anna's feet, which she only grudgingly displayed for him, they both ended up in bed with the TV on.

Then somehow, her hand ended up touching his. His leg sidled up to her leg. It was as if their limbs were doing it on their own, their bodies finally saying, *Enough of this, I'm cold. I'm lonely.*

Charles got up and locked the door. Not a word about what they were doing. He slid back into bed and embraced her, heart colliding with his ribs, kissing her and thinking how he'd really and truly missed this.

Only somewhere in the middle of becoming lovers again they became strangers. It was odd how that happened. As he was moving on top of her and beginning to enter her, his mouth searching for hers – a sudden awkwardness to their motions. They were like two jigsaw pieces refusing to match – turn them this way and that way, and they still wouldn't fit. She pushed against his chest, he fell out of her, he went to kiss her, she turned her head the wrong way. She smiled in encouragement, he moved back into her, she froze, he shrank and slunk away.

They untangled slowly and drifted to opposite sides of the bed. Neither of them said good night.

Eight

How did they get from lunch hour to the cocktail hour?

From tuna Niçoise and biscotti to cosmopolitans and salted nuts?

Lunch, after all, was something you did with a friend. Drinks was something you did with a good friend. Lunch involved a call to Lucinda, but drinks required a call to Deanna. An explanation for his lateness. It required *lying*.

And he was as bad a liar as he was a joke teller.

Then again, practice makes perfect.

'I'm working late tonight,' he told Deanna over the phone on the afternoon of their first night-time date.

'I'm working late *again*,' he told her the next time.

And the time after that.

Slowly becoming aware that life was changing for him. That he was spending most of his time more or less waiting for the *next* time he'd see Lucinda.

Temple Bar.

Keats.

Houlihan's. Where both of them finally had to acknowledge where this was heading.

Maybe it was the drinks. He'd decided to forgo his usual Cabernet and had opted for a margarita instead. Or two. At a bar where they didn't skimp on the tequila.

By his second drink, he was seeing things. Or not seeing things. For instance, the rest of the bar patrons had faded away, leaving only Lucinda.

'I think you're trying to get me drunk,' she said.

'No. I'm trying to get you drunk*er*.'

'Oh right. I forgot. I'm already wasted.'

'You look beautiful wasted,' he said.

'That's because *you're* wasted.'

'Oh yeah.'

She did look beautiful – glassy eyes had nothing to do with it. Dressed tonight in something ridiculously short and impossibly snug, stretched *this* tight over her glossy nylon thighs.

'What did you tell your wife?' she asked him.

'I told her I was having drinks with a beautiful woman I met on the Long Island Rail Road.'

'Ha,' she said.

'What did you tell your husband?'

'Same thing. That I was having drinks with a beautiful woman I met on the Long Island Rail Road.' She laughed, holding her pink cosmopolitan away from her body so it wouldn't spill on her.

Her husband. Stolid, dependable, nearly twenty years older than her, and poisonously boring, she'd complained to him. Passionate only about golf these days.

'You know . . .' he said. 'You know . . .'

'What?'

'I forget.' He was going to say something that he had the vague notion he was going to regret later, but he'd lost it when she turned to look at him with those soft green eyes. If jealousy was the *green-eyed monster,* what was love? The green-eyed angel?

'What are we doing, Charles?' she said, looking kind of solemn now. Maybe she was about to say something she was going to regret, too.

'We're having a drink.'

'I meant what are we doing after we have a drink?'

'Having another drink?'

'After that.'

He was thinking of a possible answer for that one, but suddenly there *was* someone else in the bar; they *weren't* the only two people left in the world. A man of uncertain age had pushed himself between them to get the bartender's attention.

Only his attention went elsewhere – as soon as he got a look at Lucinda's legs, that is.

'May I buy you a drink?' he said to her.

'No,' she said, showing the cosmo still in her hand.

'Okay. May I buy you the bar?'

'Sure, go ahead.'

54

'Excuse me,' Charles said; the man was nearly standing on his shoes.

'I don't want to buy *you* a drink,' the man said.

'That's funny. It is. Only I was talking to the woman here.'

'So was I.'

Charles couldn't tell whether the man was being funny or just being himself, which could be anything from rude to homicidal. It was hard to tell these days.

'You know, actually, he *was* talking to me,' Lucinda said to the man. 'So . . .'

'A needle pulling thread.'

'All right, *we*'ll leave,' she said.

'Oh, *stay*,' he said.

'Excuse me,' Lucinda said, getting up from her bar stool and trying to push past him.

'Something I said?'

'*Excuse* me.'

'Great. The cunt's leaving,' he said.

Charles hit him.

As far as he knew, he'd never hit anyone before; he was surprised that hitting someone was just as painful as being hit. He was also surprised that the man actually went down, with genuine blood on his lip.

'He said something very rude to me,' Lucinda explained to several waiters who'd suddenly materialized and stepped between them.

A flushed-looking man came rushing up from the nether regions of the restaurant – the manager, Charles guessed.

'Maybe you should all leave,' he said after ascertaining what had transpired. It wasn't difficult – the man Charles had punched to the floor was still in the process of getting up, and Charles was still rubbing the hand that punched him.

'Sure,' Charles said. 'Why not.'

He retrieved Lucinda's coat from the cloakroom, aware that all eyes were on him, though the only eyes he cared about were green and widened with gratitude.

Well, weren't they? Hadn't he just kicked sand on the bully, rescued the maiden, defended her honor?

It was blustery outside, cold enough to turn his breath to vapor.

'Get a cab to Penn?' she asked, her eyes tearing up from the chill – or was it from the emotion of the moment? From the exhibition of his *prowess*?

'Forget the train,' he said. 'I'll call a car. I'll get a car and drop you home.'

'You sure?'

'Yes.'

'Maybe that's not a good idea.'

'Why's that?'

'I don't know. Someone may see us.' The first open acknowledgment of illicit doings.

'Someone might see us on the train, too.'

'That's the train. Strangers sit on trains. It's different.'

'Okay. Whatever you want.' His arm was on her arm – he hadn't realized he'd put it there, but he had, and he could feel her body heat beneath the coat. Like the fever beneath a chill.

'I just don't think the car's a good idea.'

'Okay.'

'I might do something I shouldn't do.'

'Like pass out?' He was trying to be funny again – emphasis on *trying* – but maybe it wasn't the time to be funny, because he could almost swear she was leaning in toward him, that she'd somehow gotten closer than she'd been before.

'Like maybe *eat* you,' she said.

'That settles it,' he said. 'I'm getting the car.'

She kissed him.

But kissing doesn't quite do it justice. It wasn't kissing as much as mouth-to-mouth resuscitation, because he felt himself coming back from the dead.

When they pulled apart, and they didn't do that for what seemed like a day and a half, they both caught their breath as if just beached from the sea.

'Uh-oh,' she said.

His sentiments exactly. Or maybe just *oh*. An exclamation of wonderment and unbridled joy – okay, not *totally* unbridled, since there were just a few complications lurking around somewhere.

Yet those complications – which had names and faces and legitimate claims to his love and loyalty – suddenly seemed to recede like the bar patrons from moments ago and fade away into a peripheral world.

In the car ride home they snuggled in the backseat, *snuggling* the kind of word you generally stop using past a certain age. It felt both warmly familiar and achingly new.

They kissed again, too. And he kissed not just lips, but several parts of her, the nape of her neck, the faint scar on the inside of her arm – *playground accident* – her dark, downy eyebrows. One eye on the driver, who now and then would glance in his rearview mirror, the other eye on each other, and he'd have to say that each other looked pretty good. Flushed faces – hers for sure, and he could also feel the heat on his own, though *it wasn't the heat, it was the humidity.* As if they were enveloped in a swollen raincloud ready to drench them to the bone and him all ready to dance through the puddles afterward like Gene Kelly.

When they lip-locked over Van Cortland Avenue, when they squeezed hands past the shadow of Shea, when they nuzzled on the exit ramp to the Grand Central Parkway – he was willing to wager that no one had felt exactly like this before, even though he knew it was a lie. The number one sin of the hopeless addict: denial. And he *was* addicted, wasn't he? It seemed as if he couldn't go two exits without kissing her. That he couldn't make it through three songs on the radio – 101.6 FM, Music to Make Out By – without running his hands up and down her body.

'Slow down,' she said once they made it off Exit 8E of the Meadowbrook Parkway – no meadow, no brook, just parkway. She was saying it to the driver, but she might as well have been talking to him, because if he didn't slow down, it was possible that he would overheat – one of those unfortunate victims you see littering the highway on their way to somewhere important.

'I don't want you to drop me in front of the house,' she said. 'My husband's home.'

'Where is your house?'

'A few blocks up. Over here is fine.'

They stopped at the corner of Euclid Avenue – the name of a tree that no longer exists on Long Island.

And Lucinda said: 'Meet me on the train tomorrow.'

Nine

It was called the Fairfax Hotel. The kind of hotel that had fallen into disrepair and anonymity. The kind of hotel most people would choose to bypass for something better.

But not Charles, and not now.

He was on his way there to spend the morning with Lucinda.

He'd finally screwed up the courage to ask.

They'd had two more dinners and two more car rides where they'd made out like overly hormonal high school kids. They'd kissed and petted and snuggled, and now it was time to *take the relationship further.* He'd actually used those words. Surprised they'd actually made it out of his mouth and eternally grateful she hadn't laughed at him. Even more grateful for her response, which after several moments of silence had been: *Sure, why not.*

He'd asked her this over two cups of coffee in Penn Station, and then they'd walked out onto Seventh Avenue arm in arm and shared a taxi, even though he'd be going approximately seventy blocks out of his way to drop her off – but then that was seventy more blocks of her company – embracing and clinging to this new idea of them. And she'd said, *Where?* Good question, too. Where exactly were they going to consummate things? And they'd passed one hotel in the taxi – *No*, she said, *too close to Penn*; and then another – *too stuffy looking*; and then one more when they'd made it all the way downtown.

The Fairfax Hotel.

Flanked by a Korean deli on one side and a woman's health center on the other. Kind of dingy, yes, but wasn't that the kind of hotel made for these things?

And she'd said, *Fine, yes, that one looks fine.*

And they'd made a date.

The train ride into Penn Station.

Both of them were surprisingly quiet, he thought, like boxers before the biggest bout of their lives.

He spent most of the time counting the minutes between stations: Merrick to Freeport to Baldwin to Rockville Centre. Under the darkness of the East River, she grabbed for his hand and locked fingers. They felt ice cold, as if all the blood had rushed out of them, frozen with . . . what? Guilt? Shame? Fear?

There was something nonspontaneous about all of this. Before, they'd been sort of fumbling around in the dark,

61

but now it was all coolly premeditated. On the walk to the taxi stand, she leaned against him not so much from desire as from inertia, he thought. As if he were dragging her there – lugging dead weight up the escalator and through the entranceway.

He understood. It was one thing to make out in a car and another thing to check into a hotel with the intention of having sex.

The inside of the Fairfax Hotel looked pretty much the way the outside looked – shabby and faded and just this side of destitute. The lobby smelled of camphor.

When they walked up to the desk, he could feel Lucinda's white-knuckled grip somewhere up by his throat. He told the deskman that he'd be paying in cash and was given a key to room 1207.

They rode the elevator up in silence.

When the doors opened on twelve, he said, 'Ladies first.'

And Lucinda said, 'Age before beauty.'

So they walked out together. The floor was in need of a few more light bulbs, he thought, since the only light seemed to be coming from a half-draped window to the left of the elevator. The carpet smelled of mildew and tobacco.

Room 1207 was way down at the end of the hall where it was darkest, and Charles needed to squint just to make out the numbers on the door.

This is what they got for ninety-five dollars in New York City: a room smelling of disinfectant, with one queen-size bed, one lopsided table lamp, and one table, all pretty much within two feet of one another.

A room that was virtually equatorial – with no discernible thermostat to help.

There was a white paper sash encircling the toilet lid. Charles did the honors; he had to go the moment he entered the room. Nerves.

When he came out of the bathroom, Lucinda was sitting on the bed, playing with the TV clicker. Nothing was actually appearing on the TV screen.

'I think you have to pay extra,' she said.

'Do you want to . . . ?'

'No.'

There was an awkward politeness to their mannerisms, he thought, as if they were a couple on a blind date. Jitters masked as solicitude.

'Why don't you sit down, Charles?' she said.

'Fine.' He sat in the chair.

'I meant *here*.'

'Oh. Right.' He slipped off his coat and hung it up in the closet next to hers. Then he walked over to the bed – a very short walk given the dimensions of the room – and sat down.

I shouldn't be here. I should get up and leave. I should . . .

But she laid her head on his shoulder and said: 'So. We're here.'

'Yes.' He was sweating right through his shirt.

'Okay.' She sighed. 'Do you want to stay, or do you want to go?'

'Yes.'

'*Yes?* Which is it?'

'Stay. Or go. What do *you* want to do?'

'Fuck you,' she said. 'I think I want to fuck you.'

It happened when they were ready to leave.

They'd dressed quietly, and Charles had searched the room to make sure they hadn't left anything.

Then they'd walked to the door.

He opened it to usher her out. She moved past him, and he could smell the perfume she'd just dabbed on in the bathroom. Then he smelled something else.

There were two of them standing there – Lucinda and him, and then suddenly there were three.

He was knocked backward onto the floor.

He was kicked in the ribs, then kicked in the stomach as the air was forced out of him. Lucinda was thrown on top of him, then not on top of him, then she was lying there beside him.

The door slammed. The lock turned.

There were two of them, and then there were three.

'Make one fucking sound and I'll blow your heads off,' the one who wasn't either Lucinda or himself said.

A man with a gun – Charles could see him, could see the gun, too, something stunted looking and oily black. He was panting, as if he'd just run a long distance to get there.

'I'll give you all my money,' Charles said. 'You can have it.'

'What?' The man was black but Hispanic, Charles thought, a kind of accent, anyway. 'What the fuck d'you say?'

'My money – it's yours.'

'I told you to shut the fuck up.' He kicked him again, not in the ribs this time, but lower down. Charles groaned.

'Please,' Lucinda said in a trembling little girl's voice, a voice that didn't seem capable of coming out of a grown woman. 'Please . . . don't hurt us . . .'

'Don't hurt us,' the man said, mimicking her, taking pleasure in making fun. Of her fear. That little-girl voice . . . like she was going to cry or something. 'Oh, I ain't gonna hurt you, baby . . . uh-uh . . . Now throw me your fucking wallets.'

Charles reached for his pocket, through the folds of his down jacket saturated with sweat – reached in and grabbed his wallet with a shaking hand.

This only happens in movies. This only happens on the front pages. This only happens to someone else.

He threw his wallet to the man with the gun. Lucinda was fumbling inside her pocketbook, looking for hers, the one with the picture of a five-year-old girl on a swing somewhere in the country. Somewhere other than here – the threadbare floor of room 1207 in the Fairfax Hotel.

By the time she threw him her wallet, he was already looking through Charles's, pulling the cash out of it – quite a bit of cash, too, the cash Charles was going to use to pay for the room. But after the man took the cash, he kept looking at the wallet – grinning at something.

'Well, look at this,' he said.

He was looking at Charles's pictures – Anna and Deanna and him. The Schine family.

'Funny,' he said. 'That don't look like you . . .' talking to Lucinda. 'That sure as *shit* don't look like you.'

Back to Charles. 'That don't look anything like her, *Charles*.' Smirking at them.

Then, looking through her wallet and finding a picture of *hers*. 'Ain't that something,' he said. '*This* guy don't look like you, Charles. Uh-uh. This guy *ain't* you, Charles.'

He snorted, laughed, giggled; he'd figured something out.

'Let's see here. Know what I think? Hey' – he kicked Charles again, not as hard this time, but hard enough – 'I *said*, Know what I think?'

Charles said, 'What?'

'*What?* What? I think you guys are fucking around with each other. Stepping out on the old lady, huh, *Charles*? Getting some *strange*, my man. That what you doing, *Charles*?'

Charles said, 'Please, just take my money.'

'*Just take your money?* Just take your money? Thanks, but I already took your fucking money. See' – holding the cash out to him – 'this is your money. I *got* your fucking money.'

'Yes,' Charles said. 'I see. I promise we won't go to the police.'

'You promise, huh? That's fucking nice of you, that's real fucking *kind* of you, Charles. I can take your word on that, huh? You won't go to the police. Well then . . .'

He waved the gun around in little looping circles, first toward him, then her, then back again. Inky black, snub-nosed barrel . . .

'Well then . . . if you ain't gonna go to the police and all . . .'

Lucinda was trembling beside him, shaking like a wet stray.

'Hey, baby,' the man said. 'Hey, *baby* . . .'

'Please . . .' Lucinda said.

'How is she, *Charles*? Better than the old lady, I bet. Nice pussy, Charles? Nice *tight* pussy?'

Charles started to get up. He was back in the bar and the man was insulting her, and Charles would have to set him straight, to show him what's what. Except the man pistol-whipped him across the face and Charles went flying back again. Hearing a crack before feeling the pain – first one and then the other, first the sound of his nose being broken, then the nauseating *pain* of his nose being broken. And the blood starting to seep out on the floor.

'What was that, my man? I didn't hear you, *Charles*. What'd you say? You said you can fuck her if you want? Why, thank you, Charles. That's fucking kind of you. Letting me have your bitch and all.'

'No,' Lucinda moaned. 'No . . .'

'*No?* Didn't you hear him say that I could fuck you, *Lucinda*.' It was the first time he'd said her name – in a way, it seemed every bit as horrible as kicking them to the floor and stealing their wallets. 'That's what the man said. You giving it to him – you can give it to me. Whore's a whore, *baby*. Am I right, Charles? Am I?'

Charles was choking on his own blood. It was pouring down his throat and clogging his windpipe – he was drowning in it, sputtering for air.

'Sit up here, Charles.' The man pulled him up, led him over to the lone chair, which had fluff seeping out of a ripped cushion decorated with a faded floral design. He sat him down on it. 'Feeling better there, Charles? Take a deep breath. That's right – in, out. You'll want a good seat for this, Charles. *Championship* fucking, my man. Twelve rounder. You don't want to miss this.'

Lucinda ran.

She'd caught him by surprise – the man with the gun, lying there trembling like that, and then suddenly springing up and making a run for it. She made it all the way to the door.

She even turned the knob and got it half-open before he reached her and pulled her back in. By her hair. That dark, silky hair that tasted of shampoo and sweat, so soft you could comb it by hand – twisted in his fist as she screamed.

'You want to shut the fuck up, *Lucinda*.' He'd put the barrel into her mouth, straight in, knocking it up against her teeth. Lucinda stopped screaming.

Charles was still wheezing through his own blood, dizzy enough to pass out, a white light searing the bridge of his nose. Watching as the man laid Lucinda onto the floor as if they were engaged in some eerie kind of dance, some modern pas de deux, laying her down and standing over her. As he pulled her skirt up above her waist. As he snorted and wolf whistled and slowly, slowly pulled her black lace panties down to her knees.

As he unzipped his pants.

Ten

He passed out, more than once he passed out, but each time the man brought him back, slapping water onto his face, whispering into his ear.

Don't fade on me, my man. Round two . . . baby. Round three . . . four . . .

It was like bad porno . . . the kind you don't really want to see, but your friend just happens to have it, so you watch. Even as you pull your eyes away, you watch. The woman with the dog, the scat tape where she swallows it all – sickening, really, can't believe she's really doing that, but she is, and you're watching it. Your stomach churning, your guts heaving, makes you want to throw up, but you have to look at it. Don't know why, but you do.

Him and Lucinda. Beautiful naked Lucinda and him.

And she was beautiful. As he placed her on hands and

knees and put it into her ass. Telling Charles what he was doing, too – keeping up a kind of running commentary . . .

See, Charles – they love it in the ass. They tell you they don't, but all whores do.

Telling her to moan for him. Putting the gun up by her head as he rode her and *making* her moan. Moans of pain, probably, but they sounded like moans of pleasure. Moans were moans. Hard to tell which were which, except for the fact that her eyes were squeezed shut, her mascara streaked and running, and she was biting into her lip until it bled.

And Charles watching, sitting there in the chair as if he were tied down, even though he wasn't tied down.

See this, Charles – a born cocksucker . . . That's right, baby . . . suck that big daddy dick . . .

The tableau changed, no longer fucking her in the ass, but standing in front of her, hands cradling her face, that beautiful Lucinda face. And Lucinda choking, gurgling, the sounds spurring him on . . . *Oh yes . . . oh yes . . . you watching this, Charles, Charley . . . don't want to miss the cum shot . . . gotta see the money shot . . . oh yes . . .*

And later, Lucinda lying there – how much later? Charles didn't know, later that morning, later that afternoon. Lucinda lying there covered with sweat and cum, hardly moving. Was she dead? No, she was still breathing, if only barely. Charles looked down at the dried blood on his hands and wondered whose it was, forgetting that it was his, that his nose must be broken.

And now the man was rubbing himself, naked except for his sweat socks and sneakers, staring at Lucinda on the floor and jerking himself. For another round. Round . . . *what*? Five, six?

'Still with us, *Charles*?' the man said. 'Hang in there, bud. More to come . . .'

And there was.

The man taking her again, propping her up against the bed as if she were a marionette, all loose arms and legs, twisting her into his vision of lewd. Legs up by her ears, hands spreading herself – giggling at this. Taking his time, placing her just right, an inch here, an inch there. Lucinda slack jawed, just a prop, a blowup doll.

And Charles decided to give it one more shot – not *him* deciding, his *machismo* deciding, his reptilian cortex, maybe – pushing him up off the chair in the general direction of the man who was about to rape Lucinda for the fifth or sixth time.

The first thing was – he was dizzy. It was blindman's buff and he'd been spun around the room like a top and couldn't tell which way was which. He staggered, he teetered, he wobbled – the man not even aware of him yet because he was still positioning Lucinda and had maybe forgotten that Charles was even in the room. So Charles eventually righted himself and actually made it all the way over to him. He grabbed the man from behind, around the neck, and squeezed.

He squeezed for all he was worth, he squeezed like there was no tomorrow, a virtual *death grip* of steel. But the man calmly, almost lazily, stood up and sloughed Charles off him as if he were dumping garbage onto the sidewalk. Charles ended up splay-legged on the floor, wondering what happened, as the man grinned and shook his head.

'Charles . . . Charles . . . what the fuck's the matter with you? Giving you the show of a lifetime. *Championship* fucking – you've never seen fucking like this. And this is the thanks I get. *Shit.* I ought to kick your ass, Charles. I ought to kick the *shit* out of you.'

Charles mumbled something back at him. *What* did he say? He didn't know . . .

'Okay, *Charles.* Let's calm down. Let me count to ten. You just wanted some for yourself, that it? Watching the *fuck machine* got you hot, that it? I understand. Only not today, my man. It ain't your turn, understand?'

Lucinda was still stuck in that pornographic position, like a bored model waiting for the shutter. Only she didn't look bored as much as dead, not even turning to look at her would-be savior, who in the end had simply traded one seat for another. One in the balcony for one in the front row.

As the man – fully erect, the clumsy violence had apparently invigorated him – knelt between her white thighs, the thighs Charles had lain between not two hours before, and began again. So close to him, Charles could almost touch him, even if he couldn't hit him, even if he couldn't *stop* him.

'Oh, Charles,' he whispered, 'like velvet. Like *smooth*, fucking velvet . . .'

*

73

It took a while after the man left to *know* the man had left.

Charles heard the door slam, even saw him walk through the door before he heard the door slam, even heard the man say good-bye to them – *Hate to go, but . . .* And Charles continued to sit there on the floor as if the gun were still trained at his head. As if the man were still moaning into Lucinda's hair, that grotesque ass pumping up and down mere inches from his face.

And Lucinda, too. Still with her legs apart like something wanton, like those Amsterdam hookers who lounge in shop windows with their legs spread in an open invitation. Only their expressions not quite as horrified looking, their hair not matted to their chins with sweat and blood and dried cum.

Eventually Charles moved.

One leg at a time, tentatively, like a man testing the water. As if to prove he *could* move even if he wasn't quite willing to believe it. And then after he'd moved his legs, his arms, and then his whole body, getting up off the floor and standing, a little wobbly, but up on his own two feet again. And when he moved, so did she.

Not saying anything, nothing at all, but slowly bringing one thigh over to the other, hiding that open part of her that resembled a raw wound. And then slowly picking herself up off the floor and trudging over to the bathroom, where she went in and closed the door.

He heard the water running, heard the sound of towel rubbing skin, then what sounded like retching. A toilet flushing once, then twice.

He still hadn't cleaned himself up yet. Bloody hands, blood all over his face, too, no doubt – his nose feeling twice its normal size, as though he had a clown nose on his face. And maybe he did – maybe that was entirely appropriate. Charles the clown, getting whacked in the head and booted in the bottom while the circus master had his way with the star attraction. Who was opening the bathroom door now. Still not saying anything to him – what, after all, do you say to a clown? Still looking dazed and battered, if a little more cleaned up. Still naked, too, as if that didn't matter, as if she could never be more naked than she was fifteen minutes ago – spread open and violated, and after that, what could clothes do for you? And maybe something else – that clowns don't count, they're superfluous in the scheme of things, and it doesn't matter what they *see* if they can't act.

Are you all right? he started to say to her. He almost had the words out of his mouth until he realized how hopelessly inadequate they were. How could she be all right, how could she ever again be all right?

'I should take you to a hospital,' he said.

'No.' Her first word to him in what must have been hours.

'You should be looked at.'

'No. I've been looked at enough for one day.' Her voice sounded dead, the way bad actors sound, wooden, no real emotion there. It was scarier than screaming, more frightening than tears. If she'd cried, he'd have put his arms around her and comforted her. But there was nothing he could do for her.

She began to get dressed, slowly, one item at a time, not covering up, no coyly turning away from him like before. So Charles went into the bathroom, where he flinched at his own reflection, thinking at first that it was someone else staring back at him. It couldn't possibly be him. But this was *Charles the clown*, remember? He of the bulbous nose and red paint and fright wig.

He pressed a wet towel up against his nose, where it stung, as if he'd applied iodine. He smoothed down his hair and tried to wipe the blood away from his cheeks.

When he came back into the room, she was more or less dressed. One stocking ripped, skirt slit where it wasn't before, yet she was put back together in a reasonable facsimile of a dressed woman. The way a mannequin is a reasonable facsimile of a dressed woman – minus the thing that actually makes a woman alive.

'What do we do?' Charles asked her, not just her, but himself as well, because he didn't know.

And she said, 'Nothing.'

Nothing. It sounded so ridiculously preposterous. So blatantly ludicrous. The criminal was still at large, his victims beaten and bleeding, and what does she propose doing? Nothing.

Only the opposite of nothing is something, and he couldn't *think* of a something.

Go to the police?

Of course you go to the police. You've been robbed and raped and beaten, so you go to the police. Only . . .

What were you doing at the Fairfax Hotel?

76

Well, we were . . .

What were you doing at the Fairfax Hotel in the middle of the morning?

Well, the thing is . . .

What were the two of you doing at the Fairfax Hotel?

If I could take a minute to explain . . .

Maybe they could ask for some discretion here, maybe you were *allowed* to ask for a little discretion, and the police detective would wink at them and say, *I understand.* That he'd be sure to keep this just between them, no need to worry. Only . . .

There was a criminal here, and sometimes criminals get caught – you report them to the police, and sometimes the police actually apprehend them and bring them to court. And then there are trials, public forums that make the front pages, where witnesses have to get up and say, *He did it, Your Honor.* Those witnesses being him. Him and Lucinda.

And what were you doing at the Fairfax Hotel?

Well, we were . . .

What were you doing at the Fairfax Hotel in the middle of the morning?

Well, the thing is . . .

Just answer the question.

What do we do? *That* was the question.

Nothing. Maybe not as ludicrous as it first appeared. Maybe *not* so ridiculous.

Yet was it possible that they could just ignore what had happened to them? That she could just forget about it, like

77

rude comment or a vulgar gesture? Go to sleep and wake up and *poof* – gone.

Lucinda said, 'I'm going.'

'Where?'

'Home.'

Home. To the blond five-year-old who never met a playground swing she didn't like. To the husband with the nine handicap who might or might not notice the sudden pallor in her cheeks, the bit lip and shell-shocked disposition.

'I'm sorry, Lucinda,' he said.

'Yes,' she said.

He was sorry for everything. That he'd asked her up here in the first place. That he hadn't seen the man lurking in the stairwell opposite their room. That he'd sat and watched as the man raped her again and again. That he hadn't protected her.

Lucinda trudged to the door – that amazingly elegant gait turned plodding and ungainly. She didn't look back, either. Charles thought about offering to call a car for her, but he knew she'd turn him down. He hadn't been able to provide the one thing she'd really needed him to. She'd want nothing more from him.

She opened the door, stepped through the open space, and shut it behind her.

Attica

Sorry, I have to interrupt here.
I think I should come clean.

Three things happened.

On Wednesday, a man rang our doorbell to see the house.
He'd gotten the listing from a real estate agent, he said.

My wife answered the door and told him the house wasn't
for sale. It must be some kind of mistake.

Your husband's a teacher, isn't he? he said.

Yes, she said. But it was still some sort of mistake. The
house wasn't for sale.

The man apologized and left.

He didn't look like a man who was in the market for a
house, she told me later.

Well, what did he look like? I asked her.

Like one of your students, she said.

A high school kid? I said.

No. Like one of your other students.

Then the second thing happened.

A CO called Fat Tommy informed me in the lounge that I was going to be ass out soon.

What did that mean? I asked him.

It means you're going to be ass out soon, he said.

Fat Tommy was over three hundred pounds and had been known to sit on unruly prisoners who'd been shackled face-down on the floors of their cells.

Why? I asked him.

Cutbacks. I guess somebody finally realized they've got better things to do with our taxes than teach coons to read.

I asked him if he knew when.

Nah, he said. But I wouldn't start teaching them War and Peace.

When Fat Tommy laughed, his three chins jiggled.

Then the third thing happened.

The writer penned a note on the bottom of chapter 10. At first I thought it was just part of the story, something Charles said to Lucinda or even to himself. But it wasn't. It was to me — a kind of editorial aside.

'Like the story so far?'

That's what he wrote.

The answer, by the way, was no.

I didn't.

For one thing, the story lacked suspense.

It was missing the one crucial ingredient needed to make it suspenseful.

Surprise.

Because suspense depends on not knowing what's going to happen.

But I did know what was going to happen.

I knew, for example, what would be on the other side of the door of room 1207. I knew what was going to come in when they opened that door. I knew what that man was going to do to Lucinda over and over for the next four hours.

I remembered it all from a previous life.

In this previous life, I woke up every morning wondering why I preferred to remain sleeping.

I showered and dressed and tried not to look at a blood meter sitting on the kitchen counter. I took the 8:43 to Penn Station, with the exception of one morning in November when I didn't. The morning my daughter made me late and I took the 9:05. The morning that I looked up from my paper and was asked for a ticket I didn't have.

This was my story.

I'll take over from here.

Eleven

After Lucinda left, I went to the doctor.

It was 130 blocks uptown from the Fairfax Hotel. I walked because the man had taken my wallet and all my cash in it.

I had a broken nose and a bloodstained jacket, but no one seemed to notice. There were other things to look at, I suppose – a homeless man with no clothes on, for instance. A woman on Rollerblades dressed entirely in purple. A black man shouting about something called the Sons of Jonah. My swollen nose and bloody jacket slipped right under the average city dweller's radar.

A funny thing happened as I walked. And walked and walked.

I started counting blocks but ended up counting blessings.

Because there *were* blessings. I was alive, for instance. That was blessing number one. I'd been half-sure the man was going to shoot me. So being alive was a blessing. And then there was my wife and daughter. Blessings, both of them. My *unknowing* wife, blessedly ignorant of the fact that I'd just spent the morning in room 1207 of the Fairfax Hotel with a woman other than her. Watching that woman get brutally and repeatedly raped, of course – but still.

And Anna . . . how could I have done a thing like this to *her*? I felt as if I'd been deathly sick for a long time and that my fever had finally broken. I could think clearly again.

Dr Jaffe asked me what happened.

'I fell getting out of a cab.'

'Uh-huh,' Dr Jaffe said. 'You'd be surprised how many times I hear that.'

'I'm sure.'

Dr Jaffe set my nose and gave me a sample bottle of codeine. 'If the pain gets bad,' he said.

I felt like telling him that the pain was already bad, but then I was kind of welcoming the discomfort. Like the 130 blocks of arctic air I'd just stepped out of, it grounded me.

I walked all the way to the office. I suppose I could've gone home, but I was going to make this a day like any other. A late-starting day, a day with a morning I'd rather not think about, but wasn't there a whole afternoon ahead? And another morning and afternoon after that, and so on? I was jumping back in with both feet.

When I got to the office, I trotted out the same story for anyone who asked. And everyone who saw me did. Winston, Mary Widger, and three-quarters of my creative group. The cab, the street hole, the unfortunate fall. They were all sorry for me; they all tried not to look at my nose and the two raccoonlike rings appearing under both eyes.

When I finally sat down in my office, I felt the kind of relief that comes with being back in your own environment, an environment that had been feeling a little sad and hopeless lately, but suddenly felt warm and welcoming. Life *itself* feeling warm and welcoming – richer than I'd been willing to give it credit for. There were all my *things,* for example. My very own phone and computer and couch and coffee table. And all those industry awards I'd managed to garner – gold and silver and bronze – and who could say, despite recent setbacks, that there wouldn't be more to come? And on my desk, a photograph of *us:* Deanna and Anna and me, taken somewhere on a beach in the Caribbean. My *family,* secure in the knowledge of my love. And I did love them.

But looking at that picture made me think about that *other* picture, the one in my wallet. The one the man had ogled, then polluted by holding in his hand. The one he still had with him.

'Darlene,' I called.

'Yes?' My secretary appeared at my door, wearing a look of motherly concern.

'I just realized I lost my wallet. It must've fallen out when I broke my nose.'

'Uh-oh.'

'Can you call the credit card companies for me and cancel the cards?'

'No.'

'What?'

'No. You've got to call them yourself. They'll only listen to the cardholder.'

'Oh. Right.' I probably should've known that. I probably should've known a lot of things. For instance, that shabby-looking hotels look shabby for a reason – because they *are* shabby. The kinds of places that attract lowlifes and persons with criminal intent. Persons who loiter in stairwells, waiting for persons with adulterous intent to cross their paths. I was in my forties and still learning.

I called the card companies. American Express and Visa and MasterCard. Canceling your cards is an easy thing to do these days; you just tell them your mother's maiden name – *Reston* – and poof. Your card number ceases to be. And I pictured the man standing in some store being told that his card was no good. That one, too. And this one as well. All of them no good.

Only I suddenly pictured Deanna in a store, being told the same thing. I had to call her. It was after three – she'd be home.

She picked up on the fourth ring, and when I heard her voice saying, 'Hello,' I was overcome with a kind of gratitude. Grateful to God, I suppose – assuming that there was one, assuming that he'd care enough to see that I'd made it out of the Fairfax Hotel in one piece. Minus a whole nose, maybe, minus a *lover*, sure, but other than that, reasonably intact.

'You won't believe the day I had,' I told her. And she *wouldn't* have believed it.

'What happened?'

'I broke my nose.'

'You broke your *what*?'

'My nose. I fell down getting out of a cab and broke my nose.'

'Oh, Charles . . .'

'Don't worry. It's okay, it's fine. The doctor set it and gave me enough codeine to sedate a horse. I'm feeling no pain.' That wasn't true – I *was* feeling pain, but this pain was a kind of penance and tempered by that other thing I was feeling, which was unmitigated relief.

'Oh, *Charles*. Why don't you come home?'

'I told you. I'm fine. I have a few things to do here.' Like say three hundred Hail Marys and lick my wounds.

'You sure?'

'Yes.' I was moved by the obvious empathy in her voice, the kind of empathy made possible only through years of sticking together through thick and thin. Even if we couldn't communicate it lately – even if we couldn't physically express it – it was there. It had always been there. And I nearly felt like confessing and throwing myself on the mercy of the court. But then I'd never have to, would I? Life was back where it started, before I'd looked up from my paper and noticed a white thigh and swinging black pump.

'One other thing,' I said.

'What?'

86

'I lost my wallet. When I fell out of the cab. I told you, you *wouldn't* believe the day I had.'

'A wallet's just a wallet. I'm more concerned about you.'

'I already called the credit card companies and canceled them. Just wanted you to know – you better cut them up and throw them away. They're going to send us new ones by tomorrow – at least they say they are.'

'Fine. Consider it done.'

I said good-bye, whispered, 'I love you,' and started to hang up.

'Oh, I almost forgot,' she said.

'Yes?'

'Mr Vasquez called.'

'Mr *Who*?'

'Mr Vasquez. He said he had a business lunch with you at the Fairfax Hotel. He forgot to tell you something.

'Charles . . . ?'

'Yes?'

'Why didn't he call you at the office?'

Twelve

I called Lucinda at the work number she'd given me.

Hello, this is Lucinda Harris at Morgan Stanley. I'm not here at the moment, but if you leave your name and a brief message, I'll get back to you.

So I did leave a brief message of sorts. *Help.* Not saying the actual word, of course, but then it's the thought that counts.

'I've got to talk to you,' I said. 'That . . . *person* from the hotel called me.' I tried to keep the panic out of my voice, the same way I'd tried to keep it out of my voice when Deanna had told me that *Mr Vasquez* had called. I failed both times.

Are you okay? Deanna had asked me.

It's the codeine, I'd said. *It's making me woozy.* I had wanted to say, *It's Mr Vasquez, he's making me terrified.*

Eliot came into my office to offer condolences about my nose. Maybe to try to patch things up, too – after all, we were friends, weren't we? More than co-workers, than simple boss and employee. Eliot had been my rabbi all these years – hadn't he promoted me and talked me up and provided me with more than generous raises? I'd been mistaken to blame Eliot for my dismissal from the credit card account – that had been their doing, not his. Ellen Weischler and her gang of four. Eliot was burying the hatchet and saying let's be friends again.

And I needed a friend right now.

How much do you love me? I used to ask Anna when she was very small.

From the earth to the moon, she'd answer me. And sometimes, *To infinity.*

Which might be how much I needed a friend right now. A need as infinite as it was immediate.

I felt like unburdening myself to him. *I'd like to tell you something that happened to me,* I'd say to him. *I know it's hard to believe – I know it's kind of ridiculous. I met this girl.* And Eliot would wink and nod and smile, because Eliot had met girls before, too – three marriages to prove it and number three on life support these days.

I met this girl, I'd say, *married,* and Eliot's smile would grow only wider, if that were possible, because he'd met married girls, too. *We went to a hotel together* – and here Eliot would lean in even closer, all ears, because was there anything quite as delicious as listening to a buddy give up the details, other than recounting the details yourself?

We went to a hotel together, I'd continue, *only when we got to the room, someone else came in there with us.*

And Eliot would lose that smile. Because this story took

89

a vicious left turn and ended with this someone who came into our room raping the woman and calling my house. Talking to my *wife*.

Eliot asked me if something was the matter.

'No,' I said.

'Maybe you ought to go home,' Eliot said. 'You look a little pale.'

'The nose,' I said.

'Yeah – the nose doesn't look so good.'

'No.'

'Well, go home, then.'

'Maybe I will.'

Eliot patted me on the back – friends again, after all.

So I went home.

Why did he call you at home, Charles?

To prove that he could, Deanna.

I took money out of petty cash to pay for the train ride – the scene of the crime. The crime of coveting – another man's wife, another man's life. One night when I was eight years old and my parents' constant sniping had reached a full-out conflagration, I'd packed my football helmet with a change of underwear and announced I was running away from home. Down the block I went – one block, two blocks, long enough to realize that no one was going to be coming after me. Eventually I stopped amid the swirling autumn leaves and started back. Thirty-five years later, I'd run away from home again. But this time I was running back.

My cellular phone rang. For a second, I wondered if it

was *him* – my business associate from the Fairfax Hotel. But it couldn't be him, he didn't have the number. But someone else did.

'Hello,' Lucinda said.

She sounded different from this morning. Emotion was back in her voice after all, only a different kind from what I was used to. *Dread,* I'd say. First dead, then dread, all in the space of one afternoon.

'He called my *house,* Lucinda,' I said.

'Welcome to the fucking club,' she said.

'What?'

'He called *mine,* too,' speaking in a whisper, as if she were trying to keep someone else from hearing. Was her husband somewhere in the house?

I'd been very much hoping that Mr Vasquez hadn't called my house. Or that a Mr Vasquez had, but that it was simply someone who'd found my discarded wallet in a vestibule of the Fairfax Hotel and called as a Good Samaritan. Or for a reward. Ridiculous, maybe. But there was always hope, wasn't there?

Not anymore.

'You spoke to him?'

'Yes.'

'What did he want?' I asked. That, after all, was the million-dollar question here – you have to know what a man wants before you know what to do.

'I don't know what he wanted.'

'Well, what did he *say*? Did he—'

'He asked me how he was.'

'How he *was*? I don't—'

'Did I enjoy it? He wanted to know if I *enjoyed* it. He wanted affirmation – isn't that what men ask you after they . . .' But she couldn't bring herself to finish the sentence. I guess even false bravado has its limits.

'I'm sorry, Lucinda.'

Another apology. I had the feeling I could apologize to her every day for the rest of my life, then keep on apologizing to her into the afterlife, and it still wouldn't be enough. And then I'd have all those other people to apologize to as well.

'I think he wanted to know . . .' she said.

It suddenly occurred to me that I was speaking louder than I should've been. Either louder or softer – because I was drawing glances from the sparsely filled train – from the woman surrounded by Bloomingdale's shopping bags sitting across from me and the two girls with nose earrings holding hands on the other side of the aisle.

'What did he want to know?' I asked.

'Whether we'd done anything. Gone to the police . . .'

We won't go to the police, I'd promised him. The kind of promise most victims of violent crime probably make in the heat of terror. Only in this case, a promise *Vasquez* could more or less believe if he chose to. *This woman don't look like you*, he'd said to Lucinda. *And this man – he don't look like* you.

Vasquez might've jumped anybody this morning. But he'd gotten lucky. He'd found the perfect victims. Because we had to hide the fact we *were* victims.

'What do we do now?' Lucinda asked me now, the same

question I'd asked her back in the hotel room. Because suddenly *nothing* wasn't enough. Not anymore.

'I don't know.'

'*Charles* . . .'

'Yes?'

'What if he . . .'

'Yes?'

'Never mind.'

'What if he *what*, Lucinda?' But I think I knew what she was going to ask me. I just didn't wish to hear it said out loud – not now, not yet.

'Okay, so what do we *do*, Charles?'

'Maybe what we should've done before. Maybe we have to go to the police.'

'I'm *not* telling my husband.'

She'd gotten real emotion back in her voice after all. A sudden and undeniable firmness that brooked no further discussion. 'If *I* can manage it, then you can.' *I was the one raped,* she was saying to me. *I was the one raped six times while you sat there and did nothing. If I can choose to be quiet about it, then you can. Then you* have *to.*

'Okay,' I said. 'Okay. If he calls again, I'll talk to him. I'll find out what he wants.'

Deanna mothered me when I got home. So did Anna – maybe she was finally happy to see someone else in need of medical attention. She brought me a warm compress to lay against my swollen nose and gently rubbed my arm as I lay half-dead on the bed.

I was back in the bosom of my family – content, grateful, the very picture of domestic bliss.

Except each time the telephone rang, I flinched as if punched in the stomach.

A friend of Deanna's. A mortgage broker's cold call. My secretary wanting to know if I was all right.

But there was always the next call, wasn't there?

And they insisted on hearing about the accident. Anna wanted to know how I could have been so *spastic*. Stepping out of a cab, for God's sake. Into a *hole*?

I said I didn't want to talk about it. And I wondered if repeating the same lie was the same as telling different lies. If one was worse than the other. Neither one felt particularly good, not when my daughter was offering me a warm towel and my wife her unconditional love.

I tried to watch some basketball in the den, to root for the struggling Knicks. But I found it hard to focus; my mind kept wandering. There was a player on the Indiana Pacers, for instance, who looked a little like . . . Black, but Hispanic. Lopez, his name was – a backup guard. Taller of course, but . . .

'What's the score?' Anna asked me. She'd stopped watching basketball with me at age nine, but I supposed she was trying to be kind to her bruised and battered father.

'We're losing.' It was a safe answer these days, even if you didn't actually know what the score was.

Just then it turned up in the left corner of the screen. The Knicks had rallied within four.

'Eighty-six to eighty-two,' Anna recited.

'A close one,' I said. 'We've got a shot.'

'Daddy?'

'Yes?'

'Daddy – did you ever play basketball?'

'Sure.'

'On a *team*?'

'No. Not on a team.'

'Then how'd you play?'

'With friends. At the park – you know.' Murray Miller, Brian Timinsky, Billy Seiden. They were my best friends growing up – but slowly, one by one, they'd faded away. Years ago, I'd seen Billy Seiden in a Pathmark supermarket, but I'd left without saying hello.

I hugged Anna. I wanted to tell her something, about love and life and how it can be fleeting if you don't hold on – that you have to jealously guard what's important to you – but I couldn't think of the right words.

Because the phone rang.

Anna picked it up after the second ring.

'For *you*,' she said.

'Who is it?'

'Some Spanish guy,' Anna said.

Thirteen

The conversation:

'Hello there, *Charles*.'

'Hello.' His voice seemed out of context. It belonged in a hotel room smelling of blood, not here in the safety of my own den. Unless my den wasn't safe anymore.

'How's things, *Charles*?'

'What do you want?'

'You doin' okay, Charles?'

'Fine. What do you want?'

'You *sure* you doin' okay, Charles?'

'Yes, I'm doing okay.'

'Not getting stupid on me, Charles, right? Not running to the cops?'

Lucinda was right; he wanted to know if we'd gone to the police. 'No,' I said.

'I know you promised and all, but I don't know you that well, know what I'm sayin'?'

'I haven't gone to the police,' I said. I was speaking softly; I'd ushered Anna out of the room, but that didn't mean she wouldn't come in again. And then there was Deanna, who just might pick up the phone and wonder who I was talking to.

'That's good, Charles.'

'What do you want?' I asked him again.

'What do I want?'

'Look, I—'

'You're not going to get stupid on me, Charles, right? You tell the cops, you got to tell the *little woman*, right, Charles? You got to tell her how you're fucking *Lucinda*, right, Charles? Why you want to do that, huh?'

He'd laid it out for me. The crux of the situation, just in case I'd missed it.

'I'm not going to the police,' I repeated.

'That's good, Charles. Here's the thing – I need a loan.'

Okay. It was the question Lucinda had begun to ask me on the phone. *What if he . . .* Not exactly finishing, but if she had, she would have said: *What if he asks for money?*

'I *hate* to ask, know what I mean?' he said. 'But I'm a little short, see.'

'Look, I don't know what you think—'

'Not much, Charles. A little loan, you know. Say ten grand . . .'

'I don't have ten grand.'

'You don't have ten grand?'

'No.' I'd thought it was over, but it wasn't over.

'Shit. That's a problem.'

'Look, I don't have cash just lying around like that. Everything's—'

'That's a real problem, *Charles*. I really need that loan, see.'

'I just don't have—'

'I think you better get it for me.' Leaving unsaid *why* I better get it for him.

'Everything's tied up. I just can't—'

'You're not listening to me, Charles. I'm talking here and you're not listening. I need ten grand, Charles. Okay? That's the deal. You're a *big fucking executive*, Charles. Says so right on your business card. Senior' – saying it like señor – 'creative director. Ex-ec-u-tive vice pres-i-dent. That's pretty fucking impressive, Charles. And you don't *got* ten grand? Who the fuck you kidding?'

No one, I thought.

'Charles.'

'Yes.'

'I don't give a fuck about your *cash flow,* okay? I want ten grand from you. You understand me?'

Yes.

'If you understand, then say you will give me ten grand.'

Deanna was calling me from the kitchen. 'Do you want some chicken soup?'

'I'll get it for you,' I said.

'You'll get what for me?'

'I'll get you the ten thousand.'

98

'Great. Thank you. Hated to ask you and all, but you know how it is.'

'Where?'

'I'll call you again, okay, Charles?'

'Can you please call at the office? Can you—'

'Nah. I like calling here. I'll call you back *here*, okay, Charles?'

Click.

What if he asks us for money? Lucinda had wondered.

Even though he'd taken our money, even though he'd said, *See, I got your money, right here,* he didn't have *all* our money, did he?

And as long as we weren't going to the police, he could go ahead and ask for it.

The Knicks lost at the buzzer.

Deanna asked me what was wrong, and that's what I told her – the team lost and I'd been pulling for them.

'Poor baby,' she said.

Which is exactly what Lucinda had said to me that day on the train. *Poor baby,* as she'd patted me on the arm and whispered something into my ear. Something about me being sexy.

Which maybe I was, back before I'd turned into a clown.

Vasquez wanted ten thousand dollars.

I didn't have ten thousand dollars just lying around. It wasn't sitting under the mattress or accruing interest in a bank account, either. What I did have was approximately $150,000 worth of stock certificates sitting in a file cabinet in my office attic. Company stock, handed out to me each and every year thanks to Eliot's beneficence.

Deanna and I had a name for those stock certificates – a designation that left no doubt as to their purpose. Not our vacation fund, or our retirement fund, or even our rainy day fund. *Anna's Fund.* That's what we called it. Anna's Fund, there for whenever and whatever might come in the future. Call it a hedge against a coming depression.

An operation, for instance.

Or ten operations. Or other things I didn't necessarily want to contemplate.

Anna's Fund. Every paper penny of it.

But what else could I do but *pay* him?

I lay in bed with Deanna, Deanna already starting to doze even though it couldn't be much past nine. Those twenty-six third graders take a lot out of her – and now this, what would *this* take out of her? If she knew, that is – if she found out. If I broke down and told her, not breaking my promise to Lucinda, not exactly, not telling the *police.* Just her.

Then I wouldn't have to give Vasquez his money, would I? Unless . . .

Unless Vasquez threatened to tell someone else. Unless he said, *Fine, your wife knows – great, but Lucinda's husband – he* doesn't. Lucinda's husband, whom she'd sworn would never know, no matter what, never know she'd gone to a hotel room with another man to have sex and ended up having more sex than she'd bargained for.

If I can manage it, then you can, Lucinda had said to me.

I owed her that, didn't I? After letting another man rape her – after sitting there and *watching* another man rape her? We were in this together.

Besides, I could fantasize all I wanted about telling Deanna, but the truth was, I could no more imagine telling Deanna what I'd been up to than I could imagine telling *Anna*. I could rehearse the very words; I could imagine the burden being lifted. *See? No burden*. But it was make-believe – it wasn't real.

After Deanna was safely asleep, I went upstairs to the attic to rummage through our file cabinet. Under *A* for Anna's Fund.

Only to find it, I had to wade through a few other things first, the file cabinet having surrendered over the years to general disorganization and chaos. High school diplomas, college degrees, birth certificates – a record, more or less, of *us*. The Schines. Milestones, achievements, life-changing events. A tiny pair of footprints courtesy of Anna Elizabeth Schine. A degree from Anna's kinder-garten. And farther back – a marriage certificate. 'Charles Schine and Deanna Williams.' Promising to love and honor – a promise I'd callously discarded in a downtown hotel.

There was a surreal quality to taking my stock certificates out of the file cabinet in order to pay off a rapist. There was no manual for this sort of situation, no self-help books promising to make it all better.

On the way out of the den, I passed Anna's room – a sleeping Anna bathed in moonlight, or was it simply her night-light? She'd begun plugging it into the wall again soon after she'd gotten sick. Because she was suddenly scared to death to be alone in the dark. Because she worried she'd wake up hypoglycemic and wouldn't be able to find her sugar tablets – or maybe that she wouldn't wake up at all.

Sleep seemed to relieve her of all her anger and sadness, I thought.

I tiptoed in and leaned over her bed. Her breath brushed against my face like butterfly wings (remembering now how I'd once pinched a monarch's wings between my thumb and forefinger to show it to a four-year-old Anna before carefully placing it into a cleaned-out jelly jar). I planted a kiss on one cool cheek. She stirred, groaned slightly, turned over.

I went downstairs and slipped the stock certificates into my briefcase.

Fourteen

I met Lucinda at the fountain on 51st and Sixth.

When I called and told her what Vasquez wanted, she'd lapsed into silence and then asked to meet me there.

I'd been sitting there ten minutes when I saw her cross 51st Street.

I stood up and began to raise my hand in greeting. But I stopped – she was with another man. She continued toward me, and for a moment I was caught between sitting down and standing up, between saying hi and saying nothing. I sat back down; something made me lie low.

I stayed seated right there on the rim of the fountain as Lucinda and the man walked right by me without a glance.

The man was dressed in a respectable blue suit and recently shined shoes. Fiftyish, hair just beginning to thin, lips pursed in thought. Lucinda looked almost normal again, I thought, which was to say gorgeous, if you didn't look too closely. If you didn't peer intently at the faint rings under her eyes – not like the rings under mine, which resembled football black, but undeniably there. A woman who looked as though she hadn't slept much lately, who's tossed and turned despite the two Valiums and glass of wine.

She seemed to be speaking to the man, but whatever she was saying was swallowed up by a cacophony of New York clatter – car horns, bicycle bells, piped music, bus engines. They passed within five feet of me and I couldn't hear a word.

I waited as they headed for a side street. I was surrounded by the usual mix of tourists with craned necks, afternoon smokers puffing away with undisguised desperation, and the odd street person mumbling to himself.

I stared at the Christmas decorations on Radio City Music Hall across the street. 'Spectacular Christmas Show,' it said, the entire marquee wreathed in holly. A sidewalk Santa was ringing a bell by the front doors and shouting, 'Merry Christmas, everyone!' Here by the fountain it was cold and raw.

I waited five, then ten minutes.

Then I saw Lucinda coming back, hurrying around the corner and staring straight at me. So. She'd seen me after all.

'Thank you,' she said.

'You're welcome. For what?'

'For not saying hello. For not saying anything. That was my husband.'

That was my husband. The golfer. The one who would never know.

'Oh,' I said.

'He surprised me at the office. With flowers. He insisted on taking the cab uptown with me. Sorry.'

'That's okay. How have you been?'

'Just terrific. Couldn't be better.' The tone of her voice suggested that I was kind of stupid for asking her that, like one of those TV reporters at a scene of unimaginable tragedy asking the victim's remaining family how they're feeling these days.

'Has he called you again?' she asked me.

'Not since he asked for ten thousand dollars. No.'

'And?' she said. 'Are you going to give it to him?'

'Yes.'

She looked down at her hands. 'Thank you.'

'Don't mention it.' And I *didn't* want her to mention it, either. Because every time I mentioned it, it became realer, something that was going to actually take place.

'Look,' she said, 'I have one thousand dollars here. A little account my husband doesn't know about.' She reached into her pocketbook.

'It's okay,' I said. 'Forget it.'

'Take it,' she said as if she were trying to pay for the Milk Duds and soda and I was insisting on being old-fashioned about it and covering the entire date.

'No. I'll take care of it.'

'Here,' she said, and forced ten hundred-dollar bills into my hand. After a brief tug-of-war, I gave up. I put the money into my pocket.

Then she said: 'Do you think it's going to stop here?'

Which was the real question, of course. Would it stop here, or would it not?

'I don't know, Lucinda.'

She nodded and sighed. 'What if it *doesn't*? What if he asks for more money? *Then* what?'

'Then I still don't know.' *Then we're doomed, Lucinda.*

'How did it happen, Charles?' she said, so softly that at first I wasn't sure I'd heard her.

'What?'

'How did it happen? *How?* Sometimes I think I dreamed it. It seems impossible, doesn't it? That it actually happened to us? *Us?* Sometimes . . .'

She dabbed at her eyes – they'd turned liquid, and I thought how her eyes were the second thing I'd noticed that morning on the train. First her thighs, maybe, then her eyes. I'd seen a tenderness in them, and I'd said: *Yes, I could use that. I need that now.*

'Maybe that's the way you should think of it,' I said. 'A bad dream.'

'But it wasn't. So that's stupid.'

'Yes. That's stupid.'

'If he found out, it would kill him,' she said.

Her husband – she was talking about her husband again.

'If he found out, he'd kill *me*.'

'He won't find out.' We were in this together, I was assuring her. We may have cheated on our spouses, but we wouldn't on each other.

'What did you say to your wife?' she asked me. 'About your nose?'

'I fell.'

'Yes,' she said, as if that were what she'd have thought of, too.

'Look, I wanted to tell you . . .' Tell her what, exactly? That I'd failed her, I suppose, that I'd failed her, but I wouldn't fail her again.

'Yes?'

'I should've . . . you know, stopped him.'

'Yes.'

'I tried. Not hard enough.'

'He had a gun,' she said.

Yes, he had a gun. He had a gun he sometimes pointed at me and sometimes didn't. While he was raping her – he didn't. The gun was there on the floor, three feet from me, maybe, that's all.

'Forget about it,' she said. But I could tell she didn't mean it – that she *did* think I should've tried harder, that I should've saved her. And I remembered how I'd defended her in the bar that night and how she'd kissed me afterward for it. Bar bullies are one thing, of course, and armed rapists are another.

'I don't think we should talk to each other again, Charles,' she said. 'Good-bye.'

'Happy so far?' David Frankel was asking me.

'*What?*'

'Happy so far? With the commercial?'

We were finally shooting the aspirin commercial. Stage ten at Silvercup Studios in Astoria.

'Yes. It's fine.'

'Yeah. Corinth's an old pro.'

Well, he is old, I felt like saying. Robert Corinth was the director of the aspirin commercial. He was short and balding, with a silly-looking ponytail beneath a half-moon of sun-burnished skin. The ponytail said: *I may be succumbing to the indignities of aging, but I am still cool, I am still with it.* We were on take twenty-two.

'Who's doing the music for the spot?' I asked him.

'Music?'

'Yes, the track. Who's doing it?'

'T and D Music House.'

'I never heard of them.'

'Oh, yeah. They're good.'

'Okay.'

'They do all the tracks for my stuff.'

'Okay. Fine.'

'You'll like them. They always give us a good price.'

I was going to ask him why he was smiling at me like that. But I was interrupted by Mary Widger whispering in my ear.

'Charles,' she whispered, 'can I have a word with you?'

'Sure.'

'Mr Duben thinks the aspirin bottle should be higher.'

'Higher?' Mr Duben was my new client. He'd greeted me by saying, *So you're the new blood.*

Yes. Type O, I'd answered him, and he'd laughed and said, *Great, that's just what we need.*

'Higher. In the frame.'

'Sure. Can you tell Robert to put the bottle higher in the frame, David?'

'No problem,' David said. 'I live for stuff like that.'

Later in the afternoon, somewhere between takes forty-eight and forty-nine, Tom Mooney cornered me by the craft service table.

'Hey, buddy,' he said.

Tom wasn't my buddy. He was the rep for Headquarters Productions, and his modus operandi was to make himself annoying enough to cause clients to give him work in an effort to make him go away. He'd been fairly successful at it, too.

'How are you, Tom?'

'Me, I'm fine. The question is how are you?' He was looking at my face.

'I fell,' I said. For the hundredth time.

'I meant workwise.'

Tom knew exactly how I was, workwise. He knew, for instance, that up till just a few weeks ago, I'd been in charge of a showcase credit card account but now was solely in charge of this aspirin account. He knew this because advertising was a small community, and as in most small communities, news traveled fast, and bad news faster.

'Great,' I answered him.

He asked me if I'd gotten his Christmas card.

'No.'

'I sent you a card.'

'I didn't get it.'

'No?'

'No.'

'Well, Merry Christmas. Christmas gift to follow,' he said.

'No gifts necessary, Tom.'

'Don't be silly. Uncle Tommy never forgets a client.'

'If it's a Headquarters hat – I've got one,' I said.

'Who's talking hats?' Tom said. 'Did I say anything about hats?'

'I've got a Headquarters T-shirt, too.'

'Hey, you're a Headquarters *client* now.'

'Yes, that's me.'

'So think of me as Santa Claus.'

'That's funny. You don't look like Santa Claus.' With his slicked-back hair and hyperkinetic mannerisms, Tom resembled Pat Riley on amphetamines.

'How do you know? Did you ever *see* Santa Claus?'

When Anna was small, five and a half, maybe, she'd asked me how Santa shopped at Toys R Us if he lived in the North Pole. I'd inadvertently left the store sticker on a My Little Pony.

'Nice to meet you, Santa.'

'And what does little Charley want for Christmas?'

If Tom had all day, I could've told him.

'Nothing, Tom. I'm fine.'

'Hey, you're shooting with me, right?'

'Right.'

'You're working with Frankel, right?'

'Frankel? Yes, sure.'

'Okay. Ask him what he gets for Christmas.'
What did that mean?
'All I want for Christmas is a good spot, Tom.'
'Then why'd you use *us*?' he said.
But when I didn't laugh, he said: 'Just kidding.'

That night, Vasquez called my house and told me to meet him in Alphabet City at the corner of 8th Street and Avenue C.

Fifteen

They called it Alphabet City because it stretched from Avenue A to D in lower Manhattan. It used to be the stomping ground for Hispanic gangs, till it was invaded by an artsy crowd and became both dangerous and hip. Bodegas and galleries coexisted side by side, serving empanadas and op art.

I hadn't been down here since I was in my early twenties. I vaguely remembered a cab ride to no particular destination that had ended here – seven of us stuffed in one cab looking for a good time. I couldn't remember how the night ended.

Today I wasn't looking for a good time.

I was looking for Vasquez.

Deanna had picked up the phone when he called. *How are you, Mrs Schine?* he'd said to her. She'd looked just a little puzzled when she'd handed it over to me.

Business call, I'd told her later.

Vasquez had asked me if I had the money: yes. He'd asked me if I was still being a good boy (translation – no police): yes. He'd told me to meet him here in Alphabet City.

When Deanna left the room, I told him it was ten thousand and no more, did he understand? This was it.

Vasquez said sure thing, bro.

The corner of Avenue C and 8th at eleven in the morning was an accurate reflection of the neighborhood. Five Latino kids were killing time on the hood of a high-rider while a street artist was putting up a sign offering henna tattoos. No Vasquez yet.

A black man bumped into me.

'Why the fuck you don't look where you going?' he said.

I hadn't been going anywhere, of course; I'd been pretty much just standing there. 'Sorry,' I said anyway.

'Sorry, huh?' The man was bigger than me, approximately the size of a typical SUV.

'Yes,' I said.

'What if sorry ain't good enough?'

'Look, I didn't see you . . .'

The man laughed.

'That's okay,' he said. 'That's fine. *Charles*, huh?'

He knew my name – the man who'd accused me of not looking where I was going knew my name.

'Charles,' he said again. 'Right?'

'Who are you?'

113

'Didn't I just ask you a question? You Charles or not Charles?'

'Yes, I'm Charles.'

'They call you *Chuck*? If you were my crimey, that's what we'd call you.'

'No.' *Chuck, Chuck, bo buck, banana fana fo fuck* . . . A song other kids in the neighborhood used to have a lot of fun with when I was eight. 'Where's Vasquez?' I asked him.

'I'm gonna bring you to him. What the fuck you think I'm here for?'

I didn't want to be brought to him.

'Why don't I give you the money and—'

'You ain't givin' me nothin', understand? We're gonna take a little walk.'

'How far?'

'*How far?*' imitating me. 'Just up the street.'

He started walking, looking back to make sure I was following him, and I remembered how I used to do the same thing when Anna was small, walking with her but not with her, making sure she wouldn't wander off in a dangerous direction. Only I was already going in a dangerous direction.

When we passed an alley between two renovated tenements, the man stopped and waited for me, then began steering me into the narrow passageway. I tried to stand my ground, until the man's grip threatened to crush my arm and I gave up.

He threw me up against the wall. *This is what happens in alleys, isn't it*, I thought: *beatings and stabbings and robberies. Sometimes in hotel rooms, but mostly in alleys.* I waited for the inevitable, which was going to be swift and brutal and complete.

Only the beating never came.

'Let's see here,' the man said. And he groped me instead, running his hands up and down my legs, chest, and back. He was patting me down.

'No fuckin' wire on you, Charles, that's good . . .'

'I told him I didn't go to the police.'

'Yeah. And he believes you.'

'Look, I really need to get back,' I said, hearing the panic in my own voice and trying to inch away from the wall.

'Come on,' he said, 'just over here . . .'

I'd gone *just over here* when I first sat down next to Lucinda, and then just over a little more when I took her to the Fairfax Hotel, and now I was being asked to go just over here again, when all I really wanted to do was go back to that place called yesterday.

I followed the man out the other side of the alley and down a block that smelled of sauerkraut and pomade. We passed a hair salon specializing in dreadlocks and hair tattoos. The man took a left into the vestibule of a partially renovated tenement.

He buzzed a name and was buzzed back.

'Come on,' he said, holding the scratched glass door open for me. *Come on* again. I was taking orders these days, a new recruit in the army of the morally dispossessed. Aware that I was treading deeper into enemy territory with

115

each and every step, but not at liberty to refuse. In this army, deserters were subject to possible execution.

Vasquez was in an apartment on the first floor. He was there, just behind the door when it opened and let us in.

I flinched when Vasquez put out his hand. I'd seen that hand do other things – to Lucinda and me. But Vasquez wasn't looking for a handshake.

'Money,' he said.

He was dressed in do-rag chic – low-slung pants with a hint of Calvin Klein peeking out of the waistband – a ratty green sweater hanging off his shoulders. I was getting my first good look at him. And I was surprised how different he appeared from what I'd remembered, at least in the overall impression. He seemed less physically imposing, thinner and distinctly bonier. And I wondered how many criminals had gone to the chair on erroneous eyewitness testimony – plenty, probably, it being hard to get a fix on someone when he's beating your brains in or raping your girlfriend.

I handed over the ten thousand dollars in crisp hundred-dollar bills. Feeling as if I were making another domestic purchase – a washing machine, a big-screen TV for the den, patio furniture – only this domestic purchase, of course, purchasing domesticity itself. Five thousand for Anna and five thousand for Deanna. No money-back guarantee, either. A strictly good-faith purchase when there wasn't any.

'Nine thousand nine hundred . . .' Vasquez diligently counted to the last bill, then looked up at me with that awful smile, the one I remembered from the hotel room.

'Almost forgot,' he said, and punched me in the stomach.

I went down.

I couldn't breathe; I began to claw the air for breath.

'That's for canceling your cards, Charles. It was kind of inconvenient for me, seeing as how I was in the middle of buying something.'

The other man thought the whole thing was funny – he started laughing.

Then Vasquez said: 'We'll be leaving now, Charles.'

It took me five minutes to breathe normally again, then another five minutes to actually get up, using the wall as support. The five minutes I spent on the floor trying to breathe was spent crying, too, partially from the punch to my solar plexus and partially from the realization of where I was.

Down on the floor next to a roach-infested container of two-day-old Chinese takeout.

Sixteen

I stayed late at the office the next day.

I was feeling kind of jumpy and ashamed at home these days – not in any particular order. Every time I looked at Anna, I'd think about the ten thousand dollars I'd robbed from her fund; and every time the phone rang, I suffered through that interminable pause before someone actually answered it – imagining actual dialogue that always ended with Deanna tromping into the bedroom or den or basement to accuse me of ruining her life and killing our daughter.

I preferred that moment happen over the phone – seeing that I couldn't imagine actually having to look her in the eyes as she recited my litany of crimes. In the office I could shut the door and turn off the lights and stare at my reflection in the computer screen, which was stuck in perpetual sleep state – which was the state I wished I could somehow place myself. I could think about ridding myself of this awful thing that threatened to derail my life. At home I could only suffer its consequences.

At the moment, I was trying to look up the T&D Music House.

I wanted to call them tomorrow about the track for the aspirin spot. Something emotional without being maudlin. Something that might disguise the banal dialogue and wooden delivery of the actors.

I couldn't find a listing for them, though. T&D – wasn't that what Frankel had said? Or was it some other letters? No – I was pretty sure it was T&D.

Maybe the postproduction guide I was using was out-of-date. Maybe—

I heard a loud bump.

It was past eight, and the custodial staff had already finished their rounds. I was fairly certain nobody was burning the midnight oil but me.

I heard it again.

A kind of scraping now, a few clinks, a thud. Someone next door – Tim Ward's office, and I'd seen Tim with my very own eyes sprinting off for the 6:38 to Westchester.

Then something else.

Someone was whistling 'My Girl'. Temptations, 1965.

Maybe it was a member of the custodial staff after all – some piece of unfinished cleaning up that needed to be taken care of while the office slept – custodians, like a shoemaker's elves, appearing mostly at night to magically leave behind the fruits of their labor. A new carpet, freshly painted walls, a renovated air-conditioning system. Sure, it was just one of the elves.

Clink. Thud. Boom.

I stood up from my chair and walked across my paper-strewn carpet to see. When I opened the door, the noise stopped. So did the whistling. I thought I heard a sharp intake of breath.

There was a light on in Tim Ward's office – the desk light, I guessed; a cool yellow was radiating through the glazed glass like sunlight caught behind morning fog. For a moment, I was unsure what to do. You don't *have* to do anything when you hear someone whistling late at night from the office next door. You can, but you don't have to.

I opened the door to Tim's office anyway.

Someone was doing something to Tim's computer – an Apple G4, same as mine.

'Hello,' said Winston Boyko. 'I'm fixing it.'

Only Winston didn't seem to be fixing it.

He seemed to be stealing it.

'Tim said it was flickering on and off,' he said, but he looked flushed and his voice was unsteady. The computer was connected to the wall with a thin steel cable Winston must've been in the process of cutting. I figured this out because Winston had what looked like a wire cutter in his hand.

'Tim asked *you* to fix it?' I said.

'Yeah. I'm pretty good with computers, didn't you know that?'

No, I didn't.

'We've got a computer department, Winston. To fix computers.'

'Well, what do you know? Guess I don't have to, then.'

'Winston?'

'Yes?'

'Tim didn't ask you to fix his computer,' I said.

'Not in so many words. No.'

'You don't know anything about computers, do you?'

'Sure I do.'

'Winston . . .'

'I know how much they sell for.' And then he shrugged. *Okay, the charade is up,* he was saying. *Can't blame a guy for trying.*

'Why are you *stealing* computers, Winston?' Maybe that was an odd question to be asking the person stealing it. After all, why does anyone steal anything? To make money, of course. But why Winston – the human baseball encyclopedia and all-around agreeable guy. Why *him*?

'I don't know. Seemed like the right thing to do at the time.'

'Jesus . . . Winston . . .'

'You know what a G4 sells for? I'll tell you. Three thousand used. How about them *Apples*?'

'It happens to be illegal.'

'Yeah – you got me there.'

'And I *saw* you stealing it. What am I supposed to do?'

'Tell me not to do it again?'

'Winston . . . I'm not sure you—'

'Look. I didn't steal it, right? See – the computer's still here. No harm done.'

'This is the first time?'

'Sure.'

But now I remembered hearing something about missing computers. That's why they'd fastened them to the wall with steel wires in the first place, wasn't it?

'Look,' Winston said. 'It would really be inconvenient for me if you said anything.'

And for the first time, I felt a little uncomfortable. A little nervous. This was Winston here – my baseball trivia partner and mailroom buddy. But this was also a *thief*, standing here late at night with no one else around, with a wire cutter in his hand. I wondered what kind of weapon it'd make and decided probably a good one.

'So can we just forget about it? Okay, Charles? Promise I won't do it again.'

'Can I think for a second?'

'Sure.' Then, after that second went by, and then another one: 'Tell you what,' Winston said. 'I'll tell you why it would kind of fuck me over. Aside from getting fired from this job, of course, which wouldn't be the biggest deal in the world, relatively speaking. I'll be honest with you, okay?'

'Okay.'

'Here's the deal.' He sat on Tim's chair. 'Sit down, you look like you're going to jump through a window.'

I sat down.

'The thing is . . . ' Winston said.

*

Winston had served time.

'Nothing major,' he assured me. 'I was a recreational drug user.'

'That's it?'

'Well, I was also a recreational drug *pusher*.'

'Oh.'

'Don't look at me like that. It wasn't like I was dealing H. Mostly E.'

When did drugs become designated by letters of the alphabet? I wondered. Was there one for each letter now?

'It was my college job,' Winston said. He scratched his upper arm over by his tattoo. 'I suppose I could have worked in the school cafeteria. This seemed easier.'

'How much time did you . . . ?'

'Sentenced to ten. But my bid was five. Five and a half up at Sing Sing. Which is like a hundred years old.'

'I'm sorry.' But I wasn't sure if I was sorry about Winston going to prison or sorry about catching him in the act of stealing a company computer, which might necessitate his having to go to prison again. Maybe both.

'*You*'re sorry. Talk about a bad career move. I came out and I'm six years behind everybody else. I've got no college degree. I've got no work experience except for stacking books in the prison library, and I don't think that counts. Even if I did have a college degree, no one would exactly be welcoming me into the executive ranks. I carried a three-point-seven GPA my first year and now I'm pushing mail.'

'Do they know you served time?' I asked him.

'You mean *here*?'

'Yes.'

'Sure. You should come down to the mailroom sometime. We're a liberal's wet dream. We got two ex-cons, two retards, an ex-junkie, and a quadriplegic. He's our quality control man.'

'When you came out – why didn't you go back to college?'

'Were you going to pay my tuition?'

Winston had a point there.

'Look, I'm on parole,' Winston continued. 'They have these rules when you're on parole. You can't go out of state without permission. You've got to check in with your parole officer twice a month. You can't associate with any known criminals. And – oh yeah – you can't steal computers. I may have fucked up on that one. On the other hand, there's this *other* rule they have when you're on parole. You can't earn a living – not really. Know what they pay me to deliver your mail?'

We could talk sports all we liked, but we were on two different sides of the socioeconomic spectrum, Winston was saying. I was an executive, and he was just a mail boy.

'How many computers, Winston?'

'Like I told you, this is the first time—'

'You got *caught*. I know. How many times didn't you get caught?'

Winston leaned back and smiled. He flexed his arm – the one with the wire cutter in it. He shrugged.

'A couple,' he said.

'Okay. A couple.' I suddenly felt tired; I rubbed my forehead and looked down at my shoes. 'I don't know what to do,' I said out loud. I might have been saying that about everything now.

'Sure you do. I just bared my soul to you, man. I was stupid, I admit it. Won't happen again. Promise.'

'All right. Fine. I won't say anything.' Even as I was saying this, I wondered exactly why I'd come to that decision. Maybe because I felt like no less of a thief than Winston. Yes. Hadn't I stolen money from Anna's Fund? Late at night, too, when no one could see me – just like Winston? Wasn't that criminal etiquette – never turning in a fellow criminal? Do the same for me, wouldn't he?

'Thanks,' Winston said.

'If I hear about another computer being stolen . . .'

'Hey – I'm larcenous. Not stupid.'

That's right, I thought. *The stupid one is me.*

Seventeen

'Daddy . . .'

The word you almost never tire of hearing during the day, becoming the word you dread waking to in the middle of the night. It came like a fire alarm in a pitch-black movie theater, and right in the middle of the film, the current feature a kind of domestic drama involving me and Deanna and a woman with green eyes.

'*Daddy!*'

I heard it again, and this time I woke up for good and nearly fell off the bed.

Memories of other nights like this clamored for my undivided attention even as I tried to deflect them, to concentrate on the physical act of standing up and running barefoot across a dark and frigid hall.

To Anna's room.

I flipped on the lights even as I entered it – one hand

pressed against the switch, the other already reaching out for her. Even with my eyes squinting from the sudden brightness, I could see that Anna looked exceptionally and spookily weird. She was, I was fairly certain, smack in the middle of hypoglycemic shock.

Her eyes were rolled back, to that part of her brain that was reeling from lack of sugar, her body caught in one unending stutter. When I put my arms around her, it was like holding on to a frightened puppy, all shake and quiver. Only if Anna was frightened, she was incapable of telling me.

When I shouted at her, she refused to shout back. When I shook her head and whispered into her ear, when I slapped her gently – no response.

I'd been told what to do when this happened. I'd been prepped and trained and reminded and warned. I just couldn't remember a word of it.

I knew there was a syringe sitting in a fire-engine-red plastic case. I thought the case was downstairs in a kitchen cabinet. I believed that the case needed to be opened and the syringe filled with a brown powder that was also in the case. And water – some amount of water was to be added.

These things were flying through my mind like a dyslexic sentence I couldn't quite grasp. I caught the general drift, though, which was horrifying and merciless.

My daughter was dying.

Suddenly Deanna was right behind me.

'The shot,' I said to her, or possibly yelled.

But she already had it in her hand. I felt a momentary

surge of pure love for her, this woman I'd married and created Anna with, even in the midst of terror feeling like falling to my knees and hugging her. She opened the case for me, calmly plucked out the syringe, and studied the bold-lettered directions on the way into Anna's bathroom. I cradled Anna in my lap, whispering that it would be okay, Anna, yes, it would, *you'll be fine, Anna, yes, my darling*, as I heard the water running in there. Then Deanna was back out, shaking the syringe in her hand.

'Deep,' Deanna said, handing the shot to me. 'Past the fat into the muscle.'

I'd dreaded this moment – had imagined over and over what it'd be like. When they'd first trained me on the fine art of insulin giving, pricking thin quarter-inch needles just into the fatty tissue on hip, arm, and buttock – they'd also mentioned *this*. That eventually there would come a moment when I'd probably have to use it. Not *every* parent had to, but given that Anna had an especially virulent case and given that Anna had gotten it so young ... This needle *not* a quarter inch long, more like four inches, and thick enough to make you turn your eyes away. Because it had to get its pure sugar mix into the brain cells fast enough to keep them from starving.

This syringe was in my hand now, only my hand was quivering as much as Anna was, because it was like stabbing her, even if it was with the gift of life. I placed it by her upper arm, but since we both were shaking, I was afraid to push it in, afraid I'd miss and blunt the needle, waste the liquid.

128

'Here . . .' Deanna took the needle from me.

She put it against Anna's hip, hand steady, and stuck it all the way in. Then she slowly pushed the plunger down till all the brown liquid was gone.

It was almost instantaneous.

One minute my daughter was lost. Then suddenly her eyes rolled back into focus, and her body gently quieted and settled back onto the bed.

And she cried.

Anna cried, worse even than the morning she was diagnosed and we told her more or less what was in store for her. Worse than that.

'Daddy . . . oh Daddy . . . oh Daddy . . .'

So I cried, too.

I took her to the hospital – the children's wing of Long Island Jewish, just to be on the safe side. I hadn't been back since those first excruciating weeks, and the very smell of the place was enough to take me back to the time when I'd paced the halls at four in the morning, knowing that the best part of my life was over. Anna felt it, too; she'd managed to calm down on the twenty-minute ride to the hospital, but the moment we entered the waiting room, she'd shrunk back into my body and hid there, so that I nearly had to carry her inside.

It was 2:00 A.M.; we were given an Indian intern who seemed overworked and distracted. Deanna had been calling Anna's doctor when we'd left the house.

'What happened, please?'

129

'She was hypoglycemic,' I said. 'She had an episode.' Anna was sitting on the examining table, virtually slumped against me.

'You administered the shot?'

'Yes.'

'Uh-huh . . .' He was examining her even as we spoke, doing all the things doctors do – heart, pulse, eyes, ears – so maybe he was competent after all. 'We'd better take her blood sugar, no?'

I wondered if he was asking me for my medical opinion or simply being rhetorical.

'We took it before we came. One forty-three. I don't know what it was before she . . .' I was going to say *passed out, fainted, became unconscious* but felt reticent to say it in front of Anna. I noticed a bruise had already formed where Deanna had given her the shot and thought that other parents who bruise their children are brought up on charges and locked away.

'One forty-three, yes?'

'Yes.'

'Well, we'll see . . .'

He asked for Anna's hand, but Anna had no intention of giving it. 'No,' she said, and meant it.

'Come on, Anna, the doctor has to take your blood sugar to make sure everything's okay. You do this four times a day – it's no big deal.'

But of course it was a big deal. *Because* she did it four times a day and now they were asking her to do it a fifth – actually sixth, since I'd taken it before we came here. It was a big deal because she was back in the hospital where she'd first been told she wasn't like everyone else, that her body had this terrible deficiency that could kill her. It might not be a big deal to the doctor, or even to me, but it was to her.

Still. She was sitting in LIJ at two in the morning because she'd almost died, and now the doctor needed a blood sample. 'Come on, Anna, be a big girl, okay?' remembering back to those first days at home when I'd have to beg her to give me her arm, sometimes having to take it from her, brute force preceding brute pain, each time convinced I was committing the worst kind of assault.

'I'll do it *myself*,' Anna said.

The doctor was losing patience now; so many patients and so little time. 'Look, miss, we have to—'

'She said she'll do it herself,' I said, remembering something else about back then. How after her diagnosis, Anna had spent two weeks here learning how to deal with this thing called diabetes, with hospital protocol demanding that all patients administer one insulin shot to themselves before they could be discharged. And Anna, who feared needles the way other people fear snakes, or spiders, or dark cellars, had made me promise that she wouldn't have to do that. And I'd said, *I promise*. And on the day she was due to be discharged, the nurse had come in and asked Anna to do it – to fill up the shot with two kinds of insulin and inject it herself into her already bruised arm. And at first both parents, Deanna and me, had said nothing, letting the nurse gently and then not so gently cajole the patient into doing what she was so clearly terrified of. And finally, with the silence from her only allies nearly deafening, Anna had looked over at me with pure naked pleading. And even though I knew that it probably was a good thing for Anna to give herself a shot, I still told the nurse, *No. She doesn't have to do that.* I'd made a promise to her and I kept it. Her body might have betrayed her, but her father hadn't. It was the kind of moment you feel like bronzing – the one you take out of the cabinet and hold up to the light later on, when you've betrayed everything else.

'She'll do it herself,' I repeated.

'Okay,' the Indian said. 'Well then, please let her do it already.'

I gave her the lancet pen and watched as Anna shakily brought it up to her middle finger and snapped the top, a bright bubble of blood already forming as she took the pen away. I offered to hold the blood meter for her, but she took it from me and managed it herself – little Anna not so little anymore, a fighter if there ever was one.

Her blood sugar was fine – 122.

I told the intern that my daughter's endocrinologist, Dr Baron, would be coming by any minute.

But Dr Baron wasn't coming by. The intern's beeper sent him scurrying out of the ER, and when he came back, he said: 'Dr Baron says she can go home.'

'He's not coming?'

'No need. I told him her numbers. He said she can go home.'

'I thought he would come to see her.'

The intern shrugged. *Doctors,* he was saying, *what are you going to do?*

I said, 'That's great.'

'Could I please have a word with you?' he said.

'Sure.' I followed the intern to the other side of the ward, where a Chinese man was sitting in a chair, looking down at his bloody hand.

'How is her sit, please?'

'Her *what?*'

'Her sit.'

Her *sight.* 'Okay,' I said. 'She uses glasses for reading. She's supposed to, anyway,' thinking that it had been a while since I'd actually seen them on her. 'Why?'

He shrugged. 'There is some damage there. It's no worse?'

'I don't know. I don't think so.' Feeling that familiar ache in the pit of my stomach again, as if something were lodged in there that even Long Island Jewish Hospital couldn't surgically remove.

'Okay,' the intern said, and gave me a pat on the shoulder. Overworked, a little impatient, maybe, but friendly after all.

'Is there something I should be telling Dr—'

'No, no.' The intern shook his head. 'Just checking.'

After I signed a few papers and handed over my new credit card, we were told we could leave.

Outside in the quiet winter air, our breath merged on the way to the car, one vaporous cloud that followed us all across the parking lot. *It should be a* black *cloud,* I thought – wasn't that the metaphor for ill luck?

'Hey, kiddo,' I said, 'you seeing okay these days?'

'No, Dad, I'm blind.'

Well, her blood sugars might be running wild, but her sarcasm was intact and healthy.

'I was just wondering if you noticed anything, that's all. With your eyes.'

'I'm fine.'

But on the ride home, Anna snuggled against me, the way she used to when she was small and needed to nap.

'Remember that story, Dad?' she asked me after several blocks.

'What story?'

'The one you used to tell me when I was little. You made it up. About the bee.'

'Yes.' A story I'd put together on the spot, after Anna had been stung and I'd told her the bad bee was dead to make her feel better. Only it hadn't made her feel better; she was horrified that bees *die* when they sting, even the bee who'd stung her.

'Tell it,' Anna said.

'I don't remember it,' I lied. 'What about the one about the horses? You know, the old man who goes looking for adventure?'

'No,' she said. 'I want the bee story.'

'Gee, Anna, I don't even remember how it starts.'

But she did. 'There was a little bee,' she began. 'Who wondered why he had a stinger.'

'Oh yeah. That's right.'

'Tell it.'

Why that story, Anna?

'He wondered why he had a stinger,' I said.

'Because . . .' Anna said impatiently.

'Because he saw that every time the other bees used their stingers, they died.'

'His best friend' – she nudged me – 'and—'

'His best *bee* friend,' I corrected her, 'his aunt Bee, his uncle Bumble, all of them used their stingers and then died.'

'He was very sad about this,' Anna said softly.

'Yes, he was sad about this. Because he wondered what was the point, then. Of having a stinger, of being a bee.'

'So then . . .'

'So then. He asked everyone this question. All the other animals in the forest.'

'In the *garden*,' Anna corrected me.

'In the garden. But no one could help him.'

'Except the owl.'

'The *wise* owl. The owl said, "When you use it, you'll know."'

'And . . .'

'One day, the bee was in the forest – the garden – and he saw a peacock. Of course he didn't know it was a peacock. He didn't know what a peacock was, exactly. Just an ordinary-looking bird, apparently.'

'You didn't say *apparently* when I was little,' Anna said.

'Well, you're not little anymore. Apparently.'

'No.'

'Just an ordinary-looking bird. So he thought. Until he

landed on it and asked it the same question he'd asked all the other animals. Why do I have a stinger?'

'Why?' Anna said, as if she really wanted to know the answer to the question, as if she'd forgotten and needed to hear it again.

'And the peacock said to the bee, "Buzz off." Whereupon the bee got angry.'

'And stung the peacock,' Anna said, finishing for me. 'And the peacock went ouch, and all its feathers stood out. All of them. All the colors of the rainbow. And the little bee thought it was the most beautiful thing he'd ever seen. And died.'

When we turned into Yale Road, Vasquez was there. Standing like a sentinel under a street lamp.

I drove right past him and almost up onto the facing sidewalk.

'Daddy!' Anna was suddenly not snuggling anymore, but up and alert and maybe even alarmed.

Somehow I managed to steer the car back into the street, then up the driveway to 1823 Yale.

'What's wrong?' Anna said.

'Nothing.' As insincere a 'nothing' as ever left a person's mouth. Certainly mine. But Anna was too polite to question me any further, even when I grabbed her by the arm and nearly yanked her into the house.

Where Deanna was up and waiting. Coffee brewed, lights on, kitchen TV set to the Food Channel as she waited for the loves of her life to return home safely.

Anyway, we'd returned.

It's possible she mistook my expression of dread for the night's events – waking up to find our daughter unconscious and in shock. What else would she think caused me to turn white and pace up and down the kitchen floor?

'Is she all right?' Deanna asked. She'd already directed this question to Anna herself, who with her teenage sullenness back in full working order had simply tramped by her and up the stairs to her room.

'Yeah,' I said. 'Fine. Her blood sugar was down to one twenty-two.'

'How is she? Scared?'

'No,' I said. *I'm scared.*

Anna was a trooper, and Anna was going to be a-okay. But *Charley* here – that was a different matter. I was trying to deflect my wife's attention from the door, where any minute now the man who was blackmailing me might ring the bell.

Vasquez was no more than forty yards away from my wife and child.

I walked to the window and stared out into the dark.

'What are you looking at?' Deanna asked me.

'Nothing. I thought I heard something . . .'

She was behind me now. She laid her head against my neck and stood there half leaning on me, one of us thinking the danger had passed, the other one knowing it hadn't.

'Is she really okay?' Deanna asked me.

'What?' I felt momentarily calmed by the warmth of her body.

137

'Maybe I should sleep with her tonight.'

'She wouldn't let you.'

'I can slip in after she falls asleep.'

'I think it's okay, Deanna. She'll be fine tonight.' The operative word being *tonight,* of course. Couldn't vouch for tomorrow night or the night after that. Of course, it was possible *we* wouldn't be fine tonight.

Why had Vasquez come here? What did he want?

'Why do you look so worried, Charles? I thought that was my department.'

'Well, you know . . . the hospital and all.'

'I'm going to sleep,' she said. 'I'm going to try.'

'I'll be up later,' I said.

But after Deanna walked up the stairs, I counted to ten, then went over to the fireplace and picked up a poker. I swung it back and forth a few times.

I opened the front door and went outside.

It was approximately twenty-five steps from my front door to the beginning of the driveway. I knew this because I counted every one. As something to do – anything to do – instead of panic. Of course, it was possible I was *already* panicking. After all, I was walking down the driveway with a fireplace poker in my hands.

When I made it all the way down to the sidewalk, I took three deep breaths and saw that Vasquez wasn't there.

The streetlight illuminated a starkly empty corner.

Was it possible I'd imagined it? Was I starting to see Vasquez even when Vasquez wasn't there – my very own personal spook?

I was honestly willing to believe it – in fact, desperately *wanted* to believe it. But it wasn't until I dutifully walked all the way to the corner and even called out his name – not loudly, no, but loud enough for the neighborhood setter to start barking – then reversed field and walked back past my driveway to the opposite corner and *still* saw no Vasquez, that I was willing to embrace it as gospel.

Maybe I *was* seeing things. I'd had a near death experience tonight – my daughter's, maybe, but still. You have one bad fright, you're due for another. Chalk one up for my old pal fear. Or my *new* pal – we were spending so much time together these days.

But when I passed the oak tree that established the borders of my property, I noticed a wet stain running down its gnarled trunk. And I smelled something.

Acrid, tart – the smell of Giants Stadium at halftime. So many beers consumed and so many beers given back, the stadium like one enormous urinal. That's what it smelled like here.

Courtesy of a passing canine? Fine, except for a simple law of physics. A dog just couldn't reach that high on the trunk – not Curry, not the neighborhood setter, not even a Great Dane. Dogs pissing on trees is a very solemn ritual, or so I'd read – a way of marking their territory.

That's why Vasquez had done it.

I hadn't been imagining things. No.

Vasquez had come calling and had left a calling card. *See,* he said, *this is my territory – your home, your life, your family.*

It's mine now.

Eighteen

'Hello, Charles.'

It was 10:15 Wednesday night. I was sitting in the den, where I'd been standing guard over the telephone. It was unnerving – every time it rang I'd pick it up and wait to see who'd say hello. The fastest answering machine in the West – one ring and it was sitting in my hand. I knew he'd be calling; I didn't want Deanna picking it up first.

'Why were you outside my *house*?' I said.

'Was that me?'

'I'm asking you what you were doing here.'

'Must have been taking a walk.'

'What do you want? What?'

'What do *you* want?'

Okay, I was a little taken aback – this answering a question with a question.

'What do I want?'

140

'That's right. You tell me.'

Well. For one thing, I wanted Vasquez to stop coming by my house. For another thing, I wanted him to stop calling my house. That would be nice.

'I want you to leave me alone,' I said.

'Okay.'

'I'm not clear what you mean—'

'Something about *okay* you don't understand? You said you want me to leave you alone, I said okay.'

'Great,' I said, stupidly letting some vague tenor of hope enter my voice, even though I knew, I *knew*—

'Just give me some more money.'

More money.

'I gave you money,' I said. 'I told you—'

'That was then. This is now.'

'No.' The till was empty, the cupboard bare. I'd taken once from Anna's Fund. No more.

'You fucking stupid?'

Yes. Probably.

'I don't have any more money for you,' I said.

'Look, *Charles*. Pay attention. We both know you got the money. We both know you're gonna give it to me, 'cause we both know what's gonna happen if you don't.'

No, I didn't know. But I could guess.

So I asked him how much he was talking about. Even though I didn't really care how much he was talking about, because it was already too much.

And Vasquez said: 'Hundred thou.'

I shouldn't have been surprised, but I was.

141

That was inflation for you – ten thousand to a hundred thousand in the blink of an eye. But then – how much is a life worth, exactly? Are *three* lives worth? What *is* the going rate for a wife and daughter these days? For being able to look them in the eye without seeing disgust staring back? Maybe a hundred thousand was cheap. Maybe I was getting a bargain here.

'I'm waiting,' Vasquez said.

He would have to keep on waiting. It was a bargain I simply couldn't afford.

Besides, it was never going to stop *here* anyway. Wasn't that the point of blackmail? Wasn't it governed by its own immutable laws, like the universe itself, and, just like the universe, never ending? Vasquez might say it would stop, but Vasquez was lying. It would stop only when I stopped Vasquez. A simple truth even an idiot could understand – even someone *fucking stupid* could grasp that. Only I couldn't stop Vasquez – I didn't know how. Other than to say no and take my chances.

'I don't have it,' I said.

And hung up the phone.

When Winston delivered my mail the next morning, he found me slumped over the desk.

'Are you dead,' Winston asked me, 'or just pretending?'

'I don't know. It feels like I'm dead. Could be.'

'Can I have your computer, then?'

I looked up, and Winston put up his hands and said: 'Just kidding.' Since the night in the office, Winston had

142

been exactly like the Winston *before* the night in the office. No tiptoeing around, no bowing and scraping, no false humility. If I'd scared Winston straight, you wouldn't have exactly known it. On the other hand, I hadn't heard about any missing computers lately, so maybe Winston had reformed.

'Seriously,' Winston said, 'something wrong?'

Where to begin? Then again, much as I might want to, I couldn't tell Winston a thing.

'What was it like?' I asked him instead.

'What was what like?'

'Prison?'

Winston's face darkened – yes, a definite change from sunny to cloudy, with possible thunderstorms lurking in the area. 'Why are you asking?'

'I don't know. Just curious.'

'It's hard to describe unless you've been there,' he said flatly, maybe hoping I'd just say okay and leave it at that.

But I didn't say okay. And though Winston was under no obligation to answer me, maybe he *saw* himself as having an obligation to me now. Because he did answer me.

'You really want to know what prison was like?'

'Yes.'

'What was it like? It was like . . . walking a tightrope,' he said, letting that simple statement lie there for a while. 'Walking a tightrope, but you can't get off. All that concentrating on not falling and getting yourself killed. Constantly – twenty-four hours a day, understand? You tried to not get involved in things – that was your mantra, because if you did get involved in things, it was almost always trouble. So you tried to ignore everyone, to walk around with your head up your ass. But that takes enormous concentration. To act like you're blind. Because all kinds of shit is going on around you – the worst kind of shit. Rapes, beatings, stabbings – all this gang warfare. You try to be invisible. You know how *hard* it is to be invisible?'

'I can imagine,' I said.

'No, man, you *can't* imagine. It is the hardest possible thing to do. It's not doable. Sooner or later, you're going to get involved, because someone is going to make you get involved.'

'And someone made you?'

'Oh yeah. I was prime meat in there. I was unaffiliated, and so I was prime meat.'

'You were . . . ?'

'Bitched up? No. But only because I fought someone who tried, and did two months in lockup. You can't go out of your cell. Except for showers. No rec. Nothing. Which was kind of okay, since I knew when I *did* get out of my cell, I was in trouble, since the guy I fought was affiliated.'

'So what did you do?'

'I got affiliated.'

'With who?'

'A gang. Who do you think runs things in there?'

'Just like that?'

'No. I had to earn it – you don't get anything for nothing there, Charles. There's always a price.'

'What was the price?'

'The price? The price was I had to stick a shank in someone. Like a blood initiation, only the blood was someone else's. That's how you get into a gang. You make someone else bleed.'

'Who were they?'

'Who was who?'

'The gang?'

'Oh, just a bunch of guys. Nice guys, really, you'd like them. They had some very pronounced beliefs, though. Like for instance, they believe all blacks are subhuman. And all Hispanics – them, too. They don't like Jews much, either. Other than that – they're terrific.'

And now I noticed something again. Winston's tattoo. AB. Maybe not Amanda Barnes after all.

'You got that tattoo in prison, didn't you?'

Winston smiled. 'Can't put anything over on you. Proud member of the Aryan Brotherhood. We have a handshake and everything.'

You had to admire Winston, I thought. He found himself in a terrible situation, and he did what he had to. Maybe there was a lesson in that.

'See you this afternoon,' Winston said. 'But no more questions about prison, okay? It kind of ruins my day.'

Nineteen

When I disembarked at Merrick station I called Deanna to pick me up. I thought about walking, but a steady wind was whipping in from the ocean and I was nearly blown back into the train when I stepped off onto the platform.

But when Deanna answered the phone, she asked me if I could wait ten minutes. The chimney guy I'd hired was there, and she didn't want to leave him alone in the house with Anna.

So I told her I'd walk after all.

Christmastime had turned what was generally a quiet and reserved residential street into something akin to the Vegas strip. All those flashing lights. All those plastic reindeer pulling plastic Santas on their plastic sleighs. A plastic manger or two. Several stars of Bethlehem precariously perched on once stately arborvitaes.

I pulled in gulps of air that felt strangely heavy and

saturated with moisture as I walked past and took in the show.

And then, suddenly, rescue.

A car horn beeped, then beeped again.

I turned and saw my neighbor's Lexus purring by the side of the curb.

I walked up to the passenger door as my neighbor Joe cracked open the window.

'Hop in,' he said.

You didn't have to ask me twice. I opened the door and slid into a kind of primal warmth – what the first cavemen must have felt when they created those first licks of flame and finally, miraculously, stopped shivering.

'Thanks,' I said.

'Cold out there, huh?' said Joe, who was nothing if not observant.

'Yes.'

Joe was a chiropractor, which either was or wasn't a legitimate profession. No one had ever been able to explain it to my satisfaction.

'How's the kid?' Joe asked.

'Okay,' I answered, thinking I sounded like Anna now. One-word answers to any question. 'And yours?' Joe had three children spaced a year apart, including a girl around Anna's age who was academically oriented, athletically gifted, and disgustingly healthy.

Joe said they were fine.

'How's things at the office?' he asked me.

'Fine.' People politely asked you things that they didn't

actually want answers to, I thought – but what if I did answer him? What if I said, *Glad you asked, Joe,* then gave him an earful about Eliot and Ellen Weischler. *I was fired off the account I worked on for ten years, and now they have me working on a shit account that no one cares about.* And while I was at it, I could fill him in on Vasquez and Lucinda, too. What would he say then?

But instead I said: 'How are things with you?'

'People always have bad backs,' Joe said.

Even after they've gone to you for treatment, I felt like saying. But didn't.

'Doing anything for the holidays?' Joe asked me. We were stopped at a traffic light that was generally acknowledged to be the slowest traffic light in Merrick. Whole days would pass and this traffic light would stay red. Kingdoms rose and fell, presidential administrations came and went, and the light obstinately refused to change.

'No. Going over to Deanna's mom like we do every year.'

'Uh-huh.'

Then after I asked Joe the same thing, and Joe told me he was going down to Florida for a few days, the car went quiet as we both realized that was pretty much it – we'd run out of small talk.

'Boy, it's cold,' Joe finally said, repeating his comment from earlier in the ride.

'Go through the light, Joe,' I said.

'What?'

'*Go through the light.*' Something had just come to me. 'Why should I—'

148

Deanna had asked me to wait at the station. Because the chimney cleaner I'd hired was there and she didn't want to leave him alone in the house.

'Go through the *fucking light*.'

I hadn't hired a chimney cleaner.

'Look, Charles, I don't want to get a ticket and I don't see what the big rush is—'

'*Go!*'

So Joe did. The evident panic in my voice finally spurred Joe into action; he gunned the engine and went right through the traffic light, swinging into Kirkwood Road just two blocks from our homes.

'If I got a ticket, you'd pay it,' Joe said, trying to regain a little of his dignity now that he'd blindly obeyed his neighbor for no good reason. *What did I mean, coming off like that, ordering him around?*

'Stop here,' I said.

Joe had obviously intended to steer the car into his own driveway and let me walk next door. But I couldn't wait. For the second time in two minutes, Joe did as he was told. He stopped the car in front of 1823 Yale and I jumped out.

When I flung open my front door, I saw Deanna leaning against the banister, in the middle of telling someone that Curry didn't like everyone this way, that he was selective with his affections.

And then the person she was telling this to.

'Mr Ramirez said he's giving us a special price,' Deanna was saying.

We were sitting in the living room, the three of us.

'But only because he likes Curry and vice versa,' Deanna continued. She was talking about the price of cleaning the chimney. Deanna always managed to settle into an easy rapport with handymen of one kind or another, befriending them, regaling me later with stories about their wives and children.

'Yeah,' Vasquez said. 'I'm just a dog lover.' He was smiling, the same smile he'd had when he was propping Lucinda up against the bed to rape her for the last time.

'Mr Ramirez—' Deanna said, but she was interrupted.

'Raul,' Vasquez said.

'Raul said our chimney has a broken . . . what was that again?'

'Flue.'

'Yes, we have a broken flue.'

'Yeah. It's an old chimney,' Vasquez said. 'When was this house built?'

'Nineteen twelve,' Deanna said. 'I think.'

'Yeah. It's probably never been touched.'

'Then I guess it's about time,' Deanna said.

'That's right. Sure.'

I hadn't said anything yet. But now they were waiting for me to say something, some acknowledgment of the problem at hand and what I was going to do about it. I hadn't said anything yet because I couldn't imagine what to say.

'So,' Deanna continued, 'Raul is prepared to fix it and clean the chimney. But it's up to you.'

'You don't want to live with a broken flue,' Vasquez said. 'The thing could be dangerous. All that carbon dioxide can back up, man – it'll *kill* you while you're sleeping, understand?'

Yes, I understood all right.

'There was this family I knew that didn't fix their flue,' Vasquez said. 'One night they went to sleep, and in the morning they didn't wake up. All of them, dead. A whole family.'

'So, what do you say?' Deanna asked me, looking alarmed now. 'What do you want to do?'

Anna wandered into the living room, dressed in pajamas.

'What's the capital of North Dakota?' she asked me.

Two questions before me now, but I only felt like answering one.

I'll take state capitals for one hundred, Alex.

'Bismarck,' I said.

'Anna, this is Raul,' Deanna said, always the hostess.

'Hi,' Anna said, flashing him her most polite smile, the one she trotted out for distant relatives, old friends of her parents, and, apparently, handymen.

'Hello,' Vasquez said, and reached out and tousled her hair. That hand on my child's head.

'How old are you?' Vasquez asked her.

'Thirteen,' Anna said.

'That right?'

He hadn't taken his hand off her head. Instead of coming off the way it was supposed to, it was lingering there uncomfortably, five, then ten, then fifteen seconds; Anna was starting to squirm.

'Look just like your mom,' Vasquez said to her.

'Thanks.'

'You like school?'

Anna nodded. My daughter, who generally tried to refrain from offending anyone, obviously wanting that hand off her head now, but evidently unsure just how to accomplish that. She looked at me for help.

'Look . . .' I said.

'Yeah?' Vasquez stared right back at me. 'You say something?'

I said: 'Why don't you run upstairs and finish your homework, Anna.'

'Okay.' She wanted to do that, yes, but the problem was that Vasquez hadn't taken his hand off her head yet. So she stood there, her eyes still beseeching me for assistance.

'Go *on*, honey.'

'Okay.'

But Vasquez was *still* not removing his hand, still standing there and smiling at me as the room finally went quiet. One of those awkward moments – like watching a friend of the family kiss your wife just a little too intimately at a drunken party and not knowing whether to stand by and watch or challenge him to a fistfight.

'I have to do my homework,' Anna said.

'Homework? Aww . . . pretty girls like you don't have to do homework. You gotta get the boys to do it for you.'

This was where I was supposed to act. Where I was supposed to say please get your fucking hand off my daughter's head because it's fucking making her uncomfortable and she wants to go upstairs, understand fucking English?

The silence was loud enough to split eardrums.

Then: 'She likes to do her homework herself,' Deanna said. Ending it. And finally, mercifully, insinuating herself between Vasquez's arm and Anna's head, physically and decisively ushering our daughter out of harm's way.

When Anna padded out of the living room, she glanced back at me with an expression that seemed to admonish me. Apparently, her face said, she'd been looking to the wrong parent for help.

I heard her footsteps going up the stairs at double speed.

Quiet again. Then:

'So . . . ?' Deanna said, clearing her throat. 'Maybe you want to think about this, honey?' Apparently this was one hired help she wasn't going to befriend after all.

'I wouldn't take too long,' Vasquez said, still smiling. 'You don't want to take chances with your family's safety, right?'

I felt something acidic deep in my guts, something ice cold and broiling hot at the same time. I thought I might need to throw up.

'No,' I said. 'I'll get back to you soon.'

'Okay, you get back to me, then.'

'Yes.'

'Why don't you see Raul out,' Deanna said, evidently eager to get him out of the house.

So I walked him to the front door, where Vasquez turned and put his hand out, just as you'd expect from your friendly neighborhood chimney cleaner.

'Know what they taught us in the army, Charles?' he whispered. 'Before I got kicked out?'

'What?'

Vasquez showed me.

Leaving one hand exactly where it was, proffered in friendship, but using the other one to grasp my testicles. Crushing them in his fingers.

My knees buckled.

'*Grab 'em by the balls. Their hearts and minds will follow.*'

I tried to say something but couldn't. I wanted to cry out but couldn't. Deanna was not twenty feet behind me and completely oblivious to the excruciating pain radiating down my legs and threatening to make me scream.

'I want the money, Charles.'

I felt my eyes begin to water. 'I'll . . .'

'*What?* Can't hear you . . .'

'I'll . . .'

'*I'll never hang up on you again?* That's cool, apology accepted. I want the fucking money.'

'I can't breathe . . .'

'A hundred thousand dollars, okay?'

'I . . .'

'*What?*'

154

'Plea . . .'

'A hundred thousand and I give you your balls back.'

'I . . . pl . . .'

And then he did.

He did give them back. At least temporarily. He opened his fingers, and I slumped against the doorjamb.

'Honey,' Deanna said, 'can you bring the recycling bin out to the curb?'

Twenty

I was looking over the bid for the aspirin job.

Think of this as a kind of avoidance therapy. If I was looking over the bid for the aspirin job, I couldn't be asking myself *What was I going to do? How was I going to survive this?*

So that's what I was doing.

Meticulously going over that aspirin bid; something was wrong with it, but I didn't know what. What *was* wrong with it?

This avoidance strategy was only partially successful.

In the middle of scanning down a line of neatly typed-in figures, I saw Vasquez with his hand on my daughter's head.

If he didn't get one hundred thousand dollars, he would be coming back.

I thought about telling Deanna.

But as much as I tried to say, *She will forgive me, she will.* As much as I told myself that Deanna loved me, and wouldn't that love survive an indiscretion? As many times as I postulated the theory that every marriage has its ups and downs and that okay, *this* down might be subterranean, but wouldn't it naturally be followed, after much anguish and restitution, by another upswing? As much as I rationalized, ruminated, debated, and what have you — I couldn't quite convince myself that I could for one minute withstand that look in Deanna's eyes. The one that would inexorably come immediately after she found out what I'd been up to.

I'd seen that look before. I'd seen it the morning they'd diagnosed Anna in the emergency room. The look of being utterly and hopelessly betrayed. I'd had to stare it full in the face as the news slowly sank in and she'd fastened on to me like a swimmer being pulled off by an undertow.

I didn't think I could bear to see it again.

Back to the sheet in front of me. It listed every expense associated with the commercial.

Director's fee, for instance. Fifteen thousand dollars day rate. Which was about average for a B director, A directors being somewhere up at twenty or twenty-five. Then there was set construction. Forty-five thousand — pretty much the going rate for one suburban kitchen on a New York stage set.

All these thousand dollars reminding me of the thousands I myself didn't have. Why was I looking at this estimate, anyway? There was something wrong with it. What, exactly? I didn't know.

There was editing. Film-to-tape transfer. Color correction. Voice-over costs. And there was music. Yes, T&D Music House; that was the name all right. Forty-five thousand dollars. Full orchestra, studio record, mix. Seemed okay.

I called David Frankel.

'Yep,' David answered.

'It's Charles.'

'I know. It says your extension on my phone.'

'Right. I've been trying to call the music house, but I can't seem to find the number.'

'*What* music house?'

'T and D Music.'

'Oh. What are you calling them for?'

'What am I calling them for? I wanted to talk to them about the spot.'

'Why don't you talk to me about the spot. I'm the producer of the spot.'

'I've never heard of T and D Music,' I said.

'You've never heard of T and D Music.'

'No.'

'Why are we having this conversation, exactly?' David sighed. 'Did you talk to Tom?'

'You mean ever?'

'Look, what do you want the music to be? Just tell me.'

'I'd rather talk to the scorer.'

'Why's that?'

'Because I want to convey my feelings directly.'

'Okay, fine.'

'Okay, fine, *what*?'

'Convey your feelings directly. Go ahead.'

'I need their *number*.'

Another sigh now, the kind of sigh that said he was dealing with an idiot here, a complete and utter moron.

'I'll get back to you on that,' David said.

I was going to ask why David needed to get back to me since all I was asking for was a number. I was going to ask him why he was acting as if I were brain-damaged. I was going to remind him that a producer's job was to produce, and sometimes that meant producing something as simple as a phone number.

But David hung up.

It was only then, as I heard that familiar question whispering in my ear again – *What are you going to do, huh, Charles?* – that I realized I was a little brain-damaged after all. That I'd been a little slow on the uptake here.

T&D Music House.

Tom and David.

Tom and David Music House.

Of course.

I followed Winston for five or six blocks in subzero temperature.

Winston smoked a cigarette. Winston window-shopped – a Giuliani-ized video store – once plastered with triple-X-rated posters promising the raptures of the flesh, now plastered with kung fu posters promising the pulverizing of it. Winston leered at two teenage girls in miniskirts and woolen leggings.

I hadn't intended to follow Winston. What I'd intended to do was walk right up to him at closing time and ask him if he wanted to have a beer with me. But I'd felt strangely reticent about doing it.

It was one thing to joke around twice a day with a man who delivered your mail, to ask him what left-handed baseball player had the highest batting average in history, to trade wisecracks and earned run averages. It was another thing to go drinking with him. I wasn't sure Winston would *want* to go drinking with me.

On the other hand, hadn't we traded confidences? Or hadn't *one* of us done that? And now the other ready to do the same? But that brought me to the other reason I hadn't been able to just walk up to Winston and suggest a drink.

Winston blew on his hands. He waltzed through a traffic light, narrowly avoiding a taxicab seemingly intent on mayhem. Winston stopped at a pretzel man and asked how much.

I was close enough to make out the words. I wished Winston would turn around and acknowledge me. A few more blocks and I was in danger of freezing to death.

Across the street was a Catholic mission with a biblical statement I remembered from Sunday school emblazoned over its door: 'Oh Lord, the sea is so large and my boat is so small.' *True enough*, I thought.

When I looked back toward Winston, he wasn't there. I ran over to the pretzel man and asked him where his last customer had gone to.

'Eh?' the pretzel man said.

'The tall guy you just sold a pretzel to. Did you see where he went?'

'Eh?'

The man was Lebanese, maybe. Or Iranian. Or Iraqi. Whatever he was, he couldn't speak English.

'One dolla,' he said.

I said never mind. I walked away and thought: *I will talk to Winston tomorrow. Or maybe tomorrow I will change my mind and not talk to him at all.*

Someone grabbed me by the arm.

I don't want a pretzel, I started to say. But it wasn't the pretzel man.

'Okay, Charles,' Winston said, 'why the fuck are you following me?'

Twenty-one

On Christmas Eve I got drunk.

The problem was my mother-in-law's special eggnog, the special part being that it was two-thirds rum.

'Come to Daddy,' I said to Anna after I'd finished one and a half of them, but she didn't seem to like that idea.

'You look dopey,' she said to me.

'Are you drunk, Charles?' Deanna asked me.

'Of course not.'

Mrs Williams had an upright piano that must've been seventy years old. Deanna had taken lessons on it until she'd mutinied at ten years old and said enough. No more 'Heart and Soul' and 'Für Elise'. Mrs Williams had never quite forgiven her for that; her punishment was having to bang out Christmas songs on the piano we were all forced to sing to. 'Hark the Herald Angels Sing', for instance. Neither Deanna nor I was particularly religious, but there

162

are no atheists in foxholes. I belted out, 'God and sinners reconcile . . .' as though my life depended on it, my syncopation slightly askew, as I was already into my third eggnog.

'You *are* drunk, Daddy,' Anna said dourly. She liked singing songs with Grandma about as much as she liked giving herself shots.

'Don't talk to your father like that,' Deanna said, stopping in midchord. Deanna, my defender and protectress.

'I'm not drunk – both of you,' I said. 'Want to see me walk a straight line?'

Apparently not.

Instead Anna snorted and said: 'Do we have to sing these stupid songs?'

'. . . in Bethlehem,' I sang, focusing on the Christmas star on top of the tree. It was faded from years of use, no longer sparkling the way it'd been when Anna needed to be held up in my arms during the Christmas sing-alongs to see it. A tarnished star now; you could see that it wasn't a star at all – just papier-mâché pockmarked with glue.

'Well, that was fun,' Mrs Williams said when we finished. Then when no one answered her, '*Wasn't it?*'

'Yep,' I said. 'Let's sing another.'

'Get bent,' Anna said.

'What does that mean?' I asked.

'It means *no*,' Deanna said.

'That's what I thought it meant,' I said. 'Just checking.'

'No more eggnog for you,' Mrs Williams said.

'But I *love* your eggnog.'

'I think you love it too much. Who's going to drive home?'

'I will,' Deanna said.

'When are we going?' Anna asked.

After dinner, we opened Mrs Williams's presents. Anna would get hers tomorrow morning: two new CDs, including one by Eminem. Two tops from Banana Republic. And a cell phone. These days if you didn't have a phone of your own, you were some kind of dweeb. After all, you never knew whom you'd need to call: a girlfriend, a boyfriend, an ambulance.

Mrs Williams received a lovely new sweater from Saks. She dutifully thanked us all – even me, who of course had no idea what was going to come out of the box.

'I'd like to propose a toast,' I said.

'I took away your eggnog,' Deanna said.

'I know. That's why I want to propose a toast.'

'Geez, Charles, what's gotten into you?'

'I know what's gotten into him,' Mrs Williams said. 'My eggnog.'

'Damn fine eggnog, too,' I complimented her.

'*Charles.*' Deanna looked mad.

Anna giggled and said: 'Oh my, Daddy said "damn". Call the police.'

'No,' I said. 'No police. Not a good idea.'

'Huh?'

'Just kidding.'

164

Mrs Williams had put up some coffee. 'Coffee, anyone?' she asked.

'I'm sure Charles would love some,' Deanna said. As it happened, I wouldn't have loved some. It was clearly a plot; they were trying to sober me up.

Meanwhile Anna was whispering to Deanna. Something about getting off her back. 'I'm behaving fine,' I heard her say.

I'd sunk into the living room couch and was wondering if I'd be able to get up when the time came to leave.

'How's your nose, Charles?' Mrs Williams asked me.

'Still there,' I said, and touched it for her. 'See?'

'Oh, Charles . . .'

Mrs Williams had put on the TV station with the yuletide log. I stared into the flames and started to drift. It felt warm and pleasant. Until I began drifting into dangerous waters and it became unpleasant. That frozen street corner in the city.

The Charles that was all liquored up with the holiday spirit was screaming at me not to think about it.

But I couldn't help it.

I don't want a pretzel, I'd started to say. Remember?

I'd wanted something else.

Okay, Charles, why the fuck are you following me?

Winston with his arm casually around my shoulder, although I could feel the strength in it, and what's more, I thought Winston *wanted* me to feel that strength.

'I wasn't following you,' I said. Lying seemed to be my

first instinct here – and besides, I wasn't following Winston as much as procrastinating about following him.

'Yes, you were. Sing Sing gave me eyes in the back of my head, remember?'

'I was just going to ask you to have a beer. Really.'

'Why? You finally figured out the seven players with eleven letters in their last names?'

'I'm still working on that one,' I said, not exactly sure how to proceed.

'So why didn't you just ask me? If you wanted to have a beer so badly?'

'I saw you walking a block ahead. I was just trying to catch up.'

'Okay,' Winston said. 'So let's have a beer.'

And he smiled.

We went to a place called O'Malley's, which looked very much like what you would expect a place called O'Malley's to look like. It had a pool table in the back, a dartboard in the corner, and a TV tuned to an Australian football match. It had two resident drunks, at least I assumed they were more or less regulars, since one of them had his head laid flat on the bar and the bartender wasn't bothering to wake him. The other one Winston knew, because he said, 'Hey, man,' and briefly clapped him on the back when we walked by.

'What'll you have?' Winston asked after we took our seats at the bar.

'I'm buying,' I said.

'Hey, you did me a favor, remember?' Winston retorted.

Yes, I remembered. Enough to think Winston might do me a favor in return.

'A light beer,' I said.

Winston asked the bartender for two. Then he turned back to me.

'So, everything okay?' he asked. 'You looked a little depressed the other day. Is it your kid? Isn't she sick or something?'

I'd never told Winston about Anna, but word gets around, I suppose.

'No, it's not that,' I said.

He nodded and watched as the bartender put two beers in front of us.

'I have this problem,' I said, finding a certain comfort in that word. Problems, after all, were manageable things. You had problems and then you figured out a way to solve them.

'Look, if it's a pang of conscience about that night, forget it. Have you heard about any more computers being stolen? I told you I wouldn't, and I haven't.'

'Yes, I know,' I said.

'So what is it?'

Winston took a long sip of beer. I hadn't touched mine yet – there was an ever-widening pool of water under the glass, making the bar beneath it look dark as blood.

'I did a stupid thing,' I said. 'I went a little crazy. With a woman.'

Winston looked just a little confused. I understood – he

167

was probably wondering why someone who wasn't a friend in the strictest definition of the term was talking to him about other women, about things you talked only to *best* friends about.

'You had an affair or something?'

'Or something.'

'Okay. So, it's over, or what?'

'It's over, yes.'

'So what is it? You're guilty about it. You wanted to unburden yourself? Fine. Don't worry about it. Everybody in the office is having an affair. Even with each other. What do you think we talk about down in the mailroom? Who's screwing who.'

I sighed. 'It's not that.'

'Okay,' Winston repeated. 'So what is it?'

'Something happened.'

'What? She's pregnant?'

'No. We were caught by someone,' I said.

'Huh?'

'In the hotel room.'

'Oh,' Winston said. The wife, he was thinking.

'A man came in and attacked us,' I said.

'*What?*'

'He jumped us as we were leaving the room. He robbed us and . . . raped her.'

I had Winston's full attention now. Maybe he was still asking himself exactly why I was telling him all this, but at least he was interested in what I was saying.

'He raped her. In a hotel?'

'Yes.'

'What hotel?'

'Just a hotel. Downtown.'

'*Fuck*, Charles. What happened? Did he get away? They didn't catch him?'

No, they didn't catch him. In order to have caught him, they would have had to be told that he'd done something that necessitated his having to be caught.

'We didn't report it,' I said.

'You didn't report it.' Winston had fallen into the unfortunate habit of repeating every other thing I said. Probably because every other thing I was saying was a little hard to believe.

'We *couldn't* report it,' I said. 'Understand?'

'Oh,' Winston said, finally comprehending the situation. 'Yeah. Okay, sure. So he took your money and disappeared?'

'No. He *didn't* disappear.' I finally took a sip of beer – it tasted flat and warm. 'That's the problem.'

Winston looked confused again.

'He's blackmailing us,' I said. 'I guess that's what you call it. Asking us for money so he won't tell Deanna. My wife. And her husband.'

Winston sighed and shook his head. *That's some situation you've got yourself into,* this sigh said. *I feel for you.*

I wanted Winston to do more than feel for me. I wanted him to *act* for me. And that would take more than sympathy. It would take a kind of quid pro quo; it would take *another* kind of blackmail.

169

'So – did you pay him what he wanted?' Winston asked.

'Yes and no.'

'Well, did you or didn't you?'

'I did. He wants more now.'

'Uh-huh,' Winston said, taking another sip of beer. 'I guess that's kind of par for the course, isn't it. Don't they always want more?'

'I don't know. It's the first time I've ever been blackmailed.'

Winston almost laughed. Then he caught himself and said: 'Sorry, Charles. Really, it's not funny, I know. It's just that it's kind of hard to imagine – I mean, *you*. In this kind of shit?'

He lifted his glass again and sucked down foam. 'So . . . what are you going to do?'

Winston had finally reached the million-dollar question.

'I don't know,' I said. 'There isn't much I *can* do. I can't pay him. I don't have the money.'

'Uh-huh. So you're going to let him tell your wife,' he said, adding up all the variables but coming up with the wrong answer. 'Sure – fuck him. She loves you, doesn't she? So you fucked around – who hasn't? She'll forgive you.'

'I don't think so, Winston. I don't think she will forgive me. I don't think she could. Not with our daughter and all . . .'

I explained the rest. How Lucinda refused to let her husband know, either. How I felt I owed her that.

'Shit,' Winston said. Then, after a long moment of

silence: 'Been a great couple of months for you, Charles, hasn't it?'

He was referring to losing the credit card account, I guessed – even the mail department must've weighed in on that one.

'So,' Winston said softly, 'what do you do now?' as if asking himself that question, putting himself in that situation, maybe, and wondering what *he*'d do. And it's possible that it was then, that very moment, that he finally understood why I'd asked him here, why I'd followed him four blocks in the freezing cold to get him to have a beer with me. Maybe because he said to himself, *If it was me, I'd kick that blackmailer's ass. I'd kill him. I would.* Dismissing that as a reasonable alternative for me, of course, since I wasn't exactly the violent type. No, you had to have a little muscle to do something like that, you had to have a little experience in these matters, gotten your hands dirty now and then, or at least your fists bloody. Didn't you?

Winston put his glass down – midswallow he put it down and looked at me.

'What the fuck are you asking me?' he said. He'd finally put two and two together; he'd finally figured it out.

'I was hoping—'

'You were hoping *what*?' Winston cut me off. 'What?'

'You'd help me.'

'You were hoping I'd help you.' There he went, echoing me again, but this time not because he couldn't believe what I was saying, but because he *could*.

'. . . and the Sydney Swans take the ball upfield . . .' The TV was still tuned to the Australian football match, which had evidently reached the do-or-die point of the game, because the crowd was roaring now, on their feet screaming for victory.

'Look,' Winston said, 'I like you, Charles. You're okay. I'm sorry about your daughter, man. I'm sorry about this blackmail thing, I am. But you're not my brother, okay? You aren't even my best friend. I have a best friend, and I'd do just about anything for him, but even if he asked me what I think you're about to – I'd say, *Go fuck yourself.* Do we understand each other?'

'I just thought maybe you'd . . . see him.'

'*See* him. What the fuck does that mean? And when I see him, what would I be supposed to say to him? Huh? "Could you be a nice guy and stop bothering my friend?" Is that before or after I kick his ass for you?'

Winston was no dope – a 3.7 GPA, and even with a history of drug abuse, his brain cells were still more or less intact.

'I'd pay you,' I said.

'You'd pay me. How nice of you. Great.'

'Ten thousand dollars,' I said, plucking the figure out of the air. I'd paid ten thousand to Vasquez already, hadn't I – ten thousand seemed about right. Out of Anna's Fund again, but maybe there'd be a way to replenish it – that I *had* been giving a little thought to.

'Ten thousand,' Winston said. 'Or *what*?'

'What do you mean?' I said, even though I knew exactly

172

what Winston meant. I'd been trying to leave that part of it unsaid.

'Or what?' Winston repeated. 'If I don't take the ten thousand. And ten thousand is a lot of money for me – I'll admit it. But if I turn you down anyway. *Then* what?'

'Look, Winston . . . all I'm asking you—'

'You're asking me to commit a felony. I'm just wondering why you thought I'd say yes.'

Then, after I didn't answer him: 'How did *he* put it to you, Charles? The rapist. The blackmailer.'

'What?'

'When he asked you for money – he said you pay such and such to me. Or else. Isn't that how he said it? More or less? So that's what I'm asking you. I'm asking what the *or else* is.'

'Look, I think you misunderstood—'

'No, I understand perfectly. You're not asking me for money – you're *offering* it – I understand, very generous of you. But if I turn it down, if I say no thanks – then what? What's my alternative here?'

He wanted me to say it out loud. That's all.

I caught you stealing. I caught you stealing, and I can tell. Delivering mail is no great shakes, but prison is a lot worse. Right?

I might have offered to buy him a beer like a long-lost friend, but it wasn't friendship I was banking on.

But I couldn't bring myself to say the words.

I'd hoped Winston might do it as a favor – I'd let him off the hook once, and now Winston would get me off

173

mine. That ten thousand dollars might do the trick here. But now that Winston was forcing me to issue the actual threat, I found I couldn't.

And I thought: *I'm not Vasquez.*

'Ten thousand dollars, huh,' Winston said. He turned back to the football match: '. . . ball kicked upfield, Dover has it in the left corner . . .' He looked over at the sleeping drunk, who'd momentarily roused himself before sticking his head back down on the bar. He tapped his fingers on the edge of his beer glass – *tink, tink, tink,* like a wind chime caught in a sudden breeze.

And then he turned back to me and said: 'Okay.'

Just like that.

'Okay,' he said. 'Fine. I'll do it.'

Twenty-two

I called Tom Mooney and told him I wanted to talk to him about something.

About music production.

It was the three-day work week between Christmas and New Year's. The time of year when people attempt to put their affairs in order and make a New Year's resolution or two. To lose those few extra pounds, for instance. I was formulating a weight-loss plan of my own. I had approximately one hundred and eighty extra pounds sitting on my neck. I needed to get rid of it.

Tom showed up five minutes early and made an elaborate show of taking off his coat and closing the door.

'Okay,' Tom said when he sat down, 'so what do you want to talk about?'

'Kickbacks,' I said.

But maybe I'd been too blunt, because Mooney suddenly

edged back in his chair. Was it possible there was a kind of code you were supposed to use for these things, a language of men in the know?

'Kickbacks – what's that?' Tom said. 'Are we in the Teamsters or something? The last time I looked, we shoot commercials.'

'T and D Music,' I said. 'So you also write songs.'

'Hey, we're a full-service production company. Whatever it takes.'

'And that's what it takes?'

'Have you seen Robert's reel lately?' He was trying to be funny, I guess, because he seemed to be waiting for me to laugh.

I didn't feel like laughing today.

'How long has this been going on?' I asked. 'You and David?'

'Look, Chaz. Did you call me over here for an interrogation? Because maybe I missed something when you called me. I thought you called me over here for another reason. Correct me if I'm wrong.'

I blushed. Maybe there *was* another language, or maybe I knew the language but was incapable of speaking it. First with Winston in the bar and now here. I had called Mooney over here for another reason, not to condemn him, not even to sweat all the dirty little details out of him. Just to put out my hand and say, *Count me in.*

So maybe it was time I dropped the air of moral superiority – that's what Tom was saying. And what's more, he was right.

'Twenty thousand,' I said.

Kind of amazed that the words had actually made it all the way out of my mouth. *Twenty thousand* as a bald statement of fact – no equivocation, no rising consonant lilting into a plea. Twenty thousand – for the ten I owed Winston and the ten I'd already given out. And I wondered if this was the way it was done – or if I'd been expected to slide a scrap of paper across the table with the figure scrawled in pencil.

But Tom smiled again – the kind of smile that says, *You are one of us, aren't you?*

I felt a bit queasy – but less than I expected. Was this how it happened? Losing yourself a little at a time until suddenly there was no *you* there anymore? Someone who used your name, slept with your wife, hugged your kid, but wasn't actually you anymore?

'Hey,' Tom said. 'I told you I was Santa Claus, didn't I?'

The next day, I met Winston one block north of the number seven subway tracks in the mostly empty parking lot of a Dunkin' Donuts in Astoria, Queens.

Winston's idea. *Aren't you supposed to meet in out-of-the-way places?* he'd said after asking me if I knew the only pitcher with five Cy Young Awards.

Roger Clemens, I'd said.

Winston was waiting for me in a white Mazda with nonmatching hubcaps and a busted taillight. The windshield was covered with spiderweb cracks.

I drove up in my silver Mercedes sedan and felt

embarrassed about it. I parked at the far end of the lot, hoping Winston wouldn't see me. But he did.

'Over here,' he yelled.

When I made it to the car, Winston leaned over and opened the passenger door.

'Hop in, bud.'

Bud hopped in.

'Know my favorite song?' Winston asked.

'No.'

'"Money". By Pink Floyd. Know my favorite artist?'

I shook my head.

'Eddie Money.'

I said: 'Yes, he's good.'

'My favorite movie? *The Color of Money.* Favorite baseball player of all time – Norm Cash. Second favorite – Brad Penny.'

'Yes, Winston,' I said, 'I have your money.'

'Hey, who was asking for *money*?' Winston said. 'I was just making conversation.'

A number seven train rumbled over the el, showering sparks down onto the street.

'But now that you mention it,' Winston continued, 'where is it?'

I reached into my pocket. *It's burning a hole in my pocket* – isn't that the expression? A messenger from Headquarters Productions had dropped off the manila envelope yesterday.

'Five thousand,' I said. 'The other half after.'

'You see that in a movie?' Winston asked, still smiling.

'What?'

'The "other half after" stuff? You see that in a movie or something?'

'Look, I just thought—'

'What's the deal, bud? I believe, when I said I'd do this, from the goodness of my heart, by the way – because you're a pal and you're in trouble – you said *ten* thousand.'

'I know what we—'

'A deal's a deal, right?'

'I understand.'

'What were the terms?'

'I think one-half—'

'Tell me what the terms were, Charles.'

'Ten thousand,' I said.

'Ten thousand. Right. Ten thousand for what?'

'What do you mean?'

'What are you giving me ten thousand for? Because you like me? 'Cause you want to send me back to college?'

'Look, Winston . . .' I suddenly wanted to be somewhere else.

'*Look*, Charles. I think maybe there's some kind of confusion. I want to review the terms with you. You ask someone to do something like this for you, you have to know what the terms are.'

'I know the terms.'

'You do? Then state them for me so there's no confusion. What are you giving me ten thousand for?'

'I'm giving you ten thousand to . . . make Vasquez go away.'

Winston said: 'Yeah, right – that's what I thought the

terms were. Ten thousand to make Vasquez go away.' He pulled something out of his pocket. 'Here's my *argument* to make him go away,' he said. 'What do you think? Think he'll listen to it?'

'A gun.' I felt myself recoil; I edged back against the window.

'Hey – you're good,' Winston said. 'You sure you haven't done this before?'

'Look, Winston, I don't want . . .'

'What? You don't want to look at it? Neither will he. What did you think I was going to do, Charles – ask him nicely?'

'I just want . . . you know . . . if at all possible . . .'

'Yeah, well, just in case it's not at all possible.'

'Okay,' I said. 'Okay.' I had been thinking in euphemisms all this time – *making Vasquez go away*. Doing something about him. Taking care of him. But this was the way a Vasquez was taken care of, Winston was saying. Sometimes it was this way.

'Okay what?' Winston said.

'Huh?'

'"Okay, here's your *ten thousand*, Winston"?'

'Yes,' I said, giving up.

'Great,' he said. 'For a second there I thought you were only giving me half.'

I took the envelope out of my pocket and handed it over.

'You're too easy, Charles,' Winston said. 'I would've settled for three-quarters.'

Then, after he'd counted it all, he said: 'Where?'

Twenty-three

Under the West Side Highway.

One week into the new year.

I was sitting next to Winston in a rented metallic blue Sable with leather seats. Winston had his eyes closed.

I could see a lone tugboat chugging its way up a Hudson River so black, it was as if it weren't there. Just an empty black space where the river ought to be. It was cold and sleeting; thin slivers of glass were exploding onto my face through the open window.

I was shivering.

I was trying not to think about something. I was trying to stay calm.

There was a hooker standing on the corner across the street. She'd been standing there ever since I entered the car.

I was looking at her and wondering where her customers were.

A fair question, since it was only a little past ten, and she was wearing a sheer red negligee and shiny black boots. She'd been dropped off by a Jeep with New Jersey license plates and was waiting for some other car with New Jersey license plates to come along. But it had been ten minutes and she was still stuck out there in the sleet. Doing nothing much but looking across the street at the blue Sable, which didn't seem to be moving, either.

She looked as if she were freezing. She had a small fake fur wrap around her shoulders, but other than that nothing, lots of pasty white flesh out there where her customers could see it and put a price tag on it.

But where *were* her customers?

The insurance salesman from Teaneck, the broker from Piscataway, the truck driver on his way to the Lincoln Tunnel?

I was under the West Side Highway because that's where Vasquez had told me to meet him.

Do you have the money? he'd asked me.

Yes, I did.

You'll meet me ten o'clock at Thirty-seventh and the river.

Yes, I would.

You'll tell nobody – understand?

Yes, I did. (Well, maybe just one other person.)

You'll show up alone.

Yes, I would. (Well, maybe not exactly alone.)

How long *had* the hooker been standing there without a customer? I thought again. How long, exactly?

Then she began to walk over to me.

In the middle of the street now, closer *to* me than away from me, so I knew that she wouldn't be turning back. Her boot heels echoing as she made a beeline for the blue Sable that had been sitting there all this time without moving an inch.

'Want a date?' she asked me when she reached my window. I could see actual goose bumps on her breasts and legs, because her breasts were only half-hidden by the red negligee and her legs were naked save for those calf-length boots.

No, I didn't want a date. I wanted her to leave.

'No.'

'Uh-huh,' she said. Her face was young but old, so it was practically impossible to tell her age. Anywhere from twenty to thirty-five. 'You got a cigarette?'

'No.'

But there was a pack of cigarettes sitting on the seat between Winston and me – Winston's cigarettes. She could clearly see them there, one or two cigarettes even peeking out of the torn wrapper.

'So what are *those*?' she asked me.

'Wait a minute,' I said. I reached for the pack, but when I picked it up I got a piece of Winston's brain matter on my hand – the pack was smeared with it. I pulled one cigarette out anyway and handed it to her through the window.

'Thanks,' she said, but she didn't sound as though she meant it.

Then she asked me for a light.

'I don't have one.'

'What about him?' She meant Winston, who still had his eyes closed.

'No,' I said.

'Maybe *he* wants a date?'

'I don't think so.'

'What's wrong with him? He drunk?'

'Yes, he's drunk. Look, I gave you a cigarette, so—'

'What good's a cigarette without a light? What am I supposed to do – *eat* it?'

'We don't have a light, okay?'

I saw the reflection first – a flickering puddle of red in the middle of the street and then the sound of tires crunching glass.

A police cruiser.

'Get out of here,' I told her.

'*What?*'

'Look, I just want to be left—'

'Go fuck yourself,' she said. 'You don't go telling me to get outta *nowhere*. Understand?'

'Yes, okay . . . I just don't want a date, okay?' trying to be nice now, trying to be polite about this so that maybe she'd go away. Because Winston still had his eyes closed, and the police cruiser was almost up to our car. And the hooker – she wasn't leaving, now that I'd made her good and mad at me.

'I'll stay where I damn please,' she said.

And the cruiser rolled right up to the car; and the side window rolled down.

I expected the policeman to yell at me. Tell me to get out of the car, maybe – me and Winston. I expected the policeman to get out of the cruiser and shine a flashlight into the front seat, where he'd notice that Winston had his eyes closed and, if he looked closer, something else. That half of Winston's head was gone.

'Hey,' the policeman said.

'Hey yourself,' the hooker answered. Like old friends.

'How you doin', Candy?'

'How d'ya think,' she said.

'Great night to work, huh?'

'You got that right.' Just making conversation, one pal to another.

I was sitting there listening to them. But I wasn't actually hearing them.

I was remembering.

When I'd arrived at the pier, I saw Winston sitting in the rented blue Sable, just as he was supposed to be. I watched him sitting there for ten minutes, then fifteen, before I noticed that a window was open. That Winston wasn't moving a muscle – hadn't moved his head in all that time. Hadn't lit a cigarette, hadn't coughed, or yawned, or scratched his nose. Stock still, still as a still-life: *Man in Blue Car.* Something was wrong. That open window, for instance – the sleet blowing straight in. Why was that?

I crossed the street finally to take a quick look, *quick* because I was expecting Vasquez any minute, and I was supposed to have come alone. Winston's eyes were closed as if he were sleeping. Except he didn't appear to be actually *breathing*. And the window *wasn't* open; it was broken.

I got into the car and tapped Winston on the shoulder, and Winston ignored me. And then I leaned across the front seat to get a better look at Winston's hat, which was when I realized that it wasn't a hat. It was pulp. Half of Winston's head was gone. I threw up – my vomit mixing in with the various pieces of Winston's head. And I was about to run out of the car screaming when I saw the hooker being dropped off by that Jeep. So I stayed put.

Did you see anyone get in or out of the car? they'd ask her.

And she'd say no.

Unless she decided to walk across the street and ask for a cigarette.

The Sable was starting to smell. Even with the broken window letting in steady gusts of frigid air.

'You're keeping safe, right, Candy?' the policeman was saying.

'You know me,' she said.

No one had bothered to say anything to me yet.

I was tempted to turn the ignition and take off. There were two problems with that, of course. One was that Winston was sitting behind the wheel. And the other was that the policemen, who so far were still ignoring me, would more or less have to *notice* me if I suddenly gunned the engine and took off.

But now, finally, one of them did look inside the car.

'You,' he said.

'Yes?'

'You conducting a transaction with Candy here?'

'No. I just gave her a cigarette.'

'Something wrong with her?'

'What? No . . . she's fine.'

'That's right, Candy's a honey.'

'I just was . . . having a smoke.'

'Are you married?'

'Yes.'

'Your old lady know you go around looking for hookers?'

'I told you. I was just—'

'What about your buddy here? He married, too?'

'No. No . . . he's single.' He's *dead*.

'Both of you out looking for hookers and you aren't doing any business with Candy? Why's that?'

'Officer, I'm sorry if you misunder—'

'What are you apologizing to me for? Tell *her* you're sorry. Freezing her ass out here and you two guys don't give her the time of day. What's with your friend over there?'

'He's . . .' *Dead, Officer.*

'Maybe you should show Candy some appreciation.'

'Sure.'

'Well?'

'Oh . . .' I fumbled for my wallet. My hand was shaking so hard, it was difficult to actually get it into my back

187

pocket. I finally managed to grab an indeterminate bunch of bills and held them out to her.

'Thanks,' Candy said listlessly, taking them and stuffing them into the top of her negligee.

'What about him?' the policeman asked. 'What's your name?' he asked Winston.

Winston didn't answer him.

'I *said*, What's your name?'

Winston still didn't answer him.

I was picturing myself in the back of the police car, being driven *downtown* – wasn't that the expression? I was picturing myself being booked and fingerprinted and given one call. I didn't even know a lawyer, I thought. I was picturing facing Deanna and Anna through a scratched plastic partition and wondering where on earth to begin.

'Okay. Last time,' the policeman said. 'What's your *name*?'

And then.

A sudden crackle, and a staticky voice broke through the excruciating silence like a clap of thunder on an oppressively humid afternoon.

'. . . we have a . . . uh . . . ten-four . . . corner of Forty-eighth and Fifth . . .'

And suddenly the policeman was no longer asking Winston what his name was. He was saying something to Candy instead – 'Catch you later,' it sounded like. And the police car left – just like that, *vroooom*, gone. Mere seconds from discovering a man with half a head and another man sitting calmly next to him in a front seat covered with vomit and brain matter, and it was suddenly, inexplicably, over.

And finally, at last, I could let it out.

I could cry for Winston.

Twenty-four

It occurred to me almost by accident. I was driving to nowhere in particular. I was following the West Side Highway and trying to keep from shaking.

Winston was dead.

Winston was dead, and I'd killed him.

Hadn't I cornered him in the bar that night and more or less *forced* him into doing this?

I tried to work it out – what happened, exactly? Vasquez had said come alone, but maybe Vasquez hadn't trusted me to come alone, so he'd come early to sniff around. Is that what happened? There was Winston in a blue Sable just sitting there, and maybe Vasquez got suspicious and confronted him, and maybe Winston got belligerent – remembering this was a man who'd been in prison, who was used to doing things to people before they did it to him. Only not this time. And Winston had ended up with half a head.

That made sense, didn't it? It was hard to tell if it *really* made sense, because I was scared senseless.

I was almost suffocating from the stench inside the car now. And it was then that I remembered *another* awful smell sniffed from the front seat of a moving automobile. The mind worked like that sometimes, playing a kind of charades with you – *stench* and *car* and what do you get?

Memories of Sunday afternoons spent motoring down to Aunt Kate's house in southern New Jersey. To get there, we had to take the Belt Parkway down to the Verrazano Bridge, then go straight through the heart of Staten Island. Passing not much of anything along the way, just a supersize mall here and there with a megaplex cinema showing seventeen different movies all playing at once. Then, smack in the middle of nowhere, it would hit with terrifying swiftness. A vomitous odor would suddenly assault us through the cracked-open windows, through the air-conditioning vents and sunroof. The odor of garbage, the stench of landfill. Huge mounds of dun-colored earth on either side of the highway circled by clouds of screaming gulls. Fishkill.

I'd close the windows, Deanna holding her nose right next to me and Anna screeching in the backseat. I'd turn off the air-conditioning and make sure the sunroof was locked tight, but the odor would still come in. It was like sticking your head in a garbage pail, and no matter how fast I drove – and I'd hit the accelerator for all it was worth – I couldn't drive fast enough. I couldn't outrun the smell, not until I'd traveled a good fifteen minutes or so and the landscape turned sweetly suburban.

An hour later, drink in hand on Aunt Kate's backyard deck, I could still sniff it on my clothes.

That's where I headed.

I took Canal down to the Manhattan Bridge, then up the Belt to the Verrazano. Traffic was light this time of night – a good thing, considering Winston was decomposing right next to me. *Have you got half a brain?* I used to complain to Anna when I lost my temper. And Winston did have half a brain, the other half spread in pieces around the car.

I was thinking ahead to the tollbooth. If it would be a problem paying – if the toll collector would be able to see inside the car. If he or she would be able to *smell* the car. Trying to take this thing one obstacle at a time – like Edwin Moses, whom I'd once heard on ESPN explaining his method in the hurdles as just that: one hurdle at a time and never look at the finish line.

The finish line for me was Winston safely disposed of and me back in bed. And Vasquez paid off in full – oh yes, a hundred thousand was seeming kind of cheap right at the moment – all of Anna's Fund, maybe, but still kind of cheap, things being what they were.

The toll collector was humming vintage James Brown – 'I Feel Good'. Not if she sniffed the car, she wouldn't be. Not if she took a peek at my traveling companion and noticed the brain schematic sitting on his shoulders. I'd pulled out the money in advance and had it out there

192

waiting for her. She'd had a kind of cool rhythm going with the cars in front of me – arm out, arm in, money in, change out, like one of those funky dances from the sixties, the *swim* or the *monkey*. But when I rolled up to her window with cash in hand, she told me to wait a minute. She started to count bills inside the booth and left my money sitting right where it was – in my sweaty palm.

It was maddening. I began to worry about the other toll collector now, the one to my right and therefore closer to the dead body. I wondered if they carried guns – toll collectors? It didn't really matter, since I knew they carried radios. A simple message to the police station up ahead and I was dead meat.

Finally, after another half a song – Little Stevie Wonder circa 1965 – she reached out and took the money from me.

And I breathed again – shallow breaths, of course, head turned toward the window because the stench was enveloping me like steam. Winston was the second dead person I'd ever seen. I'd attended an open-coffin funeral when I was fourteen – a friend of the family who'd succumbed to cancer – and I'd more or less kept my eyes on my shoes, peeking just once at a face that seemed oddly happy. Not so with Winston, his mouth half-open as if caught in midscream, his eyes squeezed shut. He'd gone complaining about it.

I killed Winston, I thought again.

Just as if I'd pulled the trigger myself. Adultery, fraud, and now murder? It didn't seem so long ago that I'd been one of the nameless good guys. It was a little hard to reconcile that Charles with this one – this one driving a dead man through Staten Island on the way to the dump. It was a little difficult to digest. Yet if I could only make it to the dumping grounds without being apprehended by the police; if I could dispose of Winston's body and the bloody car; if I could make Vasquez go away with one hundred thousand dollars . . .

One hurdle at a time.

First I had to find a way into the landfill. It had to be close; the stench in the car had been joined by another one that was even worse.

I reached the exit for the dump. At least I thought it was, because the next exit said Goethals Bridge. I exited onto a deserted two-lane road with no street lamps. Winston slumped against the window as I turned right.

I followed the road for five minutes or so, not a single other car in either direction. I imagined the only traffic that found its way here was either coming or going to the landfill, and at this time of night no one was doing either of those things. Except for me.

I squinted into the blackness, looking for a gate that might let me in, slowing to a crawl so I wouldn't ride past and miss it.

There.

Just up ahead, a gate all right – a barbed-wire fence ending in two swinging doors and a sentry box. A gate in – which might have made me weep for joy, or shout in exultation, or at least sigh in relief, if it wasn't for the fact that it was locked solid.

Well, what had I expected? This was city property, wasn't it, not a public dumping ground for anyone with a dead body to get rid of.

I got out of the stinking car only to find that it smelled worse outside the car than in it. It was as if the air itself were garbage, as if all the putrid smells of New York City were dumped here, too, along with all that solid stuff. Landfill and airfill both, and the seagulls feeding on all of it and crying out for more. *Rats with wings* – wasn't that what they called them? And now I understood why.

An entire flock of them had descended by my feet – lifting their wings and cawing at me as if I were after their food. As if I *were* their food. Sharp yellow beaks all pointed at me, and I wondered if they could smell Winston's blood on me, if, like vultures, they could sniff out the dead and dying.

I felt hemmed in, surrounded by encroaching seagulls and stench, and I yelled and flapped my arms, hoping to scare them away. But the only one scared seemed to be me; the gulls hardly moved, one or two of them beating their wings and lifting an inch or two off the ground. I retreated to the car, where I sat in the front seat and stared at the locked gate.

I reversed the car and began to meander up Western Avenue again, tracking the fence and looking for anything that might constitute a way in.

'Come on, surprise me,' I said out loud. Life had thrown me a few nasty ones lately – thinking that maybe I was due some good ones. Even *one* good one, right now, here in the asshole of Staten Island, where all the waste exited and lay rotting.

And then my headlights caught a piece of torn fence as the road curved right. Just big enough for one man to get through – even one man dragging *another.*

He must have a mother somewhere, I suddenly thought. I pictured her as a typical suburban mom. I didn't know where he'd grown up, so maybe she wasn't a suburban mom at all. But that's the way I imagined her. Divorced, maybe, disillusioned by now, but still proud of her grade-school son with the 3.7 GPA. That pride tested through the years, of course, as Winston got into drugs, then into dealing drugs, and then, God help her, into *prison* for dealing drugs. But wasn't he putting his life back together again? Wasn't he the owner of a legitimate job these days – okay, just delivering mail for *now*, but you couldn't keep a good man down for long, could you? Not with his brains. Before you knew it, he'd be running that company, sure he would. And such a good-hearted boy, too, and likable – everyone but everyone liked Winston – and he never forgot her birthday card, not once. She still had that lopsided clay ashtray he'd made her in second grade, didn't she – sitting up somewhere on the mantelplace. Winston's mom, who wouldn't be getting a birthday card from him this year or any other year from now on.

I wished I'd asked Winston more about his life. Anything about his life. If he *did* have a mom waiting for his Christmas cards every year, or a girlfriend sitting up tonight and wondering just where Winston was exactly, or a brother or sister or favorite uncle. But all I'd asked him about was baseball and prison, that's it, and then I'd asked him to do something that had gotten him killed.

I stopped the car right by the section of torn fence, then sat there for a while to make sure I was really alone. Yes, as far as I could tell, I was very much alone, alone at the dump, alone in the universe. 'Deanna,' I whispered, my partner in life, but only the one she knew about – Charles the nine-to-five adman, as opposed to Charles the adulterer and accessory to murder.

I got out of the car, I walked around to the other side, I opened the door and watched helplessly as Winston fell over onto the ground. I would try to think of it as the *body* – the thing that's left behind when the soul, what made Winston Winston, had already departed. It was easier that way.

I lifted the body by its arms and began dragging, and I immediately realized that the term *dead weight* was not a misnomer. Dead weight was the immovable object, panic the irresistible force, but who said the irresistible force wins out? I could barely move the *body*; an inch or three at a time. It felt as though it were pulling back – tugging at my shoulder sockets, at my elbow joints and aching wrists. At this rate, I'd have the body through the fence by daybreak, just in time for a fleet of sanitation workers to point me out at the police lineup. *That's him,* they'd say – the man pulling the deceased into the garbage dump.

But slowly, torturously, I made progress, working out a kind of routine: one huge pull, then a dead stop to catch my breath, shake my hands, and rev up for another. In this fashion, I got the body all the way to the torn section of fence without suffering a single heart attack. And still hours from sun break, too – twelve-thirty, according to my luminescent-dial Movado, a forty-second-year birthday gift from Deanna, who was probably starting to wonder where I was. She *worried*, and she did it better and with greater dedication than anyone I knew.

I fished my cellular phone out of my coat pocket, flipped it open with a now throbbing wrist, and pressed 2 – my home number. Number 1 in automatic dialing was Dr Baron's office.

'Hello?' Deanna, sounding, yes . . . upset.

'Hi, honey. I didn't want you to worry – it's taking longer than I thought.'

'Still at the office?'

'Yeah.'

'Why are you calling on your cellular?'

Yes, why was I?

'I don't know. I walked down the hall for coffee and suddenly realized how late it was.'

'Oh, okay. How much longer do you have?'

Good question. 'An hour or so, maybe . . . we have to show these stupid aspirin boards in the morning.' I was kind of surprised how adept I'd become at telling lies, surprised too that I was having this perfectly normal domestic chat – *I'm working late, dear* – while standing over a man with half a head.

'Well, don't work too hard,' Deanna said.

'Yes, I won't.' Then: 'I love you, Deanna,' saying her name this time, which on the scale of I love yous ranked somewhere near the top, uttered as something meant as opposed to just another way to end a conversation. Love you – love you, simply a more intimate version of good-bye, but *not* when you put a name there. Not then . . .

'I love you, too,' Deanna said, and I knew she meant it, no name necessary.

I put the phone back in my pocket, put one foot through the open hole, reached down, and began to drag Winston through.

The stench was worse over here – hard to imagine, but it was. Outside the fence I was smelling it, but inside the fence I was *eating* it, ingesting it smell by smell and beginning to turn sick to my stomach.

I pulled the body farther into the dump, closer to the edge of the enormous mound of ground-up garbage. Now that I was this close to it, it looked like one of those temples to the sun I'd seen in Mexico City on a long-ago trip with Deanna. Pre-Anna, and we'd spent the mornings sight-seeing and the afternoons soaking our livers in tequila. Lots of lovemaking, followed by long drunken naps.

Now what?

You could think in the general all you wanted, but sooner or later the specific starts snapping at you for answers. I'd gotten the body to the dump, I'd dragged it through a barbed-wire fence, I'd brought it to the very foot of the temple of the garbage god.

I looked down at my hands, the very hands that hugged Deanna, that gave insulin shots to Anna, that once upon a time had explored every inch of Lucinda, now being asked to moonlight on a very different kind of job. To shovel a grave.

I dug in, scooping out handfuls of ground-up waste, sharp pieces of tin and bone, glutinous pieces of gristle and fat, man-made fibers of cardboard and Sheetrock.

If I'd been trying to remain dispassionate before, I took it up like religion now. As if my soul depended on it, my very life, this objectification of tonight's events. Merely smells, merely hands, merely a body. Focusing solely on the act of digging – so much material removed at such and such a rate, leaving an ever widening hole.

By now, I had garbage all over me, up to my elbows in garbage – dangerously close to *becoming* garbage.

I heard something from far off, the sound of a thunderstorm that might or might not be coming this way – but maybe it wasn't a thunderstorm after all. The sound was a little too thin for thunder – and as far as I could tell, it was a more or less cloudless night. I heard it again – ears wide open this time – and finally recognized it for what it was. And in recognizing it, I pictured it, too: black pointy ears, snub tail, and sharp white teeth practically dripping with saliva.

And it was getting closer. The junkyard dog of my nightmares.

I dug quicker, scooping out the worst kind of shit with broken-nailed fingers like a dog digging for bones. And every passing minute I could hear the *real* dog getting louder – distinct barks and growls drifting around the mounds of garbage and over to me, just as my scent must have been drifting back the other way.

The hole was big enough. I stood up and breathed once, twice – getting myself ready for my last physical expenditure of the night.

A cloud of seagulls suddenly passed in front of my eyes – a screaming thundercloud of them, swollen with panic. I could see two glowing eyes staring at me from across the dump.

All those clichés of fear – of where real fear first makes itself known to you: *in the pit of your stomach . . . up and down your spine*. They were all true. And I could feel it in places you might not expect, either. The back of my neck, where it felt as if each little hair were standing on end. The hollow of my chest, which was vibrating like a bass woofer.

The two eyes advanced and with them a sound that grated on what little nerve I had left. Not a bark, no, one low, sustained growl. The kind that said, *I am not happy to see you.*

I began to back up, slowly, one baby step at a time, even as the dog – I couldn't make out what breed, exactly; let's say human retriever – padded closer and closer.

Then I turned – and ran. Maybe I shouldn't have; maybe it would have been wiser to stare it down. *Never show a dog fear* – wasn't that the old wives' adage you're taught from youth? It makes them mad, gets their blood up, stirs up their carnivorous impulses.

But something else stirs up their meat-eating instincts even more. Meat. And I had magnanimously left the dog a lot of it. In the person of Winston.

It took several minutes – several minutes I spent scurrying out through the fence hole and into the car – to realize that the dog wasn't following me.

And then I heard it. A sound of gnashing teeth – of tearing flesh – of lascivious guttural consumption.

The junkyard dog was eating Winston.

Twenty-five

I had to get rid of the blue Sable.

It had been rented from Dollar Rent A Car by one Jonathan Thomas. One of the four driver's licenses Winston had stuffed in his otherwise depleted wallet.

The easiest thing to buy – identities, Winston had confided in me. And Winston had four of them. Back when I was young and idealistic, searching for your identity was an expected rite of passage. Winston, on the other hand, simply bought his – or stole it – making sure he had a few extras just in case.

Just in case someone asked him to get rid of someone else.

Now I had to get rid of the car.

That sort of took care of itself. On the way back down Western Avenue, I passed the highway; it was dark, and I was replaying the sounds of canine feeding in my head –

hitting the rewind button against my better judgment and listening to it over and over again. When you're hearing the sounds of someone being eaten, it's easy to miss things like highway signs. I ended up in a part of Staten Island I hadn't known existed – farmland, actual rows of fallow field with an honest to God silo sitting in the distance. Two ticks from every sin of urban congestion, and I was suddenly in Kansas.

But not *every* sin of urban living was missing. I passed a massive car dump. It looked like a watering hole for wrecks, being as they were all grouped around a mud pond, some of them half-submerged in it. One more wreck would hardly be noticed, would it?

I gently swerved off the road and into the bumpy lot, driving the car to the very edge of the water. I took one last look around the car – trying not to touch the pieces of flesh stuck to carpet and leather, opening the glove compartment, and finding a surprise in there. A gun. Winston's, I remembered, the one that must've never made it into his hand because another gun took his head off before it could. I delicately placed it into my pocket. Then I put the car in neutral, stumbled out of the front seat, and with a gentle push forward let the car slip quietly into the pond, where it finally came to rest with just its antenna poking out of the muck.

I wasn't much for religion – I didn't know any prayers to really speak of. But I stood there for a minute and whispered something anyway. In his memory.

I turned away and began to walk.

How I was going to get home?

I could have called a car service, I suppose, but I knew they kept records. I needed to find my way back to midtown, where Charles Schine taking a car ride home would be like any other late night at the office.

I passed a gas station. I could see a lone Indian-looking man reading a magazine in a barely lit cubicle. I walked around the side, looking for a bathroom. I found one.

Gas station bathrooms were much like bathrooms in Chinatown, which were much like black holes in Calcutta, or so I now thought. There was no toilet paper. The mirror was cracked, the sink filled with sludge. But I needed to wash up. I would have to find a bus or train that would take me back into the city, and I smelled like garbage.

The sink had running water. Even a little soap left in the holder, a thick scummy yellow. I washed my hands – I threw water on my face – I took my shirt off even though the bathroom was frigid and I was exhaling clouds of vapor every time I breathed. I rubbed my chest and under my arms. *A whore's bath* – isn't that what they called it? And I was a whore in good standing these days. I'd prostituted every single thing I'd believed in.

I put my shirt back on. I zipped up my jacket. I went back outside and began walking.

I just picked a direction. I wasn't going to ask the gas station manager, who just might remember a shell-shocked-looking white man who'd showed up without his car.

A half hour later I discovered a bus stop. And when an empty bus came to a stop there a half hour after that, I took it. I was lucky. It was headed to Brooklyn, where it eventually let me off by a subway station.

I made it back to Manhattan.

Home.

Something I appreciated after a night of grave digging. Four solid walls of clear yellow shingle and black-pitched roof with one impressive chimney poking through. The real estate agent who'd sold it to us described it as a center hall colonial. A substantive ring to it – nothing much could happen to you in a center hall colonial, now could it? Of course, outside the center hall colonial, all sorts of things.

When the car dropped me off, I walked to the back door and tried to open and close it as silently as I could, but I could hear Deanna stirring from our upstairs bedroom.

I made one more foray to the bathroom – this bathroom a lot cheerier than the previous one. Cleaner, too. Nice fluffy yellow towels hanging from the wall and a Degas print over the toilet – *Woman Bathing*?

This time I undressed down to my boxers and used a towel generously soaked in soap to rinse myself down. That was more like it – I smelled almost bearable. I took the gun out of my pants and put it into my briefcase.

Then I went upstairs to the bedroom, where I maneuvered my way through the pitch black – one stumble over a high-heeled shoe – and into bed.

Deanna said: 'You washed up.' Not as a question, either.

Of course; she smelled the soap, she'd heard the faucet, too. Now, why would a working-late husband wash himself before climbing into bed? That's what she was asking herself – and I was having trouble coming up with an answer.

Don't be silly, Deanna, I could say. *I haven't been with another woman.* (See: Lucinda.) *I've been busy burying a body. This hit man and friend I hired to get rid of someone who was blackmailing me because I was with another woman before. Got it?*

'I worked out today,' I said, 'and I never took a shower.'

Not a great excuse when you thought about it – not at this hour of the night. I mean, why couldn't I have just waited till morning? But maybe it would do.

Because Deanna said: 'Uh-huh.' Maybe she was suspicious about it, maybe she was suspicious about a lot of my recent behavior, but maybe she was too tired to hash it out. Not at two in the morning. Not when she'd stayed up all night waiting for me to come home.

'Good night, sweetheart,' I said, and leaned over to kiss her. Milky and warm: home.

I had a dream that night, though – when I woke in the morning I could remember several details.

I'd been visiting someone in the hospital. I had flowers with me, a box of candy, and I was in the reception room waiting to be called up to the sick person's room. What sick person, though? Well, the patient's identity changed

207

several times in the dream, which is what happens in dreams – first they're one person and then they're someone else. At first I was visiting Deanna's mom, but when I finally got up to the room it was Anna lying there. She was plugged into a spider's web of IVs, and she barely acknowledged me, and I demanded to see the doctor. But when I turned to look at her again, it was Deanna who was lying there in just this side of a coma. Deanna. I remembered the next part of the dream clearly: shouting in the hall for the doctor to come see me, even though there *was* a doctor there – Dr Baron, in fact, who kept explaining that they couldn't get hold of the doctor, not possible, but I was having none of it.

Finally my shouting seemed to do the trick; the doctor *did* come to see me. But he changed identities, too – first Eliot, my boss, then someone who might've been my next-door neighbor Joe, and finally and last, Vasquez. Yes, I woke up remembering Vasquez's face there in the hall with me. By turns impassive and malevolent and snide, but consistently deaf to my pleas. Deanna was dying in there and he was doing nothing to help her. Nothing.

In the morning, after Deanna left for work and Anna for school, I made another trip into the file cabinet, another furtive visit into Anna's Fund.

208

Twenty-six

On the train in the morning, I did *not* read the sports page first. Did not read about the Giants' last lamentable defeat, about the Yankees signing yet another platinum-priced free agent, about the Knicks' eternal search for a point guard.

For one day, at least, my Hebraic reading of the daily newspaper (that is, back to front) was put aside, and I read the paper like a concerned citizen. Concerned about the festering situation in the Middle East, the ongoing congressional gridlock, the roller-coaster tendencies of the Nasdaq. And, of course, the recent upswing in urban crime. Murder, for instance.

I had listened to the 1010 on your dial morning news flash in the shower and been pleased to hear nothing of the sort. Someone was murdered all right – someone was always getting murdered in New York City. But this someone was female, twenty-one, and French. Or Italian. A tourist, anyway.

The *Times* 'Metro' section yielded no male victims. Likewise the local Long Island paper. Of course, even if someone *had* been discovered, it would've been too late to make it to print.

But these were modern times. The first thing I did when I arrived at the office, after saying hello to my secretary, was to get on the Net.

I searched the on-line editions of two newspapers. There was nothing about a male murder victim in New York City.

Good.

I spent the rest of the morning trying not to think about Winston's body. Trying not to think about the hundred thousand dollars of Anna's Fund that was no longer Anna's. About how I was giving up – finally and futilely giving up.

It was easier said than done – at lunchtime I made another visit to David Lerner Brokerage on 48th Street.

It helped that I had to go to an editing house to look over the nearly finished aspirin commercial with David Frankel. He had the editor play it several times for me. It wasn't the best testimonial commercial ever done. It wasn't the worst, either. I took particular notice of the music bed, which sounded like something borrowed from a stock music house – or thrown out by one. It probably *was* stock, of course – something purchased for three thousand dollars, then billed at forty-five.

David, the D of T&D Music House, seemed much more personable today. As though I were a true partner in this endeavor now. Maybe because we *were* partners now. Partners in bilking the agency and client out of their dubiously earned cash.

'Trust me,' David said after the editor – Chuck Willis, his name was – had played the spot another three or four times, 'the client will love it.'

And I thought how on the accounts I *used* to work on, it didn't matter if the client was going to love it. That was always secondary to whether or not *we* loved it. But it was hard to love a spot where a housewife basically read the product's attributes off an aspirin bottle.

Still, I had to look it over and act like I cared. Like it was worth looking over and making helpful hints about, suggestions for improvement.

I pointed out places where I thought the film could be trimmed. I asked them to look for a better voice-over. I would've mentioned doing something about that saccharine music bed, but then someone might've discovered we'd illegally made over forty thousand dollars off of it.

When I got back to the office around two, someone I'd never seen before was placing my mail onto Darlene's desk. Of course – my new mailroom guy.

I asked him where Winston was. I would've been expected to ask him that.

The man smiled and shrugged. 'He didna come in,' having trouble pronouncing each word correctly. I wondered if this was one of the disadvantaged people Winston had told me about.

'Oh,' I said, acting surprised. 'I see.'

Darlene smiled at the new mail deliverer and said: 'You're better looking than him, anyway.' *Than Winston*.

The man blushed and said: 'Tank you . . .'

I watched him walk away with a sickening feeling. *Life goes on*, people say when someone dies, *it goes on*. And there was the proof right in front of me. Winston had been gone just one day, and his replacement was making the rounds already. It both belittled and magnified what had transpired last night – it did both. It made me sick.

Later that afternoon, I held a creative briefing.

Just the thing to get my mind somewhere else, I hoped. The meeting took place at three-thirty in a conference room dutifully reserved by Mary Widger.

My band of unhappy creatives dutifully listened to me – with pads and pencils, too, no less, managing to look halfway interested in what I was saying. They were unhappy because it was another assignment for their new account – a combination cold and headache pill – instead of an assignment for their *old* account, which might've meant a commercial worth doing and putting on their reels. And they were also unhappy because I was more or less reading verbatim from a strategy statement prepared by Mary Widger. Strategy statements much like Foucault's theorem – obtuse, complex, and understood by no one. In my bygone halcyon days, I'd simply ignored them; we'd write the commercial, fall all over ourselves laughing, and write the strategy statement from that.

Not anymore; now I read words like *target audience,* like *comfort level* and *saturation,* without once turning red. A dutiful drone doing what drones do – droning on interminably, or until the said strategy was read down to the last period.

I went back to my office and closed the door. I called Deanna.

'Hello,' I said. I wasn't sure why I was calling her, but I remembered the days when I used to call her *daily* from work, and more than once, too.

When we'd stopped talking to each other, really talking, when we'd started talking about inconsequential things only – I'd stopped calling her three times a day. And there were days I didn't call her at all, entire twelve-hour periods when not a single word passed between us.

And now there were so many things I couldn't talk to her about, too – things I was ashamed of, things I could barely bear to think of.

But I called her anyway.

'Hello yourself,' Deanna said. 'Everything okay?'

'Yes, fine.'

'You sure, Charles?'

I wouldn't realize till later that Deanna wasn't merely making small talk here. That she *knew* things weren't okay with me – not the details, but enough.

But I didn't take advantage of the opportunity – not yet. I couldn't.

'Yes, everything's fine, Deanna,' I said. 'I just wanted to say . . . hi. I just wanted to see how you're doing today. That's all.'

'I'm doing okay, Charles. I am. I'm worrying about you, though.'

'Me? I'm fine. Really.'

'Charles . . . ?'

'Yes?'

'I don't want you to think . . . well . . .'

'Yes?'

'I don't want you to think you can't *talk* to me.' There was something heartbreaking about that statement, I thought. Talking – surely the easiest thing two people can do with each other. Unless they can't. And then it's the *hardest* thing two people can do with each other. The most impossible thing on earth.

'I . . . really, Deanna. There's nothing. I was just going to say hi. To say . . . I love you. That's all.'

Silence from the other end of the line. 'I love you, too.'

'Deanna, do you remember . . . ?'

'Remember what?'

'When I played the magician at Anna's party? I bought those tricks from the magic store. Remember?'

'Yes. I remember.'

'I was good, too. The kids loved it.'

'Yes. Me too.'

'When I turned over the hat, remember? And they thought they were going to get soaked with milk. Confetti came out. Oohs and aahs.' I'd been thinking about that for some reason today, maybe because I was searching for another kind of magic now.

'Yes, David Copperfield has nothing on you.'

'Except a few million dollars.'

'But who's counting.'

'Not me.'

'Thinking of changing careers?'

'I don't know. It's never too late, is it?'

'Yeah. Probably.'

'That's what I thought.'

'Charles?'

'Yes?'

'I meant what I said. About *talking* to me. Okay?'

'Sure.'

'Be home normal time?'

'Yes. Normal time.'

'See you then.'

When I hung up the phone, I thought it might actually be possible to make everything turn out okay. Not everything, but the important things. I knew what the important things were, too – they were staring at me from the ten-by-twelve picture frame on my desk.

But that's when everything began to go wrong.

Twenty-seven

The phone call came maybe two minutes later.

Two minutes after I'd hung up with Deanna, after I'd stared at the picture of my family and thought that maybe I could make it all work out in the end.

The phone rang. And rang again. Darlene was probably down the hall swapping boy stories with her fellow executive assistants – which is what secretaries liked being called now in lieu of decent salaries.

So I picked it up.

There were over one hundred people who could have logically been on the line – much later, I counted them as an excuse for something to do. Everyone I knew, basically – maybe a hundred people, all in all, who could reasonably be expected to pick up a phone and call me. Not that I wasn't expecting this call, of course. In many ways, it was the only call I *was* expecting. But I imagined it very differently. I imagined it was going to be *Vasquez* on the line.

But it wasn't Vasquez.

It was her.

Only her voice was strangely reminiscent of another time, another place. That little-girl voice again. Terribly cute when it's coming from a little girl, but nauseating when it's not.

'Please, Charles,' the voice pleaded. '*You have to come here. Now.*'

I was thinking several things at once. For instance, where *here* was. Her home, her office? Where? For another, I was wondering what it was that was causing her to sound like a frightened child again. Even though I knew what it was. I knew.

'You *have* to . . . *Oh God . . . please,*' she whispered.

'Where *are* you?' I asked her. A good logical question, one of the four Ws they teach in journalism. What, When, Why, Where? Even if I was asking it in a voice that sounded as panicked as hers. Even then.

'*Please . . .* he followed me . . . he's going to . . .'

'What's going on, Lucinda? What's wrong?' Which, after all, was the real question here.

'He's going to hurt me, Charles . . . He . . . he wants his money . . . he . . .' And then her words got muffled and I could picture what was happening. I saw the phone being yanked out of Lucinda's hand, the receiver covered by a large black fist. I pictured the room, which looked like the room in Alphabet City even if it wasn't. And I imagined her face – even as I tried to avert my eyes, I did. Don't look . . . don't . . .

And then someone was speaking again. But not her. Not this time.

'Listen to me, *motherfucker.*' Vasquez. But not the one I was used to. That phony ingratiating tone was gone, the carefully controlled fury. Fury had been let out for a stroll, and it was kicking up its heels and break-dancing on whoever got in its way.

'You thought you could fuck with me. You thought you're gonna set *me* up? You miserable piece of shit. *Me*? You put some pansy in a car, and he's gonna what? Kick *my* ass? You fucking crazy? I got your *girl* here, understand? I got your whore right here. Tell me you understand, motherfucker.'

'I understand.'

'You understand *shit*. You think you're some kind of gangsta or something? You send some clown to fuck me over? *Me*?'

'Look . . . I understand. I—'

'You understand? You get your ass over here with the hundred grand or I will fucking kill this stupid whore. You understand *that*, Charles?'

'Yes.' After all, who couldn't understand that? Was there anyone on earth who couldn't grasp the gravity of that statement?

Now we were down to Where again. I asked for an address.

This time it was uptown – Spanish Harlem. A place I'd never been to except in passing while on my way to somewhere else – Yankee Stadium or the Cross Bronx Expressway.

I called Vital for a car. I opened my locked drawer and stuffed the money into my briefcase – I had it sitting there, waiting for the moment to arrive. I saw something else sitting there, too: Winston's gun. For a second I thought about taking it with me, but then I decided against it. What, after all, would *I* do with it?

On the way downstairs I passed Mary Widger, who asked me if anything was wrong.

Family emergency, I explained.

In fifteen minutes I was traveling up Third Avenue. The car slithered, it squeezed, it maneuvered its way excruciatingly through an obstacle course of stationary refrigeration trucks, FedEx vehicles, moving vans, commuter buses, taxis, and gypsy cabs.

But maybe we weren't moving as slowly as I thought – maybe I was simply picturing what Vasquez was going to do to Lucinda and thinking that I couldn't let it happen again, not twice in one lifetime. It seemed that I'd look up at a street sign – 64th Street, for instance – and five minutes later I'd still be looking at the same sign.

Halfway through the ride, I realized the hand that was holding my briefcase had gone numb. I was gripping the handle so tightly, my knuckles had taken on the color of burnt wood – ash white. And I remembered a game Anna used to play with me, a kind of parlor trick – asking me to hold her forefinger in my fist and squeeze for five minutes, not a second less, and then release, always giggling as I tried to open my now paralyzed fingers. That was the way I felt now – not just my hands, but all of me: paralyzed. The way I'd felt back in that chair in the Fairfax Hotel. The woman I'd fallen in love with being raped not five feet from me, and I like a victim of sleeping sickness, able to perform all the functions of life save one. To act.

Eventually, the tonier sections of the East Side fell away. Boutiques, handbag stores, and food emporiums turned into thrift shops and bodegas as more and more Spanish words began showing up on passing storefronts.

The apartment building was on 121st Street between First and Second Avenues.

It was surrounded by a check-cashing place, a hairdresser, a corner bodega, and two burned-out buildings. A man selling roasted chestnuts and what looked like unpeeled ears of corn had set up shop in the middle of the block. Another man who looked suspiciously like a drug dealer was checking his beeper and talking into a fancy-looking cellular phone in front of the building.

I asked the car to wait for me. The driver didn't seem very happy with the idea, but he had the kind of job where you couldn't exactly say no.

'I may have to circle,' he said.

I didn't answer him – I was staring at the building and wondering if I could make it through the door. There were three men loitering in the entranceway, and none of the three looked like anyone you'd ask for directions. They looked like three-fifths of a police lineup, men you don't put your hand out to unless it contains your wallet.

And I was carrying more than my wallet today; I was carrying my wallet plus one hundred thousand dollars.

As soon as I eased myself out of the car, I heard the click of the door locks. *You're on your own*, they said. And I was; and on 121st Street between First and Second Avenues, I was pretty much the center of attention, too. I imagined that Lincoln Town Cars made very few stops here, as did well-dressed white men carrying expensive leather briefcases. The chestnut seller, the drug dealer, the three men guarding the entranceway of building number 435, all were looking at me like a hostile audience demanding something entertaining.

I didn't know whether to run up the steps like a man in a hurry or walk up the steps like a man on a stroll, and I ended up somewhere in between – a man who's not quite sure where he's going but is still anxious to get there. When I reached the landing where the cracked asphalt was liberally scribbled with chalk and spray paint ('*Sandi es mi Mami*; *Toni y Mali . . .*'), I ended up acknowledging the three doormen the way most New Yorkers acknowledge anyone: I didn't. I kept my eyes averted – on the doorstep, an island of worn tire tread separating brown cement from curled yellow linoleum.

'Hey . . .'

One of the men had said something to me. I was hoping the man had been addressing one of his friends, but I was pretty sure he'd been talking to me. A man

wearing oversize yellow basketball sneakers and dress
pants – all that I could actually see of him, since I had my
eyes trained down by my feet.

I looked up into a middle-aged Spanish face that
might have been okay behind the counter at McDonald's
but not in the middle of Spanish Harlem with one
hundred thousand dollars sitting in my briefcase.
Besides, the face looked upset with me, as if I'd just
complained about the Happy Meal having no French
fries in it, and where exactly was the pickle on my
burger?

I kept moving, continued to make like a halfback in the
opposing secondary as I kept those legs pumping. Just
about through the door, too – since the door was
permanently half-ajar and offered no resistance.

'Where *you* going?'

The same man as before, speaking in heavily accented
English, with the emphasis on *you*, the intonation
important here, since I might've thought the man was
being helpful otherwise: *Tell me where you're going and
maybe I can help direct you there.* No – the man was
questioning my very validity for being there.

'Vasquez,' I said. The first thing that entered my head
besides *Help*. If you gave a name, it sounded aboveboard.
Maybe they knew that name, and maybe they wouldn't
want to fuck with it. And maybe even if they didn't know
that name – *Vasquez, who's that?* – they'd still be leery of
poaching in someone else's territory. A man alone was fair
game, but when he wasn't alone, who knew?

222

Anyway, it worked.

I kept walking through the doorway, and they didn't stop me. There was no elevator, of course; I took the steps two at a time. Lucinda was waiting for me – *He's going to hurt me, Charles*. Maybe the end was waiting for me, too.

The stairway smelled of bodily fluids: piss and semen and blood. I slipped on a banana peel that turned out to be a used condom and nearly fell down the stairs. I could hear ghostly laughter coming from somewhere I couldn't see, the kind of laughter that might be funny or might not be. It was impossible to tell.

When I knocked on the door, Vasquez opened it. I got one word out before I was dragged in and slammed up against the wall. He slapped me across the face. I tasted blood. I dropped the briefcase onto the floor and tried to cover up. He slapped me again. And again. I said, 'Stop it – I have it, there . . . there.' He kept slapping me, open-handed wallops that sneaked in between my upraised arms.

And then, suddenly, he stopped.

He dropped his arm, uncurled his fist, took a deep breath and then another. He shook his head; he exhaled. And when he finally spoke, he sounded almost normal. As if he'd just needed to vent his anger a little bit before coming back to himself.

'Shit,' he said, as if he were saying glad that's over with. 'Shit.' Then:

'You got the money?'

I was breathing too fast, like an asthmatic searching for air. My face stung where Vasquez had slapped it. But I managed to point to the floor. To the briefcase. The apartment had at least two rooms, I thought – I could hear someone from the room next door. A soft sniffling.

'Where is she?' I said, but my lip was swollen and I sounded like someone else.

Vasquez ignored me. He was opening the briefcase and turning it upside down, watching as stacks of hundred-dollar bills slithered across the floor.

'Good boy,' Vasquez said, the way you might to a dog.

I could hear her clearly now from the next room. The apartment – what I could see of it – had almost no furniture. The walls were streaked with dirt and scarred with cigarette burns. They were painted the color of yolk.

I said: 'I want to see her.'

'Go ahead,' Vasquez said.

I walked through the half-open door, which led to the rest of the apartment. The room was dark, the window shades pulled down. Still, I could make out a chair against the back wall. I could see who was sitting on that chair.

'Are you okay?' I said.

She didn't answer me.

She was sitting very still, I thought. Like a child on a church pew who's been told repeatedly to be quiet. She didn't look hurt, but she was sitting there dressed only in a slip.

Why was she in a slip?

I could hear Vasquez counting the money from the next room: 'Sixty-six thousand one hundred, sixty-six thousand two hundred . . .'

'I gave him the money,' I said.

But maybe not soon enough. I'd said, *Sorry, I don't have it* – and Winston had ended up dead and Lucinda had ended up here in her underwear. I wanted her to move, to answer me, to stop sniffling – to understand that no matter what had happened to her, no matter how many times I'd failed her, the end was within sight. I wanted her to walk across the finish line with me and not look back.

But she wasn't moving. She wasn't responding.

And I thought: *I have to do something now*. I'd taken Anna's money, I'd gotten Winston killed, I'd let Lucinda be snatched off the street. I'd done this all to keep a secret, and even if Lucinda was one of the people who'd wanted me to keep it, I had to do something.

Vasquez walked into the room and said: 'It's all here.'

I was going to get out of here, and I was going to go to the police. It had gone too far. It was the right thing to do. Only, even as I told myself in no uncertain terms what was necessary here, even as I steeled myself for what would be an unpleasant – okay, even horrible – duty, I could hear that *other* Charles beginning to whisper into my ear. The one who was telling me how close we were. The one who was saying that what's past is past, and now I was *this* close to getting out of it.

'Okay, Charles,' Vasquez said. 'You did good. See you . . .'

225

He was either waiting for me to leave or was about to leave himself.

'I'm taking her with me,' I said.

'Sure. You think I want the bitch?'

Lucinda still hadn't said anything. Not one word.

'Maybe you better stay home from now on, Charles. Back in *Long Island*.' He had my briefcase in his hand. 'Do me a favor, don't try some crazy shit like before – you ain't gonna find me anyway, see? I'm . . . relocating.'

And he left.

I stood there listening to his footfalls growing softer down the stairs, softer and softer till they disappeared completely.

I'm . . . relocating.

For some reason, I believed him, but maybe only because I wanted to. Or maybe because even Vasquez knew you could bleed someone only so much before the body was declared officially dead.

'I thought he was going to kill me this time,' Lucinda whispered slowly. She was staring at a point somewhere over my head. Even in the darkness I could see she was trembling. There was blood on the inside of her thigh. 'He held the gun to my head and he told me to say my prayers and he pulled the trigger. Then he turned me over.'

'I'm taking you to a hospital, Lucinda, and then I'm going to the police.'

Lucinda said: 'Get out of here, Charles.'

'He can't get away with it. He can't do this to you. It's gone too far. Do you understand me?'

'Get out of here, Charles.'

'Please, Lucinda . . . we're going to report this, and—'

'*Get out!*' This time she screamed it.

So I did. I *ran*. Down the stairs, out the front door, back into the waiting car, feeling all the while one distinct, overpowering, and guilty little emotion.

Overwhelming relief.

Twenty-eight

For two weeks or so, I believed.

Believed that possibly the worst was over. That, okay, I'd been tested, tested severely – a modern-day Job, even – but that it was entirely possible things were going to work out in the end.

Yes, it was *hard* to look Anna in the face these days, very hard. Knowing that the money I'd painstakingly accumulated for her was, for all intents and purposes, gone. That my carefully constructed bulwark against her insidious and encroaching enemy was virtually depleted.

It was hard, too, looking at Deanna – who trusted me, maybe the very last thing in life she *did* trust – knowing what I'd done with that trust.

Hardest of all, of course, was thinking about the people I couldn't look at. Lucinda, for instance – whom I'd failed not once, but twice. And Winston. Whom I'd failed right into the grave. Their pictures clamored for my attention, like needy children demanding to be seen. *Look at me . . . look.* I tried not to, I tried tucking Winston away in places where I couldn't find him. But I always did. When I picked up an ordinary piece of office mail, or read an article about the winter baseball meetings – he'd say hello. I'd see him lying there the way I'd left him. I'd close my eyes, but the pictures wouldn't go away. Like the flash of a camera that remains seared on your eyelids.

Still, I was hopeful.

Hoping for two things, really. That Vasquez had actually meant what he said, that he realized the well was good and dry now and he wouldn't be coming back. That he *had* relocated.

And I was hoping that I could rebuild Anna's Fund. That through diligent and constant *cheating*, through the auspices of the T&D Music House, I could build it back to where it was before. That I could do this before I might actually need it. Before anyone noticed it, either.

For two weeks, then, this is what I clung to.

Then there was a man waiting for me in reception. That's what Darlene said.

'What man?' I asked her.

'He's a detective,' Darlene said.

I thought of Dick Tracy. At first I did – remembering the Sunday comics I used to press into Play-Doh, then stretch into funhouse mirror versions of their former selves.

'A detective?' I repeated.

'Yeah.'

'Tell him I'm not here,' I said.

Darlene asked me if I was sure.

'Yes, Darlene. I'm sure.' Letting just a touch of annoyance into my voice – because annoyance covered up what I was actually feeling, which was, okay, fear.

'Fine.'

And the detective left. After which Darlene informed me that it was a *police* detective who'd been waiting for me.

The next day he was back.

This time he was sitting there in full view as I exited the elevator. I wasn't actually aware he was the police detective until he got up and introduced himself as such.

'Mr Schine?' he said.

And I immediately noticed that if he was a rep, he was devoid of reels, and if he was someone seeking employment, he was minus a portfolio.

'I'm Detective Palumbo,' he said, just like in the movies and TV. That New York accent, the kind that always seems somehow phony in the darkness of a movie theater.

Purpetration . . . dufendunt . . . awficcer.

That's how Detective Palumbo sounded – only no matinee looks here. A genuine double chin and a stomach that never met the Ab Roller +. Of course, he carried a real badge.

'Yes?' I said. A dutiful citizen just trying to be helpful to an officer of the law.

'Could I have a word with you?'

Of course. No problem. Anything I can do, Officer.

We walked past Darlene, who gave me a look that seemed somewhat reproachful. *I asked you if you really wanted me to tell the detective you weren't there, didn't I?*

We walked in, I shut the door behind us, we both sat down. And all that time, I was having a disturbing conversation with myself. Asking myself myriad questions that I couldn't answer. For instance, what was the detective here for? Had Lucinda reconsidered and gone to the police herself?

'Do you know Winston Boyko?'

No. Detective Palumbo was here about someone else. He was here about Winston.

'What?' I said.

'Do you know Winston Boyko?'

Okay. What were my options here? *No, I don't* wasn't one of them. After all, there were a number of people who could swear just the opposite – Darlene, Tim Ward, and half the sixth floor.

'Yes.'

Detective Palumbo was scribbling something in his little notebook that he'd produced almost magically out of his coat, scribbling away and seemingly waiting for me to embellish a little.

(A detective comes to see you and asks you if you know this obscure mailroom employee and you say . . . what is it? *Yes*. That's it. No curiosity about *why*?)

'Why do you want to know, Detective?'

231

'He's missing,' Detective Palumbo said.

A lot better than *He's been found dead.* I could cry all I wanted about this unexpected interrogation, but a Winston missing was better than a Winston found.

'Really?' I said.

Detective Palumbo had a red mark on the bridge of his nose. Contacts? A slight nick on his chin where he'd cut himself shaving? I checked out his face as if it might hold a few answers for me. For instance, what he thought I knew.

'For over two weeks,' Palumbo said.

'Hmmm . . .' I was down to monosyllabic responses now, being as my brain was off somewhere else furiously constructing alibis.

'When was the last time you saw him?' Detective Palumbo asked.

Good question. Maybe even a trick question, like who was the last left-handed batter to win the American League MVP award? Everyone says Yastrzemski, everyone, but it's a trick – it's really Vida Blue, left-handed wunderkind pitcher for the Oakland As. The kind of question Winston would have loved, too.

When did you last see him?

'Gee, I don't know,' I finally said. 'A few weeks ago, I think.'

'Uh-huh,' Palumbo said, still scribbling. 'What exactly was your relationship, Mr Schine?'

What did *that* mean? Wasn't *relationship* the kind of word you used for people who *had* one? Lucinda and me,

232

for instance. If Palumbo was asking me what kind of relationship Lucinda and I had, I would've said *brief*. I would've said sex and violence, and you can forget the sex.

'He works here,' I said. 'He delivers my mail.'

'Yeah,' Palumbo said. 'That's it?'

'Yes.'

'Uh-huh.' Palumbo was staring at the picture of my family.

'So I guess you're interviewing . . . everyone?' I asked, hoped.

'*Everyone?*'

'You know, everyone who works here?'

'No,' Palumbo said, 'not everyone.'

I could've asked him, *Why me, then?* I could've asked him that, but I was afraid of the answer I might get back, so I didn't. Even though I was wondering if Palumbo was *expecting* me to ask him that.

'So . . . is there anything else I can—' I began, but was interrupted.

'*When* was that again? The last time you saw him?' Palumbo asked, pencil poised and waiting – and I was reminded of an image from one of those British costume dramas that continuously turn up on Bravo: the Crown's executioner holding the axe above his head, only awaiting the signal to strike.

'I don't remember, exactly,' I said. 'Two weeks ago, I guess.'

I guess. Couldn't hold someone to a guess, could you?

233

Couldn't drag them downtown and haul them before the court on a wrong *guess*.

'Two weeks ago? When he delivered your mail?'

'Yes.'

'Did you ever get together with Mr Boyko, you know, socially?'

Yes, once in a bar. But it was business.

'No.'

'Did Mr Boyko ever talk to you about himself?'

'How do you mean?'

'Did Mr Boyko ever talk about himself? To you?'

'No, not really. About mail . . . you know.'

'*Mail?*'

'Deliveries. Where I wanted something sent. Things like that.'

'Uh-huh. That's it?'

'Pretty much. Yes.'

'Well, what else?'

'Excuse me?'

'You said *pretty much*. What else did he talk to you about?'

'Sports. We talked about sports.'

'Mr Boyko is a sports fan, then?'

'I guess. Kind of. We're both Yankee fans,' trying hard to keep in the present tense when I was talking about Winston – not so easy, when I could picture him lying stiffly at the foot of the mound of garbage.

'That's all, then. You talked about mail and sometimes about the Yankees?'

'Yes. As far as I can remember.'

'That's it?'

'Yes.'

'Would you know how Winston came into ten thousand dollars, Mr Schine?'

'What?' *You heard him.*

'Mr Boyko had ten thousand dollars in his apartment. I was wondering if you had any idea how he got it.'

'No. Of course not. How would I . . . ?' I was wondering something: if the police were allowed to check with David Lerner Brokerage and see how much stock I'd sold. It wouldn't look good, would it? It would look, okay, suspicious. But then, why would they suspect me of giving ten thousand dollars to Winston? I was panicking for no good reason.

'There were some computers stolen from your agency. One from this floor.'

'Yes, that's right.'

'Did you ever see Mr Boyko up here when he wasn't supposed to be?'

Computers. Palumbo was asking me about computers. Of course. *Winston the thief.* Winston the ex-con. He was talking to me because he suspected Winston had gotten that money from stealing some computers. He needed witnesses. Winston had stolen some computers and he'd made some money and taken off.

'Now that you mention it, I did see him up here one night when I was working late.'

'Where, exactly?'

'Just around, you know. In the hall here.'

'Was there any reason for him to be up on this floor after work?'

'Not that I can think of. I thought it was kind of strange at the time.' I was killing him again, I thought. First when he was alive and now when he wasn't.

'Did you challenge him about that? Ask him what he was doing there?'

'No.'

'Why not?'

'I don't know. I just didn't. He was down the hall – I was in my office. I really didn't know if he was supposed to be here or not.'

'All right, Mr Schine.' Palumbo shut his notebook and placed it back into his hip pocket. 'I think that's all I have for you today. Thank you for taking the time to talk to me.'

'You're welcome,' I said, even as I wondered about that word. *Today*.

'I hope you find him.'

'So do I. You know, Mr Boyko was pretty good about seeing his parole officer. He hadn't missed a meeting. Not one. You *did* know he'd been in prison, right?'

'I think I may have heard something about that. Yeah, sure. Is *that* who told you he was missing? His parole officer?'

'No,' Palumbo said. Then he looked straight into my eyes, the way lovers do when they want you to acknowledge the sincerity of their feelings.

'Mr Boyko and I had a kind of working relationship,' he said. 'Understand?'

No, I didn't understand.

As I walked Detective Palumbo out into the hall, wondering if the detective was going to go interview someone else – he didn't. Still not understanding that statement: *Mr Boyko and I had a kind of working relationship.*

And what kind of relationship was that?

It was only when I replayed the interview later in the day, wondering if I'd been okay with my answers, meticulously going over each Q&A to see if I'd slipped up, given the detective any cause, no matter how minute, to distrust me, that it occurred to me what kind of relationship any ex-con can have with any police detective.

What were the terms?

Because something else was bothering me. Something that didn't make sense. It was this. People are reported missing all the time – isn't that the usual quote you hear from bored and jaded police detectives on the evening news? The distraught parent complaining about police inaction, how their teenage daughter or son was missing for God knows how long, and the parents knew something was wrong, of course, they *knew,* but still the police did nothing much but take a report. Because people disappear all the time. That's what the bored detectives say. And if they looked for every kid who didn't come home, they'd have no time left to go after the serious criminals.

And these are kids they're talking about – *kids* that they don't exactly jump into action after. And Winston was not a kid. He was a grown man – and by the usual social standards, not a very important one. In fact, on the scale of important people, of people the police need immediately to start looking for, he'd probably be next to last, just above black transvestite heroin addicts, maybe.

Yet just two weeks after this ex-con doesn't show up for work, a police detective is there looking for him.

What were the terms?

So I replayed the detective's words again. *Mr Boyko and I had a kind of working relationship, understand?*

And yes, I *was* beginning to understand now.

What were the terms?

I'd seen all the movies, I'd watched the TV shows, I'd read the papers. Police detectives were allowed to lean on ex-cons for information. Ex-cons were inclined to give it to them so as not to be leaned on. So that maybe they'd look the other way when they were trying to supplement their income with, say, a little computer theft.

What were the terms?

I know the terms, Winston.

Why don't you state them for me so there's no confusion.

That night in Winston's car by the number seven train.

Why don't you state them for me.

And why was that? Why *did* Winston need me to state them for him, need to hear me say the words out loud? Because in the end, it's the words that'll set you free. You need to give them the words if they're ever going to believe you.

State them for me.

Policemen and ex-cons with only one kind of working relationship, really, and this is the way it works. This way. They ask and you tell. You whisper. You snitch.

State them.

If you don't have the words, if you don't have them sitting there on some tape somewhere, how will they ever believe you? A company big shot, a bridge and tunneler, an honest to God white-collar commuter, and he wants you to *what*? Say again, Winston . . .

State them.

No, not everyone, Palumbo said.

Just you.

Twenty-nine

Things happen for a reason. That's what Deanna believed. That things aren't as random as you might expect – that there was some kind of unseen and only hinted-at plan out there. That the orchestra might be out of tune and all over the place, but there was a maestro somewhere in that hidden orchestra pit who knew exactly what he was doing.

I'd always treated that kind of thinking with a healthy skepticism, but now I wasn't so sure.

Take the Saturday after my interrogation. Freakishly warm, pools of soft mud sucking at my shoes as I meticulously picked up after Curry in the backyard. I was concentrating on this task – covering every inch of the yard with eagle-eyed dedication – as a way to keep from concentrating on other things.

I was holding in fear and panic; I was trying not to let them out.

So when Deanna called out to me from the back door – something about auto insurance – I barely acknowledged her.

She needed to renew our insurance, she was saying. Yes, that's what it was. I nodded at her like one of those bobble dolls they stick on the dashboard of cars – reflexive motion caused by the slightest disturbance in the air. She needed to renew our insurance, and she wanted to know where our policy was.

So I told her. And went back to the business at hand.

It was ten or fifteen minutes later when she appeared at the back door wearing an expression I was all too familiar with. The one I'd hoped to never see again.

At first, of course, I thought, *Anna. Something happened to Anna and I must throw down my garbage bag and run into the house.* Where I would no doubt find my daughter comatose again. Only at that very moment I saw Anna pass her upstairs bedroom window, where the latest from P. Diddy was streaming through the closed sill. She looked fine.

What, then? So my mind backtracked, scurrying down the recent road to *here* – searching furiously for clues that might explain the nature of this particular disaster.

I'd been cleaning the yard; she'd come out to tell me something – yes, our insurance needed renewing. She'd asked me where our policy was; I'd told her.

In the file cabinet, of course. Under *I* for insurance. Right?

Except this was *auto* insurance. Automobile insurance

that needed renewing. So in the haphazard and admittedly chaotic filing system of the Schines, it was possible that this policy wasn't under *I* after all, but under *A*. *A* for automobile. In the *A* file.

All this occurring to me at lightning speed and, as lightning would, leaving me dazed and scorched. Possibly even *dead*.

Which is when I wondered about things happening for a reason. Why, for instance, our auto insurance had needed to be renewed now, right this minute, *today*. Why? And why at the very moment she'd asked me for help in finding our policy, I'd been so preoccupied with staying preoccupied that I hadn't had the wherewithal to tell her I'd go get it myself.

'Where's Anna's money, Charles?' Deanna asked me. 'What have you done with it?'

Maybe I'd always known the moment would come.

Certain things were just too massive to be hidden successfully – their very dimensions make them impossible to conceal. Their edges stick out in the open, and sooner or later someone is bound to notice them.

Or maybe I *wanted* to be found out – isn't that what any psychiatrist worth his salt would say? That I might've been cleaning up the garden, sure, but at the same time I was yearning to clean up my life.

Hard to believe that I would've gone through all I had only to throw it all away on purpose. But then, things weren't that simple anymore.

'What have you done with it?' she asked me.

And at first, I was rendered speechless. Deanna stock still on the back stoop and me standing there with a garbage bag reeking of excrement.

'I brought the certificates to a safety deposit box,' I lied through my teeth. *I will take one stab at extricating myself from this*, I thought, *one outright denial*.

'Charles . . . ,' she admonished me with my own name. As if that kind of blatant lying weren't worthy of me. And I wanted to say, *Yes, Deanna, it is. You don't know what I've been up to – it* is.

But I couldn't say much of anything – not yet, not when it concerned the truth. I was dead in the water, and I knew it.

'Charles, why are you lying to me? What's going on?'

I suppose I could've denied I was lying to her. I could've stuck to my ridiculous story about the safety deposit box – ridiculous not because it wasn't possible, but because even if she had believed me, I would have had to produce the stock certificates on Monday, and that *was* impossible. I could've said this is my story and I'm sticking to it, no matter what. But in the end, I had too much respect for her. In the end, I loved her too much.

So even though I knew what I was about to do, knew that now that I was about to take a stab at the truth I was going to be stabbing *her* – I went ahead anyway.

I started with the train. That hurried morning, the lack of cash, the woman who'd helped me out.

When I mentioned Lucinda, I could see Deanna's

expression change – her features flattening, the way animals' faces do at the first sign of danger.

'Then I had a bad day at the office,' I continued. 'I was kicked off the credit card account.'

Deanna was obviously wondering what getting kicked off an account had to do with $110,000 missing from Anna's Fund. And with the woman on the train.

I was wondering about that, too. I knew there was a connection, but I couldn't remember what it was. Something about needing to talk to someone, maybe – or had it simply been a precursor to what followed? One step taken off the ledge before the other foot followed?

'I ran into the woman again,' I said. What I should've said was that I ran after, sought, meticulously looked for, this woman. But wasn't I allowed to soft-pedal just a little?

'What are you *talking* about, Charles?' She wanted the Monarch Notes version now – she wasn't interested in a prologue or an introduction, not when she could tell that her future with me was hanging in the balance.

'I'm talking about a mistake I made, Deanna. I'm so sorry.' A *mistake*. Was that all it was? People made mistakes all the time, and then they learned from them. I was hoping she might look at it that way, even though common sense and everything I knew about Deanna after eighteen years of marriage told me there was no chance of that. Still.

Now Deanna sat on the stoop. She pushed her hair back from her face and straightened her back like someone about to be shot who still wants desperately to keep her dignity. And me? I raised the gun in my hand and pulled the trigger.

'I had an affair, Deanna.'

P. Diddy was still seeping through the window. Curry was barking at a passing car. Still, the surrounding world was about as silent as I'd ever heard it. A silence even worse than the kind that had permeated the house ever since Anna got sick, silence so black and hopeless that I thought I might start crying.

But she did instead. Not loudly or hysterically, but the tears suddenly there, as if I'd slapped her hard in the face.

'Why?' she said.

I'd expected she would ask questions. I thought she might ask me if I loved her, this woman – or how long it had been going on, or how long it was over. But no – she'd asked me *why* instead. A question she was entitled to, absolutely, but a question I was unprepared to answer.

'I don't know, exactly. I don't know.'

She nodded. She looked away, down at her bare feet, which seemed strangely vulnerable on the green step of our back stoop, like naked newborn mammals. Then she looked up again, squinting, as if looking directly at me were hurting her eyes.

'I was going to say, *How could you*, can you believe it? I was. But I know how you could, Charles. Maybe I even know *why* you could.'

Why? I thought. *Tell me . . .*

'Maybe I even understand it,' she continued. 'Because of what's happened with us lately. I think I can understand it,

I do. I just don't think I can *forgive* it. I'm sorry about that. I can't.'

'Deanna,' I began, but she waved me off.

'It's over now? This affair?'

At last a question I could more or less handle.

'Yes. Absolutely. It was once, just one time, really . . .'

She sighed, cracked her knuckle, wiped her eyes. 'Why is *Anna's money* missing, Charles?'

Okay. I'd told half of it, but there was still a whole other half, wasn't there?

'You don't have to tell me anything else about the affair – I don't want to know anything else about it,' Deanna said. 'But I want to know that.'

So I told her.

As sparingly as possible, as linearly as I could remember it – one thing leading to another leading to another – and I could tell that while it had all made sense to me, in a horrible, albeit panicked, way, it wasn't making any sense to her. Even when I reached the part where we'd been attacked and beaten and I could see actual sympathy in her eyes. Even when I reached the part where Vasquez entered our home and put his hand on Anna's head. Still it made no sense to her. Perhaps she could see what I hadn't been able to – could spot the moments in this tortured tale when I could've done something different, when this different course of action was *crying out* to be tried. Or maybe it was because I'd left something out, something significant and necessary to any true understanding of events.

'So I paid him the money,' I finished. 'To save her.'

'You never thought about going to the police? About going to *me*?'

Yes, I wanted to say. I had thought about going to the police, or going to her, which was pretty much the same thing, really. But when I'd thought about it, I'd pictured the way she'd look – which was the way she looked *now*. So I hadn't. And now I *really* couldn't go to the police, even though it might not make much of a difference, since it was entirely probable the police were coming for me.

'That money,' she whispered. 'Anna's Fund . . .' saying it the way I'd heard investors mention one fund or another these past couple of years while perusing the stock pages on their way to work. *That Dreyfus Fund . . . Morgan Fund . . . Alliance Fund . . .* As if reciting the names of the dearly departed. Gone and never to return.

'You have to go to the police now, Charles. You have to tell them what happened and get our money back. It's *Anna's*.'

I'd told her a story with a hole in it, a hole I'd hoped would be big enough to sneak through. But no. She was making a perfectly reasonable request, only I didn't have a perfectly reasonable answer. Protecting Lucinda from her husband's anger wouldn't do now – not for Deanna, not when protecting her was costing our daughter over a hundred thousand dollars.

What she didn't know was that I was protecting *me*.

'There's more,' I said, and I could see Deanna deflate.

247

Haven't you told me enough already? her expression seemed to say. *What more can there possibly be?*

'I asked someone to help me,' I said, thinking that I was still lying, since I hadn't asked Winston as much as *coerced* him. On the other hand, Winston hadn't actually helped me as much as set me up. 'I asked someone to help me scare off Vasquez.'

'*Scare off?*' Deanna might be in semishock, but she was still smart enough to see the inherent flaws in my plan, and she was calling me on it. That when you ask a man to scare off someone else, there was a volatility factor of plus ten. That what starts out as a fist in the face can end up as a knife in the heart. Or a bullet in the head.

'He was threatening this family, Deanna. He came to our *house.*'

When something loves me I love it back, Deanna had said to me once. That was her rule to live by, her credo, her own *semper fidelis*. But she was in the battle of her life now, with bomb after bomb falling all around her, and it was anyone's guess if that love could actually survive. Judging by the expression on her face, I would've had to say no. She was having problems recognizing me, I imagined – recognizing this man as the generally loving and gentle husband she'd known for eighteen years. Not this guy, who'd had a seedy affair and paid blackmail money because of it and even enlisted someone to get rid of this blackmailer for him. Was it possible?

'I didn't know what else to do,' I said lamely.

'What happened?'

248

'I think Vasquez killed him.'

A sharp intake of breath. Even now, when I'd no doubt ripped apart every illusion she once cherished, I was still capable of surprising her. An affair – bad enough; but then *murder*.

'Oh, Charles . . .'

'I think . . . I believe, this man, the man who died, may have been taping me. Setting me up, sort of.'

'What do you mean, *setting you up*?'

'He was an ex-con, Deanna. He was an ex-con and an informant, I think. He was obligated, maybe.'

'You're telling me . . . ?'

'I don't know. I'm not sure. But I'm worried.'

And so was she. But maybe the biggest thing she was worried about was where love goes when it *goes*. This steadfast devotion of hers, which had been pummeled and knocked around and stomped on. Where?

'I knew something was wrong, Charles. I thought some money was missing before – when you took the first ten thousand, I guess. Maybe it's my imagination, I thought. So I didn't say anything. Maybe I was imagining *everything* – the way you were acting. The hours you were keeping. Everything. I thought it might be a woman. But I didn't want to believe it. I was waiting for you to come tell me, Charles . . .'

And now I had told her. But more than she could have actually imagined.

She asked me a few more questions – some of the ones I'd expected she would. *Who was this woman, exactly? Was she married, too? Was it really just that one time?* But I could tell her heart wasn't really in it. And then other questions that maybe her heart *was* in, or what was left of her heart – how much trouble was I really in with the police, for instance, things of that nature.

But in the end, she told me to leave the house. She didn't know for how long, but she wanted me out of there.

A few weeks later, weeks I spent avoiding Deanna and retiring to the guest bedroom after Anna went to bed, I found a furnished apartment in Forest Hills.

Thirty

Forest Hills seemed to be made up of Orthodox Jews and unorthodox sectarians. People who seemed alone, or who were without a visible means of support, or who didn't seem to really belong there. In that particular apartment or particular building or that actual neighborhood. I fit in perfectly.

For instance, I looked like a married man, but where was my wife? I was undoubtedly a father, but where exactly were my kids? And then I even became a little shaky on the means-of-support thing.

On the first Tuesday after I moved out, I took the train into work at Continental Boulevard.

I was called down to Barry Lenge's office. That itself was unusual, since office hierarchy dictated that bean counters – even the head bean counter – travel to *your* office when a face-to-face was needed.

I went anyway. After all, I think I was suffering from a kind of post-traumatic stress syndrome, and whatever self-confidence I had left was down to the approximate level of a whipped dog.

Barry Lenge looked even more uncomfortable than me. That should have been my first clue.

His triple chin made him appear physically agitated, in any case – as if his head couldn't find a position where it wasn't imposing on another part of his body. But today he looked worse.

'Ahem,' Barry cleared his throat, which should have been my second clue; there was something in there he was going to have a little trouble getting out.

'I was just looking over the production bills,' Barry said.

'Yes?'

'This Headquarters job. There's something I wanted to talk to you about.'

Now it must have been me who looked truly uncomfortable, because Barry looked away – at his set of silver pencils – and I remembered how Eliot had doodled on his stationery the morning I was fired off my account by Ellen Weischler.

'The thing is . . . something's been brought to our attention.'

'What?'

'You see, there's forty-five thousand here for music.' He was pointing to a piece of paper sitting on the desk in front of him. The same bid form I'd looked at before.

'*See* that?' Barry asked. 'Right there.'

I pretended to look, if only because that's what whipped dogs do when given a command – they obey. I could see a number there all right; it looked like forty-five thousand.

'Yes?'

'Well, Charles . . . there's a problem with that.'

'Yes?' Was that all I was going to say – answer each of Barry's revelations with a yes?

'Mary Widger heard the same music on a different spot.'

'What?'

'I'm *telling* you this same piece of music was on another spot.'

'What do you mean?'

'Correct me if I'm wrong. Forty-five thousand dollars was for *original* music, right?'

'Right.'

'So it's not original.'

'I don't understand.' But I did understand, of course. Tom and David Music had found a piece of music in a stock house, and they hadn't bothered to see if someone else had used it before. Someone had.

'Well, maybe it just sounds the same. It's just a bed, really.'

'No. She brought it to the musicologist. It's the same piece. Note for note.'

She brought it to the musicologist. Musicologists were generally consulted to make sure that any music we did wasn't too close to any other existing piece of music we might be trying to imitate. For instance, we might cut a commercial to Gershwin's "S Wonderful', but if the

Gershwin estate wanted an arm and a leg to let us use it, we might attempt to rip it off, but not too closely – because the musicologist would say no. Only in this case, of course, it wasn't Gerswhin who was being ripped off.

'I'll talk to the music house,' I said, trying to sound as officially indignant as Barry did. Instead of scared.

'I talked to the music house,' Barry said.

I didn't like the way Barry said that – *music house* – with a noticeable derision. A pointed sarcasm.

'Yes?'

'Yeah. I talked to the music house. So the question I have for you is *this*. How much?'

'How much *what*?'

'How much? If I was to give you a bill of what you owe this agency, how much should I make it out for?'

'I don't understand.'

'You don't understand.'

'Yes.'

'I think you do. I think you understand perfectly. The music house is a paper company, Charles. It doesn't exist. It exists only to make illegal profits from this agency. So if I want those profits back – how much do I need to ask you for?'

'I don't know what you're talking about. If you've uncovered some kind of scam here . . .'

'Look, Charles . . .' And now Barry didn't seem the slightest bit uncomfortable anymore. He seemed right in his element. 'Look – if you pay us back the money, there's a chance this won't end up in court. That *you* won't end up in court. Are you following me? Not that that would be my decision. If it was up to me, I'd throw you in jail. But since I'm the company comptroller, money's kind of close to my heart, right? Eliot feels differently. Fine.'

Eliot feels differently. I'd been wondering if Eliot knew anything yet.

'Look, maybe I suspected something . . . I thought maybe something was . . . Shouldn't you be talking to Tom and David?'

'I *talked* to Tom and David. They both had plenty to say. So you want to keep fucking with me, fine, but you should know that if you keep this up, Eliot will reconsider his decision. Why? Because I'll *tell* him to. They don't want the bad publicity – I understand. But they want their money back. And you know something? When it comes to money versus a momentary smudge on their reputation, they'll take the money. Trust me on this.'

It was clear I had a decision to make. I could admit taking the twenty thousand dollars. I could even pay the twenty thousand dollars back – if Deanna let me go near Anna's Fund again, which might not be so easy. On the other hand, I had the distinct feeling Tom and David had implicated me to a greater degree than the facts actually warranted – and that Barry wasn't going to believe twenty thousand dollars was the extent of my fraudulent activities. No, the bill was going to be higher. If I admitted anything, I decided, I was done.

'I didn't have anything to do with this,' I said as forcefully as I could. 'I don't know what Tom and David told you, but I wouldn't necessarily trust the word of two guys who've apparently been cheating you for years.'

Barry sighed. He tried to loosen his collar, an impossible task since it was already two sizes too small.

'That's the way you want to play this,' he finally said. 'Fine. Your decision. You say you're innocent, we institute company procedures. Fine.'

'Which are . . . ?'

'We suspend you. We hold an internal investigation. We get back to you. And if I have any influence on the powers-that-be at all – we fucking *arrest* you. Understand, pal?'

I got up and left the office.

Thirty-one

Time passed. One week, two weeks, a month.

Time I spent mostly wondering in lieu of working. I was wondering, for instance, if Deanna was ever going to forgive me and whether or not I was going to be arrested for murder or indicted for embezzlement. None of those things had happened yet. Still, there was always tomorrow.

I decided after my first day as a jobless person that I was a creature of habit and was habitually programmed to go to work in the morning. So I rode the train into Manhattan just like I always did and commuted back in the afternoons. My depressing environs had something to do with it; the furnished apartment was like a motel room without maid service. I felt a little like Goldilocks sleeping in someone else's bed. Someone who was about to show up at any minute and demand my immediate departure.

There were clues who this someone was – little relics of actual habitation left behind in this now sterile desert.

A paperback, for example. A dog-eared copy of *Men Are from Mars, Women Are from Venus*. But was it a Martian or a Venutian who'd once owned it? It was hard to say.

A toothbrush discovered behind the stained toilet. One of those fancy ones with a curved brush for those hard-to-reach areas. Lavender. Was that considered a feminine color or a masculine color, or neither?

And in my one desk drawer: a sheet of lined paper filled with what appeared to be New Year's resolutions. 'I will try harder to meet people,' was the first one. 'I will be less judgmental.' And so on. I decided the writer of this list and the owner of the book were probably one and the same, since both pointed to a devotee of rigorous self-improvement. I wondered, if Deanna was from Venus, was I from Pluto?

I visited the 42nd Street Library. I strolled the Met. I spent an entire day half sleeping in the Hayden Planetarium, waking periodically to a canopy of stars – like an astronaut coming out of suspended animation, alone in the universe and so far from home.

I made sure to call Anna every afternoon – always from my cell phone, since the elaborate cover story we'd worked out to explain my absence was that I was shooting a new ad campaign in Los Angeles. Once, I'd spent two months out there doing just that; it seemed like an excuse that might actually work.

Where are you now? Anna would ask me.

The Four Seasons pool, I'd reply.

A studio in Burbank. A street in Venice. In a rented car at the intersection of Sunset and La Cienega.

Cool, Anna would say.

Deanna had told me she didn't wish to speak to me for a while. The torture involved how long a while that would actually turn out to be. Occasionally she would pick up when I called and I'd hope that a *while* had ended right then. But she'd call out for Anna and wait silently until our daughter picked up the phone. In a way, it wasn't that different from all our years AD – after diabetes – that stifling silence about things we couldn't mention. Only there was a terrible reproof in her silence now, as opposed to just plain grief. And where before silence had been filled with the inconsequential and bland, it was now filled with the kind of quiet western movie heroes were always running into just before an ambush. *It's quiet*, they'd say to their amigos, too *quiet*.

It was late February, the Monday of my third week of banishment and joblessness, when I saw Lucinda again.

My first instinct was to hide and duck back farther into the faceless crowd. My second instinct was to say hello. Possibly because it was good to see her up and about again; it alleviated my guilt a little. Up and about and even talking to someone.

I'd wondered about her, of course. If she could ever recover from what Vasquez had done to her. I hoped so.

And now I thought that maybe she could. The rings under her eyes had gone away. She looked beautiful again; she looked like Lucinda.

259

I was so entirely fixated on her, it was probably a minute or so before I even took notice of whom she was talking to. Was that her husband – glimpsed briefly that day in front of the fountain at the Time-Life Building?

No. It wasn't her husband she was talking to. This man was shorter, younger, frumpier. A fellow broker, perhaps – a friend from the neighborhood.

They seemed to be on good terms with each other, at least. They'd stopped in front of a newsstand and were engaged in a lively discussion.

I was in a kind of no-man's-land, I realized. Neither far enough away to be invisible, nor close enough to be conversational. One look to the left and Lucinda would see me for sure – stuck in limbo, the man who'd failed her, a reminder of all she'd been through.

I wanted to spare her that. Mostly, I wanted to spare *me* that.

So I turned tail. I skirted the fringes of the slowly moving crowd and tried to keep my face forward to avoid any accidental eye contact.

I made it through the crowd, a piece of flotsam moving with the tide. All the way over to the stairway leading to Eighth Avenue. Home free.

Only, I'd peeked. I couldn't help it. I'd peeked over at Lucinda and her business associate to see if I'd remained unnoticed.

And noticed something.

I mulled it over on the cab ride to the National Museum of the American Indian and decided I didn't know what. Whatever it was had been picked up in one quick, furtive glance. And there'd been all these people between us, too. *Foreground crosses*, we call it in shoot-speak. Where you walk the extra back and forth between camera and actors to ensure it looks real, that it doesn't look like some sound stage in Universal Studios.

Only sometimes you put too many extras into the mix, and they obliterate the actors entirely. It becomes impossible to see them, and they themselves become extras in the shot. Then you have to thin out the extras and rework the blocking so the actors can be seen again.

That's sort of what I was doing in the cab.

I was trying to push the faceless crowd of commuters off to the side so I could see Lucinda clearly. Lucinda and that business associate of hers, or neighborhood friend. Or . . .

Her brother. Yes, maybe it was her brother, only I couldn't remember if she had a brother or not. It seemed to me we'd spent a lot more time talking about my family than hers. I'd poured my heart out to her, hadn't I? About Anna and Deanna? I didn't remember whether she had brothers or not.

But it seemed to me now that it must have been her brother. Or perhaps her cousin. Yes, it could have been her cousin.

It had to do with what I'd noticed.

I was trying to push those other people out of the way to get a clear look, but they were getting annoyed and pushing back. They were telling me to get lost or busy looking for a cop.

Their hands.

I thought I saw their hands touching. Not interlocked, not intertwined, but touching.

Something you might do with a brother, wasn't it?

And even if it wasn't her brother, even if it was a friend of hers, a *new* friend of hers, could you blame her? I'd never asked her if I was the first. Why should I assume I'd be the last?

She was still stuck in the same awful marriage. She was desperately in need of someone to talk to. Now especially. Maybe she'd gone and found someone.

And for the briefest moment, I felt something suspiciously like jealousy. Just a quick pang, a phantom ache from a long healed wound.

Then I forgot about it.

Thirty-two

It was Anna's birthday.

I'd never missed one. I couldn't imagine missing one now. She might give a sullen shrug of her shoulders when I brought up things like birthdays – *Birthday, what's that?* – but I genuinely believed she'd never forgive me if I didn't actually show up for one. And then I'd have two Schines in an unforgiving mode, and I was having a hard enough time with one.

So when I phoned home and Deanna picked up, I said: 'Please don't call Anna yet. I need to talk to you.'

She sighed. 'Yes, Charles?' she said.

Well, she'd used my name, at least.

'Anna's birthday is coming up,' I said.

'I know when Anna's birthday is.'

'Well. Don't you think I should be home for it? She'd hate me if she thought I'd stayed in California on her birthday.'

263

'I'm not ready for you to come home, Charles.'

Yes, that was a problem – Deanna not being ready. As for me, of course, I was more than ready.

'Well, couldn't we . . . what if I say I came back just for her birthday and then I have to leave again?'

'I don't know . . .'

'Deanna, it's Anna's *birthday* . . .'

'Look . . . you can stay the night, okay? But in the morning, Charles, I want you to leave.'

'I understand. That's fine. Thank you.'

It felt a little odd thanking my wife for letting me stay overnight in my own home. Not unjust, just odd. The important thing, though, was that she'd said yes.

When I arrived at the kitchen door, present in hand – I'd bought her three CDs based on the recommendations of a clerk at Virgin Records – Anna was sitting at the counter munching cereal and staring zombie-eyed at MTV.

'Daddy!' Anna, who normally liked to keep her childish enthusiasm under control, seemed unabashedly glad to see me. Only not as glad as I was to see her. She popped up off her stool in a flash and straight into my arms, where I clung to her as if my very life depended on it. And maybe it did.

I was about to ask her where her mother was, but just then she walked into the kitchen. I had no idea what to do – I felt as awkward as someone on a blind date. I wasn't sure how to greet her, what to say to her, and it occurred to me that she was probably a little confused on the issue as well. We both hesitated, then settled on a perfunctory embrace with all the warmth of a postgame hockey handshake.

'How was California?' she asked me, evidently determined to see the charade through.

'Fine. Not done yet, either. I have to go back in the morning.'

This was evidently news to Anna. She immediately pouted and said: '*Daddy* . . .'

'Sorry, honey. There's nothing I can do about it.' And here, at least, I was telling the truth.

'I wanted you to see me sing at the spring concert. I have a solo.'

'Well, don't turn professional till after high school.'

The attempt at levity failed; Anna turned back to MTV, looking hurt and upset with me.

'Can somebody get me some juice?' she said. Her hands were suddenly shaking; she was holding the TV remote, and it was jiggling up and down.

'Are you low, honey?' Deanna said, quickly opening the refrigerator.

'No. I'm shaking because I *like* to.'

Deanna shot me a look: *See what I've been going through*, this look said. *She's getting worse.*

Deanna pulled out some orange juice and poured Anna half a glass. 'There you go . . .'

Anna took it and swallowed a little.

'I think you should drink a little more,' Deanna said.

'Oh, is that what you think?' Anna, ever vigilant against

265

any suggestions concerning what she should or shouldn't put into her own body. She was still shaking.

'Come on, sweetie,' I said.

'I'm fine,' Anna said.

'You're not—'

'*All right!*' Anna said, grabbing the glass and striding out of the room. 'I wish both of you would get *off* of my back already.'

After she left the room, Deanna said: 'She's scared. She's been going up and down like a roller coaster. When she gets scared she gets angry.'

'Yes,' I said. 'I know.'

Why did you call me Anna? our daughter Anna used to ask when she was very small.

Because you're part of me, Deanna would answer. *De-Anna, see?*

'I have to get back to the bills,' Deanna said. Which suddenly reminded me that we might soon be having a problem paying those bills. Deanna left the kitchen.

I still needed a birthday card. Since my daughter and wife were both mad at me, I decided it was a good time to go to the stationery store on Merrick Road and buy one.

When I walked into the store, an older woman was buying Lotto tickets at the counter.

'. . . eight . . . seventeen . . . thirty-three . . . six . . . ,' listlessly spitting out a seemingly endless litany of digits. '. . . nine . . . twenty-two . . . eleven . . .'

I walked to the back where the greeting cards were. Of course, there weren't just greeting cards; there were anniversary cards, get well cards, condolence cards, Valentine's Day cards, thank-you cards, graduation cards, and birthday cards. I planted myself in front of the birthday section, momentarily dazzled by all the subcategories: Happy Birthday, Mom, Son, Wife, Mom-in-law, Grandmother, Best Friend, Cousin. And Daughter – it was there somewhere. Of course, once I found the category, I had to decide on the tone. Funny? Respectful? Sentimental? I was inclined to go sentimental here, since that's how I felt these days. There were a lot of sentimental cards, too, most of them with flowers on the cover and little poems on the inside. Only the poems weren't sentimental as much as trite – the *roses are red, violets are blue* genre of poem writing.

For instance:

> To my daughter on her birthday
> I have this to say
> I love you very much
> Your smile, your spirit and such
> Even though we may be apart
> You have your daddy's heart.
> The end.

I was worried Anna might throw up if I brought that one home for her. On the other hand, if I wanted to be sentimental *and* halfway intelligent, the pickings were slim. There were cards with nothing on the inside, for instance, allowing you to be as intelligent or sentimental as you'd like. These cards tended to have moody black-and-white photographs on the cover – of a snowfield in Maine, say, or a lonely mountain stream. They basically said stupid poems are for the unenlightened masses – these are for the more soulful of you. I couldn't decide if I was up to soulfulness today, though. So what was it to be?

Just past the card racks there were more elaborate gifts. Ceramic hearts saying 'World's Best Mom.' A golf ball 'Fore a Great Dad.' Fake flowers. A bell that said 'Ring A Ding Ding.' And some picture frames.

I didn't notice it immediately.

I looked here and there, sifted through the ceramic and cheap plastic, picked up the golf ball, gently rang the bell. I even turned back to the card rack, intent on finally making a decision. Only I had what you might call an episode of peripheral vision – you *might*, except it wouldn't be strictly true. It wasn't that I saw anything out of the corner of my eye, just that I remembered seeing it.

The bell, yes. And the silly golf ball. And the ceramic hearts. Keep going. There.

It was in the second picture frame.

And the third one, too.

And three miniature ones set behind it. And the large frame decorated with a metal trellis of flowers.

'Can I help you with anything?' The voice seemed to be coming from far away.

The picture in the picture frames.

They put them there to show you how nice they'll look

once you get them home and put *your* pictures inside them. You and your wife at that wedding in Nantucket. The twins as Hansel and Gretel from a long-ago Halloween. Curry, the sweet-faced pup. Because people lack the necessary imagination otherwise. They need surrogate faces in there so they'll know what to expect when it's sitting back home on the mantelpiece.

'Can I help you with anything, sir?' The voice more insistent now – but it was as if it were speaking through glass.

Behind the glass of the picture frames was the picture of a little girl. She was on a swing somewhere in the country, with her tawny blond hair caught in midswirl. Freckle faced and knobby kneed and sweet smiled. The very model of carefree youth. Because she *was* a model. Behind the swing were makeup artists and hairstylists and wardrobe people – only you couldn't see them.

'Sir, are you all right?'

I'd seen this picture before.

I showed you mine, now you show me yours.

Remember?

She'd seen Anna peeking out from the inside of my wallet, so I'd asked to see hers.

I showed you mine, now you show me yours.

And she'd laughed. I'd made lovely Lucinda laugh out loud, and she'd reached into her leather bag and shown me.

The little girl on the swing. Out in the country somewhere.

She's adorable. That's what I'd said.

And she'd said thanks. *I forget sometimes.* Two parents complimenting each other on their respective progeny, commuter small talk, nothing to it.

Nothing at all.

I forget sometimes. Because maybe that was an easy thing to do, to forget something that you didn't actually have.

She'd shown me a picture of her child, only it wasn't *her* child. It was someone else's child.

'*Sir? Is something wrong?*' The clerk again, wondering just what had come over me.

Well, I would tell him. Amazing grace, that's what.

Was blind but now I see.

Thirty-three

I was helping Deanna clean up the plates smeared with half-eaten cake and dollops of melting ice cream.

I was asking myself how it was possible.

The birthday celebration had been strained and awkward. Anna had invited just one friend, possibly her only friend these days. It felt more like a wake than a birthday celebration, but then I was kind of preoccupied.

I was thinking about that resident in the ER who'd asked me about Anna's eyes. I was thinking he should've asked me about my own. *Are you having problems seeing?* And I would've said, *Yes, Doctor, I'm blind. I can't see.*

But not anymore.

My life had turned into a train wreck. I could hear the screams of the dead and dying. But all that time it had been Lucinda at the wheel. I knew that now. Lucinda. And him.

How was it possible?

A lie. A farce. A con – trying to stick a label on something that was clearly out of my experience. As Anna waited patiently for us to stop singing 'Happy Birthday'.

A setup. A hoax. As she opened her presents and read her cards. My card said: 'Can't you stay thirteen forever?'

An out-and-out robbery. As Anna thanked each of us for her presents and even gave me a hug.

And this, too: *That man at Penn Station.*

He wasn't her brother, her neighbor, or her favorite uncle.

He was *next*.

Deanna and I had managed to put up a decent front. We'd smiled, we'd talked, we'd clapped our hands when Anna blew out her candles.

But now that Anna and her friend had been dropped at a movie and we were alone, it had grown deathly quiet again. Just the steady splash of the faucet and the sour clinks of plates and glasses being laid to rest in the dishwasher tub. And the awful shouting going on in my own head.

'Well,' I said, trying desperately to tug my thoughts in another direction, *any* direction, and at the same time cleave the silence, 'one year older.'

'Yes,' Deanna said without much enthusiasm. Then she placed the last plate into the dishwasher, walked to the kitchen table, and sat down. And, for the first time in God knows how long, *really* began talking to me.

'How have you been, Charles?'

'Okay. Fine.' *Liar,* I thought.

'Really?'

'Yes. I'm okay, Deanna.'

'I was thinking,' she said.

'About?'

'I was thinking as we sang "Happy Birthday" to her. To our Anna.'

'Yes . . . ?'

'You said something once. About us, about being a parent. I wonder if you even remember it?'

'What did I say?'

'You said' – she closed her eyes now, trying to conjure up the exact words – 'that it was like making *deposits.*'

'Deposits? I don't remember . . .'

'Anna was three or four, somewhere around there, and you'd taken her someplace she wanted to go – the zoo, I think. Just you and her, because I was sick. I don't think you were feeling so hot yourself – I think I'd caught your cold. And you just wanted to stay home and lie down on the couch and watch football all day, but Anna pestered you and you gave in and took her. You don't remember?'

I did remember now, vaguely, anyway. A Sunday long ago at the Bronx Zoo. Anna and I had fed the elephants.

'Yes, I remember the day.'

'When you came back, I thanked you. I knew you were feeling shitty and you didn't really want to go. It wasn't a big thing, but I remember being really happy that you did it.'

273

Deanna was looking right at me now – *directly* at me, as if she were searching for something missing. I wanted to say, *I'm here, Deanna. I never left.*

'You said something to me. You said that every day with Anna, every good moment you spent with her, was like a *deposit*. A deposit in a bank. If you made enough of them, if you diligently kept putting money away in that account, then when she was older and on her own, she'd be rich enough to get by. Rich with memories, I guess. I thought it was kind of sappy. I thought it was kind of brilliant. She's going to need dialysis soon,' Deanna said.

'No, Deanna.' All thought of zoos and elephants, of Lucinda and Vasquez, immediately disappeared.

'Dr Baron did some tests. Her kidneys are failing – one of them is barely there at all. Very soon our daughter is going to have to be strapped up to a machine three times a week so she can stay alive. That's what he said.'

'When?'

'What does it matter? It's going to happen, that's all.'

Then Deanna was crying.

I remembered wondering not too far back if Deanna was all cried out. But then I'd learned differently – that day in the garden. And now.

'I think you were right, Charles.'

'What . . . Deanna . . . how do you mean?'

'I think we did okay with her. I think we gave her a very nice bank account. I think we never forgot to put something in. Never. Not once.'

I felt something itchy under my eyes, something hot and wet on both cheeks.

'I'm sorry, Charles,' she said. 'I never closed my eyes to what was going to happen. But I did in a way. Because I wouldn't let you talk about it. I didn't want to hear it said out loud. I'm so sorry. I think that was wrong now.'

'Deanna . . . I . . .'

'I think we *should* talk about it. I think we should talk about what a remarkable daughter we have, for as long as we have her. I think that's very important.'

And somehow, in some magical and unexplained way, we ended up in each other's arms.

When we stopped crying, when we finally disentangled and sat across from each other, holding hands and staring out the window into the black-as-ink night, I thought that Deanna was about to ask me to come home now. I could almost see her forming the words.

I deliberately broke the mood; I got up and said it was time to leave, to go back to Forest Hills.

I couldn't come home. Not now. Not yet.

Something had just been made clear to me. Crystal clear.

I had unfinished business to take care of.

I was out of one job, fine. Now I had another one. An even more important one.

I had to get Anna's other bank account back.

Somehow I had to find them.

Somehow I needed to get back my money.

Thirty-four

It was impossible to miss Lucinda's legs.

I hadn't missed them that first morning on the train.

And I didn't miss them *now* when I saw them emerging out of the morning crowd at Penn Station. Striding forward from a sea of denim, serge, and English wool – sleek and sexy and belonging solely to her.

Her and that man.

I'd been waiting to see them for days. I'd taken the 5:30 into Penn each morning. I'd planted myself at approximately the same spot I'd seen them the last time. I'd diligently stood guard. When the morning crowd dissipated and they didn't show up, I'd walked from one end of the station to the other.

I'd done this day after day.

I'd told myself it was my only chance. I'd crossed my fingers and said my prayers.

But now that I'd spotted them, I had trouble looking at them.

I felt naked and vulnerable and scared.

I couldn't help looking at that man, for instance, and seeing myself. Once at an office friend's bachelor party, I'd turned away from the nubile young stripper in a gold lamé thong just long enough to see everyone *else* staring at her and thought with sudden dismay: *I look like them.*

This man was so evidently besotted with Lucinda – or whoever she was. He kept grabbing for her hand and gazing lovingly into her eyes.

I hadn't been wrong about who he was. She was playing him just as she'd once played me. He was *next.*

How pathetic, I thought. *How pitiable.*

How exactly like I'd been.

When I'd looked into the picture frame that day in the candy store, I'd asked myself what it was that had made me such a target. But only briefly. Because I knew the answer. In the cold light of day, it was so easy to see just how much I'd been asking for it. For something. Anything. Anything at all to come rescue me from me.

I'd spent a lot of time replaying all the moments I'd spent with her, too, my rescuer. Only now remembering them just a little differently from before. Running them back and forth and back in my head, the way, in the days before computer editing systems, I used to have to run strips of celluloid through Moviolas until they frayed and split. I had to patch them with tape again and again and again, until the images formed actual cracks and nearly disintegrated into dust. Take the first time I met Lucinda. *Here, I'll take care of it*, she'd said sweetly on the train that day, but when I looked closely now, I could already see ugly fissures crisscrossing her face as she offered a ten-dollar bill to the pissed-off conductor.

She'd picked me that day.

Lucinda and the man had worked their way over to the open coffee shop, where they sold fat-free peach muffins and doughy bagels. The man ordered coffees, and they stood elbow to elbow across a small table. Steam sometimes obscured their faces.

I kept my back to them. I flipped through newsstand magazines and peeked. I was worried about her seeing me, but less worried than I might have been.

My face had changed.

It had happened gradually, bit by bit. I'd lost weight. As my life seemed to implode, my appetite had lessened, waned, disappeared. My clothes began to hang on me. When Barry Lenge administered the coup de grâce and sent me into the ranks of the unemployed, I'd stopped shaving, too. My goatee had become a beard. A few days ago, I'd looked into the bathroom mirror and seen the kind of face you see in hostage dramas staring back. That haunted-looking overseas government official who's finally been released after months of dark captivity. I looked like that.

Only I was *still* a hostage.

I kept peeking now.

It became hard watching them without actually being able to go over and confront them. Because now, in addition to feeling scared and naked and vulnerable, I felt angry. It welled up in me like sudden nausea. The kind of anger I'd up to this point reserved solely for God – on those days I believed in God and on the days I didn't – for Anna's disease. The kind of anger that caused me to clench my hands into fists and imagine landing them in Vasquez's face. And hers.

But I resisted the urge to walk over and tell her that I was on to them. That I knew what she'd done to me. I needed to bide my time. To get Anna's money back, I needed to find Vasquez; and to find Vasquez, I needed Lucinda.

That was my mantra. This was my mission.

She would lead me to him.

I guessed that Lucinda wasn't a stockbroker anymore.

I overheard a conversation Lucinda had with the man at Penn Station on Wednesday morning the next week. The man mentioned *selling short* for a client, how this client was a veritable *meal ticket* for him, which meant that he was a stockbroker and Lucinda wasn't. Because another stockbroker might be inclined to know people in other brokerage houses and might be inclined to ask them about their co-worker Lucinda, who, it would turn out, didn't exist. No, Lucinda obviously had another occupation these days. A lawyer, an insurance agent, a circus clown. And Lucinda, no doubt, wasn't even her name.

I knew the name of the man she was about to con out of his money, though. I knew this because another man had come up to them while they were having coffee together that same morning and said: *Sam, Sam Griffen, how are you doing?*

Not too well, actually. Mr Griffen blanched – his face turning the color of soap, as Lucinda turned away and stared at the price list on the wall.

When Mr Griffin regained his voice, he said: *Fine*.

Then Lucinda got up and walked off with her coffee cup – just another commuter on her way to the subway. And Mr Griffen sat and talked with this unwelcome intruder for five minutes. When he left, Mr Griffen sighed and wiped his face with a stained napkin.

I thought it was unnerving being this close to a victim without being able to warn him. Like standing next to a child who can't see the speeding car bearing down on him but being forbidden to tell him to get out of the way. Watching this horrible accident unfold in close-up and super slow motion. The worst kind of voyeur.

I thought she saw me once.

I'd followed them to a coffee shop north of Chinatown one morning.

They'd taken a table by the window, and I saw Sam Griffin reach for her hand and Lucinda give it to him.

I couldn't help remembering the way that hand had felt in my own. Just briefly. Remembering the things the hand had done to me, the pleasure it had conjured up for me that day at the Fairfax Hotel. Like opening up one Chinese box and finding another inside, and opening that one up, too, and then the next box, each box smaller and tighter than the previous one, opening them faster and faster until there were no boxes left and I was trying to catch my breath.

I was still trying to catch my breath, still lost in memories of guilty pleasure, when they exited the coffee shop. I had to turn and dart across the street. I had to hold my breath, count to ten, then slowly turn back, fingers crossed, and see if I'd been spotted.

No. They'd gone off somewhere in a taxi.

Then I lost them.

One day.

Two days.

Three days.

A week. No Lucinda. No Mr Griffen. Nowhere.

I scoured Penn Station from one end to the other, coming early, staying late.

But nothing.

I started to panic, to think maybe I'd missed the boat. That she'd already taken Mr Griffen off someplace for an afternoon of sex and Vasquez had already caught them in the act. That he'd already taken their wallets and asked Mr Griffen why he was fucking around on his wife. Maybe even called Mr Griffen at home and stated his dire need for a loan. Just ten thousand dollars, that's all, and he'd be out of his hair.

When the next week came, and I still couldn't find them, I was ready to give up. I was ready to admit that a forty-five-year-old ex-advertising executive had no business thinking he could win here. That I was hopelessly out of my element.

I was ready to throw in the towel.

Then I remembered something.

Thirty-five

'Okay,' the deskman said. 'How long you want it for?'

This deskman was the very same one who'd given me the key to room 1207 back in November when I'd stood in front of him with Lucinda on my arm.

I was back at the Fairfax Hotel, and the deskman was asking me exactly how long I'd be needing room 1207 for.

Good question.

'How much is it for two weeks?'

'Five hundred and twenty-eight dollars,' the man said.

'Fine,' I said. So far, I was on paid suspension. And $528 was a bargain in New York City, even if the room had bloodstains on the carpeting and the stink of sex in the mattress sheets.

I paid in cash and received my room key. There was a pile of magazines sitting on top of a beat-up couch, the only true piece of furniture in the lobby. I stopped to peruse them: a *Sports Illustrated* from last year, a *Popular Mechanics*, two issues of *Ebony*, and an old *U.S. News & World Report:* SHOWDOWN IN PALM BEACH COUNTY. I took the *Sports Illustrated*.

I rode the elevator with a man wearing a University of Oklahoma jacket who actually looked as if he were from Oklahoma. He had the slightly bewildered look of a tourist who'd fallen for the picture on the cover of the brochure – the one taken in 1955, when the Fairfax wasn't being subsidized by federal welfare checks. He'd probably tried his hand at three-card monte and already purchased a genuine Rolex watch from the man on the corner. He looked like he was ready to go home.

So was I.

But I was on a mission now, so I couldn't.

For just a moment as I was opening the door, jiggling the key inside the somewhat resistant door lock, I couldn't help tensing up and waiting for someone to blindside me into the room. No one did, of course, but that didn't stop me from sighing in relief as soon as I made it inside and shut the door.

It looked a little smaller than before, as if my imagination had given it a size more commensurate with what had gone on there. But it was just a room in a cramped downtown hotel, big enough for two people who pretty much intended to stay glued to each other, conducive to sex if for no other reason than its restrictive dimensions. The kind of room where two is company but three's a disaster – remembering what it was like to be stuck in that bird's-eye seat on the floor.

I lay down on the bed without taking my shoes off and closed my eyes. Just for a few minutes.

When I woke, it was nearly dark.

For a few seconds, I had no idea where I was. Wasn't I home in bed? Wasn't Deanna next to me or downstairs whipping up something tasty for dinner? And Anna – chatting away on-line in the next room, homework spread out on her lap like a prop to throw me off the scent?

There was a musty odor in the room, mustier even than my furnished apartment; the mattress felt hard and lumpy at the same time; the ghost images of a chair and table I didn't recognize were hovering precipitously by the foot of the bed. And I finally woke to my current surroundings as to a radio alarm that's been set too loud – I groaned, winced, and looked furtively for a stop button that didn't exist.

I got up and made my way into the bathroom to splash some cold water onto my face. My body felt like pins and needles, my mouth dry and pasty. I looked down at my watch: seven twenty-five.

I'd slept the whole day away. When I walked back to the bed, I saw the *Sports Illustrated* I'd taken from downstairs lying on the floor.

I saw the date.

November 8.

One week before I'd walked onto the 9:05 to Penn Station and my world had come tumbling down.

Thirty-six

I was sitting on the beaten-up couch in the lobby.

I was wearing a baseball cap pulled down low over my eyes.

I was tracking human traffic like an eagle-eyed crossing guard.

How long do you want it for? the deskman had asked me when I checked in.

Why did I want it in the first place?

That day when we walked out of Penn Station and into a taxi, that day when she'd finally said yes. When she'd asked me, *Where?*

I'd gone and dutifully picked our hotel from a moving taxi.

But maybe not.

Now it seemed to me that I'd pointed one out to her, but she'd said, *Uh-uh*, then picked out another one she didn't like the look of; and then finally, when we'd made it nearly all the way downtown to the vicinity of her office, I'd pointed to the Fairfax and she'd said, *Okay.* So when you really thought about it, maybe I hadn't picked our hotel after all.

Maybe *she* had.

The hotel where I'd run into the wrong person at just the wrong time. Only I hadn't really run into anyone. They'd set a trap, and I'd walked into it.

Which brought me to my hunch. An idea that occurred to me when I was standing empty-handed and frantic in Penn Station.

There was no reason on earth for her to think I would ever find out about her and Vasquez. The last time she'd seen me, I'd been running for my life down that stairway in Spanish Harlem.

They didn't need to change addresses.

Just victims.

When she relieved Mr Griffen of most of his cash and all of his dignity, odds were it was going to be in the very same place they'd done it to me.

So I sat on the couch in the lobby.

I waited.

I had a dream.

I was on the train again. The 9:05 to Penn Station.

I was looking through my pockets again because the conductor was standing over me, asking for money.

One hundred thousand dollars, he said.

Why so much? I asked him.

The fare's gone up, the conductor replied.

When Lucinda offered to pay for me, this time I said no.

I made it through both issues of *Ebony*.

Patience, I told myself as another morning went by without a sighting. Patience. After all, look how much patience Lucinda had exhibited with me. All those chummy lunches and romantic dinners she'd had to suffer through in order to get me to go upstairs to that room. If she could do it, so could I.

From *Popular Mechanics* I learned the basics of hot-water piping. Which wrench was voted best overall value. How to tile a floor. Roofing made simple.

One afternoon, I called Barry Lenge from the room to see how the investigation was going. To touch base with the *real* world – isn't that what Vietnam grunts used to call the world back home, the one that existed far away from the front? Which is where I was now – on the front lines, pulling guard duty to prevent any enemy incursions.

And the military reference was entirely apt. Wasn't I exercising each morning now? Push-ups, sit-ups, jumping jacks, isometrics – the works. So the next time Vasquez said, *Good boy,* maybe I'd show him how good I really was.

And something else. I still had Winston's gun. I kept it up in room 1207 wrapped in a towel and hidden behind the bathroom radiator.

As far as the real world went:

Barry Lenge got on the phone and said there was no point in my calling him. They were still conducting their investigation. They were still crossing the *t*'s and dotting the *i*'s. It didn't look very good for me, though. I should've taken him up on his offer – that's for sure. He'd be calling me soon enough.

I thanked him for his time.

Then I checked my cellular for messages and found a voice mail from Deanna.

A Detective Palumbo called for you. He said it was important. I told him you were out of town.

Time was running out.

I knew that. Running out for me and Sam Griffen both. If it hadn't run out on Sam Griffen already.

It was Friday morning.

I was browsing through the out-of-date *U.S. News & World Report,* whose headline was SHOWDOWN IN PALM BEACH COUNTY.

Occasionally the deskman would glance over at me, the deskman and the bellman, too, look me over, up and down, all without saying a word.

It was that kind of hotel. People who came here had nowhere else to go, so no one expected you to go anywhere or do anything. You could loiter in peace here, sit on a couch all day and read out-of-date magazines to your heart's content.

'Gore is confident of ultimate victory,' the magazine reported solemnly.

When I looked up again, the bellman had multiplied. He had some help for the afternoon rush; a black man dressed in a similar nondescript green uniform was leaning on the desk, talking to him.

I'd left my cell phone upstairs, and I wanted to call Anna. I got up and walked to the elevator. The bellman nodded at me, the black man who'd been talking to him momentarily stopped, turned around, then resumed his conversation.

I was thinking that I knew that bellman – the black one. That I must've seen him that day months ago when I'd entered the very same elevator with Lucinda. The elevator doors opened; I walked inside and pressed twelve. I got off on my floor, I hummed a song whose words I couldn't remember, I opened the door to my room and walked inside. Which is when I realized that I was wrong, that it wasn't that day I'd seen him after all.

I walked back into the elevator and pressed Lobby.

The black man was still yapping at the bell captain – his back directly toward me, so I couldn't actually tell if I was right.

They call you Chuck?

I took a loping circle over to the front desk, looking sideways the whole time, holding my breath as the man's face slowly came into view, a quarter moon into a full half, his features starting to fill in.

If you were my crimey, that's what we'd call you.

Remember? Biding my time that day on the corner of, what . . . 8th Street and Avenue C? Waiting for Vasquez in

Alphabet City, but it wasn't Vasquez who'd walked up to me – or actually *into* me.

Why don't you look where you're going?

The face three-quarter now, and I was beginning to feel clammy and light-headed.

It was him.

Yes, it was.

The black man who'd frisked me up against the alley wall, who smelled of blood and pomade.

I quickly turned away – toward the deskman, who looked up as if waiting for a question. This question being, *How smart is Charles?* Very smart – or at least smarter than I was seven months ago.

Then again, even fools have their day.

After all, for once I knew something they didn't.

I knew how they did it.

I knew where they'd be doing it again.

Thirty-seven

I bought a pair of sunglasses from the Vision Hut on 48th Street. I was pretty sure the black man hadn't recognized me the other day, that he hadn't matched the bearded and undernourished-looking man he'd seen sitting in the lobby to the man he'd led into that alleyway in Alphabet City.

Still, it wouldn't hurt to take precautions.

I completed fifty-two push-ups and seventy-five sit-ups before 7:00 A.M.

When I got downstairs, I walked over to the bellman's desk and said hello.

'Hi,' the bell captain said.

'Not too busy today, huh?' I said.

'Nope.'

Then I was pretty much out of things to say.

'How long have you worked here?' The good conversationalist will always ask the other person about himself.

The bellman looked kind of suspicious. He was about forty or forty-five, I guessed, greasy hair combed in a kind of pompadour, a style about forty years out-of-date.

'A while,' he said.

'Get any days off?'

'*Why?*'

'Excuse me?'

'Why do you want to know if I get any days off?'

'I don't know. Just making conversation.' That, at least, was what I was attempting to do.

'Oh, I get it,' he said.

'Huh?'

'What kind you looking for? You want white, black, spic . . . *what?*'

'Excuse me?'

'You looking for a date or not?'

I blushed. 'No. I was just . . . talking . . .'

'Right,' the bellman said. 'Fine.'

In this hotel, apparently the bell captain did a little more than carry your bags.

'Are you the only bellman?' I asked, trying to steer the conversation where I needed it to go.

'Why?'

'I was just wondering if you had any—'

'What *exactly* you looking for, mister?' He sounded irritated now. 'You got something going with Dexter, ask him, okay?'

Dexter. That was his name. Dexter.

'When does . . . Dexter work?'

293

The bell captain shrugged. 'Wednesdays and Fridays.'

'Oh.'

'You need your bags put somewhere?'

'Bags? No.'

'Right. Well, I'm the bell captain. So if you don't need your bags put somewhere . . .'

He was asking me to shut up. I retreated back to the couch, where I sat for another half hour or so, or until lunchtime.

When I came back in from my 7:00 A.M. coffee run a few mornings later, Dexter was standing behind the desk.

I sat on the lobby couch and opened my coffee cup with trembling hands.

I was afraid Dexter would recognize me, and I was feeling kind of scared again; I might look like a dangerous man with my oversize shades, but looks can be deceiving. For instance, Dexter looked more or less harmless reading a magazine in that pale green uniform. He looked like a guy who might even help you with your bags if you asked him nicely. Not like a guy who'd slam you up against an alley wall and laugh when you were punched in the stomach.

I could feel a vague pain there, the vestige of that wallop to my solar plexus, which might have been the body's way of warning me. *What are you doing, Charles?* my body was saying. *Don't you remember how much it hurt? You were crying. You couldn't breathe, remember?*

I remembered just fine.

There was another reason my hands were trembling.

Wednesdays and Fridays, the bellman had answered me when I'd asked about Dexter's work schedule.

But today was Tuesday.

Thirty-eight

I got the gun out from behind the radiator – it was hot to the touch. I just wanted to know it was still there, that it hadn't disappeared, hadn't fallen down the hole in the bathroom wall or been stolen by the maid.

I held it like a rosary – something that just might grant me my dearest wish.

I put it back into the hole.

When I exited the elevator into the lobby, I could see Dexter sitting behind the bell captain's desk with his head in his hands. He appeared to be reading a women's muscle magazine.

I walked slowly over to the front desk and perused an old stack of tourist brochures. 'Ride the Circle Line,' one said. 'Broadway Tours.' All the things New Yorkers themselves never get around to doing.

The lobby was fairly quiet this morning. There was a

couple who seemed to be waiting for a cab; every minute or so, the man poked his head out the front doors and announced there were no taxis yet. His wife nodded and said they were going to be late. The man said you can say that again. When the man announced that there were *still* no taxis two minutes later, she did.

The man in the University of Oklahoma jacket I'd seen on the elevator was complaining to the deskman that there was no King James Bible in his room.

'Are you kidding?' the deskman said to him.

An old man stood hunched over his walker just to the left of the elevators. He might've actually been moving, but if he was, it was too slowly to register on the eye.

I was happy for the company. It was hard to imagine anything really bad was going to happen to you while an old man was shuffling along next to you in a walker and someone else was complaining about there being no Bibles in his room.

Dexter looked directly at me and asked if I had the time.

'Eight o'clock,' I said.

And then I tensed up and waited for Dexter to recognize me.

Wait a minute, I know you – what the fuck are you doing here?

But Dexter went back into his magazine.

The old man seemed to be suffering from some kind of emphysema in addition to his leg problems; he wheezed, gurgled, and heaved with each tiny shuffle.

A woman with six-inch heels, who wasn't suffering from any walking problems, sashayed into the lobby with a fat little man in a bad suit. She detoured past the front desk without actually stopping and grabbed a room key the deskman had already laid down on the counter.

'Come on, sweetie,' she said to the fat man. 'Come on.'

The fat man kept his face trained on the worn carpeting in the lobby. He remained that way until the elevator opened up to rescue him.

Two young couples walked in with luggage and asked how much a room was. But the two women – girls, really – spent the entire time peering around the lobby with obvious distaste. They looked at the old man as if he were walking around without any clothes on. They didn't seem to like the sight of me, either.

I heard them whispering to their boyfriends, who seemed interested in staying – the price was right, wasn't it? But the women won out – the guys shrugged and said no thanks, then all four of them left.

'Next month . . . is my . . . birthday,' the old man in the walker said.

He'd maneuvered his way over to me. I remembered a game I used to play as a kid. It was called red light, green light, and the object of the game was for you to sneak up on someone without ever actually being seen to move. Whoever was 'it' had to close his eyes and say, *Red light, green light, one, two, three*, then quickly turn around and attempt to catch the pursuers in the act of advancing. It wasn't fun being it. It was eerie – seeing someone twenty feet back, then turning and seeing them frozen not five feet from you. It was like that with the old man, who every time I'd looked had seemed stuck in place yet was suddenly there by my right shoulder.

'Eighty . . . three . . .' he said again. He had to pause before every word or two in an effort to get enough air in his lungs. Vegas would've given you attractive odds on his making it to eighty-four.

'Happy birthday,' I said.

'Lived here . . . twenty years,' the old man said between gasps.

I imagined that was just about the time the hotel began its precipitous decline.

'Well, good luck,' I said.

Ordinarily, I found it hard talking to old people. I resorted to hand motions and condescension, as if they were foreigners. But this morning, talking to anyone was better than not talking at all. Because I was harboring two terrible fears. One that Lucinda and Vasquez and Dexter had already robbed and beaten Mr Griffen; the other that they hadn't.

The old man said: 'Thanks.'

I needed to go to the bathroom. Nerves. I'd needed to go for the last hour but kept telling myself I couldn't leave my post. Now I had to. I walked to the elevator and pressed the button.

The doors opened with a loud sigh; I entered and pressed twelve. I jiggled my legs. *Come on . . . come on . . .*

trying to will the elevator doors to shut. Finally they began to close, the hotel lobby starting to narrow by inches, less and less of it until it was just about gone, a mere sliver of a view. I'd estimate ten inches – no more.

Just wide enough to see Lucinda and Sam Griffen enter the hotel.

Thirty-nine

It's what I'd come for.

Even if I felt like shouting, *No, not today!*

Even if I wasn't ready.

Still, I made it up to the twelfth floor without passing out. So far, so good. I made it into my room without being assaulted. I was on a roll. I paced around the room, back and forth, like the big cats in the Bronx Zoo, only the truth was, I was more like that lion in *The Wizard of Oz,* the one searching for courage.

I *had* courage, though, didn't I – it was there somewhere, wasn't it? Yes, of course. Courage was hidden behind the bathroom radiator in a towel. I went in and got it, unfolded the towel and took courage out.

I glanced at the mirror and saw a blind man staring back at me. A blind man with a gun.

I walked out of the room again, but this time I took the

fire exit down – the dark stairway, which would enable me to *peek* once I made it downstairs. I shoved the gun into my pocket.

The stairway had strips of what looked like asbestos hanging from the walls; rats were scurrying back and forth in the dark corners of the landings. When I reached the lobby floor, I slowly opened the door wide enough to put one eye there. Only there was nothing to see. Lucinda and Sam were gone.

I walked back out into the lobby. Dexter was still behind the desk, but he appeared to have just gotten there. Maybe because he looked jumpy. As if he were worrying about his tips.

I walked over to the front desk, although I couldn't actually feel the ground.

'Excuse me?' I said to the deskman. 'Can I ask you something?'

'What?'

'That woman who walked in before?'

'Yes? Which woman?'

'The woman who walked in with the man. Just before. Dark hair. Very pretty. I think maybe I know her.'

'So?'

'Well, I'm curious if that's her. What's her name?'

He looked as if I'd just asked him for his wife's phone number or the exact measurements of his prick. 'I can't give out that information,' he said dourly.

'Fine,' I said. 'Just tell me what room she's in and I'll call her.'

302

'You'll have to tell me her name first,' he said.

'Lucinda?'

The deskman looked down at his register. 'Nope.'

'How about the man. Sam Griffen.'

'Nope.'

For a second, I was ready to tell the deskman to check again and, if he still said *nope*, to accuse him of lying. That it *was* Sam Griffen, no mistake about it. Then I realized it wasn't the deskman who was guilty of lying.

Sam Griffen wouldn't have registered under his own name.

'Never mind,' I said. I walked over to the glass doors and stared out at the sunlit sidewalk.

This is how they do it, I thought. *Dexter knows the room number in advance.*

Lucinda picks the hotel. Then after Lucinda tells Vasquez when, Dexter tells Vasquez where. The exact room number. So Vasquez can be there waiting for them in the stairwell. Dexter is paid off, probably – each time he gets paid off. Dexter works Wednesdays and Fridays, but sometimes he works Tuesdays. If that's when Vasquez tells him to.

I went back to the front desk. Dexter was still reading his magazine over by the bell station.

I had to get that room number.

'Excuse me,' I said.

'Yes?'

I leaned forward and whispered, 'That woman I asked you about before. She's my *wife*.'

'What?'

303

'I've been waiting to see if she'd come here. You understand?'

Yes, he understood. He was a hotel deskman, so he understood perfectly. Only he still wasn't talking.

'I can't give out room numbers.'

'Maybe for a hundred dollars you can.'

But even though he hesitated, licked his bottom lip, and looked around the lobby as if for eavesdroppers, he still said no.

I had approximately $280 in my wallet.

'Two hundred and eighty dollars,' I whispered, and then, after the deskman still didn't say anything: 'And I won't tell anyone you run whores out of here.'

The deskman of the Fairfax Hotel turned red. He stuttered. He sized me up. *How much trouble can this guy actually make?*

He whispered: 'Okay.'

'For two hundred and eighty dollars, I'd like the *key,* too,' I said.

And the deskman said: 'Room eight oh seven.'

And when I slid the money across the counter, he slid the room key back to me.

Forty

I went back up the stairs.

But this time I heard someone in there with me.

Not at first, though. I was concentrating too hard on simply walking up the stairs. Putting one foot in front of the other and eerily conscious of my own labored breathing. I thought I sounded like the old man in the lobby – like someone with one foot already in the grave.

Then I heard somebody else in there with me.

At least several floors above me and maybe drunk, because whoever it was was stumbling around up there and occasionally cursing at himself.

In Spanish.

Lucinda and Mr Griffen would be in the room by now, I thought. Lucinda would be demurely removing her clothing. Turning her back to Mr Griffen as she removed her dress and stockings. And Mr Griffen would be thanking a benevolent God.

Vasquez? He would be positioning himself in the stairwell opposite their room.

I pulled the gun out of my pocket and took a few deep breaths and kept coming.

When I turned the corner between the seventh and eighth floors, I saw him wedged against the hall door, panting and sweating.

'Who are you?' Vasquez said when he turned around to see who'd come up the stairs. He looked stoned.

'Charles Schine,' I said.

'Huh?'

'I need that loan back.'

'This room's occupied.'

The first words out of Sam Griffen's mouth.

I'd carefully opened the door to 807 with my room key, keeping my gun trained on Vasquez. I'd made sure he entered the room first.

Sam's statement had been directed at Vasquez. But when he saw me following him in with a gun, his expression turned from annoyed to panicked.

'What . . . who are you?' he said.

'Charles!' Lucinda answered for me. She was lying on the bed dressed in a lacy black thong, or undressed in a lacy black thong. She'd evidently gotten the show on the road already.

Four of us – a horrified-looking Sam Griffen dressed in

pale blue boxers, Lucinda in her black thong, Vasquez in a turquoise velour sweatsuit, and me in sunglasses, holding a gun.

'Hello, Lucinda,' I said.

It felt strange holding a gun like that. Pointing it at the people who'd cheated me out of over one hundred thousand dollars – moving it back and forth between them. It felt powerful, like an extension of my hand, except my hand had mythological powers now – it could suddenly throw thunderbolts. They were all scared of the gun, even Mr Griffen.

'Look,' Mr Griffen said in a very shaky voice. 'You can have all my money.' *You can have all my money* – isn't that what I'd said to Vasquez that day?

'I don't want your money,' I said. 'She does.'

'What?'

'*She* wants your money.'

Now, in addition to looking terrified, Mr Griffen looked confused. My heart went out to him – sympathy for a kindred soul, for someone who was about to go through the same shock and disillusionment I had.

'I don't understand,' Mr Griffen said. 'Who are you?'

'It doesn't matter,' I said.

'Look, I don't want any trouble,' Mr Griffen said.

'They were going to take you for everything you have,' I said. 'You're already in trouble.'

Lucinda said: 'I don't know what you're talking about. Me and Sam fell in love . . . we—'

'You met on the train, didn't you, Sam?'

Sam nodded.

'By accident – it just happened. I understand. You talked and talked about everything. She was pretty and sweet and understanding, and you couldn't believe how attracted she was to you. She was too good to be true. Wasn't she, Sam?'

Sam still looked scared of me, but at least he was listening.

'Ask yourself that question. *Wasn't* she too good to be true? Ask yourself if she ever told you where she lived. Did she? The *address*, Sam. If she ever seemed to know anyone else on the train – her friends and neighbors. Most people know someone on the train, don't they. Even one person?'

'He's been stalking me, Sam,' Lucinda said. 'We had a thing once, before you. He's jealous. He's out of his mind.'

You had to give her points for trying, I thought. She was good and she was desperate and she was trying.

Vasquez had moved a little. He seemed definitely closer to me than he'd been before. He was playing red light, green light with me.

'Get back,' I said to him. 'One giant step back.' I pointed the gun at him. Vasquez took a step back.

'I don't know who this crazy *fucker* is,' Vasquez said to Mr Griffen. He was playing along – he'd seen where Lucinda was going with this now, so he was playing along. 'I was just walking in the hall, man, and this asshole pulls a gun on me.'

Sam had a small potbelly and thin, blue-veined arms. He'd crossed them tightly over his pale, hairless chest, as if he were trying to keep himself from crying. He obviously didn't know whom to believe – maybe it didn't even matter now. He wanted to get out of there.

'Listen to me, Sam. What does she do for a living? Has she told you where she works?'

'She's an insurance agent,' he said, but not too convincingly.

'What company, Sam?'

'Mutual of Omaha.'

'Shall we call them, Sam? There's a phone right over there. Why don't you call Mutual of Omaha and ask for her. Go ahead.'

Sam glanced at the phone sitting on the night table by the bed. Lucinda glanced at it, too.

'Did she show you the picture of her little girl, Sam? The cute little blond girl on the swing? The one you can get for yourself at any stationery store?'

'We got to take this crazy fucker down,' Vasquez said. 'He's out of his fucking mind – he's gonna *shoot* us. You with me, Sam?'

But Sam wasn't with him. Sam looked forlorn. He was still confused, but he was being worn down by logic. Maybe he *had* asked himself if Lucinda was too good to be true – maybe he'd always known she was too beautiful and too smart and too available.

'Whatever she's told you is a lie, Sam. All of it. You're being set up, understand what I'm saying to you? You were going to get a surprise. You were going to walk out of the room and Vasquez here was going to jump you in the hall. He was going to rob you. He was going to rape *her*. Only it *wouldn't* have been rape because she's already given her consent. They're in this together.'

Vasquez was on the move again. He was edging forward.

'I don't understand why raping her . . . ,' Mr Griffen said.

'The rape is to make it look legitimate, Sam. And to make you feel guilty that you didn't stop it. That you didn't protect her. So when he starts blackmailing you – you and *Lucinda*, or whatever she calls herself – when he asks you for a little loan and then a not so little loan, you'll pay up. Even if you start having second thoughts about it, even if you start thinking about going to your wife and telling her everything. Because that would still leave her husband, wouldn't it? And she would've told you no, she would've *begged* you not to do it – that she couldn't have her husband know about it – about you and her and the *rape*. Even though she doesn't have a husband, Sam.'

Mr Griffen believed me now. Maybe not 100 percent, but enough.

'Can I . . . go?' Mr Griffen said. 'Can I just . . . get out of here?'

But Vasquez said: 'Are you stupid? You gonna take off and leave us with this crazy motherfucker?'

'Look,' Sam said, 'I just want to go home. I don't know what's going on here, and I don't care. Really. I just . . . just let me go, okay?'

Vasquez reached back into his pocket and hit him across the mouth with something black, and Sam went down. That fast. His mouth began to leak blood.

Another gun.

I'd done just about everything right. I'd gotten the room key and surprised Vasquez on the staircase. I'd made it into the room. I was going to get my money back. Even if my plan was just a little bit murky on *how* I was going to get my money back. Maybe by keeping Lucinda at gunpoint until Vasquez came back with it – maybe by all going for the money together. But I'd made one mistake. I'd forgotten that Vasquezes carry guns. I hadn't searched him or patted him down or made him throw his gun away.

There were a few seconds when all wasn't lost. When I still had the advantage. Vasquez had a gun and Sam was down and bleeding, but I was still the only one in the room with his gun actually pointed at someone.

I could tell that Vasquez was thinking that it was one thing to hold a gun on somebody and an entirely different thing to pull the trigger. He didn't think I had it in me.

But he didn't know something. They say money is the great equalizer, but it's really, truly, desperation. It had leveled the playing field.

I pulled the trigger.

Nothing happened.

In the millisecond it took for Vasquez to realize his good fortune, to begin raising his gun hand, I understood *why* nothing had happened.

I'd forgotten to click off the safety.

I launched myself at Vasquez, using the only advantage I had going for me. Surprise.

My initial charge knocked the gun right out of Vasquez's hand, and it skittered somewhere under the bed. So now we were more or less even.

Maybe I even had the edge. Because there was a chance my desperation was even more terrible than Vasquez's. I had nothing much to lose. Detective Palumbo would be calling back any day now, and even if *he* didn't, Barry Lenge would. So I did have desperation on my side. And something was not quite right with Vasquez. He *was* drunk, or stoned, or something.

Vasquez had gasped from the initial shock of body contact, then immediately tried to separate himself from my grasp. But he seemed like a punched-out heavyweight in round twelve, sluggish and wobbly kneed. It gave me courage.

I could see Sam out of the corner of my eye – up on his knees and looking down at his hand, which was bright red because he'd just touched his mouth with it. He looked dazed and confused.

'Mother . . . *fucker* . . .' Vasquez said, grunting now from the exertion of trying to get me off him but not having much success. I had my arms firmly around him, and I wasn't letting go.

Vasquez staggered into the wall. I had him in a bear hug, so he was doing what bears do when they want to get something off their backs. They rub themselves against the nearest tree trunk. Vasquez was using the nearest wall.

I held fast as I crashed into the plaster wall and dislodged a yellowed reproduction, my sunglasses spinning off onto the floor.

Then we fell to the floor with a loud crash; I could smell Vasquez now – the stink of garlic and cigarette smoke and fried eggs. The carpet was so thin that it was like rolling around on playground cement. And for the first time, I was absolutely convinced I was going to win. I'd moved my right arm around Vasquez's neck and was squeezing for all I was worth – and right at this minute I was worth a lot. One hundred and ten thousand dollars, at least.

Vasquez was sputtering, and I wondered if I was going to kill him. And I thought: *If I have to, I will.*

Vasquez gave one last effort at getting me off his back, but one of his arms was pinned between me and the floor, and I had the other one wrapped up tightly, so even though Vasquez gave an awkward lunge forward, he couldn't dislodge me.

He collapsed; I felt all the strength go out of him – whatever strength booze or drugs hadn't sapped from him already.

I hadn't killed him, but I'd won.

I'd won.

There were a pair of shoes standing just at eye level. At first I thought they belonged to Sam, but Sam was over there on the other side of the room, bleeding into his hands.

So I peered up.

'Lookit here,' said Dexter, 'it's Chuck.'

Forty-one

Dexter had slipped in during the heat of the battle.

We'd been rolling around on the floor, and neither one of us had heard the door open. That allowed Dexter to enter the room, pick up my gun, click off the safety, and point the barrel at my head.

I was leashed and muzzled. My hands were tied behind my back with my own belt. They took off my shoes and socks and stuffed one clammy sock into my mouth.

They did the same thing to Sam. Sam resisted momentarily, and Vasquez kicked him in the head.

I could smell Sam's blood.

It smelled almost sweet, but since I knew where it was coming from, it was a nauseating sweetness. That was a problem. Because it made me want to throw up, and the thought of throwing up with a sock already stuffed into my mouth made me want to panic.

Not panicking was easier said than done. I was wondering, for instance, what they were planning to do with us, with Sam and me. I had the strong feeling *they* didn't know yet.

They seemed at loose ends. They kept muttering and whispering to each other – sometimes in Spanish, sometimes not.

'*Nosotros tenemos que hacer algo,*' Lucinda was saying now.

I'd taken just one year of high school Spanish, and the only word I actually remembered was *gracias* – but I could intuit their confusion anyway.

I overheard Vasquez whispering something in English to Lucinda.

'Afterwards . . . we can go . . . Miami and . . .' They were taking off.

It made sense. After all, Sam was useless to them now, a would-be cash cow that had been irrevocably damaged. All that time and effort put into leading him here and nothing to show for it.

They were legitimately upset. They were unhappy I'd shown up. I was the reason it hadn't worked out the way they'd planned. Me. I'd gummed up the works and left them with a problem they hadn't counted on. Their weapons, after all, were fear and deception, but now I'd made those weapons useless.

Which left what?

'You stupid *fuck* . . .' Vasquez was sitting on the bed with his hands on his knees. He was talking to me. 'I told

315

you not to pull this kind of shit again. I told you to go back to Long Island and stay there, right? You lost *money* before, motherfucker. *Money*. You should've thanked God. *Now* what you gonna do, huh?'

Perhaps pray.

It wasn't merely the words that were frightening, that made me think praying was in order – it was the fact that Vasquez himself seemed frightened saying them. *Now what you gonna do, huh?* As if it were a question they'd asked themselves, then come up with an answer they hadn't liked. When scary people start sounding scared, that's when it's okay to be scared yourself.

The three of them went into the bathroom together. Someone – I thought it was Dexter – was arguing against doing something. I could hear his raised voice.

When they came out of the bathroom, Dexter didn't look very happy. It appeared he'd lost.

But Vasquez and Dexter were going somewhere now.

'Ten minutes,' I heard Vasquez whisper to Lucinda, 'and then we'll go down to . . . Little Havana . . . my cousin . . .'

Vasquez and Dexter left the room.

Which left the three of us. Sam, Lucinda, and me.

'What are you going to do with us?' Sam said through the sock in his mouth. The words muffled, but understandable.

But Lucinda didn't answer him.

'I won't tell,' Sam said. 'If you let me go, I won't say a thing, I promise. Please . . .'

Still no answer from Lucinda. Maybe she'd been told not to say anything – no fraternizing with the enemy. Maybe after having had to talk to Sam Griffen for months, it was nice not to say anything to him now. Or maybe she knew exactly what they were going to do with us and thought it better not to tell.

'The sock . . . it's choking me,' Sam said. '*Please* . . .'

Lucinda finally responded, but not with words. She got up and walked over to Sam – a short walk of five feet, maybe.

'Please,' Sam said, 'take it out of my mouth . . . *please . . . I'm choking* . . .'

So Lucinda reached down to pull out the sock.

As soon as her hand reached into his mouth, he bit down on it, and Lucinda screamed.

Maybe he'd been asking himself the same questions I had and come up with the same answers. So maybe he'd decided he had nothing to lose.

She kicked out at him – '*Motherfucker!*' – trying to get her hand out of his mouth, but Sam was holding on like an attack dog, the kind trained to take down robbers and not let go, even if you shoot them dead. Lucinda, screaming and punching at Sam's head with her free hand, but Sam *still* not letting go, holding on for dear life.

I tried to get over there, but I had to worm my way to them, because my hands were tied behind my back. I had to move in sections. I was trying to help Sam. Because something bad was going to happen now. I could see that.

For one thing, Lucinda had managed to get her hand out of his mouth. Finally. For another, she was raising the gun in her left hand and beginning to bring it down on Sam's head. Sam's mouth was bloody, her blood and his seemingly mixed together, as Lucinda brought the gun down on his face again. Then again and again.

'Please,' Sam said, 'please, I'm a *father* . . . I have *three children*,' as the gun smashed into his cheekbone. As it smashed into his nose. Hoping, I guess, that this might give her pause, might make her stop hitting him. But it only seemed to make her madder. Sam kept pleading, 'Three children . . . please . . . a *father*,' but Lucinda kept hitting him. Harder and harder – I could hear the sound of metal hitting bone. As if he were saying, *Hit me*, and she was just going ahead and obliging him.

I'd managed to get eight inches, ten inches, a foot closer to them, when I finally realized it didn't matter.

Not now.

Sam was dead.

Vasquez and Dexter walked back into the room.

Dexter was carrying two garbage bags – the large, industrial-strength kind, big enough for an entire lawn of leaves. Or a couple of bodies.

Maybe that's why when they saw Sam was dead, when Vasquez kicked him softly with his shoe and actually confirmed this, no one seemed particularly upset about it.

'He bit me,' was all Lucinda said, and Vasquez nodded.

Then Vasquez picked up a pillow and said to me: 'Time to go to sleep.'

Vasquez has a gun, but he can't take the chance of someone hearing it.

They were going to suffocate me.

I'd been doing something while Lucinda killed Sam. While she'd gotten up and gone into the bathroom to wash the blood off her hands. While Sam lay there without breathing. I'd remembered something. Dexter had come in and picked up my gun, and then he'd given the gun to Lucinda when they went out.

Which still left one other gun.

Vasquez's gun. Where was it?

Under the bed. Where it had come to rest when I'd knocked it out of Vasquez's hand.

Maybe five feet away from me. That's all.

They were going to suffocate me.

I'd begun to inch my way over to it.

Something else. I'd begun to test the quality of the knot that Dexter had tied with my belt. It wasn't meant to be used as a rope; it wasn't supple enough to make a good knot. There was some give there.

They were going to suffocate me.

By the time Vasquez and Dexter re-entered the room, I'd opened a tiny hole in the knot. I'd moved myself to within two feet of Vasquez's gun.

Close enough to reach it. If I could get my hands out in time.

'Bedtime,' Vasquez said.

319

Your life does not flash in front of your eyes.

I would like to tell you that now.

That's what they say happens to you when you face your own death, but it's not true. Not for me – my entire life did not play itself out before my eyes. Just one small part of it.

When I was seven years old and at the beach.

I'd been playing in the surf and not paying attention, and a rogue wave had come along and knocked me under. By the time they pulled me from the water, I was purple, cyanotic, and – if not for the ministrations of a first-year lifeguard – *dead*. From that day on, I was forever scared of drowning. From that day on, when I had dreams about dying, it was always that way. With no air in my lungs.

That's the part of my life I saw now.

Before Vasquez placed the white pillow down over my mouth, I managed to gulp in one deep breath.

There was a game we used to play as a kid. It was called No Breathing. A game I played with nearly maniacal devotion after that incident at the beach – as if I knew it just might save me one day.

I used to be able to do three minutes. Maybe even four. Go.

The pillow smelled of sweat and dust. I began to work my hands back and forth against the knot in the belt.

I pushed outward with both wrists. Then relaxed. Then pushed. Then relaxed.

It was like a painful isometric. Vasquez had all his weight pressing down on me. It was hard to move my hands.

I kept my wrists pushing, though. Even though the belt was cutting into my skin like a dull blade.

It was slow going. I heard someone pacing a few feet from me. The bed squeaked. Lucinda cleared her throat. Someone turned on the radio.

My hands were going nowhere. I kept pushing and pushing, but it was like pushing against a locked door. Like running in quicksand. I was pushing, but nothing was giving. My chest was starting to ache. My arm sockets felt as if they were being pulled apart. They were screaming at me.

No, they screeched. *Not on your life. Not possible. Forget it.*

Stop!

My lungs were on fire now. I couldn't feel my hands.

Then the belt began to give.

Just a little.

Just loose enough to get a little piece of my hand through.

I pushed with all my strength. Then again and again.

My wrists were bleeding. I kept pushing.

I got my hands halfway through. Both hands were sweating. The sweat and blood was helping them slide through the belt. That was good, that was *wonderful.* I kept pushing.

My hands were three-quarters out. I needed to push just a little bit more, just a little bit. It was my knuckles, though.

They were a problem. *Please.*

I gave one last push – one last push for everything. For everything I needed to make it back to. For Anna. For Deanna.

Now.

I pushed and pushed and pushed . . .

One hand came free.

I'm dying.

My left hand, the arm closest to the bed.

It's black. I can't see. I'm dying.

I heard Vasquez say, 'Huh.'

I heard Dexter say, 'Watch out.'

I frantically felt for the gun under the box spring. My lungs were bursting. I slid my hands this way and that way under the bed. Where was it?

I felt the gun. I got my fingers around it.

What's this? What's happening?

I brought it out from under the bed.

And at that very moment, at that very instant in time when I might've turned the tide, I died.

Attica

Fat Tommy was right.

They'd sent me notification in the mail.

'Dear Mr Widdoes: This is to inform you that State budget constraints will no longer allow for an adult education program in State prisons. Classes will end on the first of next month. A formal notice of termination will follow.'

This meant I had two classes left.

Just two.

The COs kept their distance from me now, as if I had a communicable disease. Was it possible state layoffs were contagious? When I slipped into the COs lounge for coffee, they gave me a wide berth – wider even than before, when it was simply my job that had rubbed them the wrong way. Now it was my lack of one.

I sipped my coffee alone, over in the corner of the room known as the museum.

323

The museum *had been so dubbed by a long-ago correction officer whose name no one remembered. It was a loosely arranged collection of prison-confiscated weapons. Bangers, shanks, gats, and burners – what the cons call knives. Forged from bedsprings, hollowed-out pens, smuggled-in screwdrivers – whatever the prisoners can get their hands on. But there were also crude guns – ingenious things put together with odds and ends from the machine shop, capable of putting a reasonable facsimile of a bullet into a man at close range.*

It was constantly being added to. After each clear-out there'd be one or two more donations.

I stared at these crude instruments of death until the silence at my presence there grew intolerable, or until it was time for class.

Whichever came first.

The writer had kept it up with monotonous and painful regularity.

Every class I found another installment sitting there on my desk.

My own story slowly being fed back to me, chapter by painful chapter. It was a torturously slow indictment of Charles Schine. I was convinced that torture was exactly what the writer had in mind.

There were other things, too. Another note appeared at the end of chapter 20.

'Time we got together, don't you think?'

Written in brown ink, except it wasn't brown ink. It was written in blood. It was meant to scare me.

*And I thought, Yes, it is time we got together. Even if I felt
my palms grow sweaty and my collar tighten like a noose.*

The writer wasn't in my classroom. I knew that.

The delivery boy was.

*A few classes after I received the last note, I dismissed the
class and someone stayed behind.*

*When I looked up, he was sitting there and smiling at
me.*

Malik El Mahid. His Muslim name.

Twenty-five or so. Black, squat, and tattooed.

'Yes?' I said, even though I knew what was coming now.

*'Like the story so far?' he said, still smiling. Repeating the
first words the writer had scrawled to me.*

'You,' I said. 'You've been leaving it for me.'

'Thas right, dawg.'

'Who?'

'Who what?'

'Who's giving the chapters to you?'

'You sayin' I ain't the writer?'

'Yes. I'm saying you didn't write it.'

'Fuckin' right. I didn't read none of it either.'

'Who?'

'You know who, dawg.'

Yes.

'He wants to see you now, 'kay?'

He wants to see you now.

'All right,' I said as calmly as I could.

*But as I gathered the papers on my desk, I noticed my hand
was trembling. The papers were clearly fluttering right there*

in full view of Malik, and even though I willed my hand to stop shaking, I couldn't get it to listen.

'Next week,' Malik said. 'All right?'

I said yes. Next week was fine.

But I have to get back to the story now.

I have to explain what happened.

Forty-two

When I brought the gun out from under the bed, the world collapsed. It ended.

There was a flash of light, a blast of heat, and then the earth imploded and went black.

Then I woke up.

I opened my eyes and thought: *I'm dead.*

Vasquez has killed me. I am dead. I am in heaven.

Only I couldn't have been in heaven.

Because I was in hell.

Pick up Dante's *Inferno* and go right to the sixth circle. The black sulfurous fumes. The inferno of boiling oil. The screams of agony. I opened my eyes and couldn't see. It was still morning, but it was night.

This much was clear. The eighth floor of the Fairfax Hotel had somehow become the basement. The seventh floor down had become a grave.

The room itself was half standing. It was spring, but it was snowing (plaster powder, I discovered when I tasted it on my tongue). An entire air-conditioning unit was lying on top of my left leg.

This is what I know now, but not then. What I pieced together from newspapers and TV and my own limited observations.

That women's health center next door to the Fairfax Hotel provided federally subsidized abortions, which meant that to certain people out there it wasn't a women's health center as much as an *abortion* center.

That man in the University of Oklahoma jacket whom I met in the elevator the day I checked in and then later saw in the lobby, complaining about having no Bibles in his room? He was one of those people out there. A muscular Christian, a devout right-to-lifer, but one with an aggrieved sense of injustice and a fascination with explosives.

It turned out he wasn't spending his time playing three-card monte and buying fake Rolexes on the street. He was spending his time up in his room, painstakingly putting together a bomb made out of fertilizer and acetates. When it was done, he strapped it carefully to his body.

He took the elevator down to the lobby of the Fairfax Hotel with the intention of walking into the women's health center next door and blowing it and himself up.

Let me explain the volatility of this kind of bomb. According to later reports in the papers, it is not your most stable kind of explosive. Not like dynamite, for instance, or plastic explosives. It's extremely volatile, very trans-mutable.

He never made it out of the elevator. Something happened. The elevator stopped short. Or he was jostled. Or he pressed the detonator by mistake. Something.

The bomb exploded at the very epicenter of the building. If you were trying to take down the Fairfax Hotel and not the abortion center next door, and you were smart about blast ratios and shock indexes and structural weaknesses, this is where you would do it.

In the elevator directly between floors five and six.

And the Fairfax ·Hotel was a structural weakness waiting to be put out of its misery.

Its bones were cracked and creaky and brittle. Peeling asbestos made it a model firetrap. It had several leaks in its gas heating system, or so it was later determined. In short, it was a disaster waiting to happen.

Steel beams. Sections of roof. Plaster wall. Plate glass. People. All hurtling up in the air and then, true to Newtonian physics, *down*. On top of what was left of the Fairfax Hotel. Flattening it like a crushed wedding cake.

One hundred and forty-three people died that morning in the Fairfax Hotel and four surrounding buildings.

One hundred and forty-three and, eventually, one more.

I heard a voice.

'Anyone alive down there? Anyone?'

'Yes,' I said. *If I hear myself*, I thought, *then maybe I'm alive.*

'Yes,' I said, and heard it.

Arms grasped my arms. Lifted me out of the rubble and carnage and blackness, and I was suddenly alive and breathing.

This is what I know now, but not then.

Two rooms had remained intact – or mostly intact. Who knows why? When someone decides to strap a bomb to his body and obliterate himself, rhyme and reason take a holiday. Some people that morning went to the left and survived. Some people went right and didn't. One person lay this close to death on a hotel floor and made it out alive.

And pretty much unscathed.

They brought me out of the rubble and laid me down on a stretcher at the side of the street, and they went in and brought out anyone else they could find. Including Vasquez and Lucinda and Dexter and Sam. Of the four, three of them were dead and the other one almost. Dexter and Sam and Lucinda had blankets pulled up over their faces. Vasquez was unconscious and bloody and barely breathing.

They laid him next to me on the sidewalk, and a fireman took his pulse and shook his head. When someone with a red cross on his arm came running over, the fireman said, 'Take care of the old woman over there,' and pointed at a woman whose clothes were smoldering.

'He's not going to make it.'

Eventually I decided to get up and leave. To just walk away.

Even though I must have been suffering from some sort of shock, I felt terrifyingly lucid.

Visibility was almost zero. But I could see Lucinda's body not five feet from me. I could touch Vasquez. Firemen and policemen were running back and forth in a choking maelstrom of black smoke.

I got up. I began walking. I vanished in that maelstrom.

I walked quite a while. I was wondering if Deanna had been right all along, that things happened for a reason. I wasn't sure now. People stared at me as if I'd just landed from another planet. But no one stopped me – no one asked me if I was hurt or needed a doctor or an ambulance. Maybe they were immune to this kind of thing now. I walked straight down Broadway. I thought my hair was singed – when I ran my hands through it, it crackled like static. I ended up hailing a taxicab somewhere near Central Park.

I went back to my apartment in Forest Hills. The taxi driver had the radio on. Someone was talking about the explosion. Possibly a gas leak, a woman was saying – she was interviewing a fire captain. It would be a while before they'd find evidence to the contrary. The taxi driver asked me if I was all right.

'Yes,' I said. 'Couldn't be better.'

When we got to Forest Hills, the street I lived on was deserted. Maybe everyone was glued to the news. No one saw me enter the building, go into my apartment, fall into a stupor.

I slept an entire day.

When I woke the next morning, I went into the bathroom and didn't recognize myself. I was in blackface – I belonged in a minstrel show.

I turned on the news. Three talking heads were debating figures. What figures, exactly? It took me a while to figure it out. The number of dead – that's what they were talking about. Somewhere around 100 was the consensus. On another channel they claimed it was 96, 150 on another. The hotel dead and the peripheral casualties in the four surrounding buildings. But who knew how many died, really? That's what the talking heads said. The bodies were burned up, crushed, incinerated. It was impossible to tell, one man said, they might never know. If someone who was in the hotel showed up, they were alive – he said. If they didn't they were dead. People had already begun scouring hospitals and Red Cross shelters, putting up pictures on walls and fences and street lamps – a hollow-eyed and desperate army of bereaved.

I watched for an entire day without moving.

I didn't call anyone – I didn't speak to anyone. I was more or less paralyzed. All that horror. I couldn't move – I couldn't eat. I couldn't speak.

The illusion of invulnerability I used to carry around like a birthright – the one Vasquez and Lucinda had stripped me of – had now been taken from 143 others. No one was safe anymore. No one.

The rubble from the explosion was taken by truck to the city dump. To the dump in Staten Island. To the place you can get to by following the stench straight down Western Avenue.

To make room for the tons of debris, they first had to move other tons of debris. Move those piles of debris from one place to another. And amid the pile of twisted steel, crushed cardboard, tin cans, broken bones, rotten food, cracked brick, and human waste – they found a wasted human.

They finally found Winston.

This was all the police had been waiting for. A body. They had me on tape telling Winston what I wanted him to do, but they didn't have *Winston*.

Now they did.

I discovered this when I finally called Deanna three days after I stumbled away from the blown-up buildings. From what looked like downtown Beirut. She was happy to hear from me.

'Thank God, Charles,' she said. 'I thought you were *dead*.'

Forty-three

That's when it first occurred to me.

When Deanna got on the phone and said, *I thought you were dead.*

Or maybe it wasn't exactly then. Maybe it was later, after I'd told Deanna what I'd been up to – what had happened to me in the Fairfax Hotel – and she gasped and went silent and then told me the police had come to the house with a warrant for my arrest. Because they'd found Winston's body in the Staten Island dump.

Or it might've been later that day, when a somber and pale-looking city spokeswoman read a list of the dead on a news program. The confirmed dead and the *presumed* dead – otherwise known as the still missing.

My name was on it.

It was kind of surreal, listening to myself be declared officially missing. It was like attending my own funeral –

my very own memorial service. The city spokeswoman said this list was carefully compiled from the hotel's computer hard drive, recovered in the rubble – people who were known to have been registered guests at the time of the explosion. And from belongings found here and there, scattered around the blast site and stored in the hotel safe. Briefcases, PalmPilots, engraved watches, and jewelry. My watch, for example, was missing. 'To Charles Schine with all my love,' it said on the back. The spokeswoman explained they'd matched this list to the people who'd made it to emergency rooms and hospital beds.

I was picking up the phone to call someone – anyone – and explain that I wasn't dead after all, that I was still here. I was getting dressed at the same time, because maybe a phone call wouldn't be enough, it was possible I would have to show up and produce myself in the flesh. I was rummaging through my sock drawer, and I came across Winston's wallet.

Which is when the idea *really* occurred to me.

When it changed from the ridiculous to the possible. From a wishful notion to an actual plan. I'd buried Winston's wallet in my sock drawer and forgotten about it. But I remembered something Winston told me now.

The easiest thing to get – new identities, he'd said.

His wallet, for instance, had four of them. Driver's licenses.

A Jonathan Thomas. A Brian McDermott. A Ste Aimett.

And a Lawrence Widdoes. The only one of the four who looked even remotely like me – younger, of course, but the same basic coloring.

I thought you were dead, Deanna said.

So did a few other people.

I'd checked into the Fairfax Hotel, but I'd never checked out. Or maybe I had, but only in the vernacular sense of the term. As in, *Did you hear what happened to Charley? He, well, checked out. He* died.

Which reminded me of one other popular saying.

I'd be better off dead. Yes, we've all heard that one, too. An expression we use in times of crisis, when things are absolutely hopeless and there seems to be no way out.

Unless there is. Unless you think that you're good and trapped, but there is a way out after all.

Being dead.

Maybe that was the way out.

If I showed up, I'd be alive.

But what if I *didn't*?

Forty-four

I was standing on the corner of Crescent and Thirtieth Avenue.

In front of a place called the Crystal Night Club. It didn't look like a nightclub. It was just an ex-VFW lodge – the pale imprint of 'VFW Lodge 54' still lingered on the brick facing. But it was past midnight, and I could hear music inside. A Latin-looking man was throwing up on the sidewalk.

When I walked in, I was immediately aware that I wasn't exactly in my element.

Remember that scene from *Star Wars* where the hero strolls into that alien bar? I felt like that. Only these aliens were of the terrestrial variety – the kind you see on the evening news when the INS conducts its perio^{...} roundups on the border. The kind you see on any ^{...} crew on Long Island. If I hopped a plane to

Domingo and stepped off onto the runway and into the nearest bar, it might look like this.

I was pretty sure I was the only white American in the place. Possibly the only legal American, too.

Salsa music was blaring from two enormous speakers. Spanish was flowing freely around the room.

Everyone seemed coupled up, but they were oddly paired. The women were dressed up – short flashy skirts and high heels. The men wore dirty jeans and T-shirts. It took me a while to understand what was going on.

The women were hostesses. That's the way one of them introduced herself – first in Spanish, *huéspeda*. Then in English, when I looked perplexed and she got a good look at me and realized I wasn't her usual clientele.

For a moment she hesitated, as if she expected me to realize my mistake and leave. But when I stood there and waited politely for her to continue, she did.

'I'm Rosa,' she said. 'Want a hostess?'

'Yes,' I said. 'Fine.'

Return for a minute to that moment I was taken out of the hole in the ground that had once been the Fairfax Hotel.

I was laid on the sidewalk as they waited for the ambulances and doctors to arrive. They came out with other bodies; they placed a dying Vasquez next to me on the ground.

The fireman who laid him there was covered in soot. eyes were like white ash on burning charcoal. He me if I was okay.

I said yes. I could hear the faint wail of a rushing ambulance. I knew I had just a few minutes.

When the fireman went back in for more bodies, I leaned over Vasquez as if I were comforting him. Seeing if he was all right. I put my hands into his pockets. First the front pockets, then the back.

In his front pockets was some change. A vial with white powder in it. Some matches.

His back pocket was bulging with his wallet. I quickly removed it and put it in my pocket.

I got up and left.

In the taxi to Forest Hills I rifled through it, returning the favor Vasquez had done for me in the Fairfax Hotel.

In this wallet: a phony police badge; a suspicious-looking driver's license; more white powder wrapped in aluminum foil; two hundred dollars; a business card for something called the Crystal Night Club. Proprietor listed as Raul Vasquez.

On the back was some Spanish writing. *Veinte-y-dos . . . derecho, treinta-y-siete izquierdo, doce . . . derecho.*

The next morning, the morning I woke in blackface, I looked it up on-line. Google.com – Spanish Dictionary.

Once I translated the first word, I knew they were numbers.

Twenty-two right.

Thirty-seven left.

Twelve right.

I was pretty sure it wasn't a football play.

*

This is the way it worked in the Crystal Night Club.

You ordered overpriced drinks, and Rosa talked to you.

That's what the other men were doing.

Rosa explained it to me, as something to talk about.

'You ain't no wetback,' she said. 'That's what we get in here. Usually,' she added, not wanting to offend me.

'Where do you come from?' I asked her.

'America,' she said. '*Where do you think?*'

'No. I meant where do you live?'

'The Bronx,' she said. 'All of us do. We get bused in.'

'Oh.'

'These guys' – she pointed around the room with evident disdain – 'they live on crews. You know . . . like six to a room.'

'And they come here to drink.'

'Right,' she said with a little smile, as if I'd said something funny. 'To drink. Want another?' she asked me, reminding me that that's exactly what I was doing. Drinking.

I'd barely touched my ten-dollar tequila sunrise, but I said sure.

'They're lonely,' she added after making a hand signal to the man behind the bar. He had a thick neck festooned with tattooed crosses. 'They come here to like . . . you know, bullshit. They got no one to talk to. No one *female*,' she said. 'They like, fall in love with us, you know. They ▚ow all their *dinero*.' And she laughed and rubbed her ▚rs together.

'▚h,' I said. 'I understand.'

'Oh yeah . . . you understand. So what's your story?'

'Nothing,' I said. 'I don't have one. I just wandered in.'

'Yeah, well, that's cool.'

Rosa was thick hipped and fleshy – most of the hostesses were. I was picturing Lucinda. I was wondering if she'd worked here, too; I took a gamble.

'Actually,' I said, and Rosa leaned closer, 'I came in once before. I think.'

'You *think*?'

'I was drunk,' I said. 'I think it was the same place. Not sure.'

'Okay,' she said.

'There was this girl here.' I described Lucinda in detail, all the detail someone who'd spent countless hours staring at a woman would know. I left out things like her sexy pout and liquid eyes.

'Oh,' Rosa said. 'You're talking about *Didi*.' But she said it in a way that made me think she hadn't exactly liked Didi.

'Didi? Yeah . . . I think that was her name. Sure.'

'She was a fucking *puta* . . . a player, you know . . .'

'No.'

'Oh yeah. She comes in and sees what's what in like two minutes, right? Sticking her tits out . . . her skinny little ass . . . parading it for the boss. I could see what she was doing. I'm down like James Brown on this bitch, right? She's here like two days, two fucking days, and she's doing him.'

The boss. Raul Vasquez.

'Where is the boss?' I said.

Rosa shrugged. 'Don't know. He hasn't been around. Why?'

'No reason.' And I thought: *They don't know.* I had his wallet, and he wasn't registered at the hotel. They had no name and no one to notify. No next of kin to break the news to.

'So, you married?' she asked me.

'No.'

I was trying to put it all together. I was trying to picture how it started. These poor wetbacks came into the Crystal Night Club to blow all their cash on hostesses who basically looked down on them. Lucinda was one of those hostesses. That faint accent I'd asked her about on the train – Spanish? But Lucinda hadn't remained a hostess for long. She'd flashed her *skinny ass* instead and hooked up with Vasquez. You could see why he'd want to. She didn't look like the rest of them here. She looked like someone who spent her day buying low and selling high in some office tower downtown. The kind of woman other white-collar commuters would drool over behind their morning papers.

Was it his idea, I wondered, or hers? Who got the idea – who looked around the depressing environs of the Crystal Night Club and saw the possibilities?

'You ain't drinking,' Rosa said. 'The rule is, if you don't drink, I gotta talk to somebody else, okay?'

'I'll order another,' I said, and Rosa smiled.

Maybe it was her. Didi. Maybe she saw how ridiculously it was to make these day laborers far from home fall in love with her and knew it would be even easier with guys like me. Married guys who weren't far from home, but maybe were wishing they were. Guys who wanted someone to talk to just as much as these guys. Guys with *real* cash.

When the bartender brought over another tequila sunrise, I opened my wallet to pay.

Rosa said: 'Widdoes? What kind of name is that?' She was looking at a piece of my new driver's license. Yes, my first night as a new man. Charles Schine was dead.

'Just a name,' I said.

'It's depressing,' she said. 'Like *widows*, you know . . .'

'Yes, well, it's spelled differently.'

'That's true,' she said seriously.

'Where's the bathroom?' I asked her.

'Over there—' She pointed to a back hall. 'Most of them use the sidewalk,' she said, and snorted. 'You should smell it at four in the morning. They don't know no better.'

'Well, I'll use the bathroom,' I said.

'Sure. Go ahead.'

When I got up from the table, I saw the thick-necked man behind the bar staring at me. I walked to the back of the room, passing Colombian, Mexican, Dominican, and Peruvian men engrossed in conversation with their respective hostesses. The conversations were kind of one-sided, though, the men leaning over the tables and talking in slurred Spanish. I thought that my conversations with Didi had been pretty much like that, too.

One of the bathrooms said 'hombres' on the door

I walked in that one. There was a man kneeling over the toilet. I could smell his vomit.

I walked into a stall that had graffiti over every inch of it. Mostly in Spanish, but some English, too.

'I have an ten-inch dick,' someone had written.

I sat on the toilet and took a deep breath. I'd seen a third door here in the back hallway. His office?

I waited till the other man left, then I got up and walked back into the hallway.

There was no one there. I walked to the third door.

It wasn't locked. When I opened it, its rusty hinges shrieked at me and I stopped and waited, my heart somewhere in my throat.

Nothing. The salsa music was pounding away out there.

I slipped inside and closed the door.

The room was dark. I felt for the light switch and found it just behind the door.

Yes, it was his office. Had to be. It wasn't *much* of an office, but there was a desk, a swivel chair, a beat-up couch, a file cabinet.

I was thinking about the man behind the bar. How he'd stared at me when I walked to the back hallway. The tendons on his neck had looked like thick strands of rope.

I scanned the walls – they were made of fake wood. Nothing there. No wall safe, for instance. No picture that ʌld be hiding a wall safe. Those numbers on the back of ard – they had to be the combination to a safe. If not here, somewhere. He was dead, and I needed that money back. I had to chance it.

There was a ripped calendar hanging on the wall, but when I pushed it to one side there was nothing behind it.

I heard footsteps outside the door. I held my breath.

They kept going; I heard the bathroom door open and shut.

I tried the file cabinet – it was locked. The desk drawer was open. In the back of the drawer was a sheaf of yellowed newspaper. It was a bunch of clippings. The first was an old cover of Newsday. COMMUTER JUMPS OFF LIRR was the headline. There was a picture of a body wrapped in a white sheet, lying at the side of the railroad tracks in Lynbrook, Long Island. A somber-looking policeman was standing guard over it.

The actual article was there, too.

'A Rockville Centre man apparently committed suicide last night by jumping off a Long Island Rail Road train,' the article began. It went on to say that he was married with three children, that he was a corporate lawyer, that he'd left no suicide note. He'd been experiencing some unnamed personal problems, a family spokesperson said. Other than that, there was no explanation. Witnesses on the train said the man – his name was John Pierson – was walking to the back of the train with other commuters in order to find a seat when he simply, and without warning, jumped.

I might've stopped reading right there, except one of the witnesses' names caught my eye. The last person to see him alive – the one who actually saw him jump.

Raul. No last name given. It listed his occupation as bar owner.

The door opened.

The thick-necked man was standing there staring at me.

I was standing behind the desk with the newspaper clippings in my hand. The desk drawer was open.

'Astoria General,' he said softly.

'What?'

'The nearest hospital. So you know what to tell the ambulance driver.'

'I'm sorry . . . I was looking for the bathroom . . .'

'I'm going to have to fuck you up bad,' he said, still in that soft voice. 'Two, three weeks in the hospital before you get out, okay?'

'Look, really, I was just . . .'

He closed the door behind him. He locked it.

He began to walk toward me.

I stepped back, but there was only wall behind me.

He stopped and took something out of his pocket. A roll of coins that he wrapped his right fist around.

He walked around the desk; he was close enough to smell.

Then I remembered what I had in my pocket. I pulled it out and flipped it open.

He stopped.

'Detective, NYPD,' I said. Vasquez's phony police badge.
stuffed it into my pocket and almost, but not quite,
~tten about it.

'We have reports of illicit drug activity,' I said, wondering if that was how policemen actually spoke. I tried to remember the way Detective Palumbo had spoken to me that day in the office.

'There's no drugs here,' the man said. 'You got a warrant?'

I didn't, of course, have a warrant.

'You just *threatened* me. Do I need a warrant to *arrest* you?'

'There's no drugs here,' the man said. 'I'm going to call our lawyer, okay?'

'Go ahead,' I said. 'I'm done.'

And I walked out right past him.

I counted in my head. *One, two, three, four* . . . wondering how many seconds it would take me to get out of the bar and onto the street. And how many seconds it might take him to reconsider letting me walk out without checking my badge again or asking me to wait for his lawyer to arrive. I was up to ten when I passed Rosa, who said, 'Hey, where you goin'?' . . . fifteen when I walked through the door without answering her.

Forty-five

I came back to Merrick later that same night.

When no one could see me. When I could scurry up the driveway and sneak in the back door. Curry whimpered and mewled and licked my hand.

Deanna rushed into my arms and we held each other until my arms went numb.

'Do you know you've been listed as missing?' Deanna said.

'Yes, I know. You didn't . . . ?'

'No. I told the detective who came here that we were separated, that I hadn't heard from you, that I didn't know where you were. I thought I should probably keep to that story until you told me differently.'

'Good.' I sighed. 'Look, I need to talk to you about something.'

'Wait a minute,' she said. 'They found something of ~urs, Charles.'

'My watch?' I said.

'No.' She went into the den and came back with it in her arms.

'They told me to come down and pick it up today. It was in the hotel safe.'

It was big, black, and bulging.

My briefcase.

The one I'd handed to Vasquez in Spanish Harlem with one hundred thousand dollars of Anna's money in it.

What was it doing here?

'They found it in the safe. It had your name on it.'

My name, in embossed gold, as plain as day, even though the briefcase was covered in fine white powder. *Charles Barnett Schine.*

'It's really heavy,' Deanna said. 'What do you have in there?'

I went to open it, to show her what I had in there, but it was locked. It *was* heavy – heavier than I remembered.

And I thought: *Yes, of course. If you had a lot of money and you wanted to put it somewhere other than a bank, because you weren't exactly bank material and you maybe didn't trust banks anyway, maybe you would pick a hotel safe in the care of your friend and partner, Dexter.*

'They didn't want to break into it,' Deanna said. 'Not unless it went unclaimed.'

I'd never used the lock before, of course. I seemed to remember that you had to program it yourself, put your own three-digit code into it. I'd never bothered to.

I started to walk to the kitchen drawer where we kept the knives I would use to force it open, when I remembered something.

I reached into my pocket and pulled out Vasquez's business card. I turned it over.

Twenty-two right.

Thirty-seven left.

Twelve right.

I moved the tiny cylinders. It clicked open.

In the briefcase was the $110,000 of Anna's money. And hundreds of thousands more.

Things happened for a reason, Deanna always believed. And now, finally, I agreed with her.

We talked.

And talked.

Straight through the night.

I told Deanna what was on my mind.

At first she was incredulous; she made me repeat it because she didn't think she'd heard it right.

'You're not serious, Charles?'

'As far as anyone knows, Deanna, I'm dead, understand? I think I should stay that way.'

I told her everything I hadn't before. The T&D Music House. The investigation they were conducting at my company. The charges that would no doubt soon be filed.

Deanna still resisted. She put up coffee; we huddled in the basement so we wouldn't wake Anna.

We imagined the future. But we imagined it two ways.

We imagined me walking down to the police station in the morning and giving myself up. We imagined it first that way. Giving myself up to the police and getting a lawyer and going to trial. And possibly losing. Conspiracy to commit murder, with exhibit A being an audiotape where a jury of my peers would hear me asking Winston to more or less go kill someone for me. A tough thing to explain your way out of. So I might end up looking at fifteen years, possibly ten with time off for good behavior, even with that *separate* indictment hanging over my head for embezzlement.

Ten or fifteen years. Not the longest time in the world. Maybe even doable time. Maybe. Only there was another sentence to consider here.

Anna had been handed a sentence, too. An uncertain sentence, true, a reprieve from the governor always a possibility. But not likely. Probably, more than possibly, a death sentence. Which meant that when I'd finished serving my ten or fifteen years, when I came out to find my family waiting for me outside the walls of Attica – it would be diminished by one. It would be just the two of us. And maybe sooner rather than later. Because there would be other nights where Anna would be found unconscious and shaking; other injections given with a trembling hand to my comatose daughter. Keeping Anna alive was a two-person job – it had always been a two-person job.

And since we were both sitting there and imagining this kind of future, I imagined all of it. Getting the news in

351

prison, by letter, maybe: 'We regret to inform you that your daughter, Anna, passed away yesterday.' Begging for permission to attend her funeral. Being turned down. Having to see Deanna's ravaged face through the plastic partition the next time she came to visit me.

We imagined that future first.

Then we imagined another. A different kind of future.

A future someplace else. With other names. A future that would include both of us there to share in it.

With $450,000 to support it. To support Anna.

That's how much was in the briefcase. One hundred and ten thousand dollars of Anna's Fund and $340,000 from the other men they'd taken to the cleaners.

Which was another reason to consider this second future. That briefcase. Someone might come looking for it.

There were times that night it seemed like we were talking about someone else. That it couldn't be *our* family we were discussing, that it had to be someone else's. A more or less ordinary middle-class family suddenly becoming a *different* ordinary middle-class family. Was that possible? Sometimes things like that happened, didn't they? Entire families whisked off into witness protection programs, new identities, new lives. This was different, of course.

We weren't going to be hidden by the government. We were going to be *hiding* from the government. From the New York City Police Department.

Hiding from everyone from now on.

In the end, it came down to a simple question. It came down to Anna. What was her best chance? What promised a longer future for her? With me or without me? It was possible I could beat the charges. After all, even with adultery thrown into the mix, I might have sympathy on my side – and a clever lawyer, too. I *might* beat the charges, but it was only fifty-fifty at best.

Could we take the chance? Could we roll the dice?

The reason to do it was Anna.

The reason not to do it was Anna.

I would have to disappear first – tonight. And Deanna? She might have to wait a long time to join me. Six months, maybe even a year. And all during that time, Anna couldn't know – we both realized that. She might say something, give me away. For an entire year or so, Anna would have to believe that her father was dead.

We went round and round, back and forth.

Maybe it was simple fatigue that finally beat us down. We kept hammering away at the rational and logical until they both finally switched sides.

By five in the morning, the most logical, the most reasonable thing in the world seemed to be to disappear off the face of the earth.

I never turned myself in.

I died.

Forty-six

I left that night.

But before I walked out, before I held Deanna for what seemed like twenty minutes with neither of us saying a word, I tiptoed upstairs and looked in on my daughter.

She was fast asleep, with one arm thrown over her face as if she didn't wish to see something. Bad dream, maybe. I whispered good-bye to her.

I didn't have a destination.

My destination was anywhere far from there.

I took a Greyhound bus at 6:00 in the morning that was headed to Chicago. It seemed as good a place as any.

I sat next to a thin and restless prelaw student who was on his way back to Northwestern.

'Mike,' he said to me, and put his hand out.

'Lawrence,' I said. 'You can call me Larry.' It was the

first time I'd really used my new name – that I'd said it out loud. It felt odd, like seeing myself with a beard. I would have to get used to it.

Mike was a sports junkie; he wanted to be a players agent when he graduated, he told me. I was going to tell him that maybe I could help him, that I *knew* one or two agents, having used athletes in commercials for years, but I stopped myself. From now on, I wasn't in advertising. From now on, I'd *never* been in advertising. Which got me thinking about what I did do if someone asked. And what I would do whenever I got to where I was going.

Except for a teaching degree I'd gotten from Queens College – not because I particularly wanted to be a teacher, but because I didn't know what else I was going to do back then – advertising had been it. How was I going to make a living now?

I fell asleep a few times on the way to Chicago. And dreamed. About Winston. He was sitting with me in my old office, and we were talking about the Yankees' chances in the coming season. Then Winston heard a dog barking – he got up and left. When I woke, Mike was looking at me oddly, and I wondered if I'd talked in my sleep. But Mike just smiled and offered me half of his tunafish sandwich.

When we got to Chicago, I shook hands with him and wished him luck.

'You too,' he said, and I thought that I would probably need it.

*

I found an apartment over by the lake.

I'd brought enough money to tide me over for as long as it might take. More than enough, anyway, for one month's security and one month's rent.

The neighborhood was largely Ukrainian.

Neighbors sat on brown stoops when the weather was nice. Kids rode bicycles in the street and played stickball. One month after I moved in, they held a block party. A bald, sturdy-looking Ukrainian man knocked on my door and asked me if I wanted to chip in.

I gave him twenty dollars, and he seemed very happy. He made me promise to come down and join them later.

I wasn't intending to; I was going to stay put up in my apartment and read the *Chicago Sun-Times*. The torrent of articles about the Fairfax bombing had slowly lessened to one or two a week. But there was an updated death list in today's issue. Even though I was expecting to see it there, even though I was *looking* for it, the sight of my own name in stark black and white caused me to turn pale and nearly drop my coffee. My name had migrated from the missing to the dead. It was official now.

And someone else's name had finally shown up on the list of victims as well. *Raul Vasquez* – they'd finally ID'ed him.

I got up and walked to the window. I could hear music and laughter drifting in from the street below. I suddenly realized how lonely I was.

I went downstairs.

A local band was playing Ukrainian folk songs – at least I assumed they were, since everyone seemed to know the words and at least twenty people were in the middle of the street dancing to them. Portable grills were set up on the sidewalk. A young woman offered me a kind of sausage wrapped in sourdough, and I thanked her and dug in.

Then a policeman came walking toward me.

'Hey you,' he said.

I froze. Every fiber in my body told me to run, to throw down the sandwich and take off.

'Hey.' The policeman held something out to me.

A beer.

He was off duty and lived in the neighborhood. He was just being friendly.

I let the air go out of my body; for the first time since I'd come to Chicago, I relaxed. I stayed down there till midnight. I drank beer and ate sausages and clapped to the music.

The second hardest part of all this was not seeing them. Deanna and Anna.

The *hardest* part was knowing what Anna was going through.

Once a week, I called Deanna's cell. From a public pay phone, just to be on the safe side.

Once a week, I asked Deanna how Anna was dealing with it, and Deanna would sigh and tell me.

'It's so *hard* not telling her, Charles. The other day . . .' But she didn't finish.

She didn't have to.

I could picture Anna clearly. I spent hours and hours up in that apartment doing nothing else. I tried not to, but it was like trying to keep those pictures of Winston out of my head.

'Maybe we can—' I started to say, but Deanna interrupted me.

'No, Charles, not yet.'

'They want me to hold a memorial service for you,' she told me a few weeks later.

'Aunt Rose and Joe and Linda . . . I told them you were *missing*. That until they officially declared you dead, I was going to hold on to the hope that you were still alive. Joe thinks I'm delusional, of course. He thinks it's been long enough and I have to face reality. I told him to mind his own business. He didn't take it very well. I think the family's starting to choose sides, Charles. All of them against the lunatic.'

'Good,' I said.

That, more or less, was our plan.

In five months, six months, seven months, Deanna and Anna would be coming to join me. And leaving all family behind. They belonged to our other life. They couldn't be part of this one. It would help, we thought, if they were all estranged from each other. Deanna's refusal to face facts and her family's insistence she do just that gave us an unexpected way to accomplish that. The flood of sympathetic phone calls from close and distant relations had already thinned to a trickle. Walls were being erected, barriers put in place. The one exception was Deanna's mom. We'd agreed that at some point we'd have to cross our fingers and tell her.

It was becoming more and more apparent that disappearing off the face of the earth wasn't easy – ties had to be cut, loose ends knotted up. It was like planning a long and complex vacation, only a vacation you weren't intending to come back from.

'Oh, your company called about your insurance, Charles,' Deanna said. 'I was all ready to tell them that I wasn't ready to admit you were dead yet. That they could keep their insurance, but she said she was calling to say they were *fighting* it. Because of your suspension – they'd stopped payments. She wanted me to know.'

Life was nothing if not ironic, I thought.

There were other ways I passed the time up in my apartment.

I set about creating more ID.

I had a driver's license. I wanted more.

Winston had said getting a false ID was the easiest thing in the world, and he wasn't far wrong. These days you just needed the Internet.

When I logged on at an Internet café and typed in 'False ID,' I found at least four sites all too willing to help.

The secret was simply getting that first piece of ID. That one enabled you to get more. And thanks to Winston, I already had the first piece. A driver's license, which, according to a Web site called Who Are You, is considered primary ID. That is, it enables you to get everything else. A Social Security card, for example, obtained through a simple application in the mail.

Slowly, I built up an identity.

A credit card. A voter's registration card. A bank card. Discount cards for Barnes & Noble and Costco. A library card. All the things you would be expected to carry in your wallet.

But now that I had an identity, I needed a job.

One day the *Chicago Tribune* ran an article about the education crisis in the state. Apparently there was a dearth of teachers in Illinois. Qualified people were going into other, more lucrative fields and leaving schools terribly short-handed. Classes were being piggybacked with other classes. Programs were being cut. The state was considering running a TV recruitment campaign. And something else. They were down to letting even unlicensed people teach – anyone who'd taken some teaching courses in college and promised to complete the necessary credits concurrent with their teaching job.

It seemed like an opportunity for me.

The hardest-hit area, according to the article, was called Oakdale – about forty miles outside of Chicago. Once a mill town, it was now largely destitute. Mostly blue-collar and minority, and struggling along with sometimes seventy kids to a class. They were virtually begging for teachers.

I went there one day to look around.

I got off the bus and wandered down its main street.

There were a lot of shuttered stores and broken windows. Parking meters had no heads on them. Only the bars seemed to be doing a decent business. It was just early afternoon, but they seemed filled with out-of-work men. I heard someone shouting from inside a bar called Banyon's.

'*Motherfucker!*' Then the sound of breaking glass.

I hurriedly walked on.

I went into a luncheonette and sat at the counter.

'Yeah?' the luncheonette owner asked me. He was fat and tired looking; his apron looked as if it hadn't been washed in years.

'A hamburger,' I ordered.

'How you want it?'

'Medium.'

'Okay.' But he didn't get up from his seat.

After a few minutes, I said: 'Are you going to make the hamburger?'

'Waiting for the cook,' he said.

'Where is he?'

But just then a woman came out through the doorway behind the counter. His wife, I guessed. She was smoking a cigarette.

'Burger,' the luncheonette owner said to her. 'Medium.'

She took a frozen pattie from under the counter and placed it on the grill.

'Want fries with that?' she asked me.

'Sure.'

'Just move in?' the owner asked me.

'No. Maybe. Thinking about it.'

'Uh-huh. Why?'

'Excuse me?'

'Why are you thinking about it?'

'There might be a teaching job for me here.'

'Teaching, huh? You're a teacher?'

'Yes.'

'I was never good at school,' he said. 'Didn't have the head.'

'Well, it looks like you're doing all right.'

'Oh sure. It's okay.'

His wife placed the burger in front of me. It looked pink and greasy.

'What happened to the parking meters?' I asked them.

'Oh those,' the man said. 'Someone stole them.'

'They never replaced them?'

The man shrugged. 'Nope. Wouldn't matter. We don't have any meter maids or anything, so no one was using them anyway.'

'No meter maids. Why not?'

'Because we don't have anything. The city's broke. We share a police force with Cicero.'

'Oh,' I said. Most citizens would be alarmed at having no police force to themselves, I thought, but not me. I found that piece of information comforting.

Oakdale, Illinois. It was seeming more and more like a place I might like to hang my hat.

I sent out a résumé and letter to the Oakdale School District.

I wrote that I'd taken teaching courses back in college but had gone in a more entrepreneurial direction after graduation. I'd run several successful businesses out of my home. Now I'd gotten the urge to give something back. To mold and shape young minds. Oddly enough, I wasn't being untruthful here. I'd spent most of my life attempting to sell another credit card or slice of pizza; the thought of doing something that would actually benefit someone other than me was genuinely appealing.

I kept the résumé purposely vague. I wrote down 'City University,' not specifying what *college* in the city university system I'd actually attended. I was banking on the fact that beggars can't be choosers. That an underfunded and overworked school system in desperate need of teachers is not going to have the time or inclination to check facts.

I sent out the letter and résumé in July.

By August 10 I had my answer.

They requested I come in for an interview.

Forty-seven

I started teaching the day after Labor Day.

Seventh-grade English. They gave me a choice of grades, and I picked the one closest to Anna's age. If I couldn't help her at the moment, I thought, I could help kids like her.

It was balmy, but I could already feel hints of fall in the intermittent breeze, like icy currents in an August ocean. I stood outside in shirtsleeves on the steps of George Washington Carver Middle School and shivered.

My first day was the worst.

The bell stopped ringing, and I found fifty-one skeptical students staring up at me.

The class was two-thirds black and one-third black wannabe. Even the white kids wore those low-slung dungarees with the elastic bands of their underwear showing. They practiced the strut that seemed to come naturally to their black peers; they'd stand in the schoolyard before first bell, making up raps.

When I wrote my name across the blackboard, the nub of chalk broke and the entire class laughed. I opened my desk to find another piece of chalk, but there wasn't any – something I would discover with all my school supplies that first year.

'Mr Wid' remained on the blackboard.

So that's what they began to call me. Mr Wid.

Hey, Mr Wid, what's shakin'? Yoh, Wid . . .

I didn't correct them. It broke the ice that first day, and as time went on I grew almost fond of it, with the exception of a certain piece of graffiti I read on the wall of the boys' urinal one day.

I'm holding Wid's head in my hand!

I became fond of them, too – even the graffiti writer, who sheepishly admitted it when he was caught adding to his collection and spent two afternoons in detention for it. His detention supervisor, as it happened, was me. I volunteered for it; I had nowhere to go and no one to go home to. So I supervised detention, I taught an after-school study hall, I helped out the school basketball team.

The graffiti artist was named James. But he liked being called J-Cool, he told me. He came from a one-parent household – just *his mama*, he said, and I instantly thought about Anna.

I told him if he stopped writing that he was holdi Wid's head in his hand on the bathroom wall, I would calling him J-Cool.

Deal, he said.

We became friends.

I became kind of popular with everyone. Not just with the kids, but with the faculty, since I was always volunteering for things they themselves would otherwise have had to do.

Being liked, however, had its drawbacks.

When people like you, they invariably ask you questions about yourself. They're curious about where you came from, what you did before, if you're married or not, if you have any kids.

Lunch hours became awkward for me. An obstacle course I had to negotiate for forty-five minutes every afternoon, maintaining just enough concentration to avoid tripping up. At first, I'd be talking to someone and would forget what I'd told someone else – Ted Roeger, eighth-grade math teacher, for instance, who'd invited me to play weekend softball with him in his over-forty league. I politely declined. Then there was Susan Fowler, a thirtyish fine arts teacher who seemed unattached and desperate, who always seemed to find an empty chair at my lunch table and turn the conversation to relationships and the difficulties thereof.

Eventually I went home and wrote out my life as Lawrence Widdoes. From childhood to now. Then I practiced it, asking myself questions about myself and answering them.

Where did you grow up?

aten Island. (Close to home, yes, but I needed to pick I would at least know something about. And since

I'd passed through there a million times on the way to Aunt Kate's, I knew enough about Staten Island to avoid looking stupid if a Staten Islander decided to ask me questions about it.)

What did your parents do?

Ralph, my father, was an auto mechanic. Anne, my mother, was a housewife. (Why not? Auto mechanic was as good an occupation as any, and housewife was what most women did back then.)

Did you have brothers or sisters?

No. (Absolutely true.)

What college did you go to?

City University. (That's, after all, what I'd put on my résumé.)

What did you do before this?

I ran a beauty care products business out of my house. Hairsprays. Facial creams. Body lotions. (A friend of mine had done that back in Merrick, so I knew something about it – enough, anyway, to get by.)

Are you married?

Yes. And no. (This was the tough one. There were no wife and children with me in Chicago now, but if things went according to plan, soon there would be. Suddenly they would just appear. Why? Because we'd suffered the great malaise of the twentieth century – marital difficulties – and we'd separated for a time. But just for a time. We were working at a reconciliation – we were hopeful it woul
happen and that they would join me.)

Do you have any children?

Yes. One. A daughter.

I stayed close to the truth in almost everything. It made it easier when my mind went blank, when someone cornered me with a question I wasn't prepared for. The life of Lawrence Widdoes was different from the life of Charles Schine, yes, but not *that* different, and those differences slowly and haltingly became second nature to me. I became familiar with them, nurtured them, trotted them out and took them for strolls around the park, and finally adopted them as my own.

'She's begun dialysis,' Deanna said.

I was standing at the public pay phone two blocks from my Chicago apartment. It was October now. Wind was knifing in off the lake and rattling the phone booth. My eyes teared up.

'When?' I asked.

'Over a month. I didn't want to tell you.'

'How . . . how is she taking it?'

'Like she's taking everything else these days. With this horrible silence. I beg her to talk to me, yell at me, scream at me, *anything*. She just looks at me. After you left, she just closed up, Charles. She's holding it in so tightly I think she's going to explode. I took her to therapy, but the therapist said she didn't say a word. Usually you can wait them out – the silence becomes so uncomfortable they ecome desperate to fill it. But not our Anna. She looked the window for fifty minutes, then got up and left. this.'

'Jesus, Deanna . . . does the dialysis *hurt* her?'

'I don't think so. Dr Baron says it doesn't.'

'How long does she have to sit there?'

'Six hours. More or less.'

'And it doesn't hurt her? You're sure?'

'Your being gone is what's hurting her. It's killing her. It's killing me not being able to tell her. I don't think I can *not* tell her anymore. Charles . . .' Deanna started crying.

I suddenly felt as if every useful part of my body had stopped working. Someone had just plucked out my heart and left a hole there. It was waiting for Anna to come and fill it. Anna and Deanna both. I began to calculate. It had been, what . . . four months?

'Have you put the house up for sale yet?' I asked her.

'Yes. I told anyone I'm still *talking* to that I have to get away. There are too many memories. I have to start fresh.'

'Who are you talking to?'

'Hardly anyone. Now. My aunts and uncles have given up on me – I had another fight with Joe. Our friends? It's funny . . . at first they give you the song and dance how nothing's going to change – you'll still get together for Saturday night dinners and Sunday barbecues. But it does change. They're all coupled up and you're alone and they feel awkward. It becomes easier to just not invite you. We were worried how we'd manage to cut ties with them, and it's happening on its own. Who do I talk to? My mother mostly. That's it.'

'The first decent offer you get on the house – sel' said. 'It's time.'

Forty-eight

I found a house outside Oakdale.

It wasn't much of a house, a modest ranch built sometime in the fifties, but it had three bedrooms and a small garden and lots of privacy.

I rented it.

And waited for them to come join me.

Deanna sold the house.

It wasn't the best price we could have gotten, but it wasn't the worst, either. It was expedient.

When Deanna told Anna they were going to be moving, she had to weather a storm of protest, however. Deanna was ostensibly moving to be rid of the mories – Anna wanted to hold on to them. Deanna said s done; there was no going back. Anna retreated into ilence.

She left most of the furniture. We didn't want a moving company having an address of delivery.

They packed up the car and left.

Somewhere between Pennsylvania and Ohio, Deanna pulled the car over and told Anna I was alive.

We'd agonized over this.

How exactly do you go about telling your daughter that her father isn't dead? That he didn't die in that hotel explosion after all? I couldn't just pop out of the woodwork when she got there. She had to be prepared for something like that.

We'd also wondered *what* should be told to her. *Why* was I alive? Or, more to the point, why had she been allowed to think I was dead all these months?

She was fourteen – half kid and half not.

So we decided on a story that was half true and half not.

Deanna pulled the car into the parking lot of a Roy Rogers along Route 96. Later, she told me how it went.

'I have something to tell you,' she said to Anna, and Anna barely looked at her. She was still on a kind of speaking strike, using silence as a weapon, the only one she had.

'It's something you're going to have a hard time believing, and you're going to be very, very angry at me, but I'm going to try to make you understand. Okay?'

And now Anna did look at her, because this soun serious.

'Your father is alive, Anna.'

At first, Deanna said, Anna looked at her as though she'd lost her mind. And when she repeated it, as if Deanna were maybe playing some kind of sick joke on her. A look of near disgust passed over Anna's face and she asked her mother why she was doing this to her.

'It's the truth, darling. He's *alive*. We're going to meet him now. He's waiting for us in Illinois.'

And it was at that point that Anna finally believed her, because she knew her mother *hadn't* lost her mind and wouldn't have been cruel enough to joke about it. She broke down, finally and completely and spectacularly broke down. She cried rivers of tears, Deanna said, cried so hard and so much that Deanna didn't think the body could contain that much water. She cried out of happiness, out of sheer relief.

Then, with Deanna stroking her hair, came the questions.

'Why did you tell me he was dead?' Anna said.

'Because we couldn't take the chance you would tell somebody. Maybe that was wrong – I'm so sorry you had to go through that. We thought it was the only way. Please believe me.'

'Why is he pretending to be dead? I don't understand . . .'

'Daddy got into some trouble. It wasn't his fault. But they might not believe him.'

'They *who*?'

'The police.'

'police? *Daddy*?'

'You know your father, Anna, and you know he's a good man. But it might not have looked that way. It's hard for me to explain. But he got into trouble and he couldn't get out.'

Deanna told her the rest. Their names would be different. Their lives. Everything.

'I have to change my *name*?' Anna asked.

'You always said you hated it, remember?'

'Yeah. But . . . can't I just change my last name?'

'Maybe. We'll see.'

All in all, Deanna said, she thought the overwhelmingly good news that I was alive canceled out the overwhelmingly bad news that her life was being turned upside down. And that we'd lied to her all these months.

Anna said, 'Jamie.'

'What?'

'My name. I like Jamie.'

I was waiting for them in Chicago.

The car rolled up to the curb and Anna jumped out before the car actually stopped and flung herself into my arms.

'Daddy,' she said. 'Daddy . . . Daddy . . . Daddy . . .'

'I love you,' I said. 'I'm so sorry, honey . . . I'm so—'

'Shh,' she said. 'You're alive.'

Forty-nine

Our new life.

I got up at six-thirty and made breakfast for Deanna and Anna. For Jamie. She went off to school with me. I was able to enroll her at George Washington Carver. When the principal asked if they could have her previous academic records forwarded to them, their favorite new teacher said sure – he'd notify her last school and they'd be there in a few months or so. The principal said fine and never asked me again.

I'd scouted out a local endocrinologist named Dr Milbourne, so Anna could continue her dialysis without interruption. He asked for her records. I gave him the same ~wer I gave the school. He didn't seem overly concerned ~se Deanna had Anna's blood journals for the last five ~hat and her current blood sugar reading and medical ~eemed to tell him all he needed to know. He put her on dialysis in the office, and wrote her a prescription for a portable machine we could use in the house. My new medical insurance, courtesy of the Illinois Board of Ed, took care of everything.

I managed to find a drugstore in Chicago that carried the special insulin Anna needed, the one made from pig cells that was slowly being phased out in favor of the synthetic insulins that Anna didn't respond to as well.

Deanna, who used her previous middle name of Kim, took a part-time job as a receptionist to help out with the family finances.

And an odd and wondrous thing happened.

We became happy again.

It dawned on us gradually, in small increments here and there, until we could finally and fearlessly say it out loud.

We'd been given another chance at this thing called *family*. We grabbed it with both hands and held on for dear life. It felt a little like when we'd first started out, newly married and imbued with passion and hope. We didn't know how long we'd have Anna for, that's true, but we were determined to appreciate every single minute we did. We talked about it now, comforted each other, found strength in each other. Silence was forever banned from our doorstep. We became a kind of poster family for communication.

And slowly, intimacy came back as well. The first nigh we were together again, with Anna safely asleep in bed tore into each other with a kind of desperate abando had taken on a new edge and, with it, a new excitem mauled each other, we banged bodies, we screwed ourselves sweaty, and in the end we looked at each other with a kind of amazement. Was that really us?

Two months later, Deanna announced she was pregnant.

'You're what?' I said.

'With child. Knocked up. Preggers. So,' she said, 'what do you think? Should I have an abortion?'

'No,' I said.

We'd wanted another child once. Anna's getting sick had changed our minds. But now, I believe I wanted it as much as I've ever wanted anything.

'Yeah,' Deanna said. 'I kinda feel that way, too.'

Seven months later, Jamie had a brother. We called him Alex. Call it a homage to Jamie's previous incarnation – and to my grandfather Alexander.

I had one close call.

I was coming out of Roxman's Drugs with Anna's prescription. I was marveling at the actual severity of a Chicago winter; Windy City didn't quite do it justice.

Frigid City. Subzero City. Frozen Stiff City. Yes.

I was wearing a parka, knit cap, earmuffs, fur-lined gloves. I was still quivering. Strands of frozen moisture sat on my upper lip. I was looking for my car in an outdoor parking lot and hoping it would start.

I walked past an office building and bumped into one with blond hair.

'Excuse me,' I said, turning around to face her.

It was Mary Widger.

'That's okay,' she said.

I whipped back around and kept walking. I remembered – one of our packaged goods clients had its headquarters here. She must've been coming from a meeting. When I turned the corner and peeked, she was still standing there.

Did she recognize me?

I don't think so. I still had my beard. I was bundled in leather and fur. Still, it felt like my heart went on hiatus for a while. I found it hard to breathe.

I waited a few minutes, enveloped in my own clouds of hot vapor, then walked back to the corner and peeked again.

She was gone.

Fifty

Alex was two.

He was talking up a storm, doing calisthenics on the living room furniture, and generally delighting, amusing, and captivating us on a daily basis.

Kim was back to working as a receptionist.

Jamie was holding her own. Medically, scholastically, even socially. She'd made friends with two girls who lived down the road. They had sleep-overs and pizza parties and went to the movies together.

Mr Wid? He was teaching *A Separate Peace* and several works of Mark Twain in seventh-grade English.

One of Twain's classic lines seemed remarkably apt these days.

The reports of my demise are greatly exaggerated.

Jamie wasn't the only one who'd built up a social circle. keeping a low profile for a good part of a year, I'd taken some of my colleagues up on their invitations.

Slowly, we began to see people. A dinner. A movie. A Sunday get-together.

My previous life began to fade. Not just because time had passed, but because this life was better in so many ways – all the ways that really counted, I now knew. I'd made more money before, that's true. By all the usual standards of American success – a prestigious job, a nice salary, a large house – this life was a come-down. But in *this* life I could measure job success in something other than dollar signs. My annual bonus was seeing children who came into my class struggling and unmotivated leave it on track and engaged. It was good for the soul. And I didn't have disgruntled and demanding clients looking for my head every day, either.

And married life? It continued to surprise in ways big and small.

Lawrence Widdoes was a happy man.

One Saturday in the summer, I took Alex with me into Chicago.

I had to pick up another prescription for Kim, and I thought I'd take Alex to the Children's Museum.

First, we went to Roxman's Drugs.

The druggist greeted me by name. We were old pals now. He asked me how I was doing.

Fine, I said.

He said the weather was too hot.

I agreed with him – we were stuck in the middle unrelenting heat wave. Something I was only too a<del>

since I was teaching summer school in a building with no air-conditioning. At the end of each day, I came home drenched.

The druggist slipped a lollipop to Alex, whose eyes went wide, the way kids' eyes do when you present them with their version of money. He made me unwrap it for him, then popped it into his mouth and smiled.

Then the druggist's assistant walked over and said: 'Mr Widdoes? I'm sorry, I thought you understood. I said the insulin won't be in till Monday.'

'What?'

'Remember, I said Monday.'

'You said Monday when?'

'When you called. I told you that.'

'When I called?'

'You asked me if the insulin was in. I said Monday.'

'You mean my wife. She must've called you.'

He looked puzzled, shook his head, shrugged. 'Okay. Well, it's not in till Monday.'

'Fine. I'll come back.'

We went to the Children's Museum.

There were several hands-on exhibits. Alex climbed through a giant left ventricle and into a model of a heart itself, where he sat down and refused to budge. He knew couldn't climb in there with him, and he relished this mentary independence. I had to wait him out.

ntually he appeared from the right ventricle.

w what his weight was on Mars.

He tapped in Morse code.

He finger-painted on a computer.

He put on bird's wings.

I took him to the museum café, where I bought him a hot dog and fries – but only if he promised not to tell Mommy, who was waging a personal crusade against junk food these days.

Sitting there eating, I had what you might call a flashback.

Something was bothering me. It was sitting on my shoulder and buzzing in my ear. I tried swatting it away, but it wouldn't leave. I couldn't kill it. It was maddening.

I remembered sitting and eating with Lucinda, Didi, whatever her name was. I remembered pouring my heart out to her the day she'd asked about my daughter. About Anna. I remembered telling her something.

I suddenly felt cold.

I took my cell out and called Kim.

'Honey?' I said when she picked up.

'Yes, hi. How's it going?'

'Fine. After this we're going to the museum of dead parents. I feel like I've run a marathon.'

'Then he must be having a good time.'

'You could say that. Look, I wanted to ask you something.'

'Yes?'

'Did you call Roxman's this week? About A insulin?'

'Roxman's? No. Why?'

'You didn't call? You're sure?'

'Yes, Charles . . . woops . . . yes, *Larry*, I'm sure.'

'It isn't possible you did and forgot? Isn't that possible?'

'No. I didn't call Roxman's. I would remember. You want me to sign an affidavit? Why?'

'Nothing. Just something they said to me . . .'

I said good-bye. I hung up.

I stared at my son. He was munching on his last piece of frankfurter. Voices were echoing off the museum walls, a child was screaming bloody murder at another table. He looked up at me.

'Daddy . . . okay?' he said.

Fifty-one

I went on-line.

I went back three years. I went back to the day of the explosion.

There were 173 entries for 'Fairfax Hotel'.

Everything from newspaper articles to magazine articles to mentions in TV shows and even Internet jokes.

Did you hear about the new rate policy at the Fairfax? It bombed.

Most of the articles were what you might expect.

Stories of heroic firemen and innocent victims. And among the stories of innocent victims, I saw my name there again – among the missing at first, then onto the li^s of the dead.

Charles Schine, 45, advertising executive.

And Dexter's and Sam's and Didi's names, too.

And his – placed alphabetically right at the end of the roll call.

I kept reading. There were other stories there, stories about the bomber.

RIGHT-TO-LIFER BOMBER'S HOMETOWN REMEMBERS, one of them was titled. Jack Christmas was born in Enid, Oklahoma. He was a friendly boy who washed blackboards, his third-grade teacher said. Though one school friend remembered him as *kind of spooky*.

There was an article about the hotel itself.

HOTEL'S UN-FABLED PAST GAVE NO CLUE. It was built in 1949. It originally catered to a mostly business clientele. It fell into disrepair and became a haven for short-rate prostitutes and low-income residents.

There were several entries about domestic terrorism.

An article about an organization called the Children of God. A manifesto from an army of anti-abortionists. Several items about survivalists. A recounting of the Oklahoma City bombing and its similarities to the one at the Fairfax Hotel.

And later on, another list of the dead – with brief obituaries this time.

Charles Schine was employed as a creative director at Schuman Advertising. He worked on several major accounts. 'Charley was an asset to this company, both as a writer and a human being. He will be greatly missed,' Eliot Firth, president of Schuman Advertising, said. Charles Schine leaves a wife and daughter.

Samuel M. Griffen was touted as 'a shining star in the world of financial planning'. His brother said, 'He was a generous and loving father.'

There was something about Dexter. 'He was one of our own', the holding company for the Fairfax Hotel said. 'A dedicated employee.'

Even Didi received an obituary – at least I assumed it was her.

Desdemona Gonzalez, 30. A loving sister to Maria. Daughter to Major Frank Gonzalez of East Texas.

I took a detour. I looked up East Texas newspapers. I knew the hometown papers would have been falling all over themselves to write up the stories of their local victims.

I found her. An article from a *Roxham Texas Weekly*.

Retired Major Frank Gonzalez sits on his front porch nursing a very private pain for his youngest daughter, killed in the Fairfax Hotel bombing. Desdemona Gonzalez, 30, had lived in New York City for the last ten years, her father said. 'She didn't keep in touch much,' he said, but she'd 'call on holidays and things like that.' . . . Family friends admitted that the elder Mr Gonzalez and his daughter had been estranged for a number of years . . . There had been a drug arrest when Desdemona was a teenager and allegations of child abuse against her father. A family friend who wishes to remain anonymous added that these charges were all 'unsubstantiated'.

I clicked back to the general obituaries.

There was one missing.

I felt something in the small of my back. A trickle of ice water in reverse – it began crawling up my spine.

I went back and clicked each entry again. I reread everything. Nothing. Not one mention.

I logged on to the *Daily News* Web page. I typed in 'Fairfax Hotel'.

Thirty-two articles.

I started with the one written on the day of the explosion. There was a picture of the bomb site. An old woman crying on a corner curb, firemen standing in the middle of the street with their heads down. I scanned the entire article. I went on to the next one.

Pretty much the same stuff I'd read elsewhere, except in chronological order. The bombing, the dead, the heroes, the villain, the investigation, the funerals.

It took me two hours. Still nothing.

I was beginning to think I was wrong. I'd misinterpreted an offhand comment, that's all. The kind of thing that happened all the time.

I would look at one more week – the week of the last article, four weeks after the actual bombing. That's it.

Then I would log off and go and kiss my sleeping children good night. I would crawl into bed with Kim and mold myself against her warm body. I would fall asleep and know that everything was okay.

I started with Monday. I went on to Tuesday.

I almost missed it.

It was a small item – buried in an avalanche of the Middle East war, a triple murder committed in Detroit, a marital scandal involving the New York City mayor.

HEROIC SURVIVOR NOT SO HEROIC, it said.

I clicked on it, held my breath, and read.

It was kind of a human-interest story, the kind they start running when they run out of stories about heroes and victims, a story meant to make you shake your head at the sad ironies of life.

Body pulled from wreckage . . . no identification . . . in a coma for several weeks . . . brain surgery . . . fingerprints revealed him to be . . . previously identified as dead . . . his car in hotel parking garage . . . hadn't shown for sentencing . . . police spokesperson . . . prison infirmary . . .

I read it slowly, from the beginning to the end. Then once more, making sure.

Anna's insulin.

It was made from a pig's pancreatic cells, which is the way all insulin used to be made. Until they figured out a way to make it synthetically in the laboratory. This was a fairly recent development; Anna had been using pig insulin since she'd gotten diabetes. When she'd tried t synthetic stuff, her numbers had strayed high and s there.

That happened sometimes, Dr Baron had

people responded better to the real stuff. So he'd kept her on it.

Even though they'd begun phasing it out – even though it was becoming very hard to get hold of. But there was no need to worry. There would always be some drugstores that carried it, he said.

I was talking to Jameel Farraday, a guidance counselor, in the school lunchroom.

Once a year, Jameel brought convicts from state prison into the school auditorium in an effort to scare George Washington Carver's students straight. The convicts, some of whom had even grown up in the neighborhood, would talk about drugs, about the wrong choices they'd made, about life behind bars.

Then they'd take questions from the audience.

Ever kill anyone? one student asked an ex-junkie who had a scar running the entire length of his jawbone.

He said no, and the student body groaned.

'I'm thinking about having my class write letters to men in prison,' I said to Farraday. He was eating milky mashed potatoes and greasy chicken fingers.

'For what purpose?' he asked me.

'Well, kind of like the thing you do – but in writing. My kids can practice their penmanship, and these men can ovide some life lessons, maybe.'

kay,' he said.

s wondering . . .'

'I *knew* someone who ended up going to prison – from my old neighborhood. I thought I might start with him.'

'What did he do?'

'I don't know, exactly. Drugs, I heard.'

'Uh-huh.'

'You have any idea how I could find out where he is?'

'You mean which prison?'

'Yes.'

Farraday shrugged. 'I don't know. I can ask my contact in Chicago Corrections, I guess.'

'Would you?'

'Sure. If I remember. Where's he from?'

'New York.'

'Uh-huh. What's his name?'

'Vasquez.'

'*Vasquez?*'

'Yes. Raul. Raul Vasquez.'

Fifty-two

He knew where I was.

They'd pulled him half-dead from the rubble, but only half.

He was in a coma for weeks. They didn't know who he was.

His car had been parked in the hotel lot. He hadn't shown up at work. He was listed as dead.

They ran his fingerprints in a last-ditch effort to find out his name. Raul Vasquez. He had a 'did not show' for sentencing for two counts of assault and battery and one for pandering.

He was transferred to a prison infirmary until he ~~ov~~ered sufficiently enough to be brought into Bronx ~~jun~~ior Court for sentencing.

~~I~~ knew from the article. The rest of it I imagined.

He'd sat there in prison. He'd thought and he'd remembered.

What Didi had told him. About my daughter. About the special pig insulin she needed to survive. *Why pig insulin? she had asked me, remember?* Like a concerned lover, instead of an extortionist wheedling the details out of me.

Vasquez sat there in prison and fumed. I was hiding from him. I was gone. But then he understood there was something I would have to do. No matter how carefully I was hiding, I would have to do this thing.

This is Mr Widdoes. Is my insulin in?

How many drugstores must have said no. Must've said, *Widdoes who?*

But he kept going. He kept calling. He had all the time in the world. He had all the motivation necessary.

Maybe he started in New York. Then on to Pennsylvania. And so on.

One day, he'd reached Illinois.

Roxman's Drugs.

And this time when he asked if his insulin was in, the druggist's assistant didn't say no.

He said not yet.

But it'll be in Monday.

Two weeks after I'd talked to Jameel, he found me after class and handed me a sheet of paper.

'What's this?' I said.

'Your guy,' he said. 'But there's three of them.'

'Three?'

'Yeah – three Raul Vasquezes. But if he's from New York, I'd imagine he's this one.' He pointed to the first name on the sheet. 'I'd imagine he's here.'

I lay upstairs in bed. I couldn't sleep.

Kim was attuned to my nightly rhythms and knew without even looking that I was lying there wide awake and staring at the ceiling.

'What's the matter, honey?' she said. 'What's wrong?'

I couldn't tell her yet. I didn't have the heart. We'd escaped from catastrophe once; we'd made a new life. We were happy. I couldn't tell her that we hadn't escaped after all. That the past was reaching out for us with icy fingers.

'Nothing,' I said.

I was thinking.

What was parole for a twelve-year sentence?

When would he be getting out?

He would come for me then – I knew that. For my family. And then he would do what he'd done to Winston and Sam Griffen and the man he'd pushed off the train in Lynbrook, Long Island, and God knows how many others.

That day he came to our home as a chimney cleaner.

I heard about a family that went to sleep and never woke ?.

es, he would be coming for me.

ess – I whispered it like a fervent prayer.

I get to him first.

392

He didn't know that I knew he was alive. He didn't know that I knew he'd found me.

But what did that matter?

He was in prison. He was locked up.

To get to him, I would have to get inside Attica.

Now – how could I do that?

Attica

It was my last class.

I'd circled it in my calendar. I'd rehearsed it in dreams.

When I walked through the metal detector, a CO named Stewey said, 'Last day, huh,' and I thought he looked almost despondent. Maybe people get used to the people they belittle, and who knows if they'll ever find anyone as good again?

Before I went to my classroom, I stopped off in the COs lounge.

It was just a room with folding chairs and tables and a thirteen-inch TV usually tuned to Dukes of Hazzard reruns. The COs evidently had a thing for Daisy Duke – those high-cut shorts of hers, probably – because an old poster of her still hung on the wall. Someone had penciled in nipples on her ̇ite blouse.

̇̇oured myself some coffee. I put powdered milk into my ̇̇ d stirred it with a plastic swizzle stick.

I casually walked over to the COs museum situated in the left corner of the room.

'You got your twelve oh-one, brother,' Fat Tommy said. He was spread across two metal chairs with a Jenny Craig TV dinner on the table in front of him.

It's only natural that employees pick up the lingo of the workplace; Attica guards often talked like Attica prisoners. And 12:01 meant gaining your freedom – getting your walking papers.

Maybe, I thought. We'll see.

I sipped my coffee, I perused the collection of gats and burners, as Fat Tommy chomped away on a meal he could only find ultimately dissatisfying. He was the only other person in the lounge.

When I finally turned and left, Fat Tommy looked up but didn't say good-bye.

From the lounge to the classroom, I first had to go through a black locked door – knocking twice and waiting for another CO to clear me. Then I walked down the 'bowling alley', what they call the prison's main walkway. It's dissected down the middle by a broken yellow line, like a state highway. One side is for prisoners. The other side is for COs. Or for people who fall somewhere in between.

I passed a CO called Hank.

'Hey, Yobwoc,' he said. 'I'm gonna miss you. You were best boon coon.'

Translation: best friend.

'Thank you,' I said, but I knew he hadn't mea

When the class settled in, I told them it was the last time I'd be seeing them. That it had been fun teaching them. That I hoped they'd keep reading and writing on their own. I told them that in the best classes, the teacher becomes the student and the students the teachers, and that that's what had happened here – I'd learned from them. No one looked particularly moved; but when I finished, one or two of them nodded at me as if they might even miss me.

Malik wasn't one of them. He'd passed me a note last time. Where the writer would be waiting for me.

I told the class we might as well use this last class for creative reflection. I wanted each of them to write an essay on what the class had meant to them. This time, I told them, they could even put their names to them.

Then I excused myself to go to the bathroom.

I passed the black CO who was supposed to be stationed outside the door and who, this time, actually was. I said I'd be back in ten minutes, and he said, 'I'll alert the media.'

He'd be waiting for me near the prison pharmacy, the note said.

He worked there.

A pharmacy job gave you shine, a student had explained to me, since it gave you access to drugs.

It also gave you access to something else, I knew. Drug manufacturers. You could call them up to find out things if you wanted to. Like maybe where a certain rare insulin was distributed.

ably hadn't taken him years to track me down after

I walked back down the bowling alley. I followed the signs.

The pharmacy consisted of one long counter protected by steel mesh. There are prisons within prisons, I noted, an axiom also true of life. The kind of insight I might've pointed out in my class, if I still had one.

I continued past the pharmacy, striding down an empty hallway that veered sharply left and seemed to lead to no place in particular. But it did.

Malik had told me where he'd be waiting for me, and I'd gone and scouted it.

An alcove in the middle of the hall.

A kind of blind. In an older institution like Attica, there were lots of them, hidden little corners where the prisoners conducted business, where they sold drugs and got down on their knees. Where they evened scores. A blind. An appropriate description, except I was walking in with my eyes wide open.

I walked into the alcove where it was quiet and still and stopped.

'Hello?'

I could hear him breathing in there.

'Hello,' I whispered again.

He stepped out of the shadows.

He looked different — that's the first thing I thought. That he looked different from the way I remembered him.

His head. It seemed smaller, reshapen, as if it had bee_ squeezed in a vise. He had a scar running down from forehead. That was one thing. And he had a tat on his shoulder. A prison blue clock face without hands – doing time. And farther down on his arm a tombstone with numbers – twelve – his prison sentence.

'Surprise,' he said.

No. But that's what I wanted him to think.

'How you doin', Chuck?' he said. He smiled, the way he'd smiled at my front door the day he'd come to my house and put his hands on my daughter.

'Larry,' I said.

'Larry. Yeah, I'm down. That was some cool shit you pulled off – playing dead like that. Had everyone fooled, huh, Larry?'

'Not everyone. No.'

'No, not everyone. You're right. You shouldn't have let my girl see your wallet, Larry. Bad move. Stupid.'

The hostess in the Crystal Night Club. Widdoes . . . what kind of name is that? she'd said.

'I thought you were dead.'

'You wish.'

Yes, I thought. I wish. *But there comes a time when you have to stop wishing.*

'I've been looking for you, Larry. Like all over. You took something of mine, you know. I want it back. So I've been looking for you. And I found you, too. I found you twice.'

'Twice?'

'Once in Chicago. Oh yeah . . . that's right. Surprised by *_hat, huh? Yeah, I knew exactly where you were. Oakdale, _nois. Then you moved on me.'*

'_s.'

'Bennington. Right down the fucking road. How's that for lucky?'

'That's lucky.'

'Uh-huh. You know how I found you?'

'No.'

'Your kid. Through the drugstores. First Chicago. Then Bennington. And then the next thing I know, the very next thing I know, you're waltzing in through the fucking front door.'

'Yes.'

'I said to myself, Here's your twelve oh-one, nigger. Here it is on a platter.'

'Why didn't you say hello?'

'I did. I did say hello. I got my boy to write up my hello for me.'

'Your boy? He can't even read.'

'Not Malik. My boon. A Jew literary professor who eighty-sixed his wife. Writes all the pleas for parole here. And very cool jerk-off stuff. "Charley Schine Gets Fucked" – his latest. He thinks I made it up in my head. He thinks I'm creative.'

'Yes – it was very effective.'

'I thought you might run. Seeing your life story and all.'

No, I thought. If I was going to run, I would have done it back in Oakdale. It's what Deanna said to do – Let's run, and I said, Okay, but if we run, we will have to keep running. For all time. So maybe we shouldn't. So I'd taken a leave of absence and we'd come here.

'You have something of mine, Larry,' he said.

'Some of it was mine first.'

Vasquez smiled. 'You think this is a fucking negotiation? You think I'm bargaining with you? You're fucked. It's your role in life. Accept it. Get down on your knees and open your mouth and say please, Daddy. I want my money.'

Someone was shouting in the pharmacy: 'The doc says I need this shit, understand?'

'You're in prison,' I said.

'So are you. You're locked up. You're doing time. You think you're safe out there? Think again, motherfucker. I can turn you in – I can tell them, Here's Charley. If you're lucky I could. 'Cause I might send someone to your house to fuck your wife instead. I might. How old's your daughter now – ready to get stuck with something else now, huh?'

I went for him.

Reflex simply took over my body and said: Listen up – we're going to stop this man, we're going to shut this man up forever. We are. But when I lunged at him, when I went for his throat, his knee came up and caught me in the stomach. I went down to my knees. He stepped behind me and slipped his arm around my neck and squeezed. He whispered in my ear.

'That's it, Charley. That's right. Got you mad, huh? Here's the thing. How lucky was it that you showed up in Bennington? Forty miles from here. In my own fucking backyard? And then, if that isn't lucky enough, you walk in the goddamn door and start teaching here. How lucky is that? that lucky or what? Or is that like, too lucky? What do think, Charley? You think that's too lucky? I don't know. ›t something for me, Charley, do you?' He reached his hand down and patted my right pocket. He felt it there – the gat, the one I'd taken from the COs museum. 'You got something you want to stick me with? Huh, Charley?' He took it out of my pocket – he showed it to me.

'You ought to know me better by now, Chuck. Sure I'll meet you by the river. Sure I'll come alone. Sure. But I met your mail boy at the river first, huh? Took his head off, huh, Charley? Who the fuck you think you're dealing with here? You think this is punk central?' He put the knife against my throat. He pressed it against my jugular. Then he smiled and pushed me to the floor. I could smell something acrid – urine and ammonia.

I wanted to answer him now.

To tell him yes, I did know who I was dealing with. To tell him that that was why I'd waited six months in Bennington before applying for the teaching job here. Why I'd made sure he'd found me there first, living in Bennington and teaching in high school, so that it would just seem like some kind of fortunate coincidence that I'd later taken a teaching job here. In the very prison he was incarcerated in. And I wanted to tell him that's why I'd purposely left my keys in my pocket that day I walked through the metal detector – to see if it would be possible to smuggle in a weapon. A gun. And that when I learned it wasn't possible to smuggle in a gun, how I'd started making visits to the COs lounge because I'd heard they had a kind of museum there.

I wanted to tell him that it was true – I hadn't known I was dealing with when I sat with Winston by the ri *later back in the Fairfax Hotel – even then I hadn't. But that I did now. That I'd learned.*

And one last thing. One very last thing. How when I stood there in the COs museum with my back to Fat Tommy, I'd whispered this thing I'd learned to myself. Like a prayer to the God of screwed plans. Because I'd learned if you want to make God laugh, that's what you do – you make a plan; but if you want to make him smile, you make two.

Two.

I reached into my left pocket. I took out the spring-loaded gun made of soapwood and tin that I'd carefully loaded in the COs lounge.

I shot Vasquez directly between both surprised eyes.

Times Union

Prisoner killed in Attica attack.

by Brent Harding

Raul Vasquez, 34, an Attica prisoner, was killed yesterday when his intended victim managed to wrest a prison-made gun away from him and fatally wound him. Lawrence Widdoes, 47, who teaches English to Attica prisoners two nights a week, was assaulted by Mr Vasquez near the prison pharmacy. A witness who works in the pharmacy saw Mr Vasquez physically attack Mr Widdoes. 'He was choking him good . . .' Claude Weathers, an Attica prisoner, stated. 'Then pop – Vasquez goes down.' Mr Widdoes, who suffered a bruised neck, is unsure what provoked the attack, but believes it might be related to some negative criticism he leveled at a student who is the cellmate of Mr Vasquez. Mr Widdoes, whose teaching duties are ending due to state budget cuts, is simply glad to be alive. 'I feel like I've been given a second chance,' Mr Widdoes said.

Fifty-three

I came home.

Kim came rushing out of the kitchen and stopped and stared. As if I were an apparition.

I nodded at her, I whispered, 'Yes.'

She slowly walked toward me and curled herself around my body like a blanket.

It's okay, she was saying, *you can rest now.*

Alex came running down the stairs, crying, 'Daddy's home.' He tugged at my shirt until I picked him up and held him. His cheek was sticky with chocolate.

'Where's Jamie?' I asked Kim.

'Doing her dialysis,' she said.

I kissed her on the top of her head. I put Alex down. I went upstairs to Jamie's bedroom.

She was hooked up to the portable dialysis machine. I ⎵on the bed next to her.

'We'll be going back to Oakdale soon,' I said. 'Back to your friends, okay?'

She nodded.

She did this three days a week now.

There was some talk of getting her on a list for a kidney-pancreas transplant – the newest hope for diabetics like her. But then there would be anti-rejection drugs to worry about for the rest of her life, so it was hard to know if it would really be better for her. As for now, we hooked her veins up to this terrible machine three days a week, and I sat there by her bed and listened to its whir and hum as it pumped blood through her failing body.

Sometimes I drift off to this sound, and Anna is suddenly four years old again and I'm back at the zoo with her on that long-ago Sunday morning. Feeding the elephants. I lift her up into my arms, and I can feel her tiny heart running to greet me. There's a soft chill in the air, and the leaves are drifting down from a swaying canopy of dark russet. Just Anna and her dad, walking hand in hand together in search of memories.

And I know I will sit here forever.

I will sit here as long as it takes.